NO BOUNDARIES

when Two Worlds Collide

Kevin Geise

Paperback ISBN: 978-1-965092-12-5
Hardcover ISBN: 978-1-965092-13-2

    1. Main category— Historical Fiction › 20th Century
    2. Other category— Black & African American

Published by: AR PRESS
Roger L. Brooks, Publisher
roger@americanrealpublishing.com
americanrealpublishing.com

This book is dedicated to the memory of Madeleine Thompson, my Northrop High School Literature and Composition teacher. She always went above and beyond the call of duty, inspiring her students to dive beneath the surface and search for greater purpose and meaning. Through her mentorship, I have fostered a greater appreciation for literature and its usefulness as a tool for enlightenment.

Prologue

H IS LIBRARY WAS A SAFE haven, an inner sanctum where he could be alone with his thoughts and relish his accomplishments. He could sit at his mahogany desk and feel the power of his status, or he could gaze out the window and admire the expansiveness of his estate.

His four-acre property, purchased a decade ago, was acquired to establish a permanent residence, a manor that would signify his standing in the community. Surrounded by wrought-iron fencing, the elegant enclosure was lined with blue spruce trees, forming a barrier that looked as majestic in the summer as it did in the winter when the trees were glistening with freshly powdered snow.

But it was late in the evening and the darkness of night matched the darkness of his mood. There would be no window gazing tonight, only the vision of a defeated man slouched woefully in his full-grain leather chair.

Surrounded by collectibles, the opulence of his possessions did nothing to warm his spirits. Not even the Georgian curio cabinet that proudly displayed his collection of antique firearms, like the .60-caliber English Flintlock dueling pistol, or the nickel-plated Colt Derringer from the 1870s.

Still dressed in his dark gray Stanley Blacker suit, he was alone and self-absorbed by the realization of defeat. The man whom everyone looked upon for leadership was now in a cocoon of self-doubt and despair.

The Waterford crystal decanter, typically the centerpiece of celebratory toasts, was half empty as he poured his fourth glass of single malt scotch. Spinning around his head like a carousel, the shelves of leather-bound books were nothing more than a hazy kaleidoscope of abstract colors, muddling his state of confusion and defeating his sense of purpose.

He was in surrender mode now and there was no turning back.

Baby Boomers

Growing up in the 60s

S O MUCH HAS BEEN WRITTEN about the baby boomer generation, a demographic defined as newborns between the late 1940s and early 1960s. By definition, it was a midcentury period of higher-than-normal birth rates, but beneath the surface, the story was more complex.

After years of cataclysmic warfare and global economic depression, burgeoning optimism was gathering momentum, an expectation that future generations would achieve greater prosperity and more fulfilling lives. For Americans, the age of sacrifice and survival was turning into a memory. The future was all about raising a family and achieving a higher standard of living. It was, quite literally, the rebirth of a nation.

For boomers born in the late 50s, the lion's share of their growth and development took place during the turbulent 60s, prepping and grooming them for adulthood in the 70s. But if the 60s represented a foundation for their future, it's easy to see why these boomers were on shaky ground, reaching maturity in a world of conflict and confusion.

As college enrollments swelled during the 60s, a new generation of thinkers sought solutions to the growing number of quandaries in America. No longer living in the vacuum of their homes, students viewed their independence as an opportunity to share ideas, explore new possibilities, and challenge authority like never before.

College curricula, unlike the remedial fundamentals of reading, writing, and arithmetic, served to enlighten students through broad-minded humanities courses. Instead of memorizing facts and figures and learning a trade, students were seeking a way to succeed and be socially responsible at the same time, creating a society that was more righteous and benevolent.

Delving into the successes and failures of fallen empires, college students were learning from history's mistakes, going far beyond the traditional patriotic lessons they learned in high school: Columbus discovering America, Washington defeating the British, and Davey Crockett's heroic stand at the Alamo. Instead of celebrating war heroes and their conquests of new territories, baby boomers were coming to terms with the disgraced chronicles of American colonialism and imperialism.

The US had come a long way from the original thirteen colonies as it expanded into an economic and military juggernaut. Along with this growth came the realization that indigenous people, both home and abroad, had been exploited and victimized, their cultures sacrificed for the sake of conformity.

Capitalism, solely for the purpose of prosperity and world dominance, would eventually be challenged with new ideals of peace, justice, and equality. Unbridled corporate greed could not prevail in perpetuity without considering its consequences to a world seeking harmony.

As manufacturing plants churned out their products and generated huge profits, industrial smokestacks pumped carcinogenic pollutants into the air, and factories discarded their contaminated waste into lakes and rivers, turning them into sacrificial dumping grounds.

Like never before, the 60s represented a period of recognition, bringing an acute awareness to pollution and other crimes against humanity. As the decade concluded, the growing concern for the environment resulted in the establishment of the Environmental Protection Agency (EPA), and "Keep America Beautiful" became the new campaign slogan.

One of the more memorable TV messages featured an Indian (Native American) paddling his canoe down a river surrounded by factories and pollution. After exiting his canoe, garbage is tossed at him from a passing vehicle, and a teardrop trickles down his face, a poignant ending to a public service announcement filled with symbolism.

In the 1960s, the evolution of television played an increasingly influential role in American lives, steadily expanding their awareness and changing their perspectives. Although TV had become more common in the late 50s, it didn't become a staple of middle-class homes until the 60s. Like never before, families were gathering around their television sets each evening to soak up the network news, a virtual pipeline of world events. Walter Cronkite, the *CBS News* anchor, became more iconic than the president himself, recurrently visiting the living rooms of America to assure them: "That's the way it is."

Investigative journalism, the new world order, enlightened Americans to view authority as nonconformists, enabling them to distinguish between reality and government-backed propaganda. Instead of glorifying war, saluting the flag, and pledging allegiance, Americans were learning about their government's indiscretions and hidden improprieties.

The Vietnam War, unlike any in history, was reported with excruciating detail. From coast to coast, households witnessed the horrific tragedies of jungle warfare as news correspondents risked their lives to expose the brutality. Their on-the-scene reports provided an up-close-and-personal view of what it was like to be a soldier.

Through television, social issues like pollution, poverty, corruption, and racism were exposed in ways that people could no longer ignore or deny. Even sitcoms dared to explore some of the inherent flaws of American culture by exposing the ignorance and hypocrisy of citizens living in their bubbles. By the end of the decade, the most popular TV show in America, *All in the Family*, was bringing greater awareness to bigotry and sexism as Archie Bunker hilariously unveiled his prejudices in front of millions of viewers.

In 1960, the first nationally televised presidential debate ushered in a new decade. John F. Kennedy was elected the thirty-fifth president of the United States and became the second youngest man ever to take office at 1600 Pennsylvania Avenue. The decade started out enthusiastically enough as this young, charismatic leader inspired the next generation with the words "Ask not what your country can do for you; ask what you can do for your country."

For boomers born in the late 50s, their first recollection of a US president was the powerful image of a youthful and handsome President Kennedy inspiring a nation to conquer space and land a man on the moon by the end of the decade. Tragically, the age of inspiration and innocence came to an abrupt halt on November 22, 1963, as an assassin's bullet delivered a devastating blow to the country's hopes and dreams.

The mindset of America's children on that fateful afternoon is difficult to fathom. Instead of coming home from school to find their mothers preparing for the Thanksgiving holiday, they were confronted with the grisly TV reports out of Dallas and the harsh reality of their dead president. Although the nation would grieve as a whole, the children were the biggest victims, struggling to understand nonsensical violence for the first time in their young lives.

Shortly after President Kennedy's death, Vice President Lyndon Baines Johnson (LBJ) was sworn in as the thirty-sixth president of the United States. Thrust into the spotlight of a grieving nation, LBJ was forced to embrace the enormous responsibility and tackle the country's unfinished business. Unbeknownst to most, that unfinished business included a growing involvement of US troops in a small Southeast Asian country called Vietnam.

By November 1963, a total of sixteen thousand American military personnel had been deployed to prevent a communist insurgency from North Vietnam into South Vietnam. After the construction of the Berlin Wall in 1961 and rising tensions from the Cuban Missile Crisis, relations between President Kennedy and the Soviet Union's Nikita Khrushchev had deteriorated to a new low. Drawing a line in the sand with Vietnam seemed to be the best option if the United States was going to stop the spread of communism.

As tensions continued to escalate, the breaking point occurred on August 2, 1964, when three North Vietnamese torpedo boats attacked a US destroyer in the Gulf of Tonkin. This provocation prompted President Johnson to seek and receive congressional approval to attack all perceived threats. Viewing this as the authorization he needed to coordinate full-scale offensives, LBJ launched Operation Rolling Thunder in March of 1965, marking the beginning of a lengthy and sustained aerial bombing campaign. Before the war was over, the United States and its allies would drop over 7.5 million tons of bombs on Vietnam, Laos, and Cambodia, more than double the amount dropped in World War II.

As the war continued to drag on, American troop levels grew to over five hundred thousand. With no end in sight, a growing resentment toward Vietnam was taking its toll. From coast to coast, young men lived in constant fear of being drafted into the army and dying in a jungle halfway around the world in order to defend a country they knew nothing about.

Unwilling to relinquish on principle, the establishment defended its prowar positions as patriotic battles for the preservation of democracy. Antiwar protesters and their opposing views were denigrated as cowardly and un-American. Neither side was willing to budge as public sentiment continued its downward spiral.

Despite the government's efforts to justify a proliferating war and mounting death tolls, public protests became larger and more violent. On October 21, 1967, an estimated one hundred thousand protesters surrounded the Lincoln Memorial in Washington, DC, in what became the largest and most organized effort to date. The antiwar movement had gone mainstream.

No longer dominated by political activists, the crowd was a mixture of college students, scholars, clergymen, middle-class professionals, and high-profile celebrities. When the speeches ended, nearly half the crowd began its march toward the Pentagon armed with daisies, symbolic of the 60s peace movement.

Confronted by rifle-bearing National Guardsmen, the protest turned violent as more than seven hundred arrests were made and dozens of injured were taken to local hospitals. The most iconic image of the event was captured and published by photojournalists: the picture of a protester peacefully placing a daisy down the gun barrel of a National Guardsman.

With no victory in sight, President Johnson's popularity continued to plummet. Caught between a rock and a hard place, the president had to choose between expanding the war and withdrawing disgracefully in defeat. As protesters chanted, "Hey, hey, LBJ, how many kids did you kill today?" Johnson's reelection possibilities continued to dwindle.

On March 31, 1968, President Johnson delivered a rare Sunday evening address on live television. Blindsiding his most ardent supporters, LBJ announced that he would no longer seek reelection to the nation's highest office. In his place, Vice President Hubert Humphry would soon announce his candidacy. But he would not go unchallenged. Standing in his way was a young senator from Massachusetts, the former attorney general and brother of President John F. Kennedy. At forty-two years old, Robert Kennedy possessed the youth and pedigree that could energize the Democratic Party and lead the country out of its doldrums.

But many questions remained. Could Bobby Kennedy gain enough momentum and inspire the country the same way his older brother did? Could he capture enough votes with his antiwar rhetoric, his support for civil rights, and his fight against poverty and corruption?

Notwithstanding the answers, the race was on: a choice between establishment and antiestablishment, staying the course versus a new direction. As Kennedy enthusiasm swept the nation, it reached a fever pitch on June 4, 1968, the evening of the California Primary.

Delivering a rousing speech at the Ambassador Hotel in Los Angeles, Bobby Kennedy celebrated his milestone victory, a major step toward capturing his party's nomination. Finishing with "it's on to Chicago," a reference to the Democratic Convention, the senator exited the stage and shook hands with well-wishers as a barrage of bullets sprayed through the crowded room.

Surrounded by screaming worshippers, Bobby Kennedy lie on the floor in a pool of blood, never again to inspire his followers or lead his country to glory as so many had hoped. Five years after the assassination of his brother, another Kennedy was slaughtered in a senseless act of brutality. Once again, the nation was in shock.

As the Vietnam War raged on, tearing the country to pieces, another war was being waged at home: the ongoing battle for racial equality. One hundred years after the Civil War and the end of slavery, there was still a large disparity between the rights of Black people and those of their former slave owners. Despite the pervasive myth that racial persecution had ended, the ugly truth began to unravel in the 60s, exposing the South's continuous efforts to preserve White privilege. Although the former Confederate states promoted equality under the facade of "separate but equal," it was clear that segregation and equality were anything but synonymous.

While Whites enjoyed the privilege of public parks, libraries, and theaters, admittance for Blacks was often denied with signs that read, No Colored People. Public transportation, restrooms, and drinking fountains were almost always segregated by race, available to Blacks on a restricted basis only. If restaurants didn't refuse service altogether, they would make Black people sit in a separate section. Even then, they were encouraged to enter and leave through a back doorway and order from an inferior menu.

Education, the key to a better future, may have been the biggest disadvantage. White schools almost always received more funds for newer buildings, better facilities, and teachers with advanced certifications. College, while largely available to White students, was nothing but a pipe dream for Black students. In the South, public universities had unwritten policies against admitting Blacks, denying their applications regardless of their qualifications.

A monumental turning point in higher education occurred in September of 1962, when the Supreme Court intervened and ruled on behalf of a Black applicant to the University of Mississippi. The nation's highest court ruled the university must allow the enrollment of James Meredith, a Black Air Force veteran who was initially accepted but later denied admittance after the discovery of his race.

When Attorney General Robert Kennedy summoned the Department of Justice to intervene on Meredith's behalf, the school board refused to give in. Unwilling to compromise, Mississippi Governor Ross Barnett officially stepped in to block Meredith's admission. After many failed attempts to reach an agreement, President Kennedy chose to send federal marshals onto the Ole Miss campus to protect and facilitate Meredith's peaceful admission.

As it turned out, peace had nothing to do with the transition. Instead, thousands of White segregationists orchestrated an angry mob that threatened to bomb Meredith's dormitory, lynch him, and replace the American flag with a Confederate one.

After President Kennedy authorized additional military support, the situation was brought under control, but not until a hundred federal agents were wounded and dozens of National Guardsmen injured. After fifteen hours of rioting, the violent mob was finally brought under control, and on October 1, 1962, James Meredith became the first Black person to attend classes at the University of Mississippi.

Later that year, a man by the name of George Wallace won the governorship in Alabama, stating his mission quite clearly in his 1963 inaugural address: "Segregation now, segregation tomorrow, segregation forever."

His first opportunity to act on that pledge occurred in June 1963, when two Black students attempted to break the racial barrier at the University of Alabama. Flanked by state troopers, Governor Wallace made a big show of blocking the entrance to the University of Alabama's enrollment office. Once again, President Kennedy intervened by federalizing National Guard troops and deploying them to clear the path for admission. Although Wallace yielded to the intervention and the University of Alabama was successfully desegregated, the governor clearly stated his commitment to segregation by saying that it would not be dismantled without a fight.

In a few short years, the popularity of George Wallace would grow dramatically, grabbing national attention as a force to be reckoned with. Inspired by broad-based Southern support, Wallace launched his bid for the presidency in 1968 as a third-party candidate. Although his candidacy was considered a long shot against Republican Richard Nixon and Democratic candidate Hubert Humphry, many experts were proven wrong when Wallace successfully captured the electoral votes of five states: Alabama, Mississippi, Georgia, Louisiana, and Arkansas.

As racial struggles continued to make headlines, the early 60s marked the rise of a prominent Black minister from Atlanta by the name of Martin Luther King (MLK). After Rosa Parks, a Black woman, was arrested for refusing to give up her seat to a White person in Montgomery, Alabama, MLK organized a boycott of the entire bus system that lasted 385 days. During the boycott, King was arrested and jailed, and his house was bombed by White segregationists.

After the bombing, MLK drew national attention by speaking from his front porch, where he preached nonviolence and urged his fellow citizens to love their enemies. When the US district court issued a ruling that prohibited racial discrimination on all Montgomery buses, the boycott came to an end. MLK's successful stewardship of nonviolent civil disobedience would catapult him into the national spotlight as a powerful and charismatic leader for civil rights.

In April 1963, MLK, as president of the Southern Christian Leadership Council, organized a series of marches and sit-ins on public properties, attempting to raise awareness of racial discrimination in Birmingham, Alabama. Many of these protests were captured on national television as the Birmingham police department used attack dogs and high-powered water jets to disperse the protesters into submission.

But when the Birmingham campaign resulted in the removal of discriminatory signs and the eventual desegregation of public domains, MLK's reputation continued to grow. As the momentum expanded, MLK's career reached its pinnacle on August 28, 1963, during the March on America in Washington, DC. In front of an estimated two hundred and fifty thousand people, MLK captured the world's attention by delivering his famous "I Have a Dream" speech.

> *"I have a dream that one day this nation will rise up and live out the true meaning of its creed: We hold these truths to be self-evident, that all men are created equal."*

The tide was beginning to turn, and on July 2, 1964, President Johnson signed into law what many consider to be his crowning achievement, the Civil Rights Act of 1964. The act prohibited discrimination based on race, color, religion, sex, or national origin, while strengthening the enforcement of voting rights and the desegregation of schools. Shortly thereafter, on October 14, 1964, MLK, at age thirty-five, became the youngest ever recipient of the Nobel Peace Prize.

Progress was being made, but not without resistance. Although the Civil Rights Act was passed, it barely survived an eighty-three-day filibuster in the Senate and a unanimous rejection from the twenty senators in the ten-state "Southern bloc."

The dominance of the Democratic Party in the South was coming to an end, the result of President Kennedy's fight for equal rights and the perceived betrayal of LBJ, a Southern Democrat who promoted and signed the Civil Rights Act into law. The precedent had been set and there was no turning back. Southerners were abandoning their roots and rejecting the party that had ruled Dixie for the greater half of a century.

Despite the accomplishments of the Civil Rights Act, the inability of Southern Blacks to cast their votes continued to prevail. In 1965, a march from Selma to Montgomery, Alabama was organized to protest the continued use of literacy tests as barriers to Black voters. Led by John Lewis, chairman of the Student Nonviolent Coordinating Committee, the demonstrators were met with brutal resistance as they attempted to cross the Edmund Pettis Bridge.

State Troopers, along with hundreds of deputized civilians, attacked the parade of protesters with billy clubs, as television cameras captured the brutal beatings for all to see. As a result, John Lewis, a future US Congressman, suffered a fractured skull on a day that became immortalized as "Bloody Sunday."

In March of 1968, the city of Memphis, Tennessee, was in the midst of a labor dispute with its Black sanitation workers. Complaining about lower wages and fewer benefits than their White counterparts, the Black workers organized a labor strike against the city. Looking for an opportunity to lobby on behalf of the disgruntled workers, MLK traveled to Memphis to participate in the protest, and on April 3, MLK made his last speech at the Mason Temple, delivering what became known as the "I've been to the mountaintop" speech.

Toward the end of the speech, King refers to threats against his life:

> "We've got some difficult days ahead. But it really doesn't matter with me now, because I've been to the mountaintop. And I don't mind. Like anybody, I would like to live a long life; longevity has its place. But I'm not concerned about that now. I just want to do God's will. And He's allowed me to go up to the mountain. And I've looked over. And I've seen the Promised Land. I may not get there with you. But I want you to know tonight, that we, as a people, will get to the Promised Land. Mine eyes have seen the glory of the coming of the Lord."

Standing outside of his hotel room the next day, MLK was shot in the head by an assassin's bullet. At age thirty-nine, the greatest leader in the history of American civil rights was dead, the victim of another violent murder, dashing the hopes and dreams of an entire race.

Although war, racism, and violence played prominent roles in defining the 60s, society was evolving in many other ways, challenging conventional wisdoms of the past and exploring new possibilities for the future.

Whether it was deserving or not, the decade became synonymous with a new movement that was publicized and sometimes overexposed as the sexual revolution. Often blamed upon the introduction of the birth control pill in 1960, women were allegedly exploring their sexuality more freely and more frequently, uninhibited by the fear of unwanted pregnancies.

In reality, the much-ballyhooed profusion of sexual intercourse may have been exaggerated. The fact is, the distribution of the birth control pill was closely regulated and only available through a doctor's prescription. As a result, most teenagers would not have access to this revolutionary contraceptive without parental consent. And the chance that Mom and Dad would approve of their daughter having sex was about as likely as a priest or minister extending his blessing.

Mainstream society was still deeply embedded with traditional Christian doctrine. Since the pervasive belief was that sex should only occur within the sanctity of marriage, most adolescents received no formal sex education. As far as the Catholic Church was concerned, the Vatican had clearly stated its opposition to any form of unnatural contraception, either within or outside the confines of marriage. Abstinence, by process of elimination, was still the modus operandi. As a result, the perception of an emerging society that was more sexually active was mostly blown out of proportion.

Although clothing styles traditionally change from one generation to the next, the 60s brought about a more daring approach to women's clothing, covering less of their bodies and empowering them with freedom of expression. As skirt lengths became shorter, exposing women's knees for the first time, the miniskirt fad took off and became a cultural icon of the 60s.

Teens no longer wanted to dress like their parents, and the miniskirt was yet another way to rebel against the establishment. The shorter the skirt, the more daring a woman could be as miniskirts turned into microminiskirts, all part of the sexual revolution, or so the headlines read. Fashion magazines promoted the trend as clothing pictorials became more risqué and models posed more provocatively.

Swimwear changed dramatically too, no longer embodying the images of mother and grandmother picnicking at the beach. Instead, bikinis had become the bathing suit of choice as young women continued to challenge the traditional, more prudish values of their mothers. Taking America by storm, the bikini was showing up everywhere, not only in magazines and movies, but in the lyrics of popular songs. After all, who could ever forget the smash hit: "Itsy Bitsy Teenie Weenie Yellow Polka Dot Bikini."

Challenging the Beatles for supremacy, the popularity of the Beach Boys soared as their music promoted free-spirited youth and their proclivity for beach life. Singing about surfer girls, the Beach Boys cashed in on the trend the same way that Hollywood did when they featured former Mouseketeer, Annette Funicello, and Frankie Avalon in the 1965 box-office hit: *Beach Blanket Bingo*.

Perhaps the biggest influencer of the 60s sexual revolution was a magazine that unabashedly flaunted pictorials of nude women. *Playboy*, the brainchild of Hugh Hefner, promoted nudity as an artistic form of expression, giving it a sense of legitimacy when surrounded by quality journalism. In addition to nude centerfolds, the magazine reported on politics, sports, music, and world events. The *Playboy* persona promoted a lifestyle that was for the educated and culturally sophisticated male who appreciated the finer things in life, including beautiful women. By the end of the decade, *Playboy* magazine was one of the most subscribed to periodicals in the US, with a circulation of close to seven million.

Sexual innuendos were much slower to take root in 1960s television. Monitored closely by the Federal Communications Commission (FCC), television writers were conscious of America's conservative values and hesitant to produce segments that would tempt people with impure thoughts. One of the most popular TV shows in the 60s, *The Dick Van Dyke Show*, led no one astray as husband and wife, Rob and Laura Petrie, retired to their bedroom each evening, separated by twin beds.

Cinema, on the other hand, dared to be more provocative, as nudity appeared in mainstream movie scenes like never before. Married couples and lovers routinely appeared in bed together, often performing acts of intimacy that were tastefully displayed for public consumption. The top grossing movie of 1967, *The Graduate*, took things a step further as a sexually frustrated, middle-aged housewife, Mrs. Robinson, aggressively seduced a young college-grad with nudity and perversion.

After *The Graduate*, the boundaries were being challenged more frequently, and in 1968, studio and theater owners agreed to a voluntary ratings system that would give parents the information they needed to decide whether a movie was appropriate for family viewing. The new ratings system used G, M (later PG), R, and X as identifiers to determine suitability by age.

Skimpy clothing, bikinis, nudity in magazines, sex in the cinema, all were symptoms of the 1960s sexual revolution. Nevertheless, many studies and surveys throughout the decade indicated that young people weren't really having any more sex than previous generations. Although that is open to debate, there's little doubt that baby boomers growing up in the 60s had an increased awareness of sexuality and were being tempted like never before.

As Americans became more sexually charged, casting aside their inhibitions and exploiting their libidos, women discovered that they were no longer being judged by their character, personality, or intellectual capacity. Sex appeal had become the number-one criterion, creating the biggest dichotomy of the sexual revolution, that women who were supposed to feel empowered were actually being exploited.

As a result, the sexualization of the 60s only seemed to pigeonhole women deeper into traditional support roles, serving at the pleasure and convenience of their male counterparts. Men, inspired by Hugh Hefner, still controlled the business world, and women were brought into the office as eye candy, primarily employed for their sex appeal.

In reality, a majority of married women in the 60s were housewives and stay-at-home mothers. Even television portrayed these women as apron-wearing homemakers who cooked and cleaned, took care of the children, and made sure that dinner was waiting for their husbands as they walked through the door. Daytime television shows—often called soap operas because they were supported by detergent commercials—

were designed to appeal to these homemakers by advertising a plethora of household products and appliances.

And so the stereotype had been cast. A woman was supposed to stay at home, manage domestic affairs, and be sexy for her husband when he came home from work. As a result, the growing discontent of women who wanted to be treated as equals evolved into a women's liberation movement in the late 60s. Although it was not a large-scale, nationally organized movement with well-attended marches, the momentum was gathering steam. These women no longer wanted to be treated as second-class citizens. Like the civil rights movement, they wanted respect, equal opportunity, and freedom from discrimination.

One of the first high-profile "women's lib" protests occurred at the 1968 Miss America beauty pageant. Robin Morgan, a self-proclaimed feminist who led the "New York Radical Women" society, organized the event to bring awareness to sexual exploitation. Prior to the pageant, Morgan and her associates released a pamphlet entitled "No More Miss America."

Listing the beauty pageant characteristics that degraded women, the pamphlet compared the Miss America runway to a 4-H club fair where animals are paraded around and judged on their bodies, hair, teeth, grooming, and overall appearance. Not unlike a beauty pageant, the fair awards a ribbon to the finest farm animal specimen.

One of the publicity stunts held outside the pageant on the Atlantic City Boardwalk was the creation of a "freedom trash can," where protesters dumped a number of women's beauty-aids, including high heels, makeup, curlers, hairspray, false eyelashes, girdles, and bras.

Inside the pageant hall, a few protesters made their way to the balcony where they unfurled a large banner emblazoned with "Women's Liberation." After thirty seconds of chanting "No more Miss America," the protesters were removed by the police, but not before attracting worldwide attention to the women's liberation movement.

Surrounded by conflict, Americans growing up in the 60s had many landmines to navigate. Sprinkle in a few high-profile assassinations and you have a scarred society, a society trying to heal its wounds and carve out a path toward the future. With so many issues to address, so many wrongs to right, it's no wonder the youth of America were rebelling. And born from this rebellious movement came the labels of counterculture and antiestablishment.

The mission of this new counterculture was to do things differently than their parents. This meant new attitudes, new clothing, new hairstyles, and new music. When the Beatles played their rock 'n' roll style of music on *The Ed Sullivan Show*, millions of screaming fans validated the next wave of rebellion. Teenagers were looking for a more raucous style of music that would energize them and represent their youthful exhilaration. Rock 'n' roll was going mainstream, and along with it came the birth of the mop-top hairstyle.

Striking a chord with young novice musicians, the success of the Beatles launched a new revolution in music. If four commoners from Liverpool, England, could pick up their guitars, form a band, and write and perform their own music, then why couldn't anyone else? Suddenly garage bands were popping up all over the United States and music had reached a whole new level of creativity.

By the midsixties, many musicians were taking up the same causes that dominated the political landscape. More songs were being written with antiwar and antiestablishment messages, challenging the so-called status quo. One of these artists, Bob Dylan, mixed his folk-style music with poetry and symbolism, challenging America to look at the world through a different lens.

As music became more antiestablishment, teenagers began to look at musicians as role models. Longer hair, beards, blue jeans, and T-shirts were all ways to rebel against their well-groomed, clean-cut elders. Rock 'n' roll headliners were setting the fashion trends and exploring their artistic creativity by experimenting with marijuana and psychedelic drugs. As the rebellion became more extreme, the music scene of the 60s took on the label of "Sex, Drugs and Rock 'n' roll." Whether or not that theme was authentic, there was no denying that a whole new subculture of extreme behavior was sweeping the nation.

This new subculture, referred to as hippies, reached its peak in the late 60s. The label came from a derivative of hipster, a term used to describe beatniks—groups of people originating in New York's Greenwich Village and San Francisco's Haight-Ashbury district. Beatniks dressed differently, experimented with drugs, and talked with a unique slang; in essence, walking to the beat of a different drum.

Similar to beatniks, the hippie culture often congregated, separating themselves from regular society by living in communes or traveling to destinations where they would spend their summers together. The men had long hair, beards, and often wore their faded jeans with tie-dye T-shirts and beads around their necks. Women typically wore flowered dresses and sandals, frowning upon high heels and makeup as symbols of a sexist society.

Testing the boundaries of expression, hippies were known to experiment with drugs and engage in free love, or in other words, sex without monogamy. The so-called Flower Power culture believed in peace, love, and freedom of expression, rejecting conventional wisdom and widening the generation gap even further.

As the hippie culture exploded, West Coast college students began migrating to the epicenter of the movement, the Haight-Ashbury district in San Francisco. When the Monterey Pop Festival drew one hundred thousand people in June 1967, with such acts as Jefferson Airplane, Jimmie Hendrix, Janis Joplin, Grateful Dead, and The Who, many of the attendees decided to stay in San Francisco the entire summer. As a result, the Bay area was inundated with hippies from all over the country.

Maybe it was rebellion, or maybe it was the availability of hallucinogenic drugs, or maybe it was the opportunity for free love; regardless the intent, they came in droves. Like never before, the hippie culture was thrown into the national spotlight and the summer of 1967 was forever immortalized as the "Summer of Love."

Later that year, inspired by the Monterey Pop Festival and the Summer of Love, a new publication was launched in San Francisco called *Rolling Stone*. *Rolling Stone*, a biweekly periodical, reported on rock 'n' roll music and the hippie subculture. In addition to its critical reviews on music, cinema, and theater, the magazine became well known for its celebrity interviews and the way it tackled high-profile politics.

Unlike the radical politics of the underground press, *Rolling Stone* embraced traditional journalistic standards and was sold at conventional newsstands. As the circulation continued to grow, the universal acceptance of *Rolling Stone* seemed to legitimize the rock 'n' roll scene by attracting a broader, more diversified group of followers.

In April 1968, the hippie culture reached a whole new audience with the launching of the Broadway musical *Hair* in New York City. Although the play was a sensational hit and ran for four consecutive years, it sparked a whole new wave of controversy. A far cry from traditional Broadway musicals, the multiracial cast featured long-haired hippies using drugs, experimenting with free love, and protesting the Vietnam war. But the passage that sparked the most criticism was the contentious nude scene before the intermission. To conservative mainstream America, there was no valid reason why the entire cast needed to parade around naked before exiting the stage.

In 1969, The 5th Dimension recorded one of the more popular songs from *Hair*: "Aquarius/Let the Sunshine In." It spent six weeks at number one on the Billboard charts and eventually made Billboard's top one hundred list of "Greatest Songs of All Time."

With momentum continuing to build, the pinnacle of the countercultural revolution occurred in August 1969, on a dairy farm in Bethel, NY, about forty miles southwest of Woodstock. Originally billed by its promoters as "three days of peace and music," the Woodstock Rock Festival would feature thirty-two different musical acts performing on an outdoor stage in the middle of a giant field.

Planning for a crowd of fifty thousand, the promoters offered advance ticket sales at New York City area record stores, and by mail through a Radio City post office box. But when ticket sales swelled to over one hundred and eighty thousand, overwhelmed promoters scrambled to accommodate the unprecedented onslaught, failing to deploy adequate fencing and crowd-control measures.

When it was all said and done, an estimated crowd of five hundred thousand arrived from all over the country, more than challenging the limited infrastructure of a small town in a rural farming community. Despite grossly inadequate restroom facilities, limited food, water and medical supplies, the crowds continued to pour in, backing up narrow country roads for dozens of miles.

Most authorities were baffled as to how that many people could endure such horrific conditions, especially after torrential rainstorms soaked them to the bone. Nevertheless, some of the greatest musical acts in the world continued to arrive around the clock via helicopter for three straight days. Somehow the massive crowd was able to tolerate the untold hardships until the bitter end, and the legend of Woodstock grew into a defining moment in the history of rock 'n' roll and hippie folklore.

If Woodstock represented the epitome of the counterculture, it's safe to say the antithesis occurred one month earlier, on July 20, 1969, when the United States successfully landed the first man on the moon. Despite a decade of turmoil and unrest, the country delivered on President Kennedy's 1961 pledge to land a man on the moon before the end of the decade, a crowning achievement for mankind and a tribute to American ingenuity.

It only seemed fitting that the decade would end with two events on opposite ends of the spectrum, the establishment's incredible scientific achievement, and the antiestablishment's devotion to rebellion.

Chapter 1

Brian Johnson had just put the lawnmower away and was going inside to grab some lunch. Now that his assigned chore was complete, he had the rest of the day to himself. Cutting the grass, trimming around the chain-length fence, taking out the trash, picking up after the dog, washing the family car; these were the tasks that earned Brian his weekly three-dollar allowance, a remuneration his father would often neglect to give without his son's reminder.

Brian knew how to complete his chores and he knew when to do them without being asked. After all, they were his responsibility, and you don't neglect your responsibilities without the shame that comes along with being lazy. Oh sure, there were the gentle nudges that kept him on his toes. "Hey, Brian, that lawn's lookin' a little shaggy. It's not gonna get any shorter by itself." He'd grown to expect the parental sarcasm and the fact that his definition of long grass was not the same as his father's.

Brian took off his sweaty shirt and waltzed into the kitchen. "Hey, Mom, got anything good for lunch today?"

"Whatever you can find," was his mother's response. "You know, the usual stuff, bologna and cheese, peanut butter and jelly, potato chips. Suit yourself."

Brian opened the fridge and quickly scanned the shelves as if something special might jump out. There was leftover pot roast from last night's dinner and a bowl of two-day-old egg salad, neither of which he found appealing, so he pushed them aside and grabbed the cheese and mustard to go on his bologna sandwich.

Spotting only two slices left of the individually wrapped Kraft American singles, he peeled back the cellophane and slapped the cheese on a slice of soft white bread he pulled from the loaf of Sunbeam.

Sunbeam or Wonder Bread, his mother would usually buy the one that was the cheapest, but there was a certain affinity toward Sunbeam bread since it was baked in Fort Wayne at the Perfection Bakery on Pearl Street, famously known for the giant billboard with rotating slices of bread that endlessly dropped onto a goliath-sized plate. The tantalizing aroma of fresh-baked bread was irresistible anytime you were within a ten-block radius of the Pearl Street bakery.

Grabbing a giant bag of Seyfert's potato chips, Brian dumped a huge cluster onto his plate and munched away, unabashedly smacking his lips. He would always remember the field trip his class made to the Seyfert's factory back in the fourth grade.

Touring the entire plant, the grade-schoolers marched single file along the elaborate configurations of conveyor belts that transported the potatoes from peeling machines to slicers and ultimately into giant vats of oil, where they would magically turn into crispy potato chips. When the tour was completed, each child was rewarded with a lunch-pail-size bag of chips, all of which were consumed on the bus ride back to school.

Ready to reward himself with desert, Brian went back to the pantry and grabbed both packages of Archway cookies. Recognizing his two favorites, Oatmeal and Windmill, he decided to have one of each. After gulping down his milk and letting out a large belch, it was time to clean up after himself and map out the rest of his day.

Summer days could drag on and bore a teenager to death. How ironic that kids would anxiously anticipate the arrival of summer, only to be rewarded with the monotony of nothing to do.

It was the summer of 1971. Brian, at fourteen years old, would soon be entering the ninth grade, his last year at Jefferson Junior High. His neighborhood, the Coldwater Creek subdivision, consisted of 125 single-family homes constructed on former farmland, all of which were built in the past eight to ten years. It was quintessential middle-class suburbia, a series of cookie-cutter lots aligning streets that ran horizontal and perpendicular to each other.

Described as midcentury modern, the homes of Coldwater Creek represented a phase of architecture that dominated the 50s, clean and simple lines that appeared pristine and homogeneous. Although most of the homes were ranch-style with three bedrooms, two baths, and two-car garages, an occasional two-story or split-level house would separate itself from the pack. And regardless of the design, they all shared one thing in common, exteriors that were wrapped in aluminum siding. Brick was expensive and used sparingly, mostly as a decorative trim to dress-out the front and add curb-appeal, and landscaping was unimaginative, consisting of three or four identical shrubs and an occasional tree.

Except for the incidental senior citizen, most of the home-dwellers were middle-aged parents with two or three children, baby boomers around every corner. Brian was fortunate to have a number of buddies in his age group he could pal around with, some of whom were entering the ninth grade along with him in the fall. And that is exactly what he planned to do for the rest of the day—hang out with his buddies.

Walking back into the kitchen, he found his mother chatting away on the telephone, the only phone in the house. That meant he couldn't call anyone to arrange an impromptu gathering. No problem, he thought, as he put on his Converse All-Stars.

Brian headed out the door and down the street to check in on Scott Clever. Scott lived seven houses down, an easy five-minute walk. If no one answered the doorbell, he'd walk around the corner and see if Bob was home.

There were options, and Brian would explore them thoroughly. Anything was better than sitting around the house and twiddling his thumbs.

Chapter 2

FORT WAYNE IS A MIDSIZED city located in the northeast quadrant of Indiana, the so-called heart of the Midwest. The official 1970 census reported a population of 177,671, the second largest city in Indiana and the seventy-second largest city in the United States. Fort Wayne sits at the confluence of three rivers—the Saint Joseph, Saint Mary's, and Maumee, with the latter flowing northeast to Toledo, Ohio, where it empties into Lake Erie.

The original fort was completed in 1794 under the direction of Revolutionary War General Anthony Wayne. General Wayne was tasked with settling the ongoing disputes between the French, British, and Native Americans, in what was then considered the Northwest frontier. After defeating an army of Native American tribes, the resistance was brought under control and the construction of Fort Wayne established a permanent presence for the US government.

Surrounded by rich farmland and anchored by three rivers, Fort Wayne grew into a major trading post in the 1800s. By 1840, the population had grown to over two thousand when it was officially incorporated as a city, and in 1854, the completion of a railroad line launched a period of rapid growth that transformed the town into a major midwestern industrial center. Fueled by manufacturing jobs, the population grew to over fifty thousand by the turn of the century. Much of the growth was driven by an influx of German and Irish immigrants, as well as African Americans fleeing the South for higher wages.

During that period, the late 1800s, a significant number of churches were constructed that were considered architectural achievements for their time. The Gothic Revival churches and their towering steeples dominated the city skyline for over a century, earning Fort Wayne the title "City of Churches."

In 1897, the city tasked itself with constructing a courthouse that would solidify its standing as an influential leader in government and commerce. Consisting of limestone, granite, and Italian marble, the courthouse, with its massive dome, was completed in 1902 and stands today on the National Register of Historic Places. Almost three decades later, the city would build its first skyscraper, the Lincoln Tower. Standing at twenty-two stories high, the Art Deco building was completed in 1930 and remained the tallest building in Indiana until 1962.

The 1960s represented a period of prosperity in Fort Wayne. With a booming economy, industries were expanding, and citizens were reaping the benefits of good, high-paying jobs. International Harvester, the city's largest employer, boasted that it was the most prolific heavy-duty truck manufacturer in the world. In 1961, the company expanded its product line when it launched the Scout, one of the first mass-produced SUVs in America. During its peak, International Harvester employed over ten thousand people in Fort Wayne, Indiana.

Because of its proximity to Detroit, the epicenter of the auto industry, Fort Wayne became a leading supplier of automobile parts to Detroit's Big Three: Ford, General Motors, and Chrysler. Dana Corporation, another major employer in Fort Wayne, produced drivetrains and transmissions, while Zollner Corporation became one of the largest producers of pistons. The owner, Fred Zollner, carried his passion for business over to sports when he launched the Fort Wayne Zollner Pistons in 1941, a professional basketball team that competed in the National Basketball League. The Pistons captured league championships in 1944 and 1945 before merging with the NBA in 1949 and moving to Detroit in 1957.

Inspired by the creation of the fuel pump, largely credited to Fort Wayne inventor Sylvanus Bowser, the city quickly evolved as the leading pump manufacturer in the world. Gas stations all over the country were utilizing pumps that were manufactured in Fort Wayne by Tokheim and Wayne Pump, two of the city's largest employers. Other major employers included General Electric, Phelps Dodge, and Magnavox, a major defense contractor.

Although industry produced the bulk of the city's jobs, another large employer emerged as Lincoln National Life grew into one of the largest life insurance companies in the United States. Anchoring a two-block area in downtown, the office building's plaza features a twelve-foot bronze statue of a youthful Abe Lincoln sitting with his dog on a tree stump, a vivid reminder that America's sixteenth president spent the bulk of his youth in Indiana.

When a city thrives like Fort Wayne did in the 1960s, its residents can bask in the fruits of their accomplishments. This meant an abundance of theaters, restaurants, department stores, and a nationally recognized zoo. And when the Memorial Coliseum was constructed, the city had its very own state-of-the-art venue for concerts, trade shows, and professional sports, serving as home ice for the Fort Wayne Komets of the International Hockey League.

Although its citizens took their city for granted, Fort Wayne had blossomed into a prototype for middle-class living, representing mainstream USA and a lifestyle as American as apple pie. Whenever corporations introduced new ideas or launched new products, Fort Wayne would usually surface as a likely test-market. If the people of this all-American city embraced the idea, there was a good chance the product would experience widespread acceptance and popularity.

Although economic prosperity can be a soothing anecdote for social problems, Fort Wayne was not immune to the emerging issues that were gripping the nation. Like the rest of the country, they were sending boys off to Vietnam, fighting for equal rights, battling with employers for higher wages, and rebelling against the establishment. Baby boomers were growing longer hair, protesting the war, attending rock concerts, experimenting with drugs, and reading *Rolling Stone* magazine. Fort Wayne, in many ways, was a microcosm of the United States.

Chapter 3

SCOTT CLEVER WAS IN HIS garage tinkering with his Schwinn ten-speed bicycle. At five feet, nine inches, Scott was about average height for a fourteen-year-old, but his long legs were disproportionate to the rest of his body. One look at him and you knew he was on the verge of a big growth spurt. His father, at six feet, three inches, played high school basketball for the North Side Redskins in the late 1940s. Affectionately referred to as Big Red, Robert Clever had reddish-orange hair and a magnetic personality that suited him well as sales manager at the local Oldsmobile dealership.

With few basketball scholarships handed out in the 40s, Robert Clever solicited an opportunity to try out for the Zollner Pistons. It didn't last long. Although he was a dominant player in high school, he wasn't considered to be a sharpshooter, and he wasn't tall enough to compete against the big forwards in the National Basketball League. With no money for college, Robert Clever knew his basketball career was over. Being somewhat of a local celebrity in basketball crazy Indiana, his preordained success in car sales allowed him to stay active in the community and provide well for his family.

Scott had features similar to his father, although his gangly frame made his shoulders look narrow, not nearly as brawny as his dad, and his hair was more strawberry blond than orange. Being somewhat of a jock, Scott was more concerned about sports and being cool than he was about academics. Like many boys in the neighborhood, Scott had a basketball goal set up on his driveway and could be seen launching hundreds of shots on the days he wasn't hanging out with his buddies.

When the neighborhood boys were younger, they often filled their summer days with an abundance of time-wasting activities. Nothing could kill a couple of hours like opening up the cabinet in the garage and sorting through the stockpile of board games: Monopoly, Life, Stratego, Trouble, Operation, Yahtzee, Mouse Trap, etc. If the boys were looking for some more lively action, Scott would reach under his bed and pull out his hockey board, a game where he and Brian had mastered the art of pulling, pushing, and twisting long rods that controlled the players and how well they passed the puck.

With the exception of little league baseball, there were very few organized youth sports in those days. For the Coldwater Creek boys, this was not a problem. If they weren't playing basketball on the driveway, the boys were putting together a backyard game of football, soccer, dodgeball, or kickball. When a backyard wouldn't do, they could be seen hauling their bats and gloves to the nearest vacant lot where they would carve out a makeshift baseball diamond.

As the buildout of Coldwater Creek grew closer to completion, vacant lots became scarcer, which meant the boys had to abandon baseball and settle for backyard wiffle ball. Needless to say, neighborhood parents were less than enamored with the idea of baseballs bouncing off roofs, through windows or banging against aluminum siding where dents would become lasting reminders of unsupervised horseplay.

After reaching puberty, fourteen-year-old boys no longer spent their summers playing pickup games or sorting through baseball cards. Instead, they were more likely to hang out on their driveways and play it cool by shooting the breeze about cars, girls, and music. If someone had purchased the latest *Three Dog Night* album, they could kill a whole afternoon by gathering around a record player and debating the merits of pop music versus the psychedelic rock of English bands like Pink Floyd.

"Hey, what's happenin'?" asked Brian as he walked up Scott's driveway. "Takin' your bike for a spin?"

"Well, I was thinking about it," said Scott. "There's nothin' else going on around here. Got any other ideas?"

"Not really," came the reply. "Is your brother at work?"

"Yep, still workin' second shift. Usually gets home around midnight."

"How about sneakin' into his room and playin' his stereo or messin' around with his guitar?" suggested Brian.

"I guess we could," said Scott. "Mom ran over to Maloley's to grab some groceries, so no one's around."

Scott's brother, Dave, was twenty years old and still living at home. Always a bit of a rebel, he wasn't much for school and didn't inherit his father's athletic prowess. He played a little basketball in junior high but wasn't good enough to make the high school team. With features favoring his mother, Dave Clever had long brown hair and a beard. The boys rarely saw him, but when they did, he was usually lollygagging around in faded bell-bottom jeans and moccasins. He somehow earned a diploma but didn't have any plans beyond high school. His parents told him he could live at home as long as he got a job, saved some money, and enrolled at the local college.

When Dave Clever was in the sixth grade, his parents bought him an electric guitar for Christmas. He briefly took lessons but didn't have the mental fortitude it takes to practice and become an accomplished player. He only played because he liked to listen to music and thought it would be cool to be in a rock band. After a few years, he became fairly proficient at playing chords and basic riffs, the kind of simple backup rhythms a bass player can dole out when accompanying a lead guitar.

As a result, Dave made his way into a couple of garage bands, but they were never good enough to play at parties or dances. Most of the time their practice sessions would break down into smoke sessions, distinguished by the unmistakable scent of herbal weed. They said it stimulated their creative juices, but most of the time it just made them lazy.

Dave Clever's reputation grew to legendary status in the neighborhood when he disappeared for a whole week the summer after his graduation. When he returned, he was filled with stories about Woodstock, free love, psychedelic drugs, and the greatest rock bands in the world. He talked about a new revolution, and how it was alive and well, and how they were all going to change the world. Soon after, his parents laid the ground rules on what was required to remain living at home.

Entering the Clever house through the garage door, the boys assertively made their way to Dave's bedroom, approaching his inner sanctum as if it were a temple. Once inside, Brian went right to the stack of *Rolling Stone* magazines and grabbed the latest issue.

"All right, Elton John's on the cover. Okay if I look at this?"

"Sure, I doubt if he even reads them," said Scott. "He just thinks it looks cool to have them laying around."

Brian's eyes scanned the room, looking for any updates since his last visit. It didn't take long for him to realize that nothing had changed. But then again, why would he mess with perfection? He still had the large Beatles poster from the *Let it Be* album hanging above his bed, and on the opposite wall, he proudly displayed a giant tie-dyed sheet, the one he brought back from Woodstock, emblazoned with a peace sign. But to Brian, the coolest feature was the lava lamp—a token from Spencer Gifts—and the way the colors faded in and out, producing a psychedelic vibe that could only be described as groovy.

But the holy grail of the room was his stereo system, a true hi-fi goldmine that featured a Marantz receiver, Garrard turntable, and four large JBL speakers. To Brian, nothing could replace the magic of pulling a vinyl disk out of its album cover, placing it onto the turntable, easing down the stylus and waiting for the crackling static to convert to music, instantly transforming the room into a vibrant concert venue.

With a speaker in each corner of the room, the boys would sit in the middle and absorb the reverberating notes like onstage sound technicians. Accustomed to dual-speaker stereo systems, the boys were familiar with two-channel separation, which meant detecting sounds in the left speaker that were distinctly different from the right. But 1971 was the first year that recordings were released in quadraphonic sound, or four-channel separation. With quadraphonic albums, unique sounds were produced in each of the four speakers. Although Dave's bedroom contained over a hundred albums, only a couple of his records were actually recorded with quadraphonics.

"So what do you wanna listen to?" asked Scott. "Pick one out and we can really crank it up before my mom gets home."

After flipping through the stacks of albums, Brian handed over *LA Woman* by the Doors.

"Again?" questioned Scott. "They play this stuff on the radio all the time. How many times can you listen to *Love Her Madly* and *Riders on the Storm* before you're sick of it?"

"Hey, cool it," said Brian with a grin. "Sometimes you just gotta go with the flow. Besides, they don't play *LA Woman* on the radio."

Brian knew that listening to the eight-minute album cut of *LA Woman* on a great stereo system was a guilty pleasure that far exceeded any music on the radio. Leaning back on his beanbag chair with hands behind his head, he soaked it all in.

"You think if I grow my hair as long as Jim Morrison, all the chicks will dig me too?"

"I think you're dreaming again," said Scott. "Besides, it don't matter how long your hair is if you ain't got that funk. With you, it's more like, what you see is what you get."

"Take it easy, man," said Brian with a grin. "You know I have good vibes."

As soon as the music kicked in, the banter came to a halt. With glazed-over eyes, the boys entered into an altered state of consciousness, their brains taken hostage by the intoxicating rhythm of keyboards and bluesy guitars. Brian looked over at Scott and nodded his head in affirmation, confirming the greatness of the Doors.

Two weeks later, Jim Morrison would die of a drug overdose.

Chapter 4

LYNDA LACEY, TWO DOORS DOWN from Scott Clever, lived in one of the few split-level houses in Coldwater Creek. Sitting on a perfectly manicured lawn, the Lacey house stood out from the rest of the homes. The family room, or lower level, was used for hosting evening gatherings around the RCA console television. Three steps up from the family room, the elevated level contained a living room, kitchen, and formal dining area. To the neighborhood kids, the split-level concept was cutting edge, much trendier than the two-story boxes and rectangular-shaped ranch-style homes.

Lynda, with silky blonde hair and blue eyes, was both cute and pretty at the same time. Outgoing and charming, her infectious personality put her at the forefront of the social scene. Although she ran with the popular crowd, Lynda had the unique ability to exhibit confidence without appearing arrogant, a trait that enabled her to blend into most any setting.

As an only child, Lynda received plenty of attention from her stay-at-home mom, who kept her fully engaged by chauffeuring her from one event to the next. It started at the age of seven when Lynda joined the Girl Scouts and continued as she advanced her status from Brownie to Cadette, dutifully fulfilling her obligations along the way. In between, there were piano lessons, choir practices, and Sunday performances at the Lutheran church. By the time she reached the fifth grade, Lynda's mother started her with lessons in both clarinet and dance, preparing her for junior high band and cheerleading. Entering her last year at

Jefferson Junior High, Lynda Lacey was the irrefutable sweetheart of the freshman class.

Sitting on her patio on a sunny afternoon, Lynda was hanging out with her neighborhood friend, Nancy Garber. With hazel eyes and dishwater blond hair, Nancy looked plain in comparison to Lynda, lacking the kind of femininity that turned boys' heads. Coming from a family of Mennonites, she was self-conscious and timid around others, hesitant to participate in any fad that might violate her strict upbringing. Although the Garbers were not part of the ultraconservative sect, Nancy's mother made sure her clothes were plain and loose-fitting, creating the drab wardrobe herself on an old sewing machine.

Relaxing on her chaise lounge, Lynda was wearing a pair of white shorts with a spaghetti-strap top. Nancy, standing behind her, was rubbing Coppertone lotion on her neck and shoulders.

"What's this stuff supposed to do, anyway?" asked Nancy.

"It gives you a deeper, darker tan."

"You think it really works?"

"I hope so. Haven't you seen the billboards where the dog is tugging on the girl's bikini bottoms? It clearly shows the contrast between her pale bottom and her perfectly bronzed back."

"Yes, I've seen them," said Nancy with an embarrassed grin. "My mother says they're inappropriate, but I think they're kinda funny. Anyway, I don't wear bikinis and I don't get out in the sun very much. As you've probably noticed."

"Yeah, I wish we lived near a beach," said Lynda. "And since we don't have a swimming pool nearby, there's not much of a reason to buy a bikini."

"I remember when we used to run through the sprinklers," said Nancy.

"Me too," said Lynda. "And when my mother would put out that pink inflatable pool and supervise us while we splashed around. That seems like a lifetime ago."

"Yesterday, I saw Jackie lying out in her white bikini," said Nancy, referring to one of the high school girls in the neighborhood.

"Yeah, and Jeannie and Beth are always sunbathing too," acknowledged Lynda. "I think they just do it hoping the boys will walk by and see them. Anything to get a little attention."

"Well, I wouldn't want any boy to see my body in a bikini," blushed Nancy.

"Yeah, me either," said Lynda. "But my mom said I can start wearing makeup this year. Afterall, we're gonna be ninth graders."

"What kind of makeup?" asked Nancy.

"She said I could try some lipstick, but only if it's not too bright. And maybe some blush. But she's not big on eye shadow, so that isn't gonna happen."

"Well, none of that is gonna happen for me," said Nancy. "You know how my family is about that stuff."

"No big deal," said Lynda. "Hey, let me run inside real quick and grab some nail polish. I think I'm gonna do my nails. Why don't you find something good on the radio and I'll be right back."

Lynda jumped up and opened the sliding patio door as Nancy fiddled with the radio. When she returned, Lynda was holding three different shades of nail polish and the latest *Tiger Beat* magazine.

"What's your mother doing?" asked Nancy.

"Right now, she's baking a cake and watching one of her soap operas."

"Which one?"

"I don't know," frowned Lynda. "She usually watches *All My Children* or *Days of Our Lives*. I couldn't care less. It's all boring to me. Just a bunch of old people with lots of problems."

Nancy giggled and grabbed the *Tiger Beat* magazine. "Bobby Sherman again?"

"Don't you think he's cute?" said Lynda. "I loved him on *Here Come the Brides*. I think he's adorable."

"Nah," grunted Nancy. "He doesn't do anything for me."

"Oh c'mon," said Lynda. "What if he was singing directly to you?"

Oh, oh, Nancy, Nancy, Nancy, do ya love me?

"Very funny," she giggled. "I think I'd rather have *you* sing it to me. You're more entertaining."

Interrupted by a blast of loud music, Nancy paused to listen. "Where's that noise coming from?"

"It's probably Scott Clever. Whenever he's home alone, he starts playin' his brother's stereo as loud as he can. I don't really mind, but I probably would if I lived next door."

"Here's a good one," said Nancy, as she turned up the radio volume to Carole King's number-one hit, "It's Too Late."

"They've been playin' that song over and over again all summer long," said Lynda. "Her *Tapestry* album is gonna be the biggest selling album of all time."

"Yeah, I'd like to hear the whole album sometime," said Nancy.

Grabbing her Cutex nail polish, Lynda brushed her toenails with the soft pink paint and rubbed some more Coppertone tanning lotion on her legs. "I'm ready for school to begin," she said. "This has been a long, boring summer."

Chapter 5

A T FIVE O'CLOCK ON A Tuesday morning, the digital alarm clock delivered its electronic pulses with a methodical rhythm. Outside, it was cool and damp, dew on the grass and pink skies to the east. Even though the sun wouldn't officially rise until 5:12 a.m., it was starting to get light. Indiana was one of the few remaining states that did not honor Daylight Savings Time, making it easier to roll out of bed early in the morning, but annoyingly bright for those wishing to sleep in. For Bob Wills, sleeping in was never an option. He had been managing the morning paper route for the past four years, ever since he turned ten.

Feeling numb with grogginess, Bob stumbled to the bathroom and splashed some cold water on his face. After slipping on his sweatshirt, he headed to the garage to put on his tennis shoes and Detroit Tigers baseball cap, a hat that did little to disguise the mussiness of his long, shaggy hair.

Grabbing his Sting-Ray bicycle customized with a large wire basket, Bob made his way to the end of the driveway where a stack of fresh newsprint was waiting. Before he could begin his deliveries, he needed to piece together the sections, fold them into rolls, and secure them with rubber bands, a task he could normally complete by five thirty. Not bad for a hundred newspapers.

Although Bob had ninety-six homes on his delivery route, four spares were provided as a margin for error. Since nearly every house in

Coldwater Creek subscribed to *The Journal Gazette*, he only needed to remember the houses to skip.

The Wills family was proud of their working-class heritage, keeping their noses to the grindstone and never complaining or feeling sorry for themselves. Since both of Bob's parents needed to work to provide for their middle-class standard of living, their schedules could be very hectic.

Eddie Wills worked the first shift as a foreman on the production line at Dana Corp, working five eight-hour days, from eight to five. Those were good hours, allowing him to be at home in the evening to look after Bob. That was important, considering his wife, Martha, worked evenings at the neighborhood Pizza Hut. Starting out as a waitress, she eventually worked her way into the kitchen before rising up to assistant manager. Except for Sundays, it was extremely rare for all three of them to be home together.

Bob's older brother, Danny, had been gone for over a year, drafted into the army right out of high school. Watching their beloved son ship off to Vietnam was like a bad dream for Mr. and Mrs. Wills. The thought of him fending for himself in a world he knew nothing about kept them awake at nights, fearful for the worst. But they would persevere, using prayers and letters as a coping mechanism, and trusting that their correspondence would somehow get delivered in the vast jungles of Southeast Asia.

Unlike his brother, Bob was not blessed with good looks. With sandy-brown hair, sallow skin and rings under his eyes, Bob always appeared tired. Like a crooked old man, his scrawny frame made him appear brittle, incapable of wielding any brawn.

Since both of his parents smoked, Bob's clothes always reeked of stale cigarettes. It was the nicotine that kept them going, they said. Some people drank coffee; they smoked cigarettes.

The neighborhood boys liked to joke about Mr. Wills and his evening ritual of sitting on the front porch, cracking open a cold beer, and lighting up his last cigarette of the day. "There goes another Falstaff," they would say, referencing Eddie's affinity to the local beer that was produced at the old Berghoff Brewery on Grant Avenue.

Chapter 6

MIDSUMMER EVENINGS IN INDIANA ARE fairly predictable, with warm and humid conditions prevailing until the wee hours of the morning. On this particular evening, the air was heavy and still, not even the slightest breeze to relieve the stickiness.

Strolling through the neighborhood, Bob Wills and Scott Clever heard the faint sound of music coming from a lighted garage. Approaching curiously, they detected the sound of iron clanking against cement, along with a series of low-pitched grunts and groans.

It didn't take long to determine that Brian Johnson was back into his summer routine of pumping iron. Brian played halfback for the Jefferson Patriots eighth-grade football team and was serious about preparing for the upcoming season, his last chance to make an impression before entering the competitive world of high school sports. Spotting Brian on the bench press was his neighborhood buddy and teammate, Mark Carter.

Standing a solid six feet tall, Mark sported a large mop of curly brown hair. At first glance, he appeared rugged and burly, but a closer examination revealed a smooth, unblemished complexion that softened his appearance. Clearly, his boyish face had never touched a razor. But beneath the fair skin and baby blue eyes was a sturdy skeletal structure that contributed to his natural brute strength.

Mark didn't follow sports very much and wasn't considered a jock, but playing football was a macho thing that seemed to be in his wheelhouse. He was more interested in the great outdoors, which meant camping, hunting, and fishing. His father, a captain in the Fort Wayne Police Department, had taught him the importance of survival skills at an early age. After devoting most of his youth to scouting, Mark was well on his way to achieving his Eagle Scout badge, a title his father expected him to earn.

Walking up the driveway, Scott Clever initiated the banter. "Well, well, it looks like muscle beach is officially open."

"Spoken like a skinny basketball player," rebutted Mark. "Maybe if you lifted something heavier than a Hostess Cupcake, you might get rid of those toothpicks you call arms."

Scott grinned with appreciation, reassuring everyone that a little spirited heckling was all well and good.

"You should put a mirror in your garage," continued Scott. "Then you could flex your muscles and pose in front of it with your glistening skin."

Bob Wills had to chuckle at that remark. Even though he was mostly serious, he still enjoyed the camaraderie of hanging out with the guys.

"How often are you boys doing this?" he asked.

Staying on cue, Brian explained the regimen. "Weightlifting on Mondays, Wednesdays, and Fridays; endurance running on Tuesdays and Saturdays; wind sprints on Thursdays. Sunday is my day off."

"Well, that's pretty lazy," quipped Scott.

"Gotta put on five pounds of muscle," Brian continued. "I need to be stronger and faster. Who knows what the competition will look like this year. I can't sit back and rest on my laurels."

Suddenly the tone had turned more serious. It was clear that Brian was referencing the inevitable change that would take place when school resumed in the fall.

Under growing pressure to end racial segregation, the Fort Wayne Community Schools (FWCS) had closed some of the older, inner-city schools with plans to bus those students to newer schools in the suburbs. Beginning with the fall semester, Jefferson Junior High would transition from 0 percent Black enrollment to 15 percent.

Except for the impact on football and basketball, the boys had few concerns, but that was not the case with their parents. It was no secret that desegregation was a controversial topic that stirred up many strong emotions.

"I guess I should get off my lazy butt and start working out," said Scott. "I'm afraid that shootin' a few hoops on my driveway ain't gonna compete with the brothers playin' pickup games at Reservoir Park. I hope we can add some good players, but I don't want my ass ridin' the pine."

"Yeah, my feelings exactly," said Brian. "I look at the NFL and most of the really good running backs are Black. I'm all for a little competition, anything that will make us better, but I don't want to lose my starting job."

"C'mon man," retorted Mark. "You guys sound like a bunch of pussies. They put their pants on the same way you do. If you're scared of a little competition, then you're already defeated."

"I don't think it's about being scared. It's more about being prepared," said Brian.

"Well, my dad's pissed off about the whole thing," said Mark. "He says he spends ninety percent of his time arresting these dudes and dealing with their shenanigans, and now they're invading our schools. He says there's a reason why he moved to the suburbs and pays higher taxes, all to make a better life for us. But now there's no boundaries."

"I don't think there should be any boundaries," said Brian. "I mean, this is America, right? Why should I care if they come to our school?"

"They're not coming because they want to," said Mark. "Just ask them. They're being forced to come and mix in with our people; it's not what they want."

Trying to dial it down a notch, Scott interjected. "Your arguing isn't gonna make any difference. Meanwhile your muscles are shrinking."

"Always the smartass," railed Mark.

"He's right," said Brian. "We need to work in a few more sets before we're done."

Scott walked over to the radio and fiddled with the dial. "Maybe you need to play some music that will fire you up a bit."

Pausing at WLYV, he turned up the volume to listen to Marvin Gaye's *What's Going On.*

"Wait—stop," said Brian. "I like Marvin Gaye."

"Holy shit," chimed in Mark. "Now we gotta listen to their music too?"

"You just need to boogie on down the road." Scott laughed.

Chapter 7

ALTHOUGH RACIAL EQUALITY HAD CLEARED some major hurdles in the 60s, Blacks and Whites were not competing on a level playing field when it came to education. Despite the Supreme Court ruling (*Brown v. Board of Education of Topeka*) declaring that segregation in public schools was unconstitutional, widespread disparities in the quality of education continued to exist. No longer able to enforce statutory segregation, the default for many school districts became de facto segregation, meaning a natural occurrence that results from socioeconomic differences.

While African American families were migrating to the North to escape the hardships of the past, they soon discovered that discrimination was not unique to the South. Achieved in more subtle ways, discriminatory practices in the North were more difficult to prove or challenge in a court of law.

The availability of housing, for example, was often restricted, predicated on discriminatory lending practices and the unavailability of insurance policies for minorities. Realtors would often restrict the sale of properties by excluding buyers who were considered undesirable to a community. These practices, referred to as redlining, were largely successful in suppressing the mobility of Black families. In essence, the White majority had created a system of restraining Blacks to neighborhoods that were aging and less desirable.

As Black families moved into the older, more affordable inner-city homes, White people were flocking to the suburbs. This migration to the suburbs required new homes, new infrastructure, and new schools. Once established, the suburban neighborhoods were considered a safe haven from urban blight, largely impenetrable to inner-city African Americans. This meant that inner-city schools were primarily Black, and suburban schools were mostly White; segregation not by design, but the result of demographic evolution.

In the late 60s, Charlotte, North Carolina, became the focal point of de facto school segregation when the Mecklenburg Board of Education was sued over racially imbalanced enrollments. As a result, US District Judge James McMillian heard the case and ruled the school district must pursue all possible means to achieve integration, including mandatory busing.

The school board, along with many parents, expressed their disdain for the ruling and appealed to the Supreme Court, but the Supreme Court eventually upheld Judge McMillian's ruling and ordered the Charlotte-Mecklenburg Schools to submit an integration plan for the 1969 to 1970 school year. When an outside consultant created a plan that included compulsory busing of both Black and White students, the court approved the measures, marking the first time in US history that a school system was ordered to implement mandatory busing in order to achieve racial integration.

Fort Wayne, Indiana, served as a classic example of de facto segregation. It's first high school, Central, opened in 1864. By 1921, Central High School's enrollment grew to over fifteen hundred and could no longer meet the needs of a burgeoning population. With the addition of South Side High School in 1922 and North Side in 1927, the Fort Wayne Community School system was positioned to accommodate another forty years of growth. But the evolving exodus of people from the inner-city to suburbia resulted in a shrinking enrollment at Central High School in the 60s. By 1968, the enrollment at Central had dropped to a meager 927 students, mostly African American.

As school desegregation made headlines across America, the FWCS began to realize the inadequacy of a school building that was over one hundred years old and largely segregated from the rest of Fort Wayne. Adding to the mounting pressure, the Black community had become more vocal, raising its concerns over aging facilities that were vastly inferior to suburban schools.

The heat was on, and the school board needed to act, but not without due diligence. After numerous studies and countless meetings, they finally announced their decision. The FWCS would build two new high schools, Wayne to the south and Northrop to the north, making them available for enrollment in 1971, the same year that Central High School would close its doors forever.

The decision had been made, but the execution would be complicated and controversial. Desegregation could not be achieved without a complex rezoning plan, one that enabled the redistribution of inner-city students to suburban schools in a manner that was both fair and equitable.

Despite their best efforts, the school board's plans were met with opposition from both Black and White parents. Rezoning would mean that urban students who previously walked or made short drives to school, would soon be faced with long bus rides, resulting in commutes that could last up to forty-five minutes. The commuting issue would be especially burdensome to students who participated in sports and other extracurricular activities.

How would these students get rides home from school when the buses were no longer running? How would they adjust to a whole new culture and compete in an environment that was completely foreign to them? How would they get a fair shake in schools that were dominated by students and educators who were mostly White and more affluent? The questions and concerns were considerable, and tensions continued to rise.

Suburban White parents had their own list of concerns—concerns that increasingly turned to trepidation. Although their children wouldn't be bused to far away schools, they now feared for their safety. Suddenly they were exposing their children to the very dangers they had sought to escape, the menacing element of inner-city youth and the high rates of crime and violence they represented. Protecting their children was now a priority, creating a sense of anxiety that never existed before.

But the lines had been drawn and there was no turning back. Fort Wayne was boldly moving forward, and the opening act would be fall semester of 1971. With so many uncertainties, the outcome was impossible to predict. But one thing was for sure, the stage had been set, and the students and teachers would be the experimental guinea pigs.

Chapter 8

I T WAS SEPTEMBER 3, THE Friday before Labor Day. Recognized as a federal holiday since 1882, Labor Day was largely spearheaded by labor unions as a day to honor the hard-working people who represented the backbone of this great nation. Rewarded as a day of rest and relaxation, it served up a valuable opportunity to spend time with family and friends.

In Coldwater Creek, Labor Day was typically celebrated with backyard picnics, badminton, lawn darts, tubs of ice-cold beer, and hamburgers on charcoal grills. For students, it marked the unofficial end of summer. Classes would resume on Tuesday, signifying the beginning of a new school year, a year that promised many changes at Jefferson Junior High.

Just past 10:00 a.m., Bob Wills made his way toward the TV to waste some time. He had finished his morning paper route hours ago and was done cleaning up the kitchen, a task his mother required when he was done with his bacon and eggs. The worst part was cleaning up the bacon grease that splattered all over the stovetop, but Bob knew that midmorning brunch was a luxury he could no longer afford once school started, meaning cleanup duty was a minor inconvenience. Once classes began, he would barely have time to wolf down a bowl of Frosted Flakes or Fruit Loops in between his paper route and the arrival of the school bus.

Turning the TV dial, he clicked his way through three channels, clunk-clunk-clunk, landing on ABC. Monty Hall was interviewing a crazy lady dressed up like *Little Red Riding Hood*. He handed her a hundred-dollar bill and asked, "Do you want to keep the hundred dollars for yourself, or trade it for what's behind the display case where the lovely Carol Merrill is standing?" Bob was sucked in and sat down to watch his favorite game show, *Let's Make a Deal*.

His mother was in the middle of her normal routine, running the vacuum, dusting, doing the laundry, and hanging it out to dry on the backyard clothesline. There would be no rest and relaxation for her. Labor Day weekend was always extra busy at Pizza Hut. Today's goal was to have the house in ship-shape order before leaving at three o'clock for her evening shift. Hustling around from task to task with a Virginia Slim cigarette in her hand, Martha scribbled down a note for Eddie, her husband, something he could quickly read when he got home from work. She liked to leave a few meal suggestions for her family. It was the least she could do to compensate for her absence.

"Bob," called Mrs. Wills. "Did you hear that? The doorbell just rang. Can you answer the door?"

Bob strolled casually to the front door, thinking it could be Scott, or Brian, or any of his buddies. Afterall, it was the last day of summer. Opening the door, Bob was surprised to see two military men, standing at attention, impeccably dressed in their formal regalia.

"Good morning, is this the Wills household?" asked the soldier on the right.

"Yes, it is...sir," responded Bob, thinking he should address them with respect.

"Is your mother home? Mrs. Martha Wills?"

"Yes, I'll go get her."

Bob left them standing on the porch with the door wide open. As he walked away, he wondered if he should have invited them in, not knowing the protocol. Heading toward the kitchen, his mother had just rounded the corner. "Mom, there's someone here to see you."

Before she could reply, she looked up and saw the two soldiers standing at the door. Her heart sank to her stomach, a million thoughts racing through her brain.

Somehow, she managed to walk toward the door, her knees weak and shaky. Feeling an almost out-of-body sensation, she dropped her cigarette in an ashtray and tried to steady her quivering lip. "Can I help you gentlemen?"

"Mam, I am Corporal Adam Downing, and this is Private First Class Benjamin Stewart. May we come in?"

Martha backed away from the door without saying a word. The soldiers took the gesture as an acceptance of their request. "Please sit down, Mrs. Wills."

Martha slowly lowered herself onto the living room sofa, her hands trembling. "Is this what I think it is?"

Corporal Downing continued, "Mrs. Wills, can you ask your son to give us a moment alone?"

Martha nodded her head at Bob to leave the room as his nervous expression turned to indignation. He couldn't believe they had the gall to exclude him from his very own living room. He was about to object until he saw the tears trickling down his mother's cheeks. Now was not the time to make a scene. Quietly slipping around the corner, Bob continued to glare at the soldiers.

Corporal Downing placed his hand on Martha's wrist, gently squeezing it, "Mrs. Wills, the Secretary of the Army has requested us to inform you of the unfortunate passing of your son, Private Daniel Wills. He lost his life while serving his country. He was a true Patriot."

Mrs. Wills felt her body cave in. Slumping down, she put her face into the sofa pillow, the tears flowing profusely. She didn't know what to say. There was nothing anyone could say or do now. It all seemed so pointless. In a split-second, her whole life had changed.

The soldiers remained silent, allowing her to weep. It was never easy.

"What happened?" she muttered softly, continuing to sob. "He only had six weeks left on his tour of duty. How could you let this happen?"

Corporal Downing kept it professional and polite by staying on script. "My report tells me that Private Wills was on a mission with his company to flush out some Viet Kong. Unfortunately, he stepped on a land mine while serving his mission. His commanding officer immediately summoned for medical assistance and he was flown to the nearest surgical hospital. Unfortunately, he lost too much blood and could not be saved."

Private First Class Stewart finally spoke, "Can I get you some Kleenex, ma'am? I'm so sorry for your loss."

"My sweet, sweet Danny," she mumbled. "He had no business being over there. He was just a boy."

Her body began to tremble as she sobbed uncontrollably. "He was my firstborn. And for what? To be sacrificed in your stupid war like a piece of meat."

Her voice firmed up as the anger kicked in. "He didn't have a choice, you know. Why would he care about some stupid little country on the other side of the globe? Now he's gone, and for what? He had his whole life ahead of him."

There was no response. The soldiers sat still as they allowed her to vent. That was her right. They would not rob her of her liberty.

Perceiving their indifference, Martha grabbed a sofa pillow and heaved it across the room, knocking over a lamp. She stood up quickly in an act of defiance but collapsed back down to the sofa with a head-rush of dizziness. Sobbing once again, she began to grind her fingers through her hair, tugging at the follicles as though she might rip them from her scalp.

Abruptly entering the room, Bob addressed the soldiers, "I think you should go now. Your work is done here."

The soldiers had witnessed many different reactions when performing this most dreaded of duties. They did not want to appear cold-hearted, but they needed to keep it professional. Deviation from protocol was not an option.

"Within the next twenty-four hours, you will be contacted by a survivor assistance officer," the corporal continued. "He will help you with all the necessary arrangements, including any personal problems you may experience. He will also assist you in notifying the next of kin. Your son's remains will be honorably delivered within seventy-two hours."

The soldiers stood up and headed toward the exit. As the door opened, they both turned around. Corporal Downing spoke in his most sympathetic tone.

"Mrs. Wills, I am deeply sorry for your loss. Private Wills was a brave man. He served his country with honor and dignity. You should be very proud."

And with that they were gone.

Chapter 9

BOB WALKED TO THE FRONT window and watched the soldiers drive away in their black sedan. He didn't know what to say or do; his body felt numb. He decided to go into the kitchen and grab a box of Kleenex. Sitting next to his mother on the sofa, he took her hands and pulled them from her hair. As her hysteria subsided, she fumbled through the tissues. Bob grabbed a waste basket and sat it by her side.

"What am I gonna do?" she whispered. "How do I continue from here?"

Bob wrapped his arms around her, and she hugged him like she would never let go. Feeling overwhelmed with pity, Bob could no longer hold it in as the tears streamed down his cheeks. He couldn't remember the last time he had cried, not since he was a little boy.

"Should we call Dad?"

"No, we need to wait until he gets home. I don't want him to find out with a phone call."

Regaining her composure, she said, "I need to call in to work and tell them I can't come in today."

Then suddenly, with a look of determination, she added, "Maybe I should go in. Maybe it would keep my mind occupied. What good is it for me to sit around here crying all day? I still have to take care of my family."

And then with a distant stare, she whispered, "At least what's left of my family."

"You're not going into work, Mom. They can survive without you for one day. We all need to be together this evening as a family."

Martha stared off into the distance as she contemplated how the evening would play out. Picking up her cigarettes, she clumsily pulled one out with her shaky hands. She needed to start planning.

Labor Day weekend in 1971 would not be the same for Coldwater Creek. Bob would call Scott Clever to inform him of his brother's death. Scott would then call Brian Johnson, who would then contact Mark Carter. The news would spread quickly. The boys would gather at Scott's house that fateful afternoon, just a few doors down from the Wills residence. There would be no playful banter, no back-and-forth jabs, no sarcastic heckling. Even Scott would play it straight, sticking with the solemn mood out of respect for the Wills family.

Sitting on lawn chairs in front of Scott's house, the boys wanted to be together, even though they weren't in a talkative mood. Somehow, camaraderie seemed like the best way to deal with this sudden hitch in the road. Out of respect for the Wills family, neighborhood gatherings and picnics would be canceled. Instead, the neighborhood association would coordinate the preparation of casseroles and cakes and deliver them to the Willses' front door out of honor and respect. Martha, in no condition to receive guests, would allow Bob to act on her behalf, a duty he despised, but graciously accepted in order to honor his mother's wishes.

"Look, he's home," whispered Scott.

Brian looked up and got a sickening feeling in the pit of his stomach as he saw the Pontiac Bonneville pull up into the Wills driveway. The boys watched as Mr. Wills opened the car door and grabbed his lunch pail. He was whistling as he headed toward the front door, no doubt looking forward to a long holiday weekend. The boys could only imagine how this dreadful scene would play out.

There would be no front porch sitting for Mr. Wills tonight, no cold Falstaff, and no taking in the night air. On this fateful evening, Eddie Wills would soon come to terms with the loss of a son, a young boy who would never again spend time with his family.

Chapter 10

O N THE FIRST DAY OF classes, a slew of yellow school buses rolled through the student drop-off area, filling the air with diesel, and rumbling away in black clouds of smoke. Isolated in farmland, Jefferson Junior High seemed to be in the middle of nowhere, even by suburban standards.

Not fitting the mold of a school in the country, the building was only three years old and looked modern compared to the traditional brick-and-mortar schoolhouses of the past. The classroom wing of the building was a simple, rectangular box, two stories high and running parallel to Wheelock Road. Composed of rock aggregate, the exterior surface consisted of thousands of white stones compressed together and crystalized to unveil a sparkling effect in the sun. In between the stone facades, the smoked-glass windows ran from ground to roof, resulting in an exterior veneer of stone and glass, alternating in panels of white and black. It was certainly unique, if not aesthetically pleasing.

At seven forty-five that morning, the outdoor concourse was packed with students waiting for the eight o'clock bell to ring. Except for the conspicuous absence of inner-city students, everything appeared normal.

"It looks awfully vanilla around here," remarked Scott. "I guess they're all gonna be late?"

"I wouldn't be surprised," said Brian. "They have a long commute."

"Maybe they changed their minds." Scott laughed. "They decided they didn't wanna be farmers after all."

"Well, they're running out of time," said Brian. "I wonder how many buses they'll have. Even if it's just two or three, this school's gonna be jam-packed."

Brian had barely completed his sentence when several school administrators waved the students into the building, hoping to minimize the chaos and avoid the potential for friction.

As the herd began its reluctant move toward the building, the first inner-city bus rolled to a stop. When the doors popped open, the migration came to a halt as the masses looked over their shoulders with curiosity, hoping to catch a first glimpse of the invasion.

Deboarding the bus methodically, the inner-city kids stared straight ahead, trying to appear unmindful of their surroundings. But there was no denying their wide-eyed looks of trepidation. Like a herd of antelope surrounded by lions, they cautiously measured their habitat, leery of the imposing stares and their own vulnerability.

As Brian Johnson and Mark Carter waltzed into their homeroom together, they instantly recognized Lynda Lacey in the front row. In the back, they noticed two Black students sitting next to each other, a boy and a girl. Brian immediately sized up the boy to see if he looked like a football player.

"Ready for your last year of junior high?" asked Lynda.

"I was born ready," said Brian, trying to be clever. "We'll have to compare schedules and see if we have any classes together."

"My only concern is algebra," said Mark. "I'm gonna need all the help I can get."

Interrupted by the morning announcements, the casual chit-chat came to an end with the voice of Dr. Goodwin booming over the intercom.

"Good morning, Jefferson Patriots! Let me take this opportunity to welcome back all the returning students and issue a special, warm greeting to the newcomers. You are now part of the Patriot family and we want you all to feel at home."

It was the standard stuff, explaining why everyone should be excited about the new year and how they should rise up to the challenges and prepare for their futures.

When the principal was done, the homeroom teacher, Mrs. Pratt, proceeded to consume the remaining twenty minutes with the obligatory administrative tasks: attendance, rules and regulations, documents for parents to sign, cafeteria meal tickets, etc.

Saving the item of greatest concern for last, Mrs. Pratt distributed the class schedules. Eagerly poring over their itineraries, the students quickly identified their assigned teachers. When the bell rang, Brian, Mark, and Lynda compared their schedules and determined that none of them would be in class together.

"At least we have the same lunch period," said Brian.

"Okay, I'll meet you in front of the cafeteria at eleven thirty," said Mark. Then he turned around and quickly blended in with the masses.

Meanwhile, Brian stayed close to Lynda, attempting to prolong the conversation. Although she was out of his league, it was not like him to pass up an opportunity to talk to the prettiest girl in the school. He decided to take his chances.

"So it looks like band class doesn't start until next week," said Brian, stating the obvious. "Monday, Wednesday, and Friday, fourth period. Is that what your schedule is showing?"

"Yep, that all checks out," said Lynda, shortly. "I gotta make a left turn here. I'll talk to you later." And with that, she was gone, quickly disappearing into the crowd.

Although Brian and Lynda were both in the band, the similarities ended there. Lynda took up the clarinet because it was something to do, another accomplishment on her checklist, while Brian played the trumpet because of his genuine interest in music, a passion he shared with his father.

Growing up, Brian frequently listened to his dad's records of Tommy Dorsey, Benny Goodman, Artie Shaw, and the big band sound of Glen Miller. He knew most of the big hits: "In the Mood," "A String of Pearls," "Stardust," etc. Unfortunately, his enjoyment of big band music was not something he could share with his buddies. They weren't about to show any appreciation for music their parents listened to, which meant that Brian would continue to listen to Glen Miller on his father's collection of 78 rpm disks, the ones that spun around almost twice as fast as his 45s.

At eleven twenty-five, Brian exited his American history class and headed to the cafeteria. Feeling a big smack on his back, he spun around fearfully, only to see that it was Scott holding a folder in his hand.

"Oh, it's just you. You scared the shit out of me," said Brian.

"What you see is what you get." Scott laughed. "Looks like you're a little jumpy today."

"Only when someone sneaks up and smacks me on the back. I'm heading to lunch. I'm supposed to meet Mark there."

"Cool, that's where I'm heading," said Scott. We can all break bread together."

As they approached the cafeteria, they spotted Mark and waved him over.

Mark looked at Scott and fired a preemptive strike, "Oh no, not you too."

"Yep," said Scott. "Looks like the three musketeers all over again."

"Anyone see Bob today?" asked Brian.

"Not since the bus ride," said Scott. "He's gonna be in school all week except for Friday. Friday is the funeral. Did he tell you about the newspaper this morning?"

"No, what about it?" asked Brian.

"Well, he said he was getting ready to fold the sections together when he saw a picture of Danny on the Metro page. I guess it was a picture of him in his army uniform along with an obituary. He said it made him feel kinda creepy riding around the neighborhood and tossing pictures of his dead brother on everyone's driveway."

"I can't even imagine what that poor dude is going through," sympathized Brian.

"Sometimes life just ain't fair," agreed Mark.

Approaching the service area, they saw what was being served up for lunch: Salisbury steak, mashed potatoes, mixed vegetables, and corn bread.

"Gag me with a spoon," quipped Scott. "Looks like we're starting out the year with a healthy dose of mystery meat."

"I don't mind," said Brian. "It looks better than the bologna sandwiches I've been eating all summer."

"I just wish the portions were bigger," complained Mark. "How's a football player gonna get any bigger, eatin' like a bird?"

KEVIN GEISE

Looking for a table with vacancies, they settled into an area with a dozen other boys. In the cafeteria, segregation was alive and well. The boys were clearly separated from the girls, unwilling to venture outside their comfort zones, at least not on day one. As the year would progress and familiarity would breed comfort, some of these boundaries would get blurred, but there would always be a recognizable distinction between girl tables and boy tables in junior high.

That was not the case in the Black section, and it was clearly a section in and of itself. The inner-city students had chosen to congregate at the back of the cafeteria, no deviation whatsoever, but with one major difference, the boys and girls were evenly mixed, displaying no apprehension over each other's company. A few of the girls were even sitting on the boys' laps, casually exhibiting flirtatious gestures for all to observe.

This was an eye-opening experience for Brian, Mark, and Scott. Never before had they witnessed this type of relaxed, uninhibited behavior between the sexes.

"What's that one girl doing?" asked Mark.

"Which one?" said Scott.

"The one sitting behind the dude with her hands in his hair."

"Oh, it looks like she's braiding his hair. I think they call them corn rows."

"Corn rows!" exclaimed Mark. "That's a stupid name."

"Maybe we should take them outside and show them what a real cornfield looks like," quipped Scott.

"What about those metal prongs they have sticking in their hair?" continued Mark. "What do they call those?"

"Those are picks. Or at least I *think* that's what they're called. That's how they keep their Afros all fluffed up."

"It looks like they could use them as weapons," said Mark. "I'm not sure I'll ever get used to this."

"What's the big deal?" asked Brian. "It's just some cultural differences. They're probably looking at us and laughing at how we run combs through our long hair."

"Yeah," said Scott. "We can probably learn some things from them. At least the girls could learn how to sit on our laps. That would be a better world."

"Good idea," chuckled Brian. "Maybe the glass is half-full after all."

54

Chapter 11

THE SECOND DAY OF SCHOOL seemed almost routine compared to the novelty of day one, although navigating the overcrowded hallways continued to be an adventure. When the school board decided to desegregate in 1971, the move corresponded logically to the opening of two new high schools, but it failed miserably at the junior high level.

Blackhawk, a new junior high, would not be completed until the following year, which meant that Jefferson would suffer a whole year of overloaded congestion. The stopgap measure was to bring in portable classrooms, which were nothing more than giant trailers parked in the back of the school connected by gravel walkways. Although journeying to the mobile units could be a minor inconvenience, once inside, it was apparent the teachers had done their best to simulate the look and feel of a real classroom.

As Brian and Mark exited their homeroom, they slowly shuffled their feet through the horde of humanity, incapable of taking full strides without tripping over someone.

"This is a good drill for you," said Mark.

"How so?" replied Brian.

"Well, a good running back has to follow his blocking, look for an opening, and then shoot through the gap."

"You're right." Brian laughed. "That's exactly what we're doing."

Negotiating their way through the crowd, they slowed down, sped up, and slowed down again, not finding any rhythm. Suddenly, a large commotion broke out at the end of the hallway. Difficult to identify, the disturbance soon revealed itself as a cluster of bodies rotating around like a mini tornado, clearing out a small gap in the sea of humanity. Then the shouting began, followed by a few shrill screams, as people scrambled for safety from the thundering sound of bodies banging against metal lockers.

As mob anxiety ensued, escalating the situation, three male teachers flew out of their classrooms and elbowed their way toward the scuffle. And then, almost as quickly as it started, the crowd settled to a murmur, the whole episode lasting less than a minute. Brian and Mark, as distant spectators, could only stand by and wait for an outcome, not knowing what had really happened or who was involved.

As the culprits and their captors made their way toward the office, the crowd began to part like the Red Sea, allowing Brian and Mark to get their first glimpse of the perpetrators.

Two male teachers were escorting a Black male student to the principal's office, firmly grasping each arm. Alongside them, another male teacher had the arm of a Black female student, followed by another teacher escorting a White male student. With a bloody face and ripped clothing, the White student stared straight ahead, void of any expression.

As the students began to question one another, desperately trying to gain a firsthand account, the loud buzz of the building's intercom interrupted the chaos.

"Everyone, please proceed to your first period classes as quickly as possible," announced the principal. "We will continue to honor the standard bell system. Teachers, anyone arriving more than two minutes after the bell, should be marked tardy."

"Well, that was exciting," said Brian. "I guess things are gonna be different this year after all."

"Yeah, but not in a good way," said Mark. "You just better watch yourself. I don't trust any of these assholes."

"I'll try to keep a low profile," said Brian. "I don't want my face all bloodied up."

"See you at lunch?" asked Mark.

"You got it."

Later, as Mark came out of his third period English class, heading to the cafeteria, he decided to make a quick pitstop in the restroom. Spotting Bob Wills near the urinals, he attempted a greeting. "Hey, Bobby, how's it hangin'?"

Bob, his face as white as a ghost, looked up at Mark with a visible uneasiness.

"Can you help me out?"

Before Mark could respond, two Black students stepped between him and Bob.

"Nobody needs your help around here," said one of them. "Why don't you just go about your business."

Mark got a sudden sinking feeling in his stomach as his senses surged to high alert.

"They asked me if I have a quarter," said Bob. "I told them I don't have one."

"I know you have a wallet," said one of the Black kids. "I just need to borrow some lunch money."

Mark could sense by the look on Bob's face that he was the subject of a heist.

"The restroom is not a lending office," said Mark, trying to be clever. "C'mon Bob, let's get out of here."

As Mark stepped forward, the two Black kids took a firm stand, bowing up to him in a threatening manner. Mark could feel his anger surge. He wanted to shove them away, establish his dominance and put an end to this showdown, but his better judgment prevailed as he decided to restrain himself. Although he was considerably bigger, there were still two of them and only one of him. Realizing he was in uncharted territory, Mark took a less confrontational, more strategic approach.

"Just walk around them," said Mark. "I'm sure the vice principal and dean would like to know about guys asking for wallets."

Easing around the blockade, Bob joined forces with Mark as the Black kids continued their menacing glare. Exiting the restroom together, Mark looked over his shoulder and offered one last stare, as if to issue a warning.

Mark Carter had never walked down a dark alley before, but that was his mindset as he came to the realization that danger could be lurking around every corner. The landscape was clearly changing; the school corridors were no longer the friendly confines he had grown up with.

It was only the second day of school, but the signals had been sent. Now there was a need for survival, an instinct that had never been triggered in him before, at least not at Jefferson Junior High. Although Mark had learned survival skills from the Boy Scouts, this was a different kind of survival, a different kind of wilderness.

Chapter 12

T HE FIRST WEEK OF SCHOOL was in the history books and Lynda Lacey was busy making plans for her first slumber party. It would be the usual Saturday evening affair with the girls setting up their sleeping bags in the basement, eating popcorn and pizza, playing records, and watching TV. After an eventful week of school, the girls would have plenty of fodder for gossip, and with upcoming cheerleader tryouts, Lynda would lead the discussion on potential competition and strategy.

As captain of the squad, Lynda took her role seriously. Junior High cheerleaders usually held their positions all three years, as long as they performed well and maintained positive attitudes, but if personalities and egos clashed, the coach had the authority to shuffle lineups in the interest of harmony, especially when worthy challengers were waiting in the wings.

Lynda's two best friends, Mindy Harper and Karen Gadby, were arriving at six o'clock. Although the three cheerleaders were unique in many ways, they shared a collective energy that generated a contagious enthusiasm, attributes that proved to be invaluable when leading pep sessions. Mindy was the cute and bubbly one, Karen was graceful and elegant, while Lynda exuded the kind of confidence and composure to be expected from a captain.

On this evening, they would relax, have fun and be themselves. The odd one out, Nancy Garber, was invited because she was one of Lynda's best friends and lived a couple doors down. Nancy's mother would not allow her to spend the night, but she was usually allowed to visit with Lynda as long as Mrs. Lacey was supervising.

Mindy Harper, the adorable one, was a round-faced little gal, with warm brown eyes and chestnut hair. People often described her with the expression "cute as a button." With bangs in the front and a wedge cut in the back, she kept her hair short, proudly displaying an assortment of pierced earrings. Thick, shiny, and full of body, her hair would always fall back in place no matter how much she bounced around. A few years later, US figure skater Dorothy Hamill would make the same hairstyle famous on her way to a gold medal. But Mindy was always ahead of her time, a trendsetter in many ways. She didn't care about traditions or what other people thought. She had a lot of spunk and did her own thing, or as the saying went in those days, "she let it all hang out."

"Someone's at the door," yelled Mrs. Lacey.

"I'll get it," said Lynda, exiting the kitchen. Opening the front door, she saw Mindy grinning from ear to ear. "Hey, Min, come on in."

"Don't mind if I do. Where should I dump my things?"

"Just drop them by the door that leads to the basement. We'll take them down later. Nancy and I were putting the finishing touches on the pizza. We already rolled the dough and added the sauce and cheese. Now all we gotta do is add the pepperoni."

"Is Karen here yet?" asked Mindy.

"Not yet. Would you like a Coke?"

"Sure, I'll take it on the rocks."

"Hi, Mindy," said Nancy. "Wanna help me with the Jiffy Pop?"

"Let's do it," replied Mindy. "Nothing like the smell of popcorn."

Nancy peeled off the cardboard top and settled the aluminum pan on the front-plate electric burner. Turning the burner to the medium setting, she asked, "How long does this usually take?"

"That burner doesn't heat up very fast, at least five minutes," said Lynda. "As soon as you hear the first popping sound, you need to start shaking the pan."

"This is good training," teased Mindy. "Someday you'll be able to make your husband popcorn for dinner."

"I don't think anyone will marry me for my cooking," said Nancy. "Although Mom is always teaching me the basics of being a housewife, which usually means cooking, cleaning, and sewing."

"My husband will cook for me," joked Mindy. "I'll be out shopping."

As the first few pops sounded off, Nancy started sliding the pan around on the burner using a hot pad to grip the flimsy wire handle.

"How do you know when it's done?" she asked.

"The popping will start to slow down," said Lynda. "Then you should pull it off the burner when the pops are further apart. If you leave it on too long, it will burn."

Nancy continued to shake the pan until the pops slowed to a halt and the aluminum foil top was ready to burst. Lynda grabbed a bowl and Nancy peeled back the foil, emptying the contents.

"Nothing like the smell of Jiffy Pop," said Mindy, reaching for a handful.

Before they could gather their refreshments and head for the basement, they heard the doorbell ring. Lynda opened the door as everyone greeted Karen with the usual pleasantries. Then it was down the basement stairs where they would enjoy their privacy and indulge in the latest girl talk.

Karen Gadby was an attractive girl of average height, medium brown hair, and blue eyes. She was pretty, but not in a flashy sort of way. Her angular face and prominent nose lent her a degree of sophistication. With curvy hips and a burgeoning bosom, she looked mature beyond her years, handling herself with the confidence of a young lady. Although opinionated, she could be fun and jovial, comfortably mixing into most social settings. On this particular evening, she was ready to enjoy time with her friends, albeit with a dose of misgivings over the developments at school.

"I thought we'd start out playing a few records, then pop the pizza in the oven so we can eat it while watching *The Mary Tyler Moore Show*," suggested Lynda. "Who knows, if things get really crazy, we can even break out the Twister game."

"That's what we need," joked Mindy. "A good game of Twister would stretch us out before tryouts next week."

"Anything is fine with me," said Nancy. "As long as I'm home by nine o'clock. You know how my mother is."

"No worries," said Lynda, while fumbling through her records. "How about we listen to the Carpenters?"

"Perfect," said Nancy with a smile. "My mother would approve. She says that's the only good music on the radio."

"She doesn't like *Chick-A-Boom* by Daddy Dewdrop?" teased Mindy. Mindy started singing:

Chick-A-Boom, Chick-A-Boom, don't ya just love it, Chick-A-Boom, Chick-A-Boom, Boom, Boom

Laughing at Mindy's little performance, the girls appreciated her propensity to amuse. Even Nancy got a kick out of the frivolity, indulging in the guilty pleasure of silliness while away from her mother's watchful eyes.

As the girls continued to joke around and make small talk, Lynda allowed the chit-chat to run its course, waiting for the right moment to address the looming business at hand—cheerleader tryouts.

"Karen, do you have your routine all set for next week?" asked Lynda.

"Pretty much, it's gonna be the standard stuff, isn't it? At least that's what my mother said."

"Your mother?" asked Lynda.

"Well, it's kind of a long story," confessed Karen. "She was concerned about how tryouts would be conducted this year. You know, with the Black girls arriving and everything. She was wondering if they'd be given special consideration."

"How so?" inquired Mindy.

"Well," said Karen, "we have the same six girls returning from the eighth-grade squad, right? It wouldn't be fair for the school to change the rules and decide that one of the six needs to be Black. I mean that's what they call a quota system, right?"

"I don't know," said Mindy. "I've never heard of a quota system."

"That's where the school has to maintain a certain ratio of White and Black students," said Karen.

"So what does this have to do with your mother?" asked Lynda.

"She set up a meeting last week with the principal and the cheer coach. She wanted to make sure that one of us wouldn't be dropped from the squad just because we're White."

"I never thought of that," said Lynda. "What did she find out?"

"They told her there would be no quota system, but they were considering expanding the squad from six to eight. They said they would include the same requirements as before, but maybe allow for some creativity."

"Creativity?" asked Lynda. "What does that mean? I'm supposed to be the returning captain and I'm the last to find out?"

"That's why my mother set up the meeting," said Karen. "She wanted to state her case and find out the rules before any of us got cheated out of our positions."

Mindy couldn't hold her tongue any longer. "Remember when we traveled with the basketball team to the Weisser Park game last year? Their cheerleaders weren't doing anything like us. They were playing music and doing moves that were more like dance routines."

"Yes," agreed Karen. "Swinging their arms and shaking their hips, like they were on *Soul Train* or something."

Mindy had to laugh at that. "But I kinda liked it. Except, I'm not prepared to do that."

"I'm not sure any of us is," conceded Lynda. "I guess I better talk to the coach and find out what is expected."

"I think that's where the so-called creativity comes in," said Karen. "I don't like it any more than you do, and my mother isn't happy about it. She says we're being forced to conform to their world."

"Maybe it will work out for the best," said Mindy. "We can learn from them, and they can learn from us. I wouldn't mind sassin' things up a little bit," she giggled. "It might be fun."

"I'm not interested in any of that jive stuff," Karen vented. "I think we should keep it classy."

"In all seriousness," said Mindy. "We gotta put ourselves in their shoes. Think about how they must feel being told to leave their school and come into a strange place. They might be thinking we won't give them a fair chance."

Karen rolled her eyes. "Tough toenails, they invade our school and now we're supposed to worry about giving them a fair chance? That's just too bad."

As the discussions continued, Nancy sat by in silence, wishing they would go back to the light-hearted silliness. "Hey," she said. "Look at the clock. We gotta pop the pizzas in the oven if we're gonna eat them during *The Mary Tyler Moore Show*. Don't forget, I gotta be home at nine o'clock sharp."

As the girls went up the stairs to the kitchen, Lynda's mood had changed considerably. She was not prepared for all the nuances that might come down the pipeline. Before tonight, she hadn't given much thought to her tryout routine. She had done it all before, hundreds of times. Now the landscape had changed completely. Not only did she need to work up a new routine, but her role of captain might be in jeopardy—something she had never considered.

What if the tryouts weren't fair? What if she lost her title? How could she play second fiddle to someone else? Feeling the butterflies churning away in her stomach, she barely nibbled on her pizza. Now she had to put together a new plan and there was very little time to do it.

Chapter 13

THE FIRST DAY OF BAND class was about to begin, and the students filed through the door, one at a time, checking in with their new teacher, a face they had never seen before.

"Hi, I'm Mr. Conway. I'll be your student teacher, assisting Mr. Stoops this fall. Please give me your name and tell me what instrument you play."

One by one, the band members complied as Mr. Conway directed them to the seating arrangements that aligned with their instruments. The room was already set up in a semicircle of metal folding chairs, three rows deep, each with its own music stand and facing the director's podium.

Grabbing their instruments from the nearby storage room, the students searched for their seats. Each chair was earmarked with a piece of masking tape labeled in ball point pen: six chairs labeled clarinet, four chairs labeled trumpet, three chairs for trombone, etc.

Brian Johnson grabbed his trumpet and made his way to the second row, just in front of the trombone section. At some point, Mr. Stoops would rank the trumpet players from one to four, with the best player earning the prestigious title of first chair. In most cases, the status of First Chair was largely symbolic since the whole section would typically play the same music. In rare cases, allegedly, Mr. Stoops would allow the First Chair musician to play a solo, or at least play a melody distinct from the remaining chairs. Since Brian had been in the concert band, there had never been a musician good enough to play a solo.

As the room reached its capacity, the students began their warm-ups, each doing his or her own thing. The saxophone and clarinet players squealed away as they moistened their wooden reeds, the trumpeters blared out scales, the snare drummers processed rolls, and the flutists twittered like birds, collectively producing a menacing sound that could only be described as pure chaos. The bedlam usually lasted five or ten minutes until Mr. Stoops took the podium and commanded everyone's attention.

While warming up, Brian's eyes surveyed the room, briefly fixating on Lynda Lacey in the clarinet section. She looked as pretty as ever in her purple blouse and tight white slacks. He even admired her cute little feet and the way her painted toenails protruded from her white sandals.

As he continued to scour the room for pretty girls and newcomers, he soon realized that he was familiar with everyone in the band, which meant the band was still 100 percent White. Not that he was surprised; in reality, he didn't know what to expect.

As the mayhem continued, there was still no sign of Mr. Stoops. With the room growing more restless, Mr. Conway finally took the podium and raised his arms, a signal for everyone to put down their instruments. After receiving a somewhat mixed response, he raised his arms again, this time more assertively.

"Quiet," he announced with a loud booming voice. "I need your attention right away."

Realizing this was a student teacher that meant business, the band responded with a collective silence.

"Allow me to formally introduce myself again. I am Mr. Conway. Although I will be your student teacher this fall, I will not be working alone. Instead, Mr. Stoops and I will be working collectively to produce the finest concert band that Jefferson has ever known."

Realizing that Jefferson Junior High had only been around a few years, the kids couldn't help but snicker.

"Mr. Stoops will assume podium duty on designated days while I work with you individually. Other days, I will be on the podium while Mr. Stoops looks over your shoulders and identifies any weaknesses that need to be addressed. Either way, we are both confident that this teamwork approach will produce the kind of quality results never before witnessed in this building."

The formality and sternness of Mr. Conway's remarks triggered more than a few suspicions. To the kids, this sounded more like a coach's pep talk than the nervous introduction they expected from a student teacher struggling to gain control.

"Without further ado, I will, at this time, relinquish the podium to Mr. Stoops."

As Mr. Conway stepped down, Stoops exited his office and strutted toward the podium with a twinkle in his eye. Bewildered by his obvious swagger, the students were sure he had something up his sleeve, but no one could venture a guess as to where this episode was heading.

"Thank you, Mr. Conway. We are certainly fortunate to have you working with our band this fall. And to the students, I'd like to say welcome back. I'm looking forward to a special year filled with many accomplishments. You'll find out soon enough that Mr. Conway is a very skilled musician with much to offer. Make sure you take advantage of his assistance whenever possible. Now, before we get started, I have one additional announcement."

After a brief pause for added emphasis, Mr. Stoops continued. "We have one new student transferring in this year. Luckily, I was fortunate enough to meet him before the school year began."

Suddenly there were waves of heads turning in every direction trying to identify the newbie.

"No," said Stoops, "he's not sitting out there with the rest of you because I have him back in my office."

Stoops paused again, allowing a detectable murmur to resonate. Playing the crowd like a virtuoso, he allowed the curiosity to build into a crescendo.

"If you're all ready," he said with a grin, "I would like to introduce to you, at this time, our new trumpet player, Antonio Jackson."

The band students looked up with anxiety as this embarrassing spectacle unfolded, half expecting a red-faced, shy little kid to sheepishly walk out in total humiliation. Instead, much to their dismay, a tall, handsome, African American male strolled casually into the room, displaying the confidence of an experienced entertainer.

With a warm smile on his face, he scanned the room, making eye contact with the band members and nodding his head like he'd been working a crowd his entire life. Impeccably dressed, Antonio displayed a degree of sophistication that was way beyond his years. His flawless, almond-colored skin seemed to glow under the sparkle of his hair, immaculately groomed to perfection. As if his good looks weren't enough, there was a certain aura about him that instantly commanded the attention of the room. Even if you didn't know who he was or what he did, his mere presence seemed to be captivating, exhibiting an innate quality that could only be described as star power.

"Antonio," said Mr. Stoops. "I think you selected a song to play for us today?"

"Yes, sir, I would be honored."

"Well, then, I will introduce your first number," said Stoops. "Allow me to say that up until a few years ago, Antonio lived in New Orleans. Tell me again, how long have you lived in Fort Wayne?"

"Just a couple years, but I still live in New Orleans during the summer with my relatives."

"Okay," said Stoops. "In honor of his New Orleans roots, I've asked him to play one of my all-time favorites, 'When the Saints Go Marching In'. Whenever you're ready, Antonio, take it away."

Antonio reached under the director's podium and pulled out his trumpet. It was a beauty. A handcrafted, silver-plated Getzen, engraved with "Antonio" on the lead pipe, just under the valves. Holding the horn up to his mouth, he moved his lips around as if to limber them up for the challenge. Then, like second nature, he effortlessly eased into the song, flawlessly hitting the notes in perfect pitch, and comfortably displaying his command of the instrument.

As he launched into the second verse, he started jazzing it up, improvising with Dixieland swing, and moving his body with energy and passion. With eyes like saucers, the kids gawked at his performance, not believing they were witnessing such wizardry by a ninth grader. They couldn't tell if he was hamming it up, or if his body instinctively moved to the rhythm, like involuntary motions driven by a sixth sense.

When the last note was played and Antonio lowered the horn to his side, Mr. Stoops stood up and started clapping his hands. Following his lead, the kids joined the applause and looked back and forth with big smiles, confirming with one another they had just witnessed something special.

Mr. Stoops nodded his head in appreciation. "Thank you, Antonio. Would you mind fielding some questions from the crowd?"

"Not at all," said Antonio, with a confident smile.

"I'm sure you have lots of questions," said Mr. Stoops, looking over his band. "If you raise your hands, I'll call on you one by one. Who's first?"

"How long have you been playing?" was the first question.

"I got my first trumpet, actually a cornet, when I was in the second grade. It took me awhile to learn how to hold my lips and blow hard enough to get a sound. I was pretty awful," he said with a grin as everyone laughed.

"Who was your teacher?"

"My father played trumpet and helped me when I was starting out. My uncle also played. He would give me pointers too, and sometimes we all played trios together. As I got better, I started taking lessons from professionals."

"Who's your favorite trumpet player?"

"That's a good question. Louis Armstrong is a legend in New Orleans, but he's kinda before my time. He played more traditional music. You may have heard that he passed away this summer. That was a big deal in New Orleans, even though the funeral was in New York. Spending last summer in Nola, I was able to experience firsthand the impact he had on that city. Al Hirt is another Nola legend, and he's a little more current. He actually has a club on Bourbon Street and I've had the good fortune to play there a couple times. And then there's Miles Davis. He's not from New Orleans, but he's widely respected as one of the greatest jazz musicians of all time. He grew up in St. Louis, which has a great tradition for music, especially the Blues. I think I admire Miles Davis most for his creativity, the way he explores and composes different types of music. So that would be my top three, each unique in his own way."

"Who's your favorite band?"

"That's a good question. I like Blood, Sweat & Tears. Lew Soloff plays a mean trumpet. I also like Earth, Wind & Fire. They've been putting out some really good stuff. But I like lots of bands, not just the ones with three-word names."

Antonio smiled as everyone laughed at his joke.

Brian raised his hand, "I like Doc Severinsen, what do you think of him?"

"He's pretty amazing. I especially like his outfits."

Everyone laughed again as Antonio showed his sense of humor.

"Do you like Three Dog Night?"

Mr. Stoops frowned at the laughter as the questions became more absurd.

"Yes, they have some great songs. I like all kinds of music. It doesn't have to include a trumpet. I would like to play the guitar someday too, but I haven't started that yet. I play a little keyboard, though. It seems like most musicians learn to play the piano because that is a great instrument for composing."

"Okay, one last question," said Mr. Stoops.

Brian raised his hand again. "This one is for Mr. Stoops. Have you decided yet who will be playing First Chair in the trumpet section?"

Mr. Stoops waited for the laughter to die down. "That's actually a good question. I'm sure many of you are wondering how we will keep Antonio occupied since his skill level seems to be in a different stratosphere. I have asked him to play with us when we perform our concerts, and that will probably include some solos. But he's also offered to spend some one-on-one time with our trumpet players, more or less giving them private lessons as needed. That should help us immensely. So during our normally scheduled class time, he may be playing with us, or he may be in one of the practice rooms helping our musicians, or working on his own material, composing music and arrangements. In summary, I will be granting him a great deal of latitude to help us when needed, but also to pursue his own goals."

Mr. Stoops looked over at Antonio, soliciting his buy-in. "Does that sound like a plan?"

"That sounds good to me," said Antonio, with a smile. "I look forward to playing with everyone and helping the band whenever I can."

"Thank you, Antonio, and thanks again for the performance. We all look forward to you sharing your talents with us the rest of the year." Stoops paused and looked over the band members. "Now that we've had our excitement for the day, it's time to take care of our normal business."

Taking this as his cue, Antonio walked back to the second row and sat down in the trumpet section, trying his best to appear ordinary. But, from that day on, there was nothing ordinary or normal about Antonio. He had become a celebrity and there was no turning back. It was clear that Antonio would never blend into a crowd, and the students wouldn't have it any other way.

When band class ended, he exited the room with an entourage of admirers, all trying to attract his attention. Boys and girls alike, there were no boundaries when it came to Antonio's attraction. The girls were clearly mesmerized by his charm and good looks, while the guys looked at him as somebody who was cool, a so-called happenin' dude.

Suddenly, there was a new definition of style, and it was not about counterculture, or bell-bottomed blue jeans and tie-dyed shirts. Instead, it was about fashion, flair, and sophistication. The 60s were turning into the 70s, and nobody had ever dreamed that the most popular kid in school would be an African American trumpet player, the new standard-bearer for trendiness.

Chapter 14

IN THE YEAR 1719, THE first ships carrying African slaves arrived in New Orleans from the west coast of Africa, a region where the River Gambie empties into the Northern Atlantic. By the end of the century, there would be close to twenty thousand African slaves in the state of Louisiana. New Orleans had become the slave-trading capital of the United States.

Many of these slaves were sold off to plantation owners who managed their properties along the Mississippi River, a hundred-mile stretch of fertile ground between Baton Rouge and New Orleans. By the mid-1800s, most of these landowners had replaced their rice, indigo, and tobacco crops with sugarcane, a product that proved to be far more profitable. Leveraged off the blood, sweat, and tears of forced labor, sugarcane production became extremely bountiful, and the slave population grew to one hundred thousand.

Hundreds of plantation homes were sprouting up along the Mississippi River, ranging from simple farmhouses to antebellum-style mansions with giant pillars and wraparound balconies. By the time the Civil War broke out in 1861, Louisiana had become the second richest state in the country in per capita wealth. The value of enslaved people alone represented tens of millions of dollars in capital, all fueled by the demand for sugar, Louisiana's white gold.

Through the years, Antonio Jackson had learned a great deal about the history of his family. Instead of studying ancestry through public archives, he learned everything he needed to know from his grandfather,

Elijah (1885–1968). Elijah had shared many stories about his father, Samba (1840–1910), and how he was born into slavery and worked on a Louisiana sugarcane plantation. Antonio was very familiar with Samba's firsthand accounts of slavery and the horrifying atrocities he was forced to endure, leaving a lasting impression on him and his perspective on life and liberty.

Samba began working on the plantation when he was only eight years old. Although he was not expected to produce at the same levels as an adult, his contributions were closely monitored. Too many times he had witnessed the lashings that were doled out for subpar performances.

When overseers identified a low performer, they would tie his or her arms to a tree and gather the slaves around to witness the brutal assault, using the incident as an example of what could happen to any one of them if they did not meet expectations.

Samba once witnessed his cousin, Leon, receive a beating so severe, he collapsed unconscious to the ground, his back reduced to a bloody pulp. Two nights later, his body writhing with infection, he became delirious with fever. Samba would never forget lying awake all night, listening to the haunting sounds of his cousin moaning and wailing as he hallucinated in agony. Three days later, Leon would die.

By the time Samba was twelve, he was considered an adult, working from sunrise to sunset, completely exhausted at the end of each day. With horrid working conditions, the death rate for Louisiana slaves was extremely high. The combination of poor nutrition, disease, and physical exhaustion took an unmerciful toll, resulting in an average life expectancy of twenty-one years.

Although many slaves pondered the potential for liberty, it was common knowledge that fugitives rarely survived. They were usually captured, brought back, and tortured for all to see, a huge deterrent for anyone with illusions of freedom. Whenever a slave talked about escaping, they were quickly reminded by their elders of the 1811 revolt.

Samba had heard the story many times. It all happened down river at the Andry Plantation during an unusually brutal harvest. After Manuel Andry, the plantation owner, refused to allow for any rest, an angry worker picked up an axe and swung it at him, knocking him to the ground. When the owner's son rushed the assailant in retaliation, he was swarmed and attacked by a group of slaves, murdered in plain sight.

Fleeing the scene, the small group of slaves made their way to the next plantation and coaxed the slave driver—an enslaved overseer of other slaves—to join the rebellion and bring his slaves with him. As the uprising grew to an estimated two hundred members, mostly between the ages of twenty and thirty, the band of rebels continued to attack plantations along the river, grabbing supplies, weapons, and more mutineers along the way.

In less than forty-eight hours, word of the rebellion had reached New Orleans, where Louisiana Governor William Claiborne quickly summoned the assistance of federal troops. In response, General Wade Hampton commissioned a portion of his troops, along with two voluntary militia groups, to quash the rebellion. Against overwhelming odds, the majority of the insurrectionists were either killed or captured within days.

Those that were captured were either returned to their plantations to be tortured or sent to trial. After an overwhelming majority were found guilty, they were swiftly executed, some by firing squad, others by public hanging. When the executions were complete, over one hundred decapitated heads were placed on pikes along the river road leading from New Orleans to the plantation district, grisly symbols of intimidation for all to see. Since then, no one had dared to organize any type of rebellion.

The only joyous times Samba ever spoke of were the Sunday afternoons he spent at Congo Square in New Orleans. During slow seasons, when the sugarcane plantations were not overwhelmed with planting, harvesting, or processing, the owners would permit their slaves to take Sundays off. This allowed the slaves from neighboring plantations to visit the city and mingle with one another, turning Sundays into a celebration of community and culture.

As the crowds grew larger, the city of New Orleans attempted to control the gatherings by restricting them to designated areas. The largest of these congregations took place at Congo Square, an area just north of the French Quarter in what would later become Louis Armstrong Park. Uninhibited by the presence of slave masters, Congo Square would soon establish itself as a mecca for African culture and freedom of expression.

The gatherings had grown so large and garnered such notoriety, that many locals of Spanish and French descent would come by to witness the spectacle, consumed by the singing, dancing, and pageantry of the ancestral clothing and jewelry. Spectators would watch in bewilderment as dancers twirled and gyrated to the pulsating beat of percussion instruments from their native lands: drums, gourds, marimbas, and tambourines.

Samba loved to participate and eventually learned to play the pan flute, an instrument consisting of bamboo pipes of varying lengths. By blowing into the individual pipes, Samba learned to play different notes and create his own melodies. Soon, he was playing basic refrains to go along with the percussion beats, constructing a style of music that was appreciated for its originality and creativity.

A few years later, at age twenty-two, Samba's life took a dramatic turn. It was April 1862, and the alarming news hit his people like a ton of bricks: the Union army had taken control of New Orleans. As word spread throughout the sugarcane region, the slaves tried to contain their emotions, wondering what impact this would have on their subjugation.

But the plantation owners were quick to inform them that nothing had changed. The war was still raging and the law of the land still prevailed. Even if the plantation owners had their authority taken away, the slaves had nowhere else to go and nothing else to do. It made no sense to run away and risk getting captured or shot by Confederate soldiers.

As the Union commanders scoured the sugarcane region and exerted their authority, General Benjamin Butler instituted a new policy that required all laborers to receive wages along with their food and housing. As a result, the uncertainty and confusion evolved into a period of chaos, with plantation owners resisting the new decree and laborers exercising their power of refusal.

Five months later, on September 22, the chaos would only get worse when President Lincoln issued his Emancipation Proclamation. Faced with November harvesting, December processing, and no forced labor, plantation owners were confronted with their impending doom.

By the end of 1862, Louisiana sugar production had fallen 75 percent below the previous year's output. The local economy was rapidly deteriorating, and so was the wealth and power of Louisiana landowners.

When the Civil War officially ended in 1865, Southern states were deeply embedded with poverty. Without slavery, the engine that powered their economy, farming could no longer be productive or profitable, and without agriculture, the Southern states had little else to fall back on.

Considering that 20 percent of the White male workforce had died during the war, Southern resources had dwindled dramatically. Although these jobs needed to be filled, business owners were reluctant to tap into the Black labor market, failing to realize the importance of symbiotic relationships. As business owners became more desperate and freedmen more destitute, the barriers were eventually broken, mostly driven by ex-slaves willing to work for wages that were much lower than their White counterparts.

Like everyone else, Samba scrambled to survive. Initially, he did farm work, jumping from one plantation to another, performing odd jobs as needed. Although his demographic was in high demand—strong healthy males in their midtwenties—farm work became scarcer as agriculture grew less profitable. As a result, much of the Black labor force, both men and women, were migrating to the city, competing for unskilled, low-wage jobs.

While the men scrambled to find the few industrial jobs that were available, Black women were employed mostly in domestic fields, working as cooks, maids, and laundresses. Samba briefly found work with the railroad, and then later at a lumber mill. Before long, he was supplementing his income by working evenings as a dishwasher at the local diner. That is where he met Celeste, a woman who would win over Samba's heart with her cute smile and good cooking.

Employed as a hotel maid during the day, Celeste would only have a two-hour window to freshen herself up before arriving to her job as a cook, trying her best to impress Samba. After several years of hard work, the two were married in 1880. Five years later, they would have their first child, a baby boy named Elijah.

By the turn of the century, the reconstruction period for the South was reaching its conclusion. Economic stability slowly returned as Black workers blended into the labor force and agriculture reemerged in the form of tenant farming, a system that allowed sharecroppers to live on smaller plots of land in exchange for crop production. Meanwhile, New

Orleans continued to evolve into a melting pot of ethnicity and culture. Indigenous people and persons of French, Spanish, and African descent, were blending together, homogenizing into a new breed of people called Creole.

This new blend of nationalities would soon have an impact on the local music scene, along with the growing popularity of brass instruments (e.g., trumpets, cornets, trombones, tubas, and saxophones). As military bands performed in parades and funeral processions, the marching band style of music became more popular and secondhand brass instruments became more widely available.

Congo Square, renamed Beauregard Square after a Confederate general, was thriving once again despite Confederate sympathizers' attempts to discourage the assembly of African culture. The music, a collaboration of different ethnicities, was dominated by brass instruments and represented a new style that was unique to New Orleans, a style referred to as ragtime.

Rising from this scene, an African American cornet player by the name of Buddy Bolden was gaining notoriety and attracting large crowds. He soon earned the nickname "King Bolden," as he and his brass band members produced improvised versions of ragtime that broke the mold and evolved into its own genre.

Samba took Elijah to Beauregard Square almost every Sunday to witness this new style of music, a brand that was so much different from when he played his pan flute. He told his son about the old days and how music had changed and how he too could be a star, just like King Bolden.

Antonio had heard the story many times from his grandfather, Elijah, about the day Samba took him into a small pawnshop and purchased his first trumpet. It was love at first sight. Elijah was soon practicing all day long and taking his horn to bed with him at night. Before long, he was playing on street corners, improving his skills, and perfecting his trade along with others.

At the age of fifteen, Elijah joined his first brass band and marched in his first parade. He loved to strut down the street and show off his skills as onlookers danced with joy. Not only was Elijah becoming a fine musician, but he was also blossoming into an entertainer.

Samba was extremely proud of his son and would rarely miss a performance. But he was never more thrilled than he was on the first day he saw Elijah play at Congo Square, a name that would never go away in the minds of African musicians. This was the venue where Samba had learned to play his pan flute, a place where slaves would go to be at one with their culture and express their individuality.

Time was marching on, and so was the sophistication of music. Samba didn't realize it at the time, but he was witnessing his son play a style of music that would someday be immortalized as New Orleans jazz, and Elijah had no idea that someday he would have a son and a grandson to carry on the family tradition of trumpet playing.

Chapter 15

THE WHISTLE BLEW, STOPPING PLAY. "Run it again," yelled Coach Riley. "And this time let's do it right!"

Brian Johnson was lined up in the fullback position, directly in front of his new teammate, Darius Williams, an inner-city transfer. They were running the offense out of the I-formation, which meant the tailback was lined up behind the fullback, who was directly behind the quarterback. In this formation, the fullback was primarily used as a blocker for the tailback, and sparingly used as a power runner up the middle. This was a new role for Brian, one he did not embrace. For the past two years he had played tailback, a position where he was able to utilize his speed to run wide and break the occasional long touchdown run.

The whistle screeched again. "Dammit, Johnson!" yelled Riley. "If you can't learn to block, you're not gonna be my fullback. You've got to pick up that defensive end, or Darius won't have any place to run. It's called teamwork. Football is a team sport."

Brian's worst fears had come true. After the first couple of days of team drills, he had come to the realization that he was no longer the fastest guy on the team. As they competed in forty-yard sprints, Darius Walker was consistently beating him, clocking in at 4.8 seconds, to Brian's 4.9. Coach Riley pulled Brian aside at the end of practice one day and told him that he wanted to use Darius at tailback because of his speed. "But don't worry," he said. "I still want you in the backfield. I think I can use both of you as a one-two punch. It just means that you'll have to do more blocking this year."

Darius Williams was a shy kid with chocolate-brown skin and a large Afro haircut. At 160 pounds, he didn't have an ounce of fat on him, which made him look somewhat brittle on the football field. But when he removed his shirt, it was easy to tell that he was all muscle; his washboard stomach looked hard as a rock. In the locker room, Darius was mostly relaxed and laid-back, but on the football field he was all business. When carrying the ball, he displayed a subtle shiftiness that enabled him to be elusive and explosive. Although he was serious about sports and loved the hard-nosed competition of football, he could also flash a big smile and enjoy the camaraderie that comes along with being part of a team.

Brian and Darius got along fine, that is to say, they tolerated each other's company. Clearly, a true friendship was unlikely considering their rivalry, but the Black and White lines in the locker room were becoming more blurred. Once the players were engaged in the daily routines of showering and dressing together, segregation was the furthest thing from their minds. In the locker room, there's no Black versus White, and on the football field, everyone bleeds red.

As the team was coming together and closing in on the first game, Malcom Mosely, a transfer student, emerged as the unlikely leader, both on and off the field. Malcom was a big, burly hulk of a guy, with medium brown skin, chubby cheeks, and a double chin. At 230 pounds, he appeared rotund, but his feet were deceptively quick, a lethal combination for a defensive lineman. He could bulldoze through an opponent on one play, then quickstep around a blocker on the next, routinely wrapping up ball carriers like a one-man wrecking crew.

But it was his magnetic personality that made him popular. With a big smile on his face, he would spew a steady flow of chatter, spontaneously engaging his teammates with playful repartee. It didn't matter whether he was on the field or in the locker room, his jocularity kept the team in high spirits, taking their minds off the aches and pains of daily gridiron beatings.

Mark Carter, on the other hand, was just getting by, not flourishing the way his coaches had hoped. It's not that he was averse to hard work, he just didn't have the same passion as his teammates. Mark played football mostly because his father encouraged it, and when your dad is a captain on the police force, you try to make him proud. There was no denying that he enjoyed game days and the attention that football players received, especially from the girls, but he was usually glad when the season was over.

Slotted as the starting offensive guard, Mark was well-suited for his position. He was big enough and strong enough to make his assigned blocks, and disciplined enough to understand any changes in blocking schemes, but he did not play with the kind of reckless abandon he sometimes faced on the defensive side of the ball. When he lined up across from Malcom, he was facing his worst nightmare: a player that was bigger, stronger, and quicker.

Malcom would overpower him on one play, then hit and spin on the next, never allowing Mark to gain any rhythm. One day in practice, Mark's frustration continued to build until Malcom finally flattened him like a pancake. With a big smile on his face, Malcom reached down to help Mark up, only to have his hand slapped away.

"I don't need your fuckin' help," screamed Mark. "Get out of my face!"

The coaches moved in quickly to prevent a skirmish, but the tension would remain. It was clear that Mark Carter was not as enamored with Malcom Mosely as the rest of the team. Brian was not sure whether it was race-related, or whether Mark was too beaten down, or both, but it was clear that Mark was not a happy camper.

Nevertheless, the team continued to make progress. With solid blocking, better timing, and crisper tackling, confidence was building. Coach Riley told them it would be a special year if they continued to work hard and master the fundamentals. Nothing could stop them if they remained focused and played together as a team.

"You gotta have each other's back," said Coach Riley, using an old cliché that meant to support and defend each other in times of need.

Brian was beginning to buy into the hype, although he wasn't completely sold on his new role. Mark, on the other hand, felt threatened, and his anxiety continued to grow. Nobody would have his back without his permission. It's called trust, and trust is something that is earned. He was still in survival mode.

Chapter 16

Inside the Jefferson gymnasium, the cheerleading squad prepared for the first pep session of the year. Used as a kickoff to the fall sports programs, it also served as the first student assembly of the year, providing an opportunity to build school spirit and recognize the students who participate in extracurricular activities.

Cheerleading tryouts had transpired mostly as expected, staying true to the prophecy of Karen's mother, Mrs. Gadby. In accordance to the judges' instructions, each of the girls performed three routines, two of which required standard arm movements, jumps, and splits. The third routine was up to the individual's discretion, allowing for creativity and expression. When it was all said and done, the squad had expanded to eight, consisting of the six returnees and two new members, both inner-city transfers with cheerleading experience.

Much to her relief, Lynda Lacey would remain the captain. She had put together a flawless audition, including a routine that she and her dance instructor had choreographed to the tune of Donny Osmond's *Sweet and Innocent*. After three days of tedious practice, Lynda had mastered the routine, performing in a cute and sassy style that wowed the judges. Lynda Lacey had delivered the goods, proving once again that she was a force to be reckoned with.

Teaming up with Mrs. Taylor, the cheer coach, Lynda's first task was to unify the group and mold them into one cohesive unit. Although Mrs. Taylor would issue the playbook, Lynda would have the freedom to exercise her discretion on how the routines were implemented and performed.

The playbook required Lynda to solicit input from the squad, specifically the new transferees. After considering all the input, both conventional and unconventional, it was her job to mold together the old with the new. It would be a daunting task, but she was looking forward to the challenge. It somehow made her feel more like a choreographer and producer than a cheerleading captain, yet another accomplishment she could add to her résumé.

In regard to the pep session, Lynda addressed her squad accordingly. "We only have a couple days to get ready, so we need to keep it simple. I've talked to Mrs. Taylor, and she has given me the program and our instructions."

Lynda wanted to clarify that she was acting on behalf of the cheer coach, not making up her own instructions.

"Between the national anthem, the principal speaking, the coaches speaking, football and cross-country introductions, there won't be much time for us to do our routines. Cheerleading introductions will be done last. Mrs. Taylor will introduce each of us and then we'll be allowed to do one routine. So we'll need to keep it simple. After that, we'll end the pep session by dividing in half, four of us on each end of the gym. Then we'll try to engage the students with the standard chant of 'We got spirit, yes we do, we got spirit, how 'bout you.' "

To Lynda, it all seemed like a good way to start out the year, simple and straightforward.

"So when are we gonna do some real stuff?" said Jada, visibly revealing her frustration. "I mean you gotta admit, this is awfully boring."

Jada Brown was one of the new additions to the squad. With medium brown skin and shortly cropped hair, she was attractive, but in a tough sort of way. Her long eyelashes and heavy makeup did little to soften her appearance. Not one to joke around, she was mostly serious, at times even edgy, rarely displaying a smile. With a mature, muscular physique and a confident attitude, Jada could be an imposing figure, not shy about asserting her opinions, and Lynda was growing wary of these signals, hoping to avoid any confrontations.

"I can't argue with that," said Lynda, trying to appear agreeable. "As soon as this pep session is over, we have one week until the first football game. Then we should put in something new. Do you wanna give us some ideas?"

Lynda was diplomatically calling her bluff.

"Yes, I'll give it some thought," said Jada, the ball suddenly in her court.

Karen looked at Lynda and rolled her eyes, signaling that Lynda had won this exchange. But Lynda turned away, not wanting Jada to pick up any bad vibes.

"Are we gonna do a pyramid this year?" asked Mindy.

As the smallest girl on the squad, she was the one who traditionally climbed to the top.

"It was pretty basic last year with six, right? A simple three, two, one. But how can we make eight work? I mean four, three, two, one makes ten," giggled Mindy. "You didn't know I was that good at math, did you?"

"We never did pyramids," said Jada. "And I'm just fine with that. I don't really want to be on the bottom, supporting all that weight with a bunch of knees and elbows poking me in the back."

"I can try to lose a few pounds," joked Mindy, trying to keep it light.

"We'll figure it out," said Lynda. "We could always do the same three, two, one, and then have someone on each end doing their routines while we build the pyramid. We certainly have options."

Putting her leadership on display, Lynda was leaving little doubt that she was the right captain for this squad. She liked being looked upon to make decisions and she was confident that she could build some chemistry. It might take a little time, but she was looking forward to the challenge.

Lynda Lacey was in her element and failure was not an option.

Chapter 17

THE YELLOW SCHOOL BUS CAME to a halt at the corner of Cedar and Elm, the first stop in Coldwater Creek. Scott looked up with a grin as he saw Bob sprinting to the corner, arriving just in the nick of time. This was his standard routine, scrambling to catch the bus each morning after completing his obligations to *The Journal Gazette*. Sometimes he would sprint to the bus stop with his books in one hand, and a pop tart in the other. Scott couldn't imagine his mornings being that hectic, especially in the winter when the mornings were dark and cold.

Waiting for the bus to stop, the boys allowed Lynda and Nancy to get in line ahead of them. Brian and Mark would get on board at the next stop.

"Anything interesting in *The Journal Gazette* this morning?" asked Scott, as they grabbed their usual seats.

"Something about a prison riot in Attica, New York. I didn't read it, but it sounds like a lot of people are dead."

"Another reason why I don't wanna go to prison," said Scott. "I'm gonna walk the straight and narrow."

Scott, ever the jokester, was careful to tread lightly with Bob. It had only been a couple weeks since his brother's funeral, and he wanted to be sensitive to Bob's feelings. Up until now, he had been keeping the dialogue simple and light, somewhere between the bookends of silly and serious. He knew, at some point, he should have a heartfelt dialogue with Bob, allowing him to open up and express his feelings, but Scott wasn't good at that sort of thing, and he didn't know how to go about it.

"So how are your parents doing?" asked Scott, deciding that was a good place to start.

"Not very good. They hardly ever talk to each other. Mom seems to be working longer hours. I guess that takes her mind off things. Dad doesn't seem to care. He parks himself in front of the TV and just sits there. If anything about Vietnam comes on, he quickly changes the channel."

"It's gotta be tough for everybody," said Scott. "I'm sure it will take a while. You can't expect things to be normal again overnight. So how's your classes going?"

"Classes are classes, no big deal. It's the between class stuff that makes me nervous."

"Are you talking about the fights?" asked Scott.

"That and the way I get harassed for money all the time."

"What are you talking about?" asked Scott.

"I can't even go to the bathroom anymore without getting harassed. The Black guys are always picking on the little White guys."

"Yeah, I've seen it happen a few times, but I didn't know it was happening to you."

"Yep, I even gave them my money a couple times. Didn't want the crap beaten out of me. Had to skip lunch one day—no money. Now I don't carry a wallet. I stick the money in my socks. When they ask me for money, I pull out my pockets to show them I don't have any. But they still don't believe me."

Scott didn't get angry very often, but his face was beginning to feel warm, his heartbeat rising rapidly. "You need to plan ahead. Let's get with Brian and Mark and put together a restroom strategy. From now on, you're not going in there alone."

"Yeah, I guess I gotta do something," mumbled Bob.

When they arrived at school, the boys got off the bus and waited for Brian and Mark to come down the steps. Scott told them what was going on while Bob listened quietly, embarrassed over all the attention.

"I'm ready to bust some heads," said Mark. "This shit has to stop."

"It pisses me off too," said Brian. "But starting a brawl won't make it any better. We need to plan on hitting the restrooms together. Make a big show of it. Strength in numbers. Then we need to somehow get their names, find out who these guys are and report them to the vice principal."

"Good luck with that," said Mark. "If they find out you ratted on them, they'll beat the shit out of you for sure."

"You got a better idea?" asked Brian.

"Yeah, maybe I should tell my dad. He'll talk to the principal and threaten to arrest some of these assholes. Maybe then something will be done."

After Mark had calmed down a bit, they all decided to plot out their restroom strategy. Bathroom visitation would be a group effort. From then on, no less than three of them would walk in together at designated times and locations. That was the least they could do for Bob.

At lunchtime, Brian, Mark, and Scott were sitting at their usual table. They had successfully executed their plan after second period when Brian and Mark accompanied Bob to the first-floor bathroom. Prepared for a confrontation, the boys were relieved when the whole episode proved to be uneventful.

As they left, Bob told them that none of the usual suspects were there. But he thanked them anyway, saying, "It's good to know you have my back."

"Anytime," said Mark. "Let's stick with the plan."

"I thought I was done with bathroom assistance when I was potty-trained," teased Bob. "Are you guys gonna wipe my ass, too?"

With a collective chuckle, the boys were relieved to see Bob's sense of humor again, probably the best signal he could've delivered.

"Do you have enough room for a couple of band members?" asked Lynda.

The boys looked up from their table to see Lynda Lacey and Antonio Jackson standing by with their lunch trays. Caught off guard, they nervously contemplated the question.

"Absolutely," said Brian, as he scooted over.

"I don't mind hanging out with my favorite trumpet player," joked Antonio.

"Yeah, right," said Brian. "I thought you said it was Miles Davis."

"Well, you're a close second," said Antonio, as he flashed that warm, confident smile. "And yours is Doc Severinsen, right?"

"I thought it was until you came around," said Brian, prolonging the flattery competition.

It was clear that Brian was elated to be eating in the presence of the prettiest girl and a guy who was rapidly becoming the most popular kid in school.

Scott, who normally led the conversations, remained silent as he viewed the exchange inquisitively. This little adventure was breaking all the boundaries. Not only was Lynda Lacey sitting at a guy table, but she had showed up with a Black male sidekick.

Extending his hand to Scott, the musician formalized the greeting. "Hi, my name is Antonio."

Scott nervously shook his hand. "My name is Scott."

This was breaking all the protocols. Nobody had ever witnessed this type of handshake introduction between two kids before. It was clearly an adult tradition, something the kids had seen their parents perform at cocktail parties and social gatherings, but certainly not in the setting of a junior high cafeteria.

Not knowing what to say, Scott was noticeably intimidated by Antonio.

"Scott lives in our neighborhood," said Brian, trying to break the ice. "He plays on the basketball team. And this is Mark, he also lives in our neighborhood and plays football with me."

Mark was standoffish, hoping that Antonio would not extend his hand.

Recognizing Mark's reluctance, Antonio obliged. "So I'm sitting with a bunch of jocks?" he quipped.

"All right, guys, let's keep it clean," said Lynda. "Don't make me move over to the girls' table."

"That's okay, Lynda," joked Scott. "If you go, can you take me with you?"

Scott finally found his opening for a little sarcasm.

"Don't you wish," said Lynda with a grin.

As the conversation continued, the atmosphere became more relaxed, and the dialogue flowed more freely. It was apparent that Antonio could be comfortable in any setting; Mark, not so much.

Brian was relishing the moment, recognizing it as a milestone event, a transition to adulthood. Heads had turned and barriers were broken. They were witnessing baby steps toward the desegregation of Blacks and Whites, boys and girls, and musicians and athletes, proving that mixed company could sit down together at the same table, break bread, and interact with each other in a civil manner.

As it turned out, Lynda had recently made Antonio's acquaintance in the gymnasium during pep session planning. Antonio had been tasked with playing the national anthem, and Lynda, as head of the planning committee, was showing him where to stand and which microphone to use. When Antonio unleashed the harmonic blare of his trumpet in rehearsal, Lynda was, once again, struck by his star power. She couldn't help but visualize the reaction that would take place when Antonio made his first appearance in front of the entire student body.

Lynda knew that Antonio was someone who could turn heads and command respect, someone she needed in her circle. That's how the world worked. You needed to surround yourself with the right people if you wanted to assume leadership, and Lynda and Antonio were preparing to lead the way.

Chapter 18

"ARE YOU GETTING ENOUGH TO eat?" asked Brian, making his way through the crowded hallway to the school cafeteria. Bob Wills looked even scrawnier than usual. His cheeks looked hollow, and his sunken eyes were deepened by the dark rings that contrasted sharply with his pale white skin. Brian almost called him a raccoon, but decided to be more considerate.

"I'm eating okay," said Bob. "If you're asking about people stealing my lunch money, that hasn't happened since we started ganging up together."

"I'm not implying anything," said Brian. "You just look skinnier than normal. That's all."

"Well, I never weigh myself, but I'm usually not very hungry. When I get home, I start the paper route and fix myself a sandwich when I'm all done."

Bob was referencing his new job as delivery boy for *The News-Sentinel,* Fort Wayne's evening newspaper. When the afternoon carrier quit his job, Bob jumped at the opportunity to add another delivery route. Now he was responsible for both the morning and evening newspapers.

"Dad and I don't really eat together anymore. In fact, none of us do anything together anymore. When Mom and Dad are home together, it's usually the silent treatment, and when they actually talk, it turns into an argument."

"Maybe you're just too damn tired," implied Brian. "Now that you have the evening route, you should dump the morning route and get yourself an extra couple hours of sleep. The evening route is a much better gig."

"Nah, I'm makin' some really good coin right now. My bank account is growing twice as fast. And I talked to the manager at the corner Marathon station, and he told me I can start pumpin' gas there on weekends when I turn fifteen. That's only two months away."

"That's just wonderful," replied Brian, in a sarcastic tone. "Then you'll be a full-time grunt monkey. When the hell are ya gonna have time for some fun? You're only young once."

"I figure I'll have enough money to buy a car when I'm sixteen. I've been checkin' out those Pontiac Firebirds and the new GTOs. Then you guys will be checkin' me out big-time when I'm layin' some rubber and cruisin' around with hot babes."

"Hmmm, I guess that's not a bad plan, after all," chuckled Brian. "Maybe I can cash in on your scraps."

"If you're lucky," said Bob with a grin. "But I'll need to keep a couple spares in reserve."

"Now you're dreaming." Brian laughed.

"Wish I had the same lunch period as you guys," said Bob. "Let's stop off at the can before you go eat."

The restroom was crowded as usual as Brian washed his hands and combed his hair, arranging his long bangs across his forehead just above the eyebrows.

While looking in the mirror, he captured the image of a commotion toward the back of the restroom. Twirling around to get a better look, he recognized the frail outline of Bob getting cornered near the back stall, surrounded by three Black kids.

As his heart began to race, Brian approached the disturbance, trying to make out the dialogue. He couldn't hear what they were saying, but there was no denying the look of apprehension on Bob's face.

"I told you I don't have any money!" announced Bob in a tone loud enough for everyone to hear.

Before Brian could intervene, one of the Black students pushed Bob against the wall.

"Shut your mouth, boy. I don't appreciate you mouthin' off."

"Hey, leave him alone," said Brian, walking toward them.

As the restroom started to clear, someone snuck up behind Brian and pinned his arms behind his back in a full nelson. Before he could respond, another guy punched him in the stomach.

Suddenly there was a mad scramble as panicky students rushed for the door, fleeing in exodus. Buckled over in pain, Brian sank to his knees, gasping for air.

Before Bob could respond, someone shoved him back against the wall.

"We ain't fuckin' around, boy," said one of the assailants.

"Hey, cut the shit!" came a loud voice from the bathroom door. "What the hell is goin' on?"

Brian looked up from the floor to see Malcom Mosely.

"It's okay, brother. We got things under control," said one of the Black kids.

"Don't you fuckin' *brother* me. I ain't your brother," said Malcom. Then, reaching down to help Brian, Malcom expressed his concern, "What did they do to you?"

"They're tryin' to take my buddy's money," said Brian, worried he might sound like a snitch. "When I tried to help him out, they punched me."

"Who punched you?"

Brian tentatively pointed out the culprit as Malcom seethed. This was a side of Malcom he'd never seen before. Although he was big and powerful, Malcom was always in control of his emotions, ever the gentle giant.

Grabbing the culprit's shirt with his huge hand, Malcom slammed the boy against the wall in a fit of anger. Then he grabbed the boy's throat with a choke hold, forcing him to gasp for air.

"How does that feel, asshole? Can't you breathe?"

Malcom then threw him to the floor, his head slamming against the metal partition. The other two boys looked as if they might respond, but Malcom wheeled around and glared.

"Seriously? You think you're man enough? I chew up punks like you and spit them into the garbage."

As the predators backed away in surrender mode, Malcom put one arm around Brian and the other around Bob, staring down the thugs.

"I let you off easy this time. The next time we'll be moppin' up your blood."

Escorting Brian and Bob to the door, Malcom turned around one last time. "If you have any ideas about increasing your numbers, I'll gather the whole damned football team. I'm sure we'd all enjoy feasting on your punk asses."

Walking down the hall together, Brian breathed a sigh of relief. "I owe you, man. Thanks for havin' my back."

Easing back into his jovial self, Malcom flashed his famous grin, acting as though nothing had happened.

"Always happy to help. That's what teammates are for, right?"

"Yep, you're right."

"You'd do the same for me, wouldn't you?" asked Malcom.

Brian hesitated, then responded reluctantly, "Sure, at least I'd try."

"Heh, heh, heh," bellowed Malcom, releasing a big, hearty belly laugh. "That wasn't very convincing."

Chapter 19

AS THE SCHOOL YEAR APPROACHED the end of the first semester, Jefferson Junior High appeared to be calming down, almost falling into a routine. The fights that seemed to be weekly occurrences were now few and far between. Most of the troublemakers were either permanently expelled or flunking out, proving that 98 percent of the problems were caused by 2 percent of the population.

Malcom Mosely once commented, "It's amazing how peaceful life can be when you eliminate all the riffraff." But, despite the waning violence, the school was still predominantly segregated in terms of who hung out together. Although most of the racial hurdles had been cleared in athletics and extracurriculars, situations that required teamwork and cooperation, little progress had been made in other areas.

Football season was over, but not before reaching a fever pitch at the conclusion of an undefeated season. With high expectations heading into the city championship, the title game arrived on a cold, wet, and windy day in November, the kind of day that can pop up unannounced in northern Indiana.

By kickoff, temperatures were hovering around freezing and the windchill factor was in the teens. With a mixture of rain and sleet, the blustery winds were creating a misery index much worse than snow.

The game started out appropriately enough as the Portage Ram kicker swung his leg through the ball and landed smack on his butt, the ball skidding along the field like a hockey puck. The rest of the game would follow suit, looking more like an Ice Capades performance than a football game.

Soaking wet and paralyzingly numb, neither team could execute their game plans or handle the football with any degree of security. When it was all said and done, the Jefferson Patriots were defeated 6-0 on a fumble recovery that was scooped up near the goal line and advanced for the game's only score.

After boarding the bus, the players had few regrets. All they cared about was getting back to the locker room, stripping out of their freezing-wet clothes, and jumping into a hot shower.

Fortunately, the cheerleaders did not suffer the same amount of misery. Lynda Lacey had done her homework, warning them of the impending weather and recommending gloves, knit caps and sweaters to go along with their letter jackets. In order to keep up appearances, they would strip off their jackets and gloves long enough to perform their routines, then quickly bundle up again between performances.

Although the added layers helped, they soon realized that keeping warm was next to impossible with bare legs, and since short skirts were part of the dress code, there were few alternatives. Lynda would not dare to challenge cheerleading protocol by covering up sexy legs with sweatpants or leggings; some things were still sacred.

But appearances became less significant as the bleachers emptied at halftime, no one willing to brave the elements for another two quarters. Jada Brown and Karen Gadby suggested they should leave too, pointing out that cheerleaders without a crowd were pretty irrelevant, but Lynda insisted their presence was required as a means of moral support for the players, a proclamation that went unchallenged.

In fact, the team chemistry of the cheerleading squad had progressed remarkably well considering the mixture of personalities and egos. Mrs. Taylor's role as coach had declined significantly, reduced to figurehead status. She saw no need to intervene as long as the girls were in lockstep behind Lynda's leadership.

Any tension that may have existed between the new and returning members seemed to dissipate as Lynda and Jada collaborated on new routines, creating a style of choreography that was both innovative and entertaining. Even Karen, who could be resistant and stubborn, was embracing the new moves and warming up to Jada as they worked together.

"You've come a long way, baby," said Jada one day using the catch-phrase from the Virginia Slims cigarette commercials. "Maybe we should celebrate with a few smokes."

"It's not so hard when you're learning from a foxy mama," quipped Karen.

The whole squad burst out laughing at this clever exchange, especially Jada. The use of Black slang by Karen caught everyone off guard. Not only was it humorous, but it paid a compliment in a good-natured way and signaled her willingness to be more open-minded.

"There'll be no smoking as long as I'm captain," remarked Lynda in jest. "You know the team rules."

"Just like Lynda to spoil a little fun with her rules," jabbed Mindy.

The cohesion was beginning to build and not a moment too soon. With the beginning of basketball season, the cheerleaders would be thrown into the limelight, for nothing could compare to the electrifying intensity of a packed gymnasium filled with rowdy fans cheering on Indiana's favorite sport.

Lynda's job was to match that intensity and create a little excitement of her own by selecting music that would energize the crowd and add to the raucous atmosphere. During practice sessions, she loved to crank the loud music over the gymnasium speakers, creating the sort of adrenaline rushes that stimulated her squad to practice harder.

Antonio, as leader of the pep band, was instrumental in Lynda's song selection. He helped her and Jada choose the kind of music that was popular, relevant, and conducive to their choreography.

Before a game would start, the cheerleaders usually did a routine to The Isley Brothers's song, "It's Your Thing," and the crowd loved to sing along.

And at halftime, they would do a whole dance routine to "Theme from Shaft," and if Jefferson went on a run and the other team called time-out, they'd play a popular Jerry Reed song, "When You're Hot, You're Hot."

And last but not least, when games were nearly over and Jefferson was assured of another victory, they would almost always fire up an old favorite from Ray Charles, "Hit the Road Jack."

But no game would ever commence without Antonio's patriotic solo of the national anthem, followed by his pep band's *oom-pah-pah* rhythms, causing the fans to sway back and forth and transform the bleachers into a sea of waves. Relishing the spotlight, Antonio and his band knew how to work the crowd into a frenzy.

On the hardwood, Scott Clever was beginning to make his mark, fueled by his growth spurt of three inches in less than one year. At six feet two inches, he was one of the taller players on the team, and his long legs suggested there was more to come.

With spindly arms and legs, Scott's coordination struggled to keep up with his height, causing him to look a bit awkward when handling the ball. Consequently, Coach Barrett played him at the forward position, where his rebounding prowess supplanted his propensity for dribbling and shooting.

The coach liked his feistiness on the boards and the way he scrapped with opponents, a rough-and-tumble style of play that drew lots of fouls and paid dividends at the free throw line.

Embracing his new role, Scott decided to dedicate himself to where the team needed him most, working in the paint and doing the dirty work. Or as Mr. Clever told his son, "You gotta bring your lunch pail to work every day, roll-up your sleeves, and get down to business."

Like a true Hoosier, Scott took his basketball seriously, and his buddies got a kick out of watching his transformation from jokester to taskmaster.

With the year winding down, the annual Christmas program took center stage, a festive occasion where band and choir members performed holiday-inspired songs in front of family and friends. Not only did it signal the unofficial end to the semester, but it served up an abundance of yuletide joy as the students departed for their holiday breaks.

Without a suitable theater to serve as host, the gymnasium took center stage once again. As a makeshift concert venue, it achieved the bare minimum of deliverables, which is to say it adequately accommodated the gallery. With its hardwood floors, metal bleachers, and cinderblock walls, the cavernous gymnasium was an acoustical nightmare, delivering a sound quality that could only be described as wretched.

Nevertheless, school administrators did their best to adapt and create a festive atmosphere.

For the choir, portable risers were set up at midcourt, along with rows of folding chairs and music stands for the band members. On one side of the risers, next to the piano, a ten-foot, fully decorated Christmas tree was on display, and on the other side, next to the band, a large Santa Claus faced the bleachers with one hand up, as if waving to the crowd.

Compared to basketball games, Christmas crowds were usually sparce, making the bleachers appear barren and hollow. But this year was different, largely driven by the star power of Antonio Jackson. In addition to parents and siblings, a large student population showed up for the first time, nearly filling the bleachers to capacity.

Determined to deliver a crowd-pleasing production, Mr. Stoops worked with the choir director, Mrs. Berghoff, to create a memorable performance, one that would feature two mystery acts.

The official program, distributed at the beginning of the show, listed two songs by the band, followed by two songs by the choir. The bottom of the program simply read: "Two Encore Performances."

When the band completed its second number, "White Christmas," the crowd responded with a warm round of applause as Antonio quietly slipped away from the trumpet section and exited the gym.

Next up, the choir performed a rousing rendition of "Sleigh Ride," followed by a soothing version of "Silver Bells."

As the applause died down, Antonio reentered the gymnasium wearing a bright, glittery jacket of red sequins. Standing up in admiration, the student section applauded and whistled, eager to see what sort of treat Antonio would deliver.

While everyone's attention was on Antonio, Mr. Stoops was busy setting up a row of chairs in front of the band, creating a woodwind section of four clarinets, two saxophones, and one oboe.

Taking his place in front of the ensemble, Antonio calmly waited for the crowd to quiet down, patiently creating an ambiance for his first number. After complete silence had been achieved, Antonio turned to his woodwind section and tapped his foot to the tempo. On cue, the woodwinds proceeded to deliver a soothing preamble that served as a perfect introduction to Antonio's brass solo, a heartfelt and moving arrangement of "Have Yourself a Merry Little Christmas."

In the past, the school had witnessed Antonio's ability to belt out loud and high-spirited solos, but never had they seen him play with this kind of sentimental emotion, tranquilizing his audience into a slow submission. Dazed into a stupor, the crowd was visibly moved by the melancholy Christmas classic.

When the song was over, there was a brief moment of silence, as if the crowd needed to snap out of its trance. But the silence was soon followed by an exhilarating round of applause that slowly materialized into a standing ovation.

Antonio bowed his head in gratitude and turned toward his woodwind section. He then extended his arm in recognition of their support, and the audience responded on cue.

As the second round of applause concluded, Mr. Stoops took to the microphone.

"Thank you very much, Antonio, and thanks to everyone for attending tonight's program. I want you to know the last piece was put together entirely by Antonio Jackson. He wrote and arranged the woodwind accompaniment all by himself, staying after school three nights a week for the past month, practicing until everyone had mastered their parts. He's truly a rare talent and we are lucky to have him."

As the audience applauded one more time, Mr. Stoops grabbed the microphone again.

"We're not done yet. We still have one more encore performance. I hope you enjoy it. Merry Christmas to everyone and enjoy your holiday season."

While Mr. Stoops was talking, six members of the choir stepped down from the risers and formed a small line next to the piano. The group consisted of three White students and three Black students, alternating in a black-white-black pattern and holding hands.

Antonio walked over to the piano to take his place at the keyboard, but before he could sit down, a little girl came running to him from the bleachers carrying a long-stemmed white carnation. As she handed him the flower, the crowd let out with a series of oohs and aahs, recognizing her gift as a gesture of goodwill.

Antonio accepted the carnation and kissed the little girl on the forehead, placing the flower stem through the buttonhole on his lapel in boutonniere-style fashion. Everyone laughed and applauded as the girl ran back to the bleachers.

Antonio then spoke into the microphone. "Thank you very much. That's the first time a girl has ever given me a flower."

Everyone laughed as Antonio continued. "We'd like to conclude our program this evening with a little song that has been sweeping the nation. I'm sure most of you have heard it, most likely from a very popular Coca-Cola commercial that's been playing on TV."

Antonio sat down at the piano and played the first chord as the black-and-white ensemble harmonically delivered the lyrics to "I'd Like to Teach the World to Sing."

Chapter 20

Antonio Jackson's father, Marquis, moved his family to Fort Wayne, Indiana, in 1968, shortly after the death of his father, Elijah. Like his father and grandfather before him, Marquis played the trumpet, occasionally performing with brass bands and marching in parades, but he did not share the same degree of passion for music as his ancestors.

As a child, he always had a knack for fixing things, a fascination for how things worked and how they were put together. Marquis loved to visit the local landfill, seeking out old, discarded items that appeared salvageable and suitable for a second chance at life. He discovered that many people threw away perfectly good household appliances simply because they had been replaced with newer versions. Sometimes he would bring them home, tear them apart, and put them back together again just to understand the mechanics. Once he restored his items, he would then turn around and sell them at secondhand stores and pawnshops.

At the age of thirteen, Marquis took his first job with a local landscaping company. He was hired mostly to cut lawns but was often pulled in to help with other jobs, like the heavy lifting that comes along with planting trees and shrubs. As his jobs became larger and more frequent, he eventually graduated from small push mowers to riding lawnmowers and tractors. Sometimes he would hang out in the shop on weekends and help out with oil changes, blade sharpening, and spark plug replacement, eventually getting involved with the mechanics of repair. As he became more of a fixture in the repair shop, Marquis was offered a position as a full-time mechanic and his wages were bumped up from twenty-five cents to thirty cents per hour.

In 1947, Marquis Jackson purchased his first automobile, a 1932 Ford Model A coupe for sixty-five dollars. He soon became familiar with its three-speed, four-cylinder engine, producing forty horsepower and a top speed of sixty-five miles per hour. His cousins were always tinkering around with cars, and Marquis learned a great deal from watching and helping them out.

With a few new parts and some fine-tuning, he soon had his Model A up and running, feeling proud of his accomplishment, and liberated by his new means of transportation. No longer satisfied with lawn mower maintenance and repair, Marquis became fascinated with automobiles. He realized there would always be a need for transportation and there was little doubt that technological advances in automobiles would be the driving force.

At the age of nineteen, Marquis took a job at the neighborhood filling station pumping gas and handling oil changes. It wasn't much of a challenge and it didn't pay very much, but he figured it was a baby step toward breaking into the auto industry. After six months of menial labor, Marquis left enough of an impact on the station owner to earn a full-time job in the garage. Although he was mostly doing engine tune-ups, brake pad replacements, and minor repairs, he was beginning to familiarize himself with a wide variety of cars and engines. Along the way, his curiosity continued to grow.

As fate would have it, Marquis Jackson's life took a sudden turn at the age of twenty-four. He was attending a small jazz concert in a local park, when he was introduced to Chantelle, the sweetest little thing he'd ever laid eyes on. She was everything he was not, well-dressed, educated, and confident. Chantelle did not talk like the other locals, the ones that Marquis grew up with. Instead, she spoke with a degree of sophistication that was completely untraceable to her humble roots.

Intimidated by her charm and refinement, Marquis struggled to carry on a conversation, feeling inferior and unqualified as a suitor. But, unbeknownst to Marquis, Chantelle was allured by his good looks, masculine physique, and shy mannerisms. She tried to make him feel comfortable as he sheepishly buried his hands in his pockets, embarrassed by the perpetual stains from the grease and grime of engine repair.

As the two became acquainted, Marquis learned that Chantelle had lived in Saint Louis for two years, where she attended a community college and earned her associate's degree in secretarial science. Through her education and training, Chantelle became proficient in shorthand and dictation, gaining employment with one of the more prestigious law firms in town, Landry & Boudreaux.

As her responsibilities expanded, Chantelle put her stenography skills to work as a court reporter, organizing her transcriptions into sources for legal research and court case documentation. Her involvement with some of the more prominent lawsuits and trials in town contributed to her astute awareness of New Orleans business and politics, a world far removed from Marquis's neighborhood gas station.

Despite all their disparities, a shared interest in music turned out to be the common bond that struck a chord. Chantelle told Marquis that she learned to play the piano at an early age and was actively involved in her church, where she performed with the choir each Sunday. When Marquis told her about his trumpet playing and the Jackson tradition of brass bands, Chantelle was intrigued. She wanted to hear him play, and he wanted to attend Chantelle's church, where he could watch her perform. The courtship was on.

Two years later, Marquis married Chantelle in her church, in front of family and friends, very much in love and excited about their future. Aside from his new state of marital bliss, Marquis's life hadn't changed very much. He continued to work in auto repair, mostly near the neighborhood where he grew up, while Chantelle commuted to the city every day, advancing her career with Landry and Boudreaux.

Together they made a decent living, comfortably managing their domestic affairs and preparing their home for a family. They especially enjoyed the freedom of going out on Saturday nights and meeting up with friends at their favorite clubs and restaurants. But they never missed Sunday morning church services. For Chantelle had become even more active in her church, taking over as choir director, and setting up a Sunday school where parishioners could mold their offspring into children of God.

In 1957, Marquis and Chantelle welcomed their very own child of God, a baby boy named Anthony. Like many firstborn babies, Anthony received an overwhelming amount of attention, especially from his doting mother, who made sure he had the best of everything.

Thriving on the attention, Anthony developed an outgoing personality, infectiously spreading his cheer and good spirits wherever he went. He especially enjoyed watching his mother perform on Sundays, swaying back and forth to the soulful sounds of gospel music. Sometimes Marquis and Chantelle would collaborate on Friday evenings, combining piano with trumpet for impromptu family performances, and Anthony would dance and sing along with his cousins.

As the Jacksons planned for Anthony's future, they became more and more concerned about him growing up in a segregated South, wondering if he would ever reach his potential in a society where Black people were routinely discriminated against.

The Civil Rights movement was gathering steam in the 60s, and Martin Luther King was leading the way. More than ever before, African Americans were protesting for equal rights and fighting for a better future, the Jacksons included. Inspired by King's "I Have a Dream" speech, they started attending meetings, organizing protests, and participating in marches. Marquis was tired of working long hours for low wages and Chantelle was certain that she was making less money than her White counterparts.

Like many before them, the Jacksons had reached a point of despair, a feeling that life wasn't going anywhere and they would never get ahead no matter how hard they worked.

For the first time ever, Chantelle raised the possibility of leaving New Orleans and moving North. She had a sister in Saint Louis, Missouri, and a brother in Fort Wayne, Indiana. Both of them talked about the North as a land of opportunity, a place where they could raise their family with more freedom, and earn higher wages from good, union-supported jobs.

Chantelle convinced Marquis they should, at the very least, explore the possibilities. She also convinced him to attend a trade school, explaining how a formal education and a certification in automobile mechanics would open up more doors, especially in the North.

Marquis not only agreed, but he soon discovered a passion for learning he never knew existed. This kind of schooling was different from reading, writing, and arithmetic. He was finally getting an education in something he loved, a chance to improve his skills and advance his career.

Although he was usually tired at the end of a long workday, Marquis would put on a pot of coffee and head off to class with a feeling of pride. He was gaining a whole new appreciation for automobiles, learning far more about technology and engineering than he ever grasped in his prior development, the age-old process of trial and error.

By the time Anthony reached the fifth grade, he was displaying a rare mastery over the trumpet, a skill level his teachers had never witnessed before at such an early age. Chantelle and Marquis were proud of the fact that they had trained him properly, raising him in a musical environment, surrounded by so many positive influences.

"No, this is different," said Mr. Davis, Anthony's teacher. "This is something special, something you can't teach. Anthony appears to be blessed with a sixth sense. There's clearly something in his DNA that separates him from the other ninety-nine percent."

Chantelle knew that Anthony was a blessing from God, this latest opinion only confirmed her intuition. There were other signals as well, characteristics that separated him from the pack. Not only was he highly skilled as a musician, but he was beginning to display sophistication beyond his years.

Anthony did not talk like the other kids his age. Instead of using common prose, he spoke with a degree of refinement, a polished diction that was more fitting of an aristocrat. Chantelle blamed it on the Hollywood influence, the old films he'd watch on their black-and-white TV with glamorous movie stars like Cary Grant and Audrey Hepburn.

Sometimes Marquis would laugh out loud at something Anthony would say. "Where did you learn to talk like that?" he asked. "You certainly didn't learn that from me. That's gotta be from your mother's side of the family."

As Anthony's sophisticated persona continued to blossom, he began to develop an appreciation for fashion, knowing that appearances were a big part of one's image. When he was preparing to perform, he would meticulously plan out his wardrobe, carefully selecting and coordinating his apparel with an instinctive flair for style.

But a particular style or image was not complete without a hairstyle to match, a coiffure that would contribute to his star power. Anthony knew his hair needed a change. He had witnessed the swagger and flamboyance of musicians like Chuck Berry and Little Richard. Their hairstyles were different, not like the Afros and flat-tops doled out at the local barber shop.

When Anthony finally convinced his mother of the need for something trendier, she took him to see her hairstylist. With a little effort and some chemical straighteners, Chantelle's hairdresser was able to recreate Chuck Berry's conk-like hairdo, longer and slicked back on top in a semipompadour style.

Just when Chantelle and Marquis thought the transformation of Anthony was complete, he came home from school one day excited about his new Spanish class.

"When we're in Spanish class," he announced, "we're required to use the Spanish version of our names. I really like mine. Now everyone calls me Antonio."

"That's nice," said Chantelle, as Marquis nodded his head. "To be clear, this is only when you're in Spanish class, right?"

"No," said Anthony. "From now on I want to be known as Antonio."

"You can't just change your name," challenged Marquis.

"I'm not," said Anthony. "It's just a different version of my name. It's no different from James and Jim, or Robert and Bob."

Chantelle and Marquis had no argument for his logic. They had always fostered their son's freedom of expression; why would this be any different?

From that day on, their son would go by his new name: Antonio Jackson. The transformation was complete.

One week later, the Jacksons received a phone call from Thomas, Chantelle's brother in Fort Wayne, Indiana. Thomas had worked for seven years on the assembly line at International Harvester. He had always boasted about his high union wages, a rate of pay that was much greater than Marquis ever earned.

"Can you get Marquis a job in the factory?" ask Chantelle.

"I have something much better," said Thomas. "O'Connor Buick is opening a brand-new Cadillac dealership in Fort Wayne, and they need mechanics to work in their service department. I have a connection that could land Marquis a job if he wants it. You know how Marquis has an eye for Cadillacs!"

"Sounds great," said Chantelle. "But what about me?"

Chapter 21

THE BIRTH OF A NEW year is traditionally a time to reflect, make amends, and set new goals. As 1972 rolled around, the country was still dealing with many of the same issues that had been around for years. Richard Nixon was in his fourth year as president, entering an election year and continuing to deal with a horrendous war in Vietnam. With no end in sight, the seemingly senseless war had been raging for nearly a decade, devastating a nation's resolve, and taking fifty thousand American lives along the way. Although peace negotiations had been taking place in Paris, they were mostly on-again, off-again as neither side relinquished any ground.

In January, Nixon announced a major troop withdrawal that would take place over a five-month period, but every time there were hints of de-escalation, new bombing missions were launched, and public sentiment turned to skepticism. As America's frustration grew into resentment, protests became more widespread and indiscriminate.

On January 10, Hubert Humphrey, former vice president under Lyndon Johnson, announced his candidacy for president, expressing his criticism of the war and saying that America's involvement would have ended if he was elected president in 1968.

In February, President Nixon embarked on a much-publicized diplomatic mission to the People's Republic of China (PRC). It marked the first time a US president had ever visited China and ended twenty-five years of noncommunication between the two countries. Nixon promoted the event as a new beginning for diplomacy and an opportunity to normalize relations with the Eastern Hemisphere.

Throughout the week-long affair, Americans were subjected to grandiose displays of diplomacy as Nixon appeared on television at lavish state dinners, wining and dining with Chairman Mao, the head of the Communist Party and leader of the PRC since 1949. The controversial meeting generated a great deal of debate given that China had been backing and funding North Vietnam's military throughout the war.

In March, the largest bas-relief sculpture in the world was officially unveiled on Stone Mountain, just outside of Atlanta, Georgia. Standing nine stories high and covering three acres of mountain surface, the carvings represented three famous Confederates on horseback: President Jefferson Davis, Generals Robert E. Lee, and Stonewall Jackson.

Previously owned by the Venable brothers, the mountain was a source of minerals for their rock quarry business until it was sold to the state of Georgia in 1958. James Venable served as mayor for the town of Stone Mountain in the 1940s and Grand Wizard for the National Knights of the Ku Klux Klan for nearly twenty-five years. More than a century after the Civil War and the end of slavery, the South was still resurrecting monuments to their history of racism.

Also in March, the world of cinema was taken by storm as Paramount Pictures released what would soon become the highest grossing motion picture of all time, *The Godfather*. Chronicling the fictional life of an Italian immigrant, the movie explored the world of organized crime and the way politicians, judges, and policemen were manipulated with money, power, and intimidation. Critically acclaimed as one of the most influential films ever made, it was nominated for seven Academy Awards.

On April 17, Nina Kuscsik crossed the finish line of the Boston Marathon with an official time of 3:10:26. After seventy-five years, women were allowed to compete in the Boston Marathon for the first time. Nina finished ahead of eight other women; the men's field included 1,210 participants.

On May 15, Alabama Governor George Wallace was shot four times in the abdomen while on the campaign trail in Laurel, Maryland, effectively bringing his third bid for the presidency to an end. Although

Wallace survived the assassin's attack, he would be paralyzed from the waist down and spend the rest of his life in a wheelchair.

On June 18, a seemingly insignificant event was reported in *The Washington Post*, barely recognizable at the bottom of the newspaper's front page. The article was entitled "Five Held in Plot to Bug Democratic Offices."

The offices were the headquarters for the Democratic National Committee and were located in a complex that housed the Watergate Hotel in Washington DC. The next day, *The Washington Post* would assign two young reporters with little experience to follow-up on the story. Their names were Bob Woodward and Carl Bernstein. Over the next couple of years, the whole country would become familiar with those two names, and investigative journalism would take center stage like never before.

With June in full swing, the recent grads of Jefferson Junior High were basking in the glory of summer vacation. Fort Wayne's first year of forced integration was in the books and considered mostly a success. With the experimental phase complete, the prospect for year two was optimistic, and for the kids from Coldwater Creek who would be entering high school for the first time, racial integration was the least of their worries.

No longer top-dogs at a small junior high, transitioning to a new environment would be a daunting task, especially considering the size and diversity of a large conglomerate like Northrop High School. The thought of mixing in with a bunch of kids they worshipped from afar— the ones they saw racing around in cars, smoking cigarettes, dating, and flaunting their independence—was somewhat intimidating. Some of them even had celebrity-like reputations resulting from their athletic achievements and the publicity they received in local newspapers.

For students like Lynda Lacey and Antonio Jackson, high school represented another opportunity to prove themselves all over again. They had been grooming their whole lives for this moment. For everyone else, the next step would be a giant leap, filled mostly with apprehension and anxiety.

In the meantime, the carefree days of summer were waiting to be soaked in, a time for teenagers to frolic and muse in the trivial pursuit of frivolous pleasures.

After all, that's what summer vacations were for, and the summer of '72 was in full swing, as celebrated in Alice Cooper's smash summer hit: "School's Out."

Chapter 22

Scott Clever was in the kitchen frying up his morning bacon and eggs, wondering how his day would play out. His dad had just left for work and his mom was already busy with her household chores.

"Looks like the new neighbors are moving in this morning," said Mrs. Clever.

"What new neighbors?" asked Scott.

"The ones that bought the Wilson house. You knew it was sold, right?"

"Yeah, I guess. I haven't paid much attention."

The Wilsons had lived across the street, a couple doors down. Scott didn't know much about them except that they had two little kids and their house had gone up for sale in May. It wasn't unusual for houses to go on the market in the spring. Summer was the busy season for real estate as families shuffled around, trying to upgrade their lifestyles and settle into their new homes before transitioning their children to new schools in the fall.

Scott looked out the front window and saw the big eighteen-wheel tractor-trailer labeled in large print: Atlas Van Lines. He watched the movers roll the dollies up and down the truck ramp, back and forth to the house. Some of the boxes made their way to the front door, where a large rug led from the front porch into the house. The remaining boxes were dumped in the garage, which served as a makeshift staging area for the refrigerator, washer, and dryer.

Trying to catch a glimpse of the new neighbors, Scott saw nothing but boxes and workers scurrying about their business. Parked in the street, he spotted an Oldsmobile Cutlass with an Indiana license plate, a vehicle that belonged to the new neighbors, he assumed. The only other items that caught his attention were a couple of hockey sticks that were wedged between all the boxes.

"Do you know anything about who's moving in?" asked Scott.

"Not much," was the reply. "Their last name sounded Italian, but I can't remember it. Mrs. Wilson said they have a son that will go to Northrop High School this fall, but I'm not sure what year he is."

"Do you know if he plays hockey?" asked Scott.

"I have no idea, why?"

"Well, there's a couple hockey sticks on the driveway."

"Maybe we can check in with them in a couple days," said Mrs. Clever. "I thought I'd bring over a cake and introduce myself. Sort of a 'welcome to the neighborhood' gesture. Maybe you can come along and meet the new boy that's going to Northrop."

"You can't be serious! I'm not showing up on their doorstep with my mom and a cake. He'll think I'm a real nerd, for sure."

"Well, how else are you gonna meet him?"

"The same way I met all the other kids in the neighborhood. Just by hangin' out. I certainly don't wanna appear anxious. And just my luck, he probably plays hockey. Nobody else in our neighborhood plays hockey."

"Well, maybe you should broaden your horizon a bit," said Mrs. Clever. "Besides, I thought you liked *all* sports."

"It's not that I don't like hockey. It's just that nobody around here *plays* hockey. You can't just gather up some kids and get a pickup game of hockey. The skating part is something you have to learn at an early age, and then you have to get your parents to drive you to the hockey rinks. Most kids who play hockey don't play other sports."

"Suit yourself," said Mrs. Clever. "It's not like you can't be friends with someone who plays hockey."

Scott decided to drop the whole conversation. Explaining the nuances of hockey and neighborhood friendships to his mother was a waste of time, but he couldn't help but be intrigued with the idea of another kid in the neighborhood, someone to hang out with and stir up a little mischief. He decided to keep his eye on the new neighbors for any clues, and notify Brian and Mark accordingly.

Three days later, the first opportunity presented itself. Bob Wills had just finished his afternoon delivery of *The News-Sentinel* and was standing on the driveway with Scott Clever. They heard a radio blasting and looked up to see an Oldsmobile Cutlass rolling to a stop in front of the driveway. Upon closer look, Scott realized it was actually a souped-up version of the Cutlass, a 442 in crimson red with a white vinyl roof and mag wheels. Behind the steering wheel was a young, rugged-looking kid with black shaggy hair and a hooked nose that looked crooked, like it might have been broken at some point.

"Which one of you is Scott Clever?" asked the kid behind the steering wheel.

"That would be me," said Scott, as they approached the vehicle.

"I think my mom talked to your mom yesterday. She brought over a cake. My name is Steve Marino."

"That sounds like my mom, all right," said Scott. "This is Bob, your local newspaper carrier."

"Nice ride," said Bob. "Is it yours?"

"Yeah, I got it last year."

"Pretty sweet," said Scott.

"It'll do. It's a sixty-nine, low mileage, four hundred under the hood. It's not a speed demon, but it can boogie pretty good when I punch it. My dad has lots of connections in the auto industry."

"Oh, yeah?" said Scott. "What does he do?"

"Well, it's kinda complicated," said Steve. "I guess you could say he works for the union. Some people call him an organizer. He had a pretty big title with the Teamsters when we lived in Philadelphia."

"You lived in Philadelphia?"

"Yeah, we moved here in '68."

"Well, that explains the Flyers shirt you're wearing right now."

"Yep, I grew up playing lots of hockey in the Philly area. Hockey's pretty big on the East Coast. But it's pretty decent here too. That's one of the reasons why my dad took the Fort Wayne job. I've been playing with the Pepsi Komets the past couple years."

"Cool," said Scott. "We like goin' to Komet games. We'll have to watch you play sometime."

"So I assume you're going to Northrop next year?" asked Steve.

"Yep, our first year. Gonna be sophomores. Where did you go last year?" asked Scott.

"I went to North Side, but I'm lookin' forward to Northrop, a brand-new school. I hear it's pretty cool. I'll be a junior, so I'm just a year ahead of you."

"Got it," said Scott. "My dad was a North Side Redskin, many years ago. He was a big basketball star back in the day."

"You play?" asked Steve. "You look tall enough."

"Yep, I played at Jefferson the past couple years—planning on playing at Northrop next year."

"Okay man, I better boogie," said Steve. "I'll talk to you dudes later."

Scott looked at Bob with a big grin as the Olds 442 pulled away.

"What are you grinning about?" asked Bob.

"Are you kidding? Don't you see? If we start hangin' out with this Marino guy, somebody with wheels, it means we can get around and not just hang out in the hood all summer. It looks like this summer may be shaping up after all," said Scott with a mischievous grin.

"He does have a sweet ride," said Bob. "But not as sweet as the one I'll be driving around next year."

"We'll cross that bridge when we get there," said Scott with a smile.

Scott and Bob decided to make the one-block stroll to Brian Johnson's house and update him with the news. Then they would knock on Mark Carter's door and bring him up-to-date. Suddenly, there were great expectations for the summer of '72.

Chapter 23

Brazil is a little town in the southwestern quadrant of Indiana, in between Terre Haute and Indianapolis. In 1913, this obscure little town gave birth to a baby boy by the name of James Hoffa. At the age of seven, Jimmy Hoffa's father died, and his mother moved to Detroit in an attempt to support her son and provide a better standard of living.

Jimmy Hoffa quit school at the age of fourteen and began working to help out his mother. As he scrambled from one odd job to another, he soon realized that most companies paid little respect to their laborers, forcing them to work long hours for little pay.

At five feet, five inches tall, Jimmy was not an intimidating figure, but he was often respected for his tenacity and resilience. Looked upon as a take-charge kind of guy, his coworkers were enthralled by his charisma and leadership.

With an abundance of unemployed laborers in the 1930s, hourly workers had little leverage to coerce management into higher pay and better working conditions. If employees were unhappy, they could easily be replaced by someone who was desperate for work.

In 1932, at the age of nineteen, Jimmy Hoffa was working on a loading dock at a distribution center for the Kroger grocery chain. He and his coworkers had grown increasingly frustrated with the way they were treated by the management. Forced to sit around while waiting for shipments to arrive, the workers received no compensation. Holding them in captivity, management insisted that laborers could not be paid for down time.

Despite efforts to negotiate on behalf of his coworkers, Jimmy realized he had no bargaining chip. So he waited until the right moment to execute his plan. It happened on the day a large shipment of ripe strawberries arrived on a hot afternoon. Their job was to pack them on ice and ship them off to the grocery stores.

Instead, Hoffa and his crew refused to work until they were offered a contract with higher pay. Suddenly faced with a labor strike and the possibility of a major spoilage loss, management gave in to their demands. As a result, Jimmy Hoffa's reputation grew into legendary status and the Kroger workers were soon absorbed into the Teamsters Union. It didn't take long before Hoffa was rewarded a full-time position with the Teamsters as a union organizer.

Jimmy Hoffa took his new job seriously and worked long hours to promote the labor movement. He was notorious for his strong work ethic and dedication to workers' rights. Not only was he a great contract negotiator, but his superior salesmanship enabled him to attract the smaller, independent unions, convincing them that one large, unified body would be more powerful and make them a force to be reckoned with.

As a result, Hoffa was instrumental in growing the Teamsters Union from seventy-five thousand members in 1933, to four hundred thousand by the end of the decade, and close to one million by 1950. He fought many battles along the way and learned the importance of building trust through alliances, using quid pro quo to leverage his partnerships. As a master negotiator, Hoffa was able to close many backroom deals via the execution of bribes, favors and collusion.

Throughout this period of growth, Hoffa discovered that many of the smaller, independent trucking unions were strongly influenced by organized crime, especially on the East Coast. If a labor dispute unfolded, management would often bribe local policemen, politicians, and criminal ruffians to break up the picket lines, battering the protesters with brute force and clearing the way for cheaper scab labor.

Seizing an opportunity, the mob used similar tactics to influence and gain control over the labor unions. In exchange for protection, higher wages, and better benefits, laborers were expected to cooperate with the crime syndicates that controlled large parts of New Jersey and Philadelphia. In addition to transporting stolen goods, truckers were increasingly involved with gambling, loan sharking, and other illegal activities controlled by the mafia.

Jimmy Hoffa learned how to rub elbows with this criminal element when making his deals, and his accomplishments were ultimately rewarded in 1957 when he was elected president of the Teamsters. At two million members strong, the Teamsters Union was the largest and most powerful labor union in the country.

As Hoffa's power and influence continued to grow, his association with notorious crime bosses became more publicized. Often linked to Anthony Giacolone, a street boss with the Detroit syndicate, and Anthony Provenzano, a New Jersey captain for the Genovese crime family, Hoffa was called upon to testify in front of the Senate Select Committee on Improper Activities in Labor and Management, commonly referred to as the McClellan Committee.

As chief counsel for the committee, Robert Kennedy took center stage during the televised hearings while interrogating Hoffa and hundreds of witnesses, many of whom refused to answer questions by invoking their rights under the Fifth Amendment.

After 270 days of browbeating and witness badgering, the hearings concluded without any formal charges from the Justice Department. Hoffa remained defiant until the end and most of the public viewed the proceedings as nothing more than political grandstanding.

In 1964, Hoffa completed one of his most significant accomplishments with the signing of the National Master Freight Agreement, bringing roughly four hundred thousand long-haul drivers under one single union contract. But trouble continued to brew for Hoffa when he was accused of illegally using Teamster pension funds for real estate ventures and loans to underworld crime syndicates.

On trial in Tennessee, where he attempted to hide his indiscretions under a shell company, Hoffa was eventually indicted and convicted for jury tampering. Sentenced to eight years in prison, Hoffa was subsequently found guilty in a second trial in Chicago for improper use of the Teamsters' pension fund, earning him another five-year sentence, thirteen years in total.

Hoffa continued to appeal the convictions for three more years before surrendering to authorities at the Lewisburg Federal Penitentiary in 1967. After Hoffa entered prison, Frank Fitzsimmons, vice president of the Teamsters, was named acting president. But Hoffa's popularity continued as he ran for president again in 1968 while in prison, successfully securing another term, and once again, requesting the services of Fitzsimmons to act on his behalf.

Under Fitzsimmons's leadership, the Teamsters changed course and pursued a softer, more progressive agenda, sympathizing with the underprivileged and the plight of African American families.

When United Auto Workers (UAW) President Walter Reuther witnessed Frank Fitzsimmons's attendance at Martin Luther King's funeral, he was so impressed that he decided to pursue an alliance with the Teamsters. As a result, on July 24, 1968, Reuther and Fitzsimmons formed the Alliance for Labor Action (ALA), a joint venture between the UAW and the International Brotherhood of Teamsters (IBT). Their charter was to combine resources and pursue the unionization of overlooked labor groups, especially African Americans, who were often oppressed by substandard wages and benefits.

Dominic Marino grew up in Philadelphia and spent most of his life in the shipping business. Dom, as his friends called him, was very active in the Teamsters Union at an early age. His hard work and willingness to "do what it takes," scored many points with Teamster associates.

At the age of thirty-seven, Dom's dedication and loyalty was rewarded with a leadership role, president of Teamsters Local 115. As expected, he excelled at his duties and received the usual perks along the way: Thanksgiving turkeys, Christmas hams, Cuban cigars, box seats at Flyers and Eagles games, a Buick Riviera, and a gold Rolex watch on his fifteenth anniversary.

Dominic Marino was living the good life and he knew it. No matter where he went—restaurants, taverns, delis, sporting events—there was always someone he knew reaching out to shake his hand or pat him on the back. He couldn't imagine living anywhere else, which made the call he received in August 1968, all the more jolting. He was being asked to move his family to Fort Wayne, Indiana. As far as he was concerned, it might as well have been Timbuktu. The last thing he wanted to do was leave the place where he had spent his entire life. But when the Teamsters ask you to do something, you do it; it's really not a question.

Dom was told about the Alliance for Labor Action and how the Teamsters were joining forces with the UAW to expand their operations. Fort Wayne was a major midwestern city but had little ties with the Teamsters. Because of its largest employer, International Harvester, the city was considered the heavy-duty truck capital of the world and its employees received some of the best pay and benefits due to their membership in the UAW.

Dom's mission was to set up a small office in Fort Wayne, meet with the local UAW president, and strategize on how to expand their operations. It was not an easy assignment. Dom was not familiar with UAW tactics, and he didn't know who his targets were going to be or who he needed to schmooze. Nevertheless, he quickly found a place to live and moved his family to Fort Wayne just in time for his son, Steven, to enroll in school.

Chapter 24

BRIAN JOHNSON PREPARED HIS LUNCH after completing the morning chores. It was a sizzling eighty-nine degrees outside, but drier than normal, not the kind of humidity that was typical for summer afternoons in Indiana. Since it hadn't rained in three weeks, the lawn was turning brown and crispy, and Brian was tasked with moving around their one and only sprinkler as a means to keep the grass alive.

As he finished up his sandwich, Brian heard the front doorbell ring. Grabbing a bag of Frito corn chips, he walked through the living room, chomping away and smacking his lips as he answered the door. Scott Clever and Bob Wills were standing on the front porch with big grins on their faces.

"What are you doing?" asked Brian. "You both have guilty looks on your faces."

"Maybe we are guilty," said Scott. "Wouldn't you like to know."

"I'm afraid to ask," said Brian.

Scott started singing:

Munch, munch, munch a bunch of Fritos, Corn Chips. It's not polite to smack your lips, but you can't help it with Frito Corn Chips.

"Don't give up your day job," said Brian, as Bob chuckled away. "C'mon inside."

"What's for dessert?" asked Scott.

"I've got some Hostess CupCakes. You want one?"

"Nah, I'm more of a Twinkie kind of guy," said Scott, prolonging the banter.

"You're a real Twinkie, all right," countered Brian.

"Hi, boys," said Mrs. Johnson, as she came in the back door. "How's your summer going?"

"Good," said Scott.

"Oh, Bob," said Mrs. Johnson. "Thanks for delivering our newspaper on the front porch instead of the driveway. You make us feel special. I'll be sure to give you a nice tip when you come around to collect."

"No problem, Mrs. Johnson, and thank you very much."

As Brian's mother left the room, Scott lowered his voice and asked Brian, "Are you doing anything this afternoon?"

"No plans," said Brian.

"Well, we have some plans, and we think you should join us." Scott looked over at Bob as the ornery grins returned to their faces.

"What kinda plans?" asked Brian.

"Well, last night we ended up in Steve Marino's basement playing ping-pong. He's got a really cool setup and we're going back this afternoon. We think you should join us."

Brian examined their mischievous looks with curiosity. "You guys are up to something, I can tell. Why are you acting like ping-pong is some kind of a rare treat? We play it in Mark's garage all the time."

"Trust me," said Scott. "Marino's basement is much better."

"Well, I'm sure it's not as hot as Mark's garage. What time are you going?"

"We told Steve we'd be over at one. He said his mom wouldn't be home until three o'clock."

"What's his mom got to do with it?" asked Brian.

"Nothing," said Scott. "Just a little more freedom for us to raise some hell."

Scott, Bob, and Brian showed up on Steve Marino's doorstep and Steve answered the door.

"Wassup?" asked Scott. "Are we still on for some ping-pong?"

"You guys are really obsessed." Steve laughed. "C'mon in. I just got back from hockey practice."

"Where do you practice?" asked Brian.

"Today was McMillen. That's where we usually practice, unless we can get ice time at the Coliseum."

"That's gotta be pretty cool, skating at the Coliseum," said Brian. "When does your season start?"

"We usually start in October. That's when I'll get busy, probably out of town every other weekend."

"Okay, let's drop all the pleasantries and get down to business," said Scott, heading toward the basement stairs.

The three boys followed Scott down the stairs as Steve flipped on the light, the temperature growing noticeably cooler as they hit the bottom of the steps. Brian was taken aback by his first impression, a room that was well-appointed with the kind of amenities he'd never seen in a basement before.

Instead of bare cement, the floor was covered with linoleum that simulated large tiles. On the back wall, an oriental rug stretched across a sitting area that replicated the coziness of a living room. Against the wall, a full-sized sofa ran parallel to the rug and a coffee table that served as a dumping ground for coasters, ashtrays, and *Sports Illustrated* magazines. Adjacent to the sofa, a La-Z-Boy recliner sat next to an antique floor lamp.

The opposite corner of the room hosted a tall filing cabinet positioned next to a writing table, complete with an office chair and desktop telephone. But the most prominent feature of the room was a sleek minibar stationed in front of a wall covered with Philadelphia Flyers posters and other sports memorabilia, most notably, an autographed picture of Bobby Clarke.

"Damn," exclaimed Brian. "I've never been in a basement like this before."

Continuing to explore the room, Brian walked over to the bar and noticed a small refrigerator plugged into the wall. "What's in the fridge?"

Steve opened the door to reveal an assortment of Miller High Life and Pabst Blue Ribbon beers.

"I'd offer you one, but my dad keeps a pretty tight inventory. He doesn't mind if I grab one for myself every now and then, but he doesn't want me contributing to the delinquency of the neighbors."

Walking over to the desk, Brian stated the obvious. "You even have a telephone hooked up. Does your dad work down here?"

"Not very often," said Steve. "He has an office on the south side of town, but he likes to come down here sometimes to make business calls. It's actually set up on a separate line from our house phone. He doesn't want his business associates calling him on the house phone."

Becoming more fidgety, Scott finally interjected, "Bob, why don't you grab a paddle and warm up Brian, then we can put together some kind of a tournament. Meanwhile, I'll kick back on this La-Z-Boy."

With a degree of disgust, Bob picked up a ping-pong ball and handed Brian a paddle. As the boys warmed up, Scott tiptoed over to the filing cabinet, opened the bottom drawer, and discreetly pulled out a magazine. He then took it over to the La-Z-Boy recliner, flipped on the floor lamp, and kicked up his feet.

After a few extended ping-pong rallies and no reaction from Brian, Scott tried to get his attention.

"This is probably the best *Sports Illustrated* issue I've ever read."

Brian gave no reaction as he kept playing, treating Scott like background noise.

Once again, Scott tried to get Brian's attention, this time more emphatically.

"Brian, have you seen this issue? I think you'd really like it."

Finally, Brian stopped and turned around to look. "Holy shit! Where did you get that?"

Scott, with a cocky grin on his face, continued to flip through the pages of his *Playboy* magazine. "There's some really good articles in here," he chuckled.

Bob and Steve broke out laughing as Brian approached Scott with a sense of urgency.

"Whoa...down, boy," said Scott. "I thought you were warming up your ping-pong skills."

"Nothing will warm him up better than a *Playboy* magazine," joked Steve.

"Where did you get that?" repeated Brian.

"There's a whole file cabinet over there," said Scott. "Every issue from the past four years. You didn't really think we came over here to play ping-pong, did you?"

"Well, I knew you were up to something," said Brian, as he made his way to the cabinet. But Bob had already beaten him there and was busy sorting through the issues, being very particular about which one to select.

"Hurry up," said Brian. "Do you really need to be that picky?"

"Calm down," said Bob with a chuckle. "You act like you've never seen a naked woman before."

"All right, you horndogs," said Steve. "You need to be careful with those magazines. Handle them with care and do *not* wrinkle the pages. Make sure you put them back in the exact order you found them. If my dad finds out we've been rummaging through his collection, he'll lock up that cabinet for sure."

"Then we'll just hire a locksmith," joked Scott. "Our work is really cut out for us if we're gonna get through all four years. That's forty-eight issues of research."

"You can continue your *research*," said Steve. "But just remember my warning. And when my mother gets back, we need to wrap things up quickly."

When Mrs. Marino came home, Steve directed Bob and Brian to start playing ping-pong again while he and Scott put the filing cabinet back to its original order. As the boys made their way out of the basement, they paid their respects to Mrs. Marino and exited the front door. With a wink of his eye, Scott signaled to Steve that he would soon be back for more.

Late Thursday afternoon, the boys were back in Marino's basement for a third consecutive day. This time, they brought Mark along while Bob was delivering *The News-Sentinel*. Since Mrs. Marino was home, Steve cautioned them to be aware of their surroundings.

"I don't want my mom walking down the basement stairs to see *Playboy*s scattered all over the place. Let's try and keep two people playing ping-pong at all times. If she doesn't hear a bouncing ball, she's likely to wonder what we're doing down here."

Mark found the whole situation humorous. "I feel like we're involved in some sort of covert operation."

"You should know all about covert operations," said Steve. "Isn't your dad a captain in the police department?"

"Yeah, but what about *your* dad?" asked Mark. "I'm sure the Teamsters are more familiar with covert operations than the police."

"Don't believe all the rumors you hear," said Steve. "Seriously, my dad should probably meet up with your father. He has a history of striking up good relationships with cops."

"Yeah, I bet he does," came the sarcastic response. "But if your father had *really* good connections, he'd hook me up with her," said Mark, holding up the Miss April centerfold.

Steve laughed. "Don't be so anxious until you've checked out the entire inventory. You need to consider all your options."

As the boys became more obsessed with their research, the ping-pong playing became more sporadic, prompting Steve to remind them, once again, of the need for bouncing balls.

Scott then responded by taking his *Playboy* over to the ping-pong table and turning the pages with one hand while bouncing the ball with the other.

"I'm not sure that's gonna cut it." Steve laughed.

Meanwhile, Brian was thumbing through his magazine. "I think she's my favorite one so far," he said, holding up Miss October. "I like brunettes with short hair. She's a real cutie."

"Cutie!" exclaimed Steve. "You don't look through *Playboys* hoping to find cuties. It's all about checkin' out hot babes. Besides, her boobs are too small. You should be more interested in this," he said, holding up his June issue. "Now those are some real knockers!"

"Nah," said Brian. "Those are too big. They look out of proportion. Besides, I'm not into dumb blondes. I'll stick with Miss October. She looks like she has a lot of spunk."

"You got your priorities all messed up," said Steve. "Dumb and sexy is an unbeatable combination. I can't believe you're commenting on cute hairstyles. Next, you'll be hoping she has a nice personality."

"Nothing wrong with a nice personality." Brian laughed.

Steve rolled his eyes with disgust. "So, Scott, what's the prognosis on chicks coming into Northrop next year? I won't ask Brian since he's probably more interested in their GPA."

"Well, I'm sure you've noticed Lynda Lacey from across the street," said Scott.

"Bingo," said Steve. "Of course I noticed her. What's her story?"

"You might as well forget about her," said Brian. "She's more interested in her reputation than getting it on with some dude. She's upper crust, always climbing the ladder."

"He's right," said Scott. "She's untouchable."

"Well, what about her friend?" asked Steve.

"Not Nancy Garber," said Scott. "She's a real plain Jane; a real prude, if you know what I mean."

"Nah, that's not the one," said Steve. "The one I saw was about medium height, medium brown hair, big boobs, and built like a brick shithouse. Someone dropped her off the other day and she walked up Lynda's driveway, moving her hips from side to side like she was really workin' it."

"That sounds like Karen Gadby." Scott laughed. "She was on the cheerleading squad with Lynda, and yes, she's pretty well-endowed."

"Now we're talking," said Steve. "That will be my target."

"Target?" asked Brian. "You act like you're hunting big game. If that's the case, you'd better get Mark's help. He's the only hunter in this group."

"I'm not experienced in hunting that kind of game." Mark laughed. "By the way, what's in that wooden cabinet hanging on the wall? It looks like it could be some kind of a gun rack."

"Yeah, my dad keeps a few guns locked in there," said Steve.

"Does he hunt?"

"Nah, he keeps a few pistols on hand for security. Sometimes he'll carry one in a shoulder holster under his jacket."

"That's pretty cool," commented Scott. "Kinda like James Bond."

"What kind of pistols are they?" asked Mark.

"I don't even know. My dad doesn't like to talk about it. He keeps it all pretty secret. I probably shouldn't even be tellin' you."

Suddenly they heard the basement steps squeaking and Scott jumped up and started bouncing the ping-pong ball with his paddle. The others hid their *Playboy*s under the *Sports Illustrated* magazines as Mrs. Marino peeked over the railing.

"Steve, dinner's gonna be ready in about twenty minutes. You need to wrap things up. It's just you and me tonight. Your father's stuck in Detroit for the evening."

"Okay, Mom."

After Mrs. Marino disappeared, the boys picked up the magazines and returned them neatly to the filing cabinet.

"Same time, same place tomorrow?" asked Scott.

"I think you horndogs better take the day off," said Steve. "Somebody's gonna get suspicious."

Chapter 25

RYAN O'CONNOR ARRIVED AT HIS office building on West Berry Street in downtown Fort Wayne right on schedule. He'd already had a busy day by most accounts, although busy schedules were standard operating procedures for Ryan. After a business luncheon at Don Hall's Gas House, he made his way to a vacant piece of land on the 200 block of Main Street, where he was invited to participate in a can't-miss photo-op with the mayor and city council.

The official ground-breaking ceremony for a new downtown park, Freimann Square, was receiving a lot of attention. *The Journal Gazette*, *The News-Sentinel*, and all three local television stations were there to cover the story. Ryan O'Connor, along with the mayor and other local dignitaries, posed with their shovels where the park was scheduled to open in another year, fall of 1973. It would become the first park located in the downtown office district and would feature water fountains and a large statue of General Anthony Wayne on horseback.

After the pictures were taken, Ryan made the two-block stroll back to his office in the Ft. Wayne National Bank building, the tallest building in town. To say he strolled is an understatement. He usually walked at a brisk pace, not only because he was in a hurry most of the time, but also to give the impression of importance. There was nothing on his agenda that lacked a sense of urgency. He didn't reach his level of affluence by approaching things casually, and he loved to whisk by his fellow citizens as they nodded their heads with respect.

Standing in front of the elevator, he pushed the button for level twenty-four, marked clearly as O'Connor Enterprises. Choosing his office with a purpose, he became one of the building's first tenants when construction was completed in 1970. Not only was it centrally located, but it served up impressive views of the Lincoln Tower, courthouse, and Ft. Wayne's three rivers. Just two floors up, the Summit Club functioned as an impressive host for business luncheons and after work cocktails, a place where he could close deals and celebrate his success with a toast of properly aged scotch.

At age fifty-two, Ryan O'Connor had spent most of his life in Fort Wayne, where he and his three siblings were raised under a strict Irish-Catholic upbringing. His father, Patrick, had built a successful law firm where he worked until he suffered a stroke in 1953. Up until then, Ryan had pretty much followed his father's plan, earning a business degree from the University of Notre Dame in 1942, and graduating from Yale Law School four years later. Upon returning to Fort Wayne, Ryan immediately went to work for the family law firm.

Two years later, Ryan O'Connor married Roselyn Gleason, a woman to whom he was introduced by one of his father's partners. Since the Gleasons were one of the more prominent families in town, Patrick endorsed the union, explaining to Ryan the importance of an O'Connor/Gleason merger. Not only would it solidify their status in the community, but it could potentially open the door for his son to branch out and pursue more lucrative business opportunities.

Patrick knew that Ryan was getting restless, too ambitious to spend the rest of his life running a stodgy, old law firm. There were visions of grandeur, and his son would never be content with settling for anything less. Although Ryan was not in love with Roselyn, he was in love with the idea of their union, recognizing the potential connections he would leverage on his way to the top. Roselyn, on the other hand, was content to raise the children and enjoy the fruits of Ryan's success, realizing he would not be around very much during his relentless pursuit of wealth and power.

Along the way, there would be three children and an abundance of business opportunities. As Fort Wayne continued to prosper, manufacturing persisted as the driving force behind the economy, influenced largely by the rapid growth of the auto industry. It was becoming clear to Ryan that families could no longer get by with just one vehicle, and for the first time in history, homebuilders were constructing houses with two-car garages.

Recognizing the opportunity, Ryan O'Connor decided to fuel this growth by opening his first Buick dealership in 1958. Five years later, unable to keep up with demand, Ryan opened his second Buick dealership on the south side of town. LeSabres, Wildcats, and Electras were rolling off the lots in record numbers. Soon everyone would become familiar with Ryan O'Connor's name and face as he appeared on local TV commercials promoting great deals on brand-new Buicks.

"Wouldn't you really rather have a Buick, a Buick, a brand-new Buick? Wouldn't you really rather have a Buick, than any other car this year."

Any good businessman knows that profits need to be reinvested. It serves no purpose for idle cash to sit around collecting dust. So Ryan O'Connor took his profits and started gobbling up real estate. Initially he purchased existing infrastructures, strip malls, and apartment buildings he could rent out to generate steady cash flows. But Fort Wayne was expanding very rapidly, and the big money was in development. Ryan soon recognized this potential and began speculating in real estate, purchasing tracts of land where the biggest growth was likely to occur.

Ryan knew he could purchase a relatively unused tract of land at a reasonable price, then work with the city to install an infrastructure— roads, sidewalks, water, gas, electricity, etc.—that would make the land functional for public consumption. Once the infrastructure was in place, he could sell off the developed land to businesses or homebuilders at huge profits. A new housing development alone could generate hundreds of thousands of dollars by splitting the land into hundreds of parcels that could be sold to prospective homebuilders.

In 1968, Ryan O'Connor opened his third car dealership, Cadillac, on the north side of town. Fort Wayne was thriving, and nothing flaunted prosperity like driving a Cadillac. Every year, Ryan would upgrade his vehicle to a new, top-of-the-line Caddy to solidify his status in the community and promote the prestige of Cadillac ownership. His current vehicle was a seventieth anniversary, Fleetwood Eldorado coupe in Sumatra Green. But for special occasions, he kept in his four-car garage, a vintage 1959 Cadillac Eldorado Biarritz convertible, in Seminole

Red, with white-wall tires and the largest tail fins ever manufactured by Cadillac. Ryan loved to drive his pride and joy at Fourth of July parades, top down, waving to the gawking onlookers.

O'Connor Enterprises had grown into a conglomerate of many interests, least of which was the flagship law firm. The legal practice was still growing and producing a steady cash flow, but Ryan was no longer involved in the day-to-day operations. He was too busy making deals, schmoozing politicians, and playing golf. If he happened to generate a new retainer while sinking a ten-foot putt, then all the more justification for writing off his green fees.

More often than not, his golf course of choice was the Fort Wayne Country Club, where he sat on the Board of Directors and spearheaded the annual Mad Anthony Hoosier Celebrity golf tournament. Each year he would sit at the head banquet table and participate in the ritual of awarding a prestigious red jacket to the Hoosier Celebrity of the Year.

As Ryan O'Connor ascended the throne of Fort Wayne aristocracy, he often defended his extravagance by reminding the critics about the number of people he employed and the jobs he created. Consequently, the standard joke among the locals was that O'Connor's payroll consisted mostly of politicians, judges, and policemen.

Although Ryan never had an interest in holding office, he was well aware of the importance that politics played in his business ventures. As a result, he was routinely sighted at the finest restaurants, wining and dining the mayor, the police, judges, zoning commissioners, or anyone who could play a beneficial role in his deal-making. Since most of these officials were elected as a result of his endorsements, it only seemed reasonable that favors would be returned. And if a few palms had to be greased along the way, that was the necessary cost of doing business.

Ryan and Roselyn's first child was born in 1949, a baby boy named Shane. By bearing a son, Roselyn had fulfilled her biggest conjugal duty—producing an heir to the O'Connor empire. She would soon find out that Shane needed to be raised according to Ryan's regimental formula, a blueprint that required her strict adherence. Often, she was reprimanded for being too soft, which forced her to compromise her maternal instincts. But whenever she was away from Ryan's watchful eye, she nurtured and doted on her son opportunistically.

In 1952, Roselyn gave birth to a baby girl named Christine. Her newborn daughter, a blessing from God, would someday give Roselyn the companionship she so richly deserved, someone to whom she could confide and share her innermost feelings, and someone she could go shopping with while the men were out playing golf, for the O'Connor household was a man's world, and women existed mostly for their pleasure.

If the O'Connor estate was hosting a party, it was Roselyn's duty to send out the invitations, plan the menu, and arrange the place settings. Most importantly, she would make sure the bar was stocked with premium liquors and paired with lavish displays of hors d'oeuvres. Dutifully by her mother's side, Christine would soon learn the importance of appearances and social graces, welcoming guests with her prettiest dress and impeccable manners.

When Christine entered kindergarten, Roselyn became pregnant with her third child, an unexpected pregnancy that was not without complications. After a series of dizzy spells, she was diagnosed with chronic high blood pressure, and when she experienced abnormal bleeding, the doctor ordered complete bed rest to lessen the stress on her cervix, otherwise she would increase the likelihood of a miscarriage.

This diagnosis put a strain on the O'Connor marriage as Ryan was expected to pitch in around the house and help out with the children. When Roselyn suggested the assistance of a nurse or nanny, Ryan would have none of it. He expected his wife to be strong and take care of their domestic affairs. As he saw it, giving in to bed rest was nothing more than a sign of weakness. Instead, they would somehow get through this ordeal together, and she would be indebted to him for his loyalty and dedication.

In the end, persistence prevailed, and Quinn O'Connor was brought into the world on August 15, 1956. Soon, Ryan would start making plans for his second son, and Roselyn would be expected to comply with another stewardship as their marriage deteriorated into one of custodial roles, lacking any terms of endearment.

In the meantime, the number-one son continued to be the primary focus of Ryan's attention. As an accomplished golfer, Shane became a fixture at the Fort Wayne Country Club, working on his swing with the local pro and perfecting his shot-making abilities. Not only was he the best junior golfer at the club, but he routinely beat the adult members, showing off his skills in front of Dad's business partners and wowing them with his confidence and precision. When Shane won his first junior city championship at the age of fifteen, no one was surprised that he defeated boys who were two and three years older than him. He was expected to win, and he delivered.

Heading into his senior year at Central Catholic High School, Shane was ranked number one in his class, president of the student council, and captain of the golf team. Ryan O'Connor had big plans for his son: a degree from Notre Dame, law school, mayor, lieutenant governor, and ultimately the governorship of Indiana.

But it was 1966, and a war was raging in Vietnam. Young boys were being drafted into the army, and many of them returned as war fodder, their desecrated remains reduced to burial plots. Ryan realized the importance of a military career in the world of politics, but he didn't want to risk his son's life in order to flaunt a few medals. As he saw it, there was no magic bullet that would keep his son out of Vietnam. He needed to weigh all the options and make a decision based upon probabilities.

Early in the war, college students were awarded draft status 2-S, which was a deferment for postsecondary education. This meant that college students could not be forced to serve. But it didn't take long to recognize the disparity between lower- and upper-income boys and their draft statuses. The exemption for college students was clearly a discriminatory practice that exposed the vulnerability of African Americans and economically depressed individuals unable to afford college.

In an effort to increase the eligible draft pool and put restrictions on college exemptions, the Selective Service System instituted academic achievement requirements as a condition for deferment. Deferment would only be granted after an evaluation of class rank and test results on a new requirement, the Selective Service Qualification Test. This meant there was no longer a blanket exemption for college students, and Ryan O'Connor feared that college deferments would soon be eliminated altogether.

The best remaining option, as Ryan saw it, would be enrollment in the Indiana National Guard. President Johnson had made it his policy to rely on the draft, resisting the urge to call in reserve units. Lessons had been learned from the Korean War, when over seven hundred thousand guardsmen had been activated, striking crippling blows to communities whose reserves had experienced heavy casualties.

The last Indiana National Guard unit to be called into a battle zone was an all-Black unit, the 915th Motor Ambulance Company, serving the Korean war in the 1950s. Since then, the Indiana National Guard had banished the practice of racial segregation, thus eliminating the existence of all-Black units. And by the midsixties, most units received little or no training in combat situations. Instead, they functioned primarily as emergency relief and civil defense forces, performing peacekeeping roles in crowd management and riot control, situations that were occurring quite frequently with the rising number of war demonstrations. Assuming these needs would continue, Ryan O'Connor decided it was extremely unlikely that an Indiana National Guard unit would ever be sent to Vietnam.

By the time Shane O'Connor graduated from Central Catholic as valedictorian in 1967, he'd already applied and been accepted into the Indiana National Guard. He was soon sent to Camp Atterbury, about thirty miles south of Indianapolis. Both he and his father assumed this would be a brief detour on his way to fulfilling a predetermined career. After a couple years in the Guard, Shane would meet his military commitments and start his education at the University of Notre Dame. Along the way, there would be ample time to work on his golf game and keep in contact with family and friends from Fort Wayne.

But January 1968, marked a turning point in the Vietnam war. North Vietnam had launched the Tet offensive, a major escalation that put South Vietnam and its US allies on their heels. Over one hundred South Vietnamese cities and outposts were under siege from a series of coordinated attacks, shocking American citizens who were led to believe the United States was winning the war. Consequently, General Westmoreland, commander of US forces, requested the immediate need for an additional two hundred thousand troops. To meet these needs, draft calls had risen to fifty thousand per month, and for the first time, reserve units were preparing for active duty.

For Shane O'Connor, combat training had become a reality. Transferred to the Rangers of Company D, the 151st Infantry, Shane was no longer receiving weekend passes, and communication with his father had diminished. But he did not tell his father about Company D's designation as SRF (Selected Reserve Force), which meant his unit was on high alert if reserves were sent into battle. Therefore, Ryan was caught off guard in March 1968, when Shane informed him that he was heading to the army's jungle warfare training center in Panama.

"No worries," wrote Shane, "I'm only going to Panama to earn the prestigious Jungle Expert Patch." But once the patch had been earned, Shane was off to paratrooper training at Fort Benning, Georgia. When Ryan O'Connor received the letter from Shane about his paratrooper training, he got very nervous. This was not normal. This was getting serious. Something needed to be done.

But Ryan did not have the same clout at the state level that he had in Fort Wayne. Although he vigorously pursued an explanation, there was little he could do to shield his son. Ryan had no military experience, and there was no one in a position of power he could call to make things right. Instead, he was forced to hold his breath and wait, hoping he would never be notified of Company D's active duty.

In April, Ryan O'Connor received a phone call he would never forget. An official with the Indiana National Guard informed him that Shane had been involved in a tragic accident. During a training exercise in Georgia, Shane's chute did not open as planned and he was unable to survive the fall. An investigation was underway, and they would inform him of all the specifics once the facts were determined. The National Guard was sorry for his loss, and they were honored that Shane had served Indiana and his country with the highest degree of patriotism.

That was it. In less than a minute, Ryan O'Connor's world had been turned upside down. His surge of anger was not enough to override his shocking anguish, leaving him desolated with grief. No amount of investigative work and no amount of blame would ever bring Shane back. Everything they had accomplished, everything they had planned for together had been wasted, pointlessly destroyed.

Laden with remorse, Ryan would regret his advice on the National Guard for the rest of his life. He felt responsible for Shane's death, and there was no turning back. Were it not for his father's bad advice, Shane would probably be in South Bend, Indiana, enjoying his sophomore year at the University of Notre Dame.

Although Ryan O'Connor's outlook on life had become tainted, he knew that he could not wallow in despair. Moving forward, he would use his mental fortitude to persevere, because that is what he did. Defeat was not an option. Instead, he would fall back on his one consolation, and that was Quinn. Moving forward, Quinn would get 100 percent of his attention, and everything they would accomplish together, they would do in honor of Shane.

On May 13, 1968, 204 Rangers of Delta Company were officially called to active duty. In December, they arrived in Vietnam and went on to serve over nine hundred patrols, killing more than one hundred enemy soldiers and earning numerous awards for their valor. But a price had been paid. Over one hundred casualties were reported during their tour of duty, including six deaths.

The untold impact on their young lives was not something that could be measured, but when the remaining soldiers returned to Indiana in November 1969, they arrived to a large welcome-home reception at the Tyndall Armory in Indianapolis. Mayor Richard Lugar had officially declared the occasion "Company D-Day," and the governor delivered a rousing speech, praising the Rangers for their courage and patriotism.

Throughout the crowd, a large number of supporters were sporting buttons with the phrase "Silent Majority," the new catchphrase coined by President Nixon in a recent speech. As antiwar protests continued to sweep the nation, Nixon insisted that protesters represented the minority. The vast majority of Americans, he believed, were patriotic and would continue to support the war.

Prior to Company D's return, Ryan O'Connor received a formal invitation from the Indiana National Guard to attend the ceremony. Nineteen months after Shane's death, he was still struggling to reconcile his son's fate. Ryan respectfully declined the invitation.

Chapter 26

Brian Johnson moved his knight to the sixth rank, pressuring his opponent's king.

"Check," he announced.

Scott Clever began to squirm. Studying the board carefully, he moved his king back one square.

"Nope, you can't move it there," said Brian.

"Why not?"

"Because you're still in check," lectured Brian, pointing to his bishop.

"There's no place I can move," said Scott. "It must be checkmate."

"No, you can move it diagonally and get out of check," said Brian, pointing to the only square where Scott's king would be safe.

Scott looked at the board again and reluctantly made the move.

Without hesitation, Brian moved his rook horizontally and zapped Scott's queen.

"Damn," yelled Scott. "You son of a bitch!"

"Tough break ole chap," said Brian, grinning ear to ear. "You wanna resign?"

"Resign? What does that mean?" asked Scott.

"It basically means that you've surrendered. That's what you do when your situation is hopeless."

"You mean quit?" asked Scott. "I'm not a quitter."

"That's what the professionals do," explained Brian. "It's more dignified to resign rather than drag out a long match when you have no chance of winning."

It was July 1972, and the world had become obsessed with chess, or at least the United States had become obsessed. The unthinkable had become a reality. Someone from the US was actually playing for the World Chess Championship in a competition historically dominated by Russians. Bobby Fischer, the brash, twenty-nine-year-old American, was challenging Boris Spassky, the reigning world champion from the Soviet Union, a country that had held that title for twenty-four consecutive years. As the so-called match of the century garnered worldwide attention, the media hyped the event as a Cold War face-off, democracy versus communism, the battle of good versus evil.

Bobby Fischer, known for his quirkiness and eccentricity almost as much as his brilliance, had taken the world by storm. At age fourteen, the child prodigy had become the youngest US champion ever, and at age fifteen, he earned the title of Grandmaster, the youngest ever to achieve that status.

As a Grandmaster, Fischer went up against the best players in the world, quickly earning a reputation for his creative but reckless approach to the game, breaking down traditional barriers with his brazen style of play. Heading into the 1972 world championships, he was the highest ranked player in the world, appearing in magazines and on television as an international celebrity.

With a world championship at stake, Fischer insisted the match needed to be played at a neutral site, as far away from the commotion as possible. Settling on Reykjavik, Iceland, the obscure city in the Arctic would certainly fit that bill, creating a logistics nightmare for the broadcast media.

The match was to be played as a best-of-twenty-four series, with wins counting one point and draws counting half a point, ending when one of the players scored a total of twelve and a half points. If the match ended in a twelve-twelve tie, the defending champion (Spassky) would retain the title.

Each day Brian and Scott would grab a newspaper from Bob Wills and look up the results from the previous day. Chess had suddenly become the national pastime, and the boys of Coldwater Creek were spending a great deal of their summer playing the game of kings, especially since the file cabinet in Steve Marino's basement had been locked up.

Looking up from their chess board, the boys saw Steve Marino's Oldsmobile come to a stop in front of the house.

"Are you nerds playing chess again?" asked Steve with a cocky grin.

Bob climbed out of the passenger seat with a Marlboro cigarette in his hand.

"Nothing else to do now that ping-pong isn't an option," retorted Scott.

"Hey," said Steve. "Just because the file cabinet is locked doesn't mean you can't play ping-pong. Besides, you can't say I didn't warn you. I told you horndogs that somebody would get suspicious if you kept hanging around our basement every day."

As the boys approached the chessboard, Scott tendered his resignation. "Okay, I officially resign. No way I can win this game. Especially with these knuckleheads hovering around."

"Just the mere thought of *Playboy* breaks his concentration." Steve laughed. "Maybe you should start lookin' at *Playboy* the same way all the other kids do."

"How's that?" asked Scott.

"They have 'em in the magazine rack at the back of the Revco Drug Store."

"You can't look at those," said Scott. "They're all sealed in plastic wrap."

"Aha!" said Steve. "So you *have* noticed them."

"I'm not blind," retorted Scott.

"So here's what you do. When no one's looking, you tear off the plastic wrap. Then you stick the *Playboy* inside one of those *Life* magazines. When people walk by, they'll think you're looking at *Life* magazine, but you're really looking at naked boobies."

The boys laughed out loud at Steve's suggestion, waiting for Scott's rebuttal.

"It would be much easier if you just learned the combination on that lock in your basement," said Scott. "Besides, it's easy to hide a *Playboy* in a *Life* magazine, but how do you hide the boner in your pants?"

They all laughed at Scott's clever response, and Steve had no rebuttal.

"So where did you boys just come from?" asked Brian.

"Been looking at cars," said Bob, as he took another puff on his cigarette. "I turn sixteen in September, and I'll be gettin' my license. I told you I was gonna get a nice ride."

"Have you been saving your money?" asked Scott. "Or are you spending it all on cigarettes?"

"Hardly," said Bob. "I've been working and saving for six years now. Unlike you boys who sit around playin' chess all day long."

"Yeah, but you can't say you're the chess champion of Coldwater Creek," said Brian, exposing his pride. "Besides, we're stimulating our brains. That's better than stimulating your lungs with nicotine."

"Hey," said Bob. "That's the stimulant that keeps me going. That's how I hold down three jobs and can afford a car."

"So what cars were you looking at?" asked Scott.

"I've narrowed it down to three," replied Bob. "I'm still looking at Pontiac GTOs, but now I'm leaning toward a Chevy Chevelle SS. We saw one today with a 454 V8 engine and a racing stripe down the middle. Pretty cool. We also looked at a Plymouth Barracuda that was kinda badass."

"Now we know what gives Bob a boner," quipped Steve. "And it ain't *Playboy* magazine."

As the boys laughed, Bob defended his position. "You can laugh all you want, but when I'm driving around in my muscle car next to a hot babe, I'll be the one havin' the last laugh."

"Looking at your arms," said Scott with a grin, "your car will be the only thing with muscle."

On August 31, 1972, the twenty-first game of the Spassky-Fischer World Chess Championship was adjourned. The next day, Spassky resigned. By a final score of twelve and a half to eight and a half, Bobby Fischer became the first American ever to be crowned world champion.

Chapter 27

IT WAS SATURDAY AFTERNOON AND Chantelle Jackson was busy distributing the hymnals, placing them in the church pews for Sunday services at Turner Chapel African Methodist Episcopal (AME) Church in Fort Wayne, Indiana, the city's first all-Black church. As choir director, she was responsible for the selection of hymns each week, coordinating with Reverend Brown the songs that would best underscore the gospel of his ministry.

Chantelle was proud of the fact that she'd taken over a small choir of seven women and expanded it to eighteen, including six men. Transforming a sleepy little group of elderly women into a lively and dynamic entertainment package was no easy task, but the pastor was convinced his congregation needed a lift, something that would stimulate his ministry far more than the slow, traditional hymns of the past. Within six months of Chantelle's arrival, the congregation had doubled in size, with crowds pouring in each week to witness the lively and soulful sounds of gospel music, a genre that was largely unfamiliar to the Midwest.

When Chantelle's brother informed her about the job opportunity at O'Connor Cadillac, he knew he needed more incentives than that if he was to convince her to move her family to Fort Wayne. After all, Chantelle had a career too, with obligations toward her job, church, and community—commitments she would not abandon just to satisfy her husband's needs. But the opportunity with Turner Chapel AME was unique, Thomas explained, outlining the church's rich history, its accomplishments, and its planned expansion efforts that would make it a leader in the community.

Sitting on the corner of Jefferson Boulevard and Harmar Street, Turner Chapel AME Church had only recently arrived at its current location, purchasing an old building from the Calvary Evangelical Church and officially relocating on January 3, 1965. Named after Henry McNeal Turner, a former bishop and pioneer for AME expansion, the church's roots go back to the city of Philadelphia and a man named Richard Allen, one of America's most influential Black leaders.

Born into slavery in 1760, Richard Allen worked on the Sturgis plantation in Delaware, where he began attending meetings for the Methodist Society, a Protestant group that followed the Christian teachings of John Wesley. Not only were the Methodists welcoming slaves into their ministry, but they were also allowing them to spread the gospel, and Richard began preaching to neighboring plantations when he turned seventeen.

Although many slave owners were not happy with Richard's evangelism, Stokley Sturgis, Richard's owner, was sympathetic to the Methodist view that slavery was immoral. Unlike most of his contemporaries, Sturgis was open to the idea of emancipation and spoke to his slaves about the possibility of freedom. As a result, in 1780, Richard was allowed to buy his way out of slavery and become a free man, officially changing his name from Negro Richard to Richard Allen.

Richard Allen was soon attracted to nearby Philadelphia, the largest city in the US at that time and a hub for freed slaves. In 1786, St. George's Methodist Episcopal Church allowed Allen to begin preaching, but only to its Black members and only at odd hours, in essence, segregating the church. As Allen's congregation grew, the church ordered his services to be performed on separate premises, forcing his followers to convene in a nearby park. Unhappy and feeling like an outcast, Allen officially withdrew his affiliation with St. George and formed the Free African Society (FAS) in 1787, a nondenominational society that assisted fugitive slaves from the South. Through the FAS and its underground railroad, Allen's influence in the African American community continued to grow.

Looking to organize a new church that was consistent with Methodist teachings, Allen and his followers converted an old blacksmith shop on Sixth Street in Philadelphia and officially opened its doors in 1794 as the African Methodist Episcopal church. As an affiliate of the Methodist Episcopal church, Allen's congregation was sanctioned and supervised by its White elders but could not distribute the sacraments of bread and wine without the consecration of a visiting White minister.

After similar congregations were organized in the neighboring states of Delaware, Maryland, and New Jersey, Richard Allen called for a conference in Philadelphia. His goal was to organize the existing congregations into one unified and independent body, free from the restrictions of White supervision. Together, in 1816, they all agreed to the creation of a new, independent denomination, the African Methodist Episcopal church, the first fully independent Black church in the United States. Richard Allen was elected as bishop and would serve in that role until his death in 1831.

In 1849, eighteen years after Allen's death, the AME church had its beginnings in Fort Wayne, Indiana. With limited resources, the small congregation was unable to secure any land for its church until 1869 when Emerine Hamilton, the wife of a wealthy Fort Wayne business owner, donated some property. In 1888, almost twenty years after the land was secured, Turner Chapel AME completed construction of a new church, making it the first ever building to be constructed by an African American congregation in Fort Wayne. The church would go through a couple more structural changes but remain at that location until moving to its final address on Jefferson Boulevard in 1965.

When Thomas told his sister, Chantelle, about the church's desire to start a nursery school and hire a new choir director, she couldn't help but feel excited and nervous at the same time. The opportunity sounded perfect for herself and Marquis, and she felt a sense of relief knowing that Antonio might continue to mature in his own way, free from the discrimination of a segregated South.

But Chantelle was a very thorough and prudent individual. She would not jump to any conclusions or reach any decisions until she and Marquis had weighed all the pluses and minuses.

As it turned out, the pluses were numerous and the minuses were few. After traveling to Fort Wayne, Thomas greeted them at the train station and drove Marquis to the new Cadillac dealership. Seeing the shiny new Fleetwoods, DeVilles, and Eldorados parked outside the showroom, Marquis instantly fell in love.

Dressed in his Sunday best and delivering the courtesy of his humble upbringings, he meticulously covered his work experience, education, and passion for automobiles, especially Cadillacs. Passing the interview with flying colors, Marquis was offered a position in the service department making one dollar per hour more than his current wage. He could only imagine what he'd do with an extra forty dollars every week.

Meanwhile, Chantelle was wowing Reverend Brown with her sophistication and charm. She talked about her college degree, her time in Saint Louis, and her work experience with the law firm. The pastor was fascinated by her worldliness and composure. He knew the position required a musical background, but he also wanted someone who could represent the church with style and grace, projecting a polished image of his ministry.

As Chantelle casually sat down at the piano and played *Amazing Grace*, she talked about the history of music in her family and the prodigious trumpet skills of her son, Antonio, a rising star in New Orleans. The reverend had made up his mind. His only remaining question: how soon could she start?

On the train ride home, Chantelle and Marquis were filled with nervous anxiety. Could they really leave everything that was familiar to them and start a new life? Chantelle was brave, but she was also cautious. Marquis, on the other hand, needed no convincing. He reminded her "from bold ideas, come bold plans," and "one can never get ahead without taking a chance."

Chantelle laughed. "Oh, look who's spinning the inspirational quotes. You always told me that I was your inspiration."

"You are, dear. You've always been my inspiration. That's why we're gonna do this together because we cannot sit around and let life pass us by. We deserve the best."

Chantelle leaned over and kissed her husband. Then she extended her hand, as if to seal the deal with an official handshake.

One month later, June of 1968, the Jacksons moved to Fort Wayne, Indiana.

Chapter 28

BRIAN JOHNSON HAD JUST FINISHED his sprint, the last of twelve consecutive forty-yard dashes. Although Mark Carter was not there to hold his stopwatch, Brian stuck to his routine of allowing only fifteen seconds of rest between each sprint. After gutting out each run, speed versus fatigue, he would count in his head: one thousand one, one thousand two, one thousand three. Back and forth he would continue, up and down the street until the last one was complete.

Hunched over in pain, forearms resting on his knees, he felt the burn in his lungs, the burn that told him he was taxing his body. "You can't get any better unless you test the boundaries," he told himself as his chest continued to heave.

It made him think of the test pilots he read about and their attempts to push the limits. They called it "pushing the envelope," and that's what he was trying to do. Even though he was training at the high school five days a week with the other football players, the competition inspired him to do more. How could he separate himself from the pack if he didn't have the drive to put in the extra work?

It was a sultry summer evening and Brian's body was covered in sweat. As his breathing slowed down, he felt the satisfaction that comes from hard work and going the extra mile. But there was something else, something beyond the normal sense of accomplishment.

Brian felt a tingling throughout his body, a special sensation he would sometimes get after intense exercise, an almost euphoric state of mind he would experience after his heart-pounding sprints. It was difficult to describe, but it usually happened after his breathing calmed down. He would feel the warm blood circulate throughout his body, and his mind would become clearer, his senses more in touch with their surroundings.

He had read about it in *Sport Illustrated*, a sensation often experienced by long-distance runners known as *runner's high*, a temporary condition that feels like unlimited endurance, like one could run forever. The medical journals credited the condition to endorphins, a hormone created in the pituitary gland to help the human body cope with physical stress. Often described as the body's natural opioid, endorphins attach themselves to receptors in the nervous system and relieve pain. The brain then releases a chemical called dopamine, a neurotransmitter that acts as a messenger, producing a response that results in greater focus, increased awareness, and happiness. At least that was the scientific explanation. All Brian really cared about was that he felt unusually good, a natural high he was going to enjoy for the next ten to fifteen minutes.

Taking a deep breath, Brian sat down on his driveway to meditate. A light breeze was blowing from the north, cooling his skin with evaporating sweat and creating a sensitivity that made the hair on his arms stand up. The sun had already set, but the western skies were still pink, contrasting beautifully with the dark purple patches of clouds. Soaking it all in, he savored the artistic splendor of nature, a landscape that was too perfect to be captured in a painting.

In the distance, he spotted a flock of geese skimming along the horizon in the shape of an arrow. Wondering where they were headed and who was leading the flock, Brian could barely detect their honks. It reminded him of distant trumpets and the incredible sounds that Antonio created with his horn.

Taking another deep breath, he put his hands behind his head and lie flat on the driveway, staring straight up into the sky. The eastern sky was mostly dark, except for a sliver of the moon and a scattering of twinkling stars. As Brian stared up at the moon, he couldn't help but think about the men who traveled there and walked on it for the first time just three years ago. Looking at it now, it almost seemed unreal, like something out of science fiction. His mind could not begin to fathom the enormity of something so foreign to his way of life, an incredibly ordinary life in Coldwater Creek.

Continuing to stare at the sky, Brian noticed a cluster of blinking lights so far away that they appeared no bigger than stars. But he knew that stars didn't blink, and these flickering lights were moving through the sky together, maintaining a steady proximity. When he realized it was an airplane, he couldn't help but ponder its altitude, so high up that it was barely detectable, and so far away that it produced no audible sounds. Brian had never flown before. To him, flying on a plane was no less foreign than flying on a spaceship. He was trying to imagine how many people were on that plane, what they were doing, and how precarious it must feel to be that high up in the sky, looking down on civilization like a distant planet.

Feeling completely relaxed and at peace with himself, Brian closed his eyes. As he took in the night air, enjoying the light summer breeze, the only detectable sounds were the rustling of leaves and the steady humming of locusts. He felt his mind begin to wander.

With his heightened focus beginning to wane, Brian's mind drifted away into a trance, and a familiar tune flowed through his head, the music of *Seals & Crofts* (Summer Breeze).

"Hey, are you all right?"

Startled by the interruption, Brian's head popped up and saw Mark Carter walking down the street. "Oh, it's you."

"Are you all right?" repeated Mark. "I thought maybe you passed out or something."

"Never felt better," said Brian. "I'm just relaxing after my workout."

"That's something I need to do," replied Mark.

"You missed a whole week of training. Where were you?"

"I told the coach I was gonna be gone. I was attending an Eagle Scout retreat at Camp Potawotami. We were teaching camping skills to the YMCA summer campers."

"Oh," said Brian. "I thought maybe you were hunting."

"Nah, there's nothing in season this time of year."

"So when was the last time you went hunting?" asked Brian.

"Not since early May. That's when wild turkey is in season. Didn't bag anything, though. It's been a couple years since I shot a turkey."

"Hey," said Brian. "Who's that?"

Mark looked down the street to see what Brian was referencing, barely detecting the muffled sounds of a conversation. It was mostly dark, but he could still make out the silhouettes of two people walking together.

"I don't know," said Mark. "Does it matter?"

"Look again," said Brian. "They're not from around here."

Mark squinted his eyes to focus better. "Oh yeah, I see what you mean. That looks like an Afro haircut. A Black dude in Coldwater Creek? Never seen that before. I think the other one is a chick."

As Brian and Mark continued to stare at the approaching couple, they casually eased their way onto the street, poorly concealing their curiosity. The couple then turned the corner, redirecting their route in an apparent attempt to avoid contact.

"Hey," said Brian. "I think I know who that is."

"Who?" asked Mark in frustration.

"That's Darius. Darius Williams."

"Are you sure?" asked Mark. "Why would he be in our neighborhood?"

"Let's catch up with them and find out."

The boys headed off at a brisk pace, then turned the corner. Not making up much ground, they started to walk faster. As they got closer, the couple nervously looked over their shoulders and picked up their pace. Brian and Mark then broke into a jog to close the gap. As they got closer, the couple suddenly wheeled around with eyes as big as saucers.

"Darius," said Brian. "What are you doing?"

"Holy shit!" cried Darius. "You scared the piss out of me."

"Whatever for?" asked Brian. "We were just trying to catch up with you."

"Damn, don't do that shit," exclaimed Darius, his heart pounding. "I thought some White boys were gonna beat the crap out of me."

"Well, you *do* look out of place around here." Mark laughed.

"I can't tell you how glad I am to see you," said Darius, finally smiling.

"Me too," said Jada Brown with a big grin. "Remember me?"

"Of course," said Brian. "What are you guys doing?"

"Well," said Jada. "Lynda Lacey called and invited me and a few of the cheerleaders over to her house. I didn't have a ride, so Darius's brother dropped us off at Coldwater Creek. He's supposed to pick us back up at ten o'clock. Unfortunately, all I have is Lynda's address and we're walking around trying to find her house."

"That's cool," said Brian. "We'll take you there. We know exactly where she lives."

As the gang approached the Lacey household, they noticed a group of girls had already gathered on the front porch. In addition to Mindy Harper and Karen Gadby, Lynda's neighborhood friend, Nancy Garber, had joined in on the fun.

Lynda looked up and noticed that Jada was part of the approaching foursome.

"Hey, glad you could make it. We were starting to wonder if you'd come or not."

"Well," said Jada. "I had to get a ride and then we got lost looking for your house."

"And apparently you picked up three guys along the way," teased Mindy. "Is that normal for you, or are you on a hot streak?"

"What can I say?" laughed Jada. "It must be my magnetic personality."

It didn't take long for the junior high grads to relax and get comfortable with the impromptu assembly, taking advantage of a rare social gathering in the middle of August. As the dialogue became more spirited and the laughter got louder, porch lights were popping on up and down the street, a sure sign that neighbors were taking notice.

"We may need to talk a little softer," suggested Lynda. "I don't want the neighbors to call the cops and charge us with disturbing the peace."

"That's exactly what you're doing," announced Scott Clever, as he approached the Lacey driveway with Steve Marino by his side.

"Oh no," said Brian. "Here comes the riffraff."

"Why weren't we invited to the party?" teased Scott. "I mean, a party's no fun without me."

"True," said Mark. "Now we have someone to make fun of."

As the conversations continued to grow, Darius and Jada couldn't help but ponder the improbability of such a scenario. One year ago, they could never have imagined themselves in the suburbs, in the middle of a White neighborhood, casually socializing with mixed company. Now they felt just as comfortable in their present setting as they would in their own neighborhood.

"Has anyone seen Antonio this summer?" asked Lynda, looking at Darius and Jada.

"No," replied Jada. "He usually spends his summers in New Orleans, but he should be back soon for school. It'll be interesting to see if he's changed at all."

"Changed how?" asked Lynda.

"Well, he spends most of the summer hanging out with other musicians, performing, and catching up on the latest trends. When he's not at Preservation Hall, he's hangin' out in the French Quarter and doin' street performances. I mean, that's a whole different world, if ya know what I mean."

"Nancy," someone hollered from a neighboring porch. "Nancy, can you hear me?"

"Yes, Mother," shouted Nancy Garber. "I can hear you."

"It's time to come home now."

Embarrassed by the interruption, Nancy looked at her friends. "No surprise. Just like my mom to put an end to me havin' a good time."

"You can stick around a little longer, can't you?" encouraged Lynda.

"Nah, I'm not gonna test my mom's limitations. I better go. Don't have too much fun without me."

After a few sympathetic goodbyes, Nancy made the walk of shame back to her house.

The teenagers, undeterred by the interruption, quickly resumed their conversations, focusing mostly on their first year of high school, which was only two weeks away. Brian, Mark, and Darius fixated on the prospects for Northrop Bruin football, while the girls speculated on the upcoming cheerleader competition.

Steve Marino, the outlier, was too obsessed with Karen to participate in the general dialogue. On a mission to enthrall her with his hockey prowess, he delivered a steady diet of bombastic bravado. Wise to Steve's motives, Brian couldn't help but remember the "targeting" comment he made about Karen in the basement, comparing her body to the *Playboy* centerfolds.

"That's my ride over there," said Steve, pointing to his red Olds 442. "It's got four hundred under the hood, power windows, bucket seats and an eight-track stereo system."

"Nice," said Karen. "So you have your license?"

"Yep, gonna be a junior this fall. I'll take you for a ride sometime."

Intrigued by the idea, Karen was flattered that an older boy would make such an offer, but wary of his motive, she suggested a compromise. "Maybe you could take us all for a ride."

"Watch out for those hockey players," warned Brian. "The ice rink is not the only place where they show their aggression."

"Warning taken," said Karen, with a twinkle in her eye.

Not amused by Brian's interruption, Steve retorted. "Brian can take you for a ride, too, if you don't mind balancing on the handlebars of his bicycle."

"Hey," said Karen, sympathetically. "That wasn't necessary. In a few more months, we'll all have our drivers' licenses. Then I'll ride with whomever I want."

Recognizing Karen's annoyance, Steve backed off and planted another seed.

"Why don't you hop in the front seat with me, and Brian and Mindy can ride in the back. Brian likes short-haired brunettes with a lot of spunk."

"I'll take that as a compliment," said Mindy. "Let's do it. I'm all in."

"Hold on," declared Lynda. "Nobody is going anywhere until I have my meeting."

Before anyone could respond, they all looked up to acknowledge a black Ford Galaxie 500 pulling to a stop in front of the driveway. As the car continued to idle, the driver lowered the window, slowly releasing the muddled sounds of a CB radio.

It didn't take long to realize it was Mark's father, Captain Carter. His unmarked police car didn't attract much attention until you looked inside and saw all the customized accessories.

Lynda recognized the captain's stern look and broke the ice, "Hi, Mr. Carter."

"Hi, Lynda. Are your parents home?"

"Yes, they're inside."

"I may need to verify that," said Captain Carter, showing that he was strictly business. "I got a call from someone about the noise around here. I didn't expect it to be coming from your house. It's no secret that you kids like to throw parties when your parents are away."

"I'll go get my mother, if you like," said Lynda.

"Hold on a second," said Captain Carter, as he stepped out of his vehicle and stared directly at Darius. "You're not from around here, are you?"

"No, I'm just visiting," came the nervous response.

"Do you have any identification?"

Darius looked around at his friends, wondering how to respond. "I don't know. What kind of identification?"

"Like a driver's license. You should know the drill."

"I don't have one. I'm not old enough to drive."

"Well, then how did you get here? We don't need any troublemakers in this neighborhood."

Suddenly feeling embarrassed, Mark jumped in. "It's okay. He went to school with us and played on the football team. Everything's cool."

Honoring his son's clarification, the captain backed off a bit. "Okay, but I still need to check with Lynda's parents."

As Lynda walked toward her house, the captain continued his line of questioning with Darius. "How did you get here? Is someone picking you up? What time will your ride arrive?"

"Sorry about the crowd," announced Mrs. Lacey, as she approached the police vehicle. "It was supposed to be Lynda and a few of the cheerleaders, but it looks like the whole neighborhood showed up. I hope they're not being too loud."

"No problem, Mrs. Lacey. I just wanted to make sure you were home and there wasn't an unsupervised party going on at your house."

"Okay, thanks for checking in. I appreciate your concern. I'll bring the girls in the house. That should keep the noise levels down."

Satisfied his work was done, Captain Carter thanked Mrs. Lacey for her cooperation and slowly pulled away. As soon as the vehicle disappeared, the girls made their way into the house and the boys moved over to Scott Clever's driveway.

Despite an attempt to keep the festive atmosphere alive, Scott was unable to inflate a mood that had fallen flat. Darius was visibly shaken, and Mark was embarrassed by his father's disrespect. An evening that started out with so much potential had ended on a sour note. Maybe the schools were accomplishing their goals for diversity and inclusion, but neighborhoods and communities still had a long way to go.

Chapter 29

SEPTEMBER 6, 1972, MARKED THE first day of school after a long Labor Day weekend in Fort Wayne, Indiana. Despite their enthusiasm, the kids from Coldwater Creek couldn't help but feel intimidated as they faced their first day of high school.

Northrop, a brand-new, state-of-the-art facility, appeared cavernous to first-time gawkers. The towering atrium, referred to as the Commons, served as the gathering area for students as they waited for the first period bell to ring. Bordered by a cafeteria, planetarium, gymnasium, and theater-style auditorium, the Commons was designed to accommodate large crowds before and after basketball games, concerts, and musicals.

Brian, Mark, and Scott staked out a position at 7:40 a.m., hoping to spot a few friends and acquaintances amid the loitering students. Feeling like naive sophomores, Brian and Mark tried to conceal their callowness by blending into the crowd with a contrived indifference.

Scott, on the other hand, was mostly indiscreet, unable to disguise his amorous glances at junior and senior girls. "I've already fallen in love four or five times this morning," he joked. "I'm gonna be a busy fella."

"You might wanna wipe the drool off your chin," teased Brian.

"Is it that obvious?" laughed Scott. "I'm sure they're all looking at me the same way."

As the boys eased into their new environment, the conversation turned to the summer Olympic games taking place in Munich, Germany. Televised around the clock by ABC, most of the country had become fixated on the Olympics, beginning with the opening ceremony on August 26, and continuing with US domination in swimming.

Suddenly, the most famous athlete in the world was a twenty-two-year-old swimmer by the name of Mark Spitz, winning seven gold medals and smashing seven world records along the way. Appearing on magazine covers around the globe, the handsome young man was the darling of the XX Olympiad, sought after by every major corporation in America as the ideal spokesman.

But the Olympics took a stunning and tragic turn the day before. On September 5, at the break of dawn, eight Palestinian militants snuck into the Olympic village and broke into the apartments where a group of Israeli athletes were staying. Two of the Israelis were killed as they resisted the assault and the remaining nine were taken hostage.

Even though the Olympic games came to a halt, television coverage continued as the world looked on in horror. Instead of watching competition between the greatest athletes in the world, viewers were confronted with the images of sweatsuit-attired terrorists wearing ski masks and brandishing assault rifles.

The demands had been issued: no hostages would be surrendered until the German government arranged for the release of Palestinian prisoners being held in Israeli jails.

"I went to bed at ten o'clock," said Scott. "At that point they were negotiating for a helicopter ride to the airport and an airplane that would take them out of Germany. Did anybody stay up to watch how it ended?"

"I did," said Mark. "Didn't get to bed until after midnight."

"So what happened?" asked Brian.

"Pretty much the worst possible outcome. The German government attempted a rescue at the airport, which resulted in a gun fight. The Palestinians then blew up the helicopter, which killed all the hostages. I think all the terrorists were killed too, except for maybe a couple that surrendered and were arrested."

"Damn," said Brian. "Did they show all of that on TV?"

"Nah, I don't think they could get any cameras close enough to the airport. They just reported it as the information became available. They also said that Mark Spitz would fly back to the US and miss the closing ceremonies."

"How come?" asked Brian.

"Since he's Jewish, they don't think it's safe for him to stay around any longer."

"That's crazy," said Scott.

"Yep," replied Mark. "We just need to round up all these terrorist a-holes and put them in front of a firing squad."

"Hey," said Brian. "Look who's coming."

The boys looked up to see Lynda Lacey and Mindy Harper approaching.

"Did you save us a spot?" asked Mindy.

"Can I see your tickets?" asked Scott.

"Nice try," replied Mindy. "Consider yourself lucky that we even acknowledged your presence."

Brian felt a nervous tingle at the sight of Mindy. It was just like her to come up with a cute and sassy remark.

"We were just talking about the Olympics. Have you been watching?"

"Of course," said Mindy. "Why wouldn't I be watching the most handsome guy in the universe take home seven gold medals? Especially while wearing a skimpy little speedo," she giggled.

"Maybe he's a little light in the loafers," said Mark. "I mean, it looks like he's wearing women's panties."

"Sounds like someone's a little jealous," teased Mindy. "Besides, they all wear swimsuits like that. He just happens to look better than everyone else."

"Where's Bob?" asked Lynda. "I didn't see him on the bus this morning."

"He's been chumming around with Steve lately," replied Scott. "I'm sure Steve's driving in this morning and Bob's riding shotgun. Plus, it gives Bob some extra time to get ready after his morning paper route."

"Hey, look who's heading this way," remarked Lynda, eyes lighting up.

"Well, well," said Antonio. "Long time—no see."

Approaching with his charismatic smile, Antonio stood out from the crowd, as usual. Sporting a pair of tan, polyester slacks that tapered down to his ankles and a pair of black pointed chukka boots, Antonio was the embodiment of sophistication. With his coordinated silk shirt and embroidered vest, he looked like someone out of *GQ* magazine.

"How was your summer?" asked Lynda.

"Monumental," he replied. "Absolutely monumental."

"You look different," commented Mindy. "I can't put my finger on it."

"Honey, you can put your finger on it anytime you like."

"Very funny," said Mindy, blushing from Antonio's innuendo.

"It might be my mustache," suggested Antonio. "The pencil-thin mustache is the latest thing."

"That's kinda weird," suggested Mark. "How in the hell do you shave around that thing?"

"It's not easy," admitted Antonio. "Sometimes waxing works best."

Mark rolled his eyes in disgust and looked away, deciding not to pursue the topic any further.

"I think you look taller," commented Lynda.

"I grew another inch. I'm now a full six feet two inches. Plus, the heels on these shoes add another inch or two."

"There they are," said Brian, pointing to Steve and Bob strolling through the crowd. "Over here," he yelled, waving his hand.

"It looks like some things never change," commented Bob. "The whole gang is together. How did you manage that?"

"It's not too hard if you arrive on time," quipped Scott.

"Hey," replied Bob. "We still have a whole five minutes to spare."

"Where's Karen?" asked Steve. "Anyone seen her yet?"

"Not yet," replied Mindy, with a hint of sarcasm. "I'll be sure to keep you posted."

"Please do," said Steve. "By the way, I've got some parlay tickets for the football games this weekend if anyone's interested."

"No surprise," said Mark. "Just like a Teamster to be running an illegal gambling operation."

"Aww, c'mon," said Steve. "You're not serious, are you? No harm, no foul. That's what I always say."

"Let me see them," said Scott. "I should do well at this. Like takin' candy from a baby."

"How does it work?" asked Brian.

"There's eight games on there," said Steve. "Four college and four pro. Each game has the latest Vegas point spreads. You have to pick the winners against the spreads, a minimum of three games picked. If you elect to pick three games, you can pick any three you want. If you get all three correct, it pays six-to-one odds. Meaning I'll give you six bucks back for a one-dollar bet."

"Piece uh' cake," said Scott. "I should be able to pick out three winners, no problem."

"Good luck," said Brian. "Six-to-one odds means you have a one in six chance of getting all three right. That's pretty slim pickin's. That's why the house usually wins."

"Don't be such a killjoy," said Steve. "It's just a fun way to keep track of the games."

"I'm in," said Scott. "Can I take it home and do some research?"

"Sure, but don't show your parents. I'll need your ticket by Thursday, along with your money. If you want to pick more than three games, you can increase your winnings. Four correct picks pay ten-to-one, five picks give you twenty-to-one, all the way up to eight picks paying a-hundred-fifty-to-one."

"I'm gonna be rich." Scott laughed. "And all I gotta do is study up on football. Why go to college when I can be a professional sports gambler."

"I'll take a ticket too," said Brian. "It might be fun trying to get three games right."

"Let me know if anyone else wants to participate," said Steve. "Just try to keep it on the sly. I don't want any teachers coming down on me."

"Hey," said Lynda. "Look over there. Do you know who that is?"

"Which one?" asked Mindy.

"The guy carrying the tennis bag."

Looking up, it was easy to spot the guy striding along confidently in topsiders and toting his tennis gear over one shoulder. Standing a solid six feet tall, he appeared slender, but athletic. His shiny dark brown hair was stylishly groomed and parted neatly on one side, not long and shaggy like the other boys. With a square jaw and dimpled chin, he appeared masculine, but in a regal sort of way, and his piercing blue eyes contrasted starkly against his dark complexion. With neatly pressed khakis and an Izod polo shirt, he looked as though he'd just arrived from the country club.

"I see him," said Mindy. "He's really good-looking."

"One handsome dude," agreed Antonio. "Very preppy. Do you know who he is?"

"That's Quinn O'Connor," replied Lynda, proud of her insight.

"From the O'Connor Buick and Cadillac family?" asked Brian.

"Bingo," said Lynda. "Try to keep up."

"How do you know these things?" asked Mindy.

"Trust me," said Lynda. "I make it my business to know these things."

"Something tells me this boy better look out," warned Antonio. "Someone's about to sink her sharp talons into her next prey."

Chapter 30

Another day in the service department ended with Marquis Jackson cleaning up his work area and pulling his timecard from its position in the J slot. After punching out for the day, Marquis headed toward the large ceramic basin to scrub down his hands with an industrial strength cleanser, which usually meant a bar of lava soap laced with gritty pumice. It felt scratchy on his skin and lacked the pleasant fragrance of bathroom soaps, but it cut through the grease, leaving his hands mostly clean, except for the grime under his fingernails.

Next, he headed to the locker area to strip out of his jumpsuit styled coveralls. Navy blue and fitted with an elastic waist, the coveralls were the official uniform of the O'Connor service department, projecting a classy image and adding to the prestige of owning a Cadillac. Initially, Marquis pooh-poohed the whole uniform concept as a little hokey, but he soon realized the convenience of peeling off his work clothes at the end of the day and tossing them into the laundry bin, unbothered by the burden of maintaining a clean wardrobe. How could he argue against the simplicity of arriving each morning in a pair of shorts and a T-shirt and slipping into his freshly laundered Cadillac coveralls?

After two months of work, Marquis was falling into a routine, comfortably performing his service requests and quickly familiarizing himself with genuine General Motors parts. He knew it was the best job he had ever had, far removed from the world of greasy old garages and beaten-down jalopies.

Marquis was beginning to acquire an acute ear for Cadillac engines, reaching a point where he could diagnose mechanical issues by sound alone. Fine-tuning Cadillacs until the sixteen-valve V8 engines purred with perfection was both gratifying and fulfilling, especially when satisfied customers drove off the lot glowing with pride.

Unfortunately, as the only Black man at O'Connor Cadillac, Marquis did, at times, feel isolated, a disadvantage he was not accustomed to. Although most of his coworkers were polite and respectful, he didn't feel the same camaraderie he experienced at previous jobs. There were days when he missed taking a break to shoot the shit with his buddies or grabbing a beer after work to chum around and blather on about sports, music, and other trivial gossip.

At lunchtime, most of the crew settled into the breakroom with their lunch pails. Sometimes Marquis would walk into the middle of a conversation and notice a sudden hush or a quick change of topic, making him feel self-conscious, wondering if they were gossiping about him or having fun at his expense.

On Fridays, it wasn't unusual for some of the crew members to go out for lunch and celebrate payday. Marquis was never invited. Occasionally they would tease him, calling him O'Connor's token Black, but Marquis would just smile and respond with "Well, if somebody's gotta be, it might as well be me."

Although "token Black" was a derogatory term, there was a history of truth behind the label. If companies had at least one African American on their payroll, they could legitimately deny discrimination, citing its Black employee as an example. Marquis didn't know if that was the reason behind his hiring, but he kept telling himself it wasn't that bad and he was better off than he was before. Besides, he had always gotten along well with his comrades, and he felt like his current situation was no different.

One Friday morning, Marquis arrived at work in a good mood, anticipating the typical good vibes before a weekend. Instead, he noticed a gathering of concerned coworkers in the locker room with letters in their hands, apparently discussing the contents. "Look in your locker," they told Marquis. "It looks like we all got memos."

Marquis nervously approached his locker, trying to anticipate the cause for concern. With a busy service department and Cadillac sales booming, he couldn't fathom what was going on. Were they laying people off? Were they cutting pay?

The first thing Marquis noticed was the letterhead: *International Brotherhood of Teamsters*. He had heard of the Teamsters but didn't know much about them. Labor unions were not common in the South, but he knew they were supposed to help workers get better pay. His brother-in-law, Thomas, was a member of the UAW and always bragged about his great pay and benefits. Marquis knew he wasn't making as much money as Thomas, but he also believed in job satisfaction. Performing the same, mundane routine over and over again on an assembly line was a beatdown he was not willing to experience.

The memo went on to explain the advantages of union membership and the possibility for higher wages and better benefits, and the legal representation they would receive when negotiating with management. It went on to cite recent examples of Teamster transitions and how the employees and their families were living better lifestyles. And best of all, the Teamsters were joining forces with the UAW, creating a stronger and more powerful bond, an irresistible force that could not be denied.

The last paragraph got right to the point. An informational meeting would take place to explain the benefits of union membership, and it would be followed by a Q&A session. All were invited to attend at the local UAW union hall and refreshments would be served. It was signed by Dominic Marino, union organizer.

After reading the letter, Marquis joined the group and tried to blend in. "I'm not sure I understand the concern," he said. "This is not a bad thing, right? I mean it wouldn't hurt to listen and see what they have to say."

"That depends," said Neil Bowers, the shop supervisor. "When management finds out about this, they could start playing hardball. They could make life miserable for the ones who are promoting the idea."

"So who *is* promoting this?" asked Marquis. "I mean, besides this Marino guy, who actually came in here and distributed these letters?"

"That's a good question," said Bowers. He then turned and addressed the group. "Does anyone know who distributed these letters?"

Looking around at each other, nobody responded.

"Just as I suspected," said Bowers. "It appears that we have an infiltrator."

On Monday morning, Marquis arrived at work, slipped into his uniform, and went about his normal routine. Before hitting the shop floor, he was greeted by Neil Bowers and a group of coworkers.

"Hold on, Marquis," said Bowers. "We're all gathering in here for a minute."

After rounding up all eighteen of the workers on duty, Bowers proceeded to announce plans for a company meeting in the showroom at eight fifteen.

"You're all invited to attend," he said. "I expect everyone to be polite and attentive. Nothing but your best manners. Let's have some fun."

Ernie, one of Marquis's coworkers, turned to him and said, "Let's have some fun? Are they kidding? We've never been allowed in the showroom before. This is very suspicious."

Strolling into the showroom together, the first thing they saw were a bunch of balloons and a large banner that read Employee Appreciation. Beneath the banner, a long, banquet-style table dressed up in white linen, served up a wide variety of breakfast items: donuts, bagels, pastries, sausages, and scrambled eggs.

Standing next to a podium, a distinguished-looking gentleman in a navy-blue pin-striped suit appeared ready to address the crowd. Ernie nudged Marquis and whispered, "That's the head honcho."

"Good morning, everyone. My name is Ryan O'Connor and I'm absolutely thrilled to be here this morning to help celebrate *your* success. I will try to be brief since the purpose of this gathering is not to listen to me speak, but to relax, enjoy some refreshments, and spend more time getting to know one another. The truth is, I don't think we take enough time to show our gratitude for all the things you do. Although our goal is to sell as many Cadillacs as we can, our biggest revenue stream comes from the work you do in the service department, servicing our customers. If we don't have happy customers, our business will suffer. That is why you are so critical to our success. From management, to back office, to sales, to service, we are all one team and we all matter. Starting today, I will be scheduling a series of quarterly meetings, where we can all communicate with each other and jointly manage our business the way it should be managed. And to the service department, I want to issue a promise. If any of you ever have an issue or concern that is bothering you or preventing you from being the best employee you can be, I promise I will listen and do my best to resolve the issue. That's why we're installing a suggestion box in your locker area. Please feel free to drop a note anytime you have an idea or a concern. You can sign the note if wish, and we can address the issue with you directly, or you can remain anonymous. Either way, I promise that we will listen and work hard to make O'Connor Cadillac the best place to work in Fort Wayne, Indiana. Now, let's all get something to eat and celebrate your success."

As the formal part of the program concluded, a long line formed in front of the banquet table. Ryan O'Connor strolled to the back of the line and began shaking hands and engaging in small talk. After a trivial dialogue with two employees about the upcoming football season and the prospects for the Chicago Bears versus the Detroit Lions, Ryan noticed Marquis in line and decided to work him into the conversation.

"What about those New Orleans Saints? Are they gonna be any good this year?"

Surprised by the reference, Marquis responded cleverly, "I think it will be a cold day in hell when the Saints have a good team."

"Oh my!" laughed Ryan. "That's a pessimistic attitude. You *are* a fan, aren't you?"

"How did you know I'm from New Orleans?"

"I know more about my employees than I get credit for," said Ryan as he extended his hand. "Marquis Jackson, right? Did I get that correct?"

"Yes, sir, pleased to meet you."

"How's your family doing? Are you all settled in now?"

"Yes, sir. We're gradually making progress."

"And your wife? How is she handling the big move?"

"We're all adjusting, but happy to be here. My wife is the choir director at our church. That is another reason why we moved. Now she's looking for a full-time job in her field."

"Which is?" asked O'Connor.

"She worked as a stenographer and court reporter and did some paralegal work, spending the past five years at Landry and Boudreaux in New Orleans. I don't know if you've ever heard of them."

"Of course I have. A very fine law firm. Almost as good as mine," said Ryan as he winked and flashed his pompous smile.

"Oh, I didn't know you had a law firm, too," said Marquis.

Ryan then reached into his jacket pocket and pulled out a business card.

"We're always in need of someone with your wife's experience. What is her name?"

"Her name is Chantelle, sir."

Ryan pulled out a pen and circled a phone number on the business card, handing it to Marquis.

"You tell Chantelle to call this number and ask for Cynthia. Tell Cynthia that Ryan O'Connor is expecting her to conduct an interview. I'll lay all the groundwork today, so tell her to make the phone call sometime tomorrow."

"Thank you, sir. I really appreciate it. Chantelle will be thrilled. Thank you very much!"

Ryan rewarded Marquis with his confident, but haughty smile, the one he typically issued when closing a deal. Although it was a welcoming smile, it was not without implications.

Shaking Marquis's hand, Ryan clarified his position, "I'll take good care of you, if you take good care of me."

Marquis nodded his head in acknowledgment, wondering if there was an insinuation or an expectation that someday a favor would be requested.

It didn't matter. Marquis felt like his cards were falling into place, and he was ready and willing to do whatever it takes to appease his boss's wishes.

Chapter 31

With a month of high school under their belts, the sophomores were easing into their routines and feeling more comfortable in their new environment. Brian and Mark were busy with football, but growing weary of the roles they played as scrimmage fodder for the upperclassmen. Spending a whole season as apprentices was a humbling experience, knowing they would never dress for a varsity game and never get any glory for all the bumps and bruises they suffered.

Mark was growing more and more disillusioned with football, wondering if all the effort was really worth it. Brian, no stranger to hard work and sacrifice, remained committed, focusing on the reward he would receive when he became a junior.

Malcom Mosely was the one exception to the sophomore rule. After four weeks of scrimmaging, he was beginning to display some of the physical attributes that led to his dominance in junior high. He was even reprimanded one day for being too physical when he overpowered the offensive tackle and rushed through to wrap up the quarterback.

"Don't you ever lay a hand on our quarterback! You hear me, son?"

The coach had issued his warning, but Malcom's emerging domination could no longer be ignored. Two days later he was officially placed on the varsity.

After cheerleading tryouts had concluded, Lynda, Mindy, and Jada were happy to find their names on the roster posted outside the gym by the selection committee. As official members of the reserve squad, they would soon be cheerleading at all the pep sessions and reserve basketball games, and Lynda, as captain, would retain her customary leadership role.

Karen Gadby, however, was left off the list, dampening the girls' spirits and hindering any thoughts of celebration. When Lynda attempted to console her, Karen rejected the sympathetic gestures.

"It's just as well," she said. "I'm ready to grow up and do other things. I asked the coach why I was not chosen, and she told me it was a tough decision. She said I did my routines okay, but it came down to intangibles. They were looking for girls that showed a lot of school spirit, girls that smiled a lot and showed enthusiasm. Can you believe it? All that work and it comes down to who has the best smile. Who cares, I think I've outgrown all this yay-yay, rah-rah crap. It's time to move on."

Lynda allowed Karen to vent unchallenged, acknowledging the truisms in her frustration. Perhaps she was right, it really was time for her to move on. Nevertheless, Lynda was determined to maintain their friendship and carry on as if nothing had changed.

If anyone was capable of making a seamless transition to high school, it was Antonio, fluently navigating his way like a thespian on Broadway. No stranger to performing, Northrop High School was merely a different stage, another opportunity to sharpen his image and expand his fan base. And when he was named the new drum major for the marching band, he strutted around the field with a flair that attracted large crowds, even those who had no interest in football.

Keeping his nose to the grindstone, Bob Wills did not allow the distractions of high school to derail him from his ultimate goal of buying a car. Still scrawny and pale with rings under his eyes, he always looked tired. Sleep deprivation was just a way of life for someone managing two paper routes and pumping gas on the weekends. To Bob, school was just a necessary evil. He knew his parents would never allow him to quit, so he continued to maintain his C average, struggling to keep his eyelids open through long and boring classroom lectures.

Steve Marino, after four short weeks, had expanded his parlay venture into a real business. With the assistance of Bob, his customer base was growing, somewhere between forty and fifty tickets per week. Steve once bragged that he was collecting one hundred dollars every week and profiting 65 percent after payouts. No one knew if that was true, or if Bob was getting a cut of the profits, or if any of the business was funneling through Steve's father. All anyone knew for sure was that Steve Marino was a street-smart shark who spoke with a slick, East Coast accent, and seemed more focused on gambling, girls, and hockey than school or social etiquette. His growing influence on Bob was becoming more and more apparent.

Scott Clever had seemed out of sorts, struggling to find something that would occupy his time. He was a little fish in a big pond now, and his buddies were busy playing football, hockey, and working jobs. Basketball wouldn't start for another month and his only preparation consisted of shooting baskets on his driveway and running through the dribbling drills he learned in junior high.

Unbeknownst to his buddies, the biggest driver behind Scott's unsettled demeanor was the mounting friction within the Clever household. His older brother, David, was testing the conditions his parents had established for living at home, an agreement that allowed him to stay under their roof as long as he held down a job and continued his education. But working second shift in a factory and attending morning classes at Indiana University–Purdue University Fort Wayne turned out to be more of a burden than he could handle.

David hated the monotonous drudgery of working on an assembly line, once telling Scott that the only way he could tolerate eight hours of misery was to get stoned beforehand, numbing his mind and dulling his senses with bags of pot.

When David turned twenty-one, he began staying out after his late-night shifts and drinking at the bars until the wee hours of the morning, often stumbling home drunk. Soon he was missing classes, falling behind, and forced to withdraw from school.

After dropping out, David became more disillusioned than ever, weary from his parents' constant nagging and despondent over his bleak future. As the family arguments grew more intense, Scott began to withdraw, isolating himself in his bedroom and covering his ears. But when the shouting became unbearable, there was no way to block out the back-and-forth arguing and threats.

"If all you're going to do is get drunk and flunk out of college, then you should probably move out of the house."

"Maybe I *will* move out of the house. At least I won't have to listen to your yelling all the time."

"You realize if you're not enrolled in college, you'll probably get drafted into the army. How would you like to go to Vietnam and get shot at like the Wills boy? Is that what you want?"

"Yeah, that's exactly what I want. That would be easier to take than listening to you yelling at me all the time. Besides, I can always move to Canada."

"You can't spend your whole life running away from responsibilities. It's time for you to grow up and act like an adult."

On and on it would go, the arguments getting louder and more intense, nothing ever getting resolved. It was beginning to take a toll on Scott and the knots in his stomach continued to churn. He began to wonder if it was possible for a high school kid to actually develop an ulcer. Maybe not, but there was no denying the nervous tension he felt at home, constantly walking around on pins and needles, wondering if his family life would ever return to normal.

As bad as it had gotten, it was nothing compared to the fireworks that took place the day Mrs. Clever found a syringe in David's room, an undeniable warning signal that called for drastic measures.

Loaded for bear, Mr. and Mrs. Clever waited for David to come home from work, ready to blindside him with their discovery. As soon as he walked through the door, the confrontation began. David wheeled around and attempted to leave, but Mr. Clever blocked the exit.

Scott could hear his brother yell, "Get away from me!" And then he heard a rumbling sound like someone had hit the floor. His mother screamed, "Stop it, stop it now!"

Hiding in his bedroom, Scott could tell the altercation had become physical, and he knew that David was no match for his father's size and strength.

Chapter 32

MARQUIS JACKSON WAS HEADING HOME from work on a Thursday evening, already thinking about the weekend. Since he was scheduled to work on Saturday, he would get Friday off, a schedule that alternated every other weekend. He was anxious to hear about Chantelle's job interview earlier in the day, but he knew she was usually at the church on Thursday evenings, so that meant he was on his own for dinner.

If Chantelle wasn't going to be around, he might just throw a TV dinner in the oven, or maybe a couple Swanson chicken pot pies. Or he might even splurge and do the McDonalds's drive-thru, indulging in a thirty-three-cent cheeseburger, fries, and a chocolate shake. Or maybe upgrade the cheeseburger to a forty-five-cent filet-o-fish.

Smiling at his sinful thoughts of indulgence, Marquis decided to abstain and head straight home. Afterall, the nearest McDonalds was ten minutes out of his way.

As the blue Ford Galaxie approached the 1300 block of Chester Avenue, Marquis made the turn and headed down the back alley. The only way to access the gravel driveways in his neighborhood was from behind. Although he had no garage, his carport served as an economical way to keep the snow and frost off his windshield during the long winters.

Built back in the 30s and 40s, these homes were starting to show their age. Lacking any uniformity, the neighborhood was a hodge-podge of different styles and designs. The Jackson home was a small, two-story structure with two bedrooms and a bath upstairs, the ground level consisting of a living room, dining area, and kitchen.

Marquis drove along the chain-length fencing that lined the alley, being careful to avoid the garbage cans that were already lined up for Friday morning pickup. He made mental notes of which houses were in need of a fresh coat of paint and which ones had long, shaggy grass along the fencing, wishing his neighbors were more responsible about maintaining their properties.

Turning into the driveway, Marquis was surprised to see Chantelle's car. Although he wasn't expecting her to be home, he was pleased that he would have company for dinner and was anxious to learn more about her interview. Climbing the three-stair back stoop, Marquis had a little extra hop in his step as he swung open the screen door.

"Surprise!" blurted Chantelle, greeting him in one of her Sunday church dresses.

"Wow, don't you look purdy!" said Marquis as he wrapped his arms around her and nibbled on her neck. "And you smell good too. What are you wearing?"

"Your favorite. Opium, by Yves Saint Laurent."

"Honey, I don't need no opium when I got you. You're the only one I'm addicted to."

"Ain't you sweet," blushed Chantelle. "Flattery will get you everywhere."

"So what are you doing home?" asked Marquis. "I thought you had choir practice on Thursdays."

"I canceled it. Tonight, we are celebrating. Wanna guess why?"

"I'm guessing your interview went well. Am I right?"

"Better than well. They offered me the job and I took it."

"Already? Wow, that was fast!"

"I start next Tuesday. I'm excited, but kinda nervous."

"I'm happy as long as you're happy," announced Marquis. "Are you sure about this?"

"I have a few concerns, but we'll talk about it over dinner. Let's focus on the celebration. I have a bottle of your favorite wine chilling right now, a Riunite Lambrusco."

"That sounds perfect. You want me to pour?"

"Absolutely," winked Chantelle.

"Is this what I think it is?" asked Marquis, noting the piles of chopped onion, green pepper, and celery on the cutting board.

"I don't know. What do you think it is?" teased Chantelle.

"You're making my favorite? Shrimp étouffée?"

"I might be. With andouille sausage? Isn't that the way you like it?"

"You're the best, honey. This is supposed to be *your* celebration and you're making *my* favorite dish."

"I just need to remind you every once in a while, how lucky you are that you married me."

Sitting down at the table, Marquis filled their glasses with another pour from the Riunite bottle. "So how late will Antonio be?" asked Marquis. "Do I need to pick him up?"

"I'm not sure," said Chantelle. "He said he was going to the homecoming bonfire after band practice, wasn't sure if he'd get a ride home with one of the football players or not. He said he'd call us if he needs a ride."

"So how's he gonna call us?" asked Marquis.

"The same way he always does, from one of the school payphones."

"Oh yeah, I forgot," said Marquis, as he scooped a big bite of the étouffée, careful to get a shrimp and some andouille sausage on his spoon.

"You did it again, honey. It's absolutely delicious."

"Nothing but the best for my man."

Taking another sip of wine, Marquis moved on to the main topic and the reason for the celebration. "So what can you tell me about your new job and your so-called concerns?"

"Oh, it's probably no big deal," she replied. "It just seems like they're being overly cautious, that's all. What we would normally call dotting your i's and crossing your t's."

"How so?" asked Marquis.

"Well, first of all, they told me they already completed a background check on me and I passed with flying colors."

"That's a good thing, right?" asked Marquis. "I mean, I don't know if that's normal, but if it shows you're squeaky clean, then it should be to your advantage."

"True," said Chantelle. "I know they're doing more of that nowadays, but my experience has been that employers only do this when they're suspicious."

"Like you said, I guess they're just being cautious," assured Marquis.

"Yes, but it was the legal document they made me sign that kinda put me off. In some circles it's called a morality clause, basically telling me that if I don't live up to a certain code, I could be dismissed."

"Seriously? Who are they to judge your morals?" asked Marquis, in an animated tone.

"Calm down," said Chantelle. "It's more innocuous than it seems. That's just what it's called sometimes. It's basically saying that if an employee conducts herself in a manner that is unbecoming to the reputation of the law firm, it could be grounds for dismissal."

"That sounds awfully vague."

"Exactly. I've seen it used with other law firms, but it's normally used when hiring lawyers. A law firm cannot have its reputation ruined by the behavior of one of its representatives. When you're sworn to represent and uphold the law, your behavior must be beyond reproach. That's basically what they're guarding themselves against."

"Okay," said Marquis. "I get it. If someone breaks the law, it makes sense that they should be dismissed."

"But it goes beyond breaking the law," said Chantelle. "It's the so-called gray area that makes it more ambiguous. And it pertains not only to me, but also my family."

"So if I do something, or Antonio does something they believe reflects badly on their law firm, they could dismiss *you*?"

"More or less. Here, hold on. I'll let you read it," said Chantelle, retrieving a file from her satchel. Flipping through the documents, she pulled out the so-called morality clause and handed it to Marquis.

The employee, or employee's family member, shall conduct himself/herself with due regard to the public conventions and morals, and shall not, either while rendering such services to his/her employer or in his/her private life, commit an offense involving moral turpitude under federal, state, or local laws or ordinances. The employee, or employee's family member, shall not do or commit any act or thing that will tend to degrade him/her in society or bring him/her into public disrepute, contempt, scorn, or ridicule, or that will tend to insult or offend the community or public morals or decency.

"I hate this legal crap," spouted Marquis after reading it and becoming more agitated. "Can you just tell me in plain English what this really means?"

"Well, I think I already attempted to explain it in plain English. I just thought you'd like to see the actual document and how it's worded."

Marquis looked at the document again and became more animated. "Why do they use words like turpitude, disrepute, contempt, and scorn? Sounds like a lot of legal rigmarole. I mean, how am I supposed to understand what they're really saying?"

Sensing her husband's agitation, Chantelle decided to lower the temperature a few degrees. Reaching under the table, she squeezed his hand and batted her eyelids flirtatiously. "Maybe they're just saying my husband needs to behave himself."

Then she slid her hand down to his thigh and winked. "Whaddaya say you and I move out of this kitchen and misbehave together?"

Marquis melted under her tender touch and provocative insinuation. Like a magic potion, she had flushed the legal jargon from his mind and instantly triggered his libido.

Marquis took a deep breath and let out a big sigh. Then he leaned over and kissed her warm lips. "What time did you say Antonio would be home?"

Chapter 33

I T WAS A FRIDAY MORNING, and the Northrop Commons was in a festive mood, but the spirited atmosphere did not preclude the student body from recognizing a distant commotion, a distraction that was vaguely audible, but getting louder by the second. Coming from the adjacent hallway, the sounds were becoming more pronounced, taking on structure and continuity like a pervasive undercurrent.

"Hup-two-three-four, hup-two-three-four" came the commands, in perfect sync with the thumping bass percussionist and the rhythmic rolls of the snare drummer. Like a military drum and fife corps, Antonio was marching his pep band into the Commons, strutting along with his exaggerated high steps.

"Ten-hut!" he shouted as they stood at attention under a large homecoming banner. Antonio turned around and faced the student body, raising his arms into the air. They responded on cue with a large round of applause. Then, waiting for the applause to die down, Antonio raised his trumpet to his lips and waited for complete silence. After receiving the desired response, Antonio launched into a rousing rendition of Reveille.

Like a military bugler waking his barracks at sunrise, Antonio belted out the tune with a commanding performance. When he was finished, he sharply lowered his trumpet to his side and stood at attention. The students broke into a thundering ovation, yelling out, "Antonio, Antonio!"

He then shouted out to the crowd. "Is everyone awake?"

After the students delivered their tepid affirmation, Antonio cried out again, "I can't hear you!"

Antonio repeated his question, this time even louder. "Is everyone awake?"

Screaming, shouting, and clapping their hands, the rejuvenated crowd delivered their response with an inspired enthusiasm.

After yelling "Go Bruins," Antonio turned to face his band. Raising his arms into the air, the band waited for his cue. With a loud tweet from his whistle and a downward swing of his right arm, the pep band launched into the Northrop fight song, and the invigorated student body clapped along in jubilation.

As Antonio led them out of the Commons the same way he brought them in, there was a noticeable buzz in the air, an atmosphere that was electrified with energy and enthusiasm.

"That was pretty cool," noted Mark Carter, understating what everyone had just witnessed. "I wish I was playing tonight."

"All in good time," said Brian. "Next year is our year."

"So you keep telling me," replied Mark. "I must admit, Antonio has a little something that makes him pretty unique. I could never do what he does, but I guess there's a role and a purpose for people like him."

"He sure makes life a lot more enjoyable," said Brian. "I'm glad you're finally starting to come around on him."

"Yeah, I guess it's time for me to step out of my bubble and recognize there's a whole different world out there."

"Yep, I think they call it diversity," teased Brian. "Life would be pretty boring if we were all plain vanilla."

"Speaking of diversity, or lack thereof, look who's coming," said Mark.

Brian looked up to see Lynda Lacey walking with her new sidekick, Quinn O'Connor.

"Just like Antonio predicted," said Brian. "It didn't take long for Lynda to stake her claim. I guess birds of a feather flock together."

Lynda was dressed in her cheerleading outfit, as was the tradition on game days. Quinn was carrying his tennis bag, dressed in khakis and a white cable-knit sweater vest outlined with navy-blue trim and bearing a patch that said Forest Hills.

"Why aren't you wearing your football jerseys today?" asked Lynda.

"Only the varsity is allowed to wear them," replied Brian. "I guess we'll have to wait until next year."

"Is there a tennis match today?" asked Mark.

"No, they had one last night against Concordia," said Lynda, not allowing Quinn to answer. "Quinn won his match six-to-one, six-to-zero. Still undefeated, right?"

"So far," said Quinn, embarrassed by Lynda's dominance.

"Captain of the team and undefeated, and he's only a sophomore," bragged Lynda.

"So what is Forest Hills?" asked Mark, observing the patch on his sweater.

"That's where they play the US Open every year. It's in Queens, New York," said Quinn, finally stringing two sentences together.

"Have you ever been there?" asked Brian.

"Yes, a couple times. My father took me there last year to watch Stan Smith."

"Is he your favorite player?"

"No, not necessarily. He plays serve and volley, which is not really my cup of tea. I prefer to watch the guy from Sweden. He could be the next rising star."

"Who's that?" asked Mark.

"A guy by the name of Bjorn Borg. He's starting to take the tennis world by storm. He, and a young American, Jimmy Connors, are starting to hit two-handed backhands. That seems to be the latest trend."

Feeling left out and bored, Lynda took charge and grabbed Quinn's arm. "Let's go down to the band room and see if I can introduce you to Antonio before the eight o'clock bell."

As they scurried off, Mark glanced at Brian, raising his eyebrows and rolling his eyes.

"What?" asked Brian.

"That was interesting," responded Mark. "I guess I figured him for more of a take-charge kinda guy. But she's the domineering one."

"Yeah, I know what you mean. I think people like him, people with status, seem to pair up with people who can advance their agendas."

"I think you hit the nail on the head," said Mark. "For Lynda, it's all about rising to the top. For Quinn, it's more about staying on top."

Chapter 34

BRIAN JOHNSON WAS LOUNGING IN his bedroom on a rainy Saturday afternoon. He was supposed to be doing homework, but procrastination was getting the better of him. Listening to the radio and flipping through a *Sports Illustrated* magazine proved to be too tempting.

Jim Catfish Hunter was on the cover of the latest issue after pitching his Oakland A's to a victory and a 2-0 lead over the Cincinnati Reds in the 1972 World Series. A big fan of the Reds, or Big Red Machine, as they were called, Brian had a large poster of Johnny Bench in his bedroom. He didn't know much about the upstart Oakland A's (an abbreviation for *Athletics*), except that they had only been in Oakland for four years after moving there from Kansas City in 1968. All he knew was they had crazy uniforms, long hair, mustaches, and were owned by Charlie Finley, a businessman who lived on a big ranch in LaPorte, Indiana.

Finley was somewhat of a rebel, known for his creative ideas on how to jazz up baseball by making it more fun and appealing to the younger crowd. With the growing popularity of professional football, baseball attendance was dwindling, viewed by many as too traditional and stodgy. In order to spice things up, Finley abandoned the conventional style of uniforms and introduced a new color scheme: Kelly green, gold, and white. Their white shoes, the only white shoes in Major League Baseball, became an Oakland trademark, and instead of ball boys, Finley employed an attractive lineup of ball girls.

Bucking another baseball tradition, the A's abandoned the clean-cut image of well-groomed ball players. Following the lead of Joe Namath, the star quarterback for the New York Jets, the A's grew long hair and mustaches and looked more like a neighborhood softball team than a Major League Baseball club. Embracing the new look, Finley encouraged his players to participate by doling out three-hundred-dollar bonuses to those who grew mustaches.

When they took the field for their season-opening game in 1972, it marked the first time a Major League Baseball player sported a mustache since the 1930s. Rollie Fingers, the star relief pitcher of the A's, became the team's poster boy when he flaunted his handlebar mustache, a style rarely seen since the nineteenth century. With its long, curled-up extremities held in place by wax, his mustache looked like it belonged in a barbershop quartet instead of a baseball team. But it drew lots of attention and the fans loved it.

As their popularity continued to grow, Finley's team became known as the Swingin' A's. By contrast, the Cincinnati Reds were the polar opposite, all smooth-faced and neatly groomed, with black shoes and matching black belts.

The media had dubbed the World Series as "Hairs versus Squares." But all Brian really cared about was that his favorite team was losing to a ragtag bunch of characters that didn't fit his image of professional athletes.

With a tapping on his bedroom door, Brian looked up to see his mother peek in.

"You have a telephone call. I think it's Scott."

"Okay, I'll be right there."

Brian walked down the hallway to the kitchen and retrieved the phone. His mom had left the receiver on the countertop next to the refrigerator, leaving the long cord dangling all the way back to the wall unit.

"Hey, what's up?"

"You gotta come over," pleaded Scott. "I just picked up the new George Carlin album, *Class Clown*."

"Oh yeah? What's so great about that?" asked Brian. "Is it any differ-ent from your Bill Cosby records?"

"Yeah, a lot different. This album has the seven words you can't say on television. Haven't you heard?"

"Maybe," replied Brian. "I guess I don't know that much about it."

"Well, it's been taking the world by storm because it's hilarious and controversial. He was actually arrested this past summer for performing the same act in front of a live audience."

"Arrested for what?"

"I don't know. For saying bad words, I guess. I think they called it obscenity or indecency, or something."

"So how were you able to buy it?" asked Brian.

"I just picked it out of the record section in Walgreens like any other album. I guess there's no censorship on records."

"Well, maybe there should be," suggested Brian. "It might help you keep your nose clean."

"Very funny. I guess it's okay to listen to dirty words, but you can't buy a *Playboy* until you're eighteen. It's a crazy world."

"Yeah, I guess you're right," agreed Brian. "Let me grab an umbrella and I'll be down in ten minutes."

George Carlin, an American comedian and actor, had spent most of the 60s doing traditional stand-up routines. Dressed in his customary suit and tie, Carlin toured the nightclub circuit and appeared regularly on TV shows like *Ed Sullivan* and *The Tonight Show* with hosts Jack Paar and Johnny Carson.

Although he made a decent living, he knew his act was getting stale and people were getting tired of the old-fashioned, somewhat corny, comedy acts of the 50s and 60s. When the 70s rolled around, Carlin grew long hair and a beard and started wearing an earring. After ditch-ing his suits for faded jeans and tie-dye shirts, he transformed himself into a hippie character, marketing himself to the younger crowd with an act that was more edgy and politically charged.

Abandoning the conventional nightclub scene, Carlin went on the road to hone his new act, drawing large crowds in New York's Greenwich Village and the Troubadour in West Hollywood. After sharpening his routine, Carlin released the album *FM & AM* in early 1972. The AM side of the record was an extension of his previous style, relatively tame, with quirky parodies of American life. The FM side marked the beginning of his new act, challenging traditional norms and making bawdy jokes about sex and birth control, symbolizing his official transition from mainstream society to the counterculture.

In the summer of 1972, George Carlin was performing a new act at Summerfest in Milwaukee, Wisconsin. During the show, he introduced his "Seven Words You Can't Say on Television" routine. The crowd of close to thirty-five thousand responded overwhelmingly with raucous laughter and thundering applause. But some of the people in the crowd were offended, including Milwaukee police officer Elmer Lenz, who was attending the event with his wife and young child. Apparently, Lenz was unfamiliar with previous court decisions that allowed for free speech at live performances under the protection of the First Amendment.

When Carlin walked off the stage, he was greeted by the Milwaukee police department and arrested for "disorderly conduct," a somewhat vague offense that allowed a degree of latitude for the prosecution. Carlin was booked and released that same evening after posting a $150 bond. But his arrest appeared in headlines all over the country the next day and made him and his new routine an instant sensation.

A few months later when his case went to trial, the prosecution played an excerpt of the routine from Carlin's album *Class Clown*, and the courtroom spectators laughed out loud, including the presiding judge, Raymond Gieringer. Ruling in favor of Carlin's innocence, the judge stated that obscene words alone are not grounds for disorderly conduct, noting that Carlin had the freedom to say them as long as he did not create a disturbance. Realizing that Carlin was a nightclub performer, Summerfest attendees should have anticipated the possibility of risqué material.

The ruling opened the floodgates for all comedians as they expanded their repertoires and ventured into topics that had long been considered salacious or too provocative for public consumption.

Brian stepped onto the Clever front porch and rang the doorbell. Scott opened the door slowly, displaying the *Class Clown* album under his chin with a big grin on his face.

"You haven't even opened it yet?" asked Brian.

"Nope, you and I are gonna break the seal on this puppy together. Kinda like poppin' the cork on some fine champagne."

"You're too funny." Brian laughed. "You're making quite a production out of this."

Seeing that Scott was in a better mood and back to his usual antics, Brian felt obligated to needle him.

Entering Scott's bedroom, the boys closed the door behind them. Scott turned on the record player and ran his fingernail along the cardboard edge of the album, breaking the cellophane seal. After peeling away the wrapper, he slid the record from its cover and inhaled the fresh vinyl, savoring the aroma like a fine wine.

Brian grabbed the album cover and chuckled at the picture of a long-haired George Carlin sitting on a barstool in front of a chalkboard, holding his hand in front of his face as if his middle finger was jammed up his nose.

"He looks like a class clown, all right," joked Brian. Then, flipping the album cover, he read about the act and how it was performed in front of a live audience at the Santa Monica Civic Auditorium in California. There were nine different tracks on the record, three on Side A, and six on Side B.

"The seven words routine is the last cut on Side B," said Brian. "Are we gonna listen to both sides? Or are you goin' right to the dirty words?"

"Let's go right to the main course," joked Scott, as he carefully eyeballed the thin groove between track five and track six.

"You better ease that needle down gently," teased Brian. "You don't wanna scratch your prized possession."

As the monologue kicked in, Carlin started talking about his passion for words and how they originate, how they often come from thoughts that run through people's minds. Although thoughts may come and go, the words assigned to those thoughts remain as a lasting reminder. People are stuck with them forever. And some people object to certain words, assigning their own rules to when the words can be used.

Although rules can be applied to words, no one can ever control your thoughts.

"There are four hundred thousand words in the English language and there are seven of them you can't say on television. What a ratio that is! Three hundred thousand nine hundred ninety-three...to seven. They must really be baaad! They would have to be outrageous to be separated from a group that large."

"All of you over here, you seven, you are baaad words."

"Shit, piss, cunt, fuck, cocksucker, motherfucker, and tits."

The live audience roared, and Scott rolled around on the floor holding his sides. Brian had a look of dismay on his face. "Holy shit! I can't believe he just said that."

"And you just used one of those words yourself." Scott laughed.

After the laughter died down, Carlin went on.

"Those are the heavy seven. Those are the ones that'll infect your soul, curve your spine, and keep the country from winning the war." (more laughter)

The live audience continued to roar with approval as Carlin went on to talk about how the list of seven excluded the so-called two-way words, the ones that are only bad half the time, in other words, they're 50 percent bad.

"Ass is one of them. For example, you can say: 'You've made a perfect ass of yourself tonight.' But you can't say: 'Hey, let's go chase some ass.'"

Carlin continued with his seven-minute act, keeping the audience in stitches and challenging them to view society's restrictions in a different light. Scott and Brian were completely absorbed with the routine, laughing over and over as they replayed it multiple times. Then they went back to the beginning of the record, laughing all over again as they played the entire album from start to finish, nonstop. A perfect way to waste a rainy Saturday afternoon.

Although *Class Clown* was groundbreaking, Americans continued to debate the ethics and pitfalls of free speech versus censorship. It didn't take long to realize that people would never agree upon what truly constitutes obscenity or indecency.

George Carlin later joked that the English language has more words to *describe* dirty words than it has *actual* dirty words: inappropriate, suggestive, off color, in poor taste, bad, filthy, foul, vile, vulgar, street talk, gutter talk, locker room talk, bawdy, naughty, raunchy, crude, lewd, indecent, profane, obscene, risqué, etc., etc.

For decades to come, George Carlin would continue to make jokes about the irony of words and hypocrisy in America. When *Rolling Stone* compiled a list of the fifty greatest stand-up comics of all time, they ranked George Carlin number two, describing him as America's greatest defender of free speech and "the thinking man's comic, demanding that his audiences fight from underneath the mountain of bullshit heaped upon them by clergymen, politicians, and advertisers."

After the Cincinnati Reds lost the World Series to the Oakland A's, Brian Johnson took down his Johnny Bench poster and replaced it with a poster of George Carlin.

Chapter 35

NOVEMBER 7, 1972, WAS ELECTION day in America, the date that would determine if Richard Nixon would serve a second term as president of the United States. His first term had been a rocky one, marked by a brutal war that continued to divide the nation and plunge it further into a chasm between old and young.

The Democratic challenger, Senator George McGovern, captured his party's nomination on an antiwar theme. Not only would he end the war and pull US troops out of Vietnam, but he would grant amnesty to all Vietnam defectors, many of whom had moved to Canada to avoid the draft. This was a controversial position considering so many American boys had jeopardized their lives to honor the draft, falling prey to their own loyalty and commitment.

But the antiwar movement had grown into a full-scale blitz, and McGovern was banking on a huge youth movement to carry him to victory. His strategy was strengthened by the passage of the Twenty-sixth Amendment in 1971, allowing eighteen-year-olds to vote for the first time. Up until the 1972 election, no one under the age of twenty-one had ever cast a ballot to determine the president of the United States. But the argument was simple: if you're old enough to die for your country, you should be old enough to vote.

Despite his solid lead in the polls and popularity with the establishment, Nixon was concerned about the potential for a new wave of voter rebellion triggered by the youth movement. To appease the antiwar movement and counter his opponent's attacks, President Nixon had been softening his stance on Vietnam, retreating from major battle zones, and announcing significant troop withdrawals. As the election got closer, peace negotiations intensified, and on October 26, less than two weeks before the election, National Security Adviser Henry Kissinger announced, "peace is at hand." Whether or not that was true, nobody knew. But Kissinger's statement offered timely credence to the possibility that Nixon was making progress.

Roselyn O'Connor cleared the dining room table where her family had finished their evening dinner. Fit for a king, the room featured twelve-foot-high coffered ceilings structured in three-dimensional grids, a pattern that reflected brilliantly against the shiny Italian marble floor. In between, two Baccarat crystal chandeliers glittered with radiance, shining down on the Brazilian rosewood table, and imposing a grandeur reminiscent of the Gilded Age.

Although the table accommodated up to fourteen guests, there were only three place settings on this particular evening, but Ryan insisted that his dinner be served each evening in style and elegance. Christine, attending her junior year at Saint Mary's College, was no longer living at home. Ryan would have liked for her to continue the O'Connor tradition and attend the University of Notre Dame, but Notre Dame was an all-male school when she left for college in 1970. Saint Mary's, a small, private Catholic school, was the next best thing.

Considered a sister school to Notre Dame, it sat on the western banks of Saint Joseph's Lake, just a stone's throw away. Even though Notre Dame began to accept female students for the first time in 1972, Christine was firmly established in her Saint Mary's curriculum and had no intention of transferring.

"I have a made-from-scratch carrot cake for dessert," announced Roselyn. "I'll bring it out as soon as the coffee's ready."

"Can you bring it into the parlor?" asked Ryan. "I want to watch the election returns."

Ryan rose from the table, still wearing his suit, but with a loosened tie, his version of casual attire. As they entered the parlor, Quinn turned on the RCA console television set. All three channels were providing around-the-clock election coverage.

"Who do you want to watch?" asked Quinn. "This is John Chancellor and David Brinkley on NBC." Then with a quick rotation of his wrist, the dial clunked to the next channel. "Or you can watch ABC with Harry Reasoner."

"Are you taunting me, or what?" asked Ryan. "You know I'm a Walter Cronkite kinda guy. He's a true American."

Quinn chuckled after getting the desired response, then changed the channel to CBS as his mother arrived with the cake and coffee. "Any projections yet?" asked Roselyn.

"They just called the state of Massachusetts for McGovern," said Ryan, as he sipped his coffee from the fine Haviland china. "But it was very close. That's a good sign. When a liberal state like Massachusetts shows forty-six percent support for a conservative candidate, we could be looking at a potential landslide. New York will be the key. If McGovern loses New York, it's all over." Roselyn handed Quinn a big slice of cake and tried to change the topic.

"So, Quinn, what can you tell us about Lynda Lacey? You've gone out with her twice now? Is that right?"

"Actually, we've gone out three times," said Quinn. "What can I say? She's pretty and she's nice."

"No, your mother is right," said Ryan. "Pretty and nice is fine, but it's important for you to surround yourself with the right kind of people. If you're spending a good deal of time with her, she'll become part of your reputation."

"I wasn't going down that path," countered Roselyn, uncomfortable with her husband's intensity. "I was simply asking about her. If Quinn is dating her, I'm sure she's a nice girl."

Before Quinn could offer any more insight, Ryan continued, "Is she smart? Is she involved in any activities?"

"She's very smart," replied Quinn, deciding to indulge his father. "She's a straight A student and captain of the cheerleading squad. She also plays the piano and is involved with her church choir."

"Is she Catholic?" asked Ryan, getting right to the point.

"Please, Ryan," pleaded Roselyn. "They've only gone out a few times. It's not like he's marrying her."

"It's okay, Mom," said Quinn, well-acquainted with his father's expectations. "Her family belongs to a Lutheran church, but Lynda is very open-minded when it comes to religion."

"Well, the Lutheran religion isn't far removed from Catholicism," consented Ryan. "Why isn't she going to Concordia?"

"I don't know," replied Quinn. "Probably the same reason why I'm not going to Bishop Dwenger. I guess we just wanted to go to a brand-new school and be surrounded by diversity."

"Diversity is way overrated," prodded Ryan. "It's better to be insulated in the virtues of success than exposed to the failures of an outcast society."

"Okay, that's enough," said Roselyn, embarrassed by her husband's aristocratic arrogance. "Let's change the topic."

"I want to meet her," said Ryan, not giving up. "Why don't you bring her over for dinner?"

"I can do that," said Quinn, as his mother looked on nervously.

Quinn was well-acquainted with his father's agenda. He didn't necessarily embrace it, but he knew how to cooperate gracefully, sometimes beating his father at his own game. He'd been around Lynda long enough to know that she would be up to the challenge.

"How about next weekend?" suggested Ryan, accustomed to taking charge.

Roselyn looked at Quinn apprehensively, "Is that okay?"

"I'll ask her," said Quinn, "but it shouldn't be a problem."

"Whoa! There it is," said Ryan O'Connor. "They just projected New York for Nixon. That should make it a done deal. Everything else is academic."

As the states continued to fall like dominoes, the conclusion appeared to be inevitable. The other big prizes, Texas and California, were a lock. Texas was firmly Republican, and California was Nixon's home state. As the trends continued to support those conclusions, *CBS News* projected a winner much earlier than anyone expected. Richard Nixon would serve a second term as the thirty-seventh president of the United States.

Ryan O'Connor stood up with a big, proud grin on his face. "I guess that settles that."

"I don't know why this makes you so happy," declared Roselyn. "You lost a son because of that stupid war, and now you have another son that'll be eligible for the draft in just two more years."

Ryan's face suddenly turned red as he glared at his wife. "Nixon has reduced the draft numbers dramatically. Besides, this is LBJ's war, not Nixon's. Please tell me you didn't vote for McGovern and his liberal mob."

"I don't want to argue," said Roselyn, realizing she had hit a nerve.

"No, let's put all the cards on the table," said Ryan, raising his voice. "You still think I'm responsible for Shane's death, don't you?"

"You know that's not true."

"I don't know what is true anymore," yelled Ryan, as Quinn slinked out of the room.

"My business, this house, this family; all of it was built on conservative values and principles. And now you're turning liberal on me? Sometimes I think we have nothing in common anymore."

"This is turning very ugly, and I don't want any part of it," said Roselyn. "I'm retiring to my room."

"Fine, just stay out of *my* room. I won't be needing your company."

Ryan poured himself a tall glass of scotch and shouted, "I'm going to the GOP headquarters to celebrate. I may not be back tonight."

When all the results were in, Nixon had garnered 61 percent of the votes, winning forty-nine of the fifty states, making it the largest Electoral College landslide in the history of presidential elections. The so-called silent majority, a label tagged by Nixon, had proven themselves, delivering a crushing defeat to the boisterous hordes of protesters demanding change.

Unbeknownst to most Americans, the sporadic revelations behind the June break-in at the Watergate Hotel in Washington DC were being swept under the rug, rarely discussed among political pundits before the election. But two brazen reporters with *The Washington Post*, Bob Woodward and Carl Bernstein, continued to peel back the onion, persistently pursuing an understanding of why anyone would want to break into the Democratic headquarters.

On June 19, just a few days after the break-in, Woodward and Bernstein reported that a GOP security aide was one of the Watergate burglars. But former Attorney General John Mitchell, head of the Nixon reelection campaign, denied any link to the operation.

On August 1, Woodward and Bernstein reported that a $25,000 cashier's check, earmarked for the Nixon campaign, wound up in the bank account of a Watergate burglar.

On September 29, just five weeks before the election, they reported that John Mitchell was in control of a secret Republican slush fund used to finance intelligence-gathering operations against the Democrats. As it turned out, their primary source of information was John Mitchell's wife, Martha.

On October 10, four weeks before the election, Woodward and Bernstein reported that FBI agents had determined the Watergate break-in stemmed from a massive campaign of political spying and sabotage conducted on behalf of the Nixon reelection campaign.

On January 30, ten days after President Nixon's inauguration, former Nixon aides G. Gordon Liddy and James W. McCord were convicted of conspiracy, burglary, and wiretapping in connection with the Watergate investigation. McCord was a former CIA officer and head of security for President Nixon's reelection campaign. Liddy, a former FBI agent, was head of a covert White House Special Investigation Unit.

As the investigations continued, attention began to swirl around the Oval Office. Only a month after his inauguration, Richard Nixon's presidency was under attack, ridiculed for his lack of transparency and scrutinized for his brazen deceit.

Chapter 36

MARQUIS JACKSON PULLED HIS FORD Galaxy slowly into the parking lot, looking for the best available spot. Crunchy ice crackled beneath his tires as he gingerly steered his vehicle over the jagged surface. It was a frigid evening in January, and with temperatures plunging below freezing, the daytime slush was quickly turning to ice.

Marquis was still adjusting to Indiana winters. The last thing he wanted to do was leave the comfort of his warm house on a Tuesday evening and venture out on treacherous roads. But this was the evening of the Teamster meeting, and his curiosity had gotten the better of him. Marquis had debated on whether to go or stay home, especially with the prevailing conditions, but he decided it was important to stay informed. He didn't want his coworkers to think he was disinterested in the prosperity of their futures.

Marquis buttoned up his coat and tiptoed across the parking lot. Even though most of the ice was rough, he proceeded with caution, carefully identifying the slick patches that could send him sprawling in an instant. Not knowing what to expect, Marquis sized up the UAW hall. From the outside, it resembled an old schoolhouse, a simple, unassuming structure made of brick and concrete. Once inside, it felt more like a gymnasium, with its high-pitched ceiling, wood plank floors, and heavily scented lacquer.

Scanning the circumference, he recognized a bar in one corner, and a partially hidden kitchen in the back. The right side of the room was cluttered with stacks of round tables, apparently shoved aside to make room for the meeting. With the proper decorations, Marquis could visualize the facility doubling as a reception hall for weddings, anniversaries, or graduation ceremonies.

Looking for a familiar face, Marquis scanned the crowd. Although most of the seats had been taken, he was surprised to see only a few employees from O'Connor Cadillac. Noticing Ernie in the last row, Marquis chose a seat next to him and took off his coat.

"Looks like a pretty good crowd," noted Marquis.

"But not much of a turnout for Cadillac," said Ernie.

"So who do you think these people are?" asked Marquis.

"Employees of the Buick dealerships," replied Ernie. "It looks like the Teamsters are targeting all of O'Connor's businesses. No wonder he was schmoozing us with breakfast the other day."

With the thumping of a microphone, the crowd's attention focused on a dark, distinguished-looking gentleman wearing a white open-collared dress shirt, and a navy-blue blazer.

"In case you haven't noticed, there's coffee up here for anyone in need of a warm pick-me-up. I thought it would taste good on a cold night like this. I didn't want to break out the beer for fear of losing everyone's attention."

Chuckling at his comment, the crowd delivered the desired response.

"My name is Dominic Marino. I represent the Teamsters as a union organizer for the Midwest territory. I'm assuming most of you are here as a result of the memo that was circulated. Is that right? How many of you received my memo?"

Almost everyone raised their hands.

"Good. Thank you for coming. Although you are not here for *me* this evening. You are here this evening to take a vested interest in yourselves and your families. I want you to know that I've been doing this for nearly twenty years now, and I got into this business because I've witnessed, firsthand, the positive impact the Teamster Union can have on the welfare of workers—workers like you who are the backbone of this great country, the engine that drives our economy."

A mild round of applause broke out as Marino paused to sip his coffee.

"But workers who are not organized, are workers with no power. They are workers who will be taken advantage of, workers who will have no say in how their jobs should be performed or how they will be compensated. Workers who will be exploited with long hours and low wages, workers who spend their whole lives servicing the wishes of their masters, masters who are only interested in accumulating wealth."

Marino paused again to acknowledge the murmur spreading across the room. Marquis looked at Ernie and nodded his head, recognizing the power of the speaker's words.

"But I'm not here to deliver a pep rally," Marino continued. "I'm here to explain how the system *should* work, and how we can all work together to make it happen. If you really think about it, each and every one of you provides a service, a service to your business and a service to your customers. And for that service, you are entitled to compensation—a fair compensation. But how does one really determine what is fair? That's a good question. Think about it."

Marino paused to sip his coffee, letting the words sink in.

"The other side of the coin is the business owner. The business owner must produce a product that will sell and make a profit. But how much profit is reasonable, and how much is too much? He knows his business will fall apart if he doesn't have good workers. Good workers are a valuable commodity. Agreed? One side does not exist without the other. There should be a balance, right?"

Marino paused for feedback and got the desired response as the crowd obediently nodded their heads.

"That's basically the role of the Teamsters Union—to achieve balance. Balance is achieved when neither side is taking advantage of the other. So contrary to rumors that we are some kind of a radical, leftist organization trying to stir up trouble, we view ourselves as negotiators, negotiating a fair and reasonable contract between labor and management, a contract that provides the best wages and benefits to workers, while delivering a reasonable profit to the business. That's it in a nutshell. It really is that simple."

"Now," Marino continued, "before I get into the specifics on the steps that need to take place in order to organize *your* labor movement, I want to open the floor to a question-and-answer session. I usually find that my audience has many questions at this stage, and it's best to address them as soon as possible."

"So let's get started. Who's first?" Marino pointed to the first raised hand.

"Can you explain how the negotiating process works?"

"Yes," replied Marino. "That's a good question. Perhaps you've heard of the term 'collective bargaining.' That's the negotiating process. The workers are the 'bargaining unit.' They elect a few representatives to assist the expert negotiators appointed by the Teamsters. These people are experienced in negotiations and are legal experts in their field. They will have access to facts, figures, and statistics to assist them in presenting their case. Once the negotiating team reaches a tentative agreement, the bargaining unit meets to vote Yeah or Nay. If a majority approves, the 'collective bargaining agreement' becomes an official contract. If it is *not* ratified, the negotiations may continue. Okay? Does that make sense? Next question."

"Can you tell us about union dues, what the money is used for and how it is spent?"

"Yes, a very common question, and a good one. On average, eighty percent of that money goes right back into your local union. The bulk of it is used for legal fees to handle employee grievances and arbitration expenses. Another piece of it goes toward research and investigative expenses related to the gathering of industry data and evidence, all critical to the collective bargaining process. And most of the rest goes toward office and administrative expenses. But the important thing to remember is that our union members earn, on average, thirty percent better wages than nonunion members, and receive, on average, fifty percent better benefits. None of that would be possible without the strength that comes from union dues."

As the Q&A session extended for another forty-five minutes, Marino continued to handle the questions with precision and authority, demonstrating a command of the issues with his articulate answers. But it was his style and charisma that left the most indelible impression. He clearly knew how to warm up a crowd by engaging them and building trust.

Measuring his audience and observing their behavior, Marino was intrigued by the spirited dialogue. The fact that this group had so many questions and concerns led him to believe that his pitch was working and his assemblage was seriously considering the consequences of union membership.

"Don't be surprised by management's attempts to thwart your labor efforts," Marino continued. "It may start out as something very subtle, almost unrecognizable. They may soften some rules, or they may display surprising acts of kindness. We call this 'extending an olive branch.' Then, the efforts become more definitive. For example, they may award everyone with a Christmas bonus, or maybe even issue a small raise. We call these efforts 'preemptive strikes.' All designed to take your eye off the prize."

"If those tactics don't work," Marino continued, "they may hold a mandatory meeting. We call these 'captive audience' meetings, meetings where employees are required to attend and listen to management make misleading or disparaging claims about unions and how they destroy company unity, and how everyone is better off when the company functions as partners."

Someone then raised his hand and asked, "What if they fire you for trying to organize? Can they do that?"

Marino responded calmly and professionally. "The first thing we do when unionizing a work force is to file a petition with the NLRB, which is the National Labor Relations Board. This petition will contain a 'just cause' clause, which means a company cannot fire you without a legitimate and justifiable reason. That will protect you from those types of intimidation."

Someone then raised his hand and asked, "Do you have some other examples of how management attempts to intimidate? I mean, I'm sure you've witnessed a lot over the past twenty years."

"Yes," Marino chuckled. "I've been around the block a few times. But it's safe to say that you should never underestimate management's creativity when it comes to intimidation. That's not to say you should ever *feel* intimidated; you shouldn't. You have rights and protections. But I've seen many tactics in play when management wants to play hardball. For example, some companies that offer benefits to full-time employees may start cutting back on hours. Instead of employing six full-timers at forty hours per week, they may hire a couple more people and cut back on hours. If you do the math, eight employees with thirty-hour work weeks make up the same number of labor hours, but now they can save on benefits because no one is considered full-time, which is defined by a forty-hour work week. You see what I mean? That's just dirty pool, and unions have a way to fight those tactics."

The audience buzzed again as more hands were raised. Dominic Marino looked at his watch and cleared his throat.

"You're all asking good questions and we've had some stimulating dialogue, but we've been here for an hour now and I'm sure some of you are worried about driving home in these icy conditions. Let me just say that this evening is the very first step in a series of steps. It won't happen overnight. If we find there is enough interest and the circumstances are conducive to Teamsters membership, we will proceed accordingly. My experience has shown that this is typically a six-month to one-year process. What I will have you do is pick up my informational pamphlet at the back of the room as you leave, share it with your colleagues, the ones that did not attend, and continue to spread the message. I will then let you know about our next meeting and what steps we will take to continue the process. In the meantime, my phone number is on the pamphlet, and you can call me anytime you like. Okay? Thanks for coming this evening and I will stick around a little longer if you want to chat."

As everyone stood up, Marquis slipped on his coat and started heading toward the exit with Ernie. "So what do you think? Is it what you expected?"

"Not exactly," replied Ernie. "It was actually much better than I expected. Everything he said made so much sense. For some reason, I didn't expect him to be so polished and prepared. He seems like a really smart guy."

"I agree," said Marquis. "By the time he was finished answering everyone's questions, I was thinking, why *wouldn't* we want to unionize? It almost seems naive to think otherwise."

"Bingo," said Ernie. "I like that word. Why should we be *naïve* about this? I think we should start spreading the word that this is a good thing. Agreed?"

"I don't disagree," said Marquis. "But maybe we should exercise a little caution, not be so open about it until there's greater participation. I mean, I only saw three other Cadillac guys there and one of them was

Neil Bowers. Do you think he's one of us? Or was he there as a spy for management?"

"That's a good question," replied Ernie as they tiptoed through the parking lot. "He's not technically considered to be management, but he's definitely a liaison between labor and management. They could be using him as an information gatherer."

"Yes, that's certainly a possibility," agreed Marquis. "It's like Mr. Marino said, never underestimate the tactics that management will use to fend off a union. All the more reason we should proceed with caution."

"You got that right," said Ernie. "Now, are you gonna scrape that frost off your windshield? Or have you still not bought an ice-scraper?"

"Hah, very funny. I bought my first ice-scraper a few weeks ago. Never knew it was a necessity until I moved to Indiana."

"Welcome to the Great White North." Ernie laughed. "See ya tomorrow."

Chapter 37

BENEATH A MOONLIT SKY, THE Buick LeSabre cruised along the heavily wooded country road, lighting up the sparsely traveled route with its high beams. It was a frigid January evening and Quinn was bringing Lynda home to meet his parents, albeit two months later than originally planned. Now that Thanksgiving, Christmas, and New Year commitments were out of the way, January seemed like the perfect time for an O'Connor indoctrination.

Quinn slowed down as he turned onto a narrow path that was barely identifiable, vaguely marked by a brick mailbox and a small sign that read Private Drive.

"Your house is back here?" asked Lynda.

"Yes, it's pretty well-hidden. It gives us more privacy."

Winding through the trees, they came to an iron gate. Quinn rolled down the window and keyed in his security code. After a brief pause, the gate opened slowly, its wheels grinding along the metal track. Keeping Lynda in suspense, Quinn eased into the accelerator slowly and deliberately.

Emerging from the dense foliage, the sky suddenly turned bright, and Lynda's jaw dropped. The O'Connor estate, in all of its splendor, was glowing in the night like a castle.

"It's beautiful," gawked Lynda. "Even more than I imagined."

"This is my humble abode," joked Quinn, unable to disguise his pride.

Lynda continued to gawk as the Buick rounded the large circular drive. Although it was nighttime, the structure was well-lit, showcasing all of its ornate detail.

The house, a classic Georgian Colonial, was all brick, with Indiana limestone quoined at the corners and precast concrete around the windows. Four giant pillars outlined the elevated porch and extended up to the second level, where they supported an upstairs portico wrapped in a latticed railing. The steeply pitched roof, made from Vermont slate, hosted two symmetrical gables that rose in unison, aligning with the highest peak in the middle. Jutting out from the slate, two large dormers emerged as window dressing, accenting the facade with the stately touch of an English Earl's manor.

Taking it all in, Lynda grabbed Quinn's hand. "It feels more like Cambridge, Massachusetts, than Fort Wayne, Indiana."

"Ah," said Quinn. "A reference to Harvard?"

"Yes, it has an Ivy League feel to it. I'm not sure I'm properly dressed."

"You need to look more preppy if you're going to be an Ivy Leaguer," teased Quinn, as they walked up the front steps. "Perhaps you should tell my father to grow some ivy on the brick."

"I don't think he's looking for any suggestions from me on my first visit."

Quinn opened both of the double doors so Lynda could get a full view of the spacious, two-level foyer and spiral staircase.

"It's absolutely stunning," said Lynda. "Now I feel like I'm in Newport, Rhode Island."

Quinn laughed out loud. "You're getting quite the world tour tonight."

"Is that you, Quinn?" came a voice that sounded far away.

"Yes, Mother," shouted Quinn. "We're in the foyer."

Quinn's mother entered the foyer through the dining room and approached the couple with a warm, engaging smile. "This must be Lynda."

"Pleased to meet you, Mrs. O'Connor," said Lynda, as she extended her hand.

Roselyn took her hand but pulled her in for a hug. "No need to be so formal, dear. We're happy to have you. Now, let me take your coat."

"Where's Dad?" asked Quinn.

"I think he's in the library," said Roselyn as she hung the coats. "Why don't you check in on him while I finish dinner. Everything should be ready in about fifteen minutes."

"See those double doors behind the staircase? That's my father's library, his natural habitat," remarked Quinn, rolling his eyes.

"I think that is so cool," exclaimed Lynda. "We don't even have a library at our house. By the way, your mother is adorable."

"Yes, but now comes the real test, meeting my not-so-adorable father."

Lynda could feel the butterflies in her stomach as Quinn tapped on the library door.

"Come in," announced Ryan.

The couple entered the sanctuary to find Ryan sitting on his high-back, tufted-leather armchair, reading a newspaper and smoking his pipe. Wearing a tweed jacket with corduroy slacks, his typical Saturday evening attire, Ryan stood up to greet them.

"Pleased to meet you, sir," said Lynda, shaking his hand. "I hope we're not intruding."

"Not at all," said Ryan, pleasantly surprised by her assertiveness. "We can sit down for a bit and get acquainted, or I can show you around."

"I would love for you to show me your library," said Lynda. "When I'm surrounded by books, it makes me want to absorb as much knowledge as possible."

Ryan looked at her inquisitively, wondering if she was serious or just laying it on thick. Either way, he admired her spunk.

"Many of these are law books and articles from various law reviews. I'm sure you'd find them very boring. I saved all my college textbooks, eight years' worth, and display them over here," he said, pointing to the middle shelf.

"But I also have an extensive collection of classic literature. What do you like to read?"

"Mostly biographies and twentieth century American fiction. I find nineteenth century literature to be a bit laborious."

"Such as?" asked Ryan, putting her to the test.

"Well, I guess Charles Dickens is a good example. I read *Great Expectations* and *David Copperfield*. They were okay, but *A Tale of Two*

Cities was excruciating. Beyond the famous introduction, the rest of the book was like watching paint dry."

Ryan laughed out loud. "You're quite the critic. I'm very impressed. And what about Mark Twain? He's a nineteenth century writer. Do you approve of his work?"

"Well, *Huckleberry Finn* is a classic, of course. And I liked *Tom Sawyer*, but some of his other works seem rather silly."

"Such as?"

"Well, I know he enjoyed humor, but I read *A Connecticut Yankee in King Arthur's Court* and found it to be mostly ludicrous."

Quinn crinkled his eyebrows with intrigue. He knew that Lynda could turn on the charm and sophistication, but her debut performance in front of his father was certainly Oscar-worthy.

Ryan looked at Quinn with approval and continued. "I must say, I do not disagree with your opinions. I have all the books you mentioned in this library."

Lynda continued to peruse the bookshelves. "Oh cool, you have a Steinbeck collection. This is one of my favorites," she said, pulling out *The Grapes of Wrath*. "Didn't this win a Pulitzer Prize?"

"Perhaps," replied Ryan. "A bit too sappy on the labor movement for my taste. It almost seemed like an attempt to smear business owners."

"And you have F. Scott Fitzgerald," noted Lynda. "I found the dialogue in his novels to be very entertaining, exposing the bourgeois attitudes of the wealthy during the roaring 20s."

Quinn felt a nervousness creep in for the first time. She was doing so well, but now he feared she was crossing some boundaries with her appreciation for the labor movement and Fitzgerald's stereotypes of the wealthy.

"You said you like biographies," said Ryan, changing the topic. "What are your favorites?"

"I like reading about women who changed the course of history. Some of my favorites were Florence Nightingale, Sacagawea, Susan B. Anthony, and Harriet Tubman."

"All great women," nodded Ryan. "I can see why you like their stories."

With a tap on the door, Roselyn peeked in and announced that dinner was ready.

"Let's move to the dining room," said Ryan. "Perhaps we can return after dinner for some billiards."

Roselyn led the way and seated them at their place settings. "I'll bring out the first course. How about a nice cup of butternut-squash soup to warm you up?"

"Sounds perfect," said Lynda. "Your home is beautiful, Mr. O'Connor. Those chandeliers are magnificent."

"Thank you," said Ryan, glowing with pride. "They were custom-made by Baccarat. I was inspired by our tour of the Baccarat crystal museum in Paris. They've been commissioning creative works for heads-of-state all the way back to Louis the XV in the eighteenth century. It took them a whole year to make these, but it was worth the wait."

"Incredible," exclaimed Lynda. "Was Louis the XV the king during the French Revolution? I sometimes get my French kings mixed up," she giggled.

Ryan O'Connor smiled at her playfulness. "I'm impressed with your knowledge of history, although King Louis the XV lived a full life at Versailles. It was his son, Louis the XVI, that succumbed to the guillotine."

"I've never been much of a history buff," said Quinn, trying to work his way into the conversation as his mother delivered the soup.

"Mmmm, the soup is delicious," said Lynda.

"Thank you, dear. Now tell us about your cheerleading. Quinn said that you are captain of the squad?"

"Yes, ma'am, I took a lot of dance lessons growing up. Much of that translates to the new routines we've been working on. But it's really just a hobby. It makes for a fun time being part of the school spirit at football and basketball games."

"That's nice," said Roselyn. "And you also play piano?"

"Yes, I started taking piano lessons in the second grade."

"What kind of music do you like to play?" asked Ryan.

"Mostly classical, but I'll mix in some pop tunes every now and then."

"Can you play any Elton John?" asked Quinn, trying to be clever.

"No." Lynda laughed. "I don't think I could ever play like him. That's a whole different genre."

"Time for the second course," announced Roselyn. "I'll bring out the salads."

"Let me help," offered Lynda. "I feel guilty sitting here and letting you wait on me."

"Not at all," said Ryan. "You're our guest. Besides, we're still getting acquainted."

After Roselyn left the room, Ryan started with a more serious line of questioning.

"So tell me, Lynda, what does your father do for a living?"

"He works for Lincoln Life Insurance as an actuary."

"That's a good company and a fine profession. Where did he go to school?"

"He went to Indiana University with a double major in math and actuarial science. He says his job is boring to most people, but he's very good at it. He's the director of his department and oversees eighteen people. He helps me with my algebra whenever I get stuck. He's a real whiz at math."

"A noble profession indeed," conceded Ryan. "What about yourself? What are your ambitions in regard to school and a career?"

"Here are the salads," announced Roselyn. "Did I miss anything?"

"Lynda was just going to tell us about her college and career ambitions," said Ryan.

"Already?" asked Roselyn. "She's only a sophomore in high school."

"Never too early to start planning," countered Ryan.

"It's a good question," acknowledged Lynda. "I'll probably go to Indiana University. At least, that's where my father wants me to go. I think I'd like to be a marketing executive. I'm fascinated with the way companies can impact their sales and profits through promotions and advertising. I think that would be a fun and challenging job. It kinda stimulates the creative juices, if you know what I mean."

"Very interesting," said Ryan. "I think that would be a great career."

"And I want to make enough money to buy a Cadillac," joked Lynda.

Ryan laughed out loud. "Now here's a girl that knows how to win my heart. Have you ever thought about being an attorney?"

"No, not seriously. Although I do like watching old *Perry Mason* shows; the way he would figure out crimes and intimidate people on the witness stand. And I liked Atticus Finch in *To Kill a Mockingbird*. Legal dramas are very entertaining."

"Maybe it's something you should consider," suggested Ryan. "I think you have a sharp mind and a quick wit. Perfect attributes for a lawyer."

"I'm flattered," said Lynda. "Maybe I *will* think about it."

"What did you think about the landmark Supreme Court decision last week?" asked Ryan.

"I don't think we need to get into that," said Roselyn, as she nibbled on her salad.

"Are you talking about *Roe v. Wade*?" asked Lynda. "That's the one that's been all over the news, right?"

"Yes, that's the one," confirmed Ryan.

"You don't need to answer that, Lynda," said Roselyn. "He's just trying to put you on the spot. Typical lawyer tactics."

But Lynda took the question as a challenge and thought about her answer carefully.

"That's a tricky one. I would say that I'm personally against abortion, but I don't think the government should infringe upon a woman's right to choose. Isn't that what the Supreme Court is saying?"

"Keep going," said Ryan.

"I mean, nobody should believe in taking the life of an unborn baby, but there's a lot of disagreement on when a fetus becomes a baby, right? That's when personal beliefs and religion can have a big influence on a woman's decision. Therefore, I think the Supreme Court is saying that government should not make the decision for her. Am I correct?"

"Those are some valid points," said Ryan. "Like I said, you'd make a good lawyer."

"I mean, I could never *personally* be in favor of abortion," continued Lynda, "but I don't think our government should interfere."

Ryan laughed and Lynda blushed. "Did I say something wrong?" she asked.

"No," said Ryan, "I'm laughing because you'd also make a good politician. You're basically saying the same thing as our senators and Congressmen. They're all straddling the fence, trying not to offend anyone."

"So what is your opinion?" asked Lynda. "You don't mind if I ask, do you?

"Well, Lynda, my opinion doesn't matter. I'm a Catholic, and the pope, whose authority is infallible, has proclaimed abortion to be immoral and a sin against humanity. So despite my legal background, I am one hundred percent against all abortions. The Catholic religion was around long before there were legal scholars. So the law of the church is the law I must live by."

"Okay," said Roselyn. "I think it's time to move on to another topic. You're putting way too much stress on this young lady."

"No, it's okay Mrs. O'Connor. I respect what he has to say, and I have a lot to learn."

"And I respect what you have to say," replied Ryan. "I didn't mean to be so stern, but I've always believed in speaking honestly, and you, my dear, have a sharp mind. You will always be welcome in our house."

Lynda's embarrassment turned to pride after receiving Ryan O'Connor's sincere and heartfelt commendation. She glanced at Quinn when no one was looking, and he nodded back at her and winked, as if to say, "You passed with flying colors."

As Lynda began to relax and feel more comfortable, the rest of the dinner was filled with light-hearted conversation. Roselyn enjoyed talking about celebrity gossip and the latest fashion trends, while Quinn and his father talked about golf and tennis. When the last bite of chocolate cake was consumed, Ryan stood up and announced, "Quinn, why don't you help your mother with the dishes, and I'll take Lynda back to the library for some billiards."

"I must confess," said Lynda, "that's a game I'm not familiar with. I've only played a few times."

"Then I will teach you," said Ryan. "You have to start somewhere."

"Quinn," said Roselyn, "you grab the plates and I'll pick up the glassware."

Back in the kitchen, Quinn began loading the plates and bowls into the dishwasher. "Dinner was very good, Mom. Thank you for putting this together."

"It was fun. I hope your father wasn't too tough on her."

"Oh, I think Lynda handled herself quite well," said Quinn. "I'll be honest with you; I didn't expect anything less."

"I agree," said Roselyn. "Your father seems to be enamored by her."

"I really know how to pick 'em." Quinn laughed.

"Are you sure?" asked his mother in a more serious tone.

"What do you mean?"

"I mean, did you pick her out for your father or for yourself?"

"What's that supposed to mean?"

"I don't know," said his mother. "I just didn't sense any chemistry between the two of you."

"Why do you say that? I think we go together perfectly."

"See…that's exactly what I mean," said his mother. "You never say things like 'she's adorable,' or 'she's a real sweety,' or 'I'm crazy about her.' Isn't that what guys say when they really like a girl? Instead, you say you go together perfectly."

"Mom, we've only been going out a few months. I'm not a real lovey-dovey kinda guy."

"That's fine," said Roselyn. "I know you're still young and the last thing you need to do is fall seriously in love. But don't ever settle for a girl because she impresses your father or because you think she'll be good for your career. You need to do what makes you happy. Love and happiness are the most important things in life."

Quinn gave his mother a big hug. Somehow, he knew she was talking about something much deeper and more meaningful than the girl he was dating. She was delivering a message that should have been delivered to her many years ago.

Chapter 38

S COTT CLEVER STEPPED OUT THE front door and headed toward the driveway. Taking a deep breath, he inhaled the cool, crisp air on a brisk Saturday morning in February. Although a fresh inch of powdery snow had fallen overnight, the skies had cleared, making for a bright sunny day, so bright that Scott felt blinded by the brilliant white snow.

With his eyes watering, Scott grabbed the snow shovel and elected to continue his mission without sunglasses. Shoveling a thin layer of dry, powdery snow was an easy task. It really wasn't shoveling at all, at least not in the traditional sense. There would be no thrusting, lifting, and hurling of heavy loads. Instead, all he needed to do was guide the steel blade along the surface in long strips until enough snow had accumulated to make quick, sideways flings. Once the snow was cleared, the sun would quickly evaporate the remaining moisture, leaving the cement completely dry for shooting hoops, which is Hoosier slang for playing basketball.

The Indiana High School basketball tournament was in full swing. In a few short hours, more than ten thousand people would pour into the Memorial Coliseum to watch the final day of sectional play. The Northrop Bruins, in only their second season of existence, would play in the semifinals at noon, hoping to advance to the championship game later that evening. For those who weren't lucky enough to get a ticket, Hilliard Gates would broadcast the games on WKJG-TV, NBC's affiliate in Fort Wayne.

For Scott, the day would have a special significance. He had scrimmaged with most of the Northrop varsity players and earned enough playing time on the sophomore team to average seven points and five rebounds a game, an accomplishment that gave him a good shot at playing varsity ball as a junior. On this day, however, Scott was preparing to host his annual sectional party, a tradition that would start with three-on-three driveway hoops, followed by snacks and refreshments around the television set.

Long before there was March Madness, there was Hoosier Hysteria, an annual ritual where every Indiana high school would compete for the same prize, a state basketball championship. Although basketball was invented in Massachusetts by a Canadian named James Naismith, Indiana was the state that popularized the sport, turning it into a cultural phenomenon and elevating it to folklore status.

When Naismith created the earliest version of the game back in 1891 using peach baskets, he was looking for a sport that would burn off the endless energy of his YMCA boys. Restless from the long Massachusetts winters, the boys were tired of calisthenics, so Naismith created an indoor sport that would offer both recreation and competition.

Twenty years later, Indiana would crown its first state basketball champion when Crawfordsville defeated Lebanon 24-17. By then, Naismith had already coached nine seasons at the University of Kansas, where he was instrumental in launching one of the first college basketball programs. Later he would become the Kansas athletic director and a member of the faculty, where he authored his book *Basketball: Its Origin and Development.*

In 1936, at the age of seventy-five, Naismith traveled to Indianapolis to fulfill a lifelong ambition of watching an Indiana state championship basketball game. Regarding Indiana as the epicenter of basketball, he wanted to witness Hoosier Hysteria firsthand before meeting his maker.

After viewing fifteen thousand screaming fans at Butler's Fieldhouse, Naismith was overwhelmed and described it as a thrill he would never forget. In that game, Frankfort defeated Fort Wayne Central 50-24, but Central's leading scorer, Steve Sitko, would go on to win the Gimbel

Prize, awarded each year to the athlete best symbolizing sportsmanship and scholarship.

After graduation, Sitko would go on to lead the University of Notre Dame's football team as their starting quarterback. A few years later, Steve's cousin, Emil "Red" Sitko, would also graduate from Fort Wayne Central. When he returned from his service in World War II, Red Sitko starred for four years as an All-American running back at Notre Dame, never losing a game and winning two national championships.

Between 1928 and 1971, Butler's Fieldhouse in Indianapolis served as host to the Final Four, where the Indiana state champion was crowned every year except from 1943 to 1945, when it was used as a military barracks. When the facility was completed in 1927, it was the largest basketball arena in the country and would continue to hold that title until 1950. Long known as Indiana's basketball cathedral, its name was officially changed to Hinkle Fieldhouse in 1966, after Butler University's longtime coach and athletic director, Paul D. "Tony" Hinkle. In 1983, it was added to the National Register of Historic Places, and it was designated a National Historic Landmark in 1987.

As the popularity of basketball in Indiana continued to grow, the smaller communities could no longer accommodate their throngs of supporters. Soon there were gymnasiums of monumental size popping up all over the state. Anytime someone published a list of the largest high school gymnasiums in America, the rankings were dominated by Indiana high schools, usually ten of the top twelve.

Leading the list was the renowned Wigwam, a nine thousand-seat arena that served as the home court for the Anderson Indians. New Castle Fieldhouse, with a capacity of eight thousand four hundred wasn't far behind, routinely selling out whenever it hosted the hometown Trojans. Two of Indiana's most legendary players, Kent Benson and Steve Alford, were both products of the New Castle basketball factory. Kent Benson was voted Mr. Basketball in 1973, before attending Indiana University, where he led the Hoosiers to a national championship in 1976, the last college team to complete an undefeated season. Steve Alford was voted Mr. Basketball in 1983, averaging thirty-seven points per game during an era that excluded three-point baskets. He would later win an Olympic gold medal and lead the Indiana Hoosiers to a national championship in 1987.

For decades, basketball was the sport that functioned as the great equalizer in Indiana. No matter how big or small the schools were, basketball was the common denominator. Unlike football, basketball required only five starting players and a few substitutes, making it possible for virtually every school to field a team, whether their enrollment was two hundred or two thousand. And with hundreds of schools spread all over the map, communities rallied around their teams, traveling to neighboring towns to support their local heroes. It was the perfect small-town entertainment for long Indiana winters.

Since many of the smaller schools existed in proximity to larger metropolitan areas, competition against big city schools was not unusual, creating David versus Goliath scenarios. If a small-town athlete could slay the mighty dragon, nothing would immortalize him more. For those reasons, Indiana was one of the few states that put every school into the same state basketball tournament, resisting the urge to categorize schools by size and create multiple tournaments.

Regardless of their win-loss records, every single school was invited to the state tournament, and brackets were determined by geography, not seedings. No school would know its destiny until tournament officials ceremoniously drew names out of a hat, determining first round matchups by luck of the draw.

In order to bring home a state title, a school would have to win its sectional, regional, and semistate brackets before advancing to the Final Four in Indianapolis, a monumental task considering the insurmountable odds of getting past seven hundred and fifty other schools.

For most schools, the ultimate goal was winning a sectional. Playing in a sectional title game meant television exposure and the opportunity for local bragging rights. Not only would sectional champions hoist a large trophy and ceremoniously cut down the nets, but their team pictures would be plastered in all the newspapers as conquering heroes, forever to be immortalized in their communities as champions.

In 1954, the ultimate David versus Goliath story ensued when a small school by the name of Milan advanced all the way to the state championship game to play perennial powerhouse, Muncie Central. Muncie Central had already won four state championships, more than any other high school in Indiana history, and was ten times the size of Milan, a school with only seventy-five boys. But Milan, led by Bobby

Plump, was a highly regarded team heading into the tournament after cruising through the regular season with a 19-2 record, albeit against an array of lesser-known opponents.

The Muncie Central Bearcats arrived to the Final Four in Indianapolis after being crowned semistate champions at Fort Wayne's Memorial Coliseum, avenging a regular season loss to Fort Wayne North Side. Averaging nearly seventy points per game in the tournament, the Bearcats were on a roll, and advanced to the championship game by cruising past Elkhart with a solid nine-point victory. But the Milan Indians were also on a roll, defeating Indianapolis Crispus Attucks in the semistate tournament and beating Montezuma by ten to advance to the championship game.

Bigger, stronger, and more athletic, Muncie Central was a heavy favorite, proving themselves against tougher opponents all season long. If Milan was to compete, second year coach Marvin Wood would need a new strategy. He knew his team could not keep up with the Bearcats' fast-paced run-and-gun style of play, so he devised a scheme to slow the game down, passing the ball around deliberately and methodically in seemingly endless attempts to create high-percentage shots.

Throwing the Bearcats off their game and keeping the contest close, Milan's strategy seemed to work. Down 28-26 late in the game, Coach Wood ordered Plump to hold the ball until he was challenged by a defender. But with a two-point advantage, Muncie Central had no need to challenge a stationary player at midcourt. Nevertheless, Plump delivered his coach's strategy, standing still and holding the ball for nearly four minutes as the restless crowd screamed for him to take action.

Finally, with three and a half minutes left, the standoff ended when Milan called a time-out. Returning to the floor, they began to run their offense again, but Plump missed a shot with 2:50 remaining and Muncie rebounded. Swarming the Bearcats with a pressing defense, Milan forced a turnover and hit a jump shot to tie the game at 28-28. After a defensive stop, Milan got the ball back and Plump was fouled. With 1:40 left, Plump made two free throws to give Milan a 30-28 advantage. But the Bearcats were not finished, feverishly working the ball around and driving to the basket for the game-tying score with forty-five seconds on the clock.

As fifteen thousand screaming fans looked on, Coach Wood called a time-out to draw up the final play. But there would be no *X*'s and *O*'s. Instead, Wood ordered Bobby Plump to dribble the ball around mid-court until there were only ten seconds left, at which point he would attack and create his own buzzer-beating shot.

As Plump patiently dribbled the ball, waiting for the right moment to make his move, the Butler Fieldhouse worked itself into a frenzy. With ten seconds on the clock, Plump attacked his defender, backing him up on his heels. At six seconds, he gave a quick head fake left and drove to his right at full speed, instantly elevating his body into a jump shot before the Bearcat defense could respond. The rest is history.

Pure bedlam ensued as fans rushed the floor in celebration. The 32-30 victory would go down in folklore as one of the greatest moments in basketball history, forever memorialized as the Milan Miracle. Thirty years later, Hollywood would commemorate the event with its own fictional adaptation, a movie called *Hoosiers*.

With Gene Hackman starring as the basketball coach of a small school named Hickory, the Indiana state championship would be won with a last-second shot by Jimmy Chitwood. During the filming, thousands of Indiana residents lined up outside Hinkle Fieldhouse for the opportunity to appear as movie extras. Inside, Fort Wayne's Hall of Fame broadcaster, Hilliard Gates, served as the movie's radio announcer, repeating the role he played in the 1954 Milan Miracle. The film would go on to win numerous awards and famous athletes would affectionately refer to *Hoosiers* as their favorite sports movie of all time.

In 1955, one year after the Milan Miracle, Indianapolis Crispus Attucks defeated Gary Roosevelt 97-64 to become the first all-Black school to win a state basketball championship in Indiana, and the first all-Black state champion anywhere in the United States. The following year, the Crispus Attucks Tigers extended their win streak to forty-five straight games, finishing with a 31-0 record and winning back-to-back state championships, the first Indiana school to finish with a perfect record. Their leading scorer, Oscar Robertson, would go on to be inducted into the Hall of Fame as one of the greatest professional basketball players in NBA history.

"Hey, hotshot. You got that driveway all cleaned up and ready to go? 'Cause I'm gonna school ya today."

Scott Clever looked up to see his two buddies approaching the driveway. Mark Carter was wearing a black sweatshirt embossed with gold letters spelling "PURDUE." Brian Johnson was wearing a red sweatshirt emblazoned with "INDIANA."

"Forget the sectionals." Scott laughed. "I'd rather watch the two of you play one-on-one. Purdue versus Indiana, a real battle for state supremacy."

"And the winner gets an oaken bucket," quipped Mark.

"Wrong sport, you nerd," said Scott. "That's football."

Scott then tossed the ball to Mark who launched a long shot from the street. The ball clanged off the rim and bounced off the overhead garage door.

"At least you caught some iron," said Scott. "But you better stick to football."

"Who all's coming today?" asked Brian.

"Bob and Steve are supposed to be here," said Scott. "We still have a half hour before the Bruins tip-off."

"How are we gonna play three-on-three with five guys?" asked Brian. "Is your brother home?"

"Actually, nobody's home," said Scott. "My dad got sectional tickets through the dealership and took Mom to the game, and David moved out of the house in January."

"How's he doing?" asked Mark. "Did your parents boot him out?"

"I think it was more of a compromise," replied Scott. "Kind of a long story, but my parents sent David to counseling. They allowed him to quit his late-night factory job if he replaced it with a part-time job and continued his schooling. He moved in with a couple friends so they could all share the rent. My parents are paying for his education."

"You think it will work?" asked Mark. "Is he off the drugs?"

"I hope so," said Scott. "I think it was the beatdown of working late nights on an assembly line and trying to go to school at the same time. Maybe doin' drugs was his way of escaping."

"Sounds like a plan that might work," said Brian, as he swished a shot from the corner. "Hey, why don't we just play a game of HORSE.

Besides, I'm not sure this driveway is big enough for three-on-three anymore."

"All right by me," said Scott. "How about Purdue versus Indiana. Then I'll take on the winner. I'll be Notre Dame."

"Let's do it," said Brian. "I'll shoot first."

After launching a series of creative shots, both short and long, mixed in with some underhand scoops and half-hooks, Brian was sitting on a commanding lead: H to H-O-R-S.

"Looks like it's gonna be Notre Dame versus Indiana in the finals," said Scott.

As Brian got ready to take the game-winning shot, his concentration was interrupted by the loud, rumbling sound of an engine. All three boys looked up to see a bright yellow Plymouth Barracuda slowing to a stop at the end of the driveway. When the passenger window opened, they were surprised to see the smiling mug of Steve Marino.

"What's happenin', losers?" asked Steve. "Bob wants to know if there's any chicks around here that wanna go cruising."

"Damn!" said Scott, recognizing Bob in the driver's seat. "Is this your new ride?"

"Yep, I finally pulled the trigger," said Bob, trying to be cool.

"It's pretty badass," commented Mark. "But I'm not sure about the color. Why did you decide on yellow?"

"It's officially called lemon twist," corrected Bob. "I wanted some-thing that attracted a lot of attention."

"I'd say you met your goal." Brian laughed. "You gonna take us for a ride?"

"Hop in," said Bob.

"Wait!" said Scott. "The game starts in fifteen minutes. Why don't we get the party started and go for a ride at halftime?"

"Suit yourself," said Bob as he shut off the engine. "What kind of a party are we talkin' about?"

"The usual," said Scott. "Snacks and sandwiches."

"What about girls?" asked Steve. "I hope you don't mind that I in-vited some chicks."

Scott looked up nervously. "Seriously? How many?"

"Relax," said Steve. "I just told Lynda to stop by and bring Karen with her."

"Oh, that's all right," said Scott. "She probably won't come anyway."

"Still trying to hit on Karen?" asked Brian. "When are you gonna give up?"

"He won't give up until he scores," said Mark. "He wants another notch on his belt."

"Ain't nothing wrong with that," said Steve. "But if I know Lynda, she'll probably show up with her trophy boy, Quinn."

Walking to the front of his new car, Bob tried to recapture everyone's attention. "Anybody wanna look under the hood?"

"Show them what you have in the trunk instead," said Steve. "They might find that more interesting. Especially if we're gonna have a party."

"Whaddaya keep back there, Mannix?" asked Mark.

"Mannix?"

"Yeah, don't you ever watch *Mannix*? The detective show? He always drives around in a Barracuda."

"Well, if he does, he's just trying to be cool like me," said Bob.

Opening the trunk, Bob unveiled a large Styrofoam cooler and three brown cardboard boxes. Steve opened the lid of the cooler to reveal a combination of Falstaff and Pabst Blue Ribbon beers packed in ice.

"Cha-ching," said Steve. "Let the party begin."

"Whoa," said Scott. "My parents may not be home, but we still have to be careful. If you drink these in the house, we need to get rid of all the cans before they come home."

"No problem," said Bob. "But they're not free. Twenty-five cents apiece."

Steve pulled out a dollar and handed it to Bob. "Give me four. I'll buy the first round."

"All right, you guys," said Scott. "You can't drink these on the driveway either or the neighbors will tell my parents that we were drinking beer. Then I'll be in deep shit."

"No problem," said Bob as he reached into a brown paper bag and pulled out a package of Coca-Cola labels. "Wrap these around the cans and everyone will think you're drinkin' Cokes."

The boys broke out laughing as they grabbed the labels and wrapped their cans.

"Here's to the sectionals," said Bob as they clinked their beers together in a toast.

"What else do you have in that trunk besides counterfeit Coke labels and illegal alcohol for minors?" asked Mark in a sarcastic tone.

"Damn," said Steve. "Just like a cop's kid. Always tryin' to do things by the book. Why don't you loosen up and have a little fun? Bob, show them what else you have in your trunk."

Bob reached in and opened the flaps on one of the cardboard boxes. He then rummaged around before pulling out a brand-new *Playboy* magazine, still in the cellophane wrapper. The boys' eyes lit up like it was Christmas.

"Holy shit!" cried Scott. "Where'd you get those?"

"I can't reveal my sources," said Bob, glancing at Steve with a sly grin.

"Is there enough for everyone in that box?" asked Scott.

"Hold your horses," cautioned Bob. "I have ten February issues and ten January issues. They're three dollars per issue, or I can sell you two for five dollars."

"Wow," said Brian. "This is quite a racket you got goin' on here. *Playboy*s are a buck a piece and you're selling them for three? That's a three-hundred-percent markup."

"A man's gotta make a living," said Steve.

"Yeah," said Bob. "Our business, I mean, *my* business is a little down right now since football season is over and I'm not selling any parlay tickets."

"I'll take one February and one January," said Scott. "Can I give you a five-dollar bill when we get inside?"

"Sold!" said Bob. "Any other takers?"

"I don't have any money on me right now," said Brian. "Maybe Scott can sell me one of his used issues for two bucks. As long as the pages aren't stuck together."

The boys laughed out loud at Brian's clever jab, but Mark was still not amused.

"What else do you have in that trunk?" he asked.

"One of the boxes is filled with cartons of cigarettes," said Bob. "There should be a steady demand for those. Some of the stores are gettin' really picky about whom they sell cigarettes to."

"You got quite a business goin' on here," said Mark. "First it was gambling, now it's illegal bootlegging. Sounds like mobster-style racketeering to me. Do you have any idea this is all against the law?"

"C'mon man," said Steve. "You just need to chill. All he's doin' is providing a service where there's a need. People wanna buy, and he's selling. He's not forcing anything on anyone. It's called free enterprise. It's the foundation of our economy."

"Nice try," said Mark. "What if I told my dad about this?"

Steve's mood suddenly took a dark turn as he stepped toward Mark and bowed up like a hockey player ready to brawl. "You're not gonna tell your dad about this because I said you're not."

"Says who?" countered Mark. "Are you threatening me?"

Scott jumped in to break the tension. "All right, that's enough. Let's all take our beers inside and watch the game. I'll even let you look at my *Playboy*s. Let's go have some fun."

"Next round is on me," said Bob, as he grabbed some more beers.

Scott led them through the front door and into the family room where he flipped on the TV. Hilliard Gates was standing at center court and introducing the starting lineups. "Let's crack open these beers and get ourselves a sectional title," said Scott. "I'll get the food and snacks all set up."

Scott went over to the refrigerator and pulled out a platter of assorted Eckrich cold cuts, then placed them on a Lazy Susan in the middle of the kitchen table.

"How traditional is this?" he announced. "Gotta go with Eckrich meats during the tournament."

Scott was referencing the fact that Eckrich was always a big sponsor of sectional and regional basketball games, appearing at almost every commercial break.

"And then a little Sunbeam bread to make sandwiches," he announced, as he tossed two loaves on the table. "I got mustard and mayo and Kraft cheese slices. Anything else? Oh yes, I almost forgot the Seyfert's," he said, as he tossed out two bags of potato chips.

"Hey!" yelled Brian. "Come check this out. Look who's playing the national anthem."

They all gathered around the TV to see the Memorial Coliseum in complete darkness except for a light beam shining on the American flag above the top row of seats. Standing alone in front of the flag was the silhouette of a trumpet player.

"It's Antonio," exclaimed Scott. "How did he get that gig?"

"Are you kidding?" said Mark. "That guy is always in the limelight. He never met a stage or a camera he didn't like."

When Antonio finished playing, the lights turned on and the crowd started cheering. Antonio faced the camera and raised his fist in the air. In plain view for the first time, the boys realized he was wearing a brown sweater with orange lettering that spelled "Northrop Bruins."

"Check it out!" said Brian. "How cool is that?"

"I'm really pumped now," said Scott. "Let's kick some butt."

Taking another round of gulps from their beers, they were suddenly interrupted by the sound of a doorbell.

"Someone's at the door," warned Bob, stating the obvious.

"Quick, hide those beers!" ordered Scott, his heart suddenly pounding.

Proceeding cautiously to the front of the house, Scott peeked out the window. Much to his relief, he saw Lynda Lacey and Mindy Harper standing on the front porch.

"It's cool everyone. It's just the girls," he announced, as he opened the door.

"We're lookin' for a party," teased Mindy.

"Let me see your tickets." said Scott, trying to be clever.

"You should be honored by our presence," retorted Mindy, confidently leading Lynda through the door.

Distracted by Mindy's surprise appearance, Brian suddenly lost interest in the game. He was not going to let an opportunity like this pass him by.

Steve, on the other hand, couldn't hide his disappointment. "Where's Karen?" he asked.

"She's working today," said Lynda. "She has a job at Foxmoor in Glenbrook, selling women's apparel."

"Oh, that's good to know," said Steve. "I'll have to stop in some time and say hello."

"Yeah," said Mindy. "I'm sure she could fix you up with a really cute outfit."

Before Steve could come up with a snide remark, Brian swooped in, always enamored by Mindy and her sassy disposition.

"Come over here and fix yourself a sandwich. Let me show you what we have."

Mindy approached the table and allowed Brian to continue.

"Let's see, we have bologna, old-fashioned loaf, smoked ham, salami, or you can make a combo."

Mindy snickered at the way Brian was falling all over himself. "I'll do a bologna and salami combo. Can you make it for me?" she asked, trying to test his limitations.

"Absolutely," confirmed Brian, not missing a beat. "You want cheese on that?

"Yes, two slices. Preferably Swiss," she requested, knowing it was not an option.

"Sorry, we only have Kraft American cheese. Is that okay?"

Mindy let out a big sigh and continued her little game. "I guess beggars can't be choosers. Do you have any lettuce?"

"Scott, do you have any lettuce?" shouted Brian.

"Holy cannoli, Batman! Do you think I'm running a deli here?"

"Sorry, Mindy," said Brian. "I think that was a no. Do you want mayo or mustard?"

"Mayo on one side, mustard on the other," she ordered.

While Brian continued his submissiveness, Mindy's eyes roamed around the kitchen and caught a glimpse of Scott's magazines. Unable to resist another playful opportunity, she walked over and picked up the February issue.

"So, Brian," she said in a voice loud enough for everyone to hear, "are these your *Playboy*s?"

Everyone looked up as Brian's face turned a bright red.

"Scott," he shouted. "You left your magazines out. I think you offended Mindy."

"I'm not offended," said Mindy, always the cool cucumber. "You don't mind if I look at them, do you?"

"But I'm making you a sandwich," said Brian, nervously trying to change the topic.

"I can eat and look at magazines at the same time," she teased. "I'm not physically challenged."

"Just don't get any mustard on them," said Scott, half-joking and half-serious.

Lynda, noticeably disgusted by the frivolous dialogue, was growing impatient. After Mindy picked up the *Playboy*, she'd had enough.

"We just dropped by to say hello. We can't stay for long," she announced.

"Let me finish my sandwich first," said Mindy. "Don't you want to watch the game?"

Steve walked over and offered Lynda a beer. "Here ya go. Relax and enjoy yourself."

"No, thank you," said Lynda. But Mindy raised her hand like she was flagging down a beer vendor at a ballgame. "I'll take one. I need something to wash down this sandwich."

"Mindy," said Lynda, in a reprimanding tone, "you know that cheer-leaders can get kicked off the squad if they're caught drinking alcohol."

"Well," said Mindy, "I don't think anyone here will tell on me."

"I know I won't," said Brian, always in Mindy's corner.

"I have an idea," announced Steve. "I can get us access to free Komet hockey tickets. Maybe I should arrange an outing. We could all go to a game together."

"Sounds good to me," said Brian.

Steve continued with his brainstorming. "If I can get six tickets, Brian could bring Mindy, I could bring Karen, and Lynda could bring Quinn. How does that sound?"

"It depends," replied Lynda. "Quinn has a pretty busy schedule. Case in point, he's up in Ann Arbor this weekend playing an indoor tennis tournament. If he can't go, can I bring someone else?"

"It doesn't matter to me," replied Steve. "But you gotta fix me up with Karen. Can you do that?"

"Well," said Lynda, "I'm not much of a cupid, but I can try."

"I'm definitely in," said Brian, his heart racing at the thought of going on a date with Mindy.

"Let's do it," said Steve. "I'll arrange for tickets and let everyone know. Stay tuned."

The Northrop Bruins won their sectional game that afternoon and advanced to the championship later in the evening. Not only did they capture the sectional title, but they also went on to win a regional championship the following week before meeting their demise at semistate, the so-called Sweet Sixteen. It was an incredible achievement for a school that was only two years old.

At the same time, another Bruin team was setting records at the collegiate level. Riding a seventy-five-game win streak, the UCLA Bruins won their seventh straight NCAA basketball championship on March 26, 1973. Led by legendary coach John Wooden, the Bruins went on to set records that would never be broken.

The following year, in 1974, the UCLA winning streak finally came to an end at eighty-eight games in South Bend, Indiana, when the Bruins lost to Notre Dame 71-70. Ironically, the winning streak began in 1971 after another loss to Notre Dame, 89-82. Consequently, Notre Dame would forever stand as bookends to the longest winning streak in the history of basketball.

UCLA Coach Wooden, a native of Indiana, led his high school, Martinsville, to an Indiana state championship in 1927. After that, he attended Purdue University where he became the first basketball player to be named a three-time consensus All-American.

In 1973, John Wooden was elected into the Naismith Hall of Fame as a coach. He had already been elected as a player in 1960, becoming the first person to receive Hall of Fame honors in both categories.

In 1977, the first John Wooden Award was presented to the most outstanding college basketball player in the country. From then on, it would be awarded annually to the nation's best player, both male and female, representing the ultimate in excellence.

Chapter 39

S WAYING BACK AND FORTH TO the choir's soulful rhythm, the congregation summoned the Lord, seeking His presence through the sweet, mystical sounds of gospel music. Like a spiritual revival, they clapped their hands and lifted their arms to the heavens, filling their souls with jubilation and praising the glory of God.

Chantelle Jackson banged away on the piano, leading the chorus of purple robes and flaxen stoles, while Antonio harmonized with his brass bravado to a rousing rendition of "Oh Happy Day."

It was Easter Sunday at Turner Chapel AME, and the church was filled to capacity. Parishioners were standing in the aisles, forming lines that flowed all the way out the back and into the vestibule.

Reverend Brown did not want his guests to leave disappointed. He recognized the importance of ending Sunday services with an uplifting hymn, moving his congregation with God's spirit and inspiring them to spread the holy gospel.

Chantelle had chosen "Oh Happy Day" as the perfect ending to Easter Sunday services. To her, it was a joyous song that perfectly symbolized the feeling of rebirth. Although the song's origin dates back to the eighteenth century, many different versions had been performed over the years. In 1969, the song became an international sensation when the Edwin Hawkins Singers released their gospel version that rose to the top of the pop charts in the United States, France, Germany, and the Netherlands.

"He is risen! Praise the Lord!" proclaimed Reverend Brown as he returned to the pulpit. The congregation responded with a thunderous round of applause. The reverend thumped his chest, kissed his hand, and extended his arms to the crowd, the symbolic gesture for heartfelt appreciation.

"Go forth and serve the Lord," he exclaimed. "Please, help yourselves to the coffee, juice, and pastries we have set up in the vestibule. But before you leave, I want to make a quick introduction. We have a special guest with us today, and he would like to talk to you about some things you can do to secure your futures and provide a better standard of living for your families. He's standing in the back right now. Mr. Marino, raise up your hand so everyone can see you."

Dominic Marino smiled and waved his hand. It was easy to spot him. He was the only White person in the church. Dressed in his Sunday best, Marino looked distinguished in his black suit, white shirt, and purple tie.

"For those who are interested," continued Reverend Brown, "Mr. Marino will be holding an informational meeting in our parish council room. Feel free to take your refreshments with you if you decide to participate. I think you'll find it both informative and thought-provoking."

Dom Marino had met with Reverend Brown earlier in the week, explaining his mission to bring better wages and benefits to underprivileged citizens. He talked about how the Teamsters and the UAW had formed the Alliance for Labor Action (ALA) and how their goal was to align with progressive politics in an effort to improve living conditions for the African American community. Marino went on to tell the reverend that although the ALA affiliation had recently been disbanded due to money and political issues, his mission had not changed. He had been assigned to Fort Wayne to help organize overworked and underpaid labor groups and he would not abandon those ideals. Marino explained to Brown the importance of meeting with his congregation so that he could enlighten them on the possibilities of a better future and identify labor groups that were in need of his services. Reverend Brown, in turn, agreed to grant access to his members, believing that Marino's mission was a noble cause.

As the Jacksons exited the sanctuary, Marquis grabbed a cup of coffee, informing Chantelle that Mr. Marino was the Teamster organizer, who had met with his coworkers. "I think you should meet him," suggested Marquis. "Let's walk over and introduce ourselves."

As the Jacksons approached, Mr. Marino beat them to the punch and extended his hand.

"How do you do? My name is Dom Marino."

"Yes, sir," said Marquis. "I remember you from the O'Connor meeting. I was there on behalf of the Cadillac dealership."

"Ah, yes, I remember it well," said Marino, firmly grasping Marquis's hand.

"This is my wife, Chantelle."

"Pleased to meet you," said Marino, extending his hand and his charm.

"Chantelle works for the O'Connor law firm."

"Oh my," said Marino. "So you're fully invested in the O'Connor empire. That's very interesting. Will you be able to join our meeting this morning? I promise it won't take very long."

"I would like that very much," said Chantelle. "Oh, here comes Antonio. Let me introduce you to our son."

Antonio extended his hand and said, "Pleased to meet you, sir."

"Incredible show today!" said Marino. "You have a very talented family."

"Thank you, sir."

"I'd love to spend more time getting acquainted, but I need to get this meeting started. It was a pleasure meeting your family," said Marino, looking at Marquis. "Can we chat some more when we're done here?"

"No problem," said Marquis. "I'd like that very much."

Dom Marino proceeded to gather the interested parties in the meeting room, handing them his business card along with informational pamphlets about the Teamsters. Once the meeting started, Marquis began to realize that Marino's presentation was similar to the one he gave to the O'Connor employees, only a little less specific. Marino continued to demonstrate his impeccable grace and charm, as well as his mastery of facts and statistics.

He told his audience that Teamster members, on average, earn 30 percent more than their nonunion counterparts. Marquis specifically remembered that statistic. But Marino added another piece of information that Marquis had not been privy to, the fact that Black workers, on average, are paid 20 percent less than their White counterparts.

That is not the case with a union contract, Marino pointed out. There can be no racial discrimination in union contracts because contractual pay grades are determined by job description, skill level, and experience, not by the color of one's skin.

This latest revelation was an eye-opener for Marquis. As Marino continued with his presentation, the only thing that resonated with Marquis was the possibility that his coworkers were making more money than him simply because of their skin color. He couldn't imagine that Ryan O'Connor would allow that to happen.

But how could he ever find out? The amount of money that someone makes was always considered to be a private matter. Asking a coworker about his salary or hourly rate of pay would be impolite and intrusive. On the other hand, if a pay scale disparity was exposed during contract negotiations, that could prove to be enlightening. The more Marquis thought about the merits of unionizing, the more it made sense.

When Marino finished his presentation, he asked everyone to record their names, phone numbers, and places of employment on the sign-in sheet by the door. He pointed out that he was merely on a fact-finding mission to see if there were any good candidates for labor negotiations. There would be no pressure or invasion of their personal lives, only good-faith attempts to identify victims of unfair labor practices. He was on a mission of goodwill.

Exiting the room, Marino continued to field questions. Spotting Marquis in the crowd, he made a point to flag him down before he could exit the church.

"Can you stick around to chat?" Marino called out across the room.

Marquis smiled and nodded his head in a gesture of confirmation. Marino acknowledged his gesture and continued to work the room until the crowd thinned out.

"Thanks for sticking around," said Marino. "I wanted to talk to you about the interest level at O'Connor Cadillac. We had a couple guys step up and take leadership roles at the Buick dealerships, but it seems the Cadillac turnout is less than substantial. Is that your understanding?"

"I would say that's a fair assessment," said Marquis. "There were only four Cadillac attendees at your meeting, counting myself, and one of the four was the shop supervisor, Neil Bowers. He's not management, but he reports directly to management, so I'm not sure what side of the fence he's on."

"And what side of the fence are you on?" asked Marino, getting right to the point.

"That's a good question. To me, organizing a labor group makes a lot of sense. Like you said, we're really in a partnership, offering our services for the benefit of the business and meeting them halfway on how the pie should be split up."

"You seem to have a solid understanding," said Marino. "A well-grounded person like yourself would serve well in a leadership role."

"A leadership role? What does that mean?" asked Marquis, hesitant to make a commitment.

"Before we get into that. How would you gauge the interest level at Cadillac? Surely there's been some discussions. Do you think you have a finger on the pulse?"

"To be honest with you, it's pretty safe to say I'm not part of the inner loop. Quite frankly, I'm the only Black guy working in the service department. Which means I don't participate in most of the group discussions. That's why I could never see myself in a leadership role. But there's one guy that I'm fairly close with, his name is Ernie, and I think I can speak for both of us when I say we're on board with the *concept* of organized labor."

"That's good," said Marino. "I will keep both of you in mind. If you can share your interest with the others, very casually, I will try to schedule another meeting. As we continue to increase the interest level, we will gain strength in our numbers."

"I suppose we could do that," said Marquis. "I gotta be honest with you, I'm a little reluctant to rock the boat, being the only Black guy."

"I understand completely," said Marino. "If you could continue the discussions with your coworkers, that would help a lot. We need to have an open dialogue. You don't have to pressure them, just express your concern for their well-being. Then I can follow-up with you and your buddy, Ernie, to gauge the overall level of interest."

"I can try," said Marquis. "Then what happens?"

"Like I said, I will schedule another meeting to ramp up our efforts and communicate the procedural steps. Typically, I like to publicize our labor efforts with a group of picketers, which is, quite simply, a group of people holding up signs to profess their interest in a better labor contract. Nothing more, nothing less. Just a peaceful display of unity."

"That makes me nervous," said Marquis. "I don't think I want to do that unless I'm part of a large group."

"Understood," said Marino. "We haven't reached that level of commitment yet; it takes time. The formal part of the process begins when we start asking employees to sign cards confirming their interest. If we can get a forty percent commitment rate, then we know we're close to holding an official vote."

Marquis nodded his head. "Okay, this is all new to me."

Marino issued his warm smile, "I don't want you to stress out over this. Like I said, it's a process. It won't happen overnight. You have my phone number. Feel free to call me whenever you want. I'm always available."

"Thank you very much," said Marquis, reaching out to shake his hand again.

"You got it," said Dom Marino. "Enjoy Easter Sunday with your beautiful family."

Chapter 40

BRIAN JOHNSON TURNED THE IGNITION key and checked the rearview mirror as he prepared to back out of the driveway. In a ceremonious gesture of goodwill, his father had handed over the keys to his Oldsmobile Delta 88.

Shifting into reverse, Brian glanced up to see his mother waving from the front door, looking as though she were saying goodbye to her son for the last time. They were certainly making a big deal over the fact that he was going on a date.

Embarrassed by all the attention, Brian pretended to downplay the event as routine. After all, he was only picking up Mindy Harper to meet some friends at the hockey game. He wasn't sure if it even qualified as an official date. At least that's what he kept telling himself. In reality, he couldn't ignore the butterflies in his stomach or the fact that he would soon be sitting side-by-side with sweet, adorable Mindy in the front seat of his car.

The obligatory preliminaries had been fulfilled: shower, shave, a few splashes of Old Spice and two rinses of mint-flavored Scope. His mother had given him a five-dollar bill, saying "Be sure to buy your date some refreshments." To which his father remarked, "I thought that's what his allowance was for."

But mothers know how to ignore husbands when their child's best interest is at heart. She had already ironed his shirt and picked out his best pair of jeans. More importantly, she tutored him on the proper way to greet Mr. and Mrs. Harper and the importance of walking his date up to the front door when the evening was over.

With the anxiety building, Brian felt the perspiration on his back sticking to his shirt as it pressed against the warm vinyl seat. Now he was worried about his shirt getting wrinkled before he even arrived.

Oh well, he reasoned, she would see the front of him before she would notice his wrinkled back. First impressions are what matter the most. Nevertheless, he leaned forward, separating his sticky back from the vinyl, hoping to minimize the damage. No detail was too minute.

Worried about his destination, Brian's eyes darted back and forth between the road and the directions he had scribbled on the back of an envelope. He'd only been driving a few months, usually by himself or with his parents, and always to locations he was familiar with. This particular occasion would be a real game-changer. Executing his novice driving skills, navigating an unfamiliar route, and entertaining his date with clever dialogue, could prove to be a perilous combination, generating far more stress than he had bargained for.

Was he beginning to have second thoughts? Maybe this whole dating thing wasn't what it was cracked up to be. Now, in the heat of the moment, it seemed less alluring than he had imagined, not like the glamorous images he had conjured up while worshipping Mindy from afar.

In retrospect, he realized how exasperating the whole process had become, even from the very beginning. After all, what could be more nerve-racking than taking the walk of shame into the kitchen, dialing the phone, and asking a girl on a date while your family pretended not to eavesdrop. It was like a clown taking center stage and setting himself up for failure.

"Come on in," said Mindy as she opened the door. "My parents want to meet you before we leave."

Brian looked up to see Mr. and Mrs. Harper make their grand entrance together, right on cue, as if Mindy had choreographed the whole affair.

"You must be Brian," said Mrs. Harper in a warm, but cautious tone.

"Hi, how are you?" responded Brian, stumbling for the right words. Not knowing the proper decorum, he thought about extending his hand, but decided against it in an awkward display of hesitance.

Luckily, Mindy's father stepped forward and extended his hand. "Pleased to meet you, Brian."

"Likewise," said Brian, as he embraced the firm grip. Was that the right response? He'd heard that somewhere before. He hoped it didn't sound too feminine.

"Brian's on the football team," said Mindy, trying to ease the tension. She knew that men could always find a common ground when talking about sports.

"Oh yeah? What position?" asked Mr. Harper, looking at his daughter.

"Position?" asked Mindy.

"Yes." Mr. Harper laughed. "Believe it or not, there are different positions on a football team. Brian, you'll have to educate her."

With the talk of sports and Mr. Harper's sense of humor, Brian felt more relaxed.

"I play running back," he offered.

Hearing a giggle, everyone looked up to see a little girl peeking around the corner.

"That's my sister Sarah," said Mindy. "She's eight years old and very shy. Apparently, she thinks 'running back' is a funny position."

Everyone laughed as Mindy continued. "Sarah, come out here and meet Brian." To which the little girl ducked out of the picture and disappeared completely. "I think that's the last we'll see of my sister," joked Mindy.

"So you're a running back?" said Mr. Harper. "You must have some speed."

"Not as much as I'd like," conceded Brian. "I clocked a four-point-eight in the forty last week. I wanna get that down to four-point-seven by next year."

"Okay," said Mindy, taking charge. "We better get going. You men could talk about sports forever."

"The Komets have a good team this year," continued Mr. Harper. "It should be a good game."

"Yes," said Brian. "If they win tonight against the Flint Generals, they'll advance to the Turner Cup finals."

"Okay, that's enough. We're leaving now," said Mindy, taking Brian's arm and opening the front door.

"What time will you be home?" asked Mrs. Harper.

"Whenever the game is over," said Mindy. "Bye."

"Nice to meet you," called out Brian, as he opened Mindy's car door. To which Mrs. Harper responded, "Drive carefully."

Brian and Mindy filtered through the crowds that were gathering around the entrances to the Coliseum. It had been a seasonally warm afternoon in April, but the air was cooling rapidly as the western skies turned pink.

"You didn't bring a sweater," said Brian, recognizing a chill in the air. "You realize it could be a little nippy in the Coliseum tonight, don't you? They have to keep it cool in there so the ice doesn't melt."

Mindy looked at Brian as though he was speaking a foreign language. "They play on ice?" she inquired, with her cute sarcasm.

"Yes, and with real skates," quipped Brian, playing along with her game. "You can borrow my jacket if you get cold."

"Do you have the tickets?"

"No, Steve has them. We're supposed to meet them at the north entrance. I hope we can find them through all these people."

"There they are," pointed Mindy, spotting Steve Marino near the door with Karen Gadby. "It looks like Lynda was able to play cupid after all."

"Here comes the cute couple," remarked Steve, never passing up an opportunity to tease Brian about his infatuation for Mindy.

"Is Lynda still coming?" asked Mindy.

"She better," said Steve. "I don't wanna waste two tickets."

Before Steve could utter another word, Mindy and Karen settled into their comfort zones and began chattering away. The ease with which the girls made conversation was a welcoming distraction to the boys, relieving the pressure of back-and-forth dialogues with their dates and justifying the merits of group-dating.

"I thought you worked on Saturdays," said Mindy.

"I have every other Saturday off," said Karen. "That gives me some flexibility for making weekend plans."

"Any sales coming up? I still need to get some spring and summer clothes."

"The summer inventory is shipping next week. Then we'll create a clearance rack for the spring items. Come on by and I'll fix you up."

The jibber-jabber continued as the boys looked on incredulously. Watching the two together, Brian couldn't help but notice the stark contrast. Mindy, the cute high school cheerleader, looked every bit her age, while Karen exhibited the maturity of a young, voluptuous woman. It made Brian think of the endless comparisons between Mary Ann and Ginger on *Gilligan's Island*.

It was impossible to ignore Karen's sensuality, especially when her tight sweater and snug jeans outlined her curves so dramatically. Steve had once described her as a brickhouse, a term that was unfamiliar to Brian. But admiring her protruding sweater reminded Brian of the description his father used for James Bond girls: well-endowed. And looking at her jeans, the way they hugged her hips, he couldn't help but think of the word *bodacious*. He didn't really know what that word meant either, but it somehow seemed appropriate for a derriere as fine as Karen's.

Steve, on the other hand, referred to Karen's backside as a hot ass. That sounded crude to Brian, but consistent for a guy who grew up looking at *Playboy* magazines. At any rate, it was easy to see why Steve had been targeting Karen since he first laid eyes on her last summer.

"Hey, where can I find some action around here?"

The foursome looked up to see Antonio Jackson strutting his stuff and grinning from ear to ear. Next to him, Lynda was glowing like the cat that swallowed the canary.

"You look out of place," said Steve, admonishing Antonio's appearance. "Have you ever been to a hockey game?"

"A hockey game? Is that what this is? I haven't seen this many White people since I saw a Klan meeting in Louisiana."

They all laughed nervously, knowing that Antonio was having fun, but it did little to ease the tension.

"Where is Quinn?" asked Mindy, trying to change the subject.

"Wait a minute," said Antonio. "Are you saying you'd rather have Quinn here than me? If I wasn't such a cool cat, I might be offended."

"Quinn's playing in a tennis tournament this weekend," said Lynda. "But it doesn't matter. I flipped a coin, and Antonio won the toss. So here we are."

"Yeah, right," said Antonio. "I'll never win that coin toss as long as Quinn has a bigger bank account."

"Relax," said Brian. "We can teach you all you need to know about hockey."

"Yeah," said Mindy. "Just keep an open mind."

Antonio faked an exaggerated expression, as if appalled. *"Moi?* Are you serious? Honey, I was born with an open mind."

"All right, girls," said Steve, looking at Antonio. "Let's get to our seats before we miss the face-off."

Steve had never shown the same admiration for Antonio as the others. He was not the kind of guy who embraced cultural diversity or artistic expression. If bringing Antonio to a hockey game was a charitable act of inclusiveness, Steve would not be a willing participant. Instead of embracing Antonio's unique qualities and proclivity for showmanship, he regarded him as more of a freak, not the special someone that stood out from the crowd. He once described him as "a little light in the loafers," and routinely referenced him as "one of the girls."

Approaching the entrance, Steve distributed the tickets and instructed them to form a line. "Follow me" he said, as he grabbed Karen's hand, leading them through the congested corridors. "I know exactly where the seats are."

Whisking them through the crowd, Steve darted around the obstructions and up a series of ramps that led to a narrow stairwell. Although they were moving quickly, it was impossible to ignore the apparent stares and menacing glances. Antonio's presence had transcended the masses. As if his height and distinguished good looks weren't enough, there was no ignoring the conspicuousness of a Black man in an all-White crowd.

Arriving to their row, Steve was insistent on having the aisle seat and Karen in the chair next to him. "I need to have easy access to concessions," he explained. "The rest of you can figure out your own seating arrangements."

Taking charge, Lynda and Mindy made sure they were sitting next to each other without disrupting the pairings. As it played out, the seating alignment, starting from the aisle, consisted of Steve, Karen, Antonio, Lynda, Mindy, and Brian, respectively. Brian would have preferred to sit next to Steve and his hockey expertise, but he couldn't complain as long as Mindy was next to him.

No sooner had they sat down than they heard Jack Loos, the Coliseum organist, queuing up his instrument for the playing of the national anthem. Rising in unison, they looked over at Antonio with inquisitive expressions.

"That should be you leading the anthem," said Lynda.

"What can I say? I'm guessing a Black trumpet player wouldn't be their first choice to play patriotic music at a hockey game."

As soon as the anthem was over, Steve bolted from his seat and disappeared through the tunnel.

"Where did he go in such a hurry?" asked Antonio.

"He said he was going to get refreshments," replied Karen.

Lynda then leaned over Antonio's lap and spoke softly to Karen, as if someone might be listening. "So how's it going?"

"Fine, he seems like he could be a lot of fun."

"Well, I just hope it works out," said Lynda. "After all, I feel responsible for fixing you two up."

"No big deal," said Karen. "It's just a hockey game."

"Well," said Antonio, "all I can say is mind your p's and q's. There's something about him that seems a little shady. I'm just sayin'."

"Listen to Antonio." Karen laughed, "trying to be the watchful big brother."

"Just a word to the wise," lectured Antonio.

"Well, I'm a big girl. I think I can take care of myself."

The crowd oohed and aahed as the players whizzed around the ice, slamming each other into the boards and flinging the puck around like magicians. After a Komet slap shot resulted in a loud ping, the crowd let out a collective gasp.

"What was that?" asked Mindy.

"The puck hit the pipe," said Brian. "Two more inches to the right and the Komets would be leading one to nothing."

"I must admit," said Antonio, "this is pretty exciting to watch. I didn't know White boys could move so fast when you put a pair of skates on them."

Giggling at his observation, the girls were enjoying Antonio's entertainment value more than the game itself, while Brian tried to earn their approval by explaining the nuances of hockey.

With the Komets preparing to face off in the Generals zone, Steve reappeared carrying a bag of popcorn and two drinks. "Did I miss anything?"

"Komet power play," said Brian. "Two minutes for slashing."

"Here's your soda," said Steve, handing Karen her drink.

"Soda? What's a soda?" asked Karen.

"You wanted a Coke, didn't ya?"

"Yeah, it's either a Coke or a pop. We don't call them sodas in Indiana. It's a pop."

"Well, that's pretty lame," said Steve. "That sounds like something Andy Griffith would say on *Mayberry RFD*."

Antonio had to laugh at that image. "So what are you drinking, Steve? That don't look like no soda."

"It's a beer. Haven't you ever seen a beer before?"

"Yes, I know a beer when I see one. I just didn't think they sold them to seventeen-year-olds."

"Mr. Jackson," said Steve, in a sharp, menacing tone. "If you don't learn anything else about me, you'll find out soon enough that I'm a man with connections. So I would tread very lightly if I was you."

The lightheartedness of the moment suddenly evaporated as Steve exerted his authority. Karen didn't know whether to be impressed by Steve's commanding presence, or leery of his sudden change in demeanor.

Antonio, usually quick with the retorts, turned silent, intimidated by Steve's bravado. Cowering in his chair, he suddenly felt like a fish out of water.

Standing up, Brian decided to break the tension. "I'm running to the concession stand. Anybody want anything?" There was no response.

"Here," said Steve, handing Antonio a dollar. "Go with Brian and buy yourself a drink. Unless you want a beer, then I can get it for you."

"No, thanks," said Antonio.

"Brian," commanded Steve, "take Antonio with you so he can buy a drink. Just be careful that nobody mugs him out there."

Brian took Antonio by the arm. "C'mon, let's go."

Antonio was not amused by Steve's warning, but he decided to go with Brian anyway so he could get away for a few minutes and regain his composure.

Lynda couldn't keep quiet any longer. "Don't you think you were a little rude with Antonio? I know you're treating us all tonight, but it seems to me like you made him feel very uncomfortable. I mean, you said I could bring anyone I wanted, right?"

"Relax," said Steve, suddenly warming up as if the whole incident was water under the bridge. "Antonio can be a little cocky sometimes. I just wanted him to understand his place. That's all. Forget about it. It's all good."

When the boys returned with their refreshments, the entire arena was in a state of bedlam, everyone on their feet, yelling and screaming.

"What's goin' on?" yelled Brian.

"We got ourselves an all-out brawl!" bellowed Steve. "A real donnybrook. At least that's what Bob Chase calls it," he said, referencing the Komet radio announcer.

With gloves and sticks scattered all over the ice, the boys stopped in their tracks, glued to the action. Deciding which fracas to home in on was confusing at best as scuffles continued to break out all over the ice.

"Why do they all take their gloves off?" shouted Karen.

"Seriously?" questioned Steve. "Don't you know that you can do way more damage with bare-knuckle punches than you can with gloves?"

"Well, that's pretty brutal," said Karen, as Steve and Brian laughed.

Then, another eruption from the crowd ensued as a Komet defensemen cornered his opponent and hammered away, blood spraying all over the ice.

"Gross!" squealed Karen. "Why do they just let 'em fight? Aren't they gonna stop 'em?"

"It's pretty hard for a few referees to stop a free-for-all," said Brian. "They're totally outnumbered. Besides, would you wanna step in between two guys with their fists flying around?"

"No, but how does it ever end?"

"That's a good question," conceded Steve. "That's what makes brawls so entertaining. You never know when or how they're gonna end."

Steve and Brian continued to cheer the fisticuffs as the girls looked on in bewilderment. Brian hadn't even made it back to his seat or delivered Mindy's drink; he was too engrossed. Watching the mayhem with Steve, and gaining his perspective as a hockey player, only added to his enjoyment.

Although Antonio returned to his seat and delivered Lynda's drink, he remained standing, fascinated by the uncivilized behavior. Viewing the whole spectacle with a degree of sensitivity, he chose to commiserate with the girls' repugnance rather than surrender himself to the male herd mentality. That was not part of his DNA.

As the action began to dwindle, and the players skated around looking for their sticks and gloves, the crowd started to settle down. Brian made it back to his seat and delivered Mindy her *Mountain Dew*.

"So what happens now?" she asked. "Do they keep playing?"

"It may take a while to figure out all the penalties," said Brian. "Once they sort everything out, they'll start up again."

"What if they don't have enough players?" asked Mindy.

"What do you mean?"

"Well, after they eject all the fighters, will there be enough guys leftover to finish the game?"

Brian laughed and looked down at Steve. "Hey, Steve, Mindy wants to know if they're gonna eject all the fighters."

"C'mon Mindy," said Steve. "This is hockey, not ballet. Fighting is a five-minute penalty. After they serve their penalties, they can start playing again."

"That's barely a slap on the wrist," quipped Mindy. "No pun intended."

"Do you ever get in fights when you play?" Karen asked Steve.

"Does a bear shit in the woods?" asked Steve.

Although Karen wasn't amused, she seemed intrigued by the whole machismo culture.

"It's hockey," continued Steve. "Fighting is part of the game. If you don't stand your ground, guys will take advantage of you. That's just the way it goes. It's a rough sport."

Antonio whispered in Lynda's ear, "That explains his crooked nose."

Lynda smiled but gave Antonio a stern look. "Be careful," she whispered. "I don't want to see him agitated again."

But Antonio continued to confide. "I didn't know I would be a witness to such barbaric behavior this evening. When you said we were going to the Coliseum, I didn't think it was the Roman Coliseum. I think there would be less blood if it was the gladiators versus the lions."

Weaving around the lines of traffic, Brian and Mindy navigated their way through the parking lot. The air had cooled considerably since the afternoon highs.

"Looks like it's gonna be a cold night," said Mindy, as she blew her breath into the air. "I can already see my breath."

"Here," said Brian. "Take my jacket. I don't need it."

"Are you sure?"

"Yep, the cold air actually feels good. It was getting kinda warm and stuffy in there in the third period. That's what happens when a sellout crowd gets all hot and bothered over playoff hockey."

"Over there," pointed Mindy. "Isn't that your car?"

"Yep, that's it. Good eye. I knew it was around here somewhere."

Brian pulled the car keys out of his pocket and unlocked Mindy's door, then he rounded the back of the car on his way to the driver's seat. That gave him a good five seconds to contemplate the rest of the evening and his growing anticipation.

Would there be more? Did she have any feelings for him?

Being alone with Mindy on a cold evening conjured up images of her cuddling with him to stay warm. But Brian's overactive imagination and reality were two different things.

Brian turned the key and fired up the engine. "Now, let's see how long it takes to get out of this parking lot."

"No hurry, as long as we have some heat," she said, reaching over and fiddling with the controls.

"If you get the heater going, I'll try to find the fastest route out of here," suggested Brian, using a ploy to coax her toward the middle of the seat.

Mindy scooched over a little bit and adjusted the heater. Then she looked at her watch. "It's ten thirty. The game lasted longer than I thought."

"That's because of the brawl and all the penalties. Was your mom expecting you home at a certain time?"

"Not really. Whenever the game ended, I guess. I'm sure she knows exactly what time it ended," she laughed.

"Okay, it looks like we're about ten car lengths away from getting out of this parking lot."

"Do you want me to turn on the radio?" asked Mindy, sliding a little closer.

"That would be good," said Brian. She was gradually getting closer, inch by inch, and he could feel his heart beat faster.

"What do you wanna listen to?"

"If you turn it to WOWO, Bob Chase should be doing the Komet game summary. Then you can change it to music."

Mindy slid a little closer and started turning the dial. "It's 1190 AM, right? Do you have it programmed in? Or do I need to find it on the dial?"

"Try the third button from the right."

"Yep, that's it," said Mindy.

Bob Chase was wrapping up, spewing an endless array of statistics: power play goals, even-handed goals, assists, saves, penalty minutes, etc.

Cruising along on Coliseum Boulevard, Brian realized that Mindy's house was only twenty minutes away. His window of opportunity was narrowing.

"Time for some music?" suggested Mindy.

"You're in charge," said Brian, granting her leeway to pursue whatever she wanted.

Mindy was now in the middle of the seat playing with the radio dial. Although she wasn't exactly snuggling, she was no longer on the passenger side either; Olds 88s had big front seats. Brian knew she didn't need to be directly in front of the radio to turn the knobs, but that's where she ended up. Choosing to recognize her maneuver for what it was, Brian figured it was an obvious attempt to be closer.

"How 'bout this?" said Mindy, settling on an FM station. "Do you like the Four Tops?

"Sure."

"This was top five on Casey Kasem's countdown last week. *Ain't no Woman Like the One I Got.* I expect you to memorize these words," she giggled.

As they approached the Harper residence, Brian was getting nervous over how the date would end.

"You can pull into the driveway," Mindy instructed.

"Do you think your mother is waiting up?"

"Ha! What do you think?"

Brian noticed the front porch light shining bright and a shadowy figure behind the living room curtains. Much to his disappointment, Mindy slid over to the passenger door.

"You don't have to walk me up," she suggested.

"Of course I do. Don't you think I'm a gentleman?"

Brian clumsily walked with her to the front door wondering if he should kiss her, especially with her mother waiting inside. He had never kissed anyone before, but he wanted Mindy to know that he cared about her.

Reaching for the doorknob, Mindy turned to Brian. "Thanks for a fun evening. We'll have to do it again sometime."

Recognizing his cue, Brian leaned into Mindy until their lips touched, then pulled away quickly.

"Good night," she said. "I'll see you at school."

Walking back to his car, Brian had a sinking feeling in his stomach. There was no getting around it. He had just delivered the most horrible kiss in the history of dating.

Hoping to avoid an embarrassingly sloppy kiss with their faces pressed together, Brian had overcompensated. His attempt at a quick and casual smooch turned out to be nothing more than an awkward touching of lips, not really a kiss at all.

"What a rookie move," he said to himself. "She must think I'm the worst kisser in the world."

The Fort Wayne Komets went on to defeat the Flint Generals and advance to the finals of the International Hockey League. Led by their popular coach, Marc Boileau, they defeated the Port Huron Wings and captured the 1973 Turner Cup, the franchise's third league championship. Every player on the roster, except for one, grew up in Canada.

Chapter 41

THE SCENT OF MOIST, FRESHLY cut grass filled the air on a warm and humid Saturday afternoon. It was Memorial Day weekend, the unofficial beginning of summer, and the O'Connor groundskeepers were fully deployed, meticulously grooming the estate for a long holiday weekend. Originally scheduled for Friday, their work had been cut short by a series of thundershowers. Now they were playing catch-up, laboring in the damp conditions to meet their employer's stringent standards.

Unlike a normal Saturday, the peace and tranquility of the O'Connor estate was amiss with the rumbling sounds of internal combustion engines. Buzzing back and forth across the lawn, two tractor-sized lawnmowers were forming a crisscross pattern that resembled the outfield of a baseball diamond. Along the house, three workers were busy grooming the holly, boxwood, and juniper shrubs with their gas-powered hedge trimmers, taking care not to trample the flower beds, for nothing fueled the ire of Roselyn O'Connor more than a careless intrusion on her prized possessions.

Every spring, Roselyn directed her crew of landscapers through the gardens as they wheeled in large trays of her favorite annuals: geraniums, begonias, primroses, snapdragons, and impatiens, strategically placing them according to their needs for sun. Once the annuals were planted, the gardeners' attention turned to the perennials, fortifying the hydrangea soil with organic compost, and enriching the azalea beds with natural acidifiers like tea, vinegar, and coffee grounds.

By Memorial Day, the O'Connor estate was in full bloom and Roselyn loved to show her guests around the grounds. Usually a festive affair, Memorial Day parties were catered events that accommodated up to one hundred of their friends and business associates. But this year would be different.

Christine had just completed her junior year at St. Mary's and was bringing her new boyfriend home to meet the family. They didn't know much about him except that she met him in Chicago three months ago during a weekend outing with her girlfriends. Since many of Christine's classmates were from the Chicago area, it was not unusual for them to spend their weekends in the Windy City, shopping along the magnificent mile during the day, and partying in the popular nightclubs at night.

Christine told her mother that she met Michael Williams in March, at the Hangge-Uppe, a popular bar in the trendy part of town. Since then, she and her friends had been making the two-hour drive to Chicago on a regular basis, staying out late and sampling the temptations of the big city.

As the trips became more frequent, Roselyn grew suspicious of how much time Christine was actually spending with her friends versus her new boyfriend. She'd always been vague on the specifics. Whenever her mother asked about where she stayed, Christine would respond with equivocal references to friends and their families that lived in the Chicago area, never divulging any names or locations.

But Roselyn was not concerned, nor was she naive. Isolating her daughter at an all-girl Catholic college had its limitations, and those boundaries were being tested. She recognized her daughter for what she was, a young woman who had recently turned twenty-one and was ready to spread her wings and explore what the world had to offer.

The only time Christine provided any specifics was earlier in the month when she called her mother to talk about the fabulous party she had attended on top of the Sears Tower. Apparently, her roommate's father was some sort of bigshot and secured tickets for them to attend a private reception. As a result, Christine had become one of the privileged few to view the Chicago skyline from the newly completed building, the tallest in the world. She couldn't contain her excitement as she rambled on to her mother about the Sears Tower.

"It was incredible, Mother! The views from up there are simply spectacular, especially at night with all the glittering lights. They say it's so high in the sky that you can see four different states. Who would've thought that I'd be one of the first to party with the see-and-be-seen crowd on top of the tallest building in the world!"

"Are you sure it's the tallest?" asked Roselyn. "I thought when New York opened the World Trade Center last month, they claimed their twin towers were the tallest in the world."

"And they were right," answered Christine. "That's what makes it so cool. Chicago and New York are always competing against each other for bragging rights. That's why Chicago made sure the Sears Tower was built a hundred feet taller. I guess it's all about the prestige of being the biggest and the best."

Amused by her daughter's obsession with the glitz and glamour of big city life, Roselyn began to realize the distinct possibility of her daughter graduating and taking a job in Chicago, a city where there would be more opportunities for her to branch out and realize her potential. If that were the case, her companionship would surely be missed, but that wouldn't prohibit her mother from weekend visits and shopping expeditions, ample opportunities to escape her husband's relentless subjugation.

As Roselyn continued her inquisitions, the mother-daughter conversations became more boyfriend-centric. When asked if the relationship was getting serious, Christine confessed that Michael was not like anyone she'd ever known before. He was tall, dark, and handsome, and had a special charisma that fueled her instant attraction. She told her mother there was an undeniable chemistry between the two of them, a bond she had never felt before with anyone else.

Roselyn took this to mean they were having sex. She told Christine they were anxious to meet him and to be careful. Christine took this to mean that she should practice birth control.

All Ryan really knew was that Michael Williams had earned a scholarship to attend DePaul University, a prominent Catholic college in Chicago. That was good enough to check the initial boxes, but he needed to find out much more.

"Honey, could you check on that pie for me?" asked Roselyn, her hands covered in flour and dough.

"Sure thing, Mrs. O'Connor," said Lynda Lacey. "How can I tell for sure that it's done?"

"The meringue should be turning brown, just barely at the tips."

Lynda grabbed a pair of hot pads and pulled out the pie. "How does that look?"

"Perfect! Just sit it on the counter to cool and we'll stick it in the fridge after an hour."

"That's a beautiful pie," said Lynda. "Lemon meringue is one of my favorites."

Quinn and Lynda were assisting in the kitchen while they anxiously awaited the arrival of Christine and her new boyfriend. The holiday gathering would be a casual affair, just the immediate family hosting a poolside barbeque. Christine would make the drive from South Bend by herself, preparing to move home for the summer, while Michael would make his way from Chicago, spending the weekend with the O'Connors before heading back on Monday.

"What time are they arriving?" asked Quinn.

"Christine said she would be home around five. Michael is supposed to arrive around six. At least that's the plan. If Christine is late and Michael is early, we might have an awkward introduction without Christine around."

"More so for him than us," agreed Quinn. "He might find us a little intimidating, especially if Dad was around."

"I'm sure Christine has everything under control," said Roselyn. "This is her big day."

"I guess Dad is gonna miss out," noted Quinn. "I know he's in Japan, but I thought he was supposed to be home for the weekend."

"Yes, I thought so too. But you know how erratic his schedule can be."

"What's he doing in Japan?" asked Lynda.

"Schmoozing the mayor again," said Roselyn. "He's heading up a Fort Wayne delegation that's meeting with government officials in Takaoka. It's basically a fact-finding mission. If the meeting goes well, the two cities will work together to establish some kind of a sister city arrangement. It's all part of an effort to open up communication and engage with different cultures, especially those with bustling economies. They're thinking a sister city relationship could stimulate new business opportunities for global commerce."

"That sounds very interesting," said Lynda. "I've always wanted to visit Japan. They're a real economic force these days."

"Well, my husband can tell you more about it. In the past, he's talked about hosting Japanese exchange students, but I think his real intent is to make some business connections."

"That's the real reason he's missing Memorial Day," said Quinn. "He can't pass up another business opportunity."

"I'm sure there's some truth to that," confirmed Roselyn. "He said he's working on a contact who will introduce him to a top Toyota executive. He's spending a couple extra days in Tokyo to secure that connection."

"That would be a big score," admitted Quinn. "I know he wants to open up a Toyota dealership in Fort Wayne. For years, he's been telling me that Toyota will be the next big player in the US auto industry."

"I'm sure your father knows what he's doing."

"It must be an awfully important meeting for him to miss the Indianapolis 500," said Quinn, directing his comment to Lynda. "He goes down there almost every year to watch the race from a private suite, hobnobbing with all the auto industry executives from Detroit."

"Who knows," said Lynda. "Someday he may be entertaining Japanese executives at the Indy 500. Anything is possible."

As Quinn's mother left the kitchen, he leaned over to whisper in Lynda's ear. "I hope he's truthfully meeting with Toyota executives, like he said, and not fraternizing with geisha girls."

Lynda looked inquisitively at Quinn and his ornery grin. "Stop it, that's not funny."

Looking out the window, they watched as Roselyn prepared the patio table for dinner, positioning the umbrella to shield the western sun. Then she rolled out two separate carts, one of them loaded with dinnerware: plates, glasses, silverware, and napkins. The second, a bar cart, featured two large glass pitchers, one with ice water, and the other with lemonade. Next to the ice bucket, she showcased a bottle of Beefeater Gin and a fifth of Absolut Vodka, one of her favorites.

Quinn reached into the refrigerator and pulled out the shrimp and steaks. "I'm in charge of grilling the shrimp on the barbie," he said, poorly imitating a rancher from the Australian Outback.

"You need to work on your accent," teased Lynda. "If it improves, I'll reward you with my Olivia Newton John impression."

Quinn opened the spice cabinet, searching for the right ingredients. "This goes on the shrimp," he said as he sprinkled Old Bay seasoning over a large bowl of giant prawns. Then he positioned eight filet mignons on a tray and rubbed them down with Lawry's seasoning salt.

"Hello!" came a shout from the foyer. "I'm home, is anyone here?"

"Is that your sister?" asked Lynda.

"It sounds like her. Let's go see."

Quinn and Lynda exited the kitchen and weaved through the dining room as they made their way to the foyer. Rounding the corner, they suddenly halted as they caught their first glimpse.

As expected, Christine had arrived on schedule, but she was accompanied by a guest the O'Connors were not expecting.

Quinn stood frozen as Lynda continued to approach them cordially. "You must be Christine. Am I right?"

Christine stepped forward and extended her hand. "You are correct. And you must be Lynda. Pleased to meet you."

Christine took Lynda's hand and pulled her in for a hug, similar to the way Roselyn had greeted Lynda the first time.

"I've heard all about you," Christine continued. "I'm so glad we have this weekend to get acquainted."

"The pleasure is all mine," said Lynda, as Quinn remained frozen.

"Lynda, I'd like you to meet my boyfriend, Michael Williams."

And there it was. Quinn's initial fear had been confirmed. Christine was introducing the guy standing next to her as her new boyfriend, a tall Black man sporting an Afro-style haircut. Was this really happening? Certainly, his mother didn't know about this or she would have said something. Thank God his father was out of town, otherwise the O'Connors would be witnessing fireworks like they'd never seen before.

"Are you just gonna stand there, little brother? Where's your manners?"

Quinn walked over nervously and extended his hand, "Pleased to meet you, Michael."

"I hear you're quite the tennis player," offered Michael, trying to ease the tension. "I play a little bit too, but I'm sure you're in a different league than me. Maybe you can teach me to play like Arthur Ashe." Then he laughed out loud, letting everyone know that he'd just made a racial joke.

"Michael plays basketball," said Christine. "He's on scholarship at DePaul, one of the top basketball programs in the country."

"Until I tore my Achilles tendon last year," confessed Michael. "I'm still rehabbing it, but there's a chance I may never play again. Time will tell. At least I still have my scholarship."

Quinn remained standoffish, still dumbfounded by what he was witnessing. Christine had never seen him behave this way before, lacking in basic social etiquette.

"What's with you?" asked Christine, confronting Quinn's awkwardness. "It looks like the cat's got your tongue."

Quinn responded by stammering over something unintelligible, adding to Christine's frustration.

"Never mind," she renounced. "Where's Mother? I know Dad's gone, but Mom's around here somewhere, isn't she?"

"She's on the back patio, setting up the table," offered Lynda, embarrassed by Quinn's incompetence.

"C'mon Michael, let's go meet my mother," commanded Christine, as she took her boyfriend's hand and led him to the kitchen.

"You go ahead," said Quinn. "I'll be in the kitchen getting the steaks ready for the grill."

As Christine and Michael disappeared around the corner, Lynda glared at Quinn.

"What's wrong with you? This may not be what you expected, but I think you should do a better job disguising your disappointment."

Quinn produced a big sigh and looked up to the heavens, as if seeking divine intervention. Then he shook his head in disbelief.

"I don't think disappointment is the right word. It's more like shock. I'm just glad my father isn't here. He would have a conniption for sure."

"Well, you just need to relax and make the best of it. I'm sure everything will work out in the long run."

Quinn took another deep breath and started laughing.

"What are you laughing about?" scolded Lynda.

"Christine told us her boyfriend was tall, dark, and handsome, she just didn't tell us *how* dark."

"Stop it. That's not funny."

"Hurry," said Quinn. "Let's go to the kitchen. I wanna look out the window and see my mom's reaction when she meets Christine's new boyfriend."

"I think you should be more discreet," lectured Lynda.

"Guess who's coming to dinner?" mocked Quinn. "I wouldn't miss this for the world."

Lynda backed away from the window, embarrassed by Quinn's obsession.

"What if they see you staring out the window? That will only add to an already uncomfortable situation."

"Oh, I don't think anyone will notice me standing at the window. I'm sure all the attention will be focused on the new boyfriend."

Lynda moved closer and took Quinn's hand, as if a little comfort might detract from the spectacle he was about to witness. If only she could soften the blow for Roselyn. She couldn't help but feel sorry for her, toiling away, unloading the dinnerware with her back toward the kitchen, oblivious to the fact that her daughter was about to rock her world.

"Surprise!" announced Christine. "We made it."

Caught off guard, Roselyn wheeled around and dropped one of the stoneware dishes, smashing it to pieces all over the patio.

"What are you doing? You startled me!"

"I'm sorry. I didn't mean to scare you," said Christine, feeling terrible about her intrusion.

Michael stood by speechless with embarrassment, while Quinn was beside himself, laughing away as Lynda pulled him from the window. "That was priceless!" he declared.

"I think you're overreacting," said Lynda. "Your mom dropped the dish because your sister startled her, not because her boyfriend is Black. Now get me a broom and a trash bag so I can go out there and help your mother."

Quinn continued to watch from the window as Lynda made her way to the broken dish. He couldn't hear what anyone was saying, but he eventually saw his mother shake Michael's hand. It was not the warm handshake followed by a hug that was her signature trademark. Instead, it was a forced, uncomfortable exchange that validated the tension. Quinn could tell his mother was rattled, caught off guard by her daughter's revelation.

"No worries," said Lynda, "I have a broom. I'll have it all swept up in no time."

Looking for a bit of relief, Roselyn made her way to the bar cart and poured a glass of vodka. Grabbing a lime wedge and squeezing it over the cocktail, her hands were visibly shaking.

"Christine, go ahead and pour your friend a drink. I don't want him to think we're *totally* dysfunctional."

Roselyn made her way to the kitchen, gulping her cocktail while Christine tended to Michael. Quinn saw his mother coming and hurried back to the steaks, acting as though he'd been there the whole time.

"Can you believe this?" she announced as she stormed into the kitchen. "What on earth was she thinking?"

"So you were surprised too?" asked Quinn.

"Of course! She told me nothing. I'm just thankful your father isn't here. Can you imagine how he'd react?"

"I was thinking the same thing."

"Okay, I want you to take the steaks outside and fire up the grill. Tell your sister that I need her assistance in the kitchen. You and Lynda need to keep her *friend* entertained while I have a word with Christine," emphasizing the word *friend* in a sarcastic, disrespectful tone.

Quinn couldn't remember the last time he'd witnessed his mother so frazzled. He'd seen her feathers ruffled before, mostly when arguing with his father, but never while entertaining guests. Her sense of composure and unflappable grace under pressure were things you could always count on. But now it was obvious she was feeling betrayed by her daughter. Not so much by her choice of boyfriend, but by the way she surprised her, failing to prepare her for this unlikely imposition.

Quinn picked up the steaks and headed out the door, obediently following his mother's instructions.

"All right, you guys, I'm gonna start grillin' the steaks. Christine, Mom needs your help in the kitchen."

"Seriously?"

"I'm just the messenger," replied Quinn. "Michael, I may need your assistance. Grilling meat is a man's job, right? Have you ever had shrimp on the barbie?"

Quinn's sudden change in demeanor was painfully obvious, a shameless attempt to segregate Christine from her boyfriend. Now that he and his mother had addressed the elephant in the room, Quinn was back in his element.

Christine walked into the kitchen to find her mother pouring another glass of vodka.

"Mom, you better slow down on the booze. I didn't mean to upset you."

"Well, you did. Why didn't you tell me your boyfriend is Black?"

"Wow! Let's get right to the point. I guess you're not holding anything back."

"Unlike you!"

"Now, wait a minute. Why should it matter if you found out ahead of time or when you met him? Are you saying you would not have welcomed him here if you knew in advance?"

"No, that's not what I'm saying."

"Then what are you saying, Mom?"

"I'm saying you should have shown me some consideration and prepared me. What if your father was here? Can you imagine what a scene that would've been?"

"But he wasn't, was he. So why should that matter?"

"Are you telling me that I don't deserve the same amount of consideration as your father?"

"No, that's not what I'm saying. I just thought you were a little more open-minded than him. Apparently, I'm wrong? Perhaps you're just two peas in a pod."

"I don't think that's a fair statement. I just feel like you've been deceiving me."

"Mom, there's been no deception. I just didn't know when the right time would be. If I had told you ahead of time, you may have developed some preconceived notions. That wouldn't be fair either. So why not find out when you meet him and judge him on who he is rather than prejudging him on who you think he is."

Roselyn O'Connor looked at her daughter and took a deep breath. Suddenly she was making a lot of sense.

"I just need to calm down. What can I say—it was such a surprise."

"Mom, I'm growing up in a different world than you. Things that seem so unconventional to your upbringing are not such a big deal to me. I know I'm pretty isolated in my all-White, all-girl college, but when I'm in Chicago, it's like there's a whole different world out there. When I met Michael, we were just two mature adults having a pleasant conversation. And then, the more we talked, the more we realized how much we enjoyed each other's company. Isn't that the way relationships should begin?"

"Yes, they should. You are correct. But that doesn't mean you should ignore the consequences."

"Mom, there haven't been any consequences until now. You're the first consequence. But a mother and daughter should be willing and able to reach an understanding, don't you think? Let's face it, up until now, you've been my dearest, most trusted friend."

"Up until now?"

"Mom, I'm not gonna lie to you. I feel that Michael and I are in a serious relationship. That doesn't mean we're getting married tomorrow. It just means that we owe it to ourselves to see where this is going."

Roselyn O'Connor grabbed a tissue and wiped the tear that was running down her cheek. Her daughter was making so much sense. Now she felt foolish and embarrassed by her own childish behavior.

There, standing before her, was a beautiful, intelligent woman, taking control of a delicate situation and using her maturity to reach a solution, forging a path toward progress. Perhaps the apple hadn't fallen so far from the tree after all.

Chapter 42

Scott Clever steered his father's car into the parking lot of Penguin Point, three blocks from his destination, the Central YMCA in downtown Fort Wayne. Not only was Penguin Point one of Scott's favorite burger joints, but it provided easy parking in an otherwise congested part of town. The last thing he wanted to do was spend his time meandering around busy downtown streets, looking for a curbside vacancy that would challenge his parallel parking skills. His dad had graciously loaned out his Oldsmobile Cutlass coupe, and he wasn't about to risk that privilege with a potential fender bender.

After wolfing down his Big Wally, Penguin Point's version of a double-deck hamburger with cheese and special sauce, Scott grabbed the remaining crinkle fries and his Converse All-Stars and headed toward the gym. Wearing basketball shoes outside was a no-no. He always carried them into the gym with shoestrings tied together and strapped over his shoulder. By keeping them free from dirt and grime, he ensured that his shoes would deliver the desired adhesion. Even then, if his quick stops and starts on the lacquered hardwood did not squeak as loud as intended, he'd wipe his feet on a courtside wet towel until his competitive edge was restored.

The summer of '73 would be critical to Scott's basketball progression. He was heading into his junior year and figured to be a strong candidate for varsity. But it wouldn't be easy—the Northrop Bruins were loaded. The roster had five returning seniors on a team that advanced all the way to the Sweet Sixteen of the Indiana state basketball tournament. There would be no easy path and Scott knew it, which only contributed to his determination and commitment. Standing at a solid six feet four inches, he was no longer the lanky kid with growth potential. Not only had he grown five inches in the past three years, but he had added forty pounds of brawn, the result of a three-day-per-week regimen in the weight room. He wanted to be a force in the paint, and his stature fit the bill.

The Indiana High School Athletic Association was very strict about practicing in the offseason. Coaches were not allowed to be involved in any organized practices, period. Authorized activities were restricted to physical fitness, which meant basketball players were encouraged to sign-up for the obligatory summer phys ed (PE) class. By attending summer PE every morning, Monday through Friday, players were subjected to strenuous running and conditioning drills designed to get them in basketball shape without ever touching a basketball. This meant that players were left to sharpen critical skills, like shooting, dribbling, and rebounding, on their own accord.

Fortunately for Scott, Mr. Clever knew his way around Indiana basketball and realized the importance of offseason competition. With a little research, he determined that much of the local basketball talent was congregating at the Central YMCA on Washington Boulevard. In order to participate, Scott would need a Y membership and reliable transportation. Mr. Clever willingly delivered on both requirements.

Sitting courtside, Scott laced up his shoes and sized up the competition. The first pickup game had already begun, and he recognized the familiar faces, some of which he knew on a first name basis. The ages usually ranged from fifteen to twenty-three, anywhere from aspiring high school players, up to and including college-level talent. In addition to two of his Bruin teammates, Scott would compete against Snider Panthers, North Side Redskins, South Side Archers, Concordia Cadets, and Wayne Generals. If Scott was to establish that he really belonged in the Summit Athletic Conference, the Central YMCA would be his proving ground, and the summer of '73 would play an integral role in determining his fate.

⚜

The Plymouth Barracuda creeped quietly through the darkness of a late summer evening in July. Steve Marino was navigating Bob Wills through an old, dilapidated warehouse district on the southeast side of town. "Turn your headlights off," ordered Steve. "Just use your low beams. We don't want to attract any attention."

"I don't like this," said Bob. "Is it even safe back here? It feels kinda creepy."

"Relax," chuckled Steve. "You can't spend your whole life hiding in the safety of Coldwater Creek."

With the car approaching a nearby alley, Steve directed Bob to stop. He then rolled down his window and pointed his flashlight into the darkness. "Yep, I'm pretty sure this is it. Let's turn down this alley."

Bob creeped slowly along the narrow path with Steve pointing his flashlight out the window.

"Stop here," said Steve, "I think this is it."

Bob stopped the car in front of a storage unit with a corrugated, aluminum barrier, similar to an overhead garage door.

"Yep, this is it—number forty-three. Now, shut down your engine and turn off the lights. This flashlight should be enough to see what we're after."

Steve stepped out of the car and reached into his pocket to retrieve a set of keys. "I sure hope these are the right ones. Otherwise, we're screwed."

Bob stood by passively, wondering how he got himself into this predicament.

"Here, you hold the flashlight," ordered Steve. "I got three keys on this chain. One of them is supposed to work. I'm just not sure which one."

Fiddling with the keys like a rookie night watchman, Steve's frustration continued to build as he failed to coerce the lock. "Shit! We're down to our last key."

Bob's eyes glazed over, subconsciously hoping for failure so they could leave and go home.

"Bingo," announced Steve, as he successfully turned the handle and raised the overhead door. "Now we gotta find the right boxes."

Bob shined his light beam into the storage unit, still skeptical over why he was there and who they were dealing with.

"Can you explain to me again how you know about these boxes and who put them there?"

"Connections, man. Ya gotta have connections."

"That's pretty vague," reasoned Bob. "Can you be more specific?"

"When your father is a bigshot with the Teamsters, you have all kinds of connections. Who do you think controls all the trucking and shipping in this country?"

Bob didn't answer the question. He wasn't familiar with the so-called underworld, but he knew it existed and he was beginning to realize how well the Marinos were connected.

"We're looking for two boxes," declared Steve. "One large box and one medium. They're supposed to be next to each other toward the back, each marked with yellow tape."

Steve pushed his way through the stacks of crates and packages while Bob continued with his flashlight duties. "Aha," proclaimed Steve, as he located the boxes with yellow tape. "It's pretty cool when everything falls into place the way it's supposed to."

Steve pulled a box-cutter out of his jeans pocket and slit around the edges of the smaller, lighter box. Then he opened the flaps, exposing an abundance of white Styrofoam packaging shells. Without hesitation, he brushed them aside, scattering them in all directions and exposing a brown garbage bag sealed with a twist tie.

Steve looked up at Bob with a big grin on his face as he flicked away the remaining shells that clung to his arms with static electricity.

Bob inched closer, trying to get a better look with his flashlight as Steve worked the twist tie.

"We just struck gold," declared Steve. "Acapulco Gold."

Sticking his head into the box, Steve took a deep breath and inhaled the rich aroma.

"Ah, the sweet smell of success."

"How much is in there?" asked Bob.

"It's supposed to be a kilo."

"How much is a kilo?"

"C'mon man," teased Steve. "You gotta catch up on the lingo. A kilo is about two point two pounds. In the metric system, a kilo is the same as a thousand grams."

Steve then pulled out a paper bag and dumped hundreds of little plastic baggies onto the storage room floor. "Our job is to break down this shipment of weed into these little baggies. They're called dime bags."

"We're gonna sell them for a dime?" asked Bob.

"You really are naive." Steve laughed. "A dime bag sells for ten dollars. Each of these baggies holds about one gram of pot. Enough for two joints, or one large doobie if you roll it like Cheech and Chong."

Even Bob had to laugh at that remark. "So how many dime bags are we gonna stuff?"

"Seriously? I realize you're no math wizard, but try to keep up. How many grams did I say were in a kilo?"

Bob thought about it for a second, then responded. "You mean we gotta stuff one thousand baggies?"

"Yep, and we can sell them at ten dollars apiece. So how much is that?" asked Steve, treating Bob like a fifth grader.

"You mean we have ten thousand dollars of pot in that box?" asked Bob, suddenly realizing the significance.

"That's the street value," confirmed Steve. "The markup is outrageous. That's why it's so profitable. It's the law of supply and demand. People want what they can't have; that's just human nature, the demand side of the equation. The other side of the equation is supply. When a product is illegal, it usually means there's a shortage in supply. High demand and short supply translate to high prices. People gotta pay the price if they want it. They can't go into stores and shop around for the best price. That's why the drug trade is so profitable."

"You mean if we sell all of this, we can make ten thousand dollars?"

"No, that's the street value. We can't keep it all for ourselves. We're allowed to keep thirty percent. The remaining seventy percent goes back to our source."

"So we can make three thousand dollars, right?"

"You're catchin' on, buddy boy."

"Okay," said Bob. "I get that it makes sense from a business point of view. But what about risk? It sure ain't worth the risk if I end up in jail."

"Relax," said Steve. "That's where we gotta be smart. The narcs aren't after the little guys. They don't care about a gram here and a gram there. They're after the big suppliers. Plus, we're considered minors, under eighteen years old. They're not lookin' to bust a kid with a gram of pot.

We just need to keep our stash locked away in this unit and be careful to carry around small amounts. If we're both smart and cautious, we stand to make some good coin. Does that make sense?"

"Yes, it makes a lot of sense. It sounds more profitable than selling *Playboys* and cigarettes."

"You got that right," agreed Steve. "But we're not giving that up, we're just diversifying our business. And when the football season starts up again, we'll be back in the parlay business. It all adds up."

"Damn." Bob laughed. "I'm starting to feel like a real businessman."

"It's the American way, Bobby boy. It's called free enterprise."

"What about accessories?" asked Bob. "You know, the things that pot smokers need. Like rolling papers, roach clips, pipes, and bongs. It seems like we should be selling those things too."

"Nah, those are available everywhere. There's plenty of supply. Have you ever been to Slatewood Records?"

"Of course," replied Bob. "That's where I buy all my albums."

"Well, you've seen what else they sell there, haven't you?"

"Yeah, I guess you're right. Rolling papers and all kinds of fancy pipes and bongs."

"It's like a head shop that sells records," joked Steve.

"I guess people who play rock 'n' roll like to get high while they're listening to music."

"Our laws are crazy," lectured Steve. "Marijuana is illegal, but it's not illegal to sell all the stuff that helps you smoke it. It's like we're all pretending it won't happen if we keep it illegal. Meanwhile, the profiteering continues."

"So what's in the other box?" asked Bob.

"Good question. I think I know, but let's open it and see."

"It's a lot bigger than the other box," noted Bob.

"And much heavier," said Steve, as he slit the seams with his box-cutter and pulled away a layer of bubble wrap to reveal its contents.

"Yep, cassette tapes. This may not be a big seller yet, but it's the wave of the future."

"How so?" asked Bob.

"Eight-track tapes are being phased out as we speak. They're just too big and bulky. Auto manufacturers will soon be offering cassette players in all their new vehicles. It only makes sense."

"Guess I'll need to get a new car," admitted Bob.

"And don't forget about the big vinyl records," reminded Steve. "Why would I want to go on playing music with a shaky turntable and a scratchy stylus when I can just pop in a tape?"

"Yeah, I guess that makes sense," agreed Bob. "But why should we try to sell them if anyone can walk into a music store and buy them."

"You're missing the best part," said Steve. "Recording stolen music on a tape is a very simple process. It's like taking candy from a baby. They can literally copy and produce thousands of cassette tapes for pennies on the dollar. By doing that, you bypass all the copyright laws that generate royalties for record labels, recording studios, and artists. Almost all the music sold in Asia is pirated. They don't care about America's copyright laws. And how would we enforce those laws in China if we wanted to?"

"So it's illegal. That's what you're telling me, right?" questioned Bob.

Steve started laughing. "Yes, you've identified the common thread. But if you're John Doe, and you want to listen to the latest Elton John album, why should you pay six dollars for a tape that you can buy for a dollar? Assuming the quality is the same, why should you care if Columbia House, or MCA Records, or even Elton John is not getting his fair share? He's rich enough as it is, and he's not even American."

"And we're just providing a service that other people want, right?"

"I couldn't have said it better myself," agreed Steve. "You're really starting to catch on. Why shouldn't we allow the underprivileged to listen to music just like everyone else? We're doing them a favor and making some money at the same time."

"It's called free enterprise," said Bob with a smirk. "It's the American way."

"Okay," said Steve with a skeptical grin. "Are you being a smartass? Or have I created a monster?"

"Just call me Frankenstein." Bob laughed.

Chapter 43

"HONEY, WHEN I WAS BORN, my body was blessed by Mother Nature," boasted Aunt Esther.

"And as you got older, it was cursed by Father Time," quipped Fred Sanford.

Marquis Jackson slapped his thigh and let out a big belly laugh. It was Friday evening, and he and Antonio had just finished another one of Chantelle's delicious dinners, chicken-and-shrimp jambalaya with dirty rice. Relaxing on his recliner in front of the TV, Marquis was watching his favorite TV show, *Sanford and Son*. After two seasons, the television sitcom, starring Red Foxx, had climbed to number two in the Nielsen ratings, a close second to *All in the Family*.

"I don't know why you like this show so much," proclaimed Antonio. "All it does is perpetuate Black stereotypes."

"Like what?" challenged Antonio's father.

"Well, for one, it portrays them in squalid conditions and making a living as junk dealers. Is that the image you want for our people?"

"You're taking it too seriously," declared Marquis. "It's just comedy. At the end of a long week, I just want to relax and be entertained. Sometimes laughter is the best medicine."

"I guess there's nothing wrong with that, but I'd like to see a TV show someday that depicts a Black man as a lawyer, or maybe even a doctor. Our people need to be inspired by the possibilities."

"You mean like Marcus Welby?" offered Marquis.

"Exactly!"

"I suppose you're right. But for now, I just wanna laugh."

Before Antonio could respond, they were interrupted by the ring of the telephone in the kitchen. "Is your mother still in the kitchen?" asked Mr. Jackson. "I don't want to miss my show."

"Marquis, it's for you," shouted Mrs. Jackson.

"Can you take a message?" yelled Marquis, perturbed by the interruption.

"I think you better take this," said Chantelle. "It's Mr. Marino."

Marquis stood up and made his way to the kitchen. He did not want to miss his favorite show, but he realized that some things were more important than his personal amusement.

Chantelle handed over the phone and eased around the corner. As soon as she was out of sight, her ears perked up. She was not normally one to eavesdrop, but it was hard to turn a deaf ear to a topic that could have such a profound impact on her and her family's livelihood.

Higher wages and better benefits were all well and good, but she was acutely aware of the inherent risks associated with organizing a union and challenging the status quo. Not only could Marquis jeopardize his employment with O'Connor Cadillac, but he could also inadvertently risk Chantelle's reputation and good standing with the O'Connor law firm.

Listening carefully, Chantelle attempted to decipher the telephone conversation based upon Marquis's input and feedback, trying to interpret the context from one side of the dialogue.

"Hi, Mr. Marino. How are you?"

"Yes, I have a minute. What can I do for you?"

"Yes, I've been communicating with Ernie, and yes, he seems to be making some progress."

"Not so much. I'm mostly assisting him as he approaches some of our coworkers and solicits their interest. As I said before, I don't really see myself as someone taking a leadership role."

"I think the interest is starting to grow, but I don't think we have the same level of participation as the Buick dealerships."

"No, I didn't know that. That might be helpful."

"No, we've been avoiding Neil Bowers. I think he's in cahoots with management."

"Yes, if you think we're at a point to solicit formal commitments, I can help distribute the cards."

"Okay, I think that's a good idea. Have you scheduled a date?"

"Sounds good. I'm writing it down as we speak. I'll see you on Wednesday, September nineteenth."

"Thanks. You too. Talk to you later."

Marquis hung up the phone and tried to return to the television, but Chantelle intercepted him. "So what's the latest?" she asked. "Any updates?"

"Not a whole lot," conceded Marquis. "We're making some progress, but mostly baby steps."

"What's going on with the Buick dealerships?" asked Chantelle.

"Basically, the same thing as the Cadillac dealership. Only they seem to have more interest and greater participation."

"What were you referencing when you said, 'No, I didn't know that'?" continued Chantelle.

"Well, well. I guess you were listening closer than I thought."

"I just overheard you say that. Nothing more. It only raised my curiosity."

"Nice try. I guess there's nothing wrong with your hearing," needled Marquis. "I was saying I didn't know that a gentleman by the name of Daniel was representing the Buick dealerships and would be meeting with Ernie about Cadillac's involvement. Mr. Marino seems to think that our Cadillac brethren will take a stronger interest when they realize the level of participation at Buick is much higher. That's what they call strength in numbers. Widespread participation creates more solidarity."

"And what were you talking about when you said you'd help to distribute cards?"

"Wow! Too bad we don't have two phones. You could've joined our call on the other line."

"Very funny."

"The cards are something the union uses when they believe that interest levels are approaching one-half. If forty percent of the employees sign the cards signifying their interest in joining a union, the Teamsters will file a petition with the National Labor Relations Board. Once the petition is filed, we have a degree of protection from employer retaliation. It's called a 'just cause' clause, meaning we cannot be fired without a justifiable reason."

"Yes, I'm familiar with that legal jargon," said Chantelle. "Just be careful. I don't want anything to happen to you or our family. We got a pretty good thing going right now and we shouldn't do anything to jeopardize that."

"I hear you," said Marquis. "I'm doing my best to remain in the shadows, but this thing is bigger than me. I'm just one of many."

Marquis Jackson slipped into his clean, crisp O'Connor Cadillac uniform and poured another cup of coffee. He was ready to head for the garage and start his day when Neil Bowers intercepted him.

"Hold up a second," said Bowers. "I'd like to introduce you to someone."

Marquis looked up to see a young kid walking alongside Bowers. With pale white skin, red hair, and flushed cheeks, the baby-faced boy looked like he was barely out of high school.

"This is Billy Thompson," said Bowers. "Today is his first day."

Marquis extended his hand and grasped the limp-wristed palm of the youngster. "Pleased to meet you."

"Billy's gonna be helping us out around here," continued Bowers. "I don't have a uniform for him yet, but I want you to show him around and get him acquainted with everything."

"Okay, I can do that," said Marquis. "I'm scheduled to work on a customer's transmission this morning. Does Billy have any experience with transmissions?"

"Let me see if I can put someone else on that job," said Bowers. "Just show Billy around and I'll see if I can transfer some of the more basic jobs over to you this morning. You know, oil changes, tire rotations, et cetera. After a few days of learning the fundamentals, maybe Billy can start pitching in."

"Okay, you're the boss," said Marquis, trying to hide his disappointment. Wasting his skills on such trivial tasks seemed like a slap in the face, but it wasn't like he had a choice in the matter.

"Bring him back to my office at ten o'clock and I'll show him some administrative stuff," said Bowers. "Good luck."

Marquis took him into the break area and showed him the clock where they punched their timecards. "Do you have a timecard yet?"

"Not yet," said Billy. "Neil told me he'd have one for me by the end of the day."

"So tell me a little about yourself. Have you worked with cars before?"

"No, this is my first job," said Billy. "I graduated from Bishop Luers high school last spring."

"I didn't know Cadillac hired anyone without experience. You must have good connections."

"My father is a cop on the police force," said Billy. "Mr. O'Connor told my dad that he was looking to hire some mechanics."

"But you're not a mechanic."

"No, but I can learn."

Unable to hide his contempt, Marquis rolled his eyes. Why were they bringing in a boy to do a man's job? This was a Cadillac dealership, for God's sake, not the local grease monkey. He had more experience than this kid way back when he worked on beat-up jalopies in New Orleans.

When Marquis signed on with O'Connor Cadillac, he believed it was predicated on his formal education and vast amount of experience. In his mind, working on Cadillacs represented the pinnacle of his career, a reward for his strong work ethic and commitment to excellence. Now he was babysitting a wet-behind-the-ears kid with a sense of entitlement, not the image he had envisioned when putting on his Cadillac uniform for the first time.

Nevertheless, Marquis carried on, deciding it was better to roll with the punches and perform his duties as expected. Some battles were not worth fighting, and this was one of them. Not willing to rock the boat, Marquis continued his little tour, showing Billy around the shop and pointing out the work schedule, tool cabinets, supply area, and parts depot.

When it came time for the first oil change of the day, he showed Billy how to operate the hydraulic lift, release the oil valve, and drain the fluid. He then removed the oil filter and handed it to Billy.

"Go over to the supply area I showed you earlier and find the matching filter replacement."

Although this was a trivial task, Marquis wanted to find out if Billy had been paying attention. Seemingly disengaged, he had been in a fog most of the morning, following Marquis around with glazed-over eyes and failing to display any resemblance of commitment.

No surprise, Marquis figured. How could a kid living at home with his parents have the same sense of devotion as a self-sustaining adult with unwavering obligations?

After a ten-minute wait, Marquis made his way over to the supply area to find Billy staring aimlessly into the cabinet.

"Any luck?" asked Marquis, deciding to be polite.

"I'm really not sure what I'm looking for," admitted Billy.

Marquis took the used filter from Billy, wiped it with a rag and revealed the parts number: S1487XL. Then he pointed to a box on the shelf with the corresponding number. Nonchalantly removing the box, Marquis handed the new filter to Billy.

"See how easy that was? It's not rocket science. Don't worry, you'll catch on."

At ten o'clock, Marquis promptly delivered Billy Thompson to the shop supervisor's office as requested. Making his way to the break room, Marquis noticed that Ernie was looking on, displaying a look of skepticism to go along with his irreverent grin.

"So I see you've been assigned training duties this morning," remarked Ernie.

"More like babysitting," replied Marquis, unable to hide his annoyance.

"That's the second new hire this week," said Ernie. "The other one starts tomorrow."

"I didn't know that," said Marquis. "I wasn't aware we were falling behind schedule. Do we really need them?"

"What do you think?" asked Ernie. "I also heard a third hire may be starting sometime *next* week. Don't you see what they're doing?"

"No, what do you mean?"

"These are the preemptive strikes that Marino warned us about. They're diluting the labor pool."

"Meaning what?" asked Marquis.

"So they hire three young kids who are thankful to have jobs. But they hire them on the condition they vote no on joining a union.

Remember when I told you we have eight of our staff committed to signing the Teamster cards?

"Yes, I remember."

"Well, eight out of eighteen is getting very close to half. But when they hire three more, that puts us further away again. Eight out of twenty-one. Now do you see what they're doing?"

"I get it," said Marquis. "How are we gonna compete against that?"

"And you know Jeff Stevens, don't you?" asked Ernie.

"Yes, I know Jeff."

"Well, he was one of our eight commitments. This week they reduced his hours from forty to thirty. He now makes less money and gets his benefits taken away because he's no longer considered full-time. Meanwhile, he has a wife and two kids to feed. These are classic examples of preemptive strikes that dilute the workforce."

"Yeah, I get it," said Marquis, feeling defeated. "I guess you need to tell Marino and see if he has any advice. Looks like management is gonna play hardball."

"Thank you for coming this morning," announced Ryan O'Connor from his microphone on the Cadillac showroom floor. "If you recall, one year ago I committed to you that we would hold quarterly employee appreciation celebrations. Let it never be said that I am not a man of my word. Today represents our third celebration of 1973. And I'm happy to announce that we truly have something to celebrate this morning. With two weeks remaining in September, O'Connor Cadillac is on pace to break a record for third-quarter service department revenue. As such, we have decided to reward our full-time technicians with a bonus. If we do, in fact, break the record, you will receive a Q3 bonus equal to two percent of your third quarter wages."

Ryan paused to recognize some scattered applause, most fervently led by Neil Bowers.

"But that's not all," he continued. "Moving forward, we've decided to set performance objectives for each quarter throughout our fiscal year. If you continue to meet our revenue objectives, and meet or exceed customer satisfaction goals, we will continue to reward you with two percent bonuses each and every quarter. Like never before, we are making a commitment to excellence at O'Connor Cadillac and reward-ing you for your contribution. Yet another example of how teamwork can lead to success and prosperity for everyone."

With a more resounding response, Neil Bowers led the applause again, representing a collective mood that was on the upswing. Ernie looked at Marquis with a frown as he felt the momentum swing against him. Management was patronizing its labor force and using a rah-rah strategy to manipulate and inspire company unity.

Even Marquis, who respected Marino and believed in the concept of negotiated contracts, was beginning to feel persuaded. Maybe he should drop the whole union idea, at least temporarily, and give management an opportunity to demonstrate their commitment to labor. Perhaps it was time to reevaluate the whole risk-reward ratio.

As the employees disbursed and made their way to the buffet table, Ryan O'Connor began shaking hands and working the crowd. Marquis decided to make himself obscure, not feeling comfortable in the pres-ence of the man that employed both him and his wife. Wondering if Ryan had any inkling of his involvement with Marino and the union effort, Marquis felt a sense of guilt. He had tried to remain in the back-ground, but he was certain that Bowers was aware of his position, which meant that Ryan more than likely knew as well.

Ernie walked toward Marquis, "I hope you're not buying into this bullshit."

"Let's not talk about it now," said Marquis. "Not here in front of everyone."

"Fine," said Ernie. "I'm heading back to the shop. Why don't you join me?"

"You go ahead," said Marquis. "I'll be there in a few minutes."

He didn't want Bowers or Ryan to see him leaving with Ernie. That could seal his fate for sure.

As the food line diminished, Marquis made his way to the table and grabbed two donuts and a sausage roll, careful to avoid any interac-tion with Ryan. Munching away, Marquis kept track of Bowers's and Ryan's presence. Waiting for the right moment to slip away unnoticed, he found his opening and took his food back to the breakroom.

There, he found Ernie, waiting with bated breath.

"What's wrong?" asked Marquis. "You act like you're all pissed off."

"I'm pissed off because I know this whole two percent bonus thing is just a ploy. And I'm afraid you and our coworkers are starting to buy into it."

"Wait a minute," said Marquis. "Slow down. I'm not buying into anything. I'm just being cautious. Remember when we agreed to approach this thing cautiously?"

Ernie paused and took a deep breath. "I'm not pissed at you. I guess I'm just frustrated. I mean, I really don't trust these assholes."

"I'm not saying I trust them," assured Marquis. "But maybe we should give management a chance to prove themselves. What have we got to lose?"

"You're just not seeing it, are you?"

"Seeing what?" asked Marquis.

Ernie took another deep breath and attempted to regain his composure.

"Let's look at this thing objectively and break it down the way Marino would."

"Okay," said Marquis. "I'm listening."

"Remember when Mr. Marino showed us all the statistics? Specifically, the ones where union employees receive wages that average thirty percent more than their nonunion counterparts?"

"Yes, I remember."

"So don't you see that a two percent bonus is a joke? Of course, they'd rather pay us another two percent. If that stops us from organizing, they just saved twenty-eight percent."

"I guess that's one way of looking at it," agreed Marquis.

"And how do you know they'll really pay it?" continued Ernie. "You heard them say that only full-time employees were eligible. I guess that leaves out Jeff Stevens. They reduced Jeff's hours to thirty last week. And now they're bringing in more young kids. I'm guessing they'll bring them on board as part-timers and continue to reduce our hours. What if Bowers came up to you tomorrow and told you your hours were reduced to thirty? You would certainly kiss away all your benefits and any chances at a bonus. Am I right? How would you like that?"

"It looks like Mr. Marino has taught you well," noted Marquis.

"And even if you are a full-time employee," continued Ernie, "there's no guarantee that you'll earn a two percent bonus. Who do you think will be setting the objectives? I'll answer that for you: management. And how do we know those objectives will be achievable? And who do you think will be making the calculations? I'll answer that for you too: management."

"You make a lot of sense," agreed Marquis.

"You know what they're doing? They're just tossing us a bone. A bone that throws us off the trail. We need to be like hound dogs, keeping our noses on the real prize."

"Sounds like you're the lead dog. What do you propose we do?"

"I'm calling Marino tonight," said Ernie.

Chapter 44

LYNDA LACEY PLACED THE LAST dish into the dishwasher. Her mother had already retired to the family room to relax and enjoy a little television. For Lynda, relaxation was the furthest thing from her mind. Her evening was mapped out and it did not include any leisure. First, she would finish her trigonometry, then she would start on her English paper due at the end of the week. The rest of the evening would be devoted to chemistry. It was her least favorite subject, but she had a test the next day and she needed to maintain an A.

Memorizing elements, compounds, and formulas was not her forte. She was more interested in things that she could relate to in the real world. The thought of chemists isolated in labs with microscopes, test tubes, and Bunsen burners, was not an image that got her juices flowing. She preferred to be in the limelight, interacting with people and making things happen. Companies like Proctor & Gamble needed people in white lab coats to create their products, but they also needed people to market them. A good product was only as valuable as its brand and image. That's where the glamour was, and Lynda wanted to be front and center.

Before she could exit the kitchen, the telephone rang.

Mrs. Lacey called out, "Lynda, can you get that?"

"Got it, Mom."

Lynda picked up the phone to find Quinn O'Connor on the other end. It was not like him to call during the week. In fact, he rarely called at all, unless he was firming up details for a scheduled outing or event.

Quinn was not one for small talk or chit-chat. He preferred to stay on point and take care of business, preferably in person.

"Do you have a minute to talk?" he asked.

Lynda felt her stomach sink. Quinn sounded serious, like something was bothering him. Did he want to break up?

"Of course I have a minute. What's up?"

"Tonight was not a good night," declared Quinn.

"What's wrong?"

"My mom finally told Dad about Christine's boyfriend."

"Well, it's about time. How did it go? Or is that a stupid question?"

"It was terrible, worse than I expected. Not only was he pissed that Christine had a Black boyfriend, but he was furious that no one told him until now."

"I'm not surprised," said Lynda. "And why *was* it that no one told him until now?"

"It was Mom's decision. I thought you already knew that."

"But was it the right decision?" challenged Lynda.

"She was trying to protect Christine. She wanted to wait until she returned to school and break it to my father gently. She didn't want her to be tormented by a horrible argument."

"I get it," offered Lynda, "but there was bound to be a horrible argument one way or another."

"Yes, but she thought it was best for my father to have a cooling-off period before confronting Christine."

"Maybe she's right," said Lynda. "I really don't know what to say."

"I don't mean to burden you with this, but things are getting pretty bad around here. My father is more pissed at Mom than he is with Christine. He was blaming her for everything. Their argument turned into a big fight. It was worse than I've ever seen. He left the house and I'm pretty sure he's not coming back tonight."

"Okay," said Lynda. "You just need to take a deep breath. Your mother's strategy included a cooling-off period, right? Well, that's what you need to do. Wait for things to cool off. Be patient, don't jump to conclusions. In time, cooler heads will prevail."

"Yeah, maybe you're right," conceded Quinn. "I just needed someone to talk to."

"I'm glad you called," said Lynda, in a softer, more sympathetic tone. "You should always feel that you can talk to me. That will only make us closer."

Quinn hesitated, not knowing what to say. He was not one for sympathy or mushy stuff. Suddenly his demeanor stiffened up and he felt compelled to end the conversation.

"Okay, I'm sorry I bothered you. You probably need to study for your test."

"No bother at all. You know that," assured Lynda. "Do you still want me to come over Thursday for the tennis match? Will things be okay by then?"

"Tennis match?"

"You didn't forget, did you? I guess you really *are* rattled. We were all gonna watch the match between Billy Jean King and Bobby Riggs, remember? You said it would be fun for you and your dad to heckle me and your mom while we cheer for Billy Jean."

"Oh yeah, I forgot."

"That's okay. I'm not sure the timing is right anymore. Maybe we should drop it."

"No," said Quinn. "Now that I think about it, that's exactly what we should do. You know how my father likes you. If you come over and we all watch tennis together, it will ease the tension around our house. Let's plan on it. I'll make sure my parents know that you're coming over."

Suddenly, Quinn's spirits were lifted. A plan was in place and Lynda would be part of it, confirming once again that she was the perfect partner.

"I'll talk to you at school tomorrow, but let's plan on Thursday for sure."

"You got it," said Lynda.

It had been building for months, starting out with a whimper, and flourishing into a storm. Something that began as a frivolous novelty had exploded into a cultural phenomenon. It was a "sign of the times" reasoned the press. The women of the world were no longer content with taking a back seat to their male counterparts. They were ready to take on all challenges, proving their competency and embracing their duty as the new standard-bearers for equal rights.

Billy Jean King versus Bobby Riggs had turned into the most famous tennis match of all time, so big that it was no longer just a tennis match. It had become the "Battle of the Sexes."

At twenty-nine years old, Billie Jean King's tennis career had reached its zenith. After winning Wimbledon, the French Open, and the US Open, she finished 1972 as the number-one ranked woman in the world. Considering her whirlwind agenda and tumultuous relationship with the tennis establishment, her accomplishments seemed even more astounding. *Sports Illustrated* magazine had named her 1972 Sportsman of the Year, the first woman ever to earn that title, causing the publication to change the award to Sportsperson of the Year.

It had not been an easy road. The tennis world, dominated by men, had long been treating women like second-class citizens. In the United States, the national governing body for tennis was the USLTA (United States Lawn Tennis Association), its name originating from the nineteenth century when the game was called lawn tennis.

Organized and ruled by men for nearly a century, the USLTA had little interest in organizing women's tournaments, and when it did, the prize money was often five to ten times less than what was offered to the men. As the women grew more frustrated, Billie Jean King became increasingly vocal, openly challenging the pay disparities and threatening to revolt.

In 1970, the rebellion reached a turning point when a group of nine women told the USLTA they would boycott the Pacific Southwest Championships in Los Angeles because the men's prize money of $12,500, was more than eight times higher than the women's prize money of $1,500.

In order to make a real statement, Billie Jean knew they needed to do something that would shift the attention away from the tournament in LA and onto the women who were rebelling, the so-called Original Nine. With the help of Gladys Heldman, founder and publisher of *World Tennis Magazine*, the women decided to set up a competing tournament in Texas, the Houston Women's Invitation, the first ever professional tournament solely for women. Heldman, a Phi Beta Kappa graduate of Stanford University and the daughter of a prominent New

York judge, leveraged her business connections in an effort to seek tournament sponsorship and funding. Her ultimate target was Joe Cullman, CEO of Phillip Morris.

Phillip Morris, one of the world's largest producers of tobacco products, had launched the first cigarette for women in 1968, Virginia Slims. Their catchphrase, "You've come a long way baby," was considered one of the greatest marketing slogans of all time. But, as the 60s came to an end, health risks associated with smoking had become more publicized, and government was beginning to intervene.

In 1970, Congress passed the Public Health Cigarette Smoking Act, banning the advertising of cigarettes on television and radio. In April, President Nixon signed the bill into law. Phillip Morris, unwilling to give up on its famous Virginia Slims campaign, needed other avenues to promote its cigarettes and prevent declining sales. A tennis tournament specifically for women seemed like the perfect venue to advertise women's cigarettes, and "You've come a long way baby" was the perfect slogan. With Phillip Morris's sponsorship and funding, the Houston Women's Invitation turned into the Virginia Slims Invitation, and the tournament offered a prize package of $7,500.

When the tournament ended, Rosie Casals was crowned the inaugural winner, and Phillip Morris decided to capitalize on its success by sponsoring an entire women's tennis tour, a circuit that became known as the Virginia Slims Tour.

Although the USLTA attempted to lure the women back with higher prize money, the "Original Nine" had lost all interest. By the end of 1970, the nine-woman tour had grown to forty, and in 1971, the Virginia Slims circuit toured nineteen US cities and paid over $300,000 in prize money. Billie Jean King became the first female athlete to earn $100,000 in a single year.

Never satisfied with her accomplishments, Billie Jean King continued her relentless pursuit to organize one uniform governing body for all of women's tennis. In June of 1973, her goal was ultimately achieved with the establishment of the Women's Tennis Association.

Finally, through King's persistence and determination, there was one official organization designed to sanction and promote women's tennis events around the world. A few months later, the US Open became the first major tournament to award women's prize money on the same scale as the men. It hadn't been easy, but women were finally getting the recognition and respect they deserved. Not only was Billie Jean King sitting on top of the world as the number-one tennis player, she had become, in a few short years, the universal symbol for women's rights.

Bobby Riggs, at fifty-five years old, was a gambler, a hustler, and a brilliant promoter. It hadn't always been that way. When he was thirty years younger, he was considered one of the best tennis players in the world. Standing at five feet, seven inches, his physical stature was less than impressive, but his scrappiness and competitive spirit made him a formidable opponent.

As a junior player growing up in Los Angeles, he quickly earned a reputation as a strategist. With his ball placement and shot-making ability, Riggs notoriously kept his opponents off guard, persistently frustrating them by not allowing them to get into a rhythm. In 1936, at the age of eighteen, Riggs began competing in men's tournaments all around the country even though he was considered a junior. By the end of the year, he had climbed to number four in the US men's rankings.

In 1939, at the age of twenty-one and still playing as an amateur, Bobby Riggs had his breakout year. After finishing runner-up at the French Championships, he headed into Wimbledon as one of the odds-on favorites. Competing in the men's singles, men's doubles, and mixed doubles, Riggs achieved an extremely rare Wimbledon trifecta, capturing titles in all three events. Unwilling to rest on his laurels, Riggs put an exclamation point on his amazing year by winning the US Championships and earning his ranking as the number-one tennis player in the world.

In his later years, Bobby Riggs had lost most of his quickness and agility, but not his competitive spirit. He continued to be a regular at tennis clubs, taking on all challengers and wagering on the results. Everyone knew that Bobby loved to gamble. For most people that would be considered a weakness; for Riggs, it was his biggest strength. He had become a master at weighing his own skills against those of his opponent, then handicapping matches so the odds would swing to his favor. Quite simply, he was a hustler.

If a player was better than him, he would first build up his ego, and then convince him to accept a handicap that would level the odds. His opponent might agree to only one serve, or he might agree to spot

Bobby a fifteen-love advantage in each game. For lesser opponents, he would swing the handicap the other way, against himself, convincing them they couldn't lose.

There was no limit to the number of obstacles Bobby was willing to entertain in order to bait his opponents and hustle another bet. With his fast-talking, persuasive charm, Riggs had become the biggest attraction wherever he appeared. Players looked forward to negotiating Bobby's terms and accepting his challenges, often in front of crowds that would gather around to be amused by the circus-like spectacles.

In one match, Riggs beat a lesser opponent while lugging around a suitcase throughout the entire match. On another occasion, he played the wife of a British Parliament member with chairs and umbrellas scattered around his side of the court, convincing her the obstacles would impede his movement enough for her to win. As the competitions grew more ridiculous, the crowds became larger and Bobby's legend continued to grow.

In 1973, Bobby Riggs decided to go after the biggest prize of all, the top women's player in the world. Although his primary target was Billie Jean King, she was not interested in taking the bait, dismissing the offer as a trivial publicity stunt. Unwilling to give up, Riggs went after the number two player in the world, Margaret Court, persuading her with a guaranteed $5,000 purse and another $5,000 if she won. When CBS kicked in another $10,000, the match was on. Margaret Court viewed the match as an easy payday, feeling unthreatened by a lesser opponent that was nearly twenty-five years her senior. Riggs, on the other hand, took the match seriously, meticulously studying Court's game, identifying her weaknesses, and developing a strategy.

Scheduled for Sunday, May 13, the match would be played on Mother's Day, which seemed like a fitting gesture considering Margaret Court had given birth to her first child fourteen months earlier. Before the match, Riggs presented her with a bouquet of roses, and she responded with a curtsy. Riggs had extended an olive branch, but it would be his final gesture of goodwill.

From the very outset, he dominated the match, throwing off her rhythm with slices, dropshots, and lobs, and easily passing her as she came to the net. As Court's frustration continued to build, her game unraveled. Riggs proceeded to dismantle his opponent with unrelenting efficiency.

When the rout was over, the scoreboard reflected the domination: 6-2, 6-1. The match would forever be known as the "Mother's Day Massacre." Bobby Riggs, at fifty-five years of age, appeared on the cover of *Sports Illustrated* magazine with the headline: "Never Bet Against This Man."

More brash than ever, Riggs went after his next target. He said he wanted to take on Billie Jean King because she was the leader of women's liberation; she couldn't hide from him any longer. Riggs taunted and baited her by saying, "Women who can, do. Those who can't, become feminists." Bending ears and stirring the pot wherever he could grab some attention, Bobby was on the offensive.

As the taunts became more provocative and personal, Billie Jean knew she needed to respond. How could she shy away? She had always embraced her role as the leader of women's rights. This was yet another obstacle and she needed to confront it head-on. There was too much at stake.

Patiently waiting for the publicity and controversy to fester, Billie Jean eventually negotiated a deal that would be lucrative for both players. The match would take place on September 20, 1973, allowing Billie Jean enough time to prepare while still meeting her commitments to the Virginia Slims Tour.

Billie Jean took her preparation seriously, studying the style of play that Riggs used against Margaret Court and developing a strategy that would counter his off-speed game. Bobby, on the other hand, spent most of his time taunting and promoting. He knew that this would be the biggest payday of his career, and the more publicity he could generate, the greater the proceeds.

Leading up to the match, Bobby Riggs was featured on the covers of *Time* and *Newsweek* magazines, and appeared on *The Tonight Show Starring Johnny Carson*, stirring up controversy wherever he went. When asked about the pay disparity between men's and women's tennis, he said that women play about 25 percent as well as men, so they should be paid 25 percent of what men make.

Shrewdly taking advantage of the political climate, Riggs said it was time to settle the score once and for all. He blatantly embraced his role as the ultimate male chauvinist, stating that, "Women belong in the bedroom and kitchen, in that order." His objective was "to keep our women at home, taking care of the babies—where they belong." And after defeating Billie Jean, he said, "women's lib will be set back twenty years."

His strategy was working. Women around the world were rallying for Billie Jean King, viewing Riggs as an arrogant little moron with a big mouth. Men, on the other hand, were mostly amused, secretly supporting Riggs's claim of male superiority.

Emphatically embracing the attention, Riggs knew he was transforming a tennis match into something much bigger than a sporting event. It had become "Battle of the Sexes," and the whole world was choosing sides.

An event as big as this could only be held at the world's most famous stadium, the Houston Astrodome. Completed in 1965, it was billed as the world's largest multipurpose domed stadium, designed to host both football and baseball. With its massive infrastructure and futuristic roof, it was one of the world's greatest architectural achievements, earning the nickname "Eighth Wonder of the World."

Over thirty thousand tickets would soon be sold, making it the largest crowd ever to attend a tennis match. Scheduled for a Thursday evening, ABC had made the risky decision to televise a sporting event on a weeknight during primetime viewing, a coveted time slot that was normally reserved for their top-tier programs.

With over fifty million Americans tuning in, ABC's gamble paid off. Along with another forty million viewers worldwide, it had become the most watched sporting event in the history of television. For the athletes, the winner-take-all purse had grown to $100,000, and each player was guaranteed another $100,000 from television proceeds, making it the biggest payday in the history of tennis.

Quinn O'Connor walked up to the French doors that sealed the entrance to his father's beloved library. He squinted his eyes, trying to peer through the semiopaque lead-crystal glass. Waiting for his eyes to focus, he vaguely recognized the profile of his father sitting at the desk. Cracking the door open, he peeked in.

"Are you coming? The tennis match is about to begin."

"I suppose," replied his father. "Are you ready to witness a good old-fashioned ass whoopin'?"

"Let's do it," said Quinn.

"Is Lynda here?"

"Yes, she and Mom are fixin' up the snacks."

"Good, that's what the women are supposed to do," said Ryan, exploiting the opportunity to exhibit a little chauvinism. Getting up from his desk, he decided he would rather show up with Quinn at his side than make a grand entrance by himself. He and Roselyn were not exactly on speaking terms.

Entering the family room, Quinn went straight toward the television set and dialed up ABC. Ryan O'Connor made his way to the wet bar and poured his traditional glass of scotch on the rocks.

"Hi, Mr. O'Connor," said Lynda, balancing a large tray. "Where would you like these snacks?"

Ryan's face lit up, appreciating Lynda's subservient gesture.

"Well, well, I think Bobby Riggs would approve of the way you're taking care of the men."

Lynda knew that he was teasing and was relieved to see him in a playful mood.

"Maybe we should have the men serve us dessert if Billie Jean wins."

"Touché," chuckled Ryan. "Are you willing to make a wager? That's what Bobby Riggs would do."

Quinn turned up the TV volume so everyone could hear Howard Cosell's dramatic introduction.

"Live from the Astrodome in Houston, Texas, it's the tennis Battle of the Sexes. This telecast is being brought to you by Cadillac, America's number-one luxury car and its authorized dealers."

"Attaboy, Howard," said Ryan. "We'll take all the publicity we can get."

As the television flipped back and forth between screenshots of Billie Jean and Bobby Riggs, ABC played a song from the popular musical, *Annie Get Your Gun*: "Anything You Can Do (I Can Do Better)."

"That's pretty clever." Lynda laughed. "Our school almost did that play last year, but they decided to do *Guys and Dolls* instead."

"I've seen it," said Roselyn walking into the room, not missing a beat. "It's loosely based on the real life of Annie Oakley. She was performing in *Buffalo Bill's Wild West* show and could shoot better than most of the guys."

"I'd like to see it some time," said Lynda.

"The music is great," continued Roselyn. "All of it is written by Irving Berlin."

"Look," said Quinn. "Someone's entering the stadium."

It was difficult to make out the commotion, but there was a loud roar from the crowd as an entourage of people made their way through a tunnel and onto the main floor.

"And here comes Billie Jean King," announced Howard Cosell. "She really has the fans here tonight. There is unquestionably an overwhelming sentiment for Billie Jean King."

Adorned with large feathers, Billie Jean was being transported into the arena like an Egyptian Pharaoh. A crew of bare-chested men carried her litter as she made her Cleopatra-style entrance. Billie Jean smiled and waved to the crowd. She seemed to be enjoying herself immensely.

"What a crazy spectacle," observed Quinn. "I thought she was supposed to be the serious one, the one who was staying focused. Now she's acting just as kooky as Bobby Riggs."

"It's called marketing," said Lynda. "She knows she has to play along with the hype. That's how they get all the endorsement money."

Howard Cosell continued with his coverage.

"Billie Jean is looking very much like she usually looks; a very attractive young lady. Sometimes you get the feeling that if she ever let her hair grow down to her shoulders, took her glasses off, you'd have someone vying for a Hollywood screen test."

"Oh my God!" howled Roselyn. "He can't be serious. Just like a man to critique Billie Jean's appearance, as if attractiveness is what really matters. Do you think he'll describe how the man looks? Whether he's handsome, or not? This is exactly what women are fighting for; to be taken seriously."

"She does have nice legs," offered Ryan. "I'll give her that. But the hairstyle's gotta go."

Roselyn O'Connor shook her head in disgust while Lynda attempted to moderate. "I think she has her hair done that way so it's easier to manage. It's hard to be a woman athlete and maintain glamorous hair."

Quinn stayed quiet. His only wish was that his parents would avoid another argument.

As the cameras continued to swarm around Billie Jean, another ruckus appeared in the tunnel. It was the Bobby Riggs entourage, slowly making its way through the massive crowd. Riggs was being pulled into the arena on a rickshaw, a type of human-powered cart popularized in nineteenth century Asia.

Surrounded by a harem of attractive young ladies in miniskirts, Riggs was wearing a jacket with *Sugar Daddy* emblazoned across his chest. Symbolism aside, *Sugar Daddy* was the name of a well-known candy, a caramel-flavored lollipop that was popular among children.

After arriving near center court, Riggs dismounted his rickshaw and was handed a giant *Sugar Daddy* by his bevy of beauties.

"Pathetic," proclaimed Roselyn O'Connor. "I guess he's gotta keep the stereotype going."

"I'd say he's doin' pretty well for a fifty-five-year-old man," countered Ryan. "Hugh Hefner's gotta be pretty jealous right now."

"This is marketing genius," declared Lynda. "Can you imagine how much money he's making just to endorse a piece of candy?"

"All very amusing," said Quinn, "but when do we get to watch some tennis? I'm starting to think this is all a big hoax."

As the players met at center court, surrounded by cameras and microphones, ABC's Frank Gifford attempted to moderate the event. Bobby Riggs officially presented Billie Jean with the giant *Sugar Daddy* lollipop, announcing, "This is for Billie Jean. I figure she's gonna be a sucker for my lobs tonight, so I brought her the biggest sucker I could find, and she can lick it for the rest of the year."

"What an ass," spouted Roselyn. "How does he live with himself?"

Quinn's father chuckled out loud as Lynda attempted to mediate. "It's all part of the show," said Lynda. "Millions of people are viewing, and most of them have probably never watched tennis before. They're watching for the entertainment value. So that's what they're delivering—entertainment."

As the cameras continued to swarm around the two players, the bedlam caused Frank Gifford's microphone to go dead, so ABC's coverage went back to the booth where Cosell was interviewing tennis star, Rosie Casals. Shortly into the interview, the cameras quickly cut back to center court, where Bobby Riggs was holding up a real, live piglet for all the world to see, apparently a gift from Billie Jean.

"Look at the male chauvinist pig that Bobby is holding," announced Cosell.

"That's too cute for him," said Rosie Casals. "He doesn't resemble that kind of a pig."

As the ceremonies dragged on, a discombobulated mixture of pageantry, chaos, and silliness, the officials attempted to clear the court. Finally, twenty-five minutes after the telecast began, it appeared that an actual tennis match was about to begin. When Billie Jean took her place on the baseline and prepared to deliver the first serve, the crowd settled down and the Astrodome turned eerily quiet, an undeniable tension in the air.

"I wonder how they determined who would get the first serve," questioned Quinn. "Normally you want to serve first so you can jump out to an early advantage, but I wouldn't want to serve first in this match. I can't imagine the pressure she's under right now with millions of people watching."

"It's the moment of truth," declared Ryan. "There's no place to hide now."

Missing her first serve badly, Billie Jean proceeded to put a weak second serve into play, allowing Riggs to deliver an aggressive return to her backhand. When her volley sprayed pathetically wide, the crowd let out a collective groan.

"Not a good start," observed Quinn. "She's gotta weather the storm and hope the nerves go away."

As Billie Jean settled down and eased into the match, she started to connect on her first serve. After a couple short rallies, Billie Jean came to the net and scored the winning point with a decisive volley. The crowd cheered loudly as Billie Jean took a 1-0 lead.

"I can't believe she's playing serve and volley," observed Quinn. "She hasn't changed her game at all. I didn't think she would come to the net that often considering his skill for hitting passing shots."

"It may take a few games for Bobby to dial it in," said Ryan. "He'll figure it out."

As the nerves continued to subside, the quality of tennis improved, and the players settled into some entertaining rallies. After four games, the score was knotted at 2-2, each player holding serve. But game five marked a turning point as Riggs broke Billie Jean's serve for the first time and took a 3-2 lead.

"That's the break he needed," said Ryan. "Now, all he needs to do is hold serve and he'll win the first set. I told you he'd figure her out."

But the lost service game seemed to spark Billie Jean's competitive spirit as she began to hit harder and play more aggressively. The crowd roared when she hit an overhead smash winner to break right back and capture game six. It was all even again, and Riggs was looking concerned.

With the first set tied at 4-4, Billie Jean proceeded to push Riggs all over the court, running him ragged as he attempted to chase down her precise volleys. Unable to score a single point, Riggs fell behind again 5-4. When the players took their seats during the crossover, Riggs looked tired and frustrated.

"He's all right," commented Ryan. "He just needs to catch his breath and hold service in this next game. If he forces a tiebreaker, she'll fold under the pressure."

With Riggs serving and the game tied at 30-30, he hit a high passing shot that appeared to be a winner, but Billie Jean leaped up into the air and flicked a brilliant backhand overhead winner. The crowd roared as Riggs, down 30-40, was suddenly facing set point. After missing his first serve, Riggs tried to aim his second serve down the middle but missed wide by a few inches. Bobby Riggs had just double-faulted to lose the first set 6-4. The crowd roared as Billie Jean smiled with appreciation. Bobby Riggs walked straight to his bench and conferred with his coach.

Unable to contain her joy, Roselyn stood up. "So who folded under the pressure that time?" she taunted.

Ryan O'Connor abruptly made his way back to the wet bar.

"That's ridiculous. How do you double fault on set point? Maybe Bobby's a bigger hustler than we ever imagined. What if he's throwing this match?"

"What do you mean?" asked Quinn. "Why would he throw a match when there's a hundred-thousand-dollar purse going to the winner?"

"Think about it," said Ryan. "Jimmy the Greek set the Las Vegas odds at five-to-two, favoring Bobby. What if Bobby decided to bet on his opponent and lose on purpose? He could generate a monster payday for himself. Not to mention the money he could collect from the mobsters who are willing to pay him for throwing the match."

"Nice try," said Roselyn. "He loses one set and suddenly you claim he lost on purpose. Maybe you can't deal with the fact that a woman beat him fair and square."

Ryan's face turned red. Quinn interjected quickly before his father could respond.

"It's only one set. And it was very close. Other than the double fault, I didn't see any shots that were badly missed. It seems like it's pretty competitive."

Ryan O'Connor took a couple gulps of scotch and paused to gain his composure. "All I'm saying is, never give the benefit of the doubt to a hustler."

Lynda looked on nervously, not knowing what to say. She'd never witnessed this sudden rise in Ryan's blood pressure. If he really liked her the way Quinn said he did, it was up to her to find the right words to ease the tension.

"I must admit, the double fault at set point was awfully suspicious," she said. "Let's watch the second set real close and see if we can detect any other signs."

Roselyn O'Connor rolled her eyes and looked at Quinn suspiciously. But Quinn kept playing the conservative middle ground. "Maybe lots of people were betting on a straight-set victory and Bobby's playing for a three-to-one victory. That way he can play to win, but still hustle a few side bets."

"You people are ridiculous," said Roselyn. "How many different conspiracy theories can you come up with? I saw the look on his face, and I saw the way he was chasing down one good shot after another. To me, he looks tired and frustrated. If he's really faking it, he should win the Academy Award."

After a four-minute break, the match resumed with Bobby Riggs looking refreshed. He immediately broke Billie Jean's serve to take a 1-0 lead. But after a long rally where Riggs was forced to run back and forth from corner to corner, Billie Jean hit a decisive winner to break right back at one game apiece.

The crowd roared as Riggs tried to catch his breath. Billie Jean, her confidence building, looked calm and relaxed, while Riggs continued to sweat profusely.

The next few games were more of the same. Although both players held serve, Billie Jean was making quick work of her service games, while Riggs struggled to hold onto his serve through long rallies and close points. Even though it was tied at 3-3, it appeared that Billie Jean was gradually taking control, wearing her opponent down and displaying her superior athletic ability. After Billie Jean held her serve to go up 4-3, Howard Cosell mentioned that Riggs needed to turn things around quickly if he wanted to survive. Rosie Casals responded, "He'll have to go back to cooking and doing the housework."

But Riggs had no answer. Billie Jean proceeded to break Riggs's serve and take a 5-3 lead. The crowd stood on their feet as she prepared to serve for the second set. As it turned out, it was noneventful. Billie Jean convincingly closed him out with a dominating service game, preventing him from scoring a single point. The crowd roared with glee over Billie Jean's commanding 2-0 lead, but she casually shook it off, strolling to her bench nonchalantly as if everything was going according to plan.

"That should pretty much do it," announced Quinn. "There's no way a fifty-five-year-old guy can come back and win three straight sets."

Roselyn attempted to hide her obvious glee, deciding it was better to maintain her composure. She didn't want to upset the applecart by being an obnoxious winner.

Ryan stood up. "I've seen enough. I'm going to retire. I have a big day ahead of me tomorrow."

When it was all said and done, the third set was more of the same. Billie Jean surgically dismantled her opponent, dictating his play with her precise ball placement and relentless volleys. Once again, the final score was 6-3. Riggs had succumbed in three straight sets, a humiliating setback for someone who had boldly predicted total annihilation.

Billie Jean King had slain the mighty dragon, the man who promised to set back women's liberation by twenty years. By winning the so-called

Battle of the Sexes, she had scored a major victory for women around the globe and solidified her status as the leader of women's rights.

Roselyn O'Connor stood up, stretched, and let out a big sigh of relief. "I guess that settles that," she said with a big smile on her face. Then she walked over and gave Lynda a big hug. "Score one for the ladies. It's another small step for women."

"But one giant leap for womankind," joked Quinn. "I don't know why Dad took it so seriously. It's just a tennis match."

"Your father doesn't like change," said Roselyn. "He wants to continue living in his perfect little world; always in charge and always in control. He doesn't understand that the world is evolving. People are trying to make things better, and women want to play a role in shaping the future. There are no set boundaries anymore, the lines are being blurred, and that's a good thing. This makes your father feel threatened. If he can't figure out how to adapt and deal with it, he's going to be a very unhappy man."

As it turned out, Bobby Riggs was gracious in defeat, praising his opponent and admitting he had underestimated her ability. The two went on to become good friends, gaining a mutual respect and a shared admiration.

In her memoirs, Billie Jean King later wrote: Bobby was a hustler and a showman, but he was honest. He took his defeats and paid his debts without complaint, and he expected others to do the same. He had honor, and he had humor. It is so important in any dialogue between opponents to maintain these two things. In our case, it led to a deep regard for each other.

When Billie Jean King last spoke with Bobby Riggs, he was in his final weeks, bedridden from cancer.

"We really did it, didn't we, Billie?" said Riggs. "We made a difference."

Then he told Billie Jean he loved her, and she said she loved him too.

Women's liberation continued to make strides in the 70s, buoyed by the popular Helen Reddy song, "I Am Woman." In December of 1972, the song reached number one on the Billboard Hot 100 and became the unofficial anthem for feminism in 1973.

Chapter 45

LIKE A GIANT RED BALL, the harvest moon rested on the eastern horizon, hovering over the landscape like an extraterrestrial invader. On the ground, glowing flames of fire lapped against the frigid air, scintillating the darkness. The sizzling firewood, with its soothing crackles and pops, emanated a cozy warmth, permeating the air with the alluring scent of smoke and charred oak.

It was late October in Indiana and autumn was taking its last breath. The red, yellow, and orange foliage that makes the season so magnificent was rapidly descending to the ground, producing the musty and earthy aroma of decayed leaves.

As much as Brian Johnson loved the fall, he despised the impending gloom of winter. A season filled with such beauty should not be displaced by a period of death and dormancy; it was a cruel juxtaposition. Soon, barren tree limbs and desolate landscapes would be stark reminders of winter's wrath, but with three football games remaining, Brian would savor autumn's last fleeting moments.

It was the Thursday before homecoming and Northrop High School was hosting its annual bonfire, a tradition that served as a pep rally for Saturday's game against the Snider Panthers. Staged on some vacant land behind the stadium, a piece of property referred to as the back forty, student volunteers spent the afternoon hollowing out a piece of dirt and stacking a cord of firewood into a large pyramid. Mr. Leavy, a biology teacher, would serve as the construction engineer, ensuring the edifice would not collapse or trigger any grassfires from stray sparks or scattered embers.

As dusk turned to darkness, a large contingent of students began to gather around the fire, taking advantage of a rare opportunity to be out and about on a school night. Although the event was mostly a social gathering, with no formal agenda, football players and cheerleaders alike were expected to attend.

Heading into the weekend, the football team was still undefeated in conference play, hoping to stay on course for a showdown with Bishop Dwenger, the Catholic powerhouse on the north side of town. Neither Brian Johnson nor Darius Williams would be in the starting lineup, but they would both see their fair share of action as they split duties with two senior running backs. Marcus Mosely would see the most action. He was a captain and leader of the Bruin defense, earning accolades as a bona fide college prospect and a surefire Indiana All-Star.

"Are you cold?" Brian asked Mindy. "Do you wanna get closer to the fire?"

"As long as it doesn't singe my hair," she joked.

Brian reached out and took her hand. "Wow, it's freezing. You should've worn mittens."

"I was expecting *you* to keep me warm," she teased.

"All right, you two lovebirds," said Mark Carter. "Let's keep it clean."

"Hey, there's Lynda," said Mindy, waving a hand to draw her attention.

Wearing her letter jacket and sporting a stylish knit beret, Lynda approached in her casual, confident way.

"Are you staying warm? Or is that a silly question, considering you're standing next to a bonfire?"

"I'm nice and toasty," said Mindy, "except for my hands. What about you? Did you just get here?"

"No," replied Lynda. "I was talking to Antonio on the other side of the fire. His pep band is going to end the evening with the fight song. That's really the only thing on tonight's agenda. When they're done, we're supposed to disperse. Then they'll try to extinguish the remaining embers."

"Is Quinn here?"

"No, he's not much for these rah-rah social gatherings. He said he had to study for a test."

"Well, that's pretty boring," said Mark. "He needs to get a life."

"Did you guys get some hot apple cider?" asked Lynda. "The student council is serving it at that table over there."

"That sounds good," acknowledged Brian.

"Look," said Mark. "What's Bob doing over there?"

Scanning the crowd, they eventually identified Bob's skinny torso underneath a heavy parka and knit cap. Standing close to another boy, Bob appeared to be speaking softly into his ear. The boy then reached into his pocket and pulled out some money, discreetly handing it to Bob in a closed fist. Stuffing the money into his jeans pocket, Bob surveyed his position, apparently concerned about detection. Then he casually unzipped his parka far enough to insert his hand, reaching under his coat as if there was a hidden breast pocket.

"Is he doing what I think he's doing?" asked Brian.

Mark didn't reply. He was beginning to stew as he glared intensely at Bob's exchange. The boy proceeded to accept the contents of Bob's breast pocket, slipping it under his jacket. Then the two boys casually eased away from each other, trying to look inconspicuous.

"Hey, Bob," yelled Mark, waving an arm to catch his attention. "Come over here."

Bob weaved through the crowd and approached his friends with a big smile.

"What's happenin'? How long have you been standing here?"

"Long enough to see what you've been up to," implied Mark.

"We're just trying to stay warm," said Lynda, attempting to deflect Mark's interrogation. "Did you get any cider?"

"Cut the shit," said Mark. "What were you selling over there?"

Startled by Mark's insinuation, Bob tried to play it off. "What are you talkin' about?"

"You know what I'm talkin' about. I can't believe you're stupid enough to sell drugs right here on school grounds."

"Where did you come up with that? You're way out-of-bounds, man."

"I saw what you were doing. Don't play dumb with me. We saw you take money and hand over the goods."

"That's ridiculous, man. I gave a dude some gum, and I didn't take any money."

Bob proceeded to retrieve a pack of Wrigley's spearmint gum from his pocket.

"What a crock of shit," continued Mark. "You think I was born yesterday? My dad arrests people like you."

"All right," said Lynda. "Let's take it down a notch. Bob, all we wanna do is help you. We're your friends and we don't want to see you get into any trouble."

"It's that Marino dude," said Mark. "He's nothin' but trouble. You gotta quit hangin' around with him."

Attempting to extend the charade, Bob continued his denials.

"Man, I don't know where you guys are comin' from, but you're on the wrong track. I'm not dealin' any drugs."

They all stared at Bob in silence, allowing his denial to sink in and manifest into guilt. Suddenly he appeared pathetically weak, unable to deflect his friends' pity.

Bob was always the underdog kid who seemed to get the bad breaks in life, but he continued to persevere, shaking off the setbacks and putting on a front. Like the Teflon man, he let things slide away, rarely showing any emotion.

Brian approached Bob and put his arm around him. "Dude, we're just concerned about you because you're our friend. You know we've always had your back. All we wanna do is help you and protect you."

Bob was silent for a second as his friends looked on with concern. His eyes welled up as he tried to speak, but he was unable to deliver a response with an apparent lump in his throat.

"What is it?" asked Lynda. "You know you can talk to us."

Trying to gain his composure, Bob struggled. "I've had a lot on my mind lately. It hasn't been easy."

"Like what," asked Brian. "You know you can tell us."

Not one to share his personal problems, Bob struggled to find the words. Then he suddenly blurted it out.

"My mom has lung cancer."

Blindsided by Bob's stunning announcement, his friends were thrown for a loop.

"They say it's pretty bad," he continued. "Just my luck, ain't it? First, I lose my brother and now it looks like I'm gonna lose my mom."

Bob then paused, waiting for the looks of shock to disappear. Lynda walked over and wrapped her arms around him, and Mark, suddenly feeling guilty about his aggression, pulled off Bob's knit cap and playfully rubbed his knuckles over his scalp.

That was enough to trigger Bob's breakdown. He quickly grabbed his cap from Mark and covered his face, trying to hide the tears.

"Hey, this is supposed to be a pep rally! Where's the enthusiasm?"

They all looked up to see Scott Clever, hopping along on a pair of crutches.

"What the hell happened to you?" asked Brian.

"Blew out my knee in practice today. My season's over before it even started."

"Holy shit," said Brian. "That really sucks."

"Tell me about it," said Scott. "All those summer workouts for nothin'."

Suddenly the pity party had moved from Bob to Scott. Oblivious to the conversation he intruded upon, Scott continued.

"Now my senior year is all I got left if I wanna play varsity ball. At this point I'm not really sure I give a shit anymore."

"Are you sure you're out for the whole year?" asked Brian.

"No doubt," said Scott. "Torn ligaments. We're talkin' surgery and a minimum of eight months rehab. And that's if everything goes according to plan."

"You can't give up," lectured Brian. "It's just another obstacle to overcome. I know you can do it."

"Fuck it. I don't even wanna think about it right now. I'm here to have a good time."

Reaching into his coat pocket, Scott pulled out a can of Pabst Blue Ribbon beer. "This is my pain killer."

"Put that away, asshole," said Mark. "Goddammit! Between you and Bob, we're hangin' out with a bunch of derelicts."

Mindy started laughing. "You got any more beer you can share?"

Lynda glared at Mindy in disbelief, but Brian was intrigued by her orneriness. He put his arm around her and squeezed her close. "I really have to keep an eye on this naughty girl."

"I hate to bring an end to this nonsense," announced Lynda, "but it looks like Antonio is ready to start his entertainment."

Next to the cider stand, the pep band had gathered to perform, waiting for Antonio's signal to begin.

"Let's go Bruins!" shouted Antonio, catching everyone's attention.

Like a flock of obedient sheep, the herd of students migrated over to the band.

"It's time to show some school spirit!" he yelled, holding his trumpet with one hand, and directing the band with the other. "A one, a one-two-three-four."

As the students clapped in rhythm to the Northrop fight song, Brian noticed the football team congregating together and grabbed Mark's arm. "C'mon, let's go join our teammates."

Cramming in together with the players, Brian felt a big bear-hug from behind, squeezing him tight and pushing the air out of his lungs.

"What the hell," he gasped. "I can't breathe!"

Then, recognizing two big Black hands clasped around his chest, he realized it could only be one person. "Malcom, you're suffocating me!"

Malcom Mosely let go and started laughing. "How did you know it was me?"

"Well, you're the only one around here with the strength of a grizzly bear."

"Heh, heh," he chuckled. "I said I'd always have your back."

"Yeah, but that doesn't mean jumpin' my back and squeezin' the life out of me. Save your aggression for Saturday night."

"Okay, homeboy," said Malcom. "I'm just tryin' to toughen you up a bit."

With the conclusion of the fight song, the crowd applauded enthusiastically as two students raised a giant banner depicting a large Bruin bear mauling a wimpy little Snider Panther.

"I know what *that* feels like," said Brian, teasing Marcus Mosely.

Marcus laughed and wrapped his giant arm around Brian's neck in a choke hold. The football players gathered around and started high-fiving

Marcus's free hand and dog-piling Brian in a giant huddle, jumping up and down in unison.

The fight song and banner had done the trick. It didn't take much to trigger the testosterone-fueled aggression in a group of seventeen- and eighteen-year-old boys. They were clearly ready to take on all challengers.

As the fire dwindled and the enthusiasm waned, Brian and Mark made their way back to their friends. The homecoming committee began to disassemble the cider stand and the crowd milled around aimlessly, contemplating its next move.

"I guess that pretty much wraps it up," noted Lynda.

Then, seemingly out of nowhere, a loud scream pierced the air, followed by a few shrieks and a series of shouts that sounded like heckling. Approaching rapidly, the unidentified commotion moved purposefully, threatening to wreak havoc upon an otherwise routine evening.

"What's happening?" asked Mindy. "Can you see what's going on?"

"I don't know," replied Brian, "but it's coming this way."

As the squeals turned into laughter and the onlookers assembled to gawk, the unfolding disturbance appeared less threatening, more like a peculiarity that had evolved into a spectacle. Nevertheless, it was unabashedly moving along with swiftness, destined to complete its mission unscathed.

"Streakers!" shouted Mindy, recognizing the thundering herd of naked runners.

Wearing nothing but tennis shoes, tube socks, and ski masks, the exhibitionists looped around the bonfire, moving as quickly as possible, trying not to slip and fall along the way. There was no mistaking their gender. With hairy legs and genitalia flopping to and fro, the all-male crew was clearly in a hurry.

"They look cold!" observed Mindy.

"It's called shrinkage." Scott laughed. "I hope no one gets frostbite."

Completing their loop around the fire, the boys sprinted away as quickly as they arrived, and the crowd enjoyed one last laugh before breaking into a round of applause.

"Look at all those bare white buns." Mindy laughed.

Lynda rolled her eyes with disgust. "Pretty stupid if you ask me. I hope they're proud of themselves."

The herd faded away into the distance, targeting a large white conversion van waiting impatiently in the school parking lot. As the last body scrambled to climb aboard, the van squealed away, its wheels spinning and smoking, and its driver obnoxiously honking the horn in celebration.

"Well, that was exciting," exclaimed Mindy. "I just witnessed my first streaker show."

"I'm sure it won't be your last," said Scott. "Apparently, it's the latest fad."

"I think Mindy really enjoyed it," teased Mark. "Maybe we can sell her tickets to the next one."

"You're a real hoot," said Mindy. "Did you guys recognize anyone?"

"How?" asked Brian. "They were all wearing ski masks."

"I thought maybe you guys might recognize someone's body parts," she suggested. "Afterall, don't you guys shower together?"

"Yeah, right," said Mark, sarcastically. "Whenever I shower with the team, I stare at their genitals, trying to memorize what they look like."

"Now you're making it sound creepy." Mindy laughed. "I just thought there might be some identifying features."

"One of the dudes was taller than the rest," acknowledged Scott. "He could've been a basketball player."

"They better hope nobody squeals on anyone," said Lynda. "Otherwise, they're in big trouble. They'll all get kicked out of school for sure."

Nobody knows where it really started. One thing is for sure, streaking—the fad of running naked through public areas on a dare, or as a prank—reached its peak in the fall of 1973, and winter of 1974. *Naked* may be an exaggeration. After all, most streakers had the decency to wear shoes, socks, and ski masks, with foot comfort and anonymity taking priority, not necessarily in that order. Although common sense would suggest it prevailed in warmer climates, intriguingly enough, streaking continued to thrive in the coldest of conditions. Perhaps it was the prevalence of ski masks, or maybe the fact that extreme temperatures glorified the act as being even more defiant, inspiring a sense of risk and adventure.

Whatever the motive, streaking had reached mainstream America, popping up in all walks of life.

One account suggests the fad earned its nickname in the fall of 1973 at a large-scale event on the University of Maryland campus in Washington DC. Broadcasting on live TV, a reporter announced that hundreds of naked runners were streaking by, proclaiming it an incredible sight. As a result, streaking had become the definitive term, and pop culture had adopted the stunt as another act of rebellion.

Although mass streaking events were drawing the headlines, individual streakers were not entirely excluded. Sole performers would occasionally pop up at shopping malls or sporting events, earning their fair share of attention. But they did not enjoy the same strength in numbers as their banded brethren, lacking the security that comes with homogeneous collaboration.

While coalitions of streakers were easily dismissed as thrill-seeking fellowships, singular streakers were often frowned upon as outcasts of society, exhibitionists engaged in public lewdness. Consequently, they were often chased down, captured, and arrested for public indecency.

Like most developing fads, proliferation occurred on college campuses, sanctities for freedom and expression. Although it was monopolized by men, streaking was not entirely immune to the female gender. Coed streaking events existed, but were mostly a rarity, with males dominating the herd. It's hard to imagine an all-female cast without some sort of male incitement, for women were far more likely to observe than participate.

And observe is what they did, in full force, laughing and cheering as the thundering herds stormed by. As attendance became more fashionable, women would invite friends, coordinate outfits, and make funny signs, adding to the circus-like atmosphere. Communication and promotion were almost always by word-of-mouth, for no one wanted to tip off school administrators or campus police.

Making plans on the sly became the modus operandi, although discreet postings would sometimes appear on bulletin boards in girls' dormitories:

STREAKING Tonight – 8:00 PM – Northwest
Quadrangle – BYO Refreshments

Streaking had become another night on the town, an opportunity for cheap entertainment on a tight budget. Since most college girls had never seen male genitalia before, their curiosities were typically more aroused than their libidos. Unlike men and their obsession with *Playboy*, women did not have their own magazines to flaunt male nudity, so spectating was more about education than sensuality. Unbeknownst to the males, seduction was never really a part of the equation.

As the popularity exploded, academia was asked to explain the phenomena. Why were our youngsters running around naked? Had they lost all their morals? Was this part of a new sexual revolution? Was this another form of rebellion? Were we losing control of society?

Psychologists were not short on opinions: freedom of expression, innocuous displays of nonconformity, liberation from the constraints of society, blowing off steam as an escape, narcissistic cravings, harmless releases of pressure, the thrill of violating social norms and getting away with it. The list went on and on.

Often overlooked was the likelihood of impaired judgment, the fact that many streakers built up their courage by consuming considerable amounts of alcohol, or the possibility that no explanation was necessary at all, the possibility that it was just another inexplicable fad, no different from goldfish swallowing in the 40s, panty raids in the 50s, or stuffing people into phone booths in the 60s.

No matter the justification, it all came to an abrupt halt in May 1974. Some say it had run its course, lost its excitement, the thrill was gone. Others say it came to an end when students studied for their final exams, packed their bags, and headed home for the summer. Or there's the possibility that it just wasn't cool anymore, especially when Ray Stevens released his recording entitled "The Streak," a novelty song that reached number one on the Billboard charts in May 1974.

Walking hand in hand, Brian led Mindy back to the school parking lot. She was in a frolicky mood, and he couldn't help but wonder how the rest of the evening would play out, even though it was a school night and football players were expected to go home after the bonfire.

Reaching for his car keys, Brian felt Mindy wrap her arms around his waist. Caught off guard by her assertiveness, Brian turned around to acknowledge the gesture with a warm embrace. Not satisfied with a hug, Mindy pressed her face against him and delivered a long, engaging kiss, sensuously molding her lips to his mouth.

Then, just as quickly as it began, it ended with Mindy pulling away and gesturing toward the car door. "Aren't you gonna let me in?" she asked with a whimsical twinkle in her eye.

Brian, trying his best to interpret the mixed signals, obediently opened her door. Mindy plopped down on the vinyl seat, looked up at him enticingly, and asked, "To be continued?"

Taking his place behind the steering wheel, Brian was glad to see that Mindy had already scooted toward the middle, no longer needing the radio as an alibi for her proximity. Sticking the key into the ignition, Brian fired up the Olds 88 and Mindy began rubbing his thigh, completely distracting his train of thought.

"That was a fun evening, don't you think?" asked Mindy.

"It was definitely unique," replied Brian, more interested in what Mindy's hand was doing.

"Would you ever go streaking?" she asked as the car exited the school parking lot.

"Hmmm, I doubt it. I think it's more fun to be one of the hecklers."

"Oh c'mon. Where's your sense of adventure?" coaxed Mindy, as she continued to rub his thigh.

It was just like Brian to give a common-sense response. He was not the kind of guy who succumbed to fleeting fads. He was more of a walk the straight and narrow kind of guy. And yet, savoring the touch of Mindy's hand on his thigh, he could feel himself relinquishing to her mystical powers. She knew how to ignite his sensory receptors, and he feared she would find out firsthand if her stroking became too adventurous.

"So what's next?" asked Mindy, as they stopped at a red light. "It's only nine o'clock. I don't have to be home until ten. What about you?"

"Well, I wasn't given a curfew, but ten o'clock seems like a respectable time for a weeknight."

"Ah yes, I forgot. You're all about respectability," she teased. Then she reached into her coat pocket and pulled out a Pabst Blue Ribbon beer. "You wanna help me drink this?"

Caught off guard by Mindy's surprise revelation, Brian searched for a clever response.

"It looks like Scott has corrupted you too."

"Corruption? Is that what you call this?"

"No, I was just teasing," said Brian, fearful he had offended her. "I probably shouldn't drink beer while I'm driving, but I think you should enjoy one if you want, as long as your parents don't smell alcohol on your breath and blame it on me."

Mindy popped the tab and took a few swigs. Feeling jilted by Brian's indifference, she turned on the radio. No longer rubbing his thigh, she sipped her beer and fiddled with the dial.

Brian couldn't help but notice her sudden indignation. Realizing he had killed Mindy's playful mood, he felt like a pathetic loser. The girl of his dreams had been rubbing his leg, drinking a beer, and suggesting there was time to kill. How could he screw up something so obvious?

His mind raced into damage control as they approached the intersection of Saint Joe and Washington Center Road, about a mile from her house. He needed to recapture the mood and regain her good graces without being too obvious. He had to think fast.

"Hey, have you ever been to Shoaff Park at night?"

"At night? I don't think so," contemplated Mindy as she took another sip of beer. "What does one do there at night?" she asked suspiciously, wondering if he was starting to come around after all.

"So you know how Mark Carter is the great outdoorsman with all his camping and hunting expeditions. Well, he brought me to Shoaff Park one night and showed me something pretty cool."

"Mark Carter brought *you* to Shoaff Park one night?" asked Mindy, unable to hide her confusion.

"Yeah. You make it sound weird."

"I must admit, it seems a little odd."

"Let me show you," said Brian as he pulled through the park entrance, bypassing the "Welcome" sign.

"It says the park hours are from 7.00 a.m. to 7.00 p.m.," noted Mindy. "Does that mean it's closed?"

"It doesn't matter. Nobody really cares."

"Aren't *you* the rebel," she teased.

"That's me," said Brian. "Now, are you ready to see some raccoons?"

"Raccoons? Are you serious?"

"Yep. I'll show you where they hang out. It's actually pretty cool."

Brian proceeded to pull the car into a gravel parking area across from the picnic pavilions. "Do you see those trash cans over there?"

"Just barely, it's awfully dark."

"That's where they hang out. If I flash my lights on those trash cans, you'll see them scurry about. And the coolest thing is their eyes. When they look into the headlights, the first thing you'll see is their eyes, and how they glow in the dark."

"You sound experienced," teased Mindy. "Just like Marlin Perkins on *Mutual of Omaha's Wild Kingdom*."

Ignoring Mindy's sarcasm, Brian proceeded to turn off the headlights and position the vehicle so that it directly faced the trash receptacles across the street. "Are you ready?" he asked.

"Ready as I'll ever be."

Brian turned on the headlights and immediately flashed the high beams, flooding the picnic area with light. Sure enough, right on cue, three pairs of twinkling lights appeared above the garbage can rims.

"Oh my gosh!" exclaimed Mindy. "There's three of them. Their eyes are like laser beams. Amazing!"

With a big smile on his face, Brian leaned back and enjoyed the show, pleased that his little spectacle had materialized as promised.

"Now I can make out their full bodies," observed Mindy, as the critters scrambled over the edges and tumbled to the ground. "Wow, they're bigger than I thought. They must eat pretty well," she laughed. "It's amazing how their eyes glow in the dark like that."

"I told you it was pretty cool," said Brian, as the coons disappeared into the woods. "They get plenty of picnic leftovers, that's for sure. Although a steady diet of garbage isn't exactly my idea of fine dining."

Mindy took the final swallow of her beer and pressed against Brian. "How 'bout a steady diet of this?" she suggested as she leaned in for a kiss.

"Sounds good to me," said Brian as he felt his heart begin to race.

"Surely you didn't bring me here just to watch raccoons."

Brian needed no coaxing. His plan had worked, and he was ready to take full advantage. Pulling Mindy against his body, he embraced her luscious curves and feverishly pressed his mouth to her lips.

Feeling Brian's uncontrolled passion, Mindy suddenly came to her senses. Slowly prying her lips away, she flirtatiously raised her eyebrows and fluttered her eyelashes.

"Shouldn't you turn off your headlights first? It's not like we want to advertise our location."

"I was gonna get around to that," reasoned Brian, "but you got me sidetracked."

"Okay, I'll shoulder the blame," she laughed. "Why don't we find a more secluded location. Then you can turn off your lights. But we need to keep the heater on, don't you think?"

Brian dimmed his high beams and pulled out of the parking lot. Mindy continued to rub his thigh. The fact that she was taking control of the situation and making prudent plans was a total turn-on for Brian. Mindy was a gal who knew what she wanted and how to get it.

"How's this?" asked Brian as he pulled the car off the side of the road, underneath a patch of tree limbs.

"Perfect," said Mindy as she squeezed his bicep. "How did you get such big muscles?"

Brian moved his hand toward Mindy's face and gently stroked her cheek, gazing into her big brown eyes. "You really are beautiful. You know that, don't you?"

"Flattery will get you everywhere," she whispered, blushing from his adulation.

Brian kissed her again, slowly and softly, patiently prolonging the warmth of her lips, content to savor this rare moment of seclusion. He then moved his lips across her cheek, nibbling his way down to her neck and inhaling the fragrance of her perfume. Mindy leaned her head back in submission, allowing him to take liberties. Brian shamelessly obliged, caressing her neck with his lips, then working his way back up, slowly nibbling on her earlobe and playfully inserting his tongue.

Mindy responded with a giggle. "Ooh, that tickles."

"I could nibble on your cute little ears all night long."

"You're crazy," she laughed.

"Crazy about you."

Mindy pressed her mouth to Brian again, this time in a fit of passion, rhythmically kneading his lips. Falling back on the seat in submission, she pulled Brian down with her, feeling the full force of his body on top. The foreplay and small talk were over. They were hopelessly locked together, succumbing to their primal urges. Brian instinctively rubbed his body against Mindy in a rocking motion, feeling her heavy breathing against his chest. Pushing the boundaries even further, Mindy slipped her tongue inside Brian's mouth, signaling her acceptance of his advances. Hopelessly engaged, they had entered into a state of rapture. There was no turning back.

Then suddenly, seemingly out of nowhere, Mindy raised her head abruptly, forcefully pushing Brian away. "What was that?" she asked.

"What was what?"

"There it is again!" she gasped.

There was no mistaking it this time, the loud rap on the window. They both sat up, their hearts pounding as they tried to gather their composure. Before they could figure out what was happening, they were suddenly blinded by a bright light. Staring reactively into the light, their eyes confronted the intrusion. Unlike the coons, they couldn't scurry away into the woods. Instead, Brian turned his head away and faced the steering wheel, shielding his eyes with his hand.

"This is the police," came the command. "I need you to open your window."

Brian slowly complied, his heart pounding with guilt.

"What's your name, son?" asked the officer, slowly lowering his flashlight.

"Brian Johnson, sir."

"How old are you?

"Seventeen, sir. Do you need to see my driver's license?"

"I need you to leave the park. That's what I need. Don't you know the park closes at seven?"

"No, I didn't know that," lied Brian.

"It's almost ten o'clock and it's a school night. Shouldn't you two be home right now?"

"Yes, sir," said Brian.

"All right, why don't you do me a favor and take this fine lady home to her parents where she belongs. Can you do that for me?"

"Yes, sir. I'll do that right away, sir."

Chapter 46

MARQUIS JACKSON LUMBERED DOWN THE steps, his morning shower doing little to alleviate the sluggishness. Halfway down the stairs, he picked up the intoxicating scent of fried bacon and rounded the corner with renewed enthusiasm.

It was six forty-five on a Friday morning, and Chantelle, still in her robe, was standing over the stove, seeing to it that her family started their day with a hearty breakfast. The O'Connor law firm did not open their office doors until nine o'clock, so she was usually the last one to leave the house. Antonio was already sitting at the kitchen table, fully dressed, wolfing down his scrambled eggs and placing strips of bacon on top of his freshly buttered biscuits. School didn't start until eight, but Antonio needed to be standing at the corner bus stop by seven. The commute to the suburbs was long, with lots of stops in between, which meant that Antonio rarely arrived at Northrop High School before seven fifty, ten minutes before the opening bell.

"Good morning," announced Marquis. "It sure smells good in here."

"Nothing is too good for my family," declared Chantelle. "Pour yourself a cup of coffee."

"Don't mind if I do," obliged Marquis, giving his wife a loving peck on the cheek.

Reaching into the cabinet, he grabbed his favorite mug and headed toward the freshly brewed pot of Folgers. Marquis couldn't determine what energized him more, the caffeine jolt from his coffee, or the stimulation he received each morning from his beautiful wife and her sunny disposition.

"I gotta get going," announced Antonio.

"Make sure you wear a warm coat and a hat," advised Chantelle. "It's twenty-six degrees out there, with a high of only forty-two today."

Exiting the front door each morning without Chantelle's weather report was nearly impossible. She never prepared breakfast without listening to the radio, and like most people in the Midwest, she turned her dial to 1190 AM, WOWO Radio. There was something comforting about the *Little Red Barn* broadcast and the soothing voice of Bob Sievers and the way he delivered the latest news, weather, and farm reports. He was practically an institution, earning the same credibility as Walter Cronkite on the *CBS Evening News*.

"What's the price of corn these days?" teased Marquis. "Have they told you the best time to plant your crops?"

"You can make fun of it all you want," said Chantelle, "but I find it to be quite interesting. You'd be surprised how many of our clients are in agriculture and the huge number of farm-related transactions that take place each year. Some of the largest financial institutions in the Midwest rely upon farmers for the bulk of their business. It's a big part of the economy."

"Okay," said Marquis. "I get it. I meant no disrespect. It's just a lot different from the kind of radio we listened to in New Orleans."

"Well, I still like to listen to music in the evenings, but for me, I like to start off the day with information. It stimulates my brain and gets me ready for work."

"Speaking of work," said Marquis, "what time do you get off today?"

"The usual, around five. What did you have in mind?"

"I thought I'd take you out to dinner. Did you forget that today is the day we get paid our bonus?"

"Oh, that's exciting, but I thought you were going to stash your bonuses away and save up for that Cadillac you always wanted."

"I'm still gonna do that," said Marquis. "But that doesn't mean I can't treat my beautiful wife to a nice dinner."

"Well, I've never been one to turn down dinner. I'm just glad you're getting paid bonuses and content with putting that whole union idea on the back burner."

"Well, it's not exactly on the back burner."

"What do you mean?" asked Chantelle, her curiosity aroused.

"I told you this union thing was much bigger than me. Just because I'm staying in the shadows doesn't mean it's not moving forward. It's not like I can prevent it from happening."

"So what's the latest?" asked Chantelle. "You haven't been talking about it at all. I assumed it was water under the bridge."

"I don't like talking about it because I know it makes you worry. And quite frankly, it makes me worry too."

"Well, I can't bury my head in the sand and pretend it doesn't exist," said Chantelle. "You need to keep me informed. After all, I spend forty hours a week at the O'Connor law firm, and I can't afford to be left in the dark."

"Okay, I get it. It's just that there's a lot of moving parts."

"I'm all ears," said Chantelle as she poured herself another cup of coffee.

"Well, as I told you before, Ernie's been meeting a lot with Marino and a guy named Daniel Myers, the leader of the Buick movement. They've been working really hard behind the scenes, trying to educate the workers about the merits of unions. They had another meeting at the Union Hall last week and there was a much bigger turnout. By the way, it was a meeting that I did *not* attend."

"Okay," said Chantelle. "I get it. You're trying to stay in the background."

"Yes, I'm trying to stay out of it, but that doesn't mean I disagree with what Marino is saying."

"So what's he saying?" asked Chantelle.

"He's saying what Ernie and I already know. The whole bonus plan is just a ploy to detract us from what matters the most."

"Which is what?"

"Which is organizing our labor so that workers are compensated fairly, instead of all the profits going to management."

"So you don't think the bonuses are fair?" challenged Chantelle.

"It's like Ernie said. If we could make thirty percent more by organizing a union, then the company is saving twenty-eight percent by offering us a two percent bonus."

"How do you know you'd make thirty percent more?"

"We don't know it for *sure*. That's just what the industry averages tell us. And here's the kicker. They only pay bonuses to full-time workers. So in the past four weeks, they've reduced the hours of three workers and brought on three more part-time workers, all of them inexperienced. It's all about saving money. They don't have to pay bonuses or benefits to part-time workers."

"Sounds like they're playing hardball," acknowledged Chantelle. "This is what I was afraid of. Things are starting to get ugly."

"And remember that kid they brought in a few weeks ago? Billy Thompson?"

"Yes, I remember."

"I had to spend a whole week training that kid, fresh out of high school with zero experience. He had no knowledge about auto mechanics whatsoever. But guess what?"

"What."

"He's the son of a cop, and he's just thankful to have a job."

"Why does it matter that he's the son of a cop?" asked Chantelle.

"Well, Marino thinks it's another ploy. A way to get the cops on the side of O'Connor Cadillac. After all, it's no secret that management uses the police to break up picket lines. Cops have a reputation for union-busting. Especially if they're being enticed."

"Okay, I get it," confirmed Chantelle. "Like you said, there's a lot of moving parts. I'm just afraid there's a chance that *you* will get moved to part-time, or worse, they will let you go altogether. Our family needs your income."

"Well, I have a couple of things protecting me," said Marquis, speaking as though he was embarrassed.

"Like what?"

"You're not gonna like this, but it's just a fact of life."

Not saying a word, Chantelle just stared at him curiously, worried about what he might reveal next. There were so many layers, it was like peeling back an onion.

"Marino and Ernie told me that I'm Ryan O'Connor's token Black."

"What? How can they say that? That's derogatory! I thought they were on your side."

"They *are* on my side. That's why they're being honest with me. They believe that O'Connor hired me as a protection against unfair hiring practices. After all, how can they be accused of racial discrimination if they hired *me*? That's why I'm probably safer than the rest of my coworkers. Management has a reason to hold on to me."

Chantelle closed her eyes and shook her head with disgust. She was beginning to feel ashamed of her own ignorance. How could she be so naive?

They had moved to Indiana to escape the racism of the South and seek a better standard of living with better jobs and better pay. Finally, after struggling to make ends meet, the breaks were starting to go their way. She thought the Jackson family had turned the corner. Now, she was second-guessing everything. The world was still a cruel place after all.

"So where do we go from here?" asked Chantelle.

"Things could get messy in a hurry. Remember when I told you about distributing cards to the workers? Soliciting their commitment to the Teamsters?"

"Yes, I remember," uttered Chantelle, fearful of the next layer.

"Well, they issued cards to all the Buick and Cadillac workers who were at the last meeting, and then those employees took the remaining cards and distributed them to the rest of the workers. From what I hear, there's already enough of a commitment to bring the issue to a formal vote. All they need is fifty percent, and they think they may have that already."

"Sounds like this thing is really going to happen."

"It ain't over till it's over," said Marquis, trying to be realistic. "But here's the best part. Because there's so much union support, Marino has filed a motion with the NLRB."

"National Labor Relations Board," said Chantelle, showing off her knowledge.

"Yep, and now we're all covered by a 'just cause' clause."

"So nobody can be fired without a just cause," confirmed Chantelle.

"That's right," said Marquis.

"Just so you know, those 'just cause' clauses are not necessarily iron-clad. If Ryan O'Connor really wants to get around that, he'll figure out a way. So you better mind your p's and q's."

"Holy shit!" said Marquis, looking at his watch. "It's almost seven thirty. I gotta get to work."

"All right, just remember what I said. Be careful out there and keep your distance."

"Honey, you don't have to worry about me," said Marquis, grabbing his coat and hat. "You're lucky enough to be married to a token Black."

"Very funny."

"I love you, dear. Don't forget about dinner tonight." And with that, Marquis was out the back door.

Marquis applied the finishing touches to William Bennington's Cadillac. He'd already replaced the brake pads, rotated the tires, and fine-tuned the engine. Now he was making sure the attendants had properly washed the exterior and vacuumed the interior according to specifications, all part of O'Connor Cadillac's white-glove treatment.

Grabbing a towel, Marquis swiped away the few remaining droplets, making sure the shiny surface was not marred by any water spots. This was above and beyond the call of duty, but nothing was too good for Bennington. He was special and he deserved the best that Cadillac had to offer.

Born and raised in Fort Wayne, William Bennington came from humble roots. His father, Edward, immigrated from England shortly after World War I, scratching and clawing to make ends meet, jumping from one odd job to another. Cutting his teeth in the local eateries, Edward performed all the obligatory duties. No task was too menial. He'd been a dishwasher, busboy, waiter, bartender, and cook, ultimately working his way up to restaurant management. On his fortieth birthday, Edward realized his lifelong dream of owning his own restaurant. His southside English pub was small and unassuming, but it was warm and quaint and attracted a loyal following that generated enough income to feed his family.

William Bennington grew up working in the pub, learning the ropes the same way his father had. Although Edward had always assumed his son would take over the family business, William had other ideas. The world was changing, and he didn't see much of a future in owning a small neighborhood pub.

In the United States, the automobile was king, producing a mobile society that was always on the go, in a hurry to get from point A to point B. With people eating on the run, families were no longer gathering around the dinner table the way they had in the past. There was a growing need for convenience; the need for tasty, fast food at affordable prices.

William Bennington recognized that need, and he recognized the fact that most of the great tycoons in American history had embraced new ideas and new technology, blazing their own trails toward success: Rockefeller with petroleum, Carnegie in steel, Vanderbilt with railroads, Henry Ford's mass production of automobiles, and Ray Kroc's mass production of fast food. These great entrepreneurs recognized trends, identified opportunities, and risked everything to achieve success. Bennington decided that he too would take a chance and seize his opportunity. The world would not pass him by.

In 1961, William Bennington convinced the bank to finance his first big break, the opportunity to purchase and manage his very own McDonald's hamburger franchise. Two years later, Bennington opened his second McDonald's franchise, and by the end of the decade, William Bennington had become the proud owner of eleven McDonald's franchises and four Pizza Huts, cornering most of the market in northeastern Indiana.

Along the way, Bennington served thousands of happy customers and accumulated a significant fortune. The mass production of fast food had been very good to him, generating esteemed wealth and widespread notoriety. A prominent fixture in the community, he had achieved a level of status surpassed by few. His power and affluence, according to some, rivaled that of the O'Connor family, although Ryan O'Connor quickly dismissed such notions as nonsense, disparaging Bennington as nothing more than a glorified burger-flipper.

It was in one of those Pizza Hut restaurants that Marquis Jackson met William Bennington for the first time. He and Chantelle were sharing a pepperoni pizza and sipping on beer when a gentleman approached their table and extended his hand. He introduced himself as the owner and wanted to know if the food and service had met their expectations.

Marquis was thoroughly impressed. He had never had a White business owner of such distinction go out of his way to shake his hand, let alone inquire if the level of service had met his standards. When

Bennington asked Marquis where he worked, the conversation quickly turned to their shared love of Cadillacs. From that point on, William Bennington insisted that Marquis Jackson would be the only technician allowed to service his Cadillac. He wanted a man of good character to take care of his vehicle, and there was no one he trusted more than Marquis.

William Bennington purchased his car from O'Connor Cadillac in the summer of 1970. He had read about Cadillac producing its four millionth vehicle in 1969, manufacturing over a million in the previous five years alone. In celebration, General Motors created a great deal of fanfare, inviting newspaper reporters and television crews to witness and capture the historic event. Hundreds of spectators were in the building as the made-to-order Cadillac, a Coupe De Ville in Astral Blue Metallic, rolled off the assembly line in Detroit, Michigan, its proud owner posing for pictures and ceremoniously accepting the keys.

Overwhelmed by this moment in history, William Bennington decided to order a replica, his very own keepsake of automotive excellence. Recognizing the significance of this manufacturing milestone, Bennington wanted his own token of remembrance. He couldn't help but relate it to the signs he proudly displayed on the golden arches of his restaurants: Over 8 Billion Served.

The price of Bennington's new Coupe De Ville was $6,499, which was a lot of money in 1970, considering the average annual income for a US citizen was around $9,000 and the median cost of a house was close to $16,000.

Although William Bennington came from humble roots and recognized the value of a dollar, he had gained an appreciation for style and luxury, and the price of his new Cadillac was a mere drop in the bucket for a man of his means. He could have purchased five if he wanted to, but extravagance was never a part of his persona. Lucky for him, his new Cadillac rolled off the assembly line just before the historic UAW strike of 1970.

The 1960s had been kind to the US auto industry, experiencing unprecedented growth. Nothing celebrated American grit and determination more than the mass production of automobiles, and in 1960, American factories churned out over six million vehicles. By the end of the decade, annual production had risen to over 8.7 million, increasing by 40 percent.

Leading the way was General Motors (GM), with Ford and Chrysler finishing a distant second and third. Producing close to 4.5 million vehicles in 1969, GM's line of vehicles dominated the industry, led by its entry-level Chevrolet, which composed nearly half of its production. But the popularity of GM's other lines contributed significantly, with each sequential model rising in prestige: Pontiac, Oldsmobile, Buick, and Cadillac.

It was a powerhouse lineup that dominated the industry, an industry that led the world. It was estimated, in the United States, that one out of every six jobs were linked to the auto industry, either directly or indirectly, and the bulk of these jobs were in the Midwest. The American economy was riding the wave and there seemed to be no end in sight.

But not everything was smooth sailing. Unbeknownst to many, the prevailing winds were shifting, and the seas were getting choppy. Factory workers were increasingly being pressed to meet aggressive production schedules, resulting in longer hours, more fatigue, and less leisure time with family. The monotony of performing routine and mundane tasks on an assembly line, coupled with the stress of unrealistic performance objectives, proved to be detrimental to workers' safety and health, both mental and physical. Compensation, a major incentive for many years, was no longer the great equalizer.

Over the first half of the 60s, inflation rates had hovered between 1 and 2 percent, barely raising an eyebrow. By the end of the decade, inflation had reared its ugly head, rising annually at 6 percent in 1969 and 1970, impacting the livelihood of working-class Americans.

For the first time in a decade, wage earners were experiencing a decline in their standard of living. Worker grievances and wildcat strikes were escalating, reaching levels not seen since the midforties. With rising tension and growing hostility, contract negotiations between GM and the UAW had reached a boiling point.

But the American worker was not the only one feeling the pressure. GM's executive leadership was increasingly under the gun to explain its subpar performance. Profits and dividends had been declining since 1965, and stockholders wanted answers. But the answers came with few resolutions.

GM's challenges were considerable and growing by the day. The rising cost of labor and raw materials were two of the biggest concerns, and borrowing costs (interest rates) were the highest in a century. Meanwhile, productivity had fallen dramatically, fueled by increased absenteeism and work stoppages. CEO James Roche announced that GM had lost over thirteen million labor hours in 1969 due to wildcat strikes. Unless labor relations improved, business wasn't going to get any better.

Adding to management's concerns were the skyrocketing costs of health care. Medical benefits, one of the signature achievements of collective bargaining, had long been a staple of UAW perks. But in 1970, health care costs were rising at double the rate of inflation. Management insisted that workers would have to share the burden, but rank-and-file employees weren't likely to offer concessions as long as their grievances were left unresolved, and their standard of living was dwindling. The prospect of a confrontation seemed inevitable.

As if rising costs and labor disputes weren't enough, the US auto industry was faced with another growing dilemma: foreign competition. In 1970, a record 1.3 million automobiles were imported to the United States, representing 16 percent of US auto sales. Led by Toyota and Honda, Japanese auto production could no longer be dismissed as a trivial sideshow. The Japanese had created a work culture that was unparalleled, producing high-quality, low-cost vehicles that were reliable, economical, and aesthetically pleasing.

As GM struggled with costs, labor, and profitability, its monopoly was shrinking. With so much at stake, management went to the bargaining table with a hardline approach. Acquiescence was no longer a virtue. If GM was to compete and survive, labor would need to make sacrifices. They needed to strike a balance.

On September 15, 1970, over four hundred thousand UAW members went on strike, shutting down 145 GM plants across the United States and Canada. As production came to a halt, General Motors, the largest corporation in the world, was brought to its knees. The strike would go on to last sixty-seven days, bringing untold hardship to working families and triggering hard feelings that would linger for years. When it was all said and done, GM would report over one billion dollars in lost profits, sending shock waves throughout the US economy and handicapping every business that relied upon the strength and prosperity of a thriving General Motors.

At the time of the strike, the average hourly wage of a US auto worker was around four dollars per hour, considerably more than the federal minimum wage of $1.60. When the strike was over, negotiators had inked a deal locking in annual wage increases of 5.8 percent over the next three years, keeping pace with the latest inflationary trends. Workers had given up on their hopes for dental insurance, but they were able to hold the line on other insurance provisions and gain concessions on management's productivity initiatives.

All in all, it was considered a victory for the UAW and its members, providing stability for years to come. While management painted a rosy picture, they were clearly licking their wounds, attempting to reconcile further setbacks in their ongoing struggles with labor, costs, and profitability. Without many options, they would regroup and go back to the drawing board, relentlessly pursuing a formula that would enable them to compete in an ever-changing world.

"Mr. Bennington, good morning! How are you today, sir?" groveled Neil Bowers.

"Doing well, thank you."

"Your vehicle is ready to go. I'll have someone bring it around for you."

"That's okay," said William Bennington. "I usually go back and get the full report from Marquis Jackson. He *is* back there, isn't he?"

"Yes, but I believe he's working on another vehicle right now."

"That's okay, he'll take the time for me," said Bennington, as he skirted around Bowers and opened the door to the service garage.

Bowers thought about intervening but backed away. Customers were not allowed in the shop area, let alone to talk with service technicians. They were supposed to get the service summary from him, the supervisor. Ryan O'Connor wanted his customers to speak with men of pedigree, not the grease monkeys doing the manual labor.

"Marquis, how are you doing?" waved Bennington, as he walked to the back of the maintenance area, weaving his way through the service bays and scattered spare parts. Marquis looked up nervously, knowing that customers were not allowed in the garage.

"Good to see you again," said Bennington, extending his hand with a warm smile.

"I don't think you want to shake this hand," said Marquis, embarrassed by the attention. "It's covered with grease and grime."

"Don't be ridiculous. Any hand that works on my Caddie is good enough for me," said Bennington, grabbing Marquis's hand and shaking it vigorously.

Marquis then grabbed a clean towel and handed it to Bennington, allowing him to clean up. "It's just part of our white-glove treatment," joked Marquis.

"I'll take it." Bennington laughed. "It's just like you to have my best interest in mind. That's why you're the only one I trust with my baby."

"Your baby is right over there," said Marquis, pointing to the Astral Blue Coupe De Ville.

"I see," said Bennington. "It looks like you got her all shined up."

"Yes, sir. I replaced the brake pads. The rear pads were more worn than the front, which is typically the case, but they all needed to be replaced. You should be good to go for another thirty thousand miles."

"Perfect," said Bennington. "And the steering. I told you it was pulling a little to the left."

"Yes, sir. It's taken care of. I aligned the front end, so it should glide along real smooth now. You could probably take your hands off the wheel and go perfectly straight for a hundred yards. That's how well it's aligned."

"That's what I wanted to hear," said Bennington. "Sounds like the ultimate in cruise control," he joked.

"I rotated the tires," continued Marquis. "The front ones were a little more worn than the back, but now you're good to go another five thousand miles before the next rotation. Looking at the treads, I think you'll get twenty thousand more miles out of those Goodyears. Unless you drive it like a race car."

"Ha, very funny. You know I treat it like a baby."

"Yes, sir. I don't blame you. She's a real beauty."

"Anything else?" asked Bennington.

"No, sir. I filled out your service record and placed it in the glove compartment. You'll be due for your next oil change in five thousand miles, the same time that we'll rotate your tires."

Marquis then handed Bennington the keys and opened the door for him, just like a full-service valet attendant.

"See you next time," said Bennington. "You take care. Tell Chantelle I said hello."

"I will sir. You have a good weekend."

Marquis couldn't believe that William Bennington remembered Chantelle's name. Of all the important people in his life, it seemed unlikely for him to remember something so trivial, the name of someone he only met once and would probably never see again. To Marquis, it spoke volumes about Bennington's character. He really cared about people.

Bennington waved one last time as he drove off in his Coupe De Ville. "Go ahead and bill me. You know the routine."

It always gave Marquis a warm feeling to see satisfied customers driving away, glowing with pride, filled with the special kind of self-esteem that comes with owning a Cadillac.

With Bennington barely out of sight, Neil Bowers swooped in. "You know I don't like this little arrangement you have. It goes against all of our policies and procedures."

"Understood," said Marquis. "I guess he just likes to be treated special. I'm only trying to satisfy another customer."

"That's my job," said Bowers. "It's important we all know our proper places."

"Understood, but I'm not the one who let him back here."

Bowers looked at Marquis indignantly, clearly irritated by his retort, then turned around in frustration, unable to counter Marquis's logic. Walking away, he looked over his shoulder and issued a directive, "Come on back to the break room. We're all meeting there in five minutes."

On paydays, checks were normally distributed at 8:00 a.m., just before the technicians hit the floor. On this Friday, they were told their paychecks would be issued at 10:00 a.m. There was no explanation as to why, but everyone assumed it was because of the quarterly bonus. Ernie told Marquis it was yet another opportunity for management to toot their own horn, to make a big deal out of something so trivial as a

2 percent bonus, something that was no more significant than tossing a bone.

With the employees gathered around, the breakroom door opened as Neil Bowers and Ryan O'Connor made their grand entrance. Bowers was carrying a pack of envelopes wrapped in a rubber band. Ryan was wearing a three-piece pin-striped suit, and looking more like a banker or a lawyer than someone who was about to address a group of garage attendants. There were a few surprised looks and menacing glances. Ryan had never set foot in this part of the dealership before. The service technicians had only seen him when they were invited into the showroom for the employee appreciation celebrations, or as Ernie called them, the dog and pony shows.

"As you can see, we have a special guest today," announced Bowers. "Thank you for joining us."

"Thank you for having me," said Ryan. "Today is a special day and I really wanted to be a part of it. I'd like to start out by thanking everyone in this room for their hard work. Your efforts have not gone unnoticed. You've earned your just reward, and I'm here to deliver on a promise. It is my hope that this is the first of many bonuses to come. As long as you continue to hold up your end of the bargain, I will ensure that you are rewarded accordingly. Now, without further ado, I will allow Neil to explain the specifics."

"Thank you," said Bowers. "As you should already know, today's paychecks will reflect a special two percent quarterly bonus. It is only available to full-time employees. You all know who you are. In addition to your normal biweekly pay, eighty hours, your paystubs will reflect a special line item for the bonus calculation. It's really very simple, it shows your total wages for the third quarter and multiplies it by two percent."

"It sounds simple," said O'Connor, "but I can assure you it took a fair amount of manipulation in our payroll systems to accommodate this new wrinkle. So I'd like to give a shout-out to our back-office people for making this happen."

There it was, management patting themselves on the back once again, making it sound like they would bend over backward to appease their rank-and-file workers. Ernie looked over at Marquis and rolled his eyes, clearly displaying his disgust.

"Okay," said Bowers. "That's all I have. I'll go ahead and distribute the checks. Make sure you check your bonus calculations. If anything appears out-of-line, let me know and I will hook you up with our payroll clerk."

"Thanks again, everyone," said Ryan, exiting the door. "Enjoy your weekend."

Bowers distributed the envelopes, telling everyone they had ten minutes to get back on the floor.

Marquis already knew what to expect as everyone ripped open their envelopes. He and Chantelle had made the calculation ahead of time (65 workdays X 8 hours X $2.75 X 2 percent). That amounted to a bonus of approximately twenty-eight bucks. He figured that would be consistent with everyone else, except, of course, the part-timers.

For Billy Thompson, this was his first paycheck ever. Although he wouldn't be getting a bonus, he anxiously ripped open his envelope, curious to see the bottom line, his so-called take-home pay.

Marquis scanned the paystub and found the bonus line. There it was, $28.60, right in line with expectations. Reassured, Marquis stuffed it back into the envelope, and headed toward his locker. Ernie was already at his locker and flashed Marquis an ornery grin. Marquis was ready for it, Ernie's perpetual skepticism and sarcastic commentary.

"Don't spend your thirty-six bucks all at once," warned Ernie. "Winter's around the corner and you might need it to pay your gas bill."

Not surprised by Ernie's cynicism, Marquis didn't respond. Then it suddenly sank in...thirty-six bucks.

"Is that what you got?" asked Marquis. "Thirty-six bucks?"

"Thirty-six and change. Are you not seeing that? It won't be *exactly* the same for everyone, but we all pretty much make the same wages around here, don't we? At least I thought we did."

Marquis became strangely quiet. Suddenly his twenty-eight bucks didn't seem so adequate. Was he getting screwed? His knowledge and experience outranked Ernie's, and he was already working at O'Connor's when Ernie came on board. Was there something wrong with his math? Something wasn't right.

"Hey, what's bothering you?" asked Ernie.

"I don't know," said Marquis. "How long have you been working here now."

"About two and a half years. Why?"

"It's been a little over three years for me," said Marquis.

"So what's your point?"

"Ernie," said Marquis, in a softer, more sincere tone. "Do you mind if I ask you a personal question?"

"You can always ask. Then I'll decide if I wanna answer."

Marquis leaned in close and whispered, "Can you tell me how much money you make? I mean your hourly wage?"

Ernie started laughing.

"I'm sorry," apologized Marquis. "I've never asked anyone that question before."

"No, it's okay," he chuckled. "I'm laughing 'cause I thought you were gonna ask something way more personal than that. Like maybe my sex life or something."

"No," said Marquis, relieved by Ernie's good humor. "I already assumed you're gettin' more action than everyone else around here."

"I wish," said Ernie. "I'm making three-fifty an hour. Isn't that what you're making?"

Marquis took a deep breath and swallowed hard. He could feel his heart beat faster and his blood pressure rise. Those sons of bitches, he thought to himself. Then he looked over at Billy Thompson, still sitting on the bench, studying his paystub.

"What's the matter Billy? Can't you figure it out?"

"I didn't expect so many taxes to be taken out," complained Billy. "Can you look at this and see if it's right?"

That's exactly what Marquis wanted to hear. He walked over and pulled the paystub out of Billy's hand like he was dealing with a third grader. His eyes zoomed in on the line item he was looking for, a line that had nothing to do with taxes. There it was, as plain as the nose on his face: three dollars per hour. Marquis tossed the stub back at Billy flippantly. "It looks okay to me. Don't you know that Uncle Sam always gets his piece of the pie?"

Marching away, he headed to the garage without uttering another word, his irritation turning to fury.

"What's gotten into him?" asked Billy.

"I'm not sure," said Ernie. "Perhaps a dose of reality."

At 5:05 p.m., Marquis was already in the parking lot. He had never been in such a hurry to leave work. His evening plans and entire weekend were now ruined. Chantelle was expecting him to come home in a good mood. How could he explain to her that he was no longer interested in their romantic dinner?

"Hey, hold up a second," said Ernie, as Marquis opened his car door. "I need to talk to you."

Marquis hesitated, allowing Ernie a chance to speak.

"What's wrong? Something is obviously bothering you."

"Is Marino still holding our union meeting next week?" inquired Marquis.

"Yep, Wednesday at seven thirty."

"Well, I'm all in," said Marquis.

"That's good. Why the change of heart?"

"How about the protest group?" asked Marquis. "Are y'all still planning on holding signs on the street corner?"

"That's in the works. Details to be continued."

"Well, I'm all in," said Marquis.

"I'm glad to hear it. Now can I ask *you* a personal question?"

"Shoot," said Marquis.

"How much is your hourly rate of pay?"

"Bingo," said Marquis. "I guess you figured out what's bothering me."

"I'm listening."

"Two dollars and seventy-five fuckin' cents! That little punk I trained last week is getting paid three dollars an hour. And you're making seventy-five cents more than me, every single hour of every single day. That ain't chump change."

"They're screwin' ya, pal."

"Tell me about it!"

"They can't do that if the Teamsters Union negotiates our contracts," said Ernie.

"When I started here three years ago, they offered me two-fifty an hour. I thought that was fair enough considering I was new and minimum wage was a buck sixty. I never got paid much more than minimum wage in New Orleans. Then they raised it a couple times to two-seventy-five. How was I to know that everyone else was makin' a lot more? I guess that's the going rate for a token Black."

"Welcome aboard the union train, Marquis. Together we're gonna make this thing happen. Then *everyone* will be better off."

Chapter 47

THE YEAR 1973 HAD BEEN tough for Ryan O'Connor. The rapid growth of his empire in the 60s had plateaued in recent years, exhibiting signs of vulnerability. For the first time in his life, expansion was no longer a priority. Instead, Ryan was coming to terms with the cold reality of economic headwinds and the distinct possibility that his businesses may contract, a concept that was foreign to his philosophy.

He knew that wealth was a product of growth, and growth didn't happen without investment, and investments couldn't be made without capital, and capital came from lenders, and banks didn't lend money without performance assurances. It was all part of the risk management process, leveraging the future with investment capital and delivering on promises.

The prime lending rate, an interest rate offered by banks to their best customers, had risen from 6 percent to nearly 10 percent in 1973. As a valued customer, Ryan O'Connor had always borrowed money at prime lending rates, sometimes below prime rates because of his excellent credit history and strong relationships with bankers.

That had all changed. As the economy became more turbulent, sparking uncertainty and fear, bankers were reluctant to lend, unwilling to increase their exposure to debt. As a result, O'Connor Enterprises was feeling the pinch. Not only were banks becoming stingier, but the cost of existing debt had increased by 60 percent, escalating expenditures, eroding profits, and creating a business climate that was challenging at best.

Ryan O'Connor, no stranger to adversity, had always risen to the challenge. As a student of economics, he understood consumer behavior and how it relates to the production, distribution, and sale of goods. He was prepared to navigate the economic turbulence and arrive at a formula that would weather the storm. But he was not prepared for the sudden turn of events that would occur halfway around the globe, sending geopolitical shock waves that threatened the very foundation of the US economy.

No longer capable of meeting its growing demand for oil domestically, the United States had become increasingly reliant upon the strength and stability of the Middle East, a region of Arab nations sitting on the planet's richest oil reserves. Their growing influence on global markets was irrefutable, controlling supply and access to the world's most valuable commodity. The United States, with its insatiable appetite for oil, could no longer operate in a vacuum.

On October 6, 1973, an Arab coalition, led by Egypt and Syria, launched a surprise attack against Israel on the Jewish holy day of Yom Kippur. Egypt, owner and operator of the Suez Canal, controlled the flow of oil from the Red Sea to the Mediterranean. By attacking the Sinai Peninsula, the canal's eastern bank, Egypt was seeking to destroy Israel and gain a stronger foothold in the region, an area that was no stranger to conflict.

The United States, a longtime supporter of a Jewish free state and a persistent mediator for Middle East peace, was stuck in the middle. But when the Soviet Union started shipping weapons to Egypt and Syria, the US felt a need to intervene. With President Nixon's $2.2 billion pledge of Israeli support, American planes started delivering weapons and supplies to Israel on October 14.

The Arab response was short and swift. Two days later, the Organization of Arab Petroleum Exporting Countries (OAPEC) instituted an oil embargo on the United States. The embargo halted all oil exports from OAPEC nations to the US and initiated a series of production cuts that would create worldwide shortages and cause prices to soar.

The global price of oil soon quadrupled, going from three dollars per barrel to nearly twelve dollars per barrel. Nobody felt the pain more than Americans. When gas stations started running out of fuel, some states enacted gas-rationing laws, but these stopgap measures only exacerbated the problem, causing long lines at the pump and adding to consumer frustration.

The price of gasoline, thirty-four cents per gallon before the embargo, almost tripled as it peaked at eighty-four cents per gallon. The widespread availability of affordable gasoline, once a foregone conclusion in the United States, had ceased to exist. Like never before, Americans were looking for ways to economize their consumption and make ends meet.

When it came to fuel consumption, Ryan O'Connor's business was at the top of the food chain. Nothing guzzled gasoline more than big, bulky, luxury automobiles, and Buicks and Cadillacs led the way. But being on top of this food chain was not an advantage. In 1973, a Cadillac DeVille weighed over five thousand pounds and delivered only seven miles per gallon.

This was no longer acceptable. Gasoline was too expensive. Americans were looking for smaller, economical forms of transportation, and Japanese imports were leading the way. Almost overnight, new-car stickers featured prominent displays of mpg (miles per gallon), a growing priority in consumer demand.

Although Ryan O'Connor had built a business on customer satisfaction, his hands were tied. He was suddenly at the mercy of the manufacturer, and General Motors could not reengineer their automobile designs and restructure their assembly lines overnight. Ryan's best option, a Toyota dealership, had proven to be fruitless. Despite his repeated attempts, he was unable to leverage his clout and reputation with the Japanese the same way he had with automobile executives in Detroit.

As new-car sales plummeted, Ryan's one saving grace was the continuous flow of service revenue. He knew that servicing existing customers had always been the bread and butter of his operations. But now that silver lining was in jeopardy too, threatened by worker dissatisfaction and their attempts to unionize. Worried about his future, Ryan had spent many sleepless nights trying to determine the best course of action.

Since most of the economic roadblocks were out of his control, he decided to focus on his own backyard. If there was one thing he could and must do, it would be to stop the Teamsters and their precipitous takeover of his labor force. He would do everything in his power to prevent such an injustice. Defeat was not an option.

But O'Connor Enterprises was more than a conglomerate of car dealerships. Ventures into real estate had generated some hefty profits over the years, diversifying the portfolio and anchoring the balance sheet with tangible assets. As Fort Wayne grew and expanded, Ryan O'Connor stayed one step ahead of the curve, purchasing unused land with borrowed money and developing it for commercial and residential use. Selling his developments at huge margins, he would then take the profits, satisfy creditors, and reinvest; anticipating a consistent, never-ending cycle.

Leveraging businesses during periods of expansion can be lucrative, but a stagnant economy can diminish a portfolio built on speculative growth. Saddled with vast parcels of vacant land, and no one willing to invest, O'Connor Enterprises had reached a crossroads. The economy had stalled, banks weren't lending, and businesses weren't expanding. For the first time in his career, Ryan O'Connor was contemplating selling off some of his assets at a loss.

Conversely, O'Connor's rental properties continued to function as his mainstay, generating steady profits and positive cash flows. As the cost of living increased, along with utilities, maintenance, and property taxes, Ryan simply raised the rent. Often, he would raise rents automatically each year—even if the cost of living was unchanged—betting that tenants would sign the new leases anyway and pay the higher fees in order to avoid the headache of relocation.

If there was one chink in the armor, it was the fact that some of his properties were growing old, requiring new investments in infrastructure. And that meant new roofs, siding, plumbing, appliances, fixtures, electrical wiring, heating, and air conditioning. But with a sluggish economy, Ryan continued to procrastinate, delaying the inevitable and forcing his tenants to deal with pesky repairs and lingering inconveniences.

It was during a December cold front that Ryan O'Connor received the kind of publicity that can destroy a businessman's reputation. As the temperatures dipped into the single digits, one of his older apartment buildings lost its heat, leaving residents in frigid conditions and deteriorating an already frosty relationship.

As if chilled-to-the-bone residents weren't bad enough, the extreme cold had caused the pipes to burst, sending gushes of water through walls and ceilings, and destroying carpets, furniture, and anything else in its path.

Forced from their apartments, dozens of damp and frozen tenants huddled together on the street corner wrapped in blankets. WANE-TV was quick to arrive and report the entire episode on the eleven o'clock news. Despite repeated attempts to get a statement from Ryan O'Connor, the local news was unable to solicit a response.

Realizing the potential to uncover a big story, *The Journal Gazette* spent the next two weeks investigating Ryan O'Connor's rental properties, interviewing dozens of tenants about their squalid living conditions and exorbitant rents.

As the investigation unfolded, exposing a long list of issues and complaints, the newspaper decided to reveal its findings in a documentary style feature that would appear on the front page of the Sunday *Journal Gazette*, a newspaper that would be delivered two days before Christmas and reach 80 percent of Fort Wayne's doorsteps. No shortcuts would be taken. This would be the kind of investigative journalism that could win them a Pulitzer Prize.

When the Sunday papers arrived, the headlines jumped off the page, plastered across the top in large, bold print: "*Ryan O'Connor—Slumlord Millionaire.*"

Underneath the heading, the subtitle characterized the story as a special three-part investigative report. The third and final installment would appear on Christmas day, a perfect way to fill the newspaper with content while journalists were home with their families, temporarily free from production deadlines.

The story proved to be comprehensive and hard-hitting, portraying landlords as greedy and merciless, while commiserating with renters as distressed victims of exploitation. The list of disputes went on and on, one example after another, from crumbling floors to leaky roofs, toilets that wouldn't flush and sockets that wouldn't produce electricity.

While some renters allowed themselves to be identified, others were not as bold, choosing to remain anonymous with their accusations. One woman admitted she was afraid to take out the garbage, as "there were always rats scurrying around, and rats carry diseases." Another woman said her stove didn't work and it took two weeks to get it fixed. "I had to eat out all the time and I can't afford to do that." Adam Wright, unafraid to identify himself, talked about his refrigerator. "I'd rather have a broken stove than a broken refrigerator. It took them ten days to repair my fridge. Meanwhile, all my food rotted." Another man complained about his rent. "I was out of town for a week and rushed to the leasing office to pay my rent. My check was only one day late. They said it didn't matter. All past due payments owed twenty dollars in late fees."

Ryan O'Connor was mortified. He had never suffered such humiliation, and he wasn't going to take it sitting down. He called the newspaper and insisted upon speaking with the editor, demanding a full retraction. Never had he witnessed such a one-sided report. It was a total smear job, and they would be held accountable. He would sue them for slander and the litigation would come swiftly; justice would be served.

But with actual witnesses, work orders, signed documents, and taped interviews, the editor insisted *The Journal Gazette* would stand behind its story. They were merely reporting factual instances and quoting real tenants.

Ryan countered with accusations of bias, inflammatory assumptions, and incendiary reporting. "Journalism is supposed to be balanced," he demanded. But the editor held his ground, citing numerous attempts for a response, with Ryan never returning his calls.

It was yet another setback in a year filled with obstacles. But this was more than a mere blemish. This had turned into a complete debacle, causing irreparable harm to Ryan's reputation as a community leader. Men like him were supposed to be immune from condemnation, or so he thought. Facing the aftermath could get dicey, especially when dealing with the doubters and naysayers, the ones who were questioning his integrity.

But Ryan's credibility had been under fire for some time, resulting mostly from his stubborn leadership in the Republican Party. As a staunch supporter of President Nixon, he continued to defend his party's leader against all charges, irrationally supporting his innocence despite growing evidence to the contrary. As the damaging testimony continued to evolve, Ryan remained defiant, insisting that Nixon was a victim of character assassination and would rise above his detractors fully exonerated.

The evidence said otherwise.

On February 5, 1973, North Carolina Senator Samuel James Irvin Jr., introduced S.Res.60: a resolution to establish a select committee of the Senate to conduct an investigation and study of the extent, if any, to which illegal, improper, or unethical activities were engaged in by any persons, acting individually or in combination with others, in the presidential election of 1972, or any campaign, canvass, or other activity related to it.

Two days later, the resolution was passed by a vote of 77-0, unanimously supported by Democrats and Republicans.

In April, John Dean, President Nixon's chief White House counsel, agreed to cooperate with the Senate Watergate committee. Nixon responded by firing John Dean on April 30. On that same day, two other Nixon confidants handed in their resignations: White House counsel John Ehrlichman, and Chief of Staff H. R. Haldeman. The resignations, widely regarded as forced, reflected Nixon's growing desperation and his attempt to maintain power. The inner circle was beginning to crumble and America was bracing for the next domino to fall.

The ensuing period, forever immortalized as the summer of Watergate, would be like no hitherto period in US history. Never before had the American people been exposed to such widespread corruption in the White House, an endearing symbol of democracy.

Starting in May and running all the way through August, the Watergate hearings were broadcast daily on live television, Monday through Friday. The three major networks, ABC, NBC, and CBS, agreed to share the telecasts, alternating their coverage with three-day rotations. As the daily interrogations unfolded, creating a spectacle that was pure Americana, the melodramatic storylines rivaled that of the most popular soap operas. Watergate had become the new *Days of Our Lives*.

When John Dean took the witness stand in June, the proceedings reached a dramatic climax. Surrounded by reporters, John Dean was thrust into a spotlight he never wanted. Soon he would become a household name, and his wife, Maureen, would become somewhat of a celebrity herself as the cameras exploited her platinum blond hair and glamorous good looks.

As the testimony unfolded, Dean proceeded to reveal the inner workings of the Watergate break-in and the subsequent cover-up, becoming the first person to implicate President Nixon directly. He testified that he had warned the president of the risk and legality of participating in a cover-up, telling him: "There was a cancer growing on the presidency, and if the cancer wasn't removed, the president would be killed by it."

But the president, he asserted, did not heed his warnings, choosing instead to abandon principle and continue down the path of deception. When John Dean's testimony concluded, the president vehemently denied all charges. Although Nixon's credibility had taken a hit, the legal impact was minimal; there was no corroborating evidence. It was still John Dean's word versus that of the president, and the debates would rage on over the virtues of honesty versus loyalty. John Dean had become the lightning rod.

In July, White House aide Alexander Butterfield informed the Senate Watergate Committee that Nixon had secretly recorded all Oval Office conversations, including those that might incriminate him and his coconspirators. If true, the Senate Watergate Committee could finally have access to the direct evidence it needed.

As leader of the investigation, Special Prosecutor Archibald Cox had no choice but to subpoena the tapes. He had been appointed to the position by Nixon's attorney general, Elliot Richardson, under the recommendation of the US Senate. Although the attorney general is considered the chief legal counsel for the president, the position also heads up the Department of Justice, an agency that represents the United States government in all legal matters. The conflicts of interest were apparent, and the boundaries were blurred. Nixon's attorney general, Elliot Richardson, had obligations to both the president and the US government.

When President Nixon received the subpoena, he refused to release the tapes, citing his right to executive privilege as president. Nixon then ordered Cox to drop his subpoena, exercising an authority that appeared to be out of his jurisdiction. Archibald Cox denied the order.

The breaking point in the Watergate investigation occurred on October 19, when John Dean pled guilty to obstruction of justice, the result of his "hush money" payments to Watergate burglars. He then surrendered himself to US Marshals and was confined to a special "safe house," where he would continue to cooperate with Special Prosecutor Archibald Cox. The next day, all hell broke loose; a day that would go down in history as the "Saturday Night Massacre."

President Nixon ordered his attorney general, Elliot Richardson, to fire the special prosecutor, Archibald Cox. Richardson refused to follow orders and resigned. When the deputy attorney general, William Ruckelshaus, rejected similar orders and resigned, Nixon directed the third most senior official at the Justice Department, Solicitor General Robert Bork, to carry out his orders. Bork fired Cox immediately, obliging Nixon's orders.

Shocked by the sudden turn of events, Americans viewed their president as a man acting out of desperation, blatantly trying to end a Senate investigation by firing those in charge. Destroyed by his own undoing, Nixon's credibility had hit rock bottom.

Infuriated by Nixon's gross abuse of power, members of Congress immediately went to work on their articles of impeachment, documenting a list of charges to be used as a basis for removing him from office. After US District Judge Gerhard Gesell ruled the firing of Archibald Cox to be illegal, Leon Jaworski was subsequently appointed as the new special prosecutor.

On November 17, during a televised question-and-answer session with the Associated Press, Nixon issued the following statement: "People have got to know whether or not their president is a crook. Well, I'm not a crook. I've earned everything I've got."

For the O'Connor family, the holiday season was unlike any in recent history. Instead of joy and good tidings, there was a sense of gloom and doom. Although the eighteen-foot Christmas tree was trimmed to the hilt and the estate was glittering with lights, it did little to ease the anxiety, creating instead a melancholy mood that only dampened their spirits.

Concerned over his businesses and reputation, Ryan O'Connor was under a lot of stress, leaving little time to relax and enjoy the holidays with his family. Besides, the very concept of family had seemingly lost its meaning, no longer existing in the image of his idealistic world. Roselyn, becoming more distant and despondent, was no longer attentive to her husband's rigid routine, let alone his every whim. Sleeping in separate quarters and barely communicating, their exchanges had become icy cold, filled with tension, and forced out of necessity. Their marriage had turned into a climate of coexistence, lacking any sense of empathy or goodwill.

But Ryan O'Connor had learned how to cope. Family had never been his first priority anyway, unless he was molding it into an image that reflected his wealth and power. More and more he was distancing himself from home, joining clients for dinner, and entertaining guests at the Summit Club.

Sometimes late at night, after too many rounds of scotch, Ryan O'Connor would come home feeling amorous. Tiptoeing up the stairs, he would approach the master bedroom and turn the doorknob. But it was always locked. Once, he even knocked on the door but received no response, making him wonder why he ever came home at all.

He knew there was no longer any love in their marriage, but they were Catholics, and the Church would never sanction a divorce. Besides, the last thing he wanted to do was go through the scandal of a broken marriage and the nightmare of splitting up his beloved assets. Instead, he would maintain the public facade, pretending that family values and the sanctity of marriage were at the very core of his being.

But the biggest barrier to any semblance of a normal Christmas was the return of Christine. Home for the holidays, it was the first time any of them had seen her since summer. For Ryan O'Connor, it was the first time he'd been in Christine's presence since learning about Michael Williams, her Black boyfriend in Chicago.

Preferring to leave the topic untouched, Roselyn had warned her husband to let sleeping dogs lie. "College romances can be fleeting," she advised. "Sometimes it's best to let these things run their course and die a natural death. Christine is a smart gal. Once the sizzle is gone, she'll look at things in a more practical manner. We have to trust her instincts and judgment."

Never one to take his wife's advice, Ryan realized there was some logic to her approach. Although he was compelled to lecture Christine about her future and the reputation of O'Connor's good name, he just couldn't muster up the energy to wage a confrontation that could turn ugly and destroy what little holiday spirit remained.

There was already a lot of tension in the air for a lot of different reasons, and Christine's presence only added to the stress. She had been moping around like a zombie, acting as though her two-week stay was more of a sentence than a vacation. Nobody knew if her moodiness was from boyfriend problems or the fact that she was back home again, insecure with the ones who had scorned her and shamed her poor judgment.

But the O'Connors would put on a front. They would gather around the tree on Christmas Eve and open their presents, putting aside their family problems for a few short hours and pretending that everything was normal, even though the past year had been anything but normal. And they would be joined by Lynda Lacey, a stabilizing force that would ease the family tension. When Ryan O'Connor insisted that she join the festivities, Quinn was only too happy to oblige. Lynda's company was always a pleasant distraction, delivering a degree of equilibrium, and like a sedative, soothing Quinn's enduring anxiety.

As far as Ryan O'Connor was concerned, the most positive development of 1973 had been the blossoming relationship between his son and the vibrant young gal with impeccable credentials. She was everything Quinn wasn't: confident, assertive, and ready to take on the world. And if she made Ryan O'Connor happy, then Quinn would be happy too.

The fact is, Quinn hadn't been receiving much attention from his father; and he was just fine with that, since attention usually meant lectures on academics, tennis rankings, and goal-setting. For Quinn, staying under the radar was his biggest goal; that and avoiding the comparisons to his older brother, who was a valedictorian and president of his class.

Even though Quinn had the pedigree and good looks, he wasn't cut from the same cloth as Shane. Shane was his father's son, whereas Quinn favored his mother. Shane was a man's man, born to lead and take charge, while Quinn was more introverted and accommodating, graciously appeasing his comrades in order to mesh into the mainstream.

The only time Quinn exhibited any traces of aggression was on the tennis court when he delivered an overhead smash or pumped his fist after a game-winning shot. But those episodes were few and far between, for Quinn's success was dictated more by style and grace than by fierce determination. Moving effortlessly, he would glide around the tennis court with the elegance of a figure skater and deliver his smooth strokes with the arm movements of a ballroom dancer. For him, tennis was more of an art than a sport, and he was the composer and choreographer.

Together, Quinn and Lynda had become the quintessential couple, the pretty and popular cheerleading captain paired with the rich and handsome tennis star. They stood out from the crowd, and they knew it. Unlike other couples, they never held hands or exhibited public displays of affection. They were too sophisticated for that. Immune from the magnetic forces of nature, their union was driven more by a sense of purpose. Quinn had the wealth and social status that Lynda desired, and she had the drive and charisma.

As a tennis player, Quinn was all too familiar with the jargon of "game, set, and match." For him, Lynda was his match.

Taking the stage, the seven-piece band looked like a mini version of the Glen Miller orchestra. The all-male crew, sporting sequined jackets and bow ties, was preparing to play all the big band classics, ushering in the new year with style and sophistication.

It was New Year's Eve at the Fort Wayne Country Club, and the ballroom was packed. Roselyn O'Connor was wearing a full-length sheath gown in classic black, embellished with silver embroidery. Hugging her curves and exposing her bare back, the dress showed off her glamour and elegance. She hadn't missed a single NYE Ball in twenty years, and she wasn't about to break her streak.

As the band broke into "A String of Pearls," the dance floor filled up with festive couples eager to celebrate. Standing in the back, Roselyn sipped on her flute of champagne and socialized with her lady friends, enjoying a welcome escape from the rigors of domesticity. Her husband had disappeared, making his way to the bar, a separate room fashioned in the style of an old English pub. That is where the men hung out, shooting pool, sipping whiskey, and puffing on cigars.

But this evening would be extra special for Ryan. His beloved alma mater, Notre Dame, would be playing against Alabama and their legendary football coach, Paul "Bear" Bryant. The scene would be the Sugar Bowl in New Orleans, Louisiana, and the winner would take home a national championship. Both teams were undefeated; the Crimson Tide ranked number one, and the Fighting Irish ranked number two.

The game would serve as a perfect alibi for Ryan to avoid Roselyn and hang out with the men. Broadcast on ABC, the game would be a back-and-forth affair, producing the kind of drama that men loved, and wives despised. As long as the bar remained packed with men, Ryan had an excuse to avoid the dance floor; not that Roselyn really cared.

As the game became more intense and the country-clubbers more inebriated, the noise levels in the bar increased exponentially. A few of the wives had tried to intercept their husbands, but with no success, and with the clock inching toward midnight, the intensity had reached a climax.

Clinging to a narrow 24-23 lead, Notre Dame was pinned down deep in its own territory. With only two minutes left, and faced with a third-and-ten from its own two-yard line, Notre Dame called a time-out to assess their situation, a precarious predicament that left them exposed on many fronts.

They could play it safe by running the ball up the middle, a play that would surely fail to generate a first down, and then they would have to kick to Alabama with their punter's heels deep in the back of the endzone, a kick that could easily get blocked and cost them the game. And even if the punter successfully converted his kick, Alabama would possess the ball again, most likely in a position to make the game-winning field goal.

Or they could attempt a dangerous pass, one that would be long enough to gain a first down but would require the quarterback to set up deep in his own endzone, risking a quarterback sack and a two-point safety that would win the game for Alabama. With no easy solutions at their disposal, and a national championship at stake, Notre Dame's chances appeared bleak.

As the Irish returned to the field, the ABC announcers staged the drama. Fort Wayne native Chris Schenkel proclaimed, "This is a dream match, the most important game of the year." And Howard Cosell emphasized the significance with: "Notre Dame and Alabama! At Notre Dame, football is a religion, and at Alabama, it's a way of life."

Breaking the huddle, Notre Dame appeared to be favoring the conservative approach. With their offensive linemen bunched together, the Fighting Irish lined up in a two tight-end formation with three running backs. Apparently, they were going to ram the ball up the middle.

Taking the snap under center, quarterback Tom Clements faked a handoff to the fullback and dropped back deep in his own endzone. With two Alabama linemen in his face, Clements launched a forty-five-yard pass down the left sideline. As the ball sailed through the air, a national TV audience held its breath. When the ball came back to earth, the cameras zeroed in on a little-known backup tight end named Robin Weber.

Weber, a sophomore from Dallas, Texas, cradled the ball into his hands as an Alabama defender smashed into him, forcing him out-of-bounds. While the delirious Notre Dame fans celebrated, ABC commentator, and legendary Oklahoma coach, Bud Wilkinson said, "I don't think I've ever seen a college quarterback make a more clutch play."

For all intents and purposes, the game was over. Notre Dame needed only to run out the clock to claim their ninth national championship, an impressive run that started with Coach Knute Rockne in the 1920s.

Ryan O'Connor was euphoric. He and his buddies gathered in a big circle for one final round of shots. Ryan insisted the round would be on him, breaking out a bottle of twenty-five-year-old Chivas Regal and lighting up a celebratory cigar. Nothing was too good for this moment in history.

As the circle of men broke into a chorus of "Cheer, Cheer for ole Notre Dame," Ryan glanced down at his Rolex watch. "Holy shit!" he exclaimed. "It's almost midnight! You boys better find your wives and drag them out on the dance floor. Otherwise, you'll all be sleeping on the sofa tonight."

After a thunderous roar of laughter, the men scrambled to find their jackets and return to their wives. Stepping into the ballroom, Ryan suddenly realized how drunk he was. Navigating his way through the glittering dresses and strobe effect of the mirrored disco ball, he struggled to maintain his balance.

He needed to find Roselyn. Certainly, she wouldn't deny him a midnight dance on New Year's Eve. Even *she* could let her hair down from time to time, especially when drinking champagne. He was ready to let bygones be bygones and so should she. It was time to celebrate.

As the clock inched closer to midnight, Ryan began to panic. His eyes had scanned the entire perimeter, but to no avail. Was he too drunk to recognize his own wife? Or had she disappeared? Maybe it was just as well. It might spare him the humiliation of rejection, an anticlimactic conclusion to an otherwise perfect evening.

And then he spotted her, already on the dance floor and moving gracefully to the band's rendition of "Stardust," an Artie Shaw classic. Smiling and chatting away, she was enjoying herself immensely. But who was she with? Squinting his eyes, Ryan intensified his concentration, trying to fine-tune his focus through the blurriness of his intoxication.

It looked like Jack Mullins, the recently divorced guy who headed up the New Year's Eve committee. Yes, it was definitely him. But that only made sense, Ryan told himself. Jack was without a date and in charge of showing everyone a good time. Even though Mullins was a better dancer, he certainly was no competition to Ryan O'Connor, the richest guy in town. Besides, he was a horrible golfer.

Watching Roselyn glide around the dance floor effortlessly, Ryan couldn't help but admire her style and grace. He had forgotten how elegant she looked in her glamorous evening attire. But it was more than glamour he was beholding. There was a seductiveness about her that he hadn't felt in some time.

Maybe it was the extended abstinence, or maybe it was the allure of desiring someone that he couldn't have. Either way, there was no denying her sex appeal, or the way her bare back was exposed all the way down to her curvy hips, or the way her perky breasts protruded delicately beneath her pectoral cleft. She was an image of desire, and she still belonged to him.

Stopping the music, the band director captured everyone's attention and took the lead on the official countdown: "ten, nine, eight, seven..." Ryan marched boldly onto the dancefloor and tapped Jack Mullins on the shoulder. "Hey, ole chap, you don't mind if I cut in, do you?"

Everyone let out a roar as a series of firecrackers popped and a barrage of balloons dropped from the ceiling. The emcee shouted, "Happy New Year!"

Mullins yelled over the deafening noise. "Ryan, your timing is impeccable. How could I deny a man a dance with his wife at the stroke of midnight?"

"You can't," bellowed Ryan. "But thanks for pinch-hitting."

The band kicked in with "Auld Lang Syne" as Ryan wrapped his arm around Roselyn's waist and pulled her in.

Should auld acquaintance be forgot
And never brought to mind?
We'll drink a cup of kindness yet
For the sake of auld lang syne

"You really are beautiful," said Ryan.

"Please! And you really *are* drunk."

"No, I mean it. I don't say it often enough."

"How about never. It couldn't be because you're drunk and feeling frisky, could it?"

"Why can't you just take a compliment for what it is?"

"I'm not that naive. Let me guess. You're in a good mood because Notre Dame won the football game. Am I correct?"

"I'm choosing to be sentimental and optimistic. Isn't that what people do on New Year's Eve?"

"I suppose, but I have reason to be skeptical."

"That's what I'm talking about. Throw your skepticism aside and be optimistic. Wipe the slate clean."

"It sounds good," said Roselyn, beginning to back off a bit. "But what about all the baggage?"

"See, that's being negative. I choose to be positive and ask, what about the future?"

"The future is what I'm worried about," said Roselyn, not giving in.

"What does anyone have if they don't have a future. The future is what we make of it."

"This sounds like one of your work speeches."

"It applies to everyone."

"Maybe the future of a business and the future of a family are two different things."

"The future's the future. I'm not willing to give up on my business or my family."

"I'm willing to try if you are," conceded Roselyn.

Ryan leaned down and kissed Roselyn on the forehead. "That's all anyone can do, is try. But let's not try to solve the world's problems tonight. Let's just celebrate and enjoy each other's company."

Ryan pulled Roselyn in close and slowly rocked her to the music. The warmth of her body felt comforting, an unfamiliar coziness in his authoritative world. He knew it was lonely at the top, a fact he had learned to live with. People in his position had to stay on guard, but now his guard was down.

She leaned her head against his chest, and he inhaled the intoxicating fragrance of her hair. "Your hair smells delicious."

"Thank you. Can you detect the scent of orange blossom?"

"Yes," he lied. "It turns me on."

Ryan pulled her in close and allowed his hand to wander below her waist. It was a fine derriere, perfectly shaped with the right amount of padding; not too plump, and not too skinny. Indulging in her curves, he couldn't help but give her right cheek a promiscuous little squeeze, followed by a gentle, but playful pat. He was going to have his way with her tonight, and it would be glorious. She would submit to him, and he would pleasure her in a way that would put aside all their differences. He would reside in the master bedroom once again, master of his domain.

For Ryan O'Connor, the nightmare of 1973 had come to an end, and what a magnificent end it was. Notre Dame was crowned national champion, and he would be a champion in the bedroom. All's well that ends well, he told himself.

The year 1974 would be different. He would rise up and meet all the challenges, becoming an irresistible force. His opponents didn't know what they were up against, but they would soon find out. They were up against Ryan O'Connor, he told himself, and the O'Connor name would always be at the top of the heap. Nothing would ever change that; not while he was in charge.

Chapter 48

QUINN WALKED INTO THE KITCHEN and immediately picked up the scent of coffee and English Leather cologne. His father was already dressed in a suit and tie and pouring his third cup of coffee. Grabbing his briefcase and car keys, Ryan was ready to exit the backdoor and fire up his Cadillac Eldorado.

"Are you leaving already?" asked Quinn.

"Big day, today. Got a full agenda."

"Can you holdup a second?" asked Quinn.

"What for?"

"Christine's in the foyer with her bags packed. She's heading back to school and Mom wants you to say goodbye."

"Okay, but it better be brief."

Ryan exited the kitchen as Quinn reached into the refrigerator to grab two eggs and a carton of orange juice. He'd already said his goodbyes to Christine, part of the normal back-to-school routine, but this time she seemed out of sorts. Perhaps it had something to do with it being her last semester of college. Girls could get sentimental about those kinds of things. Or maybe she didn't want to leave school and wished to express her desire to pursue a master's degree. Quinn wasn't sure how his father would react to that idea. Or maybe it was the boyfriend topic, a sensitive subject that had not been breached throughout the holidays.

"God, let's hope the whole boyfriend drama doesn't come up," Quinn said to himself as he scrambled his eggs. He wasn't prepared for anything *that* intense before breakfast. He would stay in the kitchen, or even go upstairs if he had to. Anything to avoid a heated argument.

Ryan rounded the corner and saw his daughter's bags sitting by the front door, but there was no Christine. He was expecting the obligatory front door hugs and goodbyes and good-lucks; nothing more, nothing less. Then he saw Roselyn standing by the entrance to the parlor with a concerned look on her face. Something was amiss, he could sense it, and he'd be *damned* if he would let this disrupt his busy morning. He had too many important things to worry about.

"Where's Christine?" he asked. "I thought she was leaving."

"She is, but she wants to talk to us first."

Then he saw Christine sitting in the parlor, looking unnerved, almost distressed. Never a good sign, he thought to himself. He wasn't prepared for any melodramatics.

"This better be brief," grumbled Ryan. "I have a meeting this morning."

"I know you do, but I think we should listen to what she has to say."

Ryan marched into the room and took control, the same way he controlled every situation, or so he thought. That was his role.

"This better be important," he began. "You've had all Christmas break to talk to us, and now you finally want to talk just as I'm heading out the door. Pretty poor timing, don't you think?"

"I'm sorry I already ruined your day," said Christine, mixing regret with sarcasm.

"Just get on with it," said Ryan.

Christine was prepared for an emotional exchange, an opportunity to pour out her heart and plea for compassion. But now, with her father's apparent annoyance, she stiffened up and felt the need to tell it like it is. A firm "take it or leave it" attitude.

"I'm here to tell you that I'm not going back to school."

"What? That's the dumbest thing I've ever heard," reprimanded Ryan. "Why would you quit school when you're only one semester away from earning a degree?"

"I'm not quitting altogether. I'm just not going back for the spring semester. At some point, I *will* go back and finish my degree."

"At some point? You just decided this all on your own?" questioned Ryan. "That's not how it works around here. You seem to forget that you're still our dependent and I'm the one financing your education. And, oh, by the way, a very expensive private education."

"What's this all about?" asked Roselyn. "I think you owe us an explanation."

Christine sat by despondently, staring off into space. There was more to the story, but she didn't know how to go about it. How could she carry on when her father had already lost his cool.

"So if you're not going back to school, where are you going?" asked Roselyn, trying to jumpstart her story. "You obviously packed your bags."

"I'm moving to Chicago," said Christine, almost in a whisper.

"You're what?" blurted Ryan.

"I think you heard me."

"Here we go! The moment of truth!" shouted Ryan as he began to pace back and forth. "I suppose this is all about that *Black* boyfriend of yours!"

"Oh yes," said Christine. "It's all about him being *Black*. That's all that matters to you."

"No," said Roselyn. "It's not about that."

"Oh yes, it is," said Ryan. "I'm not gonna sugarcoat it. Let's put all the cards on the table."

"My point is," continued Roselyn, "we wouldn't want you to quit school to be with *any* boyfriend, *period*. It's got nothing to do with his race."

Christine offered no reply. Roselyn had failed to desensitize her with logic. She knew there had to be more to the story, but she didn't know how to crack Christine's outer shell. She looked over at Ryan, but he continued to pace back and forth like a lawyer preparing his next statement.

"Something tells me there's more to the story," offered Roselyn, in her most sympathetic tone. "What's going on, honey? You need to open up."

Ryan stopped his pacing and stared at Christine with his arms crossed. He decided to wait and listen, hoping Roselyn could get her to open up and tell the truth. He was tired of being strung along.

"There's been a change of plans," mumbled Christine. "I have some things I need to take care of before finishing my education." Then she paused, as if her statement was a prelude, a delicate attempt to stage another awkward revelation.

"Can you please cut to the chase?" pleaded Ryan. "I don't have all morning."

"I'm pregnant!" blurted Christine, unable to delay the inevitable any longer.

Expecting her father to fly into a rage, Christine was stunned by his restraint. Instead of scorning her, her parents just stood there, frozen in time, staring at her in disbelief. This was even worse than hostility. She'd never said or done anything to shock her parents into silence.

"Everything is going to be okay," she continued. "I'm moving to Chicago to be with Michael. I love him and he loves me. We want to have this baby...our baby...a life created out of love."

"A life created out of wedlock," clarified Ryan. "Outside the sanctity of marriage."

"I know this doesn't fit into your Catholic beliefs, but not everything that happens in this world fits into your perfect mold. Life happens, people adapt, and people move forward. One step at a time. Life goes on."

"Not this life," said Ryan.

"Excuse me? What's that supposed to mean?"

Ryan was beginning to pace again, as if the shock had worn off and he had come back to his senses. Now he was in problem-solving mode, taking the lead. That's what he needed to do. As head of the family, he would resolve this problem, and everyone would move forward and get on with their lives.

"We need to deal with this as a family," lectured Ryan. "Our whole reputation is at stake, which means our livelihood is at risk. We can't take a hit like this."

"We?" asked Christine. "You mean *you*! This is about me and *my* life, not about *you*."

"You're wrong! You're still our daughter and you're still part of this family. This is a family decision and I'm still the head of this family."

"Oh my God! Are you listening to this, Mother?"

Roselyn was still in a state of shock, stunned by her daughter's confession. She was trying to digest everything, unwilling to comment one way or another.

"You're young and naive," continued Ryan. "You don't understand how fragile a reputation can be. Once you lose your reputation, you no longer have any credibility."

"Are you listening to yourself?" asked Christine. "You make this sound like a business proposition. It's not! This is my life we're talking about here, not your good standing in the community."

"It's about a lot of different things. You need to take your emotions out of the equation and make a sound business decision, one that's based on logic and probability."

"This is ridiculous! You're speaking about me like I'm a business case. Well, I'm not. I'm a grown woman. And I'm a woman who's in love and is going to have a baby. Guess what…women have been falling in love and bearing children ever since the beginning of time."

"Times have changed," countered Ryan. "We now have choices."

"What are you talking about?"

"I'm talking about last year's Supreme Court decision, *Roe v. Wade*. That changed everything. Women are no longer forced to bear unwanted babies. You now have the freedom of choice."

"Oh my God! I don't believe what I'm hearing! You want me to abort my baby?"

"It's not a baby. It's a fetus. We need to do what's right and put this under the rug. No one will ever know."

Christine looked at her father in disbelief and shook her head incredulously. "I don't even know where to begin. This goes against everything you've ever preached. You said that *Roe v. Wade* was a mistake. You said the Catholic Church protects the sanctity of life and that life begins at conception. You said the Supreme Court could not overturn God's law."

"I'm a lawyer first. The Supreme Court is the law of the land and I abide by the law of the land."

"I think you abide by whatever is convenient for you."

"Damn it! I will not allow my daughter to speak to me this way!"

Ryan O'Connor had lost his patience. He'd already spent way too much time on this issue. As far as he was concerned, a conclusion had been reached and it was time to go on the offensive.

"You listen to me, and you listen good! I will *not* allow you to destroy this family's reputation. For once in your life, do the responsible thing. Quit being an embarrassment to this family."

Christine stood up and started walking toward the foyer. Her father was close behind. She put on her coat and went directly toward the luggage.

"You're nothing but a hypocrite!" she screamed as she picked up her suitcase. "*You're* the one who's an embarrassment!"

Ryan ripped the suitcase from his daughter's hands and flung it violently across the room. "If you go to Chicago today, don't ever bother coming back. You'll be banished from this family forever."

Roselyn stood by silently, tears streaming down her face. At this point, she knew her opinion didn't matter. There was no reasoning with Ryan when he was enraged. All she could do was live to fight another day.

"I am leaving now," announced Ryan. "I have more important things to do, much more important than this nonsense." Then he pointed at Roselyn. "I expect you to take care of this. A decision has been made and you need to make it happen."

Chapter 49

WHEN THE FINAL BUZZER SOUNDED, the Northrop Bruin basketball team stormed the court, stunning a capacity crowd of over ten thousand people in Fort Wayne's Memorial Coliseum. After a convincing 67-53 victory over the previously undefeated and number-one ranked Anderson Indians, the Bruins were ready to be crowned semistate champions and punch their ticket to the Final Four.

Although the Bruins entered the game with a season record of 25-1, they were heavy underdogs after barely surviving the afternoon game, a 55-53 thriller over Logansport. Not many people were familiar with Fort Wayne Northrop, a school that was only in its third year of existence. Anderson, on the other hand, was a perennial powerhouse in the annals of Indiana basketball history, a school rich in tradition.

With three state championships to their credit, along with dozens of sectional and regional titles, the Anderson Indian basketball program was legendary. The 1974 version featured superstar Roy Taylor, their six-foot, four-inch sharp-shooting guard that would go on to win the title of Mr. Basketball, a distinguished award given each year to the state's top player. Their fabled arena, the Wigwam, was almost mythical in stature. Seating nine thousand fans, it was one of the largest high school gymnasiums in the country.

But there would be no tournament glory for Anderson on this March evening. Few had anticipated the Indians' season would end on such a sour note, losing to a little-known school from Fort Wayne. But this was no fluke. It wasn't a game like so many other tournament games where a basket here, or a foul there would swing the pendulum one way or another. This contest had been utter domination, a team exerting its authority in all phases of the game. As a result, there was little doubt the Northrop Bruins were Final Four worthy, a legitimate contender for the prestigious title of Indiana State Champion.

As the Anderson fans poured through the exits, WKJG announcer, Hilliard Gates, conducted his TV interviews with the victors. Most of the Bruin fans had moved courtside, trying to savor every last second of the celebration. At one end of the floor, the players lined up, waiting for their turns to cut down the nets that would live in infamy as trophy case souvenirs, along with the official semistate champion team photo, a picture that would be plastered in newspapers all across the state.

Mindy and Lynda meandered through the packed Coliseum corridors, high-fiving and hugging fellow students along the way. They had already issued their conciliatory hugs to the Anderson cheerleaders, a bittersweet gesture that did little to stop their heart-wrenching tears. But to the victors go the spoils, and the Bruin contingent was ready to continue their celebration well into the night. The electrifying postgame atmosphere and contagious energy only magnified the inevitable. They knew they had witnessed something special, and they weren't about to let the evening come to an end.

"Hey, Mindy," came a loud shout through the horde of humanity.

Mindy and Lynda turned their heads to see Brian Johnson and Mark Carter pushing their way through the mob and Scott Clever struggling to keep up on his crutches.

"So what do you think?" asked Lynda. "I told you we would win."

"Pretty amazing," said Mark. "I never would've predicted it."

Mindy looked at Scott on his crutches. "What about you? Did you expect an outcome like this?"

"It sucks," declared Scott. "That's all I have to say."

"What's *that* supposed to mean?" asked Mindy.

"It means I should've been down on the floor celebrating with my teammates. Instead, I'm stuck up in the stands like a regular pedestrian. Hell, even you cheerleaders got to celebrate with the players, and you've never touched a basketball in your life."

"Yeah, I guess that doesn't seem fair," agreed Lynda. "I never thought of it like that."

"Just my luck I get injured right before making varsity. At least if I was injured *during* the season, I would've been sitting down there with everyone else."

"There's always next year, ole chap," said Brian. "You gotta keep a stiff upper lip."

"Well, if I can't be in the locker room tonight, I'm gonna find where the parties are and drink myself into oblivion."

"That doesn't sound very mature," reasoned Lynda.

"Speaking of parties," said Mindy, "where's the action gonna be tonight? Has anyone heard?"

"There's not going to be any *action* for you," said Lynda, glaring at Mindy. "Next weekend's the state finals, the biggest event of our lives, and I'm not gonna let any of our squad members jeopardize that by drinking beer."

"You're such a killjoy," said Mindy. "We should be celebrating."

"Hey, look who's here," said Lynda, as Karen Gadby approached the gathering.

"Anybody know where the parties are?" asked Karen.

"My thoughts exactly," concurred Mindy. "You and I are on the same page."

"Where's Steve?" asked Lynda. "Did he come to the game?"

"Nah, he had a hockey game this afternoon. He said he'd meet up with Bob after work and swing by later this evening."

"Perfect," said Scott. "Steve Marino is our ticket to beer. He has all the right connections."

"I'm sure he and Bob will both have some beer," agreed Karen. "That's a pretty safe bet."

"Let's gather at my house," suggested Lynda. "I'll see if some of the other cheerleaders want to come over. If you guys wanna drink beer, you can do that outside on your driveways. I can't get caught up in that debauchery."

"What about Quinn?" asked Mindy. "What's he doing tonight?"

"I'm not sure," said Lynda. "He said he couldn't go to the game because his father had him doing some things. I'm not sure what that means, but he said he would call me later."

"All right," said Brian. "Let's all head back to Coldwater Creek."

When the boys pulled up in front of Scott's house, they saw both Karen's car and Mindy's car parked in front of the Lacey household.

"Looks like they beat us here," said Brian. "*Now* what do we do? Should we knock on the door? Or should we wait to see if Bob and Steve show up?"

"I say we wait," said Scott. "Unless you wanna go to their boring party of pretzels and Coca-Cola."

"I'm not waiting out here for very long," said Brian. "It's getting colder by the minute and my warm girlfriend is inside."

"You ain't gettin' any warmth from her tonight," teased Mark. "Not with the other girls around and Mrs. Lacey supervising."

"Wait," said Scott. "I think our ship just came in."

The boys looked up to see Bob's Plymouth Barracuda ease to a stop in Marino's driveway. With the four-barrel engine rumbling and loud music blaring, the boys approached the parked car unnoticed. Getting closer, they recognized a steady trail of smoke leaking through the cracked windows and the voice of Billy Preston on the radio singing "Nothing From Nothing."

"Can you smell that?" asked Mark. "That ain't no cigarette smoke."

Steve rolled down the passenger window and looked at them with a big grin on his face. "You boys ready to party?"

"Damn!" said Scott. "It smells like Cheech and Chong over here."

"You guys should be more discreet," advised Mark. "After all, the captain of the police department lives just one block away."

"Why should we worry about that?" teased Steve. "That's why we keep you as a friend. We need a get-out-of-jail-free card."

"Don't push your luck. Maybe a little jail time would straighten you out."

"Hey," said Scott. "You got any weed you can share with me? I need some painkillers for my leg."

"Nice try," said Steve. "This shit don't grow on trees."

"Well, I'll buy some from you if you're selling."

"Easy now. What makes you think we're selling? A fella can get arrested for that. If you're interested in buying, I might be able to hook you up with a seller, but I would never do anything illegal myself."

"Yeah, right," said Mark. "You're about as crooked as a broken-down old racehorse."

"Or Scott's bad leg," teased Brian.

"Fuck you!" said Scott.

"Actually, we were hoping you could get us some beer," suggested Brian. "Afterall, the Bruins knocked off the number-one team in the state tonight and we want to celebrate."

"You've come to the right place," said Steve as he stepped out of the passenger seat and headed toward the trunk, revealing, for the first time, the left side of his face and a huge black eye.

"Holy shit!" said Mark. "What happened to *you*?"

"No big deal," said Steve. "Just a little fisticuff. All in a day's work."

"Did you get in a street fight? Or did you get it while playin' that barbaric game you call hockey?"

"What do *you* think?" asked Steve. "I'll keep you in suspense."

"Did you score any goals?" asked Brian.

"No goals today, but I had an assist and a five-minute fighting major. I would've finished him off pretty good, but the refs pulled me away too soon. Lucky for him."

Bob popped the trunk to reveal a large Styrofoam ice chest. Pulling off the lid, the boys immediately recognized the golden cans of Miller High Life beer.

"Beautiful," said Scott. "We just struck gold."

"Help yourselves," said Bob. "The treat's on me. Let's enjoy the high life."

Mindy, Karen, and Nancy Garber had settled into the Lacey basement, relaxed in the seclusion of familiar surroundings. The excitement from the game had worn off and the girls were easing into their customary routine, which meant engaging in the latest gossip on school, boyfriends, and pop culture. They'd had their fill of basketball for one day. It was time for girl talk.

Moving gingerly, Lynda tiptoed down the basement stairs, precariously balancing a large tray of snacks. "Time to indulge," she announced.

"Here, let me help you with that," offered Karen. "What sort of delectables do you have for us this evening?"

"Mom and I made a batch of Chex Mix this afternoon in between games. There's also Bugles and French onion dip if you're interested. Nothing fancy."

"Can't go wrong with that," declared Mindy. "I love Chex Mix. Is it easy to make?"

"We whipped it up in less than a half hour. Just melted some butter and added a little Worcestershire Sauce. Then mixed it in a bowl with the other ingredients: Rice Chex, Wheat Chex, mixed nuts, and pretzels. Then you just stick it in the oven for about twenty minutes."

"That sounds pretty easy," said Mindy. "I think I can handle that."

"I don't know," teased Karen. "It sounds to me like Lynda is becoming pretty domesticated. Does anyone think she'll be making Chex Mix when she's a big-time executive?"

"No," answered Mindy. "She'll be attending company cocktail parties, sipping on champagne, and nibbling on caviar."

"Very funny," said Lynda. "Although that doesn't sound half bad."

"Just don't forget about us little people," teased Mindy.

"Okay, what do you gals want to drink?" asked Lynda, making her way to the compact refrigerator unit. "I have Coke, RC Cola, or Tab."

"I better have Tab," said Karen. "I'm watching my figure."

"Yeah, you and every other boy in the school," teased Mindy.

"I don't get it," said Nancy. "How's Tab supposed to make you lose weight?"

"It doesn't make you lose weight," explained Lynda. "It reduces your calorie intake. The sugar in regular pop has lots of calories. Losing weight is all about counting calories. Tab only has two calories, compared to sugary drinks that have a hundred and fifty calories."

"I knew you'd have all the answers," said Mindy. "But I don't like the taste. What do they put in there that makes it taste so bad."

"It's called saccharin. Saccharin is a sugar replacement. I guess it was developed in a lab somewhere. It's supposed to simulate the sweetness of sugar, but without the calories."

"Well, I don't like it. It has a funny taste."

"It doesn't matter," reasoned Karen. "You don't have to worry about your weight like I do. You could eat an entire smorgasbord and not gain an ounce."

"So what's the difference between Tab, and Diet Pepsi, and Diet Rite?" asked Nancy.

Lynda was only too willing to explain the differences. She made it her business to understand corporate branding and the way different products were marketed.

"Tab is a Coca-Cola product, and Diet Rite is made by RC, which stands for Royal Crown. And Diet Pepsi needs no explanation. Tab outsells the other products, partly because Coca-Cola outspends in advertising, and partly because of the unique design of its pink can and modern label. It was made for people who want to keep tabs on their weight. Get it? And their latest commercial is kinda catchy. Have you seen it?"

"Which one?"

"It features Sunny Griffin, one of the highest paid fashion models in the world. She's lying down and sipping on a diet soda. She says it contains seventy-two calories, more calories than all these Tabs put together. And then the camera fades away to show her surrounded by dozens of glasses of Tab. That's pretty effective advertising, don't you think?"

"Yeah, I've seen it," said Mindy. "But I like the Diet Pepsi commercial better. The one where the sexy gal is walking down the sidewalk, and all the guys are turning their heads to look at her. The whole time, they're playing "*Music to Watch Girls By.*"

"Yeah, that's a good one," said Karen.

"You should know," said Mindy. "That's the same way all the guys look at you when you walk by."

"Yeah, right. I wish."

"What's the catchphrase they use in that commercial?" asked Mindy, looking at Lynda.

"Well, they talk about how guys watch girls who keep a good figure, the kind of girls that drink Diet Pepsi, and then the final catchphrase is "The kind of girl that girl-watchers watch."

"That's it," said Mindy. "I knew you would know."

"Yeah, I remember silly things like that."

"So, Karen," prodded Mindy, "since we're talking about guys diggin' chicks with good figures, how are you and Steve getting along?"

"Well, I'm not sure how to respond to that."

"Oh c'mon, you know you have a hot bod. Isn't that what the guys are after? I'd give anything to have your boobs."

"Be careful of what you ask for. It's a real pain in the ass tryin' to harness these puppies and finding clothing that fits. I wouldn't wish this upon anyone."

"Yeah, but I bet Steve likes them," pestered Mindy. "He seems like the kind of guy who goes for large breasts. No offense."

"Wow, Mindy, you get right to the point," reprimanded Lynda. "I don't think Karen feels the need to discuss her personal life with us."

"Actually, I really don't mind," said Karen. "I feel like I need to discuss it with someone, and who better to discuss it with than my best friends? The fact is my relationship with Steve leaves a lot to be desired. There are some things I like about him and other things I don't. Sometimes he's fun to be around and I start to feel some chemistry. Other times he becomes bossy and domineering. Like I said before, he's a little rough around the edges. That kind of masculinity can sometimes be a turn-on, other times it can be intimidating."

"Sounds like you've given it some thought," offered Mindy. "What about physically? How far have you guys gone? I mean, he doesn't seem like a patient kinda guy."

"Wow, Mindy doesn't beat around the bush," said Lynda. "Karen, you don't have to answer her questions on the grounds you might incriminate yourself."

Karen laughed it off and then admitted, "Well, just the fact that I'm hangin' out with Steve might be enough to incriminate me."

"Hey, Nancy," interjected Mindy, "it's ten o'clock. Don't you have to be home at ten?"

"I do, but there's no way I'm leaving right now, not when Karen's about to confess her innermost secrets."

"Did you hear that?" said Mindy, looking at Karen. "You're gonna corrupt this poor, innocent young lady."

"Well, we all get corrupted at one time or another, don't we?"

"Whatever corruption means," offered Mindy. "That's a word that Brian likes to use."

"To answer your question," said Karen, "Steve and I have done the typical things that most couples do, I suppose. Without going into detail, we've done what 'Dear Abby' calls heavy petting. I mean, that's pretty normal, isn't it?"

"I don't *know* what's normal," replied Mindy. "That's why I'm asking. I guess we're all learning at the same time. Why don't you define what is normal versus abnormal."

"To be honest," continued Karen, "things got a little out of hand one night when we were alone in his basement. Before I tell you, you have to promise that this is our little secret. Agreed?"

Mindy and Nancy immediately concurred, while Lynda looked on silently, not willing to concede, but not willing to intervene.

"It started out with him reaching under my sweater," continued Karen. "Then I allowed him to remove it. Then he took his shirt off. I was thinking that maybe we'd gone far enough. But then he removed my bra."

"Aha!" giggled Mindy. "I knew he was a breast kinda guy. Nancy, you better go home now. I don't think you should listen to this."

"No way! Not when she's gettin' to the good part."

"So as you can imagine," said Karen, "he was super turned on by now, if you know what I mean."

"I'm starting to get turned on now myself and I'm a Mennonite," conceded Nancy.

"You're funny." Karen laughed. "We're all human, no matter what religion we follow. So anyway, as I was saying, things were starting to get out of hand. Steve then stood up and dropped his jeans. Then he pulled me up and pulled down my jeans. Now I was starting to get nervous."

"Were his parents home?" asked Mindy.

"No, that's the scary part. They had gone out for the evening, but we didn't know when they were coming home. But Steve didn't seem to care. So now we're on the sofa wearing nothing but underpants and he reaches for his wallet and pulls out a condom."

"Oh wow," exclaimed Mindy. "He was actually prepared."

"Yes, so now I'm thinking he's done this before, right? But in reality, we're not supposed to think like that. I mean, he was actually being responsible. Afterall, that's what birth control is for, right? To prevent a horrible mistake."

"Yes," agreed Mindy. "It's almost like we condemn someone for planning ahead to take the necessary precautions. If you plan for it, then you're looked down upon as someone with evil intentions."

"Exactly," agreed Karen. "You're damned if you do and damned if you don't."

"So what happened?" asked Mindy. "If you don't mind me asking."

"Oh, I don't think you mind asking." Karen laughed.

"Guilty as charged."

"So to make a long story short, I kinda freaked out," said Karen. "I told him I wasn't ready for this, at least not yet."

"And what did he do?"

"He was pissed. I was hoping he'd be sympathetic, but instead he turned on me."

"What do you mean he turned on you?"

"He just stood up. And when I stood up, he shoved me back onto the couch. He called me a big tease and started getting dressed."

"So what did you do?" asked Mindy.

"I started getting dressed too. Then he just marched up the steps without saying a word. That's pretty much the way it was the whole drive home. Hardly a word was spoken. I felt bad, like I ruined the whole evening."

"But then you went out with him again?" asked Mindy.

"The next time we were together, he took me out for pizza and acted like a total gentleman. Not a word about our previous encounter."

"Hmmm, very interesting," said Mindy. "That was a good story. Thanks for sharing."

"Now it's your turn," said Karen. "What's goin' on with you and Brian?"

"Brian is a very nice guy. We have fun together and I like him a lot. He's pretty conservative, though. We've made out a few times and he really seems to like it, but he's very cautious, always considerate of my feelings."

"Okay," said Nancy. "It's ten-fifteen and I really need to head home."

The girls broke out laughing. "I guess she's not interested in your stories," said Karen to Mindy. "She only wants to listen to the juicy stuff."

"Can't argue with that," said Nancy. "Make sure you invite me to the next gathering."

"Only if you come back with your own story," said Mindy.

"Ha, that's not gonna happen. See you gals later," she said, as she headed up the basement stairs.

Karen looked back at Mindy, "You're not gettin' off that easy. You must have something you can share."

"Nothing like you," replied Mindy. "Like I said, we've made out a few times, but nothing beyond passionate kissing. A couple times he started to move his hands toward my private parts, but he always stops himself. He's very respectful toward my feelings."

"And what *are* your feelings?" asked Karen.

"My feelings are bring-it-on." Mindy laughed. "I'm ready to experiment further, but he seems very hesitant."

"Maybe you should take the lead," suggested Karen. "Why is it that women have to play the passive role?"

"You may be on to something. I never really looked at it that way before." Then Mindy started laughing. "I'd probably scare him off if I got too aggressive."

"Oh, I don't think you'd scare him off. If he's respectful, like you say, he's probably just waiting for the right signals."

"Okay," said Mindy, looking at Lynda. "It's your turn. You don't get a free pass."

As was typically the case, Lynda did not engage in lurid details of intimacy. She considered such matters to be confidential. It's not that she was insensitive. In reality, she actually cared about people's feelings, it's just that she preferred to keep things at a professional level, resisting the urge to engage in garrulous tales of indiscretions. Afterall, she had a reputation to maintain and she would not compromise her dignity.

"My turn for what?" asked Lynda, pretending to be naive.

"I'm talking about Quinn," clarified Mindy. "You're going out with the richest, best-looking guy in the school and I've never seen the two of you even hold hands."

"We've held hands, it's no big deal. We just don't do it in public."

"And why is that?"

"I don't know. It's just that when we're in the public eye, we don't care to engage in personal matters."

"Personal Matters? Holding hands?"

"Well, I don't mean to sound snooty, but people like him, from reputable families, they have to keep their guard up. Their behavior is always being scrutinized, so they can't send off any signals that might stimulate gossip."

"All right, so what goes on when you're *not* in the public eye?"

"That's kinda personal, don't you think?"

"Come on," urged Mindy. "You're not talking to the general public here. You're talking to your best friends. It just seems like Quinn isn't very affectionate. Is that really the case?"

"Quinn and I hold hands and we kiss. Is that good enough?"

"Is that good enough for *you*? That's the question," reasoned Mindy.

"We have a very healthy relationship."

Mindy and Karen burst out laughing and Lynda blushed.

"I've never seen you blush before," declared Karen.

"So what are you laughing about?" asked Lynda.

"A healthy relationship?" asked Mindy. "It doesn't sound to me like there's any sparks flying."

Lynda was finally getting agitated and decided it was time to lay things on the line.

"Listen, my relationship with Quinn is just fine, thank you. He's smart, handsome, and professional. I think we're a perfect match. And, yes, he's a very good kisser. I know because I've kissed him a number of times. How's that?"

"You've kissed *him*?" asked Mindy. "Or he kissed *you*?"

"That's ridiculous. A kiss is a kiss."

"Sorry, I don't mean to pry. It's just that Quinn doesn't seem very affectionate."

"Quinn can be *very* affectionate. Just because you haven't witnessed it doesn't mean it never happens. Quinn's not the kind of guy that's gonna park his Buick on some abandoned road and pull me into the back seat. He's far too sophisticated for that. Maybe you two just don't understand proper etiquette."

Mindy and Karen looked at each other nervously. They had never seen Lynda get flustered. She was always the cool cucumber, never agitated or flying off the handle with emotion. Apparently, in Lynda's mind, they had crossed a boundary, hitting a nerve they never knew existed.

Lynda marched over to the refrigerator and stated her intentions. "I'm gonna pour myself another Tab, if it's all right with you. Are you two finished with your interrogation?"

Chapter 50

GROWING UP IN INDIANA, MOST children are taught the old proverb, "March comes in like a lion, and goes out like a lamb." Although the lion usually holds up its end of the bargain, the lamb rarely makes an appearance, choosing instead to hibernate long after the groundhog sees its shadow. If gentle lambs are the embodiment of peace and serenity, then March is a poor representation.

Turbulent at best, Indiana Marches are filled with storm clouds, high winds, and frigid temperatures. Admittedly, there are subtle teases along the way. A sunny sixty-degree day may inspire spontaneous optimism, only to be dashed by an overnight cold front and a fresh blanket of snow, smothering any suspicions of spring. It's a roller-coaster ride of volatility that requires strength and fortitude, a journey not meant for the faint of heart.

No stranger to storm clouds, the O'Connor domain was anything but docile, experiencing its own wave of turbulence. But this latest surge was neither fleeting or seasonal. Like an Arctic winter, there was a sense of perpetual darkness, a shadow of gloom with no spring redemption. Ryan and Roselyn's frigidity was accumulating like a glacier, steadily expanding, never thawing.

Over the years, Ryan had mastered the art of putting out fires, an occupational hazard of entrepreneurship. Problems arise, solutions are reached, and decisions are made. But decisions are an exercise in futility unless they are followed by action. In Ryan's mind, a solution had been reached and a decision had been made regarding Christine's pregnancy, but no one was following his orders. His mandate had failed, rendering him weak and vulnerable, and he would deal with it the only way he knew how, with spite and hostility.

Against her father's wishes, Christine moved to Chicago to live with her boyfriend and prepare for the arrival of their September baby, and Ryan O'Connor was just fine with that. If she was going to have a Black baby out of wedlock, she might as well deliver it far away from Fort Wayne, saving him the embarrassment of local publicity and humiliating gossip. If anyone asked about his daughter, he would obligingly expound upon her last semester at Saint Mary's and her subsequent job in Chicago. That's all anyone needed to know. It seemed perfectly logical and begged no further questions.

Ryan realized the truth would eventually leak out; he wasn't naive. But that was further down the road and he would deal with that when the time came. A Chicago marriage and baby could easily be explained away. No one would need to know the timeline or sequence of events.

Glossing over the specifics would be easy; it's called public relations, and O'Connor Enterprises had mastered the art of PR. In the meantime, Ryan would stick to his principles, which meant banishing Christine from the family. That would keep her in Chicago and punish her for ignoring his orders. If she really believed she was capable of making her own decisions, then she would have to survive on her own, no longer under the security blanket of the O'Connor payroll.

But Ryan's resolution for closure did nothing to alleviate Roselyn's pain and suffering. Robbed of her soul and consumed with depression, she was only a shadow of her former self. Without the companionship of her only daughter, Roselyn's life had become unbearable, trapped in a loveless marriage, and isolated from her own flesh and blood.

Reaching a breaking point, she knew the only solution was to go against her husband's wishes and escape to Chicago for weekend visitations. Although the hasty excursions delivered temporary relief, the return trips to Fort Wayne only reinforced her unhappiness. The wedge between she and Ryan had deepened, making her long for a different way of life, one in which she could spread her wings and explore new possibilities, far removed from her husband's manipulation and the isolation of the O'Connor estate.

Quinn O'Connor pranced through the back door and into the kitchen, anxious for the upcoming weekend.

"You're home early," noted his mother. "Wasn't today a full school day?"

"It was supposed to be, but it didn't end up that way."

"What's that supposed to mean?"

"Our pep rally started at nine o'clock this morning and lasted over three hours. Then everyone was allowed to leave the building and head to the parking lot where we were supposed to send off the basketball team. The team bus was parked out there, and we all gathered around. After the band played and the bus pulled away, some of the kids started heading for their cars."

"Nobody tried to stop them?"

"Not really." Quinn laughed. "I'm not sure they could. It was such a crazy atmosphere. I don't think they really planned for all the chaos. One thing's for sure, nobody felt like going back to class."

"Well, I hope you don't get in trouble for truancy."

"Nah, no worries. They announced that anyone who had their own transportation could leave for the day. Kinda funny considering most had already left anyway."

"So what time are you heading for Indianapolis tomorrow?"

"We're going to Bloomington, not Indianapolis. I thought you knew that."

"I thought the state finals were in Indy."

"They were originally scheduled to be there, but that was based upon Market Square Arena being finished. They announced a few months ago they would hold it at Indiana University instead. Anyway, we're leaving at seven o'clock tomorrow morning."

"Well, it should be a fun day," said Roselyn, as she walked toward the foyer. "I hope they win the whole thing. That would be quite a celebration."

Quinn followed his mother into the foyer and saw that she had accumulated a stack of items near the front door: boxes, garment bags, suitcases, etc.

"So it looks like you're headed for Chicago this weekend?"

"Yes," replied his mother. "I could use your help loading these things into the car."

"Why so much stuff? Is this all for Christine?"

Ignoring Quinn's question, Roselyn picked up two garment bags and continued to go about her business. "I hope this all fits. I guess there's only one way to find out. Can you grab that box?"

Quinn looked at his mother suspiciously. "You didn't answer my question."

"I'm sorry, what was the question?" dawdled Roselyn, pretending to be preoccupied.

Quinn approached his mother and took the garment bags out of her hands. "Can you please tell me what's going on here? You obviously don't need all this stuff for a weekend trip."

Roselyn let out a big sigh and winced in frustration. "I really didn't wanna get into this today, not on your big weekend."

"Get into what? What big weekend?"

"It's the state basketball finals. You should be enjoying yourself with your friends and cheering on your team. The last thing you should be worried about is me and my trials and tribulations."

"What trials and tribulations?"

"Things that are going on in my personal life."

"Why wouldn't I be concerned about things going on in your life? After all, you're my mother."

Roselyn paused, took a deep breath, and allowed her body to go limp. Feeling defeated, she stared into Quinn's eyes sympathetically. "Let's go sit down and talk."

Fearing the worst, Quinn stiffened up and glared menacingly. "No, I'm *not* gonna sit down. I just want to know what's going on."

"All right, then, I'll just give it to you straight. I'm moving into an apartment in Chicago."

And there it was, delivered as straight-up as possible, a real gut punch that took the wind out of Quinn's sails. Stunned into a stupor, he turned away and drifted to the nearest chair, deciding he would sit down after all.

"It's not that big of a deal," continued Roselyn. "Chicago is not that far away, and I'll still come back and visit."

"Visit? So you're living there permanently?"

"No, temporarily. I need to be there for Christine and help her with her pregnancy."

"Isn't that what Michael is supposed to do?"

"She needs to know that her family hasn't abandoned her. It's something I need to do for her *and* me. I need to get away from here for a while so I can think, take time to figure things out."

"What does that mean? Does Dad know you're leaving?"

"Not exactly. He knows I've been thinking about it for a while. I will tell him when I get there. The last thing I wanted was a big fight before I left."

"Are you guys getting a divorce?"

"No, it's just a separation. It's all for the best."

"For who's best? Yours or mine? I guess your daughter is more important to you than your son."

Now it was Roselyn experiencing the gut punch. She had tried to walk a fine line between complacency and consternation, hoping her laissez-faire approach would produce less drama. But now she realized it wasn't that simple. She still had a son to raise, and he had feelings too.

With misty eyes, Roselyn approached her son and extended her arms for a hug. But he would have none of it. Rising abruptly, Quinn turned his head and walked to the other side of the room.

"I really don't know what to say," sobbed Roselyn. "I love you and I owe you an explanation. It's just that I've been under a lot of stress. Sometimes I feel so trapped that I just want to scream. I decided I need to get away for a while. If I don't, I just might go crazy."

Quinn turned and looked at his mother, feeling ashamed of his selfishness.

"I really don't know what to say either, except that I'm a little bit afraid. Afraid for you *and* me."

"Don't be afraid for yourself, Quinn. You have your whole future ahead of you, a very promising future."

"Maybe that's what I'm afraid of the most, my future. Everyone says I have a promising future, but sometimes I feel lots of pressure, the pressure of trying to live up to unrealistic expectations...especially Dad's."

"Your father thinks the world of you. He'll do whatever he can to provide for your future. You don't have to worry about that. You'll always be his number-one priority."

"That's just it. If you're not around, I'll be his *only* priority. I don't want that kinda pressure. Maybe I don't want to do what he has planned for me. Maybe I wanna make my own decisions."

Roselyn wiped the tears from her eyes and wrapped her arms around Quinn. This time he accepted her hug and embraced her firmly.

"It sounds like you and I want the same things in life," said Roselyn. "An opportunity to prove ourselves on our own terms. Maybe we're on the same page after all. Let's make a pledge to support each other."

Now Quinn was the one getting misty-eyed, realizing his mother would soon be out the door and out of his life. She was the only one who really understood him.

"This is not goodbye," she said firmly, reassuring Quinn with renewed confidence. "This is just a bend in the road." Then she went to her purse and pulled out a business card.

"Keep this in your wallet. This is my Chicago address and phone number. You can call me whenever you want, and I will keep you posted on everything that's going on. I will come back and visit, and you can visit us in Chicago. We're not gonna let a couple hours of distance come between us. You hear me?"

Quinn nodded his head and put the card in his wallet. "I guess I don't have much of a choice."

Chapter 51

S UNDAY, MARCH 24, 1974: FORT Wayne was frozen under two inches of snow and a thermometer reading fourteen degrees Fahrenheit, heading for a low of five degrees. It was the coldest day of March, and the coldest day since January 13, when temperatures dipped below zero.

The Northrop Bruins had captured the Indiana state championship the day before, defeating the Jeffersonville Red Devils 59-56 in a contest that wasn't decided until the final buzzer. After such a monumental achievement, it hardly seemed fair that the victors' reward would be a parade through Fort Wayne on one of the coldest days of the year. But they would persevere, just as they had all year long, arriving at their destination chilled to the bone.

Climbing aboard a makeshift podium in the parking lot of Glenbrook Mall, the players waved the championship trophy before thousands of adoring fans. The drought had officially ended. Not since 1958 had a Fort Wayne school secured a state basketball title, the year the South Side Archers returned home as conquering heroes.

Now, despite the bitter cold, the city was ready to celebrate, and Mayor Ivan Lebamoff was on hand to ceremoniously sanction the event, rewarding the Bruins with his seal of approval. Declaring a citywide holiday, the mayor announced that all schools would officially be closed on Monday, March 25.

The crowd roared with approval as everyone scrambled to their cars, anxiously seeking an escape from the frigid conditions and an opportunity to thaw their fingers and toes.

After a grueling forty-eight hours, no one was more relieved than the Bruin basketball players. Their whirlwind schedule had been a pressure-cooker of events, putting them under a relentless microscope and pushing them to the brink of exhaustion. A day of recovery would be just what the doctor ordered, an opportunity to recharge their batteries before the festivities resumed on Tuesday.

School administrators, local media and students would spend all day Monday planning for the biggest celebration of all, a carnival-like jubilee to be held in the Northrop gymnasium in front of TV cameras, sportswriters, and thousands of adulating fans.

"Damn, it's cold!" said Quinn, as he jumped into his Buick LeSabre, accompanied by Lynda, Brian, Mindy, and Mark Carter.

"Crank the heater up," ordered Mindy. "My hands are frozen numb."

"You'll just have to suffer for a while," said Lynda. "It'll take a good ten minutes for the heater to kick in on a day like this."

"I don't know if I can wait that long," replied Mindy. "I can see my breath back here."

"At least give us some tunes," said Brian.

Lynda flipped on the radio just in time for the beginning of Elton John's smash hit, the song that dominated the airwaves throughout the Bruins's championship run. She turned around and smiled at the back seat. "How's that for timing? I guess I have the magic touch," she said, as the radio pounded out the familiar refrain: "B-B-B-B-B-Bennie and the Jets."

Quinn O'Connor steered his Buick through the icy parking lot. He hadn't been home since his mother left for Chicago on Friday. After their sentimental farewells, Quinn had called Lynda to fill her in on his latest dilemma. Emotionally distraught, he confessed that he didn't want to be around when his father came home and read his mom's Dear John letter, a revelation that would certainly send him into orbit. Quinn was willing to do everything in his power to avoid that kind of spectacle. But how could he make himself disappear? Where could he go?

Sympathetic to Quinn's predicament, Lynda started plotting. Knowing that Brian and Mark would be riding along with Quinn to the Final Four in Bloomington, she decided to arrange a strategy that would work to Quinn's advantage. Calling Mindy, she explained, without the gossipy details, why it would be logical for Quinn to spend the night at Brian's house so the guys could depart for Bloomington together, bright and early.

No sooner had Lynda hung up the phone than Mindy began dialing Brian's number, explaining the plan. Naturally, Brian had no issues with the scheme other than the obvious peculiarities. Wouldn't Quinn perceive the invitation as odd? Why would he unexpectedly ask Quinn to spend the night? Wouldn't someone of Quinn's stature feel uncomfortable spending the night in a middle-class neighborhood, sleeping on a fold-out sofa?

In the end, none of the conjecture seemed to matter. All that really mattered was that Mindy had made a request.

"Consider it done," said Brian, always willing to indulge Mindy's wishes. "I'll call him and say that my mother is whipping up a special dinner for us this evening as a way to thank him for driving us all to Bloomington. That should work. Don't you think?"

"Perfect," said Mindy. "I owe you."

"And I'll hold you to that," teased Brian.

Although Quinn had avoided the awkward encounter at home, he couldn't help but visualize, in his mind, the chilling reaction his father would have when he read his mother's letter, a true wake-up call to his twenty-eight-year pretense called marriage. It would be an insufferable blow to his ego, leaving him on a limb and threatening his enduring vitality.

Perhaps it was only fitting justice, Quinn thought, for someone who had always been so self-centered. For too long, his father's reign had been unchallenged; always dictating, never compromising. Now, like an aging heavyweight boxer, he would suffer a knockout punch, a dose of reality that would bring him to his knees. Quinn almost wished he had been there to witness it. It might have revealed a vulnerability he'd never seen before.

Playing through the scenarios in his mind, Quinn's emotions would swing back and forth like a pendulum. On one hand, he would feel pity for his father, home alone and abandoned by his family, dealing with rejection and isolation. On the other hand, he would envision his father's wrath, lashing out and striking his adversaries with intimidation. The version of his father that would endure was impossible to predict. He only knew that, moving forward, no one else would be around to deflect the outcome. There would be no buffer. From now on, it would be just him and his father, one-on-one, with no place to hide.

"You boys wanna come in?" asked Mark, as Quinn prepared to drop him off.

"Fine by me," said Quinn. "Does this mean I get to meet the honorable Captain Carter?"

"Well, I don't know how honorable he is, but he should be home on a Sunday."

Walking through the front door, the boys were immediately greeted by Mark's father.

"Well, I guess I should say hail to the victors," proclaimed Captain Carter. "How was the parade? I'll have you know, I had to throw together a crowd-control team on a very short notice. That's gonna cost me a pretty penny in overtime wages."

"Actually, the crowd along the parade route wasn't that big," said Mark. "I think it was too cold."

"Well, then, maybe I overspent on crowd control. But you can never be too safe. The mayor's gotta realize there's a real cost to his impromptu rah-rah sessions."

"Speaking of the mayor," said Mark, "he canceled school tomorrow. We get the whole day off."

"Seriously? That's just great. Now I gotta worry about kids gettin' into trouble; kids that are supposed to be in school."

"Well, you don't have to worry about us. By the way, I don't think you've met our friend here. This is Quinn O'Connor."

"Pleased to meet you, Mr. Carter," said Quinn, extending his hand. "Or should I call you Captain Carter?"

"That won't be necessary. You're not related to Ryan O'Connor, are you?"

"That would be my father," said Quinn, suddenly proud of his affiliation. "I guess you've heard of him?"

"More than that. A man of your father's means understands the need for police protection. Let's just say we've conducted business together more than a few times."

"No surprise," said Quinn. "My father has many business interactions."

"I would say that's a safe assumption," chuckled Mr. Carter.

"I hear you and Mark are quite the outdoorsmen," offered Quinn. "What's your favorite thing to hunt?"

"Well, that's hard to say. I guess it depends on the season. Mark, why don't you take Quinn out back and show him our hunting lodge."

"Hunting lodge?" inquired Quinn.

"That's what we call it," said Mr. Carter. "I guess it's nothing more than a glorified shed. But you can see some of our trophies back there."

"You wanna take a look?" asked Mark.

"Sure, let's do it."

Stepping out the back door, Quinn could see, for the first time, that the Carters lived on the outer fringes of Coldwater Creek. Enclosed by a five-foot chain-length fence, their backyard was spacious and private and bordered by a grove of trees.

"So waddaya think?" asked Mark.

"You have lots of room back here," noted Quinn. "Nice and private too. What's behind those trees?"

"Just cornfields. If you look closely, you can vaguely see them through the woods, only because the trees are bare this time of year. That won't be the case when summer rolls around."

"I thought you had hunting dogs. Is that what those pens are for?" asked Quinn, pointing toward a fenced enclosure with two dog houses.

"We share two beagles with my dad's partner. He's the one who trained them to be bird dogs, so they spend most of their time with him. Sometimes we'll keep them here when we come home from a hunting trip."

"Show him the hunting lodge," urged Brian.

"Lodge might be an exaggeration," conceded Mark.

"But it's a helluva lot bigger than a shed," said Quinn. "Can we look inside? Or is it locked?"

"I doubt it. We hardly ever lock it up. Let's take a look."

Mark proceeded to lead them toward a cabin-like building that almost looked like a tiny guest house. It's shake-shingle siding, made from cedar, gave the structure a rustic look, reminiscent of a Cape Cod style cottage.

"Pretty cool, don't you think?" said Brian.

"Very inviting," confirmed Quinn. "I definitely want to see the inside."

The boys followed Mark up two tiny steps and through the door.

"Let's warm this place up," suggested Mark as he made his way toward a portable space heater.

"It's actually warmer than I thought it would be," noted Quinn.

"Yeah, it's insulated pretty well, but this space heater will make it nice and toasty on a day like today."

Quinn slowly pivoted his body around, sizing the place up as his eyes scanned the perimeter. "This is pretty cool," he noted, "but it smells like moth balls." Then he plopped himself down on an old rocking chair.

"Your sense of smell is pretty keen," confirmed Mark. "At least we don't have any moths."

"I like it," said Quinn. "It feels like I'm camping somewhere in the wilderness. Not that I've ever camped before."

"That's because you spend too much time at the country club playing tennis," teased Mark.

"Perhaps," said Quinn. "Maybe I need to broaden my horizons. By the way, where did you get this old rocking chair? It looks like it belonged to Granny on the *Beverly Hillbillies*."

"Maybe that's where he got it," joked Brian. "I think the Carters are related to the Clampetts."

"Please don't tell me you hunt possum and cook it up in a stew," continued Quinn, thoroughly enjoying himself.

"Very funny," said Mark. "Although we do hunt deer and cook up the meat."

"That's called venison, right?" asked Quinn, exploiting his limited knowledge. "How does it taste?"

"We'll fix it up sometime and let you try for yourself. We have plenty in the freezer."

"So tell me about those deer heads mounted on the wall. Did you shoot those yourself?"

"The one on the left is a ten-point buck I shot two years ago in Brown County."

"It's a beauty," noted Quinn. "Is that the biggest one you ever shot?"

"Yeah, it was over two hundred pounds. It took three of us to load it onto the truck."

"It's not as big as the one on the right. What kind of deer is that?"

"That's not a deer, it's an elk. You can't find those around here. My dad shot that in Wyoming."

"And what about that bear?" asked Quinn. "Did someone actually shoot that? Or did you just put it up there to look macho?"

"My dad shot that up in Canada a few years ago. It's a brown bear, also known as a grizzly."

"Well, you won't ever catch me hunting grizzlies. I'd be afraid they might hunt me down first."

"I've never gone bear hunting," noted Mark. "But you are correct. It's considerably more dangerous than deer hunting."

"And what about all those guns hanging on the wall? Do you really need that many?"

"There's only four. Two of them belong to Dad, and the other two are mine."

"I don't know anything about guns," admitted Quinn. "Can you explain the differences?"

"It's really pretty simple. We have two rifles and two shotguns."

"I thought rifles and shotguns were the same thing."

"Nope, we use our rifles for shooting deer. They're better for long-range. That's why they have scopes." Mark reached up and took down one of the rifles. "This one is mine. It's a Winchester Model 70. I used this to take down that ten-point buck. I nailed it from fifty yards away."

"So what are shotguns used for?"

"Those are for shorter distances. Shot gun shells will spray dozens of lead pellets at your target. That makes it easier to aim on short notice. They're good for small game like rabbits and birds. We use ours mostly for dove hunting."

"That's interesting. This is all new to me. Do you hunt dove for sport? Or can you eat them?"

"Both. We go dove hunting the first two weeks of October. That's why we have beagles. They're trained to flush out the birds and retrieve them after we shoot 'em down. And, by the way, they're delicious to eat."

"That sounds like fun. Which shotgun is yours?"

Mark returned the rifle to the gun rack and reached for his shotgun, surprised that Quinn was asking so many questions. Outside of his element, Quinn had settled into the unassuming charm and folksiness of the Carter cabin. Feeling more comfortable, he continued with his inquiries, seeking an escape from his sheltered world of wealth and privilege.

"Here, hold this," ordered Mark as he handed Quinn his shotgun. "This is a Remington Model 32, one of the most popular shotguns ever made."

"Whoa, be careful. You really want me to hold this? It's not loaded, is it?"

"Nah, we never store our guns loaded. Dad keeps all the ammo locked up in the garage. Safety is always the number-one priority when handling guns."

Quinn took the gun and aimed it toward the ceiling. "I think I could get into dove hunting. What about fox hunting? Have you ever seen those movies where the English gentlemen get all dressed up in red blazers and ride their horses through the countryside with a pack of hounds?"

Mark and Brian started laughing.

"What's so funny?"

"We don't do that kind of hunting in Indiana," explained Mark. "Maybe you could organize a fox hunt through your country club."

"Maybe I will," said Quinn, playing along with the joke. "Here, you better put this back before I hurt myself."

Mark took the Remington from Quinn and returned it to the gun rack. "What do you know about handguns?"

"That's a silly question. The only thing I know about guns is what you're teaching me right now."

Mark proceeded to open a wooden cabinet mounted on the wall next to the elk head. "Let's see what we have in here. Ah yes, my dad's favorite gun."

Pulling a .38-caliber weapon from the case, Mark tossed it toward Quinn. "Here, catch."

Quinn started to make a catch, but then suddenly jumped back out of fear for an explosion. "Holy shit!" he exclaimed, allowing the gun to hit the floor. "That's not loaded, is it?"

"Don't be ridiculous. I told you we don't store loaded guns."

Quinn bent over and picked up the gun. "Ah yes, I like this. It feels good in my hand. What can you tell me about this?"

"Well, I can tell you everything my dad told me. Like I said, it's his favorite gun. When he was in the army during the Korean War, this gun was pretty much standard issue. One of the most popular handguns ever made, at least according to my dad. When the army released him in 1955, he had to return his gun, so he decided to buy one for himself at the PX, which, I guess, is kinda like a military store."

"So what's so special about it?"

"I guess he just liked the way it looked and handled. He said it was perfectly balanced, fired consistently and had a classic design." Mark then reached for the gun. "Here, let me show you."

"Just don't point it at me," lectured Quinn.

Mark took the gun and chuckled. "You're awfully gun shy for someone who wants to learn so much about guns."

"Tell me more," ordered Quinn.

"Well, this is a Smith & Wesson .38 special revolver, Model 19, with a four-inch barrel. It has a nickel finish and a walnut handle."

"Wait," said Quinn. "You're throwing too much at me all at once. What does '38' mean?"

"It's a .38-caliber weapon."

"That doesn't answer my question. What is 38? And what is caliber?"

"Okay, fair enough. I'm no expert, but caliber is supposed to be the diameter of the bore, which is the barrel of the gun. In other words, thirty-eight-hundredths of an inch."

"Okay, I think I get it. And what does revolver mean?"

Mark proceeded to swing out the cylinder and spin it around. "There are six chambers in this cylinder. The cylinder revolves to the next chamber every time a round is fired. That's why it's called a revolver."

"Okay, that makes sense. But what kind of guns are *not* revolvers?"

"The ones that don't have revolving cylinders. Instead, the ammo is fed from a magazine."

"Can I see it again?" asked Quinn.

Mark handed him the gun, and Quinn proceeded to swing the cylinder in and out and spin it around. Then he pointed the gun at the grizzly bear and pretended to fire. "This is pretty cool. I can see why your father likes it."

"You really need to point and aim with two hands. You'll have much more control that way."

Quinn took Mark's advice and pointed at the bear again, this time with two hands.

"So what's the difference between a handgun like this and the one that Dirty Harry used in *Magnum Force*? Remember? He called it a .44 Magnum, the most powerful handgun in the world."

"Well, a .44 caliber is a bigger, heavier weapon. And magnum refers to the type of cartridge. A magnum cartridge contains more gunpowder, which makes it more powerful, meaning it propels faster and farther. But my dad called it Hollywood hype. He said no police officer would ever carry a .44 Magnum because it's too heavy and has too much recoil, which makes it much harder to fire multiple rounds."

"Wow, you really *do* know a lot about guns," conceded Quinn.

"He's the man," said Brian. "You don't become an Eagle Scout overnight."

"Well, I didn't learn about guns from scouting. My dad taught me everything I know, and I don't know nearly as much as he does. I guess that comes from spending most of his life in the military and the police force."

"Hey, Mark," said Brian. "It looks like your father is waving for us to come in."

Mark walked over to the door and opened it. "Wassup?"

"Your mother just made supper and there's enough for everyone. Come on inside and wash up."

Mark looked at his buddies, gave them the thumbs-up, and said, "Let's go eat."

"Wow," said Quinn. "You're gonna feed me, too? I just might take up residence here in this little hunting lodge."

"You'd get tired of it pretty fast. You're too spoiled."

"You never know, I might like it. As long as your mother isn't feeding me venison and possum stew every night."

"You get what you pay for." Mark laughed.

After washing their hands, the boys joined the police captain at the dinner table. Walking in with a platter of fried chicken in one hand and a large bowl of mashed potatoes in the other, Mark's mother announced her intentions.

"This is going to be very casual. I call it family style. Just pass the plates around and help yourselves."

Mark immediately grabbed a piece of fried chicken and Mrs. Carter slapped his hand.

"Oh no, you don't. Guests always get first choice around here, so mind your manners. Besides, there's more to come, so be patient."

Mark looked sheepishly at his buddies while his mom went back to the kitchen. "I guess you can tell who's in charge around here at supper time."

"Not just supper time," joked Mr. Carter. "I may be a captain, but your mother always outranks me when I'm at home."

Mrs. Carter marched back into the dining room with authority, still wearing her apron. This time she had an oven mitt on each hand as she delivered two more large bowls. "I hope you like green beans and creamed corn. These bowls are very hot, so be careful."

This time nobody budged. Keeping their hands under the table, the men decided to mind their manners, politely waiting for Mrs. Carter to take her seat.

"That's much better," she announced. "For a minute, I thought I was feeding a pack of hungry wolves. Now, before we get started, we need to say grace. Quinn, since you're our special guest, we'll allow you the honors."

Caught off guard, Quinn was suddenly uncomfortable, struggling to gather his thoughts. "Well, I'm not very good at that sort of thing, Mrs. Carter."

"That's okay, dear. Most people like to express their thankfulness, but you can say anything you feel is appropriate."

Quinn felt his face turning red as everyone stared. He couldn't remember the last time his family said grace at the dinner table; this was all new. Then he suddenly remembered a Catholic prayer he learned in grade school and spewed it out as fast as he could.

Bless us, O Lord, and these Thy gifts, which we are about to receive from Thy bounty, through Christ our Lord. Amen.

Then he looked up to find everyone staring at him as if to ask, "Where did that come from?"

Feeling embarrassed, he quickly added one more line. "And thank you Mrs. Carter for putting together this lovely meal."

Feeling sorry for Quinn's awkwardness, Mark chimed in, "Amen."

Following suit, the table responded with a hearty "Amen."

Mark immediately reached for the platter of fried chicken and handed it to Quinn. "Dig in," he ordered.

"Thank you, don't mind if I do."

"You're in for a rare treat," noted Mark. "Mom's fried chicken is as good as it gets, even better than *Kentucky Fried Chicken*."

"And she's much better lookin' than Colonel Sanders," teased Mr. Carter.

Quinn laughed along with everyone else. He was starting to relax again and feel comfortable with his surroundings. There was something about a gathering of family and friends around a dinner table that made a person feel whole and enriched, with a sense of peace and fulfillment. Quinn couldn't remember the last time he had that feeling. This was far removed from his father's high-pressure world of wealth and power. He liked this world better.

"Thanks again, Mrs. Carter," said Quinn. "Everything is delicious. Thank you for sharing your home with me."

"You're quite welcome, dear. We're honored to have you as our guest."

"Of course, it comes with a price," teased Mr. Carter. "Tell your father I've had my eye on a new Buick Regal for some time now. Maybe he could cut me a good deal."

"I don't think that's an appropriate discussion for the dinner table," lectured Mrs. Carter.

"No, it's quite all right," assured Quinn. "I'm certain my father would be more than willing to offer a good deal to the captain of the police force."

"I was only joking," clarified the captain.

"No, I'm serious," continued Quinn. "When people do him favors, he takes good care of them in return. He told me that's how the business world works."

As soon as the words came out of his mouth, Quinn sensed a nervous tension.

Captain Carter gazed at Quinn suspiciously, realizing the O'Connor boy might not be as innocent as he seemed.

"Well, I appreciate the offer. I suppose nobody understands how the business world works better than your father."

Mark passed the bowl of creamed corn to Quinn in an effort to divert the context. Quinn took two large scoops, even though he didn't like corn, and Brian started talking about football. Everyone had moved on, except Quinn.

Acknowledging his own anxiety, Quinn couldn't help but wonder how the mood had shifted so rapidly. Did he say something wrong? Did he make everyone uncomfortable? Now he was feeling self-conscious, embarrassed that he had cast a shadow over a wholesome family dinner.

Maybe he was like his father after all, the kind of guy who manipulates others. No, he couldn't be like that, could he? He was only spewing the family jargon, the way he was trained, the same way he invoked the predinner prayer. It really didn't mean anything.

In his mind, Quinn told himself to forget about it. He needed to drop it and move on. Unfortunately, he was haunted by too many demons.

The state championship rally on Tuesday turned into a giant extravaganza, a celebration for the ages. Surrounded by sportswriters, TV cameras, and local dignitaries, the jam-packed gymnasium rejoiced as the players took center stage waving their giant trophy. Similar to the Final Four sendoff, the rally would last almost half the school day, but it was a fitting tribute to such a monumental accomplishment.

In only its third year of existence, Northrop had become the youngest school ever to win an Indiana state basketball title. The achievement was all the more significant considering the newly constructed school had become the focal point of Fort Wayne's desegregation plans, ground zero for racial unification. Serving as a model for equality, Northrop High School had become the new standard-bearer for integration.

The basketball team, consisting of six White players and six Black players, turned more than a few heads when it appeared at the state finals. Of the starting five (Walter Jordan, Mike Muff, James Wimbley, Maurice Drinks, and Tom Madden), only Madden was White. The other four players were from the inner-city and never would've played for a suburban school had it not been for the school board's decision to integrate in 1971.

But none of that seemed to matter in the end. Players and fans alike had become color-blind, oblivious to the cultural differences. The only thing that really mattered was that a basketball team had molded itself into a champion, overcoming boundaries and barriers to unite for one common cause, an Indiana state championship. The Northrop Bruins had become one big happy family, proudly representing the city of Fort Wayne and all of its diversity.

Northrop's Walter Jordan and his state finals opponent from Jeffersonville, Wayne Walls, would go on to have outstanding collegiate careers at Purdue University. They would also become key members of the Indiana High School All-Stars, a team that included Co-Mr. Basketballs, Roy Taylor of Anderson, and Steve Collier of Southwestern. Collier would go on to be a four-year starter at the University of Cincinnati and score over a thousand career points. Two other high-profile players were also on that All-Star team: Wayne Radford of Indianapolis Arlington, and Larry Bird from Springs Valley High School. Wayne Radford would go on to play at Indiana University and be part of the undefeated, national championship team of 1976, while Bird would become the most decorated player of them all, earning three NBA championships with the Boston Celtics, two league MVPs, and an election into the Pro Basketball Hall of Fame.

Chapter 52

BRIAN, MARK, AND SCOTT CLEVER loitered at their customary spot in the Northrop Commons, in between the gymnasium doors and the entrance to the cafeteria, a niche they had carved out earlier in the year. As the location evolved into a gathering spot for jocks, cheerleaders, and members of the pom-pom squad, they saw no need to deviate from their routine. Not only were they residing in their comfort zone, surrounded by friends and teammates, but they were segregating themselves from the pack, establishing their membership to the in-crowd, a status they did not achieve overnight.

Although there were no hard-and-fast rules for inclusion, there was one feature not easily mistaken, the color of their skin. It's not that Black people weren't allowed—the athletes and cheerleaders were mostly color-blind—it's just that people of color traditionally gathered on the other side of the Commons, partly because they enjoyed each other's company, and partly because their inner-city buses arrived in proximity to one another.

Unstimulated and uninspired, the student body seemed remarkably calm for a Friday morning. After three days of posttournament festivities, a lethargic mood had descended upon the school, like a hangover without a cure. With no basketball games on the horizon, weekends would become routine and mundane, leaving the students with few alternatives. Not surprisingly, the girls would begin making plans for the prom, and the guys would start talking about baseball. Nevertheless, spring remained a distant remedy, especially for those without sunny dispositions.

Mark and Scott had already indulged in their morning cinnamon rolls, a ritual they could not break, at least not as long as they had twenty-five cents in their pockets. Nobody knew which cafeteria cook was the pastry guru, but the reputation of the cinnamon rolls had become legendary.

These were not your average cinnamon rolls. Hot out of the oven, they were oversized delicacies of confectionery delight, wonderfully doughy and yeasty with an irresistible gooeyness. If a food chain could mass-produce the same formula, they would undoubtedly captivate a lifetime of allegiance.

Scott looked at Brian, who was still cradling his cinnamon roll on a paper plate.

"Are you gonna eat that? 'Cause if you're not, I'll take it off your hands."

"I'm saving it for Mindy. She loves these things and I'm not gonna pass up an opportunity to score some points."

"You've already racked up enough points with her," teased Scott. "But I'm guessing that *scoring* is something you haven't cashed in on yet."

"No skin off my nose, she's worth it," said Brian. Then he lifted the roll to reveal a pat of melted butter. "This is the key—gotta have warm butter."

"Did you pay your two cents for that butter?" asked Scott.

"Ha! Like anybody ever does. Surely, they know that *everyone* hides butter under their rolls."

"Look who's coming," observed Mark. "It's the magnificent trio."

Brian and Scott looked up to see Lynda, Quinn, and Antonio make their grand entrance, turning heads as they coasted in for a landing. The royal couple donned their usual ensemble of preppy attire, while Antonio strutted his dapperness in a silk paisley shirt, chocolate-brown polyester slacks, and black three-inch platform shoes. The only thing missing was Curtis Mayfield's theme from *Super Fly*.

By contrast, Lynda's clothing popped out like a spring tulip. Although Easter was a couple weeks away, her light and cheery pastels brightened up the room like a basket of Easter eggs. Quinn, tagging along like a puppy dog, sported a kelly-green polo shirt and navy-blue Izod sweater. The pullover sweater had been removed and tied around his neck as though he'd gotten too warm while walking to his Ivy League classroom.

"Well, well," chided Mark. "Look who's making their red-carpet appearance."

"Please," retorted Lynda, "no flash-photography today."

"I'll try to restrain myself," said Mark. "Quinn, why are you slumming it today with a pair of jeans? Did you run out of khakis? Or did you drop them off at the dry cleaners?"

"I'm dressed for the Carter Hunting Lodge," countered Quinn, enjoying the banter.

"And that sweater," continued Mark, "why is it tied around your neck like a scarf? Don't you know how to pull it over your head?"

"I got too warm after entering the building. But I may need it again if my classroom is too cold. One must be prepared and fashionable at the same time."

"You better hurry if you wanna grab a cinnamon roll," noted Brian, trying to wedge himself into the conversation. "I'm holding this one for Mindy."

"Not today," replied Lynda. "I need to watch my figure."

"Me too," said Antonio. "I need to maintain this slender physique for my performances."

"Are you gonna be in the musical this year?" asked Brian.

"*Annie Get Your Gun*? I don't think so, even though they asked me to try out. I'm not a very good fit for an old-fashioned musical about cowboys and cowgirls. But I told them I'd help out with the musical score."

"Why don't they plan on a musical that would feature *you*?" asked Brian. "It seems like they're wasting too much talent if they don't."

"I'll take that as a compliment," winked Antonio. "As it turns out, the drama teacher told me they wanted to put on *Hello Dolly* next year. He said they would feature me and my trumpet. I think that's something I could get into, although I could never sing *Hello Dolly* the way Louis Armstrong did, with that gravelly voice."

"You'd be a natural," said Lynda. "Just like everything else you do."

"Girl, you really know how to win my heart. Maybe I'll request you as my leading lady."

"Nice try, but *acting* is not my cup of tea."

"Suit yourself," said Antonio, glancing at his watch. "I gotta get going. The bell's about to ring and Papa Bruin's waiting on me."

Papa Bruin was the name the students had affectionately awarded to their jolly and portly principal, Paul Spuller. Ever since the announcement of his impending retirement, Spuller seemed to be on a mission to enjoy himself, whole-heartedly embracing his nickname and savoring his last fleeting moments around a generation that was forty years his junior.

Spryer than ever, the principal was determined to surround himself with his students and their youthful zest for life, creating a final chapter of lasting memories. The fact that his school had captured a state basketball championship in the final year of his career was only icing on the cake.

Continuing with his theme of student involvement, Spuller had decided to deviate from the old-school routine of monotonous morning announcements. Instead of using an administrator to deliver the obligatory essentials, he decided to spice things up by recruiting students, and since no one could deliver a performance like Antonio Jackson, there was little doubt about who would take over the morning broadcast.

Enthusiastically embracing his role as the orator of greetings and good tidings, Antonio delivered the school's agenda each day like a toastmaster. Some days he would spice things up with his trumpet, while other days he would tinker with a xylophone, but he would always deliver the daily news with witticism and good humor, hitting all the highlights with his entertaining eloquence. Mr. Spuller would merely stand by in admiration, giving Antonio free rein to create and perform as he pleased, extemporaneously producing his own brand of artistry.

When Antonio was done, he would typically surrender the microphone to the principal with, "That's all for today, let me turn it back over to our exalted and reverent Pappa Bruin." And Spuller would reply with, "Thank you, my worthy wizard of mystical powers. Go forth with your fellow Bruins, and prosper." And with those nimble-witted words, the tone would be set for the rest of the day.

Walking down the main corridor, Brian held Mindy's book bag while she nibbled on her cinnamon roll.

"Thanks again for the roll," garbled Mindy, her mouth filled with the sticky dough.

"My pleasure." Brian laughed.

"What are you laughing about?"

"You have a hunk of gooey icing stuck on the corner of your mouth."

"Oh, disgusting! Can you get it for me?" she asked, handing him a napkin. "Or do you want to lick it off?"

Brian raised his eyebrows flirtatiously. He knew that Mindy was teasing, but he couldn't help but get turned on by her sexual innuendos. He decided to reply in his normal, responsible way.

"I don't think that would be appropriate right here in the middle of the hallway. Besides, I might not be able to control myself."

Mindy smiled at his flattery, allowing him to proceed with the napkin. "Just be careful not to smudge my lipstick."

Brian carefully outlined the corner of her mouth with the napkin and then dabbed it on her lips gently, finishing with a tender kiss on her forehead.

"So what are you doing tonight?" asked Mindy. "Any chance we can hookup later?"

"I thought you were babysitting tonight."

"I am, but I came up with a plan," she said with a twinkle in her eye.

"I'm all ears," said Brian, his curiosity peaking.

"Well, I'm supposed to be at Dr. Adair's house at six thirty. They have dinner reservations at seven. Then they were hoping to catch a movie around eight thirty, which means they won't be home until ten thirtyish. That should give us enough time to be alone together if you wanna sneak over."

"Sounds kinda risky," noted Brian. "What about the kids?"

"There's only one, her name is Chelsea. She's three years old and goes to bed at eight o'clock. That means you can come over at eight thirty."

"Sounds good to me. You really think we can pull it off without anyone knowing?"

"Yes, we just need to be careful. I'll give you the address and you can park down the street so no one sees your car in front of the house."

"Sounds like you've thought this thing through."

"I think we can make it work. I'll call you at your house between eight and eight fifteen to let you know if the coast is clear."

Then Mindy grabbed her books and headed off to class. "Tootles."

Brian approached the doctor's residence with caution. Mindy had left the front porch light on, clearly revealing the street address, 3624. Yes, he was certain he had the right house. Even so, he felt the anxiety of suspicion as he rang the doorbell.

"Come on in," said Mindy, answering the door.

Brian couldn't help but get a warm sensation with the vision of Mindy standing at the door, inviting him across the threshold. Somehow, he knew that this was the way he wanted it to be the rest of his life, always coming home to Mindy.

"I don't see your car. That's a good thing."

"Yeah, I parked about five houses down. Is Chelsea asleep?"

"Yes, she's a good little girl. Very cute and easy to take care of. And the doctor pays me well. So this is one babysitting job I don't wanna lose."

"This is a really nice house," said Brian, following Mindy into the kitchen. "So what kind of a doctor is he?"

"He's a pediatrician."

"And he trusts *you* with his kid?" teased Brian.

"Hey, I'm good with kids, and Chelsea loves me. Would you like a Coke?"

"Sure. I guess a beer is out of the question?"

Opening the refrigerator, Mindy responded. "He has beer in here, but let's not go down that path. Like I said, I wanna keep this babysitting job."

"That's okay," said Brian. "I was only joking, but it's good to know that doctors drink beer too."

Mindy poured two glasses of Coke and set them down on the counter. "Before we head to the family room, I want to go over a little fire drill with you."

"Fire drill?"

"Yes, like I said, I don't expect the doctor and his wife to be home until ten thirty. But that's based upon them getting tickets to the movie. They were planning on seeing *The Exorcist*, but that's the most popular movie in the world right now, which means if they don't get a ticket, they could see another show, or they may decide to come home."

"Which means they could be home real soon?"

"I'm guessing nine o'clock is a possibility if they don't end up going to the movie."

"It's almost eight thirty now," said Brian, checking his watch. "Are you telling me I need to leave in the next twenty minutes?"

"No, I'm telling you I have a plan in place in case they come home early."

"I'm not sure I like the sound of this," said Brian, his anxiety building again.

"Follow me," said Mindy as she took Brian's hand and led him down the hallway and into a back bedroom. "See this window? Now watch."

Mindy flipped the latch and pushed the window up, leaving it wide open.

"See? No screen. All you have to do is hop out this back window and you're gone."

"You can't be serious."

"Why not? I'm completely serious."

"It seems awfully risky to me. How will we know when they're coming home and how will I have enough time to sneak out the back window?"

"They'll be coming in through the garage. I can easily hear the garage door opener from the family room. It makes a lot of noise."

"So I'm supposed to run down the hallway and jump out the back window when you hear the garage door opener?"

"You got it," smirked Mindy. "Piece of cake."

"Easy for you to say."

"Oh, c'mon! I thought you were a big, strong football player. Now you're afraid of jumpin' out a little bedroom window?"

Brian looked at Mindy and her ornery grin. This was the Mindy that turned him on. The cute and sassy Mindy. The Mindy who was willing to take a chance on mischief. The Mindy that thought things through and planned ahead, unbridled by conformity.

"I'm game if you are," said Brian, feeling energized by the challenge.

"It's only a contingency plan. Like I said, they probably won't be home until ten thirty, which means you'll leave around ten."

"And this is your little fire drill to get me prepared, right?"

"Exactly. Isn't that the Girl Scout motto? Be prepared?"

"I think it's the Boy Scout motto." Brian laughed. "But I'm not sure. You'll have to ask Mark Carter. Anyway, you don't seem like much of a Girl Scout."

"You got that right," said Mindy. "Now let's go back to the family room. You wanna watch some TV?"

Mindy fiddled with the TV channels while Brian waited impatiently on the sofa, sipping his Coke and contemplating his next move.

"Let's see, we've got *The Odd Couple* on ABC, or we can watch *Good Times* on CBS."

"*Good Times*," said Brian. "We already missed *Sanford and Son*. *Good Times* is the next best thing."

"*Good Times* it is," said Mindy, settling on CBS.

Halfway back to the sofa, she suddenly hesitated. "Oh wait, I need to turn the volume down a little lower so we can hear if the garage door opens."

Just when Brian was starting to relax, Mindy had made him uncomfortable again.

"You didn't really wanna watch TV, did you?" she asked as she parked herself on Brian's lap.

Feeling her derriere on his welcoming loins, Brian could feel his heartbeat kick up a notch. Watching TV was now the furthest thing from his mind. He was falling into surrender mode.

Wrapping her arms around Brian's neck, Mindy delivered a long, embracing kiss, enticing him with her playful tongue.

"How's that for some *Good Times*?" she giggled.

"Hmmm, it doesn't get any better than that."

Mindy could feel Brian's arousal against her jeans and decided to stand up again.

"I found an interesting book on Dr. Adair's bookshelves. You wanna look at it with me?"

"Sure," said Brian with a hard swallow, trying to ease his blood pressure back down again.

Mindy walked over to the shelves and pulled out a hardback book with a white cover and large red letters.

Brian recognized it immediately. He'd seen it in bookstore windows and prominently displayed in drugstores and department stores everywhere. It was the number-one bestseller: *The Joy of Sex*.

Despite its controversial contents, it was selling like hotcakes and the topic of many debates and discussions. He'd always wondered about what was between the covers, but he never had the nerve to pick up a copy in the store and look inside. Now, his girlfriend, the sexiest girl on the planet, was holding a copy in her hand and asking him to look at it with her.

"What's the matter?" she asked teasingly. "Cat got your tongue?"

Brian gulped and tried to think of a clever response. "Do you think the doctor cares if we look at it?"

"Well, he *is* a doctor, and this is more or less an instruction manual that was written by a doctor, so I doubt it."

"Instruction manual?" asked Brian. "And you're my teacher?"

"Ha, very funny. I doubt that I'm qualified to teach *this* topic, but we can learn together, can't we?"

Brian was getting turned on again. Mindy never ceased to amaze him. He patted the seat cushion next to him and said, "Sit down. Let's look at it together."

Mindy plopped down on the couch and took charge. "So you know the history behind this book, don't you?"

"Well, no, not exactly."

"The author is a scientist and a physician. He's taught at universities, and he's written many books. He decided to model this book after a famous cookbook called *The Joy of Cooking*. That's why it says, 'A Gourmet Guide to Love Making.' "

"So *that's* where the name comes from," acknowledged Brian. "See, you're already teaching me things."

It was beginning to seem so academic now, not like the perverted images he had conjured up in his mind.

"Yes, my mom has *The Joy of Cooking* in our kitchen," said Mindy. "We use it all the time."

"Does she also have *The Joy of Sex* in her library?"

"No way. Not in our conservative household. Besides, I don't even want to think about my parents having sex."

"Maybe they didn't," offered Brian, trying to be funny. "Maybe you were a test tube baby."

"I like that idea better," giggled Mindy as she opened the book and pointed to the table of contents. "As you can see, it's set up like a cookbook or a restaurant menu. It's divided into three major sections: starters, main courses, and sauces & pickles."

"Sauces and pickles? That's a funny name."

"The starters section," continued Mindy, "is sort of the science behind everything. It explains the male and female body parts and the basic fundamentals of sex. It also talks about birth control methods."

"Maybe we should go right to the main course," said Brian, trying to be clever.

"The main course section gets more into the specifics on foreplay, pleasure techniques and sexual positions. Plus, it has lots of pictures."

"How about pictures and pleasure techniques," suggested Brian, as if ordering from a menu.

"You might be disappointed in the pictures," said Mindy, flipping through the pages. "It's not like *Playboy*."

"They look more like drawings."

"That's exactly what they are—drawings. They were afraid real photos might be too explicit and cause the book to be banned as pornographic."

"I wonder who did the drawings."

"Good question," said Mindy, praising her student. "I read about it in *Time* magazine. The illustrator posed for all the pictures with his wife, and then made drawings of all the photos."

"Sounds like a lot of work. I wonder who the photographer was?"

"Wouldn't *you* like to know," teased Mindy. "I bet you'd like *that* job."

"Maybe." Brian laughed. "Or maybe it would be more fun *posing* for the pictures. But only if *you* were my partner."

Mindy put her hand on Brian's thigh and delivered another passionate kiss, rewarding him for his promiscuous suggestion.

"I think I would be up to the task," she finally answered. "But first we better study the different poses, don't you think?"

"Sure," said Brian, wondering how much longer she would go on tantalizing him with her playful enticements.

Mindy continued flipping through the book before stopping at page ninety-nine. "Here's where the main courses section begins. It's funny that the very first topic is about breasts. Do you consider that a main course?"

"That's a good question," conceded Brian, enjoying Mindy's proclivity for playfulness. "Some might consider them to be more of a snack," he said, chuckling over his own witticism.

"And then it covers buttocks, earlobes, feet, hair, and so on. Do you find feet to be very sexy?"

"I think *your* feet are sexy."

"And then it talks about handwork over the next couple pages, and then covers the topic of kissing."

"It doesn't seem to have any logical order," noted Brian.

"How so?"

"Well, I thought kissing would come first, followed by handwork maybe? Instead, it starts with breasts and buttocks and continues in no particular order."

"Good observation," agreed Mindy. "And the pictures seem to be randomly placed every few pages. They don't necessarily sync up to the topic."

"Agreed."

"For example," continued Mindy, "here's page one hundred sixteen talking about hair and handwork, and the opposing page shows a picture of a woman on top of her partner engaging in full-blown intercourse. It makes no sense. I mean, that picture should be used along with the topic of sexual positions, right?"

Brian couldn't take it anymore, breaking out into laughter.

"What's so funny?"

"I don't know...you. You're just funny. Just another example of why I like you so much, the way you can make a valid point, and still be funny and sexy at the same time."

"What can I say," she winked. "I guess I'm just multitalented."

"Maybe you should publish your own critique on *The Joy of Sex*," suggested Brian. "You could point out all the flaws and explain why it *shouldn't* be the number-one bestseller."

"Maybe I will. And maybe you and I could write a better book together."

"I like that idea."

"But we would have to run lots of experiments," said Mindy, pushing Brian to the brink.

With the sexual tension reaching a fever pitch, Brian couldn't take it any longer. He pulled Mindy in tight and pressed his mouth against her lips, tightly caressing her curvaceous buns. Losing control, she leaned back and dropped the book to the floor, enveloped by his aggression.

As they rolled around on the sofa, their limbs a tangled web, Mindy had the wherewithal to realize the awkwardness of their positioning and how it was inhibiting their advances. Pulling her mouth away and gasping for air, she asked Brian to sit up. Heavily breathing, he complied unwillingly, trying to regain his composure.

Mindy seductively batted her eyelashes and corrected Brian's approach. "You forgot that breasts come first, remember?" Then, reaching behind her back and under her sweater, Mindy unhooked her bra. "Now you have full access," she confirmed. "Unfortunately, the sweater needs to stay on. We have to be prepared for a quick exit."

Brian slowly reached his hands under Mindy's sweater, gently caressing her bare breasts. "They're perfect," he proclaimed, whispering in her ear.

"You have good handwork," she conceded.

"I have a good teacher."

"Now let me try *my* handwork," she said, reaching for his jeans.

Starting at Brian's knee, she slowly massaged her way up his thigh, not stopping until she felt his erection.

Succumbing to her powerful manipulation, Brian gulped a deep breath. His heart was pounding now as she rhythmically rubbed his jeans, distorting his sense of judgment. He couldn't help but wonder how lucky he was to be with someone so amazing. Mindy was everything he ever wanted and more.

Hypnotized by her intoxicating advances, Brian instinctively lowered Mindy down to the sofa and pushed her sweater up to her shoulders, delicately nibbling her tender breasts and tickling her nipples with his tongue. Mindy leaned her head back submissively as Brian worked his lips up to her neck and caressed her earlobes.

Reciprocating the stimulation, Mindy moved her hand back to Brian's jeans, searching for his bulge, and Brian enabled her quest by adjusting his hips to a more accommodative position, allowing her to settle in on her target.

With another gulp of air and a fervent exhale, Brian submitted to Mindy's magic. Now, more vulnerable than ever, he felt entranced by Mindy's beauty and splendor, surrendering to his innermost feelings.

"I love you Mindy," he whispered in her ear. "I love you very much."

Mindy responded with her cute little giggle and Brian pulled away.

"Why are you stopping?" she asked.

"Why were you laughing? What's so funny?"

"I just thought it was funny, that's all. I mean, do you really love me? Or are you just horny?" she asked, giggling again.

Brian sat up abruptly, turning his head away.

"What's wrong?" she inquired.

Brian said nothing, staring off into space, indignant to her inquisitiveness.

"I'm sorry if I said something wrong. I didn't mean to offend you."

Brian didn't reply. He had always been the cautious one. His friends had looked upon him for his prudence and common sense. Now he had let his guard down, believing that his adoration for Mindy was mutual and sacred. How did he misinterpret the signals? How did he make himself so vulnerable? Now, feeling exposed by his submission, Brian was embarrassed. No longer trusting his instincts, he decided to withdraw and reexamine Mindy's intentions.

Wrapping her arms around Brian, Mindy rested her head on his shoulder.

"I don't want to hurt your feelings. It's just that love is a very strong word and I want to be certain about it before I say it."

Brian didn't respond. Her words were not consoling. She wasn't saying the things he wanted to hear. He wanted to hear "I love you too." He wanted to hear her say "you're the only one for me."

"Please, just relax," said Mindy, trying to be reasonable. "Your heart is pounding a mile a minute. Please tell me what you're thinking."

Finally giving in, Brian decided to respond. "I'm thinking the stuff we were just doing is really special, and I'm thinking I wouldn't have done it with you if I didn't love you."

Feeling very guilty, Mindy sat still, not knowing how to respond.

Brian continued. "I'm thinking if you don't feel the same way, why were you doing those things? Does it not mean anything to you?"

Mindy took Brian's hand in hers, but he pulled it away.

"I didn't say I *don't* love you," she continued. "What I meant was I want to wait for the right moment. I just want to be absolutely sure. That's all."

Brian sat still, willing to hear her out, but not willing to pretend that everything was okay again.

Suddenly, Mindy jumped up. "Listen! Did you hear that?"

Brian looked at his watch. It was nine thirty.

"They're here!" she announced in a panic. "Let's go!"

Mindy yanked on Brian's arm and led him down the hallway. Storming into the back bedroom, she flipped the latch and raised the window. "Hurry!" she coaxed.

Brian quickly hiked up his leg and lifted his knee over the ledge. Wedging his torso through the opening, he struggled to keep his balance. Straddling the ledge and ducking his head, Brian appeared to be stuck.

Mindy panicked. This was not going the way she had planned. Brian was far too tentative. "Jump!" she ordered again in a loud whisper.

Brian proceeded to position his other leg on the windowsill so he could land on both feet. But Mindy, unable to handle the pressure any longer, gave him a firm shove. Brian flipped over and plunged to the ground with a solid thud, shoulder first. Writhing in pain, he took a second to gather his senses. Like a football player after a hard tackle, he forced himself to get back up, allowing the adrenaline to take over as he trotted through the neighbor's backyard and down the street.

His right shoulder throbbing in pain, Brian struggled to insert the car key into the ignition. The pain was not going away. He couldn't help but wonder if his injury was something serious. A dislocated shoulder, perhaps? How would he explain this to the football team? How would he explain it to his parents?

Brian checked the rearview mirror. The coast was clear. Nothing appeared to be out of the ordinary. He had made a clean escape.

Smiling at himself with a sense of satisfaction, Brian realized, for the first time in his life, he had cheated authority. Breaking decorum, he had entered a doctor's house without permission, indulged in a sexual encounter, and successfully completed a getaway without retribution. Brian couldn't help but feel triumphant, like a burglar after a well-planned heist.

But then he felt another sharp pain in his right shoulder as he attempted to turn the steering wheel. It was no use; he would have to drive all the way home steering with his left arm.

Perhaps there were consequences to his actions after all. Maybe an injured shoulder was the price he had to pay for his frivolous and selfish adventures. Or maybe it was all Mindy's fault. Afterall, the whole escapade was her idea, another example of her mischievous and deceptive behavior. He would be just fine if Mindy hadn't panicked and shoved him out the window.

Ah yes...Mindy. Now he realized his shoulder was not the only thing she had hurt. Maybe his broken heart would prove to be the biggest casualty. Maybe he was too emotional, or too sentimental, but the thought of losing Mindy seemed unbearable. If only Mindy would love him the way he loved her. All this time he thought their feelings were mutual. Now it seemed so pointless. How could he be so naive?

And then there was *The Joy of Sex*. Was it really all that joyful? The book had made it all seem so scientific and clinical, like a step-by-step guide to satisfaction. But there were some important topics the book did not cover, like the psychological and emotional impacts of a physical relationship. Could sex really be all that satisfying if there was no love? Isn't that why they called it *lovemaking*? All Brian knew was that he loved Mindy very much, and nobody in the whole world could compare to her sexiness. He only wished she would love him in return.

The Joy of Sex went on to sell millions of copies, resurrecting the topic of human intimacy from the back alleys and thrusting it into the legitimacy of mainstream media. Between 1972 and 1974, the book would spend over seventy weeks in the top five of the *New York Times* Best Seller list, confirming, in a resounding way, the existence of a sexual revolution.

As the availability and acceptance of a so-called sex manual became ubiquitous, academia began to recognize, more than ever, the need for sex education in public schools, a curriculum that was largely nonexistent. How could America's youth be prepared for adulthood if their schools weren't willing to engage in adult conversations about their bodies? How could we prevent unwanted pregnancies if we weren't educating our youth about the importance of birth control?

The concerns were significant, but the resistance and opposition were formidable. Many parents were not comfortable with the idea of a nonsectarian institution teaching their children about human intimacy. To them, sex was a personal and private matter, something to be discussed in conjunction with love, marriage, and family values. They viewed sex education in the schools as a sign of cultural permissiveness, another indication of a society in moral decay. Conflicted by their religious beliefs and traditional values, concerned parents were afraid that sex education would only encourage promiscuity.

In subsequent years, *The Joy of Sex* suffered a series of setbacks. After discovering the book's renowned author, Alex Comfort, had been engaged in an extramarital affair with his wife's best friend, the critics' concerns over infidelity seemed to be validated.

Soon after, Alex Comfort divorced his wife of thirty years and married his mistress. As if that wasn't scandalous enough, he took his new bride to live in California where they were known to frequent clothing-optional retreats and engage in free love, a discreet way of describing casual sex with indiscriminate partners. As a result, *The Joy of Sex*, as a legitimate guide to human intimacy, seemed less credible. What was once considered a doctor's guide to a normal, healthy sex life, seemed more and more like an enabler for perversion and debauchery.

Despite the ongoing controversies, the book continued to sell. It was still the most comprehensive guide to human sexuality, and for that reason, remained a valuable resource. But there was one critical subject left out entirely—the topic of homosexuality.

In the early 1970s, same-sex unions were considered taboo, representing a lifestyle that was frowned upon as immoral and depraved. Not only were homosexuals shunned from society, but they were subjected to persecution, as well as prosecution. Since most states had laws against gay and lesbian sex, violators could be arrested, fined, and jailed.

Traumatized by their innate desires and chastised as freaks of nature, homosexuals were forced to hide their identities, suffering immeasurable damage to their emotional well-being.

Chapter 53

Spring baseball was well under way and Indianapolis Clowns manager, Buster Haywood, was sizing up his team. It was April 1952, and the Clowns had just signed a skinny eighteen-year-old kid out of Mobile, Alabama. Playing baseball in the Negro American League, the Clowns discovered the kid the year before while playing an exhibition game against the Mobile Black Bears. Business Manager, Bunny Downs, was able to lure the kid to Indianapolis with a two-hundred-dollar-per-month contract. The kid's name was Henry Aaron.

Henry Aaron didn't stay in Indianapolis for very long. After only three months, he led the Negro American League with a .467 batting average. Enamored by the pop in Aaron's bat and his graceful athleticism, the Boston Braves purchased Aaron's contract away from Clowns owner, Syd Pollock, for $10,000, upgrading his monthly pay to $350. The next stop was Eau Claire, Wisconsin, the Braves minor league affiliate in the Northern League.

Playing with White people for the first time, Aaron finished the season with a .336 batting average and nine home runs. After being named Rookie of the Year, the Braves had seen enough. It was time to promote him to their Jacksonville affiliate in the South Atlantic League.

1953 proved to be a pivotal year for the Boston Braves and their nineteen-year-old phenom, Henry Aaron. The Braves would leave Boston for Milwaukee, and Aaron would go on to lead the South Atlantic League in batting average (.362), hits (208), runs scored (115),

RBIs (125) and total bases (338). Jacksonville won their league championship and Aaron was named MVP. Never again would Henry Aaron play minor league baseball. His next stop was Milwaukee, Wisconsin.

Fast-forward to 1974, and Henry "Hank" Aaron was being talked about more than any player in the history of professional baseball. At thirty-nine years old, he had finished the 1973 season with forty home runs, leaving him only one home run shy of the most iconic record in baseball: 714 home runs.

Considered by many to be untouchable, the home run record had stood for nearly forty years. The fact that it was established by the indominable Babe Ruth, the iconic New York Yankee, made it seem all the more sacred. When the 1973 season concluded, everyone expected Hank Aaron to break Ruth's record the following April, the first month of the 1974 season. Everyone, that is, except Hank Aaron.

Ordinarily consumed with confidence and conviction, Aaron had reason to be skeptical. The chance that he would never live to see the 1974 season was distinctly possible.

Although the acceptance of Black athletes in professional sports had made great strides, there were still many hurdles to clear, especially in the South. When the Braves moved to Atlanta in 1966, Georgia was entrenched in racial strife, a deep-rooted tension that had endured for over one hundred years. Two years later, in 1968, the state would go to the polls and select a segregationist, George Wallace, to be their next president, a solid indication that Georgians were not ready to patronize Black baseball players.

But Hank Aaron was accustomed to discrimination. Growing up in Alabama, he knew which establishments he could and could not attend. Complying with local ordinances was easy when venues were unmistakably labeled as "Whites only" or "no coloreds allowed." It was the so-called gray areas that created frustration and confusion.

Playing for Jacksonville in the South Atlantic League, Aaron was often rejected when the team checked into a hotel or denied service when the players went out for dinner. Lodging and meals, per diem allowances that were standard fare for White players, had become annoyingly unpredictable for Aaron. Often his teammates would deliver food to him on the team bus or to his hotel room late at night just so he could eat a decent meal.

But nothing could prepare Hank Aaron for the threats and inflammatory rhetoric he would endure while chasing the home run record of the beloved Babe Ruth.

Throughout 1973 and 1974, over nine hundred thousand pieces of mail were directed toward Hank Aaron, most of them related to his pursuit of the home run record. Some of the letters went so far as to threaten Aaron's life, causing the FBI to intervene on his behalf. It had gotten so bad that the Braves resorted to hiring armed guards to accompany Aaron to and from the ballpark.

Although the increased security added a degree of comfort, Aaron felt most vulnerable when he was at home. Fearing for his life, he became a prisoner in his own home, afraid to go out in public and afraid for his wife and children.

Adding to the fear, the FBI confirmed that they were investigating credible plots to kidnap Aaron's children. Because of the threats, his children received police escorts to and from school and Aaron was forced to miss their graduations out of fear for his life.

In his autobiography, Hank Aaron addressed that period of his life: "I had nowhere to go except home and to the ballpark. I was a prisoner in my own apartment. That whole period, I lived like a guy in a fishbowl, swimming from side to side with nowhere to go, watching everybody watch me."

Although most of the Atlanta Brave fans eventually embraced Hank Aaron and his mastery of baseball, the admiration was far from unanimous. One of the more popular bumper stickers in Atlanta read "Aaron is Ruth-less."

Recognizing the historical significance of the hate mail, the Atlanta Braves front office began to archive many of the letters. One of the letters read as follows:

Dear Mr. Nigger,

I hope you don't break the Babe's record. How do I tell my kids that a nigger did it? But it took more at bats, live ball, and other nigger tricks. I wish you the worst at anything you do "Nigger!"

(KKK forever)

With the Atlanta Braves facing the Cincinnati Reds, the opening day of the 1974 baseball season kicked off on April 4, in Cincinnati's Riverfront Stadium. After teammates Ralph Garr and Mike Lum successfully reached base, Hank Aaron approached home plate for his first at bat of the season. When Jack Billingham delivered the 3-1 pitch, Aaron drove the ball deep, forcing leftfielder Pete Rose to turn his back and sprint toward the warning track in hot pursuit.

Hopelessly out of reach, the ball sailed over the fence for a three-run homer. Hank Aaron trotted around the bases, tipping his cap to a standing ovation. As he approached home plate, the entire Braves roster and coaching staff gathered in celebration. Babe Ruth's home run record of 714 no longer stood alone.

After one game and one at bat, Hank Aaron had entered rarefied air, one home run away from breaking the Babe's all-time record.

Bowing their heads in reverence, a gathering of mourners prepared to deliver their last goodbyes. With the ceremonial closing at hand, the finality began to set in. There was no evading the unnerving conclusiveness of mortality. Pomp and circumstance aside, the final resting place, a paltry and primitive hole in the ground, served as a harsh dose of reality.

"We therefore commit this body to the ground, earth to earth, ashes to ashes, dust to dust; in sure and certain hope of the Resurrection to eternal life."

The minister closed his Bible and nodded his head in silence, assuring the bereaved of his conclusion.

Taking his cue, the flock turned away, trying to put the pieces back together. Only a few remained, unable to reconcile the past to the present, unable to walk away and leave a loved one in the ground. After all, Martha Wills was only forty-four years old.

It all happened so fast. Less than six months ago, Bob had revealed his mother's lung cancer, admitting it was "pretty bad." Since then, no one had seen much of Mrs. Wills. She had tried to continue work, thinking she could persevere with courage and determination, but the chemotherapy had left her weak and disabled.

Spotted a few times on her way to the mailbox, she appeared frail and ghostly white, her head completely bald. The cancer and chemo had ravaged her body. She had become a shadow of her former self, struggling with basic functions and surrendering to her inevitable demise.

Not long ago, Martha Wills had been the embodiment of ambition, attacking her daily chores with a zest for life. Bob had never seen his mom sit around and relax. She was always on a mission; often with a vacuum in one hand, and a cigarette in the other, jumping from task to task with her undaunted spirit and conviction. Bob could never have imagined it any other way. He always felt that his work ethic came from his mother, the DNA that gave him his drive.

Delivering the morning *Journal Gazette* and reading his mother's obituary seemed almost surreal.

> *Martha Wills, 44, preceded in death by her son Daniel, survived by husband Edward and son Robert.*

"Survived" seemed like an appropriate way of phrasing it. Bob felt like he was barely getting by, slowly living out a bad dream, day by day, hour by hour. Maybe one day he would see the light and turn the corner, but his despondency would not allow him to look that far ahead. Instead, he would wallow in despair.

Steve Marino loosened his tie and fired up his Olds 442. Compassion was not one of his strong suits, but he felt compelled to attend Mrs. Wills's funeral given his connection with Bob. There were certain protocols that needed compliance; he was not entirely callous.

"That was depressing," noted Brian, from the back seat of Steve's car. "I don't know how Bob just walks away from his mom's grave and carries on."

"Life just ain't fair," agreed Mark. "It seems like Bob always gets a raw deal."

"What's next, boys?" asked Steve, as he steered his car out of the cemetery and lit up a cigarette.

"Seriously?" asked Brian. "We just buried Bob's mom with lung cancer and you're smoking a cigarette?"

"Lighten up, man. You don't know if cigarettes caused her cancer. What about all the smokers that don't get cancer?"

"You have to look at the statistics," lectured Brian. "Listen to the medical experts."

"I'm not gonna stop livin' my life because of a few medical studies. Besides, I think the odds are in my favor."

"Suit yourself," said Brian.

"We need to stop off at Bob's house," said Scott. "They're having a reception there after the funeral."

"A reception?" asked Steve.

"I don't know, sort of an open house," said Scott. "Food and refreshments."

"That's weird," noted Steve. "Why would you have a party after a funeral?"

"It's not a party," corrected Mark. "It's a way to gather family and friends in honor of Mrs. Wills. A way for her spirit to carry on."

"I'm not sure I wanna go," said Steve. "I don't think I'd fit in."

"We need to be there for Bob," said Brian.

"We don't have to stay for very long," noted Mark. "We just need to pay our respects."

"Okay, but this tie is really choking me," said Steve, loosening his collar further.

In lockstep, the boys all followed suit, unbuttoning their collars and loosening their ties.

Hovering around the snacks, the boys looked awkward trying to appear normal in an abnormal environment. Not knowing the protocol, they didn't know whether to openly display their grief or lightheartedly engage in conversation. Feeling out of place, they were anything but comfortable.

"Let's go talk to Bob," said Brian. "He needs to know we care."

"Are you sure?" asked Scott. "It looks like he's busy with family members."

"Let's just move over there as a group," said Mark. "If he wants to talk to us, he will."

Like a flock of pigeons, the boys ambled toward Bob, nibbling their snacks and roosting nearby.

"Thanks for coming," said Bob, recognizing his friends' gesture. "I'm sorry I haven't had a chance to talk to you, but I've been surrounded by family."

"No problem," said Brian. "We get it."

"Let us know if there's anything we can do," offered Mark. "That's what friends are for."

"Okay," said Bob. "I wish we could just get out of here and share a few beers."

"All in good time," said Steve. "I'm right next door. Just say the word."

"I'm gonna hold you to that," said Bob.

Just when Bob was beginning to settle in with his buddies, a middle-aged woman swooped in and put her arm around him. "Bobby, I want you to come over here and meet someone." And then looking at the boys, she asked "Is it okay if I steal him away?"

The boys nodded their heads with approval as Bob rolled his eyes.

"Talk to you guys later," said Bob.

The boys looked at each other as though their good deed had been accomplished, their merit badges earned.

"You ready to blow this pop stand?" asked Steve. "I know I am."

"Let's do it," said Scott. "What's our next move?"

"How 'bout a few beers in my basement," suggested Steve. "My parents are still in Detroit and won't be back until tomorrow."

"Beers on a Monday?" challenged Brian. "Doesn't anyone have homework?"

"You go do your homework," ordered Scott. "I'm gonna have a few beers."

"Wait," said Brian, rethinking his strategy. "Can we watch the game in your basement?"

"What game?" asked Steve. "There ain't no Monday Night Football in April."

"No," said Brian. "Baseball. The Braves and the Dodgers. They're broadcasting all the Braves games until Aaron breaks the home run record."

"We can turn the game on if you want," said Steve. "But Ruth will always be the home run king. He did it in fewer games, with fewer at bats, and a longer home run fence. It will always be the Bambino's record. It belongs in pinstripes."

"Spoken like a true East Coaster," said Brian.

"Let's do it," said Mark. "We need to unwind after a day like today."

"Whoa, listen to this," said Steve. "The seventeen-year-old policeman's boy wants to drink beer. Aren't there laws against that?"

"Shut up, hockey boy. I won't tell anyone if you don't."

"It's unanimous," said Scott. "Let's do it."

Like a stampede, the boys stormed down Marino's basement steps with a sense of purpose. Steve went to the refrigerator, Brian turned on the TV, and Scott went right to the filing cabinet.

"Is it still locked?" asked Scott.

"You never give up, do you," teased Steve. "I think you need a girlfriend."

"I guess that means it's locked," said Scott. "But if you have a girlfriend for me, I'll give her a chance."

"That's very sporting of you." Steve laughed. "At least you're not on crutches anymore. Maybe you could actually satisfy a woman."

"I can't get no satisfaction," sang Scott, mimicking the Rolling Stones and cracking open his Miller High Life beer.

"What's goin' on with *your* girlfriend," Mark asked Steve. "Are you still molesting Karen Gadby?"

"What the hell is that supposed to mean?" asked Steve, in a surprisingly sharp tone. "Has she been blabbin' her mouth again?"

"Chill out, dude. I was only jokin'. I'm the last person Karen would ever talk to."

"Okay. My bad. I thought you were actually implying something," said Steve. "You know how chicks can be. Sometimes they have loose lips."

Mark decided to drop the topic, but not his suspicion. Steve's reaction spoke volumes. Maybe his statement had actually hit the mark. It certainly wouldn't surprise him.

"What's goin' on in the game?" Mark asked Brian, trying to change the topic.

"It's three-to-one Dodgers in the third inning," said Brian.

"Has Aaron been up yet?"

"Yeah, they're saying he walked in his first at bat. Then scored their only run. I hope they don't keep walkin' him. That's gonna make it awfully hard to hit a home run if they aren't pitchin' to him."

"They gotta pitch to him eventually," said Scott. "Or maybe they won't, now that they have a three-to-one lead."

"It doesn't matter to me," said Steve. "Baseball is boring. You boys should be following the Philadelphia Flyers. They're gonna win the Stanley Cup this year, mark my word."

"Why do they call them the Broad Street Bullies?" asked Mark.

"Well, they play in the Spectrum, and that sits on Broad Street. They call them the bullies because they're a bunch of badasses. Anyone who messes with them gets their asses whooped."

"Here we go again," said Mark. "Always preaching his macho hockey bullshit."

"It's not preaching," replied Steve. "It's just a fact. They lead the league in penalty minutes, and other teams are afraid of them because they have the league's toughest enforcers."

"That explains why they're all missing their front teeth," teased Brian.

"I'm more of a Boston Bruins fan," said Scott. "I like Bobby Orr and Phil Esposito."

"Yech...they're prima donnas," said Steve. "All grace and no grit."

"At least they're Bruins," said Scott. "Can't go wrong with a name like that."

"All right, boys," announced Brian. "Aaron's coming to bat, bottom of the fourth. Let's all get focused."

The boys gathered around the TV as a capacity crowd of nearly fifty-four thousand got on their feet at Atlanta's Fulton County Stadium.

"Can you imagine the pressure?" noted Brian. "How do you stay focused with the whole world watching?"

The first pitch delivered by Al Downing was a ball, and the crowd let out their collective exasperation, along with a few scattered boos. Would any pitcher dare to deliver a fast ball over the plate? No one wanted his name in the archives as the guy who gave up Aaron's record-setting home run.

But Atlanta Braves announcer, Milo Hamilton, stayed focused, continuing to build the anticipation:

> "He's sitting on seven-fourteen. Here's the pitch by Downing. Swinging. Here's a drive into left center field! That ball is gonna be...outa here! It's gone! It's seven-fifteen! There's a new home run champion of all time, and it's Henry Aaron! The fireworks

are going. Henry Aaron is coming around third. His teammates are at home plate. And listen to this crowd! A sellout crowd is cheering Henry Aaron, the home run king of all time!"

The Coldwater Creek boys hollered their approval, high-fiving each other as if they were Atlanta Braves fans.

"We just witnessed history, boys!" announced Brian. "The greatest home run hitter of all time!"

"Waddaya think of that, Stevie boy?" asked Mark.

"It's pretty cool. I ain't gonna lie. He ain't no Bambino, but he's pretty damn good. Gotta give credit where credit's due."

"This calls for another round of beers," proclaimed Scott.

On Los Angeles radio, the famous Dodger announcer, Vin Scully, gave his take on the historic moment:

"What a marvelous moment for baseball, what a marvelous moment for Atlanta and the state of Georgia, what a marvelous moment for the country and the world. A Black man is getting a standing ovation in the Deep South for breaking a record of an all-time baseball idol...and for the first time in a long time, that poker face of Aaron's shows the tremendous strain and relief of what it must have been like to live with for the past several months."

On his way home, Brian Johnson reflected upon the day. From Marino's house, it was a one-block walk, an opportunity for some peaceful solitude. Without regret, he had surrendered to the beer temptation on a school night. At least he curtailed his consumption to only two. One couldn't help but indulge after such a monumental achievement. A home run milestone like that only happens once-in-a-lifetime. It was easy to justify the celebration.

Celebration—a word that didn't seem appropriate after a funeral. It's funny how people justify things: two beers, once-in-a-lifetime, celebrations. There were always excuses. A few hours earlier, Bob Wills had buried his mother. How does one justify that?

Brian had never been to a funeral before. He'd never had a close family member die. The thought of death had never really been on his mind. Monday April 8, 1974, changed everything. It was one for the ages. Death and jubilation rolled into one. Sensory overload.

He couldn't help but recall the old adage among monarchs: "The king is dead, long live the king." He'd always thought that phrase was too simplistic, too nonsensical. But now it seemed logical, almost purposeful. Bob had lost his mother, but life must go on. There was a new home run king. A reason to be inspired, a reason to overcome obstacles and meet life's challenges. He would learn from this occasion and live each day to the fullest.

The Atlanta Braves went on to defeat the Los Angeles Dodgers that day by a score of 7-4. But most people don't remember who won the game or really care about the final score. All that mattered was that Hank Aaron had become the all-time home run king.

The Los Angeles Dodgers, led by league MVP Steve Garvey, went on to win the National League pennant that year, earning the right to face the Oakland Athletics in the 1974 World Series. It was the first all-California World Series in the history of Major League Baseball.

After splitting the first two games in LA's Dodger stadium, the series moved to Oakland. Led by their dominant pitching trio of Jim "Catfish" Hunter, Vida Blue, and Rollie Fingers, the Swingin' A's swept all three games, becoming the first team to capture three consecutive World Series titles since the New York Yankees won five in a row from 1949 to 1953.

Chapter 54

"IT WAS REALLY NICE OF your father to invite us to dinner," said Lynda Lacey. "Are you sure it's okay for me to tag along?"

"Are you kidding? My father wouldn't have it any other way. You're his favorite," said Quinn. "Why do you think I keep you around?"

Wondering if he was serious, Lynda looked at Quinn with a painful expression.

"C'mon! You know I'm only joking. I'd be lost without you, and you know it."

"That's more like it," said Lynda, somewhat relieved. "I always look forward to our time together."

"As do I," said Quinn.

Not entirely convinced, Lynda examined his sincerity with suspicion. Did he really enjoy her company? Or did he keep her around to ease the tension between him and his father?

Driving into town, the two were on their way to meet Ryan at his favorite restaurant, Don Hall's Gas House. Residing near the banks of the Saint Mary's River, the restaurant was steeped in history. Home to the Fort Wayne Gas Works in the mid-1800s, Don Hall purchased the old brick building in 1955, converting it into a classic white-tablecloth steakhouse. Since then, the establishment had become a fine dining destination for business luncheons and special occasions.

"He has a table reserved," said Quinn, "but we're supposed to meet him in the bar."

"I've only eaten there once," noted Lynda. "We celebrated my parents' twenty-fifth anniversary there last year."

"To be honest with you, I'm a little concerned," admitted Quinn. "I hope he's not planning some big announcement. He hasn't been the same since my mother moved out."

"Well, that's understandable. But what could he possibly be announcing?"

"Oh, I don't know," replied Quinn. "I just know how he operates. There's usually an angle to everything he does."

After a brief moment of silence, Lynda impulsively exposed her intuition. "You don't think he's announcing a divorce, or that he's seeing someone else, do you?"

As soon as she said it, she wished she could take it back. It was not her place to throw out unsupported theories.

"But of course not," she retracted. "I don't know why I said that."

"Well, I hadn't thought about it," said Quinn. "I don't think it's come to that. At least, not yet."

"I'm sure you're right," assured Lynda.

"But he's been very inquisitive lately, asking about what I'm doing all the time. How are my classes going? What am I doing to prepare for my future? Those kinds of things."

"It's only natural for a father to be concerned about his son's future."

"Yes, but you don't know my father like I do. He can be very forceful. Very intimidating. He has a way of making someone feel inadequate if he's not living up to his expectations."

Trusting her instincts, Lynda recognized the implications. The "someone" that Quinn was referencing was himself.

"Since Mom moved out," continued Quinn, "he scrutinizes everything I do. I feel like I'm under a microscope."

Pulling into the parking lot, Quinn changed his tone. "Maybe I'm too paranoid. Maybe we should just relax and enjoy a good meal. That's something I haven't done in a while."

"Sounds good to me," said Lynda. "Let's enjoy the evening. Make it a fun date."

Quinn walked Lynda up the steps and past two large torches that smelled like kerosene, lighting up the stone-laid portico like an old castle. Making their way to the entrance, Quinn opened one of the two large wooden doors that served as the gateway.

"Good evening," announced the hostess. "Do you have a reservation?"

"We're with the O'Connor party," announced Quinn, proud of his affiliation.

"Oh yes, we were expecting you," said the hostess, her face lighting up in reverence. "We're preparing a table for you as we speak. Mr. O'Connor is waiting in the bar. If you follow me, I'll take you there now."

"Perfect," replied Quinn, never tiring of the special treatment he received for being an O'Connor.

Following the hostess toward the bar, Quinn whispered in Lynda's ear. "I hope he's not too sloshed. That could be either a good thing or a bad thing."

"How so?" asked Lynda.

"Well, if he's in a good mood, it might make him more pleasant and light-hearted. If he's in a bad mood, it could make him more aggressive."

Sensing Quinn's anxiety, Lynda couldn't help but feel sorry for him, always carrying the burden of his father's relentless pressure. And yet she recognized the circumstances for what they were, prerequisites to her underlying importance. She was the go-between in the relationship. Ryan valued her influence and Quinn needed her emotional support.

Entering the bar, Lynda was relieved to see Ryan sitting alone. Her biggest fear was that he would be accompanied by a date, a revelation that would certainly throw Quinn for a loop.

"Your party has arrived, Mr. O'Connor."

Ryan O'Connor turned around and stood up at the sight of Lynda. He wanted to hug her but decided to extend his hand in a display of professionalism.

"Lynda, good to see you again. Thanks for coming."

Lynda responded with a firm handshake and her endearing charm. "Thanks for inviting me. I've been looking forward to this."

"Would you like to move to your table now?" asked the hostess.

"Yes," affirmed Ryan. "I'm assuming you have my regular spot?"

"Absolutely. I'll take you there now."

Still in his suit and tie, Ryan slapped a twenty-dollar bill on the bar and picked up his Manhattan.

Taking their seats in a cozy wraparound booth, an attendant swooped in and filled their water glasses from his frosty pitcher. As soon as he lit the centerpiece candle, a pretty, young waitress took over, announcing herself and displaying her willingness to be at Ryan's beck and call.

"My name is Stephanie. I'm honored to be your server this evening."

"Well, Stephanie. I've never seen *you* before. Where's Amanda? She's my usual."

"Amanda has the evening off, I'm sorry to say. But I will do my best to meet or exceed your expectations."

Acknowledging the pretentious groveling, Ryan gave her the once-over and decided to acquiesce.

"I'll need another one of these," he ordered. "Makers Mark Manhattan, straight-up, chilled."

"Absolutely, coming right up. And for the young lady?"

"A Coke is fine for me," said Lynda.

"Me too," ordered Quinn.

Ryan looked at Lynda and winked. "It's amazing how much attention you get when there's a sizable tip at stake."

Lynda grinned and continued the pandering. "They obviously know who they are dealing with."

The waitress brought back the drinks and delivered the menus. "Would you like me to tell you about our specials this evening?"

"That won't be necessary," said Ryan. "Give us a few minutes and check back."

"Absolutely," said Stephanie. "Take your time."

Ryan picked up his menu and announced his intentions. "Let's place our orders, and then we can get down to the business portion of the meeting."

Lynda glanced at Quinn to see his reaction, but Quinn picked up his menu, choosing not to respond.

"What do you usually order?" asked Lynda.

"Well, I'm not gonna lie," admitted Ryan. "It's hard for me to resist a good filet mignon. But if you're looking for a recommendation, look no further than their Greek Salad. It's gotta be their signature dish, truly to die for."

"Sounds awesome!"

"It's filled with tomatoes, black olives, feta cheese, peppers, beets, anchovies…I could go on and on. Needless to say, I'll have one with my steak. But I gotta warn you, it's practically a meal in and of itself."

"Perfect," said Lynda. "Sounds like a delicious, healthy meal."

"I'm guessing you can eat whatever you want," suggested Ryan. "How do you keep such a perfect figure?"

"You're too kind." Lynda laughed. "I guess I'm always on the go, burning calories along the way."

Feeling like a third wheel, Quinn watched helplessly as his father continued to gush. Although it was an embarrassing spectacle, he decided to focus on the positive. If it removed the pressure from him and delayed the inevitable, the so-called business portion of the meeting, he would gladly yield to his father. Apparently, Lynda and an abundance of Manhattans were an unbeatable combination.

After the orders had been placed, Ryan took on a stern look. "Now let's get down to business. Let me start by recognizing the importance of this critical juncture in your careers."

"What juncture is that?" asked Quinn.

"You're both in the last month of your junior year, soon to be seniors. I would say that's a critical juncture, wouldn't you?"

"I suppose," acknowledged Quinn.

"You'll soon be putting together college applications, right? So if you think about it, your senior year is the last chance to make an impact, your last chance to earn the kind of accomplishments that could be real difference makers, the difference between getting accepted into a prestigious school or attending a run-of-the-mill school."

Uninspired by his father's predictability, Quinn's eyes began to glaze over. He'd heard it all before.

"I thought I was going to Notre Dame," said Quinn.

"You see, that's what I'm talking about. How do you know Notre Dame will accept you?" asked Ryan.

"You said you could get me in," offered Quinn, matter-of-factly.

Ryan's frustration was starting to build. But looking at Lynda, he took a deep breath and forged ahead.

"I'm talking about putting forth the extra effort to be someone special. The kind of person who stands above the crowd and earns his way to the top."

Lynda listened intently, inspired by Ryan's motivational speech. These were the kind of words that fueled her ambition.

"Take Lynda for example," continued Ryan. "She's been accumulating quite a résumé. Am I correct?"

"I've been trying," concurred Lynda.

"Let's see…honor roll, captain of the cheerleading squad, piano player, church choir…what am I missing?"

"Well, I don't really want to start listing things," said Lynda, honored by his recognition, but embarrassed by the attention. She was afraid she would paint Quinn into a corner and damage his self-esteem even further.

"No, I really want to know," continued Ryan. "I'm not interested in your modesty. I'm interested in what you have on your résumé."

"Well, I'm also on the student council and I'm president of the Spanish club."

"There you go," said Ryan, looking at Quinn. "That's the kind of résumé that turns heads. Lynda is a real go-getter."

Now Lynda was feeling guilty. The last thing she wanted to do was bruise Quinn's fragile ego.

"Let's take another example," said Ryan. "Your brother, for instance."

Quinn rolled his eyes. He'd heard it a million times before.

"Shane was valedictorian, president of his class, and captain of the golf team."

"And I'm captain of the tennis team," noted Quinn. "Not to mention city champion. So what's the difference?"

"You're a damn good tennis player," agreed Ryan, deciding to throw his son a bone. "The difference is in the other credentials, or lack thereof."

"I'm in the top ten percent of my class," noted Quinn.

"I'm sorry, son, but the O'Connors are not top ten percenters. We're one percenters."

"Well, I can't move my class standing into the one percent range with only a year to go. That's impossible."

"Agreed," said Ryan. "Valedictorian or salutatorian is out of reach, but maybe top five percent is still achievable?"

"I don't see why that really matters."

"My point is, it's time to raise the bar, start separating yourself from the pack. We need to put together a plan that prepares you to be the man I know you can be, the man you *need* to be. Someone's gotta take over O'Connor Enterprises when I'm dead and gone, and the responsibility falls squarely upon your shoulders."

"Well, I don't think we have to worry about that for a while."

Ryan's frustration was becoming obvious. He'd always been good at delivering speeches and motivating his employees, but he could never find the formula that inspired Quinn. Quite simply, Quinn was no Shane.

"Is it okay if I offer a suggestion?" asked Lynda.

"Absolutely," said Ryan. "That's why we're all here together. Three heads are better than one."

"Well," said Lynda, "it's too late to become valedictorian, but it's not too late to become senior class president."

Quinn raised his eyebrows and looked at Lynda inquisitively. Where was she going with this?

"I'm all ears," said Ryan. "Do you have a plan?"

"The election for senior class president takes place in two weeks. That's plenty of time to launch a campaign."

"What makes you think he can win? It's not like he's ever been involved in student council."

"It doesn't matter," said Lynda. "These elections always turn into popularity contests."

"And you think he can win a popularity contest?"

"All right," said Quinn. "Let's just tap the brakes on this whole idea. I find it pretty amazing the two of you are making plans on *my* behalf without *my* input."

"It's just an idea," said Lynda.

"An idea that I don't find very appealing. I have no interest in student government, and I have no interest in getting up in front of the student body and making a speech. Besides, if it's really about popularity, like you say, then why do you think I would win? I'm not a popular, buddy-buddy kind of guy."

"Do you have an answer for that?" asked Ryan, looking at Lynda. He sensed that she had something up her sleeve. Lynda was not the kind of person who spouted off random thoughts without a plan.

"I have an idea. An idea that we could turn into a plan."

"That *we* could turn into a plan?" asked Quinn. "You seem to forget that *I'm* the critical piece in *we*."

"Let's hear her out," said Ryan. "All we're doing here is a little brainstorming. There's nothing wrong with that."

Quinn couldn't argue with that. Even *he* was a little intrigued by what sort of scheme Lynda might be brewing up.

"Your meals should be ready in five minutes," announced the waitress. "Can I get you anything else before they arrive?"

"Yes, I'm gonna need another one of these," declared Ryan, pointing at his empty Manhattan glass. "And refills on the Cokes."

"Coming right up, Mr. O'Connor."

"Okay, Lynda. You have five minutes to present your plan. Let's hear it," said Ryan with a twinkle in his eye.

"Well, like I said, it's really nothing more than a popularity contest. And who's more popular than Antonio?" asked Lynda, staring directly at Quinn.

"So what's your point?" asked Quinn.

"My point is you can run for president with Antonio as your running mate. That would be an unbeatable combination. The O'Connor good name running side-by-side with the most popular kid in school."

"Hold on a second," insisted Quinn. "First of all, what makes you think that Antonio would have any interest in running for student council? And even if he did, neither one of us has any experience… whatsoever."

"I thought I made that clear," said Lynda. "Experience has nothing to do with it. I've been to those student council meetings and they're nothing but a joke."

"Okay, hold on a second," said Ryan. "Just who is this Antonio guy and why is he so popular?"

"Where do I begin," said Lynda. "I guess I'll start by saying that Antonio is a guy with a ton of charisma. He plays the trumpet and is the most talented musician I've ever known. But he's far more than a musician. He's got style, grace, and leadership qualities to go along with his magnetic personality. Our principal even has him doing the morning announcements every day because he knows that everyone will listen to him. I could go on and on about Antonio, but one thing I can say without a doubt, he is easily the most admired guy in the school."

Ryan looked at Quinn. "Do you agree with that assessment?"

Quinn smiled as if it was a stupid question. "Oh yeah, he's all that and more."

"Well, if he's all that, then why doesn't *he* run for president?" asked Ryan.

"It's not his cup of tea," said Lynda.

"Then what makes you think he would play second fiddle to Quinn?"

"He will if I ask him," said Lynda. "Besides, he likes Quinn. He would do it for Quinn *and* me. He understands power and influence and he values friendships. Trust me, I can make it happen."

Ryan looked at Lynda with admiration. She was exhibiting wisdom beyond her years. This was a young lady who could take control of a situation and make things happen. She was someone to be reckoned with, a valuable asset, a real keeper. She was just what Quinn needed in his life.

Stephanie returned to the table, delivering their drinks and assisting the servers with the meal placements. "I hope everything is to your satisfaction," she stated. "Let me know if there's anything else I can get for you."

"We're all good for now," declared Ryan. Feeling a deep sense of satisfaction, he realized the business portion of the dinner had exceeded his expectations. He was proud of himself for gathering the right people and confident that a viable plan would be put into place.

"Let me propose a toast," declared Ryan O'Connor, lifting his cocktail. "Here's to the next senior class president of Northrop High School."

Lynda and Quinn lifted their Cokes.

"And here's to Lynda Lacey," continued Ryan, "Quinn's irrepressible campaign manager!"

Chapter 55

S COTT CLEVER STEPPED OUT THE front door on a Sunday afternoon and saw Lynda Lacey standing on her driveway. Loitering in front of her house, she appeared rather peculiar, as if distracted by some unknown curiosity.

"Expecting a visitor?" asked Scott.

"Yes, good observation," said Lynda. "Antonio is supposed to swing by this afternoon."

"Oh, are you no longer seeing Quinn?" asked Scott, trying to be clever and nosey at the same time.

"Why would you ask that?"

"Nothin' wrong with playin' the field," implied Scott.

Deciding to humor him, Lynda retorted. "Are you saying I can't have two boyfriends at the same time?"

Scott smirked at her cleverness, surprised that she would engage in such silliness.

"Why settle for only two? If you add me into the mix, you could have three boyfriends."

"*Please,*" said Lynda. "I don't think you meet my minimum requirements."

Scott smiled at her rebuttal and decided to end the nonsense. Walking toward her on the sidewalk, he continued with his intrusion. "So what brings Antonio to this neck of the woods?"

"He's coming over to work on the O'Connor-Jackson campaign. This is the week of the election. I'm assuming we have your vote?"

"My vote can always be bought," he teased. "What about Quinn? Shouldn't he be working on his own campaign?"

"He's playing in a tennis tournament at the club today, so I told Antonio to come over and we could work on the campaign without him."

"Does he even know how to get here?" asked Scott.

"I gave him directions and our street address. I hope he finds it."

"That might be him now," observed Scott. "What kind of a car is he driving?"

"I have no idea. He just told me he'd be driving his father's car."

"Well, here comes an old Ford Galaxie," noted Scott. "I haven't seen one of those around here."

Antonio stuck his hand out the window and waved. Pulling his car up to the curb, he came to a stop. "Okay if I park here?"

"Perfect," said Lynda.

Antonio stepped out of the car, apologized for his tardiness, and fired a preemptive strike. "I know what you're thinking—there goes the neighborhood."

"You're too funny." Lynda laughed. "You know you're always welcome here."

"Not so fast," said Scott. "I don't appreciate you steppin' in on my turf and messin' around with my girlfriend."

"Nice try." Antonio laughed. "I may be on your turf, but I don't think Lynda would ever slum around with the likes of you."

"Excuse me?" cracked Scott. "I have impeccable credentials."

"Ha, maybe so, but you don't have Quinn's bank account."

"All right," said Lynda. "I don't appreciate the two of you having fun at my expense."

"Well, you know Scott. He'll have fun at anyone's expense. And that's okay. I actually respect that." Antonio laughed.

"So what exactly will you guys be working on today?" asked Scott.

"We have our work cut out for us," said Lynda, getting down to business. "Wednesday is the auditorium debate and Thursday is the election. I've already put together Quinn's two-minute speech. Today we'll be working on Antonio's one-minute speech. Then we'll make some signs to post around the building."

"Well, I wouldn't put too much effort into it," said Scott. "There's no way you're gonna lose."

"That's the spirit!" said Antonio.

"We can't be overconfident," said Lynda. "There's no celebrating until the final vote is counted. Not while I'm running this campaign."

Antonio winked at Scott. "This is a woman you don't wanna mess with. She's on a mission and she'll trample anyone who gets in her way."

"All right," said Lynda. "That's a bit harsh."

"Well, well," said Scott. "Look who just showed up."

Lynda and Antonio looked up to see the familiar Olds 442 pull into the Marino driveway.

"Oh no," said Antonio. "That's not Steve Marino, is it?"

"Yep, that's where he lives," said Scott.

"That dude doesn't like me," said Antonio. "And he especially won't like me being in his White neighborhood."

"He's harmless," said Scott. "You're okay as long as you're hangin' with us."

"And he's got Karen with him," noted Lynda, raising her hand to gather attention. "Hey, Karen, over here!"

Karen looked up, waved, and headed in their direction. Steve pulled a beer out of his trunk and followed along reluctantly. He was wearing a Philadelphia Flyers jersey with the name of his favorite player, Bobby Clarke.

"Hi, Antonio," greeted Karen. "What brings you to this part of town?"

"That's a good question," noted Steve. "I thought we had higher standards than this."

"Stop it," said Karen.

Antonio responded with his witty sarcasm. "It's all right, I'm only here to deliver a pizza and cut someone's lawn."

"I'll take a pizza," joked Scott, trying to lighten the mood. "It looks like Steve can supply the beer. Are you gettin' ready to watch your Flyers?"

"You got that right, buddy boy. Today's the big day. Gonna bring home a Stanley Cup."

"You think they'll close 'em out?"

"Without a doubt, my man. The Broad Street Bullies are gonna mop up. There's gonna be Bruin blood all over that ice."

"My, my," said Antonio. "Spoken like a true barbarian."

"Oh, listen to the pretty boy," jabbed Steve. "Shouldn't you be playin' your horn somewhere today?"

"So are you hosting a watch party at your house?" asked Scott.

"Nope, just me and Karen and lots of beer. My parents are actually in Philadelphia this weekend. They have rink-side seats. Philly is still a Teamster kinda town."

For twenty-five years, the National Hockey League (NHL) had been a small, tight-knit group of six franchises in six cities: Montreal Canadians, Toronto Maple Leafs, Boston Bruins, New York Rangers, Detroit Red Wings, and Chicago Blackhawks. Hockey had been a sport that was dominated by Canadians and followed by few people outside the corridor of cities along the US-Canadian border.

It all changed in 1967 when the NHL doubled in size, expanding from six teams to twelve. Soon after, CBS decided to take a chance, acquiring the rights to broadcast NHL games on a national scale. Cities across the United States were soon getting exposed to hockey for the first time, largely through the CBS telecasts that occurred on Sunday afternoons.

It didn't take long for Americans to embrace the fast-paced, hard-hitting action of NHL hockey. Unlike the slow and tedious play of baseball, hockey showcased a steady stream of nonstop action. Instinctively flipping between offense and defense, hockey players were substituted on the fly, allowing for short bursts of maximum effort and an abundance of high-speed collisions.

With scarred faces and missing teeth, hockey players were a rough-and-tumble bunch, ready and willing to skirmish at the drop of a hat. Unlike other sports, fighting had become almost routine in the NHL, exposing fans to a whole new level of violence. And with the league turning a blind eye, players could exploit their savagery, pummeling an opponent into a bloody pulp with very few consequences.

No team personified this brutality more than the upstart Philadelphia Flyers, nicknamed the Broad Street Bullies. Entering the

1974 Stanley Cup Finals, the Flyers were on the verge of becoming the first expansion team to win a title. Their opponent, the Boston Bruins, had won two of the past four Stanley Cups and were solid favorites.

The Bruins, with a regular season record of 52-17, captured the Eastern Conference title and were the highest scoring team in the league. Their speed, finesse, and slick puck-handling skills contrasted sharply to the rugged, hard-hitting defensive style of the Flyers.

Leading the league with the fewest goals allowed, Philadelphia won the Western Conference with a record of 50-16. Their goalie, Bernie Parent, was awarded the Vezina Trophy as the league's best goaltender. A popular saying in Philadelphia that year was: "Only the Lord saves more than Bernie."

By virtue of the league's best record, the Bruins would have home ice advantage and host game one. As expected, Boston controlled the early stages of the game and jumped out to a 2-0 first period lead. But Philadelphia got on the scoreboard in the second period and tied it up in the third with a goal from their leading scorer, Bobby Clarke. Late in the third period, still tied at 2-2, the game appeared to be heading for overtime. But with one minute remaining, the Bruins's star defensemen, Bobby Orr, fired a blistering slapshot past Bernie Parent. Final score: Boston 3, Philadelphia 2.

Game two was a defensive struggle with the Bruins clinging to a slim 2-1 lead late in the third period. Desperate to stay alive, the Flyers pulled their goalie to gain an extra attacker. With less than a minute remaining, Andre Dupont scored the equalizer, and the game went into overtime. The two teams would go on to battle another twelve minutes before Bobby Clarke scored the deciding goal, his second of the game. Final score: Philadelphia 3, Boston 2. It was the first time the Flyers had ever won a game at the Boston Garden.

Skating on their home ice, the Flyers won the next two games decisively, 4-1 and 4-2. With a commanding 3-1 series lead, the Flyers returned to the Boston Garden confident and determined. But the Bruins were not about to roll over. With the game turning into a street brawl, the Flyers lost their composure and let the game get out of control. Once again, the Boston Garden proved to be Philadelphia's nemesis. Final score: Bruins 5, Flyers 1.

Sunday, May 19, 1974, the Philadelphia Flyers returned to the Spectrum, licking their wounds. Although they still held a 3-2 series lead, the Bruins had tested their fortitude, forcing them to rethink their tactics. In front of a national TV audience and a raucous home crowd, the team was feeling the pressure, magnified exponentially by the presence of Lord Stanley's Cup.

After fifteen minutes of scoreless hockey, the Flyers finally broke the stalemate when Rick MacLeish deflected Andre Dupont's slapshot past Boston's Gilles Gilbert for a 1-0 lead. The response was deafening, with seventeen thousand ecstatic fans raising the rafters, sensing a defining moment in hockey history.

With the teams battling back and forth for two more scoreless periods, the 1-0 lead was preserved. Turning away shot after shot, Parent had put on a performance of a lifetime, shutting down the high-scoring Bruins and bringing a Stanley Cup to the city of Philadelphia.

Along with his teammates, Bobby Clarke skated around the rink, holding the cup high above his head for all to see. With a shutout performance and thirty saves to his credit, Bernie Parent was awarded the Conn Smythe trophy, symbolic of the league's MVP throughout the playoffs. In the seventh year of their existence, the Philadelphia Flyers had become the first NHL expansion team to win a Stanley Cup. It was a defining moment in history and the city was ready to celebrate.

Taking in the cool night air, Brian stood on his driveway with Scott, reflecting upon the hockey game and the history they had just witnessed.

"Another one for the record books," noted Brian. "This has been quite a year. Even though I'm a Bruin fan, I gotta admit it was pretty fun watchin' those Philly fans go crazy."

"It didn't matter to me either way," said Scott. "But I usually root for the underdogs and it's pretty cool when you witness history."

"We should check in on Steve," said Brian. "I'm sure he's goin' nuts right now."

"I'll bet he's totally *inebriated*." Scott laughed. "I'd knock on his door, but he's probably on his way to third base with Karen by now."

"You think?" replied Brian sarcastically. "I bet he wouldn't appreciate you using a baseball reference to score his conquests."

"You're probably right." Scott laughed. "Maybe Karen should put him in the penalty box."

"That's more like it," chuckled Brian.

"Are you boys my bodyguards?" came a voice from next door.

Brian and Scott looked up to see Antonio walking toward them and the Ford Galaxie parked in the street.

"Antonio! What's happenin'?" exclaimed Brian.

"You tell me, this is your hood," noted Antonio, happy to see his friends.

"Did you watch the hockey game?" asked Scott.

"Yeah, right." Antonio laughed. "I came here to watch hockey with a White girl because they don't allow that in *my* hood."

"Don't knock it until you've tried it," teased Scott.

"I wouldn't hold my breath if I was you."

"Are you all set for the election?" asked Brian.

"As ready as I'll ever be. Lynda and I put together a pretty good speech and we made a few signs to post around the building. I better get your vote."

"It's gonna be a landslide," said Brian.

"I certainly hope so. I wasn't planning on stickin' my neck out for nothing."

"Just remember who your friends are when you're sitting on your throne," teased Scott.

"It's gonna be Quinn's throne," corrected Antonio. "I'm just along for the ride. Apparently, they think I'm good for a few votes."

"That's politics," said Brian.

"Yeah, well, I better skedaddle," said Antonio. "I don't think your neighbors want me around here after dark."

"Don't be ridiculous," said Brian. "You're always welcome around here."

Turning toward the car, Antonio reached for his pocket and pulled out his keys. Just as he unlocked the door, he paused unexpectedly. "What was that?" he asked.

Reacting to a suspicious shrieking sound, the boys looked down the street, their senses on high alert. A few seconds later, they heard it again, louder and more pronounced.

"I've heard *that* sound before," said Antonio. "That was a scream."

"Sounds like it came from Marino's house," said Scott.

"Should we check it out?" asked Brian.

"It's hard tellin' what that boy is up to," declared Antonio.

Scott and Brian looked at each other nervously, wondering if they should investigate or mind their own business. They'd never heard a scream before. It had an eerie, almost spooky sound to it.

Fully alert, the boys perked up their ears, trying to pick up any indication of distress.

"I can hear voices," noted Brian. "It sounds like an argument."

"Maybe Steve and Karen are havin' a fight," said Scott.

"Knowing Steve, he's probably beatin' the hell out of her," said Antonio, his suspicion mounting.

Another loud squeal pierced the air, followed by the muffled sound of wailing. It was dark, but the boys could pick up the image of two bodies scuffling near Steve Marino's car. Karen was clearly trying to get away, but Steve had her pinned against the vehicle, his hand over her mouth. Struggling to free herself, Karen twisted and turned, desperately trying to fend off the aggression, but Steve yanked her back by the arm and slammed her against the car with a sickening thud.

"Hey!" yelled Brian, his heart pounding. "What's goin' on over there?"

Startled by Brian's voice, Steve looked up and loosened his grip. Recognizing an opening, Karen pulled herself away, but Steve lunged, trying to regain control.

Just as Brian decided to intervene, Steve unexpectedly dropped to his knees, doubled over in pain. Karen, after a brief hesitation, spun around and ran toward the boys.

"I think she just kneed him in the balls," said Scott.

"That boy should be castrated," said Antonio.

Sobbing uncontrollably, Karen stumbled toward the boys in a state of delirium. With red swollen eyes and a tattered blouse flapping in the breeze, she suddenly turned her head away, ashamed of her appearance.

Not knowing how to react, the boys stood by in an uncomfortable moment of silence, stunned by what they had just witnessed. Antonio, exerting his compassion, moved forward and wrapped his arms around Karen, holding her tight and making her feel safe.

As the sobbing continued, the boys remained cautious, reluctant to press her on the details. Karen was clearly too distraught to cooperate with an interrogation.

"I'm gonna get Lynda," said Scott. "Karen will feel more comfortable if Lynda is here."

Antonio slowly loosened his hug and cupped his hands around Karen's face. "Let me see that beautiful mug," he said softly.

Karen looked down to the ground, embarrassed by the attention and ashamed of her appearance. But Antonio put his hand under her chin and lifted her face. He could see, for the first time, that one eye was swollen more than the other, and it wasn't from crying. Her puffy mouth was swelling up like a wet sponge and there was a stream of blood trickling from her nose.

After assessing the damage, Antonio tried to lighten the mood. "Girl, you look like you just went a couple rounds with Muhammed Ali. It's a good thing you have sharp kneecaps."

"You're gonna be all right," assured Brian. "I'm just glad we came out here when we did."

"Are you ready to tell us what happened?" asked Antonio.

Karen shook her head with a "no."

"You can't keep it bottled up inside. You need to talk to someone."

"Things just got out of hand," she mumbled. "He's *way* too drunk."

Antonio continued to probe. "What kind of things got out of hand?"

"I don't know. I guess he wasn't gonna take no for an answer."

Antonio looked at Brian knowingly and decided to press forward.

"Karen…dear," said Antonio, with an authoritative firmness. "Did Steve Marino rape you?"

Karen looked down at the ground despondently, choosing not to answer.

"Honey, you need to tell us what happened. He needs to be held accountable for his actions."

"I don't want anyone to know about this," she muttered.

Antonio and Brian looked up to see Lynda storming toward the sidewalk, followed closely by Scott.

"Are you all right?" asked Lynda.

Karen turned away, not wanting Lynda to see her face. She knew Lynda had more sense than to ever get herself into a predicament like this, which made her all the more embarrassed.

"Karen," came a shout from Marino's driveway. "Let's go! I need to take you home now."

Karen looked over at where Steve was standing, and then looked at her friends. Suddenly lucid, like a boxer after a whiff of smelling salts, Karen appeared to be contemplating the request.

"Don't even think about it," said Antonio.

"I need to go home," said Karen.

"Not with that animal," said Antonio. "I can take you home."

"C'mon, let's go!" yelled Steve.

"She's not going anywhere with you!" shouted Antonio. "You've already done enough damage."

Steve didn't respond. Instead, he seemed more determined than ever, walking toward the group purposefully, as if provoked by Antonio's insulting remarks.

Antonio wrapped his arms around Karen again and looked at Brian and Scott. "You boys better protect us. It's hard tellin' what that bully might do."

Following his cue, Brian and Scott stepped in front, forming a blockade.

Realizing the boys meant business, Steve decided to be more diplomatic.

"C'mon Karen, let's go," he said, with a trace of empathy. "This is all a big misunderstanding. Things just got out of hand, that's all."

"I think you should chill a bit," suggested Brian. "Maybe it's best to call it an evening. Besides, you're in no condition to be driving."

"Says who?" challenged Steve. "Let *me* be the judge of that."

"I don't think you're qualified to be the judge of anything," countered Antonio.

"Shut the hell up, boy!" said Steve, his temper flaring. "This is no affair of yours. You don't even *belong* in this neighborhood."

"Oh, is that right," said Antonio, taking the bait. "Apparently they allow *rapists* to live in this neighborhood."

Incensed by the accusation, Steve plowed through the boys like a bull and took a wild swing at Antonio, missing and falling to the ground.

"Stop it!" screamed Karen.

Steve struggled to regain his footing, and the boys, more determined than ever, resumed their blockade.

Sensing things were out of hand, Lynda ran back to the house for help.

Back on his feet, Steve reassessed his predicament. He wanted to teach Antonio a lesson, but Brian and Scott were unwavering.

"Steve," said Brian. "You've had a lot to drink. Don't make this any worse than it already is. Let's just call it a night and get a fresh start tomorrow."

"Karen," said Steve. "This is between you and me. I need to take you home. Everything's gonna be all right."

"Don't worry about it," said Brian. "We'll make sure she gets a ride home. Why don't you just go home and sleep it off."

"Sleep *what* off? What are you implying? I don't need any of you interfering in my business." Steve's temper was flaring again.

Lynda returned to the scene and whispered something to Karen and Antonio.

"No," said Karen, her voice rising with apprehension. "We don't need any police. I just want this to go away."

"Police?" questioned Steve. "Who's talking about police?"

"It's nothing," said Karen. "Forget about it."

"What's going on here?" pressed Steve. "Did someone call the police?"

In a moment of awkward silence, the boys looked at Lynda for guidance. Out of her element, Lynda appeared to vacillate, not knowing how to respond.

Karen reiterated her objective. "We don't need any police. We can handle this on our own."

Steve focused his ire on Lynda. "Did you call the police?"

"I called a neighbor," said Lynda, reasserting herself. "We need an intervention."

"What do you mean by that?" pressed Steve. "We've got enough neighbors here already."

"She's talking about Mr. Carter," said Antonio, perturbed by the ambiguity. "You may know him as Captain Carter."

Steve glared at Lynda. "Is that true?"

"I don't think I have to answer to you," said Lynda, more determined than ever.

"Oh yeah? We'll see about that."

"Are you gonna hit her too?" said Antonio.

"Shut up, nigger! Nobody around here was hit. If anyone's gonna get hit, it's you. Now go back to where you belong."

"You can make all the threats you want," said Antonio. "But we're gonna tell the police everything we know."

"You don't know shit!" yelled Steve, losing control. "Go back to your crime-infested neighborhood. There ain't no crime around here."

"Oh really? Since when is *rape* not a crime?"

Steve couldn't take it anymore. Exploding with anger, he blasted through the blockade and tackled Antonio to the ground. Brian scrambled to defend, but it was too little too late. Steve was already on top of Antonio, whaling away.

Pouncing on Steve's back, Brian wrapped his arms around him like a linebacker, laboring to pull him away and save Antonio from a thrashing. Antonio, helping his own cause, planted his shoe squarely on Marino's chest and drove him back with a solid thrust. Capitalizing on the turnabout, Brian leveraged his weight and flung Steve to the ground.

Stunned by the reversal, Steve sat up on the ground looking dazed and confused. Brian and Scott positioned themselves again, preparing to defend another assault, while Antonio, back on his feet, wiped the blood from his mouth.

Still on the ground, Steve glared at Antonio with an evil look, unveiling his wicked hostility. "You're a dead man," he said with bloodcurdling malice. "You crossed a line and you're gonna pay for it."

Before anyone could respond, all heads turned away as a series of siren blips arrived on the scene and halted the commotion. Captain Carter slowed to a stop and stepped out of his unmarked vehicle.

"Don't anybody move," he said, surveying his surroundings.

The crew stood frozen in their tracks, obediently complying.

Reaching back into his vehicle, the captain retrieved his two-way radio and announced his position. "Captain Carter here, reporting a minor disturbance at 8732 Norring Drive. I'll need backup as a precautionary measure."

Keeping it short and sweet, the captain returned the radio to the vehicle and resumed his examination. His eyes scanned the faces deliberately, looking for any peculiarities.

"I think I recognize everyone here except this guy," he said, pointing at Antonio. "What's your name and what are you doing here?"

"Antonio Jackson. I was visiting Lynda."

"Visiting Lynda?" asked Carter, with a hint of skepticism. "Is that true?"

"Yes, it's true," said Lynda.

"I'm guessing Lynda isn't the one who gave you a bloody lip," quipped Carter, looking at Antonio.

"No, sir, it was him," he said, pointing at Steve.

"That's a lie," said Steve. "You can't believe a word he says."

"All right, pipe down," said Carter. "I wasn't talking to you. I need to find out what the hell is goin' on here. Who can I trust to give an accurate account?"

With Antonio, Scott, and Steve all chattering at once, Carter blew his cool.

"Shut the hell up! Every one of you! If I don't get the kind of cooperation I need here, I'm gonna haul every one of you downtown! Now, let's start with Lynda. The rest of you can keep your mouths shut... unless you want to get handcuffed."

"Actually sir, I'm not the best one to give a full account," admitted Lynda. "Everything happened when Antonio left our house. I was still inside."

Carter scowled with frustration. "Okay, if everything started after he left, I need to know who was outside from the beginning, someone besides Antonio."

"Scott and I were outside," said Brian. "We were standing on my driveway talking to Antonio."

Pleased with Brian's response, Carter felt like he could get a straight story from an honest young man. "All right, let's hear it."

Brian didn't know how to begin. He suddenly realized he couldn't deliver an accurate account of what went down without incriminating Steve. Up until now, he considered Steve to be a friend. He didn't want that to end. But now he had an obligation. And for the first time ever, he found himself fearing Steve Marino, worried about the retribution he might receive from a shady underworld he knew nothing about.

"We were just standing around talking," said Brian. "And then we heard a noise that sounded like a scream."

Brian then hesitated, wondering how he could deliver the truth without incriminating anyone.

"Is that what it was?" asked Carter.

"Is that what what was?" blathered Brian.

"A scream. Was it a scream?"

"Possibly," said Brian. "Sort of a high-pitched sound of a girl."

"Where was it coming from?" asked Carter, his frustration growing by the second.

"It was hard to tell."

"For God's sake!" blurted Antonio. "Tell him what happened. It was Steve beating the hell out of his girlfriend."

"That's a lie!" shouted Steve.

"All right," barked Carter. "Everyone shut up."

Just when the situation seemed out of hand, all heads turned as the area lit up from the oscillating beams of a police siren. As requested, Carter's backup had arrived in a Fort Wayne Police Department squad car.

Two uniformed police officers stepped out of the vehicle and addressed Captain Carter. "As requested, sir. What can we do to assist?"

"I need you to stand guard of this motley crew while I continue my line of questioning. If anyone speaks out of turn or makes a wrongful move, I want you to put them on the ground and cuff 'em."

"You got it, captain."

Carter walked over to Steve and examined him closely. "Hmmm, just as I suspected. A strong scent of alcohol. Have you been drinking?"

"I only had a couple beers."

"How old are you?"

"Eighteen."

"That's odd. Why would you be drinking beer when the legal drinking age is twenty-one?"

Steve didn't respond.

"Are your parents home?"

"No."

"What time will they be home?"

"They won't be home until tomorrow. They're in Philadelphia."

"So when your parents are gone, you decide to get drunk? How convenient."

Steve remained silent.

"Were you drinking by yourself?"

"No, my girlfriend had a couple beers too."

"Which one is your girlfriend?"

Steve pointed at Karen.

"She didn't happen to be screaming, did she?"

"No, she wasn't screaming."

Captain Carter walked over to Karen while Steve glared at her ominously.

"Were you at Steve Marino's house this evening?"

"Yes, sir."

"What were you doing there while his parents were gone?"

"We were watching the hockey game."

Captain Carter took a closer look at Karen and pointed his flashlight at her face.

"Oh my, it looks like you had a rough evening. Were you playing hockey, too?"

Karen remained silent.

"How did your shirt get ripped?"

Karen looked at Steve and responded to the captain, "It was an accident."

"Well, it must've been a pretty bad accident for your face to get hurt that bad."

"He raped her!" yelled Antonio. "Tell the truth!"

Captain Carter reeled around and ordered his officers. "Cuff him! Put him on the ground and cuff him!"

The officers threw Antonio to the ground and cuffed his hands behind his back.

"I warned you," said Carter. "If anyone else speaks out of turn, you'll be on the ground too."

Carter looked over at Steve again. "Is that true?"

"Is what true?"

"Did you rape her?"

"No, of course not."

"Did you have sexual relations with her?"

Marino hesitated, trying to decide on the best response.

"It's not a trick question," said Carter. "Did you or did you not have sexual relations with her?"

Karen, completely humiliated by the public exposure, began to sob again.

"I'm not sure how to define sexual relations," said Steve. "Everything we did was completely consensual."

"Is that so?" replied Carter, unable to hide his skepticism.

The captain turned to Karen. "How old are *you*, may I ask?"

"Seventeen," replied Karen.

"Hmmm, that's interesting. You look older than that."

Carter looked back at Steve. "Did you know your girlfriend is seventeen?"

"No," he lied. "I thought she was eighteen."

"Well, we have an interesting dilemma here," said Carter. "Whether your relations were consensual or not, sex with a minor is still against the law."

"We didn't have sex," said Marino.

"All right," said Carter. "I've heard enough. We're not gonna try this case out here tonight. I'll quickly cover our options and then I'll tell you what I'm gonna do."

"Do you want us to take this guy downtown?" the officers asked the captain.

"No, stand him up and take the cuffs off."

Antonio glared at Steve as the officers removed the cuffs. Steve returned the stare, issuing his implied warning.

"Here's a list of potential charges I will write up in my report," continued Carter.

"Underage drinking, battery, rape, and sex with a minor. Depending upon how the responsible parties and their parents wish to proceed, we will continue accordingly. I want my officers to take this young lady home and explain the consequences to her parents. In the meantime, I want *you*, Steve Marino, to go home and stay there. We will continue our investigation when your parents return tomorrow. If you leave your house before then, I will have you arrested immediately. Is that understood?"

Steve nodded his head.

Antonio suddenly interjected. "May I please add something, sir?"

"Make it brief," said Carter.

"Can you add assault to your list of charges? This thug punched me in the face."

"That's a lie," shouted Steve.

Captain Carter walked over and put his flashlight in Antonio's face. "Well, it doesn't look that bad to me. Not nearly as bad as the young lady's face."

"He attacked me," said Antonio.

"My advice is to let it go. I'm not gonna file any charges. You can pursue a civil suit if you wish. In the meantime, I suggest you stay in your own neighborhood."

Chapter 56

M EMORIAL DAY WEEKEND ARRIVED IN typical fashion with most Hoosiers talking about the Indianapolis 500 and who would have the best shot at winning the fifty-eighth running of the greatest spectacle in racing. True to tradition, Ryan O'Connor was seated in the General Motors suite, a luxury box on the homestretch filled with Detroit executives and auto industry cronies.

Unlike previous years, a melancholy mood had settled over the two-and-a-half-mile oval, a hangover from the 1973 race that was marred by horrific crashes, injured spectators and three deaths. After three days of weather delays and intermittent racing, the 1973 race was finally called on a Wednesday after only 133 laps, far short of the two hundred laps and five hundred miles. The leader at the time, Gordon Johncock, was declared the winner, but it was a bittersweet victory.

Long celebrated as one of the greatest sporting events in the world, the Indianapolis 500 had suffered a black eye, with many calling the 1973 race the most embarrassing episode of its illustrious past. Criticized for its unwillingness to change and adapt, pundits had labeled the Speedway a modern-day death trap.

For too many years the racing teams had focused on speed, infatuated with the idea of producing the world's fastest racecars. In 1973, the pole winner, Johnny Rutherford, had gone faster than anyone in history, averaging 198.4 mph, trying to become the first driver to reach the elusive 200 mph barrier, a notoriety that would surely put him at the pinnacle of racing folklore.

But 1974 would be different. Instead of focusing on speed, racing officials dedicated an entire year to track reconfigurations and race car modifications, all in an attempt to avoid the catastrophes of 1973. The results were considerable. Heading into race day, the month of May had been relatively accident free, and the pole sitter, AJ Foyt, had averaged only 191.6 mph.

Scheduled for May 26, the 1974 Indianapolis 500 would begin on a Sunday for the first time in history. In the past, the race had been held on Memorial Day, a holiday traditionally recognized on May 30. But in 1971, Congress enacted the Uniform Monday Holiday Act, permanently moving Memorial Day to the last Monday in May, allowing Americans to celebrate a three-day weekend. In order to appease fans, Speedway officials decided to abandon its "no Sunday racing" policy.

After the ceremonial invocation and the emotional rendition of "Taps," a tribute to the brave Americans who died for their country, the Purdue Boilermaker Band played the national anthem. Then a large cheer went up from the two hundred and seventy-five thousand spectators as Jim Nabors took the stage for the traditional performance of "Back Home Again in Indiana." As the electricity continued to build, Speedway owner, Tony Hulman, ignited the enthusiasm with his command of "Gentlemen, start your engines."

In the world of sports, few, if any, events can match the heart-pounding stimulation that comes from the roar of thirty-three turbocharged engines firing up all at once, staging the age-old drama of man and machine versus the limitations of physics. It was a new year, a new race, a clean slate, putting to rest all the regrets of the past.

With a little extra hop in his step, Antonio Jackson waltzed into the Northrop administrative offices prepared to deliver his last morning announcements of the school year.

"Antonio!" announced the principal. "Are you ready to wrap up another year?"

"I am," confirmed Antonio. "What about you? Is Pappa Bruin ready to wrap up a career?"

"Ah, that's a good question. I still have a few weeks to go before officially handing over the torch, but there's definitely some light at the end of the tunnel."

"Good for you," said Antonio. "I wish you nothing but the best."

"I appreciate that, but let's save the emotional goodbyes for later; gotta take care of business first. I only have a couple items on the agenda for you this morning, then you can ad-lib all you want."

"Sounds good."

"Here's today's condensed schedule for our half-day of classes," said Pappa Bruin, handing over the itinerary. "If you can just run through this quickly and remind everyone that final grades will be issued next week. And then I'll need you to go over the sign-up information for summer school. Other than that, I'll start out with a few words, and you can take it from there."

"That's all?"

"Am I missing something?" asked the principal, with a twinkle in his eye.

"Oh, I see what you're doing," said Antonio. "You're just messin' with me."

"Whatever do you mean?" chuckled Pappa Bruin.

"Well, there's this tiny little thing called election results. Some people are wondering who the new senior class president will be. It may seem trivial at the moment."

"Oh yes," teased the principal. "How could I possibly forget? I should have those results here somewhere."

Pappa Bruin reached into his suit jacket and pulled out a piece of paper. "I hope you're not too disappointed."

Antonio looked at the sheet of paper with a hint of anxiety, then smiled. "Hmmm, closer than I thought."

"Very funny. I think we all knew how it would turn out. Congratulations."

"Thank you, sir."

Prepared to end the school year in a blaze of glory, Antonio kicked off the morning announcements with his trumpet and a rousing rendition of *Revelry*.

"Wake up, my fellow Bruins! Rise and shine! Let's embrace this new day and make the most of it. Before I go any further, I'd like to turn this broadcast over to our fearless leader. Take it away, Pappa Bruin."

"Thank you, Antonio. That was very uplifting. There's nothing like starting out the morning with a little inspiration. And that's exactly what I've received from this student body each and every day of the year. You've inspired me to work hard, embrace the challenges, and live life to the fullest. And by watching you grow and achieve great success; you've brought fulfillment into my life."

The principal paused for emphasis and looked at Antonio. Reigning in his emotions, Pappa Bruin struggled with the lump in his throat. Antonio nodded his head reassuringly and patted his principal on the back. Pappa Bruin took a deep breath and continued.

"For those of you who've spent the past two or three years in these hallowed halls, I want you to think about where we started and how far we've come. There were many doubters when this school opened three years ago. There were those that said it couldn't be done, that it would never work. To those people I say: 'Look at us now.'

"Now we are one big happy family, a diversified and unified force. And I would say to those doubters that we are a force to be reckoned with. They will never doubt us again. We are the future of this city, and we are the future of this country, a symbol of what can be achieved if we all work together in harmony."

Realizing he was witnessing something special, Antonio winked at his principal. Pappa Bruin winked in return and continued.

"As I end my career and ride off into the sunset, I can say, without a doubt, that I have no regrets. I am confident our future is in good hands, and I consider myself blessed to have been a part of it. Thank you for being a part of my life. I wish you all nothing but the best. Don't ever give up on your dreams. Go forth and prosper."

Overcome with emotion, Antonio couldn't resist giving his principal a big hug. Pappa Bruin returned the affectionate embrace and handed Antonio the microphone.

"Wow! I don't even know where to begin. That's a tough act to follow. Let me start by saying bravo! I truly feel honored and privileged to be in Pappa Bruin's company. And I think I speak for all the students and faculty when I say thank you for everything you've done. Best wishes to you and your loved ones for a wonderful and fulfilling retirement. You deserve it. God bless Pappa Bruin."

Antonio paused as his principal patted him on the back. Then he took a deep breath and laughed into the microphone. "Believe it or not, I have a few business items to take care of, so please bear with me."

Antonio ran through the day's abbreviated schedule and talked about sign-up procedures for summer school.

"That brings us to the last item on our agenda," said Antonio. "As you know, last week we held the election for senior class president. Today I have the results of that election. So let's get right to it. Without further ado, I would like to officially congratulate my friend and colleague, Quinn O'Connor, as the new student council president for the Class of 1975. Go get 'em, Quinn!"

"Moving forward, it will be my privilege to serve under Quinn O'Connor, making sure that next year's graduating class, the Class of 1975, has the best senior year ever."

"Now, I'd like to try something different. I decided to close out today's announcements and finish up the year with a little poem. I hope you'll find these words to be relevant and inspirational."

Life is something we should cherish,

We never know when we'll perish.

Live each and every single day,

Smell the flowers, stop and play.

Life is something we've been blessed,

Choice is yours; choose your quest

Follow your passions, and you'll be fine,

With the right attitude, you will shine.

When the school day ended at eleven thirty, Quinn caught up with Antonio near the loading zone, where throngs of students were waiting to board their buses. Surrounded by his usual entourage, Antonio was in good spirits, bantering with his cohorts and gesturing with animated gaiety.

Suddenly out of his element, Quinn felt hesitant. He wanted to celebrate his victory with Antonio but didn't want to intrude. Quinn was not the assertive type, and this was not his crowd. Rich White kids didn't mix in with brothers from the hood. That was common knowledge.

Feeling self-conscious, Quinn did an about-face, abandoning his intrusion and retreating back into his comfort zone. Another time, another place, he told himself.

"Quinn! Over here!"

Quinn wheeled around to see Antonio waving his arm.

"Congratulations," said Antonio, approaching and extending his hand.

Quinn embraced his hand enthusiastically. "Likewise, I couldn't have done it without you."

"Let's just say we make a good team," said Antonio.

"I can live with that. Are you going to New Orleans this summer?"

"I haven't decided yet. Maybe for a short visit. Gotta see if there's anything happenin' around here first."

"Well, nobody can make things happen better than you."

"Ha, you got that right. And don't you forget it," said Antonio with a mischievous grin. "But I better get back in line or I'm gonna miss my ride home."

Quinn extended his hand one more time. "Thanks again for everything."

"You got it," said Antonio with a firm handshake.

At a loss for words and feeling emotional, Quinn didn't want to say goodbye for the summer. Scrambling for a delay tactic, he suddenly blurted out, "Wait, what are you doing for lunch?"

"Lunch? I'm guessing another gourmet sandwich at the Jackson Bistro," joked Antonio.

"Let me take you to lunch," offered Quinn. "That's the least I can do. Then I'll give you a ride home."

Surprised by the invitation, Antonio hesitated, not knowing how to respond. "Are you serious?"

"Why not?" said Quinn. "A man's gotta eat lunch."

Sitting in their booth at Azar's, the diner style restaurant inside Glenbrook Mall, the boys perused their lunch menus, ogling the colorful displays of sandwiches laminated in plastic.

"What looks good?" asked Quinn. "Don't be shy. Order anything you want."

"Are you kidding me? Everything looks good."

"It's just a burger joint," noted Quinn.

"Not really. My idea of a burger joint is ordering a thirty-three-cent cheeseburger at the McDonalds drive-thru. This is different. Here I'm sitting in a booth where a waitress will take my order and hand-deliver my meal. I'm not used to that kind of service."

"Well, get used to it." Quinn laughed. "You and I are gonna be running Northrop High School next year."

"In that case I'll order the Big Boy."

"Make it a Big Boy Platter," said Quinn.

"Don't mind if I do. Let's live it up!"

Chowing down on their double-decker hamburgers with melted cheese, shredded lettuce, and special sauce, the boys chatted away like they'd been friends their entire lives. In the past, their familiarity had been casual, sharing each other's company under the tutelage of Lynda Lacey. Cordial at best, their interactions had been limited, but there was no denying their mutual admiration.

Antonio was everything Quinn wanted to be: confident, outgoing, and charismatic. Antonio had an understanding of who he was and where he was going, uninhibited by false pretenses or preordained allegiances. In short, Antonio was a guy in charge of his own destiny.

But Quinn had something that Antonio could not emulate, and that was a reputation for wealth and power. He was an O'Connor, and that was a name that reeked of privilege. The O'Connors were blue bloods; the Jacksons were descendants of slavery. Two different worlds, and never the twain shall meet.

But this was the 1970s, and the world was changing. Although Antonio knew his place in society, he still felt the need to bridge the gap, and that's exactly what he'd been doing since the public schools integrated in 1971. Antonio had been an ambassador for unification. Quinn's friendship would be no different.

But Quinn was more than just a barrier. To Antonio, there was an undeniable sense of envy, an intangible attraction. Maybe it was Quinn's good looks, or maybe it was his sophistication, or maybe it was his graceful athleticism when gliding around the tennis court. Antonio couldn't put his finger on it. It reminded him of the infatuation he had with movie stars when he was a little kid.

No longer segregated by any boundaries, the unlikely duo finished their lunch with Quinn paying the tab and Antonio offering his gratitude. As the two stood up from the table, Antonio reached for his Coke and offered a toast.

"Here's to the beginning of a beautiful friendship."

Puzzled by the familiarity of the phrase, Quinn asked, "Where have I heard that before?"

"C'mon, everybody knows that line," teased Antonio. "None other than Humphrey Bogart. One of the classic lines from *Casablanca.*"

"That's it!" laughed Quinn. "I knew I heard it somewhere before."

Quinn grabbed his Coke and toasted Antonio's glass. "Here's looking at you, kid."

With the honorable Judge Jenkins presiding, defense attorney Phillip Goldman rose to address the court. It was his third case of the morning and he still had two more to go. Uninspired by the repetition, Goldman went through the motions, stepping through the rudimentary procedures that fulfilled his obligations. Dotting i's and crossing t's was a monotonous chore, but he knew a steady case load went a long way toward paying the bills, every little bit helped.

The judge addressed the courtroom. "In regard to the charge of illegal consumption of alcohol by a minor, a Class C misdemeanor, how does your client, Steven Marino, wish to plead?"

"Guilty, your honor."

"Is the defendant in the courtroom?" asked the judge.

"No, sir. I am here on his behalf."

The judge reviewed the paperwork. "Okay, in light of the fact that it is Steve Marino's first offense and he was not operating a motor vehicle, I see you have already reached a plea deal."

"That is correct, your honor."

"I hereby sentence the defendant to a one-hundred-dollar fine. Next case."

For Karen Gadby, the past two weeks of her junior year had been painfully traumatic. When the police officers delivered her to her residence on the evening of May 19, she was forced to confront her parents with the harsh reality of her humiliating encounter.

Not willing to prolong the trauma, the officers delivered an abbreviated rundown of the evening's events and the potential charges. Stunned by the eye-opening allegations, Mr. and Mrs. Gadby were flabbergasted. All Karen could do was cry.

The officers advised the parents to have a long discussion with their daughter and pursue a course of action that would serve her best interest. Captain Carter would be in touch within forty-eight hours to review their options. In the meantime, their daughter should seek comfort in the services of a licensed professional.

Handing them the business card of a Social Services network, the officers suggested patience. Their daughter needed a few days off from school to engage in some therapeutical dialogue, counseling that would best serve her emotional well-being and assist in the decision-making process.

In the end, it was a no-brainer. The last thing that Karen wanted to do was drag her ordeal through the courts and prolong her agony. She only wanted to erase this painful chapter in her life and move on. Her parents agreed, but with one stipulation: she could never see Steve Marino again.

Steve had survived his predicament relatively unscathed. He had dodged another bullet. But people in his family's profession had been doing that for generations.

No longer in school, Steve Marino was faced with his future. He talked about moving back to Philadelphia and working on the docks where his father could get him a high-paying Teamsters job, or possibly joining the navy, a military branch that would keep him out of Vietnam. He had options and he was proud to announce that Fort Wayne was at the bottom of his short list.

Meanwhile, his relationship with the Coldwater Creek boys had become strained. Witnessing the evolution of Steve's dark side, his sidekicks were reluctant to maintain their civility. Adding to the discord, Steve was still bitter over the way the events went down on the evening of May 19.

Instead of defending his honor, his so-called friends had turned on him. There were names for friends like that, the ones who wouldn't honor their loyalty under pressure, the ones who turned tail and ran when the shit hit the fan. They were squealers, and they were rats, and they were not to be trusted. They would pay their dues in the end; there were consequences for behavior like that.

But most of Steve's wrath had been focused on Antonio Jackson. Although he could justify the actions of his neighborhood cronies, he could never condone the actions of Antonio, a disrespectful Black boy coming into his own backyard and unleashing a slew of accusations, incriminating him with charges that damaged his reputation and threatened his livelihood. That was, quite simply, unacceptable.

Chapter 57

ARQUIS JACKSON ARRIVED HOME FROM work to find an empty house. It was no surprise. He knew that Chantelle would be running late. She was swinging by the church to take care of a few business matters, and then picking up some groceries for dinner, at least that's what she told him. Normally Marquis would be eager to see his wife, anxious to pour her a glass of wine and linger around the kitchen as she whipped up her latest culinary delight.

But this day was different. Feeling a strange sense of uneasiness, he was reluctant to unwind and ease into his normal routine of rest and relaxation. The tension at work had been building and he couldn't leave it behind. He felt vulnerable, and the sanctity of his home did little to provide refuge.

Although it was payday Friday and Marquis had the weekend off, Saturday loomed like a buzzard hovering over its prey. Hoping to ease the anxiety, Marquis decided to grab a cold bottle of Schlitz. Perhaps it would dull the senses enough to take the edge off, or maybe it would instill a sense of bravado. Liquid courage, that's what his buddies called it, a therapy he had used time and again when courting Chantelle.

One thing Marquis knew for sure; no one had ever achieved any success by being a coward. He recalled the train ride home after their first visit to Fort Wayne and the nervous tension his wife was experiencing. It was *he* who had emboldened her with the quote: "one can never get ahead without taking a chance."

Now it was time for Marquis to take his own advice. He and his coworkers needed to take a chance and seize the opportunity. If they didn't, nothing would ever change. They would remain in servitude, encumbered by management's manipulation and subjugated by their relentless pursuit of power and wealth.

O'Connor Cadillac opened at ten on Saturday mornings, and that's when Marquis and his comrades would set up their picket line. A total of thirteen workers—four from Cadillac and nine from Buick—would lead the charge, the ones who were prounion and not scheduled to work on Saturday. Unlike the picket lines set up during a strike, this would not be a picket line to prevent employees from working. This would be a peaceful protest, an opportunity to promote the Teamsters and let management know that their labor force was serious about organizing.

It had taken a while, but the tide had turned. Although the official vote to join the Teamsters wouldn't take place until the following week, the latest solicitation had indicated a clear majority of workers were willing to get onboard the union train.

If a majority continued to prevail, the final tally would trigger a chain reaction. Soon the Teamsters would initiate their collection of dues and begin hammering out a proposal they would present during the collective bargaining process. If management refused to negotiate in good faith, the Teamsters would use their muscle and threaten a strike.

Marquis was no longer in the middle. He had wanted to remain uncommitted, or at least give off the appearance of neutrality, but that all changed when he discovered his peers were being paid more, even the new hires. No longer could he perform his duties with any pride knowing his compensation was substandard and discriminatory.

Despite his anger and hostility, Marquis still worried about the consequences of taking a stance against his employer. The last thing he wanted was to lose his job. His family could not afford that. But he spoke with Dominic Marino and was assured he had a legal right to unionize free from retaliation and persecution. Marino reminded him that he lived in America, he had inalienable rights, and he would never achieve any success if he didn't exercise his freedom.

Those were all the words he needed to hear. From that point on, Marquis was committed. His people had been persecuted long enough. It was time to take a stand and fight for equality.

Recognizing the squeaky hinges on the back porch screen door, Marquis went into the kitchen to greet his wife. Chantelle had already rested two large grocery bags on the Formica countertop.

"Anything I can help you with?" offered Marquis.

"Nope, I've got it. Just these two bags," said Chantelle.

"That's how you keep your arms so well-toned," teased Marquis, "haulin' around those heavy grocery bags."

"Well, somebody's gotta do it. Maybe I'll arm wrestle you later."

"I'd probably lose that battle," admitted Marquis. "What kinda goodies are you whippin' up tonight?"

"Nothin' fancy. I'm just gonna cook up a couple andouille sausages and serve them with fried okra and red beans and rice."

"Can't go wrong with that. Can I pour you a glass of wine?" asked Marquis.

"Sure. Riunite?"

"On ice?"

"That's nice." Chantelle laughed.

Marquis grabbed a bottle of wine and twisted the screw cap off while Chantelle unloaded the groceries. He wanted to discuss the upcoming events with his wife and express his concerns, but he didn't know how to broach the topic and he didn't want to dampen the mood. She was well aware of the picket line scheduled for Saturday and she was not shy about sharing her reservations. But Marquis still wanted to talk about it. He respected his wife's opinion and always felt better after seeking her advice.

Handing Chantelle her wine, Marquis spoke up. "I was hoping to talk to you about tomorrow. The whole thing is makin' me kinda nervous; I'm not gonna lie."

"Yes, we need to talk about it," agreed Chantelle.

"I just wanted to give you the latest updates," offered Marquis.

"And I have some updates for *you*."

"You do? Like what?"

"No, you first," ordered Chantelle.

"Well, we're meeting at nine forty-five tomorrow morning. That way we should be set up and ready to start when the dealership opens at ten. Like I said before, it's not a real picket line. It's more or less a protest, an opportunity to make our case for organized labor."

"Where are you setting up?" asked Chantelle.

"We'll be on the sidewalk, just outside the dealership. Marino told us we have a right to be there. It's not on company property."

"So what kind of signs will you be holding?" asked Chantelle.

"Marino had the signs made up for us, but we saw a few of them at our last meeting. A couple signs simply read 'International Brotherhood of Teamsters,' along with the official logo. Other signs read 'Unfair Labor' and 'Workers Unite.' Things like that. Pretty generic."

"So what's the mood like around there? Are the workers being mistreated?"

"I don't know if mistreatment is the right word," offered Marquis. "There's a lot of tension, for sure. Bowers has been extremely short with his people. He's been mostly impolite and no longer exchanges any pleasantries. He's been meeting with the attendants one-on-one, trying to find out where they stand on forming a union."

"Has he met with you?"

"Yes."

"What did you tell him?"

"I told him that I was neutral and that I was sympathetic to organized labor but I wasn't sure how I would vote."

"So you lied," offered Chantelle.

"I guess so. But what else was I supposed to say?"

"No, you're right. I think you gave the perfect response."

"Good," said Marquis, a bit relieved. "I'm glad you're on board. You're the only legal counsel I have."

Ignoring the flattery, Chantelle continued. "Does Bowers know you'll be in the picket line tomorrow?"

Marquis hesitated, realizing Chantelle had backed him into a corner. "No one's told him who's participating, but I'll be honest with you, I think he already knows."

"So there goes your neutrality," said Chantelle. "Right out the window."

A bit perturbed, Marquis became more adamant. "We've already talked about this. I told you how I'm getting screwed each and every paycheck. I told you how they're moving people to part-time and taking away their benefits. I told you that inexperienced teenagers are making more money than me. And now you act like I'm making a mistake for participating in the protest. I can't have it both ways. Either I stand up for my rights or I cower around like a slave."

Chantelle walked over to the refrigerator and pulled out another bottle of Schlitz. Without saying a word, she strolled leisurely over to Marquis and handed him the beer, giving him an opportunity to calm down.

"No need to get upset," she said calmly. "I'm on *your* side, remember?"

Marquis took a deep breath and let out a sigh. Then he took a couple swigs of his beer.

"So," he continued, "you said you had some updates for me? What's that all about?"

"I just wanted to relay something to you that happened at the office today," she said. "It may have no relevance whatsoever, but I thought it seemed a bit odd."

"And this relates to me?"

"I'm not sure," continued Chantelle. "Maybe I'm just paranoid, but I usually have pretty good instincts."

"Do tell," said Marquis.

"Well, this afternoon, Ryan O'Connor came into the law offices. Like I told you before, he rarely comes in, maybe once or twice a month. Most of the time he's sitting in his ivory tower on top of the Fort Wayne National Bank building."

"And you thought this was odd?" asked Marquis.

"There's more. Let me finish."

"Sorry."

"Not long after he entered his office, another gentleman showed up. I overheard the receptionist greet him with 'Good afternoon, Captain Carter. Mr. O'Connor is waiting for you.' "

"Captain Carter?" inquired Marquis. "Captain of what?"

"Well, my colleagues told me he's a captain in the police force."

"Was he wearing a uniform?" asked Marquis.

"No, he was wearing a coat and tie."

"You think he was there for legal advice?"

"I doubt it," admitted Chantelle. "If he was, he wouldn't be visiting with Ryan O'Connor. O'Connor isn't really involved with legal work anymore."

"So what concerns do you have?" asked Marquis.

"Hold on, there's more," said Chantelle. "So this Captain Carter stayed behind closed doors with O'Connor for almost an hour. When he came out, he went to the receptionist, and she handed him an envelope. He didn't say a word. He just accepted it and walked out the front door."

"Is that unusual?" asked Marquis.

"Well, I've never witnessed anything like it. It wasn't a large manila envelope that we use to hold legal documents. It was a plain, unmarked letter envelope. He just took it and stuck it under his jacket in his breast pocket."

"So…are you suggesting that it was a bribe? Like maybe there was a check in that envelope?"

"Well, I'm not familiar with the world of bribes, but I don't think bribes are typically done with checks. That would leave a paper trail. Besides, this envelope contained more than a piece of paper, and it had a rubber band wrapped around it."

"Seriously?" asked Marquis, amazed by the implication.

"Call me nosey, but this was a thick envelope, fully stuffed. *That* I'm certain of. I can only speculate what was inside."

Marquis sat down on one of the kitchen chairs with a stunned look on his face. He wasn't sure what to make of this, but Chantelle could tell the wheels were turning. Marquis was clearly trying to process the information she had delivered.

"Are you thinking what I'm thinking?" asked Chantelle.

"I don't know," replied Marquis. "What are you thinking?"

"Well, I remember you telling me about the young kid that you had to train and that he was the son of a cop. And then you told me how management tries to solicit the assistance of the police during labor disputes. And then I thought about the protest you're holding tomorrow. So you see, maybe I'm just paranoid, but I started to connect the dots."

Marquis was expressionless, neither angry nor perturbed, like a chess player whose opponent had just made a move, announcing "check." There was no need to be alarmed. He was in the middle of a chess match with Ryan O'Connor and the business magnate was attacking. Now it was *his* turn to make a move.

"So what are you thinking?" asked Chantelle.

"I'm thinking you're pretty good at connecting the dots. I'm thinking this SOB didn't get to where he is by being passive. He'll do anything in his power to get what he wants, including dirty pool."

"So what are you gonna do now?" asked Chantelle.

"Well, I'm glad you told me, but I'll be honest with you, it doesn't really change anything. We're still gonna do what we gotta do."

"I figured you'd say that," said Chantelle, not willing to rock the boat. "But…will you allow me to provide one good piece of advice?"

"Absolutely. Like I said, you're the only legal counsel I have."

Emphasizing the importance of her advice, Chantelle moved in closer and took Marquis's hand. "Whatever you do, don't tell anyone what I just told you."

"You mean about the police captain and the envelope?"

"Exactly. We don't really know what that was all about. Our little theory about bribes is nothing but pure speculation. In a courtroom, they call it conjecture, and conjecture is not the same thing as evidence."

"Who's talking about a courtroom?" asked Marquis.

"All I'm saying is that you, alone, are responsible for your words and actions. If O'Connor finds out that you're spreading rumors that damage his reputation, you could be held accountable for defamation of character."

"You think he would actually sue me?" asked Marquis.

"No. Usually, the only people that get sued are the ones with deep pockets. In your case, they'd have grounds for your dismissal, which means they would probably fire you."

"Okay, I get it," said Marquis. "Mum's the word."

Not satisfied with her husband's consent, Chantelle continued.

"This means not even a *whisper* of this to anyone. Not Ernie, and certainly not Dom Marino. The discussion we just had should never leave this room."

"If you're so concerned about this, why did you even tell me?"

"I guess I'm just worried about your safety. If the cops are on a mission to rough up some rabble rousers, I want you to stay out of the line of fire."

"Well, I'm not sure what the line of fire will be, but I'll do my best."

"I know we're not in the South anymore," said Chantelle. "But if we were, I think we both know who the police would target first. You should take that into consideration."

"Duly noted," said Marquis. "I'll try to lay low."

At nine forty-five on Saturday morning, Neil Bowers heard his office phone buzz. Pushing the flashing button, he recognized the voice of the showroom receptionist on the intercom.

"I have Ryan O'Connor on the line."

"Yes," said Bowers, "put him through."

"Good morning, Neil."

"Good morning, sir."

"Do you have any updates for me?" asked Ryan.

"From what I can see, they're just beginning to assemble on the street corner. It looks like maybe a dozen or so. Are you coming in today?"

"There's no need for that. I prefer to keep my distance, but I want you to keep me informed."

"Do you want me to call the police?" asked Bowers.

"No, absolutely not. I'll take care of that if and when it becomes necessary. Just keep me informed."

"You got it."

"I do, however, need one thing from you, and that's a list of who's participating in the protest. You should be able to identify the Cadillac employees, right?"

"Absolutely, but I'll probably need to get a little closer look. That could be awkward."

"Understood," said Ryan. "Don't be afraid to talk to them. Just make it as cordial as possible. Greet them with a 'Good morning' and ask them if there's anything you can do for them."

"What could I possibly do for them?" asked Bowers.

"Not much," said Ryan. "My point is, we want to be polite and courteous, no confrontations. Just get me a list of names."

"Will do. Whatever you say."

"And Gary Jennings should be there too. You can have him identify the Buick employees. I want you and Gary and the sales manager—all three of you—to go outside together. But remember the two most important things. Number one, be cordial, and number two, get a list of names."

"Consider it done," said Bowers.

Marquis Jackson circumvented the rally point several times before settling on a parking spot two blocks away. It was a curbside spot next to a meter, but with free weekend parking there was no need to scour his pockets for nickels and dimes. Despite the butterflies in his stomach, he couldn't help but feel satisfied about his proximity. Close enough for convenience, but distanced enough for obscurity, his car was tucked away discreetly, free of charge. So far, so good.

Approaching the corner, he immediately identified Ernie and a few of his cohorts. Ernie had set up a small card table along with a couple boxes of donuts and a giant thermos of coffee. Contemplating what kind of mood would prevail, Marquis tried to gauge the temperature. He couldn't help but wonder if this would be a spirited group of agitators, or a well-mannered group of conscientious objectors.

"Marquis! Good morning!" announced Ernie with a cheerful disposition. "Let me pour you a cup of coffee."

"That would be great."

"I'd like you to meet Daniel Hawkins. He's taking the lead on the Buick side."

"Pleased to meet you," greeted Hawkins, extending his hand.

"Daniel is our fearless leader," said Ernie, facetiously. "He's the one in charge."

"I don't know about *that*," said Daniel. "My leadership is based upon numbers alone. Nothing more—nothing less. All I do is follow Marino's advice."

Marquis slurped his coffee and grabbed a donut, using the refreshments as a ploy to mask his inhibitions. He wanted to enjoy their company and feel welcome, but the little voice inside of his head told him to lay low. Maybe no one would notice him or identify him if he kept a low profile.

But it didn't take long for Marquis to realize there were no other Black men in the group, a development he did not entirely expect, given the level of Buick's participation. Now his chances for blending in had vanished. He couldn't help but think of an old expression his mother used to employ: "you'll stick out like a sore thumb."

Back in the 60s, when Marquis was active in civil rights, it was not unusual for him to participate in marches that involved hundreds, sometimes thousands of people. It was easy to blend in with those protesters, legions of like-minded people uniting for a common cause. But this was different. This was like walking a tightrope, like managing a balancing act between justice and loyalty. It was a dizzying experience.

"It's ten o'clock," announced Hawkins. "We need to get started. I have ten signs, almost enough for everyone. Remember, this is a peaceful protest. We're going to maintain our position on this corner. No deviation whatsoever. By standing here, we're close enough to the entrance that everyone will see us, but far enough away to avoid interference. If anyone talks to us or asks us any questions, let Ernie or me do the talking. Marino has trained us on the proper things to say."

"So we're just gonna stand here and hold these signs?" asked one of the service attendants.

"That's it in a nutshell," replied Hawkins. "This is more or less a publicity stunt. A chance to advertise our brotherhood and let management know we're serious about organizing."

"We can't get overanxious," chimed in Ernie. "We need to advance our cause in stages. If we approach our objectives in an orderly fashion, there's a chance we can meet our goals peacefully."

Grabbing the signs, Ernie and Daniel began distributing them on a random basis. Marquis was handed one of the "Unfair Labor" signs, accepting it unceremoniously and retreating toward the back of the pack. Noting the sign's dimensions, Marquis thought about holding it in front of his face and hiding his identity, a viable option if confronted by management.

After the signs were distributed and the demonstration began, the ragtag bunch of Teamster recruits began to attract their fair share of attention. With heavy traffic flowing to and fro, their positioning was primed for awareness, and the reactions they received were growing by the minute, almost contagious in nature. If a passerby honked his horn in solidarity, it would trigger a similar response downstream, sort of a trickle-down effect, and the protesters would interpret the horns as a sign of support, waving to the cars in acknowledgment.

But for every three or four honking cars, there was the antagonist expressing his disgust with gestures of vulgarity and shouts of profanity. One driver went so far as to shout out his window, "Go back to work, you lazy bums!"

Marquis wanted to respond appropriately and set the record straight. He wanted to tell them: "I already worked a forty-hour week. This is my day off. This is what I have to do on my day off to seek justice!"

But that was his mind talking, the inner voice with no inhibitions. In the real world, he exhibited his restraint, following the advice of his leaders by remaining silent. He would follow the prescribed formula and recognize it as the necessary price for success.

"Good morning, gentlemen. Is there anything I can do for you?"

Startled by the interruption, the protesters looked up to acknowledge the familiar voice of Neil Bowers. On the other side of the chain-length fence, he was accompanied by two other gentlemen, Gary Jennings, the Buick supervisor, and Stewart Patterson, the Cadillac sales manager.

Ernie nodded to Daniel Hawkins, acknowledging his duty to respond.

"Is there a problem?" asked Hawkins.

"I don't know, you tell me," replied Bowers. "You're the ones protesting."

"This isn't really a protest. It's more of a public service announcement," reasoned Hawkins.

"Really?" asked Bowers. "That's interesting. Then why do the signs say 'Unfair Labor'?"

"Look, we don't want any trouble," said Hawkins. "We're just promoting the *Brotherhood of Teamsters* in an effort to organize our labor force."

"I'm not looking for trouble," said Bowers. "I'm just offering our assistance. If you have any grievances, why don't you come inside and talk it over in a civilized manner, like adults?"

"That's not how it works," replied Hawkins. "If we organize our efforts, it's better to negotiate with you through the collective bargaining process."

"Sounds like they've trained you well," said Bowers. "Suit yourself. Never let it be said that I wasn't willing to cooperate. Just so you know, we'll be inside if anyone wants to have a discussion."

"Thank you, much appreciated," said Hawkins, with a hint of sarcasm.

"May I put in a request?" asked Stewart Patterson, the sales manager.

"Certainly," replied Hawkins.

"Please don't taunt or interfere with any of our customers today. My guys have sales quotas they need to achieve. They have families to feed too, you know."

"Understood," said Hawkins. "We'll stay out of the way. No problem."

"Thank you," said Patterson. "I'm heading back to the showroom now."

Bowers and Jennings followed suit, leaving the scene as though their mission had been accomplished.

"That wasn't so bad," noted Marquis. "They were surprisingly cordial. I was expecting a confrontation."

"Not so fast," interjected Ernie. "Did you see what Jennings, the Buick guy, was doing? He had a pad of paper."

"I wasn't paying attention," noted Marquis.

"Well, *I* was. And I'm pretty sure he was taking down names; making a list."

"Not surprising," said Hawkins.

"Now we're all labeled," said Ernie. "It looks like O'Connor has his hit list."

Marquis was struck by the all-too-familiar sinking feeling in his stomach. It was yet another gut punch to his stability and he wondered how many more he could endure. It was time to realize that he was no longer in the middle of a chess match. This was a war, and wars are not won overnight. There would be battles, and there would be scars, and there would be pain and suffering. No one survives a war unscathed.

In Marquis's mind, the only glimmer of hope was that Dominic Marino would be their savior. Although Ryan O'Connor was a force to be reckoned with, Marino was a battle-tested warrior, and he had the power of the Teamsters behind him. Ryan O'Connor controlled Fort Wayne, but the Teamster empire stretched well beyond the Midwest.

Marquis couldn't help but think of General Sherman and his Union army's conquests during the Civil War, the way he terrorized the South, burning cities along the way and bringing the Confederates to their knees, relentlessly attacking until he controlled Atlanta. To Southern

Blacks, General Sherman was a hero, the man who brought justice to the plantation owners.

Now Marquis was looking at Dominic Marino as the man who would bring justice to exploited workers and liberate them from their oppressors. He was sent to the Midwest on a mission to expand the Teamsters' influence, extend their benevolence, and diminish the power of the establishment. If Marino could dethrone Ryan O'Connor, then he would be their General Sherman, and Fort Wayne would be his Atlanta.

"Don't look now," said Ernie, "but I think O'Connor has called in the cavalry."

Marquis glanced up to see two police cars arriving on the scene, slowing to a stop next to the protesters. Although their sirens weren't blaring, their lights were flashing, a clear indication they were not on a mission of goodwill.

"Well, waddaya know," said Hawkins. "It looks like O'Connor's gestapo is reporting for duty."

The officers, two per vehicle, remained seated in their cars as they chatted on their radios. Still holding their signs, the Teamster recruits sobered up quickly, contemplating how the sudden turn of events might play out. Marquis, wary of the intrusion, feared for the worse, but some of his comrades seemed to embrace the encounter, pointing their signs directly at the police cars.

"Let's just play it cool," said Hawkins. "I don't want anybody rockin' the boat. Let's hear them out and see what they have to say."

Leaving their engines running, all four of the police officers exited their vehicles and approached the protesters cautiously, as if they might need to fend off an unprovoked attack. One of the officers emerged as the leader, while the remaining three flanked him in a display of strength.

"Which one of you is in charge here?" asked the leading officer.

"That would be me," said Hawkins, reluctantly stepping forward. "My name is Daniel Hawkins. Is there anything I can do for you?"

"I'm not here to exchange pleasantries," said the officer. "I'm Lieutenant Thompson and Captain Carter has sent me here to handle a disturbance."

"There's no disturbance here," said Hawkins. "This is a peaceful demonstration."

"That's not what I'm hearing," said the lieutenant. "I've been told you're stirring up quite a ruckus."

"That's not true," said Hawkins.

No sooner had the words left Hawkins's mouth than a car flew by with the driver laying on his horn and shouting: "Police brutality! Fuck off coppers!"

"Well," said Lieutenant Thompson. "Sounds like quite a ruckus to *me.* I would say you people are disturbing the peace. Don't you know there's laws against that?"

"C'mon, lieutenant. You know that's a stretch. We can't control the traffic."

"I didn't say anything about *controlling* the traffic. But you're certainly *agitating* them, and your agitation is disturbing the peace."

"That's ridiculous," said Ernie. "We have our rights."

Hawkins extended his arm from his side as if to restrain Ernie. "It's okay, calm down. I've got this under control."

"I don't think you have *anything* under control," said the lieutenant. "You can't even control your own people. I will *not* allow this situation to escalate."

In a show of solidarity, the picketers gathered around Hawkins a little tighter, as if to offer their protection. Nobody said a word, but their actions spoke volumes.

Bolstered by their support, Hawkins decided to stand his ground. "Like I said before, this is a peaceful demonstration. You can't arrest anyone if they're not breaking any laws."

Taking their gestures as a sign of intimidation, the lieutenant nodded to his officers as if they were preparing for battle. The officers reached toward their batons and unsnapped their holsters.

Clearly disturbed by the officers' show of force, Hawkins tried to deescalate the situation. "There's no need for any violence. Let's just talk this over like mature adults."

Ignoring Hawkins's plea, the lieutenant continued. "I need to see your permit."

"Permit? Permit for what?"

"Your permit to assemble on public property."

Confused by the request, Hawkins hesitated, wondering if the cops had the right to intervene on a technicality. Meanwhile, a few more cars whizzed by, honking their horns and adding to the confusion. One of the officers returned to his vehicle and radioed for more backup.

"Why would we need a permit to stand on a street corner?" asked Hawkins. "We're not soliciting any business."

"Apparently you don't know the law," said the lieutenant. "Anyone can *stand* on a street corner, but you can't assemble a group of people without permission. It's called unlawful assembly?"

"That's ridiculous," said Hawkins, getting more and more perturbed. "We have it on good authority that it's okay for us to be here."

"On who's authority?"

"Dominic Marino's authority, the local Teamster boss."

"Dominic *who*?" laughed the lieutenant. "He has no authority around here. The Teamsters may call the shots in other places, but I'm not gonna let 'em run *my* town."

"I'd watch my step if I was you," warned Hawkins. "The Teamsters are backed by a pretty powerful legal team. You don't wanna get yourself into a bind."

"I don't like the tone of your voice," said the lieutenant. "Are you threatening me?"

"No, that's ridiculous," exclaimed Hawkins. "I think you're just *lookin'* for trouble."

Before the lieutenant could respond, two more squad cars arrived on the scene with breaks screeching and lights flashing. Jumping out of their vehicles with a sense of urgency, the policemen were champing at the bit.

"How do you like your odds now?" asked Lieutenant Thompson.

Hawkins did not respond. The police were dead set on a confrontation and he had no contingency plan. Mulling his options, Hawkins appeared to be rattled. He felt responsible for his workers' safety, but he knew a complete surrender would be a severe blow to their dignity.

Newly equipped with a megaphone and backed by the strength of seven officers, Lieutenant Thompson forged ahead.

"I'm officially declaring this protest over. Put your signs down on the sidewalk and leave the scene immediately. If you disburse in a peaceful and orderly manner, no one will be arrested."

Ernie couldn't hold his tongue any longer. "I'm not puttin' my sign down and I'm not leaving! We have our rights and you're not gonna violate them!"

"Suit yourself," said the lieutenant. Turning his head, he nodded to the officers with a gesture of authority. Taking his cue, the police unleashed their batons in a threatening manner. Two of the officers removed their pistols and stood next to the lieutenant. The others forged ahead with their batons, smacking them against the palms of their hands as if they were ready to administer punishment.

Not prepared for a beating, one of the picketers dropped his sign and took off running.

The lieutenant chuckled with satisfaction. "Now there goes a guy with some common sense."

As the officers proceeded with their assault, panic began to set in. Two more protesters laid down their signs and walked away briskly.

"Don't give in!" yelled Ernie. "Stand your ground!"

Flaunting their authority, the assailants plowed ahead, determined to exert their force. Two of the cops headed straight toward Marquis and screamed in his face. "Drop your sign, boy!"

With a stoic expression, Marquis willfully stood his ground and wiped the spit off his face. One of the cops lunged for his sign and gave it a strong yank, but Marquis jerked it back violently, refusing to relinquish.

Like a school of piranhas, the cops swooped in, mercilessly targeting their prey. Two of the cops went high, while a third went low, savagely cracking his baton against Marquis's shin. Howling in agony, Marquis went down on one knee and surrendered his grip. Tossing the sign to the curb, the officers continued their brutal assault, unleashing a barrage of blows for no other reason than to inflict pain.

"Leave him alone!" screamed Ernie. "You got your damned sign!"

"I want everyone to drop their signs and back away," ordered the lieutenant through his megaphone.

Sheepishly complying, the protesters surrendered their signs and backed away in submission.

"Restrain the show of force," ordered the lieutenant, understating the magnitude of his officers' assault.

The cops reluctantly retreated from Marquis, leaving him on the cement in a pool of blood.

"Place him under arrest," ordered Lieutenant Thompson.

"Arrest for what?" asked Ernie, dumbfounded by the lieutenant's audacity.

"He's under arrest for unlawful assembly, disturbing the peace and refusing a police officer's order. If he puts up another fight, I'll add resisting arrest to the charges."

"That's absurd," declared Hawkins.

"I suggest you keep your mouth shut unless you'd like to join him."

"All I can say is you'll be hearing from our attorneys," declared Hawkins.

"I look forward to it," said Thompson. "Meanwhile, I suggest *you* respect the law."

The police officers proceeded to roll Marquis over on his belly and pull his arms behind his back. Administering the handcuffs with a show of force, they displayed little regard for his injuries or his dignity.

"Stand up!" they ordered.

Lightheaded and gimpy, Marquis attempted to stand, but tumbled to the ground like a rag doll. Grabbing his arms and thrusting him to his feet again, the officers led Marquis back to the squad car as he hobbled along in pain.

"He needs medical attention," proclaimed Ernie.

"He'll get his treatment back at the jail," replied the callous lieutenant. "No one's ever succumbed from a few cuts and bruises."

Shoving Marquis into the back seat, the officers slammed the door, looking over their shoulders with assertion. As they whisked him away, Ernie couldn't help but notice the forlorn look on Marquis's face and the smug expressions of the arrogant cops. It was a bitter pill to swallow, and Ernie felt responsible.

Embarrassed by their submission and feeling defeated, the remaining protesters ambled away. In a final show of disrespect, the cops collected the discarded signs and tossed them into a nearby dumpster. All that was left was Ernie and Daniel, standing by with their tails between their legs and licking their wounds. The inaugural exhibition of Teamster brotherhood had come and gone. Soundly defeated, the future looked bleak. To the victors went the spoils, and on this day, it was the cops.

Lieutenant Thompson climbed into his police car and tipped his cap. "Gentlemen, my work is done here. Have a nice day."

Chapter 58

WITHOUT ANY WINDOWS OR VENTILATION to circulate the air, the stagnant heat smothered the room with the musty smell of mildew, perspiration, and urine. Surrounded by concrete and cinder blocks, Marquis stared up at the ceiling and a single, solitary forty-watt lightbulb, a stark reminder of his flirtation with darkness. Encompassed by a dungeon of despair, he felt trapped, a victim of his adversary's determination and his own limitations.

Sitting inside the city jail—referred to as the holding tank—Marquis was not alone. Across the room, on a concrete bench, a bearded man with tattered clothing, disheveled hair, and body odor had passed out and was snoring up a storm. The cops had dragged him in against his will, kicking and screaming like a psychotic maniac and threatening anyone who got in his way. Realizing the man was intoxicated and quite possibly schizophrenic, Marquis kept his distance, not relaxing until the vagrant had urinated in the corner of the room and passed out in a drunken stupor.

Marquis couldn't help but wonder how his life had reached this juncture. After all, this was not how it was supposed to be. He had migrated to the North in pursuit of a better life, an opportunity to work hard and enjoy the fruits of his labor. No longer impeded by segregation and bigotry, he was supposed to prosper. But now it seemed like he had jumped out of the frying pan into the fire. To Marquis, it felt like rock bottom.

"Hey, Jackson," shouted the guard, his keychain rattling. "Today is your lucky day."

Considering it the worst day of his life, Marquis marveled at the stupidity of the statement.

"Somebody posted your bail and I've been authorized to release you."

Marquis stood up, relieved that he wouldn't be spending the night on a concrete bench. "Is my wife here?"

"I don't know who's here. I'm just taking you to the room where you'll be processed."

Realizing the guard was not interested in conversation, Marquis followed along in silence, hoping his nightmare would end as soon as possible.

"If you step over to that window, the lady behind the glass will return your possessions."

Obediently following his orders, Marquis walked over to the glass-enclosed office, where a woman conversed with him through an intercom.

"I have your personal items in this envelope," she said, sliding it into a metal drawer that Marquis accessed from the other side of the glass. "I need you to verify that everything we inventoried is back in your possession."

Marquis dumped the contents of the envelope onto the metal counter and the woman began to itemize her list.

"One belt," she announced.

"Check," confirmed Marquis.

"One watch."

"Check."

"One gold wedding band."

"Check."

"One leather wallet."

"Check."

"How much money?" she asked.

"Three one-dollar bills."

"That checks out with my list," she confirmed. "Now you need to sign this sheet stating that everything was returned to you unharmed. Then you're free to go."

Marquis stuck the wallet into his back pocket and signed the sheet as directed. It all seemed so trivial, as though the significance of a few material possessions would somehow return his life back to normal.

Exiting the lockup with a noticeable limp, Marquis saw Chantelle in the waiting room along with Ernie and Dominic Marino. Chantelle sprang to her feet and embraced her husband with tears of joy. Holding her tight for what seemed like an eternity, Marquis allowed his wife to expunge her emotions, a much-needed cleansing that would sharpen her mind for the troubles that lay ahead.

Finally pulling herself away, Chantelle ran her hand across Marquis's face, compassionately examining his injuries. His left cheek, puffy and purple, was completely swollen around a bloodshot eye, and his eyebrow had been patched up with a large bandage.

"It was bleeding pretty bad, so they had to stitch it up," offered Marquis.

"Who stitched it up?" asked Chantelle,

"A doctor, I guess."

"More likely a witch doctor if it was done in this jail," said Ernie.

"If it was done by an amateur," reasoned Chantelle, "you'll likely have a scar. And why is there a cotton ball in your ear?"

"It was bleeding too," said Marquis.

"They probably busted up your eardrum," suggested Ernie.

"Did they take any X-rays?" asked Chantelle.

"Yeah, right," said Marquis. "I don't think they keep X-ray machines at the jail."

"I'll need to get some pictures," said Marino, holding up a Polaroid camera. "What other injuries do you have?"

"Pictures? What for?" asked Marquis.

"Evidence," said Marino. "If we're gonna prove police brutality, we're gonna need some evidence."

"So how do you feel?" asked Chantelle.

"Not too bad except for an earache and a throbbing leg."

Marquis reached down to pull up his pant leg, revealing a large knot on his shin.

"Ouch, that looks painful," said Ernie.

"I want you to see a real doctor," ordered Chantelle. "You'll need to take a few days off from work."

"No!" ordered Marino. "You'll have Sunday off, and you'll report for duty on Monday as usual."

Startled by the order, Chantelle and Ernie looked at Marino as if he'd become a turncoat.

"Are you out of your mind?" asked Chantelle. "Where's your compassion?"

"I need you to listen to me, and listen good," ordered Marino. "This is just a bump in the road and we're not gonna get all sappy. There are two kinds of people in this world: winners and losers. If you wanna be a winner, you gotta be a fighter."

"You're right," consented Marquis. "I knew this would be a battle."

"My experience tells me there are certain protocols we need to follow," continued Marino. "If you heed my advice, we'll be able to stay on course."

"And what's your advice?" asked Ernie.

"On Monday, Marquis is gonna walk into work and proudly display his injuries for all to see; gimpy leg and all. This will display his dedication to work and make his employers look like a bunch of imbeciles. He will not give them any grounds for dismissal."

"Are we still gonna conduct our final vote next week?" asked Ernie.

"No. We need to delay that a few more weeks. We don't want our supporters to have a sudden change of heart because of a little intimidation. This whole episode needs to boil over and simmer for a while. Besides, I need to take appropriate action on this recent turn of events."

"What kind of action?" asked Ernie.

"Like I said, I need to take some pictures of Marquis's injuries. Then I'll go to the newspaper and convince them they need to write an article about the Fort Wayne Police Department and how they attacked our little demonstration."

"Do you think they'll do it?" asked Chantelle.

"To be honest with you...no. The newspaper is supposed to abide by journalistic standards, which means independence. Nevertheless, they are typically biased toward the police, which means giving them the benefit of the doubt unless there's overwhelming evidence to the contrary."

"And you don't think we have enough evidence?" asked Ernie.

"Do you have any video?" asked Marino.

Realizing it was a rhetorical question, Ernie hesitated. "No, but we have thirteen demonstrators that will collaborate on what *really* happened. They will tell the truth."

"The truth based upon their coordinated efforts," countered Marino. "We also have eight police officers that will collaborate on *their* version of events. It's their word against ours."

"You're not painting a very pretty picture," admitted Marquis.

"I don't paint pictures," said Marino. "I deal with reality."

"What about the charges against Marquis?" asked Chantelle. "Are you saying his case is hopeless?"

"No, I'm not saying that at all. We will support Marquis with a very talented legal team backed by the power of the ACLU."

"ACLU?" asked Ernie.

"American Civil Liberties Union," answered Chantelle.

"That's right," said Marino. "They'll play hardball and produce enough evidence to tarnish the reputation of the Fort Wayne Police Department. The fact that Marquis is Black and the only one attacked makes them look all the more ridiculous."

"Are you suggesting we could actually win a police brutality case?" asked Chantelle.

"No, I'm suggesting the bad publicity will be enough for them to drop all charges against Marquis. Then he can get on with his life."

"I guess that's better than a kick in the ass," said Marquis.

"One other thing," said Marino. "The arresting officer's name was Lieutenant Thompson. It turns out he's the father of a kid named Billy Thompson. The same Billy Thompson that O'Connor hired a few months ago and is taking a stand against our union. Coincidence? I don't think so."

Like any other workplace, Monday mornings at O'Connor Cadillac were routinely mundane, lacking any semblance of enthusiasm. For the service attendants, this particular Monday was unusually dreary given the fallout from their failed protest. Faced with renewed uncertainty and little hope for a higher standard of living, the service attendants moped around like zombies. Underneath their solemn exteriors, however, was a degree of anxiety, concern over their job security and how they would be treated after such an embarrassing defeat.

True to form, Marquis showed up on schedule, hobbling to his locker amid a barrage of awkward stares. His ear still ached, and his leg still throbbed, but he knew he couldn't call in sick, not after Marino's warning. He trusted Marino's advice and he remained committed, for only Marino could put his legal affairs in order and rescue his fellow employees from a lifetime of servitude.

"How are you holding up?" asked Ernie.

"As well as can be expected," came the reply.

"I want you to know that I've been making the rounds this morning and talking to our comrades," assured Ernie. "Even though there won't be a vote this week, I told them that nothing has changed. We're all going to stay the course."

"And how are they reacting?" asked Marquis.

"To be honest with you, not great. Sort of a mixed bag. But we shouldn't be surprised by a little skepticism, right? Let's face it, that's why Marino wants to delay the vote."

"Understood," said Marquis. "Right now, I'm only worried about making it through the day, just baby steps."

Interrupted by the hasty arrival of Neil Bowers, the locker room conversations came to an abrupt halt. Expecting the worst, the attendants nervously went about their business.

Marquis whispered to Ernie. "Here comes the moment of truth."

But Bowers waltzed into the room in high spirits, acting as though it was the first day of a new beginning.

"Good morning, gentlemen. Let me have your attention, please. I have good news. June results are in, and we successfully met our second quarter service revenue objectives. That means we'll be paying out another two percent bonus this quarter. Congratulations!"

"Whoop-de-do," whispered Ernie.

"And so the gamesmanship continues," noted Marquis.

"Your bonuses will be paid out next week," continued Bowers. "Be sure to look for them in Friday's paychecks. In the meantime, keep up the good work!"

Ignoring the underwhelming response, Bowers cheerfully went about his business, posting the day's work orders and service assignments on the bulletin board.

Satisfied his little show of enthusiasm was a success, Bowers wheeled around and headed for the door. Then, spotting Marquis, he decided to continue the charade.

"Marquis! What happened to you? Are you okay?"

Shocked by the impudence of his remark, the room went silent, wondering how their supervisor could put on such a phony display of sincerity.

Knowing that Bowers was well aware of the circumstances, Marquis wondered if his question should be dignified with a response. But then he thought about Marino's coaching and decided to play it cool.

"I got pulled into a little altercation over the weekend; took a few bumps and bruises, but I'll be okay."

"Are you sure?" asked Bowers. "Your health is more important than perfect attendance. Maybe you should take the day off."

"That won't be necessary," said Marquis. "I'm sure I can manage."

Not letting it go, Bowers continued his masquerade. "But you don't look so good. I've got people who can fill in for you today. Why don't you go home and rest."

"I'll be okay. I'm not gonna let a few scrapes and bruises keep me down."

"Suit yourself," said Bowers. "But I want you to check in with me at noon. If I decide that you need some rest, I'm gonna send you home."

Marquis tossed his lunch pail into the back seat of the Ford Galaxie and eased his sore leg into the driver's seat. It had been a long morning. Although he was determined to make it through the day, Marquis was actually relieved when Bowers sent him home for the afternoon. He even guaranteed his pay.

"Don't clock out," said Bowers. "I'll clock out for you at the end of the day. That way you'll get a full day's wages."

Marquis wasn't sure what to make of it. He had never trusted Bowers before, so why would he begin now? Having grown accustomed to his underhanded chicanery, Marquis never expected an act of kindness.

Was Bowers feeling guilty and turning over a new leaf? Or was this just another ploy, another means to an end?

As Marquis got closer to home, he decided to let it go. Why should he continue to torture himself over Bowers's intentions? It wasn't worth the mental anguish. At this point, all he wanted to do was take a couple of aspirin, put his leg up and catch a little shut-eye.

Pulling into the driveway, he was surprised to see Chantelle's Chevy Nova resting under the carport. He knew she would sometimes run errands over her lunch hour. Sometimes she would even grab a bite to eat at home before heading back to the office. If that was the case, maybe she'd have time to share lunch with him before his nap.

Hobbling up the back steps, Marquis swung open the screen door to find his wife in the kitchen, her head resting on the table. Surprised by the sudden intrusion, Chantelle's head sprang up, revealing her watery, bloodshot eyes.

"What are *you* doing here?" Chantelle asked, blotting a tissue against her face.

"I was gonna ask you the same thing. What's wrong?"

Chantelle put her head back down on the table and began sobbing. Overcome with emotion, Marquis eased over to the table and began rubbing her back and shoulders.

"Easy now, sweetie. Tell me what's wrong. Honey…please…what's going on?"

Chantelle slowly raised her head as if it weighed a ton. Attempting to focus through the misty haze, she stared into her husband's eyes.

"I got fired today."

Blindsided by his wife's proclamation, Marquis blurted out the word like a parrot. "Fired!"

"That's what I said."

"Why would they ever fire you?" asked Marquis, more puzzled than ever.

"What about you?" asked Chantelle. "Do you still have a job?"

"Yes, of course. Why wouldn't I?"

"Well, at least one of us is employed. I never thought *I* would be the one to get the axe."

"Me either," said Marquis. "What the heck is going on?"

Chantelle pointed to a piece of paper on the table. "This is my letter of dismissal."

"Dismissal for what?" asked Marquis. "Just tell me. I don't wanna read a letter right now."

"Remember when they hired me, they made me sign a morality clause?"

"I vaguely remember something along those lines."

"It basically said that they would have grounds for my dismissal if I did something detrimental to the reputation of the law firm."

"So what did you do?" asked Marquis.

"Well, remember, it also pertained to family members."

"No, I don't remember," said Marquis. "Can you just get to the point?"

"To put it bluntly, I was fired today because your arrest reflects badly upon the reputation of the law firm."

Stunned by the revelation, Marquis could feel his blood begin to boil. He never fathomed an outcome like this. More than ever, it appeared as though Ryan O'Connor's perpetual bullying would plague him to the ends of the earth. These assholes would leave no stone unturned.

"Those sons of bitches," he growled. "Those motherfucking sons of bitches!"

"Calm down," said Chantelle. "There's no use in getting angry. That won't solve any of our problems."

"Calm down? How am I supposed to calm down?"

"You have to. What other choice do we have? The only way we can deal with this kind of adversity is to think clearly, and you can't think clearly if you're caught up in anger or revenge."

"How can I *not* be angry? People keep telling me to be patient, stay the course, mind your p's and q's and justice will prevail. Well, how far has *that* gotten me? I'll answer that for you. It got the shit beat out of me and my wife fired!"

"You can't give up. You told me that you *knew* this would be a war. You told me that you would have to fight many battles."

"Yes, I knew that it would be a war for *me,* but not for *you*! I never thought about causing *you* any pain or suffering."

"Don't worry about *me.* I will survive. Life goes on."

"Oh yeah? What kind of life? Not the kind of life we deserve. Not the kind we busted our butts for."

Chantelle realized there was no reasoning with Marquis when he was agitated. But she also knew he had every right to be angry; there was no denying that. She just needed to be patient and let this episode run its course. Only then could they begin to put the pieces back together.

Sitting in silence, it suddenly dawned upon Chantelle that her husband was home midday and he never explained why.

"By the way, why are *you* home so early? Are you not feeling well?"

"To answer your question, no, I'm not feeling well. But that's not why I'm home."

"What's that supposed to mean?" asked Chantelle.

"I'm home because Bowers insisted that I come home."

Chantelle looked at her husband inquisitively, not understanding his explanation, but not willing to pry any further; no need to poke the bear.

Marquis sat still, contemplating his wife's question and thinking about how Bowers had ordered him to take the afternoon off, concerned about his well-being.

Then it suddenly hit him. Bowers didn't send him home out of compassion. He didn't give a shit about his injuries. He sent him home to find out that his wife had been fired. It was all part of their scheme. Another way to beat him down into submission, yet another form of intimidation.

"Those sons of bitches," he muttered.

Chapter 59

NESTLED ALONG THE BANKS OF the Saint Joseph River, three
miles north of downtown Fort Wayne, rests a thirty-acre park
named after a legendary figure in the annals of folklore. Over
the years, much has been written about the life of Johnny Appleseed,
born into this world as John Chapman in the small town of Leominster,
Massachusetts. Historians, authors, and poets have published a wide
array of accounts documenting the life and times of this mystical character, from oddly eccentric vagabond to spiritually enriched preacher.

By most accounts, John Chapman was attracted to a nomadic lifestyle at an early age, migrating through Pennsylvania and settling briefly
in Ohio, where he worked on an apple orchard. Through his work experience at the orchard, Chapman gained an appreciation for nature and
a simplistic lifestyle, creating an existence he would devote toward the
cultivation and preservation of God's green earth.

Sewing his seeds, quite literally, he traveled from town to town,
acquiring small parcels of land along the way and turning them into
nurseries and orchards. Never staying in one spot for very long, he took
his seeds with him, leaving behind the fruits of his labor for others to
maintain and harvest.

Along the way, Chapman gained an appreciation for the spiritual writings of a Swedish scientist and theologian named Emanuel
Swedenborg. From his otherworldly dreams and visions, Swedenborg
wrote about his conversations with angels and demons. The book was
entitled *Heaven and Hell* and was published in 1758. From these teach-

ings, a number of offshoot religions were formed, resulting in a denomination known as the New Church. The New Church believed that all people who live good lives would be welcomed into the kingdom of heaven, regardless of their religion, and that the only true religion is kindness toward your neighbor.

Spreading his kindness and planting his apple trees, Chapman continued his travels, eventually making his way to Indiana. Along the way, he preached the gospel of the New Church to adults and told stories to the children, sometimes earning a meal in return, or a floor to sleep on at night. But most of the time he slept in the wilderness.

Living the life of a pauper, Chapman believed that a humble and simplistic life, lacking earthly possessions, would result in greater rewards in heaven.

Ohio author Rosella Rice described his appearance in a piece she wrote about the history of her Ashland County:

> He lived the roughest life, and often slept in the woods. His clothing was mostly old, being generally given to him in exchange for apple trees. He went bare-footed, and often traveled miles through the snow that way. He wore on his head a tin utensil which answered both as a cap and a mush pot.

History tells us that John Chapman passed away in Fort Wayne, Indiana, on March 18, 1845. To this day, John Chapman's gravesite is prominently displayed in Johnny Appleseed Park, where each year a festival celebrates his life by authentically recreating the period in which he lived. Attended by thousands, the Johnny Appleseed Festival represents the unofficial beginning of autumn and serves up bushels of apples, baked goods, and handmade crafts.

Lydia Maria Child, a well-known author and abolitionist, immortalized Johnny Appleseed with this poetic tribute:

> In cities, some said the old man was crazy
>
> While others said he was only lazy;
>
> But he took no notice of gibes and jeers,
>
> He knew he was working for future years...

And if they inquire whence came such trees

Where not a bough once swayed in the breeze,

The answer still comes as they travel on,

"These trees were planted by Appleseed John."

It was the Fourth of July in Fort Wayne and the fireworks celebration was scheduled to begin at 8:00 p.m. eastern standard time. In short order, tens of thousands of spectators would infiltrate Johnny Appleseed Park and swarm its proximities, bringing with them chairs, blankets, and picnic baskets. Unless you knew the best routes, or viewed the show from a distance, traffic would prove to be a nightmare.

But Brian Johnson knew his way around the fireworks. He had been going every year since he was a little tyke, and he knew his favorite spots, those that were as close to the launching pad as possible. To Brian, there was nothing better than getting right next to the action, lying flat on his back, and watching the explosions directly above his head, where the noise was the loudest and the colors the brightest.

For the teenage crowd, this was the biggest see-and-be-seen event of the summer, a chance to visit with reclusive classmates and show off their tanned and toned summer bodies. The football players, strutting around in tight, Fruit-of-the-Loom tank tops, couldn't wait to show off their muscles, and the girls, flaunting their short-shorts and halters, couldn't wait to bait them.

The past few years, Brian, Scott, and Mark had attended the fireworks together, targeting Independence Day as the highlight of their summer. Scott, referencing the event as a meat market, couldn't wait to gawk at the girls in their skimpy summer outfits and determine which ones had matured the most, thereby becoming objects of his desire. "I'm like a kid in a candy store," he once said, describing the way he fell in and out of love as the prospects paraded by.

But for Brian Johnson, this Independence Day would be different. Instead of exploiting his independence, he would proudly arrive as one-half of a couple, sharing his blanket with the one and only Mindy Harper. While his buddies scoured the masses, hunting for the apple of their eye, he would take comfort in knowing he was accompanied by the cutest girl on the planet. Unlike the young and the restless, he was mature enough to understand the importance of a commitment, and no woman was better suited for his loyalty than Mindy Harper.

"Well, ain't that sweet," came a catcall from a familiar voice. "It looks like Jack and Jill are sharing a picnic together."

Brian looked up from his blanket to see Scott Clever and Mark Carter approaching with big grins on their faces.

"How did you find us?" asked Brian.

"It wasn't hard," said Scott. "You think I don't know your favorite spot after all these years?"

"You're pretty predictable," added Mark. "Besides, we were hoping you'd share your picnic basket with us?"

"Of course," answered Mindy, as Brian frowned in frustration. "We've got a bucket of Kentucky Fried Chicken and a cooler of Cokes."

"I'll take a thigh and a breast," quipped Scott.

"Some things never change," noted Brian, embarrassed for Mindy.

Not missing a beat, Mindy handed him a drumstick. "I thought you were more of a leg man."

"Touché," said Scott. "I respect all body parts."

"Or maybe *disrespect* is the more definitive term," noted Brian.

Not allowing the banter to digress any further, Mindy changed the topic.

"So how long have you been here? Have you run across any of our compadres?"

"A few," said Mark. "We just bumped into Marcus Mosely and Darius Williams a couple minutes ago."

"Anyone else?" asked Brian.

"Yeah, a few other football players and a couple Bishop Dwenger jocks walking around in their Saints T-shirts."

"Losers," said Brian, unable to resist a jab.

Then Mindy waved her hand at a couple of girls in the crowd and shouted out their names.

"Wow! Who was that?" asked Scott.

"Just some North Side cheerleaders I trained with last summer."

"Man, I need to get out more often," said Scott. "There's a whole world out here just waitin' for me."

"More like *avoiding* you," teased Brian. "No one should ever let you out of your cage."

"Hey, Mindy, what's your pal Lynda Lacey doin' tonight?" asked Mark. "Is she with her pretty boy?"

"I talked to her a couple days ago," said Mindy. "She said she wasn't going to the fireworks this year. Apparently, Quinn is not big on crowds and traffic jams. He told her there's too much riffraff running around here."

"No surprise," said Mark. "That sounds like something an elitist would say."

"Or maybe not," said Brian. "After all, Mindy and I were doin' just fine until the two of you showed up, and you're the very definition of riffraff."

With dusk settling in and the buzz of the crowd intensifying, the loud speakers from the nearby baseball diamonds piped in the traditional ensemble of patriotic music: *Yankee Doodle, Stars and Stripes Forever, Battle Hymn of the Republic.* Soon the mayor would address the crowd with a spirited salutation and the playing of the national anthem would signal the conclusion of the preliminary rituals.

Scott had settled on top of the ice chest, using it as a makeshift stool, and Mark was on the edge of the blanket, leaving little room for Brian and Mindy, which Brian didn't mind because it forced Mindy to squeeze in closer.

"If you rub her right leg, I'll rub her left leg," teased Mark.

"Hands off the merchandise," ordered Mindy. "Just focus on the fireworks."

"Well, well," came a familiar voice. "I guess they'll let *anyone* set up camp around here."

Startled by the interruption, the crew turned around to acknowledge the commanding presence of Antonio Jackson, grinning from ear to ear and standing next to Quinn O'Connor.

"Antonio!" they exclaimed, standing up in unison. "What brings you here?"

"Why *wouldn't* I be here?" he laughed. "Isn't this where all the action is?"

"I thought you were in New Orleans," said Brian.

"I was, but I just got back yesterday. Gonna spend the rest of the summer here."

"Cool!" said Mindy. "Change of plans?"

"Not exactly; never really made any plans. I'm just wingin' it this summer. After a month of smokin', drinkin' and playin' the Bourbon Street clubs, I decided to clean up my act and get back home."

"We're glad you did," said Mindy.

"Besides," said Antonio, delivering a playful nudge, "I thought maybe Quinn could keep me on the straight and narrow."

Embarrassed by the attention, Quinn responded sheepishly, "I'm not sure anyone could keep him on the straight and narrow."

"How long have you guys been here?" asked Mark.

"I don't know, maybe an hour or so," said Antonio, looking at Quinn. "We've been strollin' all over the place. We bumped into a lot of people we know and met some new people along the way."

Quinn remained silent, nervous about the implications. Mindy couldn't help but think of Lynda and her comments on Quinn not liking fireworks. She wanted to bring up her name but didn't want to put Quinn on the spot.

Mark, not worried about etiquette, decided to rock the boat.

"So, Quinn, what's Lynda doin' tonight? I thought you didn't like fireworks."

"Who said that?"

"Lynda did," said Mark, not shy about his source.

Mindy issued a stern look, but it was too late.

Quinn hesitated slightly before offering his alibi.

"I may have mentioned my distaste for fireworks a time or two, but Antonio surprised me yesterday when he said he was back in town, so we just showed up on a whim."

"You know how it is," teased Antonio. "When you're the president and vice president of the senior class, you have to keep up appearances."

"I don't know about that," scoffed Mark. "You might be overstating your importance a bit."

"No way," said Antonio, in a playful mood. "In fact, we may need some secret service protection. Can your father arrange for that?"

"I doubt it." Mark laughed. "He's more likely to arrest you for loitering."

As the loudspeakers launched into the national anthem, an ocean of people rose to their feet in a gradual progression, spreading across the vista like a giant wave. Brian stood close to Mindy, holding her hand, thankful that she would be sharing this special occasion with him. It would be a glorious evening.

The anthem had barely finished when, thump, thump, thump, came the compression sounds of mortars pumping their shells into the sky, like artillery assaults on a battlefield. And then bang, bang, bang, came the explosions, followed by the crackles and pops of colors sprawling across the heavens.

Brian pulled Mindy down to the blanket so they could lie on their backs and stare up into the sky together, absorbing the sound, inhaling the smoke, and soaking up the colors.

Lured by the stimulation of sensory overload, Mindy would feel the magnetic attraction of patriotism and recommit her loyalty to Brian like a soldier commits to God and country. Through this magical setting, she would realize that they were meant to be together, united by pageantry and bonded by destiny.

But then again, Brian's overactive imagination had a mind of its own.

Quinn pulled up to the gated entry of the O'Connor estate and keyed in the security code. Even though it was close to midnight, he could hear firecrackers off in the distance and wondered if the noise would keep his father awake. Since the fourth of July had fallen on a Thursday, his father, in all likelihood, would be going to the office early in the morning, which meant the chances of him being awake so late were pretty slim. He had always been an early riser.

Pulling up to the house, Quinn decided to park his car on the circular drive and enter through the front door. If he pulled around back to the four-car garage, the motion detectors would trigger the flood lights, and that might awaken his father. Why take chances when he could increase his odds. He had learned long ago that discretion is the better part of valor.

Approaching the threshold, he keyed in another security code before unlocking the door. Hearing the alarm system's subtle beep as he opened the door, and then again as he closed it, he proceeded along gingerly. Under normal circumstances, he would be oblivious to the soft electronic signals, but now, in stealth mode, he pondered the absurdity of living in a fortress.

He thought about heading into the kitchen and grabbing a snack, but ever since his mother moved out, the refrigerator was mostly bare, symbolic of the emptiness he felt in a home without her presence. It had been five months since her departure and there was no indication that she would ever return. The handwriting was on the wall, and Quinn had resolved himself to the fact that his parents would never reunite.

Deciding he would tiptoe up the stairs and retire to the privacy of his bedroom, Quinn turned the corner. But there, at the foot of the stairwell, he could see the library doors wide open and an abundance of light. Could it be true? Was his father still working at midnight? Or, even worse, was he waiting up to have a chat?

Knowing his father, it would not be a chew-the-fat session. If he was planning on an encounter, he would have a reason, and his instincts told him it wouldn't be pleasant.

"Quinn, is that you?"

Realizing the inevitable was about to take place, Quinn decided to make the best of it. He would use a happy-go-lucky approach.

"Well, it better be me, or else there's a burglar roaming around the house."

Quinn strolled into the library nonchalantly. Ryan, seated on his leather armchair, was sipping on a glass of scotch.

"Very funny," said his father, not amused by Quinn's witticism.

"Why are you up so late?" asked Quinn.

"I could ask you the same thing."

"It's not that late for me. Don't you have to work tomorrow?"

"I'm always working. Some things never change."

"Anything special going on?" asked Quinn, hoping to appease his father by showing an interest in his work.

"Every day is special," came the terse response, with a hint of sarcasm. "What about you, what did you do tonight?"

"I ended up going to the fireworks. It was super crowded, and the traffic was a nightmare, as you can imagine. It took forever to get out of there."

His father took a big gulp of scotch and contemplated his next question.

"So what time did you get Lynda home?"

Starting to feel fidgety, Quinn wondered where this conversation was headed.

"Actually, I didn't take her home. She grabbed a ride with some friends."

"But you picked her up and took her to the fireworks, right?"

"Uh…yes, of course. But then we met up with some friends."

Ryan O'Connor took another gulp of scotch. "That's funny, why am I hearing something different?"

"Something different? I don't know what you mean."

"Where did you and Lynda sit when you were at the fireworks?"

This was getting weird, and Quinn wanted no part of it. He had no idea where his father was taking this dialogue, but he was certain he had something up his sleeve.

"I don't know how to describe where we sat," replied Quinn, unable to hide his frustration. "Like I said, we strolled around and ended up with some friends."

Ryan took another gulp of scotch, slammed his glass down, and stood up.

"Damn it! Quit trying to bullshit me! You think I don't know what goes on in this town?"

Quinn wanted to leave the room and escape his father's interrogation, but that would only make matters worse. Instead, he stood by in silence, allowing his father to show his cards.

"Lynda wasn't even with you tonight, was she? The truth is, you were *lying* to me."

"All right! So Lynda wasn't with me. What's the big deal? The truth is we haven't been getting along so well lately. I know you really like her, so I didn't wanna tell you."

Ryan paused and contemplated Quinn's alibi. Taking a deep breath, he went over to the wet bar and poured another glass of scotch.

"I'm gonna ask you one more time, and this time I want an honest answer. Who did you go to the fireworks with tonight?"

Feeling like he was on the witness stand and under oath, Quinn admitted the truth.

"I went with Antonio. He's the guy we told you about. The one that ran with me for class president."

"I see," said Ryan, using his best lawyer voice. "It appears that your story is changing."

"It's no big deal. Lynda and I told you about this guy," said Quinn, invoking some credibility by using Lynda's name.

"Apparently, there's a lot of things you *haven't* told me," continued Ryan.

"What's that supposed to mean? What else do you want to know?"

"For instance, you didn't tell me his last name is Jackson."

"What difference does that make?"

"And you didn't tell me he's Black."

"Oh my God! Seriously? Is that what this is all about? Don't you know that there's lots of Black kids at Northrop?"

"Don't question my integrity. I'm the one asking the questions around here."

Quinn hated it when his father showed off his lawyer skills. So far, he felt like he had performed pretty well under pressure, but he wasn't sure which direction his father was leading the witness.

"Do you have any idea who the father is of this Antonio Jackson?" asked Ryan.

"No. Why would I know anything about his father?"

"Well, I'll tell you. His father works in the service department of my Cadillac dealership. Does that mean anything to you?"

"No, why should it? And what makes you think I know *anything* about his parents? High school kids don't go around talkin' about their parents."

"Well, I'm here to tell you about his parents so you better listen up. His father's name is Marquis Jackson and he's a big part of the union efforts to bring down my company. The very company that provides you with a lavish lifestyle."

Quinn remained silent, surprised by the revelation, but still wondering what this had to do with him. He knew his father held grudges, but certainly he didn't expect him to foster the same ill will.

"Two weeks ago, this man was arrested outside of our building for protesting and disturbing the peace. The cops roughed him up pretty good and took him to the city lockup. Now he's suing the cops for brutality and the Teamsters Union has filed a grievance against us."

"Okay, okay. I get it. But this is all news to me. You know you don't share work stuff with me, so how am I supposed to know what's going on? And, to be honest with you, I'm guessing Antonio doesn't know anything either. He's been in New Orleans all summer and just got back yesterday."

Ryan paused and took another hit from his scotch. Quinn seemed to have all the right answers, but there was no way he'd let his son steer him off course. He had an objective to meet, and he wouldn't rest until it was accomplished. And, along the way, he would get a few things off his chest.

"You should know that I make it my business to research people and find out what kinda things they're into, if you know what I mean. And my sources tell me this Antonio Jackson is quite the character."

"I'm not sure what that means," said Quinn. "I already told you he's really popular."

"Well, I have witnesses that paint quite a different picture."

"Witnesses of what?" asked Quinn.

"Witnesses of his behavior."

"I don't understand. Are you saying you hired private investigators?"

"Let's just say that I make it my business to know what's going on in other people's lives, especially if it has an impact on my life."

"And how does Antonio's life impact you?"

"If he impacts your life, then he impacts mine."

"I don't get it. We're just friends."

"Well, I want you to stay away from him. And that's not a request. That's an order."

"That's ridiculous! How am I gonna stay away from him when we're on student council together?"

"Okay, I'll give you that. But once you're outside of school, you will have no contact with him. That means zero…none. Is that understood?"

Quinn began pacing around. "No, I don't understand."

"Well, I don't give a damn whether you understand or not. I have a reputation to maintain, and I will not let you damage it."

"That's odd. It just so happens that Antonio has a pretty awesome reputation himself. Whaddaya think about that?"

"You wanna know what I think? I'll tell you what I think. I think he's a little too flamboyant!"

"Huh? What's that supposed to mean?"

"Exactly what I said. Flamboyant. Do I need to spell it out for you?"

"Apparently so, because I have *no* idea what you're talking about."

"Well, I think he's a little light in the loafers, if you know what I mean. How's that for spelling it out? I don't know how I can sugarcoat it any more than that."

"Oh my God! I don't believe what I'm hearing! Your generation is *so* out of touch."

"Oh, so now you're going to chastise a whole generation? Let me tell you something, buddy boy, your extravagant lifestyle was made possible by the blood, sweat, and tears of my generation."

"All right, now I'm gonna tell *you* something," said Quinn, becoming more and more agitated. "Antonio is a musician, an extremely rare and accomplished musician. And that means he's an entertainer. Entertainers have to dress and look the part. That's all part of his style and charisma. But that sure as hell doesn't make him queer. You need to understand that. But I guess you're just too old-fashioned!"

"I don't need *you* to explain to *me* the ways of the world. I've been around the block a few more times than you. So let me make it plain and simple. You will no longer be seen anywhere around town with this guy. Is that understood?"

"No, I don't understand! I've had enough of this bullshit!"

Quinn spun around and headed for the exit, but his father grabbed him by the arm and pulled him away from the door. Quinn stood frozen in fear as his father slammed the doors shut, barricading his only outlet.

Suddenly, Quinn felt intimidated. He never thought his father would get physical with him, but now that Ryan was drunk and unhinged, Quinn wasn't sure what he was capable of, especially with no one around to intervene. Fearing for his safety, Quinn decided to surrender, using pacifism as his passport out of the library. He realized that fueling the fire would only be counterproductive. Instead, he would let his father blow off some steam and hope that he ran out of gas.

Ryan walked away from the doors and started pacing. There were issues he wanted to address, but first he needed to gather his composure.

Quinn, trying to appear less combative, sat down, demonstrating his willingness to listen. He would use diplomacy as his tool for survival.

"Have you heard from your mother lately?" asked Ryan, deciding to shift gears.

"No, she hasn't called in a few weeks."

"She appears to be pretty settled in Chicago now, don't you think?"

"I suppose so."

"She hasn't given any indication to you that she will return, has she?"

"No, but the baby hasn't been born yet. That was one of her reasons for going to Chicago in the first place, remember? To help out with the pregnancy."

Bringing up the pregnancy, Quinn could tell that he'd hit a nerve with his father. He realized he was walking on eggshells and needed to be more cautious.

"That damned pregnancy. It's made a mockery of me. You know that, don't you? Who would've ever thought that my very own daughter would give birth to a Black baby, or whatever color he turns out to be. Not to mention out of wedlock. And the fact that her mother is supporting this whole fiasco is simply deplorable. *That's* what's destroying our family."

Ryan paused, expecting his son's concurrence. But Quinn, realizing a response was expected, tried to remain neutral.

"I don't know what to say. I just wish we could go back to the way things used to be."

"Well, that ship has sailed," admitted his father. "You can't turn back the hands of time. We have to look ahead and prepare for our future."

"I suppose so."

"And that future, more and more, is looking like you and me. You may be all I have left. That's why it's important for you to listen. I cannot allow you to destroy what's left of this family the same way your sister did."

"I'm not trying to destroy anything. I'm just trying to get by."

"Speaking of getting by, what's going on with you and Lynda?"

"Nothing really. I just haven't seen that much of her lately."

"By her choice, or yours?"

"I don't know. Maybe it's just because school is out and we're not around each other that much. I guess I should make more of an effort to call her."

"Yes, you should. You can't just sit around and let a good thing pass you by. You have to make an effort."

"I suppose so."

"Let me tell you what I think. I think she's an incredible catch, and I think you need to foster this relationship. When I see the two of you together, I see a different Quinn. I see a Quinn with a sense of purpose and direction, a more confident version of yourself."

"Yes, I guess we're a good match."

"It's important to be with someone who will always be there for you. Someone who can help you be successful."

Quinn nodded his head.

"Whatever you do, don't mess this up. Don't screw up your life the way your sister did. You're all I have left, and you need to trust my instincts."

Quinn nodded his head again. There was no longer any fight left in him, just the numbness of defeat. He wished he could reveal his true thoughts and feelings the way he used to with his mother, but those days were gone. Instead, he would just roll with the punches.

"You don't understand the pressures I'm up against each and every day, trying to run my businesses and trying to fend off threats—threats from all sides. The competition never gives up, which means I never have time to rest. In this dog-eat-dog world, only the strong survive. You can't be successful if you're not willing to do what it takes. That's really what it comes down to, doing whatever it takes."

Quinn nodded his head in compliance.

Satisfied his lecture had hit home, Ryan opened the library doors.

"From now on, you need to follow my advice. Otherwise, there will be serious consequences. Consequences for both you and me, and neither one of us needs that. Do you understand?"

"Yes, I understand."

Chapter 60

O N AUGUST 8, 1974, MILLIONS of Americans gathered around their television sets, captivated by the drama that was playing out in their nation's capital. President Richard M. Nixon was scheduled to deliver an address unlike any other president in history.

Good evening. This is the thirty-seventh time I have spoken to you from this office, where so many decisions have been made that shaped the history of this Nation. Each time I have done so to discuss with you some matter that I believe affected the national interest.

In all the decisions I have made in my public life, I have always tried to do what was best for the Nation. Throughout the long and difficult period of Watergate, I have felt it was my duty to persevere, to make every possible effort to complete the term of office to which you elected me...From the discussions I have had with Congressional and other leaders, I have concluded that because of the Watergate matter, I might not have the support of the Congress that I would consider necessary to back the very difficult decisions and carry out the duties of this office in the way the interests of the Nation would require.

I have never been a quitter. To leave office before my term is completed is abhorrent to every instinct in my body. But as President, I must put the interest of America first...

...To continue to fight through the months ahead for my personal vindication would almost totally absorb the time and attention of both the President and the Congress in a period when our entire focus should be on the great issues of peace abroad and prosperity without inflation at home.

Therefore, I shall resign the Presidency effective at noon tomorrow. Vice President Ford will be sworn in as President at that hour in this office.

Three days earlier, the so-called smoking-gun tape had been released to the public, revealing, in convincing fashion, the president's explicit attempts to cover up the Watergate break-in. In the tape, Nixon spoke to his Chief of Staff H. R. Haldeman, just six days after the burglary at the Democratic headquarters. The recorded discussion addressed their need to approach CIA Director Richard Helms, and ask him to halt the FBI investigation, citing national security as a justification.

When Special Prosecutor Leon Jaworski presented the tape as evidence, the congressional response was overwhelming, leaving little doubt that President Nixon had participated in a criminal conspiracy to obstruct justice. The ten Republican members of the Judiciary Committee who had spoken against impeachment announced that they would now vote in favor of an indictment once the matter reached the House floor. Facing a certain impeachment and Senate trial, Nixon had met his Waterloo.

But it had been a long struggle. When the House Judiciary Committee originally subpoenaed the tapes in April, the White House was slow to respond. When they were finally released, the recordings were so heavily edited that it was difficult to make head or tail of the conversations. Citing executive privilege and national security, Nixon emphasized the importance of redacting the transcripts. But the Judiciary Committee did not accept the president's sleight of hand, viewing the edited transcripts as noncompliant with their subpoena.

Pressing on, Jaworski convinced US District Court Judge John Sirica to issue another subpoena for additional White House tapes. When Nixon refused to comply, Jaworski appealed to the Supreme Court. On July 24, 1974, the Supreme Court ordered President Nixon to comply with the subpoena and release the tapes. In their unanimous 8-0 judgment, the Supreme Court ruled the Judiciary Committee need not honor President Nixon's claim of executive privilege.

The "smoking-gun" tape had sealed the deal. With the president's resignation, America's long ordeal had reached a dramatic conclusion. But justice may never have been served without the far-reaching efforts of two little-known *Washington Post* reporters, Bob Woodward and Carl Bernstein. Their relentless pursuit of truth and justice had established a bold new frontier for investigative journalism. Because of a free press and a separate and independent judicial process, democracy was able to prevail over the political ideology of executive privilege.

Ryan O'Connor gazed out the window from his office on the twenty-fourth floor of the Fort Wayne National Bank building. It was a warm and hazy morning, limiting his visibility to no more than three or four miles. On a clear day, his panoramic view would extend a good ten to twelve miles, allowing him to view the whole city and the way it transitioned from downtown office buildings to industrial plants to commercial developments, and ending where the suburban sprawl abutted fertile farmland.

As the city continued to expand, Ryan imagined a day when farmland would no longer serve as a backdrop to his aerial landscape. Despite the warnings from environmentalists, he wasn't concerned. The tree-huggers could continue their crusades, oblivious to the benefits of capitalism, but he would keep on doing what he was doing. Expansion is what fueled the economy and he was proud of his contributions. There's a reason why they called it progress; progress was very profitable.

Ryan had already gone over the day's agenda with Monica, his personal assistant, but there were more pressing issues that needed his attention, which meant his itinerary would be in a state of flux.

It was nine o'clock in the morning, and Ryan had been in the office since seven thirty, but he was struggling with his concentration.

Seemingly out of sorts, he had been reluctant to attack his day with the sort of rigor he'd grown accustomed to. His focus had been as foggy as the haze that clouded his view.

Stepping away from the window, Ryan stared in disbelief at the newspapers sprawled across his desk. *The Journal Gazette*, *The New York Times*, and *The Wall Street Journal* all shared the same headline in epic bold print: "*NIXON RESIGNS.*"

Ryan never thought it would come to this; a perfectly good man completely destroyed by his enemies. This was not justice—this was political assassination. Surrendering his honor and dignity, Nixon had allowed his enemies to complete their mission, exploiting the fallibility of their commander in chief.

Ryan couldn't help but feel betrayed by Nixon's vulnerability. He should have fought for his job and reputation until the bitter end. All the incredible things he had achieved over the years had been erased. Now, instead of memorializing his accomplishments, history would record him as the only US president ever to submit a resignation.

Pouring himself another cup of coffee, Ryan could feel his dander on the rise. This is just what he needed; a little stimulation to get the juices flowing again. He would fuel his determination with anger, using the adrenaline rush to trigger his sense of purpose.

Those bastards may have gotten to Nixon, but they weren't going to defeat him, by God. They would find out soon enough that you don't mess with Ryan O'Connor. An O'Connor will never surrender; he will fight to the death.

"Monica, I need you to get Bowers on the phone right now."

"Yes, sir."

"Neil Bowers speaking."

"Bowers, I need an update on the Teamster situation."

"Yes, sir. What do you want to know?"

"I need to know the latest on the official vote. Have they set a date yet?"

"My understanding is it will take place sometime next week."

"Your understanding? Is that all you got? I need more specifics than that, damn it!"

"Yes, sir. I'll do what I can, but it's not like the Teamsters are keeping me in the loop. This is behind-the-scenes stuff they negotiate with our attendants."

"Well, what about their leader? What's his name again?"

"Dominic Marino. He's the union organizer."

"Can you get ahold of him and find out more?"

"I suppose, but his first priority is with the workers. He's not gonna share anything with me that will compromise their objective."

"Everyone has a price," said Ryan. "Just find out when the vote will take place. I need to know how much time we have."

"Yes, sir. I will do my best."

"And get the phone number of this Dominic Marino and provide it to Monica. I need to know how to reach him. We may need to schedule a negotiation."

"We can't do any negotiations until they officially unionize," said Bowers. "They call it collective bargaining."

"I'm not talking about *those* kinds of negotiations," said Ryan. "By then it will be too late. Just get me the phone number of this Marino guy and everything else I asked for."

"Yes, sir. I will do my best."

"Make it today," said Ryan. "I want everything today."

"Yes, sir."

Ryan O'Connor sat down at his desk, contemplating his next move. If the vote to unionize was taking place in a week, he needed to get the ball rolling fast.

Punching the intercom button on his desktop phone, he forged ahead. "Monica, when is my meeting with Captain Carter scheduled?"

"Tomorrow afternoon at three o'clock."

"Can you please try to move that up to today? If not today, at least try to push it up to tomorrow morning."

"Yes, sir, I will do my best."

"And if he has any questions or wants to talk, do not hesitate to put him through. I need to place a priority on our interaction. Is that understood?"

"Yes, sir, understood."

"And I want you to call Bowers in an hour. Tell him you need the phone number of Dominic Marino. I already told him this, but I want you to remind him again."

"Yes, sir. The phone number for Dominic Marino. I will call him."

"And what's the status on the grievance the Teamsters filed against us? Do you have any updates on that?"

"No, sir. Your law office is handling that. Do you want me to connect you?"

"Never mind, I can handle it. That's all for now, thanks."

Feeling restless, Ryan O'Connor stood up. In a few short moments, he'd gone from hollow and rudderless, to deliberate and determined. He knew what he needed to do and how he would go about it. But just when he was motivated to set things in motion, he felt paralyzed by inactivity, a victim of his dependency on others. It was like being frozen in time. Sometimes the world just didn't move fast enough.

Grabbing *The Journal Gazette* and *The New York Times*, he slam-dunked them into a nearby waste basket. One thing was for sure, he didn't need to be reminded anymore about Nixon's failures. Out of sight, out of mind, he told himself. No more negative reinforcement.

He would've done the same with *The Wall Street Journal*, but decided against it, realizing it would be sacrilegious to disfigure the business-man's Bible. Ripping away the front page, he wadded it into a ball, and filed it into the trash can along with the other newspapers. Then he turned to the section that reported on stock market activity.

It had been a bad year on Wall Street. In fact, it had been a bad couple of years. Since early 1973, when the Dow Jones Industrial Average hovered around one thousand, the most watched index in the world had dropped 30 percent, and there was nothing to indicate it would stop its precipitous fall. The pundits had called it a bear market, but it was more complicated than that.

During the Nixon administration, the economy was defying logic and delivering a bevy of bad news on all fronts. Not only was economic growth stagnant, but inflation was running rampant. The experts had coined the unlikely combination as stagflation, and it was a problem that nobody knew how to solve.

Flipping through *The Wall Street Journal*, Ryan found an entire page devoted to the stock market and the economic indicators during the

Nixon administration. It had been a roller-coaster ride. Now the big question was how the markets would react the day after the president's resignation. Would the financial world be spooked by the perceived instability? Or would investors be relieved by the long-awaited closure of Watergate and inspired by the possibilities of a new administration?

Searching the stock quotes for GM, the symbol for General Motors, Ryan checked on his biggest holding, a company that made up more than 80 percent of his portfolio. He had bet big on the auto industry during its heyday, gobbling up GM stock in the late 1950s and watching it double in value in the midsixties. But now it was right back to where it started, valued no more than it was twenty years ago.

It didn't take a genius to figure out that his GM holdings had been a bad investment. If only he had sold his stock in 1965, he would have doubled his money. Instead, he got greedy, ignoring the economic headwinds and gambling on permanent success. Now, in retrospect, he realized he could have buried his money in the backyard and done no worse.

Ryan had committed the cardinal sin of investing. He had put all of his eggs in one basket. Not only were his businesses centered around the auto industry, but his personal investments were too. He had become a victim of his own greed and narrow sightedness, suffocating under an industry riddled by competition and stagflation. He had always been a risk taker, but now he wished he had been more prudent and diversified some of his holdings. Better safe than sorry was the old saying. Now there was only sorrow.

Hearing the buzz of his desktop phone, Ryan punched the flashing light.

"Sir, someone is here to see you from the law firm of Hanley & Cooper."

"Does he have an appointment? I don't see anything on my calendar."

"It's not an appointment, sir. He's here to serve you with papers."

Angered by the interruption, Ryan stormed into the reception area.

"What's this all about?" he demanded. "My law offices handle all of our legal matters."

"It's not business related," said the courier, handing him a large yellow envelope. "I believe this is a personal matter. You'll understand what it's all about when you open the envelope. Have a good day."

Ryan grabbed the envelope and marched back into his office. The suspense was killing him. Why would he be served papers from Hanley & Cooper? Daryl Hanley and he were good friends, or at least he thought they were. They were regular golfing buddies at the Fort Wayne Country Club. Was this something personal? With everything he had on his plate, he didn't need any surprises.

"When it rains, it pours," he mumbled to himself.

Unable to disguise his anticipation, Ryan O'Connor closed the office door behind him and ripped open the envelope. Extracting the papers, his eyes danced across the legal verbiage in disbelief. It was a form he'd seen countless times before as a young attorney, but never had he foreseen himself as a party to such a petition; a petition for the dissolution of marriage.

Stunned by the revelation, he suddenly felt weak in the knees. How could he be so naive? How could he have been in denial for so long? Now it was inevitable, as plain as the nose on his face. A new battle had emerged in Ryan O'Connor's war of survival. It was now O'Connor versus O'Connor, and this could be the ugliest confrontation of all.

In the competitive world of business, he was resolved to defend himself against adversaries, but he hadn't prepared himself for friendly fire. But then again, friendliness had long since left his marriage.

Even though Roselyn had been gone for months, the cold hard reality of divorce seemed like an unprovoked wake-up call, a cruel slap in the face that left him feeling empty and alienated. Now, more than ever, it was Ryan O'Connor against the world. Even his golfing buddy, Daryl Hanley, had abandoned his loyalty, seditiously opposing him for his own personal gain.

Roselyn's choice for legal representation was not happenstance. She was going for the jugular, and Hanley would be the henchman. Seeking an equal division of all the marital assets, Roselyn knew that Hanley would leave no stone unturned, for he had privileged information that would give them a decided advantage. She would prove to her ex that she had the fire in her belly to engage in warfare.

Chapter 61

Brian Johnson killed the throttle on his lawnmower and grabbed the cutoff T-shirt waiting for him on the lawn chair. It was an eighty-five-degree day with 90 percent humidity, and he was using the T-shirt as a makeshift towel. He had done his fair share of sweating already, completing his last summer workout at 10:00 a.m. and family lawncare duties at noon.

Gulping down a glass of ice water and admiring his work, Brian thought about the Northrop football field and how it would be groomed even better than his backyard. It had been a rainy August, and he knew the Bruin groundskeepers were working around the clock to meticulously prepare the lush green carpet. At least that's how it would appear for the home opener in September. By November, it would be equal parts grass and dirt.

Although school didn't start for two more weeks, the first official football practice was scheduled to begin on Monday morning at eight o'clock sharp. It would be the beginning of a two-week grind the players called two-a-days, meaning they would practice twice every day, two hours in the morning and two hours in the afternoon. Even though they had been training all summer long with weightlifting and running drills, nothing could prepare them for the first day of full-contact hitting, or as the coach described it: all hell breaking loose.

Senior year varsity football and Friday nights under the lights; this is what Brian Johnson had been preparing for the past five years. But this summer, in particular, he had been living and breathing football, eagerly anticipating his last shot at glory.

Loaded with twenty-three seniors, the Bruins were expected to compete for the conference title, and Brian would play a key role in their run-oriented attack. He and Darius Williams would get a lot of touches, both on the ground and through the air, and Brian couldn't wait to be in the spotlight. There would be marching bands, pep sessions, newspaper articles, and interviews. And best of all, Mindy would be cheering him on from the sidelines, waiting for her knight in shining armor.

Leading the charge on the defensive side of the ball would be Malcom Mosely, their all-state tackle. If he could stay healthy and continue to dominate the way he had his junior year, colleges would be waiting in line to win his favor. Already entertaining offers from Indiana, Purdue, and Michigan State, Malcom's future appeared bright and his opportunities immensurable.

Earlier in the day, after their last summer training session, Malcom invited Brian and Mark Carter to a party. He described it as a summer-ending bash that would serve as a senior year kickoff. "Summer's last hurrah," he called it. "We gonna do this up right and y'all are invited."

Anytime the word *party* came up, the boys were all ears, but they had never been to a party outside the sprawling neighborhoods of White suburbia. An inner-city party was something altogether different, and they needed as many specifics as possible before making a decision.

"So whose party, is it?" asked Brian.

"Our party, man. It's our party. Don't you wuss out on us."

"Whose house?" asked Brian. "Do you have a map?"

"It ain't nobody's house, but I do have a map," said Malcom, reaching into his pocket and pulling out sheets of paper with photo-copied directions.

"If it's not a house, then what is it?" asked Mark Carter.

"It's a private club, man. We call it an after-hours club."

"I've heard about these after-hours clubs," said Mark. "Aren't they against the law?"

"No, man. Don't be givin' me that shit. Nothin' wrong with throwing a party at a private club."

"What about alcohol?" asked Brian.

"Oh yeah. There'll be plenty of that. A fully stocked bar."

"Isn't that illegal?" asked Brian.

"Not if you ain't sellin' it. What would a party be without booze? And we gonna have plenty of music too. We gonna be movin' to the groove."

"Sounds like fun," admitted Brian.

"Yeah," said Mark. "Until the cops show up. I've heard about these after-hours clubs gettin' busted."

"C'mon man! I wouldn't be invitin' you if I thought there was trouble. I know the cats who own this club and they're lettin' me have this party. We won't be allowin' no riffraff. I'll make sure everything's cool."

"What about Antonio?" asked Brian. "Will he be there?"

"Are you kiddin'? Of course he'll be there. He and his homies will be playin' the music. Then we gonna have a DJ spin some tunes."

"Cool," said Brian. "I think I'm gonna try to make it."

"You think?" asked Malcom. "There ain't no thinkin' to be done. If you wanna be my teammate, I expect you to be there."

"Who am I to say no to our defensive captain."

"That's more like it. But don't tell nobody and don't bring nobody with you. If we keep this under wraps, there won't be any trouble."

"Whatever you say," nodded Brian.

"Oh, and we gonna have some foxy mammas there too. Don't be stirrin' up no trouble by hittin' on our ladies," he said with a wink of his eye. "Not that they'd ever want any homeboys like you," he chuckled.

"Carter residence."

"Hi, Mrs. Carter. This is Brian. May I please speak to Mark?"

"Oh, hi Brian. Hold on a second, I'll call him." *Hey Mark—Brian's on the phone.*

"Hey, wassup?"

"So what's the scoop?" asked Brian. "Are we goin' to the party tonight, or what?"

"No can do," said Mark. "My pops would shit a brick if he found out I was goin' to some inner-city party."

"Well, that sucks," said Brian. "I was hoping you could drive."

"No way, Jose."

"Well, Scott wants to go too. He was invited by some of the basket-ball players."

"So let him drive if you can't," suggested Mark.

"Nope, that won't work either. He's in the same boat as me. Our fathers won't let us borrow the cars unless we give them details on where we're goin' and what we're doin'."

"Looks like you're screwed," said Mark. "Guess you'll be watching TV with your folks tonight like the rest of us."

"Unless," Brian contemplated.

"Unless what?"

"Unless we can talk Bob into goin'. He gets off work at nine. We could still be there between nine thirty and ten."

"That's a bold move," said Mark. "I can just see Bob Wills hangin' out in the hood with a bunch of jocks. Besides, didn't Malcom tell us not to bring anyone else?"

"Well, I really wanna go and sometimes you gotta do what ya gotta do to make things happen."

"Let me know how *that* works out." Mark laughed. "I'd give any-thing to see a scrawny little White dude drivin' into the hood with a bright yellow Plymouth Barracuda."

Riding shotgun, Brian Johnson held the map under the dimly lit dash-board, nervously trying to sync up his directions with the unfamiliar surroundings. "Wait a minute," he said. "Did we just pass Baxter Street?"

"I don't know," said Bob. "You tell me. You're the one with the directions."

"Do you even know where the hell you're goin'?" asked Scott Clever, from the back seat.

"No, I don't," answered Brian. "But at least I'm tryin'. We're sup-posed to turn right on Baxter. I think we just passed it. We need to do a U-ey."

Bob gunned the Barracuda to the next intersection and wheeled around sharply enough to squeal his tires.

"Perfect, just what we needed," said Scott. "Now the whole neigh-borhood knows there's three White dudes drivin' around in a yellow Barracuda."

"Slow down," said Brian. "This is Baxter Street right here. You need to turn left."

"I thought you said right."

"It would've been right from the other direction, you numbskull. Quit confusing me."

"Who's confusing who?" asked Bob, frustrated with his navigator.

"All right, we're gonna go six blocks until we reach Turner Avenue. Then we turn left. Slow down so I can read these street signs. They're hard to see in the dark."

"I'm gettin' awfully thirsty back here," said Scott. "I guess we're gonna owe you big-time for this, Bobby boy."

"Yep, you can *both* buy me drinks tonight."

"I don't think we have to worry about that," said Brian. "Malcom said everything is on the house. I just hope we can get you in."

"You better," said Bob. "Otherwise, I'll leave you high and dry."

"Slow down," said Brian. "This should be Turner… Yep, now turn left."

"Turn on Turner," quipped Scott.

"Now we need to find the address. We're lookin' for 4624. Even numbers are on the right, and they should be getting higher."

"All right," said Bob, "but you need to find it for me. I can't drive and look for street numbers at the same time."

"It's kinda creepy around here," said Scott. "Whaddaya think, Bobby boy?"

"Nah, no big deal," said Bob. "Steve Marino's taken me to scarier places than this."

"That's no surprise," said Brian. "Now slow down, here's a strip of buildings comin' up. 4616…4620…4624. Stop here."

"There's nothin' here," said Scott. "Just an empty store front. I think they played a prank on you."

"No, it's okay," said Brian. "Malcom said it would look like a vacant building from the front. We're supposed to pull around back to the alley. That's where there's an entrance to the club."

"Let's hope so," said Scott. "It kinda sounds like a speakeasy."

Bob rounded the block as the boys looked for an alley. Two cars crossed paths in front of them as they slowed down.

"Roll down your window," said Scott. "I think I hear some voices."

Looking down the alley, they saw a cluster of guys standing behind the building, smoking cigarettes and jawing away.

"That's gotta be it," said Brian, as the gang of young men looked up at the Barracuda.

"Should we turn down there?" asked Bob. "I don't see any place to park."

"Malcom said we'd have to find our own parking spot, whatever's closest. Let's just drive down the alley and make sure it's the right place."

"Are you sure you want to attract that much attention?" asked Bob. "I'm not seein' any White dudes down there."

"It's okay." Scott laughed. "You're gonna dazzle them with your fancy ride."

Bob eased his way down the alley as the street gathering focused their full attention on the Barracuda. As they got closer, they could hear the faint sound of music from inside the building.

"Whooeee!" came the catcalls. "Look at that shiny ride. What color is that? Piss yellow?" After the laughter subsided, the jeering continued. "Who is that behind the wheel? Richard Petty?" With another round of laughter, someone shouted out, "Are you boys lost?"

"Just keep going," said Brian. "Let's find a place to park."

"You still wanna go in?" asked Bob. "Those dudes looked like they were about thirty years old."

"Yeah, I noticed. But that's all right. Malcom said the club was owned by some older guys and they were letting him use it tonight."

"So you think it's the right place?" asked Scott.

"Yep, one hundred percent."

"I'm not seein' any place to park along this alley," said Bob.

"No, you need to get off this alley and park somewhere around the block," said Brian.

Bob turned the corner to find a Cadillac cruising toward them real slow, as if it was in a parade. All decked out with an array of gaudy accessories, it was a real showstopper; an ice-blue Coupe De Ville with shiny mag wheels and white sidewall tires. As if the car itself wasn't attracting enough attention, the driver had the stereo on at maximum decibels, blaring out William DeVaughn's summer hit, "Be Thankful for What You Got."

"Slow down," ordered Scott. "I wanna get a good look at this Caddy."

Following orders, Bob slowed to a crawl, enabling them to get a closer view. Decked out in a fedora, silk shirt and gold chains, the driver wore dark shades even though it was ten o'clock at night. With his left arm extended straight ahead, hand resting on the steering wheel, he positioned his right elbow on the center console, boastfully demonstrating his gangster lean.

Slowing to a stop, the driver nodded his head, respectfully acknowledging the Barracuda. Intrigued by the gesture, Bob stopped directly next to him, aligning the driver-side windows.

"Nice ride," said Bob.

"Back at ya, brotha."

And just like that, the two cars pulled away.

Brian and Scott broke out laughing.

"What's so damn funny?" demanded Bob.

"That was a stimulating conversation," teased Brian.

"You can laugh all you want," said Bob, "but he was diggin' my ride. And you guys said my Barracuda would be laughed at."

"I'm not so sure he was diggin' your ride as much as he wanted to show off *his* ride and make you feel inferior," explained Scott. "Let's face it, he was pretty badass."

"So what were those little antennas he had around his wheels?" asked Brian.

"Are you serious?" asked Scott. "You really *are* a nerd."

"They're not antennae," explained Bob. "They're called curb feelers. It warns them when they're getting close to the curb so they don't scuff their whitewalls."

"Never heard of that," said Brian. "I guess I need to get out more often."

Two blocks away from the club, Bob wedged his car in between two other vehicles, barely managing to parallel park on his third attempt.

"You boys lead the way," said Bob. "I'm really feeling out of place here."

"And we're not?" joked Scott. "Just remember, we're all in this together."

Turning up the alley, the boys approached the gathering of men with the confidence of a steer entering a slaughterhouse. Brian led the way, trying to look like a macho football player, followed by the gangly redhead and the pintsized paperboy.

"Can I help you, boys?" asked a heavily bearded Black man guarding the door.

"I'm here to see Malcom Mosley," said Brian. "I'm on the Northrop football team."

"And what about the ginger man?" asked the gatekeeper, looking at Scott.

"He's on the basketball team," said Brian.

"And the midget?" he inquired, amid a scattering of snickers.

"He's our driver," said Brian.

The gaggle of onlookers broke out into a collective round of laughter.

With a playful, but skeptical scowl, the gatekeeper continued. "You have a driver? You must be pretty big-time."

After another round of laughter, Brian tried to keep his composure. "Well, you know how it is. We're plannin' on knockin' down more than a few with Malcom, so we need a driver to get us home."

Satisfied with the response, the gatekeeper opened the door. "You need to check in with Malcom. If he's okay with it, then so am I."

Entering the club, the boys were greeted by a wave of smoke. With dim lighting and hazy conditions, they struggled to identify any familiar faces. But one thing was for sure, none of the partygoers were White, and none of them seemed to care that a few stray White boys had intruded their space.

The room, laid out like an old-time tavern, was long and deep, with a bar on one side and a makeshift music stage in the back. Except for the barstools, there were no chairs. The only furnishings were a few small tables used to accommodate cocktail glasses and beer bottles.

Brian could hear a trumpet in the background, accompanied by bass and drums. Assuming it was Antonio, he thought about milling through the crowd to get a closer look, but then he spotted Malcom behind the bar.

"I'm heading over to the bar," said Brian. "It looks like Malcom is pouring drinks."

"Okay," said Scott. "I see a couple of my teammates, so I'll head over there."

"What about me?" asked Bob. "Don't leave me alone."

"Come with me," said Brian. "I'm sure Malcom will remember you."

At the sight of Brian, Malcom unleashed his infectious smile, grinning from ear to ear. "You made it! And I was betting against you."

"I wouldn't miss it for the world," said Brian, extending his right hand and locking thumbs with Malcom in a solidarity handshake.

"And you brought half-pint with you," teased Malcom.

"You remember Bob?"

"Yeah, I used to rescue him from restroom scuffles."

"I'm the guy," said Bob. "I guess I still owe ya."

"Nah, drinks are on me tonight," said Malcom.

"I feel underdressed," admitted Brian. "You're lookin' pretty dapper in that suit jacket."

"You like it?" asked Malcom, flapping his lapels.

"Wait, what was that?" asked Brian.

"What was what?"

"That shoulder strap under your jacket."

"You mean this?" asked Malcom, opening his jacket and revealing a shoulder holster stuffed with a pistol.

"Holy shit," said Brian. "You're packin' heat?"

"Man, you can never be too careful. I told ya I'd keep you safe if you came tonight."

"Are you expecting trouble?" asked Brian, with a renewed sense of danger.

"Not with this under my jacket and my doorman out front. He's packin' heat too; in case you didn't notice."

"No, I didn't notice."

"Man, you need to get real. Look around you. This ain't no Mayberry around here."

"Yeah, I guess so. I'll just hang by you and trust you to protect me."

"Heh, heh," chuckled Malcom. "I'm glad *somebody* trusts me. None of your homies I invited bothered to show up. You're the only one."

"Yeah, it's hard to get transportation," admitted Brian. "That's why I brought Bob."

"We just need to get y'all liquored up," said Malcom. "Then you'll relax."

"I'll take a beer," admitted Brian.

"I'll pour ya a beer later. Let's start out with a little top-shelf hooch."

Malcom took Brian by the arm and pulled him behind the bar. Then he slammed two shot glasses on the counter. Feeling left out, Bob decided to light up his first Marlboro.

"Look under here," said Malcom, pointing at a shelf under the bar. "This is where I keep the good shit."

"Ah yes, Wild Turkey and Southern Comfort," declared Brian. "Not bad."

"Which one you want?"

"Let's do the Southern Comfort. I could use a little comfort."

Malcom made a big show of displaying the bottle on the bar, as if it were a thousand-dollar bottle of Dom Perignon. Carefully filling the shot glasses like he was pouring liquid gold, he handed one to Brian.

"Here's to a great football season."

"Cheers to that," said Brian, as they downed the shots together.

"Ah, smooooth," said Malcom.

"I don't know 'bout that," said Brian, his eyes watering. "That shit's got a kick to it."

"Exactly," said Malcom. "Let's do another."

"You want one?" Brian asked Bob. "Maybe I should skip a round."

"No, I'm the driver, remember? I'll stick to my pack of smokes."

"Pour him a beer," said Brian.

"Sure thing," said Malcom. "I hope you like Schlitz."

After three rounds of shots, Brian was starting to ease into his comfort zone. He and Malcom were shooting the breeze as if there was no tomorrow, but he could see that most of the people were gathering toward the back around Antonio.

"I need to get back there and pay my respects," said Brian.

"Yeah, you should do that," said Malcom. "He'll be wrappin' up pretty quick. The DJ takes over at eleven. Then it's time to boogie down."

Grabbing a beer apiece, Brian and Bob started making their way toward the back, Brian leading the way and Bob following along obediently.

Wedging their way closer to the stage, they settled into a prime spot just in time to see Antonio unleash a wicked trumpet solo, accompanied by keyboards and drums.

"That's from Blood, Sweat & Tears," yelled Brian over the noise. "That's one of Antonio's favorite bands."

Then a middle-aged gentleman took the stage and grabbed a microphone. "How 'bout some vocals?" he asked, to which the patrons applauded and whistled. Not missing a beat, he belted out the lyrics to "Spinning Wheel."

"This is really badass!" Brian yelled in Bob's ear. "I think I need a membership to this club."

When the combo wrapped up their rendition of "Spinning Wheel," the enthusiastic revelers responded with a round of applause and Antonio grabbed the microphone.

"That's all for tonight folks. Thanks for coming out. The DJ is setting up and should be ready to go in a few more minutes. So grab some drinks and get ready to boogie."

Brian took a few more gulps of his beer and waited to greet Antonio as he exited the stage. As the crowd dispersed, he struggled to maintain his position amid all the jostling. Then he felt a tap on his shoulder. Brian turned around, expecting to see Scott or one of his teammates. Instead, it was Quinn O'Connor.

"What's up, ole chap?"

"Oh my God!" exclaimed Brian. "What are *you* doing here?"

"Same as you, I suppose."

"We thought we were the only White dudes. How long have you been here?"

"Long enough."

"Is Lynda here?"

"Good *God,* no! This isn't her style. I came with Antonio."

Wearing a navy-blue polo shirt, khakis, and topsiders, Quinn looked like a fish out of water. With bloodshot eyes and a shit-eating grin, he was well beyond sobriety, bobbing and weaving around like a boxer who had just been given a standing eight count.

"You look three sheets to the wind," said Brian. "What have you been drinkin'?"

"Antonio and I have our own little stash behind the bar. A big bottle of Cognac. A guy named Malcom is guarding it for us."

"Yeah, I know Malcom. He's my teammate."

"Listen, can you guys do me a favor?" asked Quinn.

"Sure, waddaya need?"

"I need you to keep this on the sly. Whatever you do, don't tell anybody you saw me here tonight. Especially Lynda."

"I won't tell anyone," said Brian. "But there's a lot of people here. I don't think you can keep it a secret."

"I'm not worried about *these* people," said Quinn. "They don't run in our circles. I'm more worried about Lynda and my father."

"I don't know why Lynda would care that much," offered Brian.

"Maybe," said Quinn. "I guess it's my father that scares me the most. He'd kill me if he knew I was here. Especially with Antonio."

"No worries," said Brian. "Your secret is safe with us."

"Well, well," came a thundering voice. "What have we here? A pretty white rose among all these thorns."

Looking up, the boys recognized the familiar swagger of Antonio, confidently flashing his captivating smile. Brian reached out and locked wrists in a sign of solidarity.

"That was some great stuff," acknowledged Brian. "I wish you'd keep playin'."

"Nah, my time is up. Now these people wanna dance."

"I'd rather listen to *you* than dance," admitted Brian.

"I appreciate the kind words, but maybe you should find someone and cut the rug."

"Maybe I would if Mindy was here."

"How about me?" came a female voice standing directly behind Brian.

Brian turned around to see Jada Brown batting her eyelids facetiously.

"Down, girl!" said Antonio. "Give this White boy a fightin' chance."

"Oh, I think a football player can fight for himself," said Jada, clearly amusing herself. "Where's Mindy? Does she know you're here?"

"No. We just decided to come on a whim after Malcom invited us this morning."

"So *that's* your excuse." Jada laughed. "What she don't know won't hurt her, right?"

"Wait a minute," interrupted Quinn. "You're a cheerleader, aren't you?"

"Listen to this," said Jada. "The pretty boy has quite a keen eye."

Quinn ignored the jab and pleaded his case. "I'm just sayin', as long as we're keeping Mindy in the dark, why don't we do the same with Lynda."

"Ah, now I get it," declared Jada. "We have an interesting dilemma here, don't we? The boys from the 'burbs are partyin' in the hood, and they don't want their pretty White girlfriends to know about it."

"It's not like that," said Brian.

"Yes, it is," insisted Quinn. "Can I trust you to keep this under wraps?"

"I don't know," answered Jada. "How much is it worth to ya?"

"All right, I think that's quite enough," interrupted Antonio. "C'mon Quinn, we got a bottle of Cognac waiting on us."

Antonio grabbed Quinn by the arm and led him back to the bar. Jada, with a perplexed look on her face, watched them saunter away suspiciously.

"What's with those two?" she asked. "When did they become so tight?"

"Ever since they won that student council election, I guess."

"Is that it? Are you sure there's nothin' more to it than that?"

"Like what?" asked Brian.

"I don't know," answered Jada. "Maybe it's just Antonio tryin' to climb the social ladder. He's awfully ambitious, you know."

"Yeah, maybe so."

"What about you?" asked Jada, with a twinkle in her eye.

"What *about* me?"

"So what are you drinkin'?" she asked.

"We were drinkin' some *Southern Comfort* with Malcom."

"That's boring. Why don't you drink with me?" she asked as she pulled a pint of liquor out of her purse.

Embarrassed and feeling like a third wheel, Bob decided to excuse himself. "I think I see Scott over there. I'll talk to you guys later."

"I think we scared him off." Jada laughed. "You don't scare that easy, do ya?"

"What's in the bottle?" asked Brian, trying to deflect the question.

"Cherry vodka," she replied, tipping the bottle to her lips and taking a big sip.

"Does it really taste like cherry?"

"Why don't you see for yourself?"

Jada leaned in and planted a big kiss on Brian's lips.

"Could you taste it?" she asked.

Surprised by Jada's ploy, Brian played along willingly. "I'm not sure if I did or not. Could I have another taste?"

Jada laughed at Brian's response. "You catch on quickly. Maybe you're not as shy as I thought."

"Oh, I don't know. I'm pretty shy."

"Here," said Jada, handing him the bottle. "Why don't you taste for yourself?"

"Don't mind if I do," said Brian, taking a big gulp.

"So waddaya think?"

"I think it's really good. Although I liked my first taste better."

"Oh my! You *are* a player, aren't you?"

"I don't know what you mean."

"Don't play naive with me. I know Mindy, and she's no prude."

"I don't know what you're talking about," reiterated Brian.

"Let's share this vodka together and see how much damage we can do."

After a few more hits from the bottle, the DJ played his first song, and the pair were swept away by a swarm of would-be dancers. Taking Jada's hand, Brian pulled her away from the mob and kept on blathering, never missing a beat. Jada, enamored by the attention, reciprocated the dialogue, wondering if there was more to this playful encounter than frivolous merriment.

Feeling his head start to spin, Brian realized the whiskey, beer, and vodka were taking a toll, allowing him to look at Jada in a whole new light. He never imagined her to be so much fun, not to mention so attractive. How had he not noticed her before? But then again, he'd never seen her dressed this way either, a far cry from her prissy cheerleading outfit.

Donning a spandex tank top that flaunted her bountiful bosom, Jada looked both athletic and sexy at the same time. Her broad shoulders and muscular arms were a perfect accent to her curvaceous buttocks, and Brian was consumed by her sexuality. He couldn't help but think of the term "brickhouse," and if there was ever an image to represent that cliché, it would be Jada's body, without a doubt.

"I think there's one more swallow in here," said Jada, holding up the bottle. "Why don't you polish it off?"

"If you insist," said Brian, tipping the bottle upside down and swigging the last drop.

"So is it true what they say?" asked Jada.

"About what?"

"That White boys can't dance."

"Very funny! Although there might be some truth to that," he admitted.

"So when am I gonna find out?"

"I'm just waitin' for the right song."

"Well, I'm not gonna wait much longer. I'm gonna pick out a song and drag you out there."

"If you insist," said Brian, offering little resistance.

"Uh-oh. Don't look now, but I think your buddies are tryin' to flag you down."

Brian looked over his shoulder to see Scott and Bob approaching as if they were on a mission.

"Wassup?" asked Brian.

"Well," said Scott. "Mr. Party-pooper here says we need to get going."

Bob pointed at his watch and stated his case. "It's after midnight, and I gotta get up at five o'clock tomorrow morning to deliver the papers."

"Seriously?" asked Brian. "This party is really rockin' right now."

"That's what I told him," said Scott.

Brian looked at Jada helplessly. "What time does this place close down?"

"Close? Why would it ever close? I guess when the last person leaves."

"You can party all you want," said Bob. "But I gotta get goin'. How 'bout I give you fifteen more minutes. If we leave at twelve thirty, that means I won't hit the hay until one. That's only four hours of sleep."

"You can make it up with a nap," reasoned Scott.

"Wait! Here's my song," said Jada, grabbing Brian's arm. "We gotta dance to George McCrae!"

Left in the dust, the two boys watched as Jada and Brian rushed to the dance floor with a sense of urgency. Blending in effortlessly, the couple settled into the beat. Brian looked over his shoulder as if he'd been taken hostage. Bob glared back helplessly, pointing at his watch, but Brian was fully engrossed in the summer smash hit, "Rock Your Baby."

Rocking back and forth to the rhythm, Jada held her arms around Brian's neck, while he promiscuously explored her hips. Oblivious to their surroundings, the couple clung to each other with a carefree indulgence, heedlessly embracing the chemistry.

"I didn't know you were so much fun," yelled Jada over the loud music.

"I was thinking the same thing," replied Brian.

"Maybe it's just the alcohol and music," she reasoned.

"Maybe," yelled Brian. "Or maybe not."

"Meaning what?"

"Meaning we can make of it whatever we want."

As the song came to an end, Jada came back to her senses. "You better hookup with your friends. You don't wanna miss your ride."

"Wish I didn't have to go," said Brian. "I'm havin' too much fun."

"Yes, I know," she replied, ignoring his disappointment and leading him back to the boys.

"Are you ready?" asked Bob.

"Yes, he's ready," commanded Jada. "I delivered him on schedule."

Brian looked at Jada with sappy eyes, trying to determine the best way to end the evening, but she backed away as he leaned in for a good-night kiss.

"Tell Mindy I said hello," she ordered. "Guess I'll see you back at school."

"C'mon—let's hit the road," said Bob.

Once they were outside and away from the loud music, the boys began to realize how late it was, or how early, depending upon the point of view. The streets were dark and deserted, and the cool night air did nothing to sober them up.

"Are you okay to drive?" asked Brian. "Cuz I'm feeling pretty drunk right now."

"I'm fine," said Bob. "I only had two beers and a half-a-pack of ciga-rettes. I'm just tryin' to remember where we parked."

"Scott can help you with the directions," said Brian. "I'm sure he's not as drunk as I am. Or are you?"

"I'm not too drunk to remember that you and Jada were gettin' pretty hot and heavy in there."

"That was wild," admitted Brian. "Whatever you do, don't tell Mindy."

"We'll see about that." Scott laughed. "Maybe I should blackmail you."

"Did we come down this street?" asked Bob, continuing to navigate. "For some reason, I don't remember this. Everything looks different."

"You better not be lost," said Brian. "We're relying on you to get us home."

"Relying on *me*? *You're* the one who had the directions."

"Not from where we parked. Are you tellin' me you don't even re-member where you parked?"

"I think we need to turn right on this street and go down a block, and then take a left."

"You don't sound very confident," noted Scott. "I just hope we don't get mugged."

"I think Bob is right," said Brian. "But I remember cutting through an alley."

"An alley sounds familiar," confirmed Bob. "I remember parking next to one."

"Okay, let's turn here and take this alley," suggested Scott. "What've we got to lose?"

Following Scott's command, the disoriented trio turned into the dark corridor, proceeding with caution. But suddenly, at the faint sound of a mysterious commotion, the crew came to a screeching halt. Frozen in time, their eyes popped out and their jaws dropped, dumbstruck by their shocking discovery.

"Holy shit!" gasped Bob.

"Get outa here!" came an exasperating cry.

The boys instantly scrambled back around the corner, their chests heaving as though they had just run a mile. Unable to hide their revulsion, they just stared at each other in disbelief, trying to gather their composure.

Still breathing heavily, Brian finally spoke up. "Did you see what I just saw? Or am I drunk and delusional?"

"I may be drunk," said Scott. "But I will never get that image out of my head."

"I never thought I'd witness anything like that," added Bob, seemingly confused and bewildered.

"All right, that's enough," ordered Brian, trying to sober up and take charge. "We need to get ahold of ourselves. Let's just take a different route. But before we go, we need to reach an agreement."

"What kind of agreement?" asked Bob.

"Let's make a pact that we will *never ever* mention this to anyone," ordered Brian.

"Why not?" asked Scott. "We can't just erase it."

"Yes, we can," demanded Brian. "As far as I'm concerned, it never happened. And you need to do the same."

"How am I gonna do that?" asked Scott. "I can't make it go away."

"Yes, you can, and you will."

"Why?"

"There are *so* many reasons why that I don't even know where to begin. You just have to trust me," demanded Brian.

After hearing Brian's plea, the boys reluctantly surrendered to his demand. At the end of the day, all they really wanted was to forget about the whole incident and get back home where they could take comfort in their familiar surroundings.

Brian stuck his hand straight out in a sign of unity, implying that Scott and Bob should do the same.

"As of right now, we are all sworn to secrecy. No one besides the three of us will ever know what we witnessed tonight."

Like a football team breaking a huddle, all three boys locked their hands together in unison, as if they were sealing a pact. Then they disappeared into the night.

Chapter 62

IN LATE AUGUST, WHEN SUMMER reaches the homestretch, Hoosiers are still enduring warm and muggy conditions, with little relief in store until September. Two months after the summer solstice, daylight is reduced a full hour. For Bob Wills, that meant dragging himself out of bed in the morning while it was still pitch-dark. With the days getting shorter, he realized his working conditions were diminishing, but they wouldn't hit rock bottom until winter. That's when he would perform his morning newspaper delivery entirely in the dark, not seeing the light of day until he arrived at school.

During the summer months, when Bob didn't have to rush around and get ready for school, he was still expected to complete his deliveries by six thirty every morning. That was the absolute cutoff. If he fell behind schedule, he would hear about it, either directly from the customer or from the main office. If there were too many complaints, he would get fired. It was that simple. People wanted their newspapers, and they wanted them on time.

It was a Tuesday morning, and Bob felt comfortable in his routine, much better than he had felt three days earlier on Saturday morning when he was forced to complete his tasks on only four hours of sleep. Luckily, the Saturday paper was the second skinniest of the week, second only to the Monday edition. If he had partied on Saturday night instead of Friday, he would have been faced with the Sunday morning edition, a monstrosity of a newspaper that included seven different sections and multiple inserts. Piecing that puzzle together would have been a nightmare in his groggy condition.

Exiting the garage, Bob pushed his bicycle toward the piles of newsprint waiting for him at the end of the driveway. Before piecing the sections together, he usually checked the date on page one against the date on his *Timex* calendar watch. He wasn't sure why he did that. Maybe it was his way of verifying the accuracy of his timepiece, making sure that everything was in working order, or maybe he felt more assured or squared away by the harmony of equilibrium, like an accountant who balances his ledger. At any rate, he'd been conditioned to believe that no amount of stress or strain could harm his watch, that a *Timex* could take a licking and keep on ticking.

Shining his flashlight across the top of page one, everything checked out. It was August 20, 1974, a date that seemed insignificant at the time. Just another summer day, putting him one step closer to his final year of high school.

The headlines were unremarkable, more news about the new president, Gerald Ford, and how he was trying to heal the wounds of Watergate and move the country forward; not the kind of riveting reporting that attracted Bob's attention.

Moving along to the next stack of newsprint, the sports section, he scanned the featured stories. There was an article about the Notre Dame football team—fresh off a national championship—and their prospects for the upcoming season, and right below it, an update on the baseball pennant races and the odds of the Oakland A's winning a third consecutive World Series. All that really mattered to Bob was that his Detroit Tigers were in dead last.

Not wasting another minute, Bob began his assembly line, which meant inserting the sports section into the main section, then grabbing the metro section from the third stack and inserting it into the middle of his finished product; three sections rolled together and secured with a rubber band. It was a simple process that took no more than ten seconds per newspaper, and that's the pace he needed to maintain in order to stay on schedule and meet his deadline.

Rolling together his first newspaper and grabbing a rubber band, Bob noticed a small headline toward the bottom of page one: "Local Musician Found Dead."

Allowing his curiosity to get the better of him, Bob stopped and skimmed the first paragraph.

> *The dead body of Antonio Jackson, a young rising star in the music world, was found late last night in Memorial Park, apparently the victim of three gunshot wounds. Although the police have ruled foul play, no suspects have been identified at this time.*

Feeling the all-too-familiar knot in his stomach, Bob reread the paragraph two more times. No, it was not a mistake. There could only be one Antonio Jackson.

With his throat tightening and his eyes watering, Bob felt suspended in time. Like the proverbial raven, another nightmare had come to roost, haunting his soul and crushing his spirits. It seemed as though death followed him wherever he went. To Bob, it could only mean one thing. He was living his life under a curse—there was no other explanation.

Maybe some things in life could be explained away, but this defied all logic. Everybody loved Antonio. He had style, he had grace, and he had a bigger-than-life personality. But most of all, he had a rare gift—a virtuosity that brought joy and fulfillment to all the lives he touched. The world was his oyster, and the sky was the limit. Now there were only unfulfilled dreams. Why would someone rob him of such a brilliant future? It was all a colossal waste.

Now Bob was thinking about how much time he had left to pursue the things he wanted in life, even though his potential seemed far less than Antonio's. Feeling numb, he sat down on the ground and pondered the meaning of life and his sense of duty and purpose. It all seemed so pointless now, like it didn't really matter anymore. After all, it could all be taken away from him in an instant.

The powers that be would expect him to carry on, to persevere. That's what you did. "Stiff upper lip," is what they told him. "Courage and fortitude." That's how you succeed in life.

Then he thought about his brother and Vietnam, and how they told his mother that he was a good soldier and that he served his country well and that she should be proud. But what did that get him? Bob knew the answer. It got him nothing but death, plain and simple. Used as a political pawn, his whole life was stolen away. What was so honorable about that?

Bob knew he needed to be a good soldier and complete his morning obligations, but all he really wanted was a shoulder to cry on, someone who would listen to him and explain this horrific tragedy and help him to cope with the mental anguish. That's what he really needed.

Approaching the dinner hour, Bob and Scott lingered sluggishly around the Clever front porch, waiting for Brian Johnson and Mark Carter to return from football practice. They were prepared to deliver the bad news, an obligation they took seriously, unless the fateful demise of Antonio had already been communicated. Tragic stories have a way of making the rounds.

Bob had just completed his afternoon delivery of *The News-Sentinel* and should have been leaving for his next job at the gas station, but instead he called in sick, something he had never done before unless he was hopelessly bedridden. On this day, it didn't matter. He decided that some things in life were more important than work and money.

Lynda Lacey had spoken to Bob earlier, just as he was beginning his afternoon delivery. She wanted to see if *The News-Sentinel* had published any more details than *The Journal Gazette*. Desperate for information, she was no different from anyone else, but there were more questions than answers and nothing new had been reported.

"How is she handling it?" asked Scott. "Is she doing all right?"

"I'm not sure," replied Bob. "You know her, she's pretty good at hiding her emotions. But I could tell that she'd been crying."

"What did she say?"

"She said that she didn't even know Antonio was in town. She thought he was in New Orleans for the summer."

"Did you tell her we just saw him last Friday?"

"No. I almost spilled the beans but then I remembered Quinn telling us to keep everything on the sly. So I didn't even bring it up."

"Yeah, it's just as well. She would have interrogated you to no end."

"That's what I was thinking."

"Here they come now," said Scott, watching Brian pull into Coldwater Creek in his father's Oldsmobile.

The boys anxiously approached the curb as Brian and Mark slowed to a stop. One look at their faces and it was painfully obvious the news had already spread.

"So I assume you heard about Antonio?" began Scott.

"That's all anyone could talk about at practice today," answered Mark.

Brian turned off the engine and the two boys climbed out of the car, displaying their willingness to commiserate in the misery of company.

"How are you guys holdin' up?" asked Brian.

"As well as expected," replied Bob. "Are there any more details out there other than what was reported?"

"Not that I'm aware of," said Brian. "I talked to Malcom and he's just as shocked as we are. As far as he knew, Antonio had no enemies. He's just as clueless as the rest of us."

"Did anyone see him or know what he was doing last night?" asked Scott.

"Malcom said he hadn't seen him since the party last Friday. He said that Antonio didn't really go out and do anything unless he was playin' a gig somewhere, and he doubted he was doing that on a Monday night."

"Have you talked to your father?" Scott asked Mark. "Does he have any scoop from the police department?"

"I haven't talked to him yet and I don't know if he's working the case or not. Either way, he might be privy to some investigative evidence, but that doesn't mean he'll share it with me."

"Well, let us know," said Scott. "It looks like we'll be going to another funeral here pretty soon. This is gonna be a tough one, no doubt about that."

"Yeah," said Brian. "The coaches spoke to us this afternoon and paid a nice tribute to Antonio, which is pretty impressive, considering he had no connections to the football team. I guess everyone realizes how important he was to the school. They even said we could get out of practice if we wanted to attend the funeral."

"That's gonna be one big funeral," said Scott. "One for the ages."

"Hey," said Mark. "Not to change the subject, but what's that sign doin' in Steve Marino's front yard? I just now noticed it."

"It's a realtor's sign," said Bob. "They just put their house up for sale."

"Yep," said Scott. "They're movin' back to Philadelphia."

"I can't say that I'm surprised," noted Brian. "Steve is all done with school, and he talked about moving back where his dad could get him a good Teamster job."

Scoffing at the revelation, Mark let his true feelings be known. "Goodbye and good riddance, that's what I say."

"Well, you missed his goodbye this morning," said Bob. "Now he's gone."

"You talked to him?" asked Brian.

"Yep, his car was all packed and he was drivin' to Philly. He stopped by to say goodbye and wish me good luck. He starts his new job next week."

"So I assume his dad is taking a new job too?" asked Brian.

"I guess. But his parents aren't movin' out until the house is sold. In the meantime, Steve will be livin' with his uncle."

"Don't look now," said Scott, "but someone is pulling into Marino's driveway in a shiny new Cadillac."

The boys all looked up to see a top-of-the-line red Cadillac Eldorado, in pristine condition. With temporary tags and a new-car sticker attached to the rear window, it was clearly brand new, looking as though it had just been driven off the lot.

"Maybe it belongs to their realtor," said Brian. "I didn't know realtors made that much money?"

Gawking at the glamorous eye candy as if it was a golden chariot, the boys watched Mr. Marino exit from the driver's seat. All spiffed up in a three-piece suit, Dominic Marino surveyed the vehicle from hood to trunk, admiring its beauty and craftsmanship. Then he pulled out his handkerchief and shined the chrome door handle, as if the only flaw he could detect was an errant fingerprint.

"I guess that answers your question," said Scott.

"What question was that?" asked Brian.

"The question about whether Mr. Marino got a new job. Not only did he get a new job, but it looks like he got one helluva promotion."

Chapter 63

STARING INTO THE MIRROR, BRIAN Johnson untied his silk, JC Penney necktie for the third time. It was too long on his first attempt, too short on the second, and too loose and untidy on the third, resembling a knot that would inevitably fail a Boy Scout inspection. He could never get his knots to look like his father's, but then again, he didn't put a tie around his neck five days a week.

The last time he wore a coat and tie was in April at Mrs. Wills's funeral, and now he was preparing for the funeral of one of his classmates. Never in his wildest dreams had he imagined such an ordeal. What he *had* envisioned was someday wearing a tie along with Antonio and posing for graduation pictures together with the Class of 1975.

The four boys from Coldwater Creek were planning to attend the church services together, at least that was their plan. Already a tight-knit group, the neighborhood crew had bonded even closer since the loss of Antonio, leaning on each other for fellowship and emotional support. Bob, more than ever, relied upon the brotherhood as a substitute for his dwindling family, using what means he could to endure. If he had to attend yet another funeral, at least he could surround himself with the warmth and cohesiveness of lifelong friends.

"Hi, Mrs. Carter, this is Brian. May I please speak with Mark?"

"In regard to what?"

Usually congenial, Mrs. Carter's inquiry caught Brian off guard. "I just wanted to tell him that Bob is driving us to the funeral and picking us up at nine fifteen. Can he come to the phone?"

"Well, unfortunately he won't be able to go today. But hold on a minute, I'll let him tell you."

"This is Mark speaking."

"What was that all about?" asked Brian. "Your mom just said you can't go with us to the funeral."

"Yeah, change of plans. They don't want me to go anymore."

"Why is that?"

Mark hesitated as if waiting for some privacy, and then continued in a low voice. "To be honest with you, things haven't been very good around here the past twenty-four hours."

"Okay, but what's that got to do with Antonio?"

"As it turns out, it has a lot to do with Antonio."

Brian, more confused than ever, continued his probe. "Are you gonna elaborate on that? I mean, this will be our last chance to pay tribute to our classmate."

"I know, but we've decided it may not be a good idea for me to be there. There are some extenuating circumstances that you don't know about."

"Okay, but how will I know unless you tell me."

Mark hesitated again before responding. "If I tell you, you have to promise to keep it a secret."

"Okay, you got it. Your secret is safe with me."

"Well, yesterday afternoon, the homicide department took my father off the Antonio Jackson investigation. They believe they found the murder weapon, and it turns out to be a gun that's registered to my father."

"No way—that's crazy! Are they saying he's a suspect?"

"They're doing an internal investigation, and my dad has been named a person of interest."

"I don't know what to say," admitted Brian, dumbfounded by Mark's revelation.

"It's all bullshit, of course. Either a big misunderstanding or some-one's tryin' to frame my dad. Either way, he'll be fully exonerated. In the meantime, my parents are really stressed out, as you can imagine."

"Okay, I get it."

"I really wanted to be there to pay my respect, but if word leaks out that my father is a suspect, then it could get really awkward, if you know what I mean. I don't want to put myself or anyone else in an uncomfortable situation."

"Okay man, I understand. All I can say is I hope everything works out."

"Me too. I'll talk to you at football practice this afternoon."

"See you then."

Traffic around Turner Chapel AME was heavy and congested for a Wednesday morning, even more so than a Sunday service. Considering the Jacksons were prominent leaders in the church, it was no surprise that most of the congregation showed up for Antonio's funeral. When coupled with Northrop students, faculty and staff, the horde of humanity had reached epic proportions.

Stuck in a long line of bumper-to-bumper vehicles, Bob's Barracuda inched along tediously. Just as they got to within three car lengths of the church parking lot, a police officer set up a barricade of cones and waved everyone away, advising the lot was completely full. By the time the boys found a curbside parking spot, they were a good three blocks away from the church. But they were not alone. Making their way toward the church, they could see lines of people coming from every direction.

Arriving ten minutes late, the boys were glad to see that the services had been delayed to accommodate the overwhelming number of mourners. With the pews filled to capacity, the ushers were busy directing people to the standing-room-only sections, which meant along the aisles and in the back of the church behind the last row of seats.

Stranded in the back, Brian stretched his neck, looking over and around a sea of heads and shoulders, trying to locate the presence of Antonio's body. Identifying his target, his eyes settled on a shiny bronze casket nestled in a blanket of white bouquets. Except for the flowers, it was not the image of divinity he had envisioned. To Brian, the stark metal casket appeared cold and sterile, a harsh contrast to the warmth and tranquility of the floral surroundings.

Realizing the coffin was closed, Brian wasn't sure if he was disappointed or relieved. He wanted to see Antonio's face one more time, but he didn't know if he could handle the vision of him in such a lifeless state, an image that would certainly drive him to tears. Even the thought of it made his eyes well up, for Antonio had always been high-spirited and full of life, the unwaning vision of effervescence. He decided it was better to remember Antonio as he was than to bereave his corpse. After all, as an ambassador of joy, Antonio would have wanted his funeral to be a celebration of life, not an outpouring of wistful sentiments.

Glancing down at the memorial card in his hand, Brian cherished the chosen image, a black-and-white photo of a trumpet-playing Antonio, with his head tilted back and his horn pointing toward the heavens. It was quintessential Antonio, full of spirit and jubilation. Except for the historical marker, no words were necessary, the picture said it all.

Anthony (Antonio) Elijah Jackson (1957–1974)

Brian thought about the short period of time that Antonio had blessed the earth. Even though he was taken away far too young, he had accomplished so much in so little time, leaving behind a lasting legacy. His spirited music had been a unique gift, a contribution that made the world a better place. It made Brian think about his own life and what little he had accomplished. There was so much more to do and so much more to contribute. Maybe that's why God took Antonio instead of him. Antonio had already made his mark.

Feeling the sweat drip down his face, Brian realized how incredibly warm and stuffy the church had become. Packed in like sardines, the mass of humanity was generating an inordinate amount of heat, and people were fanning themselves with the memorial cards as a means to cope. Brian fought off the urge to loosen his tie as the moisture accumulated under his collar, intentionally avoiding any signs of disrespect. Putting up with a little discomfort was a small price to pay in light of Antonio's ultimate sacrifice.

Waiting for the ceremony to begin, the boys continued to scan the crowd for familiar faces. Although none of them had ever met Antonio's parents, it was easy to identify them in the front row, isolated from the masses. Marquis Jackson appeared statuesque in his black suit, silver tie, and dark sunglasses, while Chantelle sat motionless, her face concealed in a black shoulder-length veil. To Brian, it was a vivid reminder of Jackie Kennedy and the veil she wore at her husband's funeral. Although he was a young kindergartener at the time, Brian would never forget the images of Jackie Kennedy and her desolate look of despair, bravely weathering the storm as millions looked on. Like Chantelle, she had lost a loved one far too early, senselessly murdered by gunfire.

Brian contemplated the nonsense of it all, the absurdity of why people would kill other people, why a species would destroy itself. It seemed to defy the laws of nature that a human being would rob humanity of its very own future, destroying the ones with the greatest potential. Instead of self-preservation, it was self-destruction.

Allowing his mind to drift away in reflection, Brian comprehended his surroundings, a Black church in the middle of the city, far removed from White suburbia. Four years ago, he never would have imagined himself in such a setting. But now it not only seemed appropriate, it almost seemed normal, as if this was the way it was supposed to be, different people and different cultures united together in a common cause.

And then, looking over his shoulder, he spotted Lynda Lacey with a distant, forlorn look on her face, as if her mind was in a faraway land, detached from her physical presence. He knew that no one would be more devastated than Lynda, for Antonio was the apple of her eye, the very embodiment of her ambition. It was a loss from which she may never recover.

Recognizing that Lynda was surrounded by the cheerleading squad, Brian searched for Mindy, knowing her petite stature might lessen her visibility. And then he saw Jada Brown, conservatively dressed in a black skirt, silver blouse, and high heels, a dramatic contrast to the casual attire she had adorned at the club.

And right behind Jada, he spotted Mindy, a good five inches shorter. How ironic the two would be standing next to each other. Certainly, Jada didn't tell Mindy about their night together at the club. To Brian, she didn't seem like the snarky type, the kind of girl that would stir up any soap opera drama. Jada seemed a little more worldly than the other girls her age, more squared away and authentic.

And then it hit Brian like a ton of bricks. For the first time in his life, he was looking at Mindy in a different light, no longer obsessed with her presence or infatuated by her allure. Maybe he was growing up, or maybe death was taking its toll, putting things in a different perspective. It made him appreciate everything that life has to offer.

Ten days ago, he was feeling guilty about his evening with Jada, as though he had crossed a line and jeopardized his relationship with

Mindy, the girl he planned to spend the rest of his life with. But now, life itself seemed so fragile, like something that should be appreciated and enjoyed. He was young and there were so many things he wanted to experience. Maybe his conventional views of courtship were impeding him from a world of limitless possibilities. After all, he and Jada had done nothing wrong. They were just two people appreciating each other's company and enjoying life.

Scott tugged on Brian's sleeve and gestured toward the rear of the church. "Don't look now, but there's a band settin' up back there, and it looks like they're gettin' ready to perform."

Looking over his shoulder, Brian could see three musicians in coordinated outfits tuning up their instruments: a trumpet, trombone, and sousaphone. "This ought to be good," said Brian. "This is exactly what Antonio would've wanted."

As the commotion began to attract attention, Reverend Brown took to the podium and addressed the congregation.

"Ladies and gentlemen, please rise as we honor the memory of our very own Antonio Jackson. In a heartfelt tribute to his legacy, I present to you, live from New Orleans, three of the Crescent City's most celebrated musicians."

Standing up in unison, the assembly turned their attention to the back of the church, and right on cue, the trumpet player launched into one of Antonio's favorite songs: "When the Saints Go Marching In."

As the trumpet blared the lyrical refrains, the trombone responded in kind, like a soulful mockingbird, imitating and then complementing the melody. Moving to the rhythm, the musicians sashayed up the aisle, pointing their instruments to the sky and then back down again, alternating their up and down motions, while the sousaphone player, with his thundering bass, kept the band on beat, rocking his giant horn from side to side.

With watery eyes and a lump in his throat, Brian recalled the very first day he met Antonio, the day he played this song in front of the junior high band class and wowed them with his star power. Although this performance was a perfect tribute to Antonio's legacy, it stirred up so many emotions that Brian was beside himself, overwhelmed by the significance. Never before had he felt joy and sadness together at the same time. As the tears streamed down his cheeks, he quickly wiped them away before Scott or Bob could recognize his vulnerability.

Reaching the conclusion of their performance, the band faced the assembly from the front of the church, just a few steps from Antonio's coffin. The parishioners responded with a scattering of applause, producing an awkward moment of uncertainty, not knowing if they should celebrate the performance with enthusiasm or honor the solemn occasion with dignity.

Settling the confusion, Reverend Brown approached the podium clapping his hands vigorously. "It's okay," he said. "That was an incredible performance. I can feel Antonio's spirit and he wants us all to celebrate."

Relieved by the clarification, the congregation extended their applause slowly and gradually until it reached a dramatic climax, resulting in a prolonged ovation. The band members bowed their heads with heartfelt appreciation.

When the rousing ovation concluded, Reverend Brown took to the microphone and asked everyone to be seated. Waiting for order to resume, the pastor exercised his patience. Without saying a word, he transitioned his expression from one of joy to one of somberness. When total silence had been achieved, he paused another ten seconds for dramatic affect. The church remained deathly quiet as the pastor bowed his head and meditated in silence, preparing to deliver his eulogy.

Dearly beloved, we are gathered today to pay homage to the memory and spirit of Antonio Jackson, to celebrate the precious gift of his life that was so graciously bestowed upon us by the grace and goodwill of our Lord, Jesus Christ.

Six years ago, this city, this community did not even know that Antonio Jackson existed. We were not aware of the void in our lives, not aware that a change was about to occur, a change so significant that we'd soon not imagine our lives any differently. His impact has been mystifying, begging the question of how one person in such a short period of time could touch so many souls.

Ladies and gentlemen, it has been a long journey, a journey that began in the roots of slavery. For it was Antonio's great-great-grandfather, Samba, a man who persevered through his own blood, sweat, and tears, enduring the perils of bondage on the sugar plantations of Louisiana, struggling to make ends meet so that one day the Jackson family might thrive in prosperity.

Through all of his perils, the one thing that brought joy to Samba was his love of music, the music that he discovered and helped to create on the sacred grounds of Congo Square, deep in the heart of New Orleans. For Congo Square is where our African ancestors were free to connect and express themselves without persecution. A place where traditions could be cultivated and celebrated, and African heritage preserved.

When Samba first blew his precious breath through the wind pipes of his pan flute, he had no idea that he was creating a tradition that would be handed down from one generation to the next. A sound that would evolve slowly but surely, a sound that would transition from rhythmic percussion to soulful melodies, a sound that would one day be characterized by brass bands and parades, a sound that would one day take on its very own identity, a sound called New Orleans jazz. Yes, it has been a long journey, but the Jacksons were there from the very beginning, passing the torch and preserving the tradition.

It was on March 22, 1957, that our world became a better place, for it was on this date that our heavenly father blessed us with the precious gift of Antonio Jackson, and soon the world would find out that Antonio was the gift that keeps on giving. And we could not get enough. We wanted more and more and more, and Antonio would always deliver. And when he delivered, he delivered not out of duty, but out of love and devotion. His love for music and his devotion to the people.

The Jackson journey took a dramatic detour in 1968, for that was the year that Marquis Jackson moved his family to Fort Wayne, Indiana. That was the year that Marquis and his wife, Chantelle, made a big decision. The decision to take a chance, the decision to leave their homeland for a better way of life, the decision to escape the prejudice and discrimination of the South and explore new beginnings and new opportunities in the North. It was not without risk, but Marquis was persistent and persuasive, for he convinced his wife that no one could ever move ahead without taking a chance.

Ladies and gentlemen, I am here today to tell you the chance has paid off. The chance has paid huge dividends to this church and this community. From the very moment that Chantelle Jackson stepped foot into this house of worship, the lives of our parishioners were transformed, reaching a spiritual level that we never thought was possible. Through her music and stewardship, our congregation has thrived like never before. For we are united, and we are devoted, and we are full of the holy spirit and all the joy that comes from His love and mercy.

But there's more to the story than that. When the Jacksons arrived in Fort Wayne, Indiana, they had no idea that their son, Antonio, would be caught up in the middle of a firestorm. And that firestorm was called school desegregation. Not only would Antonio need to adapt to a strange new land, but he would soon be sent to schools that did not embrace him or his culture. He would soon be facing the very same intolerance and rejection his family was attempting to escape.

A lesser human being might have been intimidated. A lesser human being might have said, "Lord, why are you doing this to me? Why do you continue to challenge me? Why have you given me so much hardship?"

But Antonio was not a lesser human being, he was an extraordinary *human being. He was* not *put on this earth to do ordinary things. He was put on this earth to make a difference, and what a difference he did make. Not only did he welcome the challenge, but he embraced it. And like everything else he did in life, he excelled. For he was not a follower, he was a leader, and when it came to bridging the gap between Whites and Blacks, he was a pioneer.*

You see, Antonio Jackson had a passion for life, and that passion knew no boundaries. It didn't matter where he was, or what he was doing, or who he was doing it with. All that really mattered was his zest for life and his passion for making a difference.

Looking around this magnificent cathedral today, I can see the difference. I can see the fruits of Antonio's passion. I can see people from different walks of life, people of different races, and people of different religions. And I can see the glory of God. For we are all God's children, and we are all on the same mission, and that is a mission to love one another and spread God's goodwill.

Ladies and gentlemen, I am here to tell you the journey does not end today. The journey has only begun. We must keep our faith, and we must remain steadfast, and we must carry Antonio's mission forward. As children of God, we must rise up together and meet the challenge, for we will not *be defeated.*

For Antonio, his journey has reached the final chapter. His journey has taken him to his just reward, where he will live in eternity with our heavenly father. And his life will remain an inspiration for all of us as we continue to do God's work, as we continue to fight the good fight as soldiers of his gospel.

Dearly beloved, let us now, in Jesus's name, bow our heads in prayer.

Chapter 64

THE FIRST DAY OF SCHOOL always brings an air of excitement. For seniors especially, it triggers a broad assortment of emotions. No matter how many times they've been through it, it never gets old, but when they experience it for the last time, their perspectives change dramatically, ranging anywhere from sentimental reflections up to and including great expectations.

Heading into the fourth year of its existence, Northrop High School was the beacon on a hill, a shining example of success and prosperity. Considered a risky experiment a few short years ago, the resulting achievements spoke for themselves, exceeding all expectations.

Northrop had become the most admired high school in Fort Wayne and one of the most respected in the state. Although it was a basketball state championship that put them on the map, it was the social implications that scored points with educators. If anyone ever doubted the reasoning or intent behind desegregation, all they needed to do was look at the students of Northrop High School. They had become a diversified and enlightened community, and they couldn't imagine it any other way.

The fact that the Northrop Commons was overflowing with hundreds of students on the first day of school was to be expected. The anticipation of day one almost always inspired early arrivals. What remained a mystery was the quandary over how the student body would behave and what the prevailing mood would be after the unimaginable jolt of a homicide. It had been only two weeks since the shocking discovery of Antonio's body, and for those who attended the funeral, the emotional farewell was still fresh in their minds.

Settling upon their familiar stomping ground, the boys from Coldwater Creek surrounded themselves with the usual suspects, but their coping mechanisms were as varied as their personalities. Scott Clever, normally the most animated of the crew, played it close to the vest, reluctant to marginalize the occasion with inane gibberish, while Mark Carter, predisposed to the impending investigations, remained reserved, not willing to expose himself to any speculation, and Brian, the unpretentious leader of the pack, tried to remain casual, easing into the routine without any inclinations one way or the other.

Waiting for Mindy's arrival, Brian had already obliged her with the traditional cinnamon roll.

"I see some things never change," noted Scott.

"Why would I change a winning formula?" reasoned Brian.

"Are you gonna buy one for Jada too?" he asked.

Caught off guard by Scott's brazenness, Brian felt the urge to denounce him, but decided to remain quiet, not willing to dignify the question with an answer. Instead, he changed the subject.

"I just realized how weird this Friday is gonna be. We have our first game coming up and Antonio won't be here to lead the pep band."

"I'm guessing someone will be designated to assume that role," suggested Mark.

"Yeah, but it won't be the same," noted Brian.

"Life goes on," suggested Bob. "Nobody knows that better than me."

"It's not just the band," said Brian. "What about the morning announcements? I can't imagine them without Antonio. No one will ever replace what he did."

"They'll probably go back to using the teachers to deliver the announcements," suggested Mark.

"I wouldn't be surprised," said Brian. "After all, using Antonio was Pappa Bruin's idea, and now he's gone too."

With ten minutes to the opening bell, the Commons was filled to the brim. Brian, getting edgy over Mindy's arrival, eventually spotted her as she made her way through the crowd, side-by-side with Lynda Lacey. Tagging along in the rear was Quinn O'Connor.

"Good morning," said Mindy, forging ahead with the formalities.

"Good morning. I have your cinnamon roll."

"I'm not very hungry, but thank you anyway."

"That's okay, I guess it'll take a while to ease back into a routine."

"Yes, I'm sorry," said Mindy. "It's just that I never thought we'd be starting our senior year without Antonio. Somehow, all the joy is gone."

Remaining silent, Lynda appeared reluctant to mingle, which was somewhat out of character considering she was the one who always handled things professionally, always the one to say the right thing regardless of the circumstances. But Brian, concerned for her well-being, decided to engage her delicately.

"How are you holding up? Is there anything we can do to lift your spirits?"

"I doubt it, but thank you for asking."

"I've got an idea," continued Brian. "Why don't we plan some sort of a tribute to Antonio at halftime of the football game?"

Lynda looked up and actually made eye contact with Brian for the first time. Intrigued by the thought, she appeared to snap out of her trance. Brian knew that she was a person who needed a sense of purpose. Assigning her a meaningful task was just what the doctor ordered.

"That's actually a pretty good idea. I'll talk with the cheerleading coach and the band director and see if we can work something out."

"Great, I know you're just the person we need to make it happen," said Brian, hoping to lift her spirits.

"Maybe this is not the time or place," said Quinn. "But are there any developments whatsoever in the investigation? Has anyone heard anything?"

"I haven't heard anything," said Scott.

"Nothing's been in the newspaper," confirmed Bob.

"What about your father?" Quinn asked Mark. "Has he been involved at all with the investigation?"

"I don't know if he's involved or not," said Mark. "Even if he was, he would never bring up the topic at home. He's not allowed to discuss an ongoing investigation."

"Okay, I guess that makes sense," said Quinn. "I was just curious. We all want to find out what happened and try to understand why anyone would do such a thing."

"Yes, we all want answers," said Brian. "But I don't think we'll ever understand. There's never a good explanation for a tragedy like this."

Bob Wills, who had been mostly quiet, seemed distracted. Looking across the giant atrium, his attention was drawn to the row of glass doors at the front of the building.

"What are you looking at?" asked Scott.

"I don't know," said Bob. "There seems to be some kind of a disturbance by the front door."

Turning to look, they all focused their attention on a cluster of students gathered between the front entrance and the doors leading to the auditorium. As the concentration of bodies accumulated, they were able to recognize the focus of their attention: three uniformed police officers.

"What are the police doing here?" asked Scott.

"That's a good question," said Brian, looking at Mark.

"Why are you looking at me?" asked Mark. "Just because my dad's on the police force, doesn't mean I know what's goin' on whenever a cop shows up."

"No, but you're the closest thing we have to an inside source," noted Scott.

As they continued their observation, it became apparent the police officers were delivering a line of questioning. Fully engaged, the students listened intently and responded by pointing across the Commons.

"They seem to be looking for someone," said Scott.

"Yeah, maybe someone's car was broken into," said Brian. "Or vandalized, maybe?"

"Or maybe something was stolen," suggested Scott.

The police officers continued to mill through the crowd, pausing again toward the middle of the Commons and asking the students for more directions. Once again, the students responded by pointing their fingers. But this time it appeared the pointing was aimed directly toward the gathering of jocks and cheerleaders.

"They seem to be heading this way," noted Scott.

Mark looked at Bob and got a funny feeling in his stomach. "Bob, I hope you haven't been peddling any of that wacky weed, if you know what I mean."

"Man, don't look at me—I'm clean."

Parading through the sea of bodies, the officers' mission had turned into quite a spectacle, and the crowd was responding with a steady murmur. Stopping one more time, less than twenty feet away from the Coldwater crew, the police asked someone another question. The student responded by pointing directly toward Brian Johnson and his friends.

As the cops approached, Brian could feel his heart pounding. He had no idea what was about to occur, but whatever it was it couldn't be good.

"Which one of you is Quinn O'Connor?" asked the lead officer.

Caught off guard by the question, nobody said a word. Instead, they all looked at Quinn with shocked expressions, unable to comprehend what was taking place. Quinn responded by turning red as a beet.

All three officers approached Quinn and surrounded him.

"Are you Quinn O'Connor?"

Quinn contemplated the question for a second, then nodded his head.

"Quinn O'Connor, you are under arrest for the murder of Antonio Jackson."

"Place your hands behind your back," ordered the second officer, as he pulled out a set of handcuffs.

"You have the right to remain silent. Anything you say can and will be used against you in a court of law. You have the right to an attorney. If you cannot afford an attorney, one will be appointed for you."

Two days after the arrest of Quinn O'Connor, Lynda Lacey remained missing in action. Devastated by the turn of events, she had sheltered herself at home, refusing to go to school or take any calls.

Having taken her home that fateful morning, Mindy had not seen or heard from Lynda since. Despite Mindy's repeated attempts to talk, Mrs. Lacey could not entice Lynda to the phone, and finally admitted to Mindy that Lynda was in denial, that she continues to insist that Quinn and Antonio were good friends, and Quinn would never do anything to hurt him.

Expressing her desire to get Lynda some counseling, Mrs. Lacey was hopeful that she would return to school soon, but for the time being,

Lynda was far too embarrassed to show her face around friends, afraid she would be chastised by people who believe that her boyfriend was responsible for Antonio's death.

Hoping for an intervention, Mindy turned to the one person who would do anything for her at the drop of a hat: Brian Johnson. More than willing to assist, Brian expressed his concern, but admitted there was nothing he could do to make Lynda feel any better, that maybe she needed more time to heal so that she could come to terms with reality and resume some sort of normalcy.

But Mindy persisted, suggesting that Lynda would face reality much sooner if her friends gathered around and told her how much they cared and how much they supported her.

"Her problem is she's in denial," said Mindy. "And the longer she's in denial, the longer it will take her to face reality."

"I agree," said Brian. "She needs to know the truth."

"I think she knows the truth but isn't willing to accept it."

"Maybe she needs more proof, more evidence that will justify the truth."

"You sound as if you have an idea."

"To be honest with you," admitted Brian, "we have some information that might help explain to Lynda everything she needs to know."

"We? Who's we?"

"We, as in myself, Scott, and Mark."

"Are you saying you know something the rest of us don't?"

"Yes, that's exactly what I'm saying. The problem is, I don't know if Lynda can handle the truth."

Mindy, along with the entire Coldwater crew, Brian, Scott, Mark, and Bob, were gathered on the back patio of the Lacey residence. Mindy had convinced Mrs. Lacey that Lynda should listen to what they have to say and that it was important for her to know how much they cared. She also made it clear that there were some important details that Lynda needed to know, information that might help her reach an understanding. When Mrs. Lacey agreed to arrange for the meeting, the stage was set.

Grudgingly sitting on her patio, Lynda remained silent, willing to listen, but not fully engaged. Brian, the ringleader, would act as the appointed spokesperson, and the others would offer their support as needed.

"So let me start out by saying that we're all very concerned about you," began Brian. "That's the number-one reason why we're here. But we're also here because there are some things you need to know—things that you have a right to know."

"What do you know that I don't know?" asked Lynda. "I knew Antonio and Quinn better than any of you."

"Yes, you probably did. But some things have happened that I'm sure you're unaware of."

Lynda gave no response, but rolled her eyes as if she could barely tolerate this intrusion on her integrity.

"A couple weeks ago, I went to a party along with Scott and Bob. A party we were invited to by Malcom Mosely. It was at a private, after-hours club in some old, abandoned building. Needless to say, we were all out of our element. But the point of this story is to tell you that we bumped into Quinn while we were there."

Lynda's antennae perked up at the mention of Quinn, wondering where Brian was going with this story. "Are you sure it was him? It doesn't sound like his kind of scene."

"It was definitely Quinn. I know because we all talked to him, and he had been drinking quite a bit. In fact, we'd all been drinking."

"Especially Brian," interjected Scott.

"Yes, that is true," said Brian. "But I have no doubt that Quinn was *very* drunk."

"So what was he doing there?" asked Lynda. "Was he meeting up with you?"

"No, he was there with Antonio. Antonio was performing that night, and he and Quinn were drinking Cognac."

"Okay, now it's starting to make sense," said Lynda. "He and Quinn had become pretty good friends."

"Well, there's more to the story," continued Brian. "We ended up leaving pretty late. And when I say we, I mean myself, Scott, and Bob. Do you remember what time it was, Bob?"

"Yeah, it was twelve thirty," said Bob. "I remember because I'm the one that made them leave. I was driving and I had to get up early to deliver the newspapers."

"Okay, okay," said Lynda, revealing her frustration. "Can somebody please get to the point?"

"Yes," said Brian. "The point is, when we were heading to Bob's car, we kinda got lost along the way and stumbled into an alley. And that's where we saw Quinn and Antonio together. And when I say together, I mean they were really together, if you know what I mean."

"No, I don't know what you mean. What are you trying to say?"

"Well, I don't know how to tell you this and still be discreet. Let's just say that they were making out."

"No way! That's the most ridiculous thing I've ever heard."

"I'm not making it up," said Brian. "Scott and Bob can back me up."

Bob nodded his head in agreement and Scott spoke up. "I guess making out is one way to describe it."

"Okay," said Lynda. "It was very late, and it was dark, and you were all drunk. I'm sure it was nothing."

"It wasn't nothing," said Bob.

"You're just making a mountain out of a molehill," continued Lynda.

"Listen," said Brian. "We're all here because we want you to know the truth. So I'm not gonna sugarcoat this anymore. What we saw was Quinn and Antonio engaged in an explicit act. To be more precise, a homosexual act. And there's no two ways about it. We would never mistake anything like that. And yes, we were all shocked."

Brian's blunt admission sent Lynda for a loop. Her face turned red, and her body started to tremble. Beginning to rise, as if to stand up for her principles and abandon this assault on her sanity, she collapsed back to her chair, her knees buckling.

"Believe me," said Brian, "we were all stunned just as much as you are right now, and we all wanted to turn around and leave as quickly as possible. But they saw us. In fact, Quinn yelled at us to get out of there. And that's exactly what we did."

"Why are you telling me this?" mumbled Lynda, with an icy stare on her face.

"I want you to know that we were not going to tell anyone what we witnessed that night. Am I right?" Brian asked Scott.

"That is correct. Brian insisted that we make a pact to never tell anyone. We all swore to keep it a secret."

"And yet, here you are," said Lynda.

"Listen," said Brian. "Antonio and Quinn were our friends. We decided whatever was going on between the two of them was their own personal business. That's why we swore ourselves to secrecy. But when Antonio was murdered three days later, we started to look at things in a different light."

"And why is that?" asked Lynda.

"It all started when Mark told me the police found one of his father's guns near Antonio's body. Then they ran the ballistics tests and said it was the murder weapon."

"They took my father off the case," said Mark. "They said he was a person of interest."

"Of course, that made no sense," said Brian. "So we started brainstorming. Why would Mark's dad want to kill Antonio, and why would he be so dumb as to leave his gun near the murder scene? Afterall, Mr. Carter is a police investigator, he wouldn't be that stupid."

"Then we remembered that Quinn was in our hunting shed where we store all of our guns," said Mark. "He asked a lot of questions and even handled the gun that was used in the murder, a Smith & Wesson, .38-caliber revolver."

"When was he ever in your hunting shed?" asked Lynda.

"It was after the state championship parade. He was dropping me off at my house and he and Brian stayed for dinner."

"It's all true," said Brian. "Quinn knew exactly where to find that gun, and he knew the Carters didn't lock their shed. So we started wondering if Quinn was so embarrassed about our discovery of him and Antonio together that he might actually kill Antonio to shut him up so no one would ever find out. It sounds crazy, but it was one of our theories."

"He was under tremendous pressure from his father," admitted Lynda.

"And what would his father have done if he found out Quinn was having a homosexual relationship with Antonio?" asked Brian.

Lynda sat still, as if contemplating the scenario. "He probably would have beaten the living daylights out of Quinn. That would've been the ultimate disgrace to Mr. O'Connor's reputation."

"So when we told Mr. Carter about our theory," continued Brian, "he was able to convince his friends on the police force to treat Quinn as a suspect."

"Things started to fall in place pretty quick after that," said Mark. "It turns out that several witnesses saw Quinn with Antonio that night. Then they found out that Quinn had purchased ammunition for the Smith & Wesson revolver. Then they captured Quinn's fingerprints on the murder weapon and on the back of our shed. Then they were able to identify some small bloodstains in Quinn's Buick, blood that came from Antonio."

Surrendering to the barrage of evidence, Lynda had heard enough. Suddenly it all made sense. All of Quinn's mixed signals and all the suspicions that had haunted her were now coming into context. It was a trainwreck waiting to happen. And the sad truth was that she had been instrumental in facilitating the trainwreck, the one who had proposed the whole idea of joining forces for student council president. Now she felt naive and responsible at the same time. It was a bitter pill to swallow.

Burying her face into the palms of her hands, Lynda started sobbing. Mindy, overwhelmed with pity, put her arm around Lynda and consoled her with sympathy. Everyone else sat still, not knowing what to say.

After a few short moments, Lynda pulled herself back into the present. "So what happens next?" she asked. "Is there going to be a trial?"

"I don't think so," answered Mark. "Apparently Quinn broke down when confronted with all the evidence and confessed to the crime. As an eighteen-year-old, he can make his own decisions and will be treated as an adult. The police department has his signed confession."

Epilogue

B ALANCING THE GLASS OF SCOTCH in one hand and pushing himself out of the armchair with the other, he teetered unsteadily toward the library desk. Although his vision had become blurred, he could still make out the headline on the front page of *The Journal Gazette*: "Quinn O'Connor Confesses to Murder."

This was the epitome of ignorance, he thought to himself. You never confess to anything you can defend. It was not a cut-and-dried case, and he would have surrounded his son with the best legal team money could buy. In his mind, Quinn's life was worth way more than a boy from the hood, and a jury of his peers would have understood that.

But none of it seemed to matter anymore. He had resigned himself to the fact that all had been lost. As far as Ryan O'Connor was concerned, life as he knew it would never be the same.

Reaching into his desk drawer, he searched for his lighter. Perhaps he would indulge in one last Cuban cigar before succumbing to his scotch-induced coma. Then he noticed the ammo clip for his 9 mm pistol. He had always kept the shells in his desktop drawer, with the actual firearm stored in the bottom drawer. It would be his last line of defense if a crazed adversary ever penetrated the O'Connor compound and forced his way into the house. He had made his share of enemies over the years, and it was better to be safe than sorry.

Retrieving his lighter, he decided to remove the clip from the drawer at the same time, laying both of them on the desktop in front of him.

Contemplating their functionality, lighter versus clip, he pondered which would be more destructive, fire or bullets.

Taking another gulp of scotch, he abandoned the cigar idea and decided to apply his lighter elsewhere, igniting the newspaper with two flicks of his thumb. As the smoldering edge grew into surging flames, he thought about the insurance claim he could file if his estate burned to the ground. It would be a sizable amount, no doubt, but there was no way he could keep it for himself, for Roselyn would have her greedy little hands all over it.

Before the fire could scorch his hand, he dumped the burning newspaper into the wastebasket and watched the flames diminish, gradually dying out until there was nothing left but a smoky pile of ashes. Such a fitting tribute, he thought. It was like looking in the mirror, watching his very own livelihood reduced to rubble.

Reaching into the bottom drawer, he pulled out the pistol. He couldn't remember the last time he fired it, not since his last visit to the gun range, where he had proudly demonstrated its power and authority.

Removing the magazine, he sat it next to the clip. Eight rounds, that was the capacity. He would only need one shell to accomplish the task, but he decided to load all eight, yet another way to delay the inevitable.

Removing his handkerchief, he wiped the sweat from his brow and straightened his tie. With one last sip of scotch, he aimed the gun barrel toward his mouth.

The last announcement had been stuffed into the envelope. All that remained was a trip to the post office and the world would soon prepare itself for the next generation of O'Connors.

Tyler Anthony O'Connor

September 6, 1974

8 lbs., 4 oz., 21 inches

Christine O'Connor & Michael Williams

"Momma's very proud of you," said Christine, snuggling her bundle of joy. "You have your pappa's brown eyes and curly hair, and I'm gonna spoil you rotten."

Bob Wills parked his Barracuda in front of Slatewood Records and the boys piled out of the car.

"I hope they're not sold out," said Brian, reaching for his wallet.

"They shouldn't be," said Scott. "I called the store this morning and the manager said their shipment just arrived yesterday."

"How many?" asked Brian.

"One hundred copies."

Entering the storefront, they were greeted with the alluring smell of incense and a prominent display of *Santana's Greatest Hits*, the album cover that depicted a white dove cradled against a Black man's chest. It was the number-one-selling album in the country, on its way to eight million copies.

"We're here to buy the latest issue of *Rolling Stone*," announced Bob.

"You're in luck," said the store manager. "I've got about twenty left. They've been selling like hotcakes."

"Still a buck ninety-five?" asked Scott.

"Yeah, but I should've raised the price. I think I could sell them at five bucks a piece and still sellout."

The boys piled around the newsstand and gawked at the image. *Rolling Stone*'s feature story depicted a full-page cover of a young Black man playing his trumpet.

The Ballad of Antonio Jackson

Musical genius cut short at an early age

William Bennington applied his signature to the last document and extended his hand to Roselyn O'Connor.

"I promise I will do my duty to preserve your legacy to the best of my ability. Rest assured; the Cadillac dealership is in good hands."

"I have no doubt," said Roselyn. "I would never sell unless I thought it was in good hands. I've always been impressed with your business acumen and your passion for Cadillacs. You have my blessing."

Two weeks later, the O'Connor Cadillac sign was taken down and replaced with Bennington Cadillac. The next day, William Bennington named Marquis Jackson as his vice president of operations.

About the Author

Kevin Geise was born and raised in Fort Wayne, Indiana. He attended Jefferson Junior High and Northrop High School when the school board implemented their busing plan to achieve racial integration. Now, after a thirty-year career in corporate finance, he has written a novel that captures the essence of those events and other consequential moments from the 70s. Since 1995, he has resided near Dallas, Texas.

As a proponent of an independent and free press, Kevin Geise supports investigative journalism and literary works that retrace important moments in history, enlightening its readers with thought-provoking awareness.

Connect with the author on Facebook:
Kevin Geise - Author